Athabasca
Ice Station Zebra
Partisans

HMS *Ulysses*
The Guns of Navarone
South by Java Head
The Last Frontier
Night Without End
Fear is the Key
The Dark Crusader
The Golden Rendezvous
The Satan Bug
When Eight Bells Toll
Where Eagles Dare
Force 10 From Navarone
Puppet on a Chain
Caravan to Vaccarès
Bear Island
The Way to Dusty Death
Breakheart Pass
Circus
The Golden Gate
Seawitch
Goodbye California
River of Death
Floodgate
San Andreas
The Lonely Sea *(short stories)*
Santorini

Athabasca

Ice Station Zebra

Partisans

Alistair MacLean

Diamond Books
An Imprint of HarperCollins*Publishers*,
77–85 Fulham Palace Road
Hammersmith, London W6 8JB

This Diamond Books Omnibus edition first published 1994

Athabasca © Devoran Trustees Ltd 1980
Ice Station Zebra © Devoran Trustees Ltd 1963
Partisans © Devoran Trustees Ltd 1982

The Author asserts the moral right to be identified as the author of this work

ISBN 0 261 66272 4

Printed and bound in Great Britain by
BPC Hazell Books Ltd
A member of
The British Printing Company Ltd

Athabasca

To Sabrina and Tony

PROLOGUE

This book is not primarily *about* oil, but is based on oil and the means whereby oil is recovered from the earth, so it may be of some interest and help to look briefly at these phenomena.

What oil is, and how it is formed in the first place, no one quite seems to know. The technical books and treatises on this subject are legion – I am aware that, personally, I haven't seen a fraction of them – and they are largely, so I am assured, in close agreement – except when they come to what one would have thought was a point of considerable interest: how, precisely, does oil *become* oil? There appear to be as many divergent theories about this as there are about the origins of life. Confronted with complexities, the well-advised layman takes refuge in over-simplification – which is what I now do, as I can do no other.

Only two elements were needed for the formation of oil – rock, and the incredibly abundant plants and primitive living organisms that teemed in rivers, lakes and seas as far back as perhaps a billion years ago. Hence the term fossil fuels.

The Biblical references to the rock of ages give rise to misconceptions about the nature and permanency of rock. Rock – the material of which the earth's crust is made – is neither eternal nor indestructible. Nor is it even unchanging. On the contrary, it is in a state of constant change, movement and flux, and it is salutary to remind ourselves that there was a time when no rock existed. Even today there is a singular lack of agreement among geologists, geo-physicists and astronomers as to how the earth came into being; but there is a measure of agreement that there was a primary incandescent and gaseous state, followed by a molten state, neither of which was conducive to the formation of anything, rock included. It is erroneous to suppose that rock has been, is and ever shall be.

Yet we are not concerned here with the ultimate origins of rock, but rock as we have it today. It is, admittedly, difficult to observe this process of flux, because a minor change may take ten million years, a major change a hundred million.

Rock is constantly being destroyed and rebuilt. In the destructive process weather is the main factor; in the rebuilding, the force of gravity.

Five main weather elements act upon rock. Frost and ice fracture rock. It can be gradually eroded by airborne dust. The action of the seas, whether through the constant movement of waves and tides or the pounding of heavy storm waves, remorselessly wears away the coastlines. Rivers are immensely powerful destructive agencies – one has but to look at the Grand Canyon to appreciate their enormous power; and such rocks as escape all these influences are worn away over the aeons by the effect of rain.

Whatever the cause of erosion, the end result is the same: the rock is reduced to its tiniest possible constituents – rock particles or, simply, dust. Rain and melting snow carry this dust down to the tiniest rivulets and the mightiest rivers, which in turn transport it to lakes, inland seas and the coastal regions of the oceans. Dust, however fine and powdery, is still heavier than water, and whenever the water becomes sufficiently still, it will gradually sink to the bottom, not only in lakes and seas but also in the sluggish lower reaches of rivers and, where flood conditions exist, inland in the form of silt.

And so, over unimaginably long reaches of time, whole mountain ranges are carried down to the seas and in the process, through the effects of gravity, new rock is born as layer after layer of dust accumulates on the bottom, building up to a depth of ten, a hundred, perhaps even a thousand feet, the lowermost layers being gradually compacted by the immense and steadily-increasing pressures from above, until the particles fuse together and re-form as new rock.

It is in the intermediate and final processes of this new rock formation that oil comes into being. Those lakes and seas of hundreds of millions of years ago were almost choked by water plants and the most primitive forms of aquatic life. On dying, they sank to the bottom of the lakes and seas along with the settling dust particles and were gradually buried deep under the endless layers of more dust and more aquatic and plant life that slowly accumulated above them. The passing of millions of years and the steadily increasing pressures from above gradually changed the decayed vegetation and dead aquatic life into oil.

Described thus simply and quickly, the process sounds reasonable enough. But this is where the grey and disputatious area arises. The conditions necessary for the formation of oil are known: the cause of the metamorphosis is not. It seems probable that some form of chemical catalyst is involved, but this catalyst has not been isolated. The first purely synthetic oil, as distinct from secondary synthetic oils such as those derived from coal, has yet to be produced. We just have to accept that oil is oil, that it is there, bound up in rock strata in fairly well-defined areas throughout the world but always on the sites of ancient seas and lakes, some of which are now continental land, some buried deep under the encroachment of new oceans.

Had the oil remained intermingled with those deeply-buried rock strata, and were the earth a stable place, that oil would have been irrecoverable. But our planet is a highly unstable place. There is no such thing as a stable continent securely anchored to the core of the earth. The continents rest on the so-called tectonic plates which, in turn, float on the molten magma below, with neither anchor nor rudder, free to wander in whichever haphazard fashion they will. This they unquestionably do: they are much given to banging into each other, grinding alongside each other, over-riding or dipping under each other in a wholly unpredictable fashion and, in general, resembling rocks in the demonstration of their fundamental instability. As this banging and clashing takes place over periods of tens or hundreds of millions of years, it is not readily apparent to us except in the form of earthquakes, which generally occur where two tectonic plates are in contention.

The collision of two such plates engenders incredible pressures, and two of the effects of such pressures are of particular concern here. In the first place the huge compressive forces involved tend to squeeze the oil from the rock strata in which it is embedded and to disperse it in whichever direction the pressure permits – up, down or sideways. Secondly, a collision buckles or folds the rock strata themselves, the upper strata being forced upwards to form mountain ranges – the northern movement of the Indian tectonic plate created the Himalayas – and the lower strata buckling to create what are virtually subterranean mountains, folding the layered strata into massive domes and arches.

It is at this point, insofar as oil recovery is concerned, that the nature of the rocks themselves becomes of importance. The rock can be porous or non-porous, the porous rock – such as gypsum – permitting liquids, such as oil, to pass through them, while the non-porous – such as granite – does not. In the case of porous rock the oil, influenced by those compressive forces, will seep upwards through the rock until the distributive pressure eases, when it will come to rest at or very close to the surface of the earth. In the case of non-porous rock, the oil will become trapped in a dome or arch, and in spite of the great pressures from below can escape neither sideways nor upwards but must remain where it is.

In this latter case what are regarded as conventional methods are used in the recovery of oil. Geologists locate a dome, and a hole is drilled. With reasonable luck they hit an oil dome and not a solid one, and their problems are over – the powerful subterranean pressures normally drive the oil to the surface.

The recovery of seepage oil which has passed upwards through porous rock presents a quite different and far more formidable problem, the answer to which was not found until as late as 1967. Even then it was only a partial answer. The trouble, of course, is that this surface seepage oil does not collect in pools, but is inextricably intermixed with foreign matter such as sand and clay from which it has to be abstracted and refined.

It is, in fact, a solid and has to be mined as such; and although this solidified oil may go as deep as six thousand feet, only the first two hundred feet, in the limits of present-day knowledge and techniques, are accessible, and that only by surface mining. Conventional mining methods – the sinking of vertical shafts and the driving of horizontal galleries – would be hopelessly inadequate, as they would provide only the tiniest fraction of the raw material required to make the extraction process commercially viable. The latest oil extraction plant, which went into operation only in the summer of 1978, requires 10,000 tons of raw material every *hour*.

Two excellent examples of the two different methods of oil recovery are to be found in the far north-west of North America. The conventional method of deep drilling is well exemplified by the Prudhoe Bay oilfield on the Arctic shore of northern Alaska; its latter-day counterpart, the surface mining of oil, is to be found – and, indeed, it is the only place in the world where it can be found – in the tar sands of Athabasca.

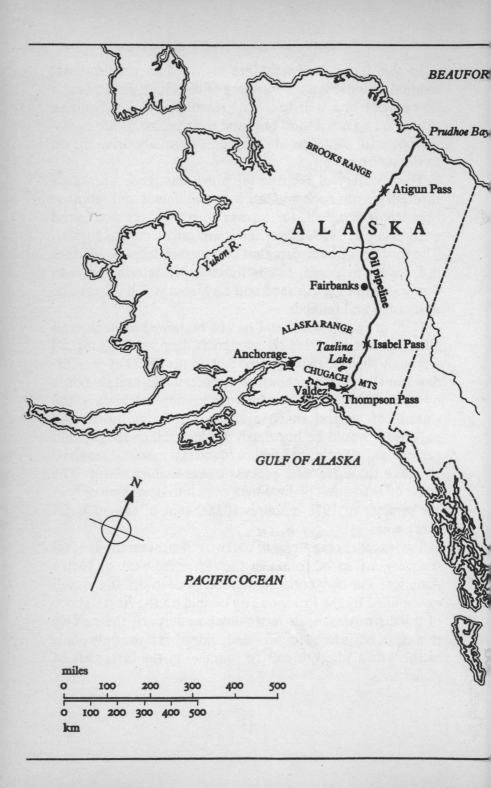

BEAUFOR[T]

Prudhoe Bay

BROOKS RANGE

✕ Atigun Pass

A L A S K A

Yukon R.

Oil pipeline

Fairbanks ●

ALASKA RANGE

Tazlina Lake

✕ Isabel Pass

Anchorage ●

CHUGACH

MTS

Valdez

Thompson Pass

GULF OF ALASKA

N

PACIFIC OCEAN

miles

0   100   200   300   400   500

0   100   200   300   400   500

km

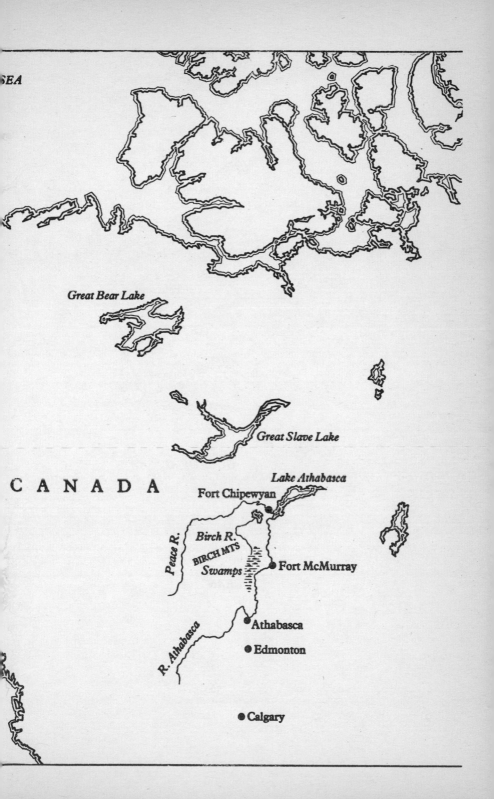

SEA

Great Bear Lake

Great Slave Lake

CANADA

Lake Athabasca

Fort Chipewyan

Peace R.

Birch R.

BIRCH MTS

Swamps

Fort McMurray

R. Athabasca

Athabasca

Edmonton

Calgary

1

"This," said George Dermott, "is no place for us." He eased his considerable bulk back from the dining-table and regarded the remains of several enormous lamb chops with disfavour. "Jim Brady expects his field operatives to be lean, fit and athletic. Are we lean, fit and athletic?"

"There are desserts," Donald Mackenzie said. Like Dermott he was a large and comfortable man with a rugged, weatherbeaten face, a little larger and a little less comfortable. Observers often took him and his partner for a pair of retired heavyweight boxers. "I can see cakes, cookies and a wide variety of pastries," he went on. "You read their food brochure? Says that the average man requires at least five thousand calories a day to cope with Arctic conditions. But we, George, are not average men. Six thousand would do better in a pinch. Nearer seven would be safer, I'd say. Chocolate mousse and double cream?"

"He had a notice about it on the staff bulletin board," Dermott said wryly. "Heavy black border, for some reason. Signed, too."

"Senior operatives don't look at staff boards," Mackenzie sniffed. He heaved his 220 pounds erect and headed purposefully for the food counter. There was no doubt that B.P./Sohio did extremely well by their staff. Here at Prudhoe Bay, on the bitter rim of the Arctic Ocean in midwinter, the spacious, light and airy dining-room, with multi-coloured pastel walls back-dropping the recurrent five-pointed star motif, was maintained at a pleasantly fresh 72 degrees by the air-conditioned central heating. The temperature difference between the dining-room and the outside world was 105°F.

The range of excellently-cooked food was astonishing.

"Don't exactly starve themselves up here," he said as he returned with a mousse for each of them and a pitcher of heavy cream. "I wonder what any of the old Alaskan sourdoughs would have made of it."

The first reaction of a prospector or trapper of yesteryear would have been that he was suffering from hallucinations. All in all, it was hard to say what feature he would have found the most astonishing. Eighty per cent of the items on the menu would have been unknown to him. But he would have been still more amazed by the forty-foot swimming-pool and the glassed-in garden, with its pine-trees, birches, plants and profusion of flowers, that abutted on the dining-room.

"God knows what the old boy would have thought," said Dermott. "You might ask *him*, though." He indicated a man heading in their direction. "Jack London would have recognised this one right away."

Mackenzie said: "More the Robert Service type, I'd say."

The newcomer certainly wasn't of current vintage. He wore heavy felt boots, moleskin trousers and an incredibly faded mackinaw, which went well enough with the equally faded patches on the sleeves. A pair of sealskin gloves was suspended from his neck, and he carried a coonskin cap in his right hand. His hair was long and white and parted in the middle. He had a slightly hooked nose and clear blue eyes with deeply entrenched crow's feet, which could have been caused by too much sun, too much snow or a too highly developed sense of humour. The rest of his face was obscured by a magnificent grizzled beard and moustache, both of which were at that moment rimed by droplets of ice. The yellow hard hat swinging from his left hand struck a jarring note. He stopped at their table, and from the momentary flash of white teeth it could be assumed that he was smiling.

16

"Mr Dermott? Mr Mackenzie?" He offered his hand. "Finlayson. John Finlayson."

Dermott said: "Mr Finlayson. Field operations manager's office?"

"I *am* the field operations manager." He pulled out a chair, sat, sighed and removed some ice particles from his beard. "Yes, yes, I know. Hard to believe." He smiled again, gestured at his clothing. "Most people think I've been riding the rods. You know, hobo on the box-cars. God knows why. Nearest railroad track's a long, long way from Prudhoe Bay. Like Tahiti and grass skirts. You know, gone native. Too many years on the North Slope." His oddly staccato manner of speech was indeed suggestive of a person whose contact with civilisation was, at best, intermittent. "Sorry I couldn't make it. Meet you, I mean. Deadhorse."

Mackenzie said: "Deadhorse?"

"Airstrip. A little trouble at one of the gathering centres. Happens all the time. Sub-zero temperatures play hell with the molecular structure of steel. Being well taken care of, I hope?"

"No complaints." Dermott smiled. "Not that we require much care. There the food counter, here Mackenzie. The watering hole and the camel." Dermott checked himself: he was beginning to talk like Finlayson. "Well, one little complaint, perhaps. Too many items on the lunch menu, too large a helping of any item. My colleague's waist-line –"

"Your colleague's waist-line can take care of itself," Mackenzie said comfortably. "But I do have a complaint, Mr Finlayson."

"I can imagine." Another momentary flash of teeth, and Finlayson was on his feet. "Let's hear it in my office. Just a few steps." He walked across the dining-hall, stopped outside a door and indicated another door to the left. "Master operations control centre. The heart of Prudhoe Bay – or the western half of it, at least. All the computerised

17

process control facilities for the supervision of the field's operations."

Dermott said: "An enterprising lad with a satchelful of grenades could have himself quite a time in there."

"Five seconds, and he could close down the entire oilfield. Come all the way from Houston just to cheer me up? This way."

He led them through the outer door, then through an inner one to a small office. Desks, chairs and filing cabinets, all in metal, all in battleship grey. He gestured them to sit and smiled at Mackenzie. "As the French say, a meal without wine is like a day without sunshine."

"It's this Texas dust," Mackenzie said. "Sticks in the gullet like no other dust. Laughs at water."

Finlayson made a sweeping motion with his hand. "Some big rigs out there. Damned expensive and damned difficult to handle. It's pitch dark, say, forty below and you're tired – you're always tired up here. Don't forget we work twelve hours a day, seven days a week. A couple of Scotches on top of all that, and you've written off a million dollars' worth of equipment. Or you damage the pipeline. Or you kill yourself. Or, worst of all, you kill some of your mates. Comparatively, they had it easy in the old prohibition days – bulk smuggling from Canada, bath-tub gin, illicit stills by the thousand. Rather different on the North Slope here – get caught smuggling in a teaspoonful of liquor, and that's it. No argument, no court of appeal. Out. But there's no problem – no one is going to risk eight hundred dollars a week for ten cents' worth of bourbon."

Mackenzie said: "When's the next flight out to Anchorage?"

Finlayson smiled. "All is not lost, Mr Mackenzie." He unlocked a filing cabinet, produced a bottle of Scotch and two glasses and poured with a generous hand. "Welcome to the North Slope, gentlemen."

18

"I was having visions," said Mackenzie, "of travellers stranded in an Alpine blizzard and a St Bernard lolloping towards them with the usual restorative. You're not a drinking man?"

"Certainly. One week in five when I rejoin my family in Anchorage. This is strictly for visiting V.I.P.s. One would assume you qualify under that heading?" Thoughtfully, he mopped melting ice from his beard. "Though frankly, I never heard of your organisation until a couple of days ago."

"Think of us as desert roses," Mackenzie said. "Born to blush and bloom unseen. I think I've got that wrong, but the desert bit is appropriate enough. That's where we seem to spend most of our time." He nodded towards the window. "A desert doesn't have to be made of sand. I suppose this qualifies as an Arctic desert."

"I think of it that way myself. But what do you do in those deserts? Your function, I mean."

"Our function?" Dermott considered. "Oddly enough, I'd say our function is to reduce our worthy employer, Jim Brady, to a state of bankruptcy."

"*Jim* Brady? I thought his initial was A."

"His mother was English. She christened him Algernon. Wouldn't *you* object? He's always known as Jim. Anyway, there are only three people in the world any good at extinguishing oil-field fires, particularly gusher fires, and all three are Texas-based. Jim Brady's one of the three.

"It used to be commonly accepted that there are just three causes of such oil fires: spontaneous combustion, which should never happen but does; the human factor, i.e. sheer carelessness; and mechanical failure. After twenty-five years in the business Brady recognised that there was a fourth and more sinister element involved, that would come broadly speaking under the heading of industrial sabotage."

19

"Who would engage in sabotage? What would the motivation be?"

"Well we can rule out the most obvious – rivalry among the big oil companies. It doesn't exist. This notion of cut-throat competition exists only in the sensational press and among the more feeble-minded of the public. To be a fly on the wall at a closed meeting of the oil lobby in Washington is to understand once and for all the meaning of the expression 'two minds with but a single thought, two hearts that beat as one'. Multiplied by twenty, of course. Let Exxon put up the price of gas by a penny today, and Gulf, Shell, B.P., Elf, Agip and all the others will do the same tomorrow. Or even take Prudhoe Bay here. The classic example, surely, of co-operation – umpteen companies working hand-in-glove for the mutual benefit of all concerned: benefit of all the oil companies, that is. The State of Alaska and the general public might adopt a rather different and more jaundiced viewpoint.

"So we rule out business rivalries. This leaves another kind of energy. Power. International power politics. Say Country X could seriously weaken enemy Country Y by slowing down its oil revenues. That's one obvious scenario. Then there's *internal* power politics. Suppose disaffected elements in an oil-rich dictatorship see a means of demonstrating their dissatisfaction against a régime that clasps the ill-gotten gains to its mercenary bosom or, at best, distributes some measure of the largesse to its nearest and dearest, while ensuring that the peasantry remains in the properly medieval state of poverty. Starvation does nicely as motivation, this kind of set-up leaves room for personal revenge, the settling of old scores, the working off of old grudges.

"And don't forget the pyromaniac who sees in oil a ludicrously easy target and the source of lovely flames. In short, there's room for practically everything, and the more bizarre and unimaginable, the more likely to happen. A case in point."

He nodded at Mackenzie. "Donald and I have just returned from the Gulf. The local security men and the police were baffled by an outbreak of small fires – small, so-called, but with damage totalling two million dollars. Clearly the work of an arsonist. We tracked him down, apprehended him, and punished him. We gave him a bow and arrow."

Finlayson looked at them as if their Scotch had taken hold too quickly.

"Eleven-year-old son of the British consul. He had a powerful Webley air pistol. Webley make the traditional ammunition for this – hollow, concave lead pellets. They do *not* make pellets of hardened steel, which give off a splendid spark when they strike ferrous metal. This lad had a plentiful supply obtained from a local Arab boy who had a similar pistol and used those illegal pellets for hunting desert vermin. Incidentally, the Arab boy's old man, a prince of the blood royal, owned the oilfield in question. The English boy's arrows have rubber tips."

"I'm sure there's a moral there somewhere."

"Sure, there's a lesson: the unpredictable is always with you. Our industrial sabotage division – that's Jim Brady's term for it – was formed six years ago. There are fourteen of us in it. At first it was as a purely investigative agency. We went to a place after the deed had been done and the fire put out – as often as not it was Jim who put it out – and tried to find out who had done it, why, and what his *modus operandi* had been. Frankly, we had very limited success: usually the horse had gone, and all we were doing was locking the empty stable door.

"Now the emphasis has changed – we try to lock the damned door in such a fashion that no-one can open it. In other words, prevention: the maximum tightening of both mechanical and human security. The response to this service has been remarkable – we're now the most profitable side of Jim's operations. By far. Capping off runaway wells, putting fires out, can't hold a candle, if you'll pardon the expression, to our security work. Such is the demand for our services that we could triple our division and still not cope with all the calls being made upon us."

"Well, why don't you? Triple the business, I mean."

"Trained personnel," Mackenzie said. "Just not there. More accurately, there are next to no experienced operatives and there's an almost total dearth of people qualified to be trained for the job. The combination of qualifications is difficult to come by. You have to have an investigative mind, and that in turn is based on an inborn instinct for detection – the Sherlock Holmes genes, shall we say. You've either got it or not: it can't be inculcated. You have to have an eye and a nose for security, an *obsession*, almost – and this can only come from field experience; you have to have a pretty detailed knowledge of the oil industry world-wide: and, above all, you have to be an oilman."

"And you gentlemen are oilmen." It was a statement, not a question.

"All our working lives," Dermott said. "We've both been field operations managers."

"If your services are in such demand, how come we should be so lucky as to jump to the head of the queue?"

Dermott said: "As far as we know this is the first time that any oil company has received notification of *intent* to sabotage. First real chance we've had to try out our preventive medicine. We're just slightly puzzled on one point, Mr Finlayson. You say you never heard of us until a couple of days ago. How come that we're here, then? I mean, we knew of this three days ago when we arrived back from the Mid East. We spent a day resting up, another day

22

studying the layout and security measures of the Alaskan pipeline and –"

"You did that, eh? Isn't it classified information?"

Dermott was patient. "We could have sent for it immediately on receiving the request for assistance. We didn't have to. The information, Mr Finlayson, is not classified. It's in the public domain. Big companies tend to be incredibly careless about such matters. Whether to reassure the public or burnish their own image by taking thorough-going precautions, they not only release large chunks of information about their activities but positively bombard the public with them. The information, of course, comes in disparate and apparently unrelated lumps: it requires only a moderately intelligent fella to piece them all together.

"Not that those big companies, such as Alyeska, who built your pipeline, have much to reproach themselves about. They don't even begin to operate in the same league of indiscretion as the all-time champs, the U.S. Government. Take the classic example of the de-classification of the secret of the atom bomb. When the Russians got the bomb, the Government thought there was no point in being secretive any more and proceeded to tell all. You want to know how to make an atom bomb? Just send a pittance to the A.E.C. in Washington and you'll have the necessary information by return mail. That this information could be used by Americans against Americans apparently never occurred to the towering intellects of Capitol Hill and the Pentagon, who seem to have been under the impression that the American criminal classes voluntarily retired *en masse* on the day of de-classification."

Finlayson raised a defensive hand. "Hold. Enough. I accept that you haven't infiltrated Prudhoe Bay with a battalion of spies. Answer's simple. When I received this unpleasant letter – it was sent to *me*, not to our H.Q. in Anchorage – I talked to the general manager, Alaska. We

23

both agreed that it was almost certainly a hoax. Still, I regret to say that many Alaskans aren't all that kindly disposed towards us. We also agreed that if it was *not* a hoax, it could be something very serious indeed. People like us, although we're well enough up the ladder in our own fields, don't take final decisions on the safety and future of a ten-billion-dollar investment. So we notified the grand panjandrums. Your directive came from London. Informing me of their decision must have come as an afterthought."

"Head offices being what they are," Dermott said. "Got this threatening note here?"

Finlayson retrieved a single sheet of notepaper from a drawer and passed it across.

"'My dear Mr Finlayson'," Dermott read. "Well, that's civil enough. 'I have to inform you that you will be incurring a slight spillage of oil in the near future. Not much, I assure you, just sufficient to convince you that we can interrupt oil flow whenever and wherever we please. Please notify ARCO'."

Dermott shoved the letter across to Mackenzie. "Understandably unsigned. No demands. If this is genuine, it's intended as a softening-up demonstration in preparation for the big threat and big demand that will follow. A morale-sapper, if you will, designed to scare the pants off you."

Finlayson's gaze was on the middle distance. "I'm not so sure he hasn't done that already."

"You notified ARCO?"

"Yup. Oilfield's split more or less half-and-half. We run the western sector. ARCO – Atlantic Richfield, Exxon, some smaller groups – they run the eastern sector."

"What's their reaction?"

"Like mine. Hope for the best, prepare for the worst."

"Your security chief. What's his reaction?"

"Downright pessimistic. It's his baby, after all. If I were in his shoes I'd feel the same way. He's convinced of the genuineness of this threat."

"Me too," Dermott said. "This came in an envelope? Ah, thank you." He read the address. "'Mr John Finlayson, B.Sc., A.M.I.M.E.'. Not only punctilious, but they've done their homework on you. 'B.P./Sohio, Prudhoe Bay, Alaska'. Postmarked Edmonton, Alberta. That mean anything to you?"

"Nary a thing. I have neither friends nor acquaintances there, and certainly no business contacts."

"Your security chief's reaction?"

"Same as mine. Zero."

"What's his name?"

"Bronowski. Sam Bronowski."

"Let's have him in, shall we?"

"You'll have to wait, I'm afraid. He's down in Fairbanks. Back tonight, if the weather holds up. Depends on visibility."

"Blizzard season?"

"We don't have one. Precipitation on the North Slope is very low, maybe six inches in a winter. High winds are the bugaboo. They blow up the surface snow so that the air can be completely opaque for thirty or forty feet above the ground. Just before Christmas a few years ago a Hercules, normally the safest of aircraft, tried to land in those conditions. Didn't make it. Two of the crew of four killed. Pilots have become a bit leery since – if a Hercules can buy it, any aircraft can. These high winds and the surface snowstorms they generate – that snow can be driving along at 70 miles an hour – are the bane of our existence up here. That's why this operations centre is built on pilings seven feet above ground – let the snow blow right underneath. Otherwise we'd end the winter season buried under a massive drift. The pilings, of course, also virtually eliminate heat transfer to the permafrost, but that's secondary."

"What's Bronowski doing in Fairbanks?"

"Stiffening the thin red line. Hiring extra security guards for Fairbanks."

"How does he set about that?"

"Approach varies, I suppose. Really Bronowski's department, Mr Dermott. He has *carte blanche* in those matters. I suggest you ask him on his return."

"Oh, come on. You're his boss. He's a subordinate. Bosses keep tabs on their subordinates. Roughly, how does he recruit?"

"Well. He's probably built up a list of people whom he's personally contacted and who might be available in a state of emergency. I'm honestly not sure about this. I may be his boss, but when I delegate responsibility I do just that. I do know that he approaches the chief of police and asks for suitable recommendations. He may or may not have put in an ad. in the *All-Alaska Weekly* – that's published in Fairbanks." Finlayson thought briefly. "I wouldn't say he's deliberately close-mouthed about this. I suppose when you've been a security man all your life you naturally don't let your left hand know what the right hand's doing."

"What kind of men does he recruit?"

"Almost all ex-cops – you know, ex-State troopers."

"But not trained security men?"

"As such, no, although I'd have thought security would have come as second nature to a State trooper." Finlayson smiled. "I imagine Sam's principal criterion is whether the man can shoot straight."

"Security's a mental thing, not physical. You said 'almost all'."

"He's brought in two first-class security agents from outside. One's stationed at Fairbanks, the other at Valdez."

"Who says they're first class?"

"Sam. He hand-picked them." Finlayson rubbed his drying beard in what could have been a gesture of irritation.

"You know, Mr Dermott, friendly, even genial you may be, but I have the odd impression that I'm being third-degreed."

"Rubbish. If that were happening, you'd know all about it, because I'd be asking you questions about yourself. I've no intention of doing so, now or in the future."

"You wouldn't be having a dossier on me, would you?"

"Tuesday, September 5, 1939, was the day and date you entered your secondary school in Dundee, Scotland."

"Jesus!"

"What's so sensitive about the Fairbanks area? Why strengthen your defences there particularly?"

Finlayson shifted in his seat. "No hard and fast reason, really."

"Never mind whether it's hard and fast. The reason?"

Finlayson drew in his breath as if he were about to sigh, then seemed to change his mind. "Bit silly, really. You know how whisperings can generate a hoodoo. People on the line are a bit scared of that sector. You'll know that the pipeline has three mountain ranges to traverse on its 800-mile run south to the terminal at Valdez. So, pump stations twelve in all. Pump Station No. 8 is close to Fairbanks. It blew up in the summer of '77. Completely destroyed."

"Fatalities?"

"Yes."

"Explanations given for this blow-up?"

"Of course."

"Satisfactory?"

"The pipeline construction company – Alyeska – were satisfied."

"But not everyone?"

"The public was sceptical. State and Federal agencies withheld comment."

"What reason did Alyeska give?"

"Mechanical and electrical malfunction."

"Do *you* believe that?"

27

"I wasn't there."

"The explanation was generally accepted?"

"The explanation was widely disbelieved."

"Sabotage, perhaps?"

"Perhaps. I don't know. I was here at the time. I've never even seen Pump Station No. 8. Been rebuilt, of course."

Dermott sighed. "This is where I should be showing some slight traces of exasperation. Don't believe in committing yourself, do you, Mr Finlayson? Still, you'd probably make a good security agent. I don't suppose you'd like to venture an opinion as to whether there was a cover-up or not?"

"My opinion hardly matters. What matters, I suppose, is that the Alaskan press was damned certain there was, and said so loud and clear. The fact that the papers appeared unconcerned about the possibility of libel action could be regarded as significant. They would have welcomed a public enquiry: one assumes that Alyeska would not have."

"Why were the newspapers stirred up – or is that an unnecessary question?"

"What incensed the press was that they were prevented for many hours from reaching the scene of the accident. What doubly incensed them was that they were prevented not by peace officers of the State but by Alyeska's private guards, who, incredibly, took it upon themselves to close State roads. Even their local PR man agreed that this amounted to illegal restraint."

"Anybody sue?"

"No court action resulted."

"Why?"

When Finlayson shrugged, Dermott went on: "Could it have been because Alyeska is the biggest employer in the State, because the lifeblood of so many companies depends on their contracts with Alyeska? In other words, big money talking big?"

"Possibly."

28

"Any minute now I'll be signing you up for Jim Brady. What *did* the press say?"

"Because they'd been prevented for a whole day from getting to the scene of the accident, they believed Alyeska employees had been working feverishly during that time to clean up and minimise the effects of the accident, to remove the evidence of a major spillage and to conceal the fact that their fail-safe system had failed dangerously. Alyeska had also – the press said – covered up the worst effects of the fire damage."

"Might they also have removed or covered up incriminating evidence pointing to sabotage?"

"No guessing games for me."

"All right. Do you or Bronowski know of any disaffected elements in Fairbanks?"

"Depends what you mean by disaffected. If you mean environmentalists opposed to the construction of the pipeline, yes. Hundreds, and very strongly opposed."

"But they're open about it, I assume – always give their full names and addresses when writing to the papers."

"Yes."

"Besides, environmentalists tend to be sensitive and non-violent people who work within the confines of the law."

"About any other disaffected types, I wouldn't know. There are fifteen thousand people in Fairbanks, and it would be optimistic to expect they're all as pure as the driven snow."

"What did Bronowski think of the incident?"

"He wasn't there."

"That wasn't what I asked . . ."

"He was in New York at the time. He hadn't even joined the company then."

"A relative newcomer, then?"

"Yes. In your book, I suppose that automatically makes him a villain. If you wish to go ahead and waste your time

29

investigating his antecedents, by all means do so, but I could save you time and effort by telling you that we had him checked, double-checked and triple-checked by three separate top-flight agencies. The New York Police Department gave him a clean bill of health. His record and that of his company are – were – impeccable."

"I don't doubt it. What were his qualifications, and what was his company?"

"One and the same thing, really. He headed up one of the biggest and arguably the best security agencies in New York. Before that he was a cop."

"What did his company specialise in?"

"Nothing but the best. Guards, mainly. Additional guards for a handful of the biggest banks when their own security forces were under-staffed by holidays or illness. Guarding the homes of the richest people in Manhattan and Long Island to prevent the ungodly making off with the guests' jewellery when large-scale social functions were being held. His third speciality was providing security for exhibitions of precious gems and paintings. If you could ever persuade the Dutch to lend you Rembrandt's 'Night Watch' for a couple of months, Bronowski would be the man you'd send for."

"What would induce a man to leave all that and come to this end of the world?"

"He doesn't say. He doesn't have to. Homesickness. More specifically, his wife's homesickness. She lives in Anchorage. He flies down there every weekend."

"I thought you were supposed to do a full four weeks up here before you got time off."

"Doesn't apply to Bronowski – only to those whose permanent job is here. This is his nominal base, but the whole line is his responsibility. For instance, if there's trouble in Valdez, he's a damn sight nearer it in his wife's flat in Anchorage than he would be if he were up here. And he's very mobile, is our Sam. Owns and flies his own Comanche. We pay his fuel, that's all."

"He's not without the odd penny to his name?"

"I should say not. He doesn't really need this job, but he can't bear to be inactive. Money? He retains the controlling interest in his New York firm."

"No conflict of interests?"

"How the hell could there be a conflict of interests? He's never even been out of the State since he arrived here over a year ago."

"A trustworthy lad, it would seem. Damn few of them around these days." Dermott looked at Mackenzie. "Donald?"

"Yes?" Mackenzie picked up the unsigned letter from Edmonton. "F.B.I. seen this?"

"Of course not. What's it got to do with the F.B.I.?"

"It might have an awful lot to do with them, and soon. I know Alaskans think that this is a nation apart, that this is your own special and private fiefdom up here, and that you refer to us unfortunates as the lower 48, but you're still part of the United States. When the oil from here arrives at Valdez, it's shipped to one of the west-coast states. Any interruption in oil transfer between Prudhoe Bay and, say, California, would be regarded as an unlawful interference with inter-state commerce and would automatically bring in the F.B.I."

"Well, it hasn't happened yet. Besides, what can the F.B.I. do? They know nothing of oil or pipeline security. Look after the pipeline? They couldn't even look after themselves. We'd just spend most of our time trying to thaw out the few of them that didn't freeze to death during their first ten minutes here. They could only survive under cover, so what could they do there? Take over our computer terminals and master communications and alarm detection stations at Prudhoe Bay, Fairbanks and Valdez? We have highly trained specialists to monitor over three thousand sources of alarm information. Asking the F.B.I. to do that would be like asking a blind man to read Sanskrit. Inside or out, they'd only be in the way and a useless burden to all concerned."

"Alaska State Troopers could survive. I guess they'd survive where even some of your own men couldn't. Have you been in touch with them? Have you notified the State authorities in Juneau?"

"No."

"Why not?"

"They don't love us. Oh, sure, if there was physical trouble, violence, they'd move in immediately. Until then, they'd rather not know. I can't say I blame them. And before you ask me why I'll tell you. For good or bad we've inherited the Alyeska mantle. Alyeska built the pipeline and they run it; but we use it. I'm afraid there's a wide grey area of non-discrimination here. In most people's eyes they *were* pipeline, we *are* pipeline."

Finlayson reflected on his next words. "It's hard not to feel a bit sorry for Alyeska. They were pretty cruelly pilloried. Sure, they bore the responsibility for a remarkable amount of waste, and incurred vast cost over-runs, but they did complete an impossible job in impossible conditions and, what's more, brought it in on schedule. Best construction company in North America at the time. Brilliant engineering and brilliant engineers – but the brilliance stopped short of their PR people, who might as well have been operating in downtown Manhattan for all they knew about Alaskans. Their job should have been to sell the pipeline to the people: all they succeeded in doing was in turning a large section of the population solidly against the line and the construction company."

He shook his head. "You had to be truly gifted to get it as wrong as they did. They sought to protect the good name of

Alyeska, but all they did, by blatant cover-ups – it was alleged – and by deliberate lying, was to bring whatever good name there was into total disrepute."

Finlayson reached into a drawer, took out two sheets of paper and gave them to Dermott and Mackenzie. "Photostats of a classic example of the way they handle those under contract to them. One would assume they learnt their trade in one of the more repressive police states. Read it. You'll find it instructive. You'll also understand how by simple thought-transference we're not in line for much public sympathy."

The two men read the Photostats.

Alyeska Pipeline Service Company	Supplement No. 20
Pipeline and Roads	Revision No. 1
Job Specification	April 1, 1974
	Page 2004

C. IN NO EVENT SHALL CONTRACTOR OR ITS PERSONNEL REPORT A LEAK OR AN OIL SPILL TO ANY GOVERNMENTAL AGENCY. Such reporting shall be the sole responsibility of ALYESKA. CONTRACTOR shall emphasise this to all its supervisory personnel and employees.

D. Further IN NO EVENT SHALL CONTRACTOR OR ITS PERSONNEL DISCUSS, REPORT, OR COMMUNICATE IN ANY WAY WITH NEWS MEDIA whether the news media be radio, television, newspapers or periodicals. Any such communication by CONTRACTOR shall be deemed to be a material breach of CONTRACT by CONTRACTOR. All contacts with news media regarding leaks or oil spills shall be made by Alyeska. If news media people contact CONTRACTOR or CONTRACTOR's personnel they shall refer news media to Alyeska without further discussing, reporting or communicating. CONTRACTOR shall emphasise the aforementioned ALYESKA news media requirements to all its supervisory personnel and employees.

Dermott rested the Photostat on his knee. "An *American* wrote this?"

"An American of foreign extraction," Mackenzie said "who obviously trained under Goebbels."

"A charming directive," Dermott said. "Hush-up, cover-up or lose your contract. Toe the line or you're fired. A shining example of American democracy at its finest. Well, well." He glanced briefly at the paper, then at Finlayson. "How did you get hold of this? Classified information, surely?"

"Oddly enough, no. What you would call the public domain. Editorial page, *All-Alaska Weekly*, July 22, 1977. I don't question it *was* classified. How the paper got hold of it, I don't know."

"Nice to see a little paper going against the might of a giant company and getting off with it. Restores one's faith in something or other."

Finlayson picked up another Photostat. "The same editorial also made a despairing reference to the 'horrendous negative impact of the pipeline on us'. That's as true now as it was then. We've inherited this horrendous negative impact, and we're still suffering from it. So there it is. I'm not saying we're entirely friendless, or that the authorities wouldn't move in quickly if there were any overt violations of the law. But, because votes are important, those in charge of our destinies rule from behind: they sense the wind of public opinion, then enact acceptable legislation and adopt correspondingly safe attitudes. Whatever happens, they're not going to antagonise those who keep them in power. They are not, with the public's eye on both them and us, going to come and hold our hands because of any anonymous threat by some anonymous crackpot."

Mackenzie said: "So it amounts to this: until actual sabotage occurs, you can expect no outside help. So far as preventative measures are concerned, you're dependent solely upon Bronowski and his security teams. In effect, you're on your own."

"It's an unhappy thought, but there it is."

Dermott stood up and walked back and forth. "Accepting this threat as real, who's behind it and what does he want? Not a crackpot, that's sure. If it were, say, some environmentalist running amok, he'd go ahead and do his damnedest without any prior warning. No, could be with a view to extortion or blackmail, which do not have to be the same thing: extortion would be for money, blackmail could have many different purposes in mind. Stopping the flow of oil is unlikely to be the primary purpose: more likely, it'll be a stoppage for another and more important purpose. Money, politics – local or international – power, misguided idealism, genuine idealism or just crackpot irresponsibility. Well, I'm afraid speculation will have to wait on developments. Meantime, Mr Finlayson, I'd like to see Bronowski as soon as possible."

"I told you, he has business to finish. He'll be flying up in a few hours."

"Ask him to fly up now, please."

"Sorry. Bronowski's his own man. Overall, he's answerable to me, but not in field operations. He'd walk out if I tried to usurp his authority. Unless he had the power to act independently, he'd be effectively hamstrung. You don't hire a dog and bark yourself."

"I don't think you quite understand. Mr Mackenzie and I have not only been promised total co-operation: we've been empowered to direct security measures if, in our judgment, such extreme measures are dictated by circumstances."

Finlayson's Yukon beard still masked his expression, but there was no mistaking the disbelief in his voice. "You mean, take over from Bronowski?"

"If, again in our judgment, he's good enough, we just sit by the sidelines and advise. If not, we will exercise the authority invested in us."

"Invested in whom? This is preposterous. I will not, I

35

cannot permit it. You walk in here and imagine – no, no way. I have received no such directive."

"Then I suggest you seek such a directive, or confirmation of it, immediately."

"From whom?"

"The grand panjandrums, as you call them."

"London?" Dermott said nothing. "That's for Mr Black."

Dermott remained silent.

"General manager, Alaska."

Dermott nodded at the three telephones on Finlayson's desk. "He's as far away as one of those."

"He's out of State. He's visiting our offices in Seattle, San Francisco and Los Angeles. At what times and in what order I don't know. I do know he'll be back in Anchorage at noon tomorrow."

"Are you telling me that is the soonest you can – or will – contact him?"

"Yes."

"You could phone those offices."

"I've told you, I don't know where he'd be. He could be at some other place altogether. Like as not he's in the air."

"You could try, couldn't you?" Finlayson remained silent and Dermott spoke again. "You could call London direct."

"You don't know much about the hierarchy in oil companies, do you?"

"No. But I know this." Now Dermott's customary geniality was gone. "You're a considerable disappointment, Finlayson. You are, or very well may be, in serious trouble. In the circumstances, one does not expect an executive in top management to resort to stiff outrage and wounded pride. You've got your priorities wrong, my friend – the good of the company comes first, not your feelings or protecting your ass."

Finlayson's eyes showed no expression. Mackenzie was

staring at the ceiling as if he had found something of absorbing interest there: Dermott, he had learned over the years, was a past-master of penning an adversary into a corner. The victim either surrendered or placed himself in an impossible situation of which Dermott would take ruthless advantage. If he couldn't get co-operation, he would settle for nothing less than domination.

Dermott went on: "I have made three requests, all of which I regard as perfectly reasonable, and you have refused all three. You persist in your refusals?"

"Yes, I do."

Dermott said: "Well, Donald, what are my options?"

"There are none." Mackenzie sounded sad. "Only the inevitable."

"Yes." Dermott looked at Finlayson coldly. "You have a radio microwave band to Valdez that links up with the continental exchanges." He pushed a card towards Finlayson. "Or would you refuse me permission to talk to my head office in Houston?"

Finlayson said nothing. He took the card, lifted the phone and talked to the switchboard. After three minutes' silence, which only Finlayson seemed to find uncomfortable, the phone rang. Finlayson listened briefly then handed over the phone.

Dermott said: "Brady Enterprises? Mr Brady please, Dermott." There was a pause, then: "Good afternoon, Jim."

"Well, well, George." Brady's strong carrying voice was clearly audible in the office. "Prudhoe Bay, is it? Coincidence, coincidence. I was just on the point of phoning you."

"Well. My report, Jim. News, rather. There's nothing to report."

"And I have news for you. Mine first, it's more important. Open line?"

"One moment." Dermott looked at Finlayson. "What

security classification does your switchboard operator have?"

"None. Jesus, she's only a telephone girl."

"As you rightly observe, Jesus! Heaven help the trans-Alaskan pipeline." He pulled out a notebook and pencil and addressed the phone. "Sorry, Jim. Open. Go ahead."

In a clear, precise voice Brady began to recite a seemingly meaningless jumble of letters and figures which Dermott noted down in neatly printed script. After about two minutes Brady paused and said: "Repeat?"

"No thanks."

"You have something to say?"

"Just this. Field manager here uncooperative, unreasonable and obstructive. I don't think we can profitably operate here. Permission to pull out."

There was only a brief pause before Brady said clearly: "Permission granted." There came the click of a replaced receiver and Dermott rose to his feet.

Finlayson was already on his. "Mr Dermott –"

Dermott looked down at him icily and spoke in a voice as cold as winter: "Give my love to London, Mr Finlayson. If you're ever there."

2

Thirteen hundred miles south-east of Prudhoe Bay, at ten p.m., Brady's men met Jay Shore in the bar of the Peter Pond Hotel in Fort McMurray. Among those qualified to pass judgment on such matters, it was readily agreed that as an engineering construction manager Shore had no peer in Canada. His face was dark, saturnine, almost piratical – which was rather an unfair trick for nature to play on him, since that same nature had made him easy-going, companionable, humorous and cheerful.

Not that he felt in the least humorous and cheerful at that moment. Nor did the man who sat beside him, Bill Reynolds, Sanmobil's operations manager, a rubicund and normally smiling man to whom nature had given precisely the kind of diabolical mind that Shore appeared to have but didn't.

Bill Reynolds looked across the table to Dermott and Mackenzie, whom he and Shore had met thirty seconds previously, and said: "You make fast time, gentlemen. Remarkable service, if one may say so."

"We try," Dermott said comfortably. "We do our best."

"Scotch?" asked Mackenzie.

"Thanks." Reynolds nodded. "Twin jet – is that it?"

"Right."

"A shade expensive, a man would think."

"Gets you around." Dermott smiled.

"Head Office – that's Edmonton – told us you might take up to four days. We didn't expect you in four *hours*." Reynolds eyed Dermott speculatively over his newly-poured glass. "I'm afraid we don't know much about you."

"Fair enough. We probably know even less about you."

"Not oilmen, then?"

"Of course. But drilling oilmen. We're not familiar with mining the stuff."

"And your full-time job's security?"

"That's right."

"So there's no need to ask what you were doing up on the North Slope?"

"Right again."

"How long were you up there?"

"Two hours."

"Two hours! You mean you can lick a security –"

"We licked nothing. We left."

"May one ask why?"

"Operations manager was . . . unhelpful, let's say."

"Me and my big mouth."

"Meaning?"

"I'm the operations manager here. But I get the message."

Dermott said pleasantly: "No message. You asked a question, I answered."

"And you decided to walk out –"

"We have a backlog of cases all over the world, and no time to waste trying to help those who won't help themselves. Let's not get off on the wrong foot, gentlemen: your company expects Mackenzie and myself to do the questioning while you do the answering. When was this threat received?"

Shore said: "Ten o'clock this morning."

"You have it with you?"

"Not exactly. It came by phone."

"Where from?"

"Anchorage. International call."

"Who took the message?"

"I did Bill here was with me, listening in. Caller gave us

his message twice. Word for word he said: 'I have to inform you that Sanmobil will be incurring a slight interruption in oil production in the near future. Not much, I assure you, just sufficient to convince you that we can interrupt oil flow whenever and wherever we please.' That was all."

"No demands?"

"No – surprisingly."

"Don't worry. The demands will come when the big threat does. Would you recognise this voice again?"

"Would I recognise the voices of a million other Canadians who talk exactly as he does? You take this threat seriously?"

"I do. We take most things seriously. How good is security at the plant?"

"Well – fair enough for normal circumstances. I suppose."

"These promise to be highly abnormal circumstances. How many guards?"

"Twenty-four, under Terry Brinckman. He knows what he's doing."

"I don't doubt it. Guard dogs?"

"None. The usual police dogs – Alsatians, Dobermans, boxers – can't survive in these extreme conditions. Huskies can, of course, but they make lousy watch-dogs – they're more interested in fighting each other than looking for intruders."

"Electric fences?"

Shore rolled his eyes upwards and looked sorrowful. "You want to equip the environmentalists with a gallows right on the site? Why, if even the meanest old wolf were to singe its mangy hide . . ."

"Okay, okay. I suppose it's pointless to ask about electronic beams, sensor devices and the like?"

"Pointless is right."

Mackenzie said: "How big is this plant site?"

41

Reynolds looked unhappy. "About eight thousand acres."

"Eight thousand acres." Mackenzie's voice was all doom. "What kind of perimeter would that make for?"

"Fourteen miles."

"Yes. We have a problem here," Mackenzie said. "I take it your security duties are twofold: the guarding of vital installations in the plant itself and patrolling the perimeter to keep intruders out?"

Reynolds nodded. "The guards are in three shifts, eight men per shift."

"Eight men, without any protective aids at all, to guard the plant itself and at the same time patrol fourteen miles of perimeter in the blackness of a winter night."

Shore was defensive. "Ours is a 24-hour operation. The plant is brilliantly lit day and night."

"But the perimeter isn't. A blind man could drive a coach and four – hell, why go on? A couple of army regiments might help, although I doubt even that. As I say, a problem."

"Not only that," Dermott said. "All the brilliant illumination in the world isn't of the slightest help. Not when you've got hundreds of workers on each of the three shifts a day."

"Meaning?"

"Subversives."

"Subversives! Less than two per cent of the work-force are non-Canadians."

"There's been a royal decree abolishing Canadian criminals? When you hire, you investigate backgrounds?"

"Well, not intensive questioning, third degree, lie-detector tests or any of that rubbish. Try that and you'd never hire anyone. We check on previous experience, qualifications, recommendations, and, most important, criminal records."

"That's the least important. Really clever criminals never *have* criminal records." Dermott looked like a man who had

42

been about to sigh, explode, curse, or quit, but had changed his mind. "Well – it's late. Tomorrow, Mr Mackenzie and I would like to talk to your Terry Brinckman and look over the plant."

"If we have a car here at ten o'clock –"

"How about seven o'clock? Yes, seven will be fine."

Dermott and Mackenzie watched the two men go, looked at each other, emptied their glasses, signalled the barman, then looked out through the windows of the Peter Pond Hotel, named after the first white man ever to see the Tar Sands.

Pond went down the Athabasca River by canoe almost exactly two hundred years before. He did not take too much interest in the sands, it appears, but ten years later the much more famous explorer Alexander MacKenzie was intrigued by the sticky substance oozing from outcrops high above the river, and wrote: "The bitumen is in a fluid state, and when mixed with gum, or the resinous substance collected from the spruce fir, serves to gum the Indians' canoes. In its heated state it emits a smell like that of sea-coal."

Oddly, the significance of the words "sea-coal" wasn't appreciated for more than a hundred years; nobody realised that the two 18th-century explorers had stumbled across one of the world's largest reservoirs of fossil fuels. But had they not so stumbled, there would have been no Peter Pond Hotel where it is today nor, indeed, the township beyond its windows.

Even in the mid-nineteen-sixties Fort McMurray was little more than a rough, primitive frontier outpost, with a population of only thirteen hundred and streets covered with dust, mud or slush according to season. By now, though still a frontier town, it had become a frontier town with a difference. Treasuring its past, but with an eye to the future, it was the epitome of a boom-town and, in terms of burgeoning population, the fastest-expanding township in

43

Canada. Where there were thirteen hundred citizens fourteen years earlier, there were thirteen thousand. Schools, hotels, banks, hospitals, churches, super-markets and, above all, hundreds of new houses were or were being built. And, wonder of wonders, the streets were paved. This seeming miracle stems from one factor and one factor only: Fort McMurray sits squarely in the heart of the Athabasca Tar Sands, the biggest such known deposits in the world.

It had been snowing heavily earlier in the evening and had still not completely stopped. Everything – houses, streets, car-tops, trees – was under a smoothly unbroken cover of white. Hundreds of lights shone hospitably through the gently falling flakes. The scene would have gladdened the eye and heart of a Christmas postcard artist. Some such thought had occurred to Mackenzie.

"Santa Claus should be here tonight."

"Indeed." Dermott sounded morose. "Especially if he brought along some of that peace on earth and goodwill to all men. What did you make of that telephone message to Sanmobil?"

"Same thing you did. Practically identical to the letter Finlayson received up in Prudhoe Bay. Obviously the work of the same man or group of men."

"And what do you make of the fact that Alaskan oil people got a threatening message from Alberta, while the Albertan oil interests received the same threat from Alaska?"

"Nothing – except that both threats had the same origin. That call from Anchorage. For a certainty, from a public call-box. Untraceable."

"Probably. Not certainly. I don't know if you can dial direct from Anchorage to here. I don't think so, but we can find out. If not, the telephone operator will have a record. There's a chance that we might locate the phone."

44

Mackenzie briefly surveyed Fort McMurray through the base of his glass and said: "That'll be a big help."

"It might be a small help. Two ways. That call came in at ten this morning. That's 6 a.m. Anchorage time. Who except a nut – or some night-shift worker – is going to be out in the black and freezing streets of Anchorage at that hour? That sort of odd behaviour, I suggest, isn't likely to go unnoticed."

"If there's anyone there to notice."

"State Troopers in a patrol car. Taxi driver. Snow-plough driver. Mailman on the way to work. You'd be surprised the number of people who go about their lawful occasions in the dark watches of the night."

"I would not be surprised." Mackenzie spoke with some feeling. "We've done it often enough in this damned job of ours. Two ways, you said. What's the second way?"

"*If* we locate this pay-phone, we have the police who have the post office remove the coin box and give it to their finger-print boys. The chances are good that the person who made the call to Fort McMurray used more high-denomination coins than anyone else who went into the pay-box that day – or night. Get two or three large coins with the same prints, and that's our man."

"Objection. Coins are handled by many people. You'll get prints, all right, a plethora, shall we say, of fingerprints."

"Objection overruled. It's established that on a metal surface the overlay, the last person to touch such a surface, leaves the dominant print. By the same token, we'd print the area round the dial. People don't dial in fur mittens. Then we'd check with criminal records. The prints may be on file. If they are, we'll get the man and ask him all sorts of interesting questions."

"You do have a devious mind, George. Low cunning, but albeit a mind. First catch your man, though."

"If we get a description or prints with history, it shouldn't be too difficult. If he's gone to ground, it would be different. But there's no reason why he should think he has to take cover. Might be awkward for him anyway: may well be a pillar of the Anchorage business and social communities."

"I'll bet the other Anchorage pillars would love to hear you say that. They'd have the same opinion of you as our friend, John Finlayson, has now. What are we going to do about Finlayson, anyway? *Rapprochement* doesn't seem advisable: it's essential. With the tie-up so obvious –"

"Let him stew in his own juice for a while. I don't mean that the way it sounds. But just let him worry a while in Prudhoe Bay until we're ready. He's a good man, intelligent, honest. He reacted precisely the way you or I would have if a couple of interlopers had tried to take over. The longer we stay away, the more certainly we're guaranteed his co-operation when we get back. Jim Brady may have been the bearer of bad news, but that call of his couldn't have come at a more opportune time. Gave us the perfect excuse to make off. Speaking of Jim –"

"I've been thinking that I don't much like any of this. Presentiments. My Scottish forebears, one presumes. You know that Prudhoe Bay and this place here contain well over half the oil reserves of North America. It's an awful lot of oil. A man wouldn't want anything to happen to them."

"You haven't worried about such things before. An investigator is supposed to be cold, clinical, detached."

"That's about other people's oil. This is *our* oil. Massive responsibilities. Awesome decisions at the highest levels."

"We were talking of Jim Brady."

"I still am."

"You think we should have him up here?"

"I do."

"So do I. Must be why I raised the subject. Let's go call him."

46

3

Jim Brady, that passionate believer in leanness, keenness, fitness and athleticism for his field operatives, stood five feet eight in his elevator shoes and turned the scales at around 240 lbs. Never a believer in travelling light, he brought with him on the flight from Houston not only his attractive, blonde wife Jean, but also his positively stunning daughter Stella, another natural blonde, who acted as his secretary on these field trips. He left Jean behind at the hotel in Fort McMurray, but kept Stella with him in the minibus that Sanmobil had sent to ferry him out to the plant.

The first impression he made on the hard men of Athabasca was less than favourable. He wore a superbly-cut dark-grey business suit – it had to be well cut, even to approximate to a frame as spherical as his – a white shirt and a conservative tie. On top of these indoor clothes, however, he wore two woollen overcoats and a vast beaver fur coat, the combined effect being to render his vertical and horizontal dimensions approximately equal. He sported a soft felt hat the same colour as his suit, but this too was almost invisible, anchored by a grey woollen scarf that passed twice over the crown and under his chins.

"Well I'll be damned!" he exclaimed. His voice was muffled by the ends of the scarf, tied across his face just below the eyes, which were the only part of him that could be seen. Even so, it was clear to his companions that he was impressed.

"This sure is something. You boys must have a lot of fun digging away here and building these nice little ol' sand-castles."

47

"That's one way of putting it, Mr Brady." Jay Shore spoke with restraint. "Not much, perhaps, by Texas standards, but it's still the biggest mining operation in the history of mankind."

"No offence, no offence. You don't expect a Texan to admit there's something bigger and better outside his own State?" One could almost feel him bracing himself for a handsome admission. "That beats anything I've ever come across."

"That" was a dragline, but a dragline such as Brady had never seen before. A dragline is essentially an engine-housing with a control cabin which operates a crane-like boom. The boom is hinged and swivelled at the base of the engine-housing, and so can be both raised and lowered and swung from side to side: control is achieved by cables from the engine-housing which pass over a massive steel superstructure and reach out to the tip of the boom. Another cable, passing over the tip of the boom, supports a bucket which can be lowered to scoop up material, raised again, then swung to one side to dump its load.

"Biggest thing that ever moved on earth," said Shore.

"*Move*?" Stella said.

"Yes, it can move. Walks, shuffles would be a better word, on those two huge shoes at the base, step by step. You wouldn't want to enter it for the Kentucky Derby – it takes seven hours to travel a mile. Not that it's ever required to travel more than a few yards at a time. Point is, it gets there."

"And that long nose . . ." she said.

"The boom. The comparison most generally used is that it's as long as a football field. Wrong – it's longer. From here the bucket doesn't look all that big, but that's only because everything is dwarfed out of perspective: it scoops up eighty cubic yards at a time or enough to fill a two-car garage. A large two-car garage. The dragline weighs 6,500 tons – about the same as a light-medium cruiser. Cost? About thirty

48

million dollars. Takes fifteen to eighteen months to build –
on the site, of course. There are four of them, and between
them they can shift up to a quarter of a million tons a day."

"You win. This is a boom town," Brady said. "Let's get
inside. I'm cold." The other four – Dermott, Mackenzie,
Shore and Brinckman, the security chief – looked at him in
mild astonishment. It seemed impossible that a man so
extravagantly upholstered and insulated, both naturally and
otherwise, could possibly feel even cool; but if Brady said he
was cold, he was cold.

They clambered into the minibus which, if a bit short on
other creature comforts, did at least have heaters in excellent
condition. Also in excellent condition was the girl who sat
down in the back seat, lowered her parka hood, and beamed
at them. Brinckman, who was much the youngest of the
men, in his thirties, had not paid much attention to Stella.
Now he touched the rim of his fur cap and lit up like
a lamp. His enthusiasm was hardly surprising, for the white
fur parka made her as cuddly-looking as a polar bear
cub.

"Wanna dictate anything, Dad?" she asked.

"Not yet," Brady grunted. Once safely sheltered from the
vicious cold, he undid the ends of the scarf that concealed his
face. Somewhere in the distant past there must have been
signs of the character that had driven him from the back
streets of poverty to his present millions, but years of
gracious living had eradicated all trace of them: bone
structure had vanished under a fatty accumulation which
had left him without a crease, line or even the hint of crow's
feet. It was a fat, spoiled face like a cherub's. With one
exception: there was nothing cherubic about the eyes. They
were blue, cool, appraising and shrewd.

He looked through the window at the dragline. "So that's
the end of the line."

"The beginning of it," Shore said. "The tar sands may lie

49

as deep as fifty feet down. The stuff above, the overburden, is useless to us – gravel, clay, muskeg, shale, oil-poor sand – and has to be removed first of all." He pointed to an approaching vehicle. "Here's some of that rubbish being carried away now – it's been excavated by another dragline on a new site.

"To impress you further, Mr Brady, those trucks are also the biggest in the world. A hundred and twenty-five tons empty, payload of a hundred and fifty, and all this on just four tyres. But, you will admit, they are some tyres."

The truck was passing now and they were indeed some tyres; to Brady they looked at least ten feet high and proportionately bulky. The truck itself was monstrous – twenty feet high at the cab and about the same in width, with the driver mounted so high as to be barely visible from the ground.

"You could buy a very acceptable car for the price of one of those tyres," Shore said. "As for the truck itself, if you went shopping for one at today's prices, you wouldn't get much change from three quarters of a million." He spoke to his driver, who started up and moved slowly off.

"When the overburden is gone, the same dragline scoops up the tar sand – as the one we've just looked at is doing now – and dumps it in this huge pile we call a windrow." A weird machine of phenomenal length was nosing into the pile. Shore pointed and said: "A bucketwheel reclaimer – there's one paired with every dragline. Four hundred and twenty-eight feet long. You can see the revolving bucketwheel biting into the windrow. With fourteen buckets on a forty-foot diameter wheel, it can remove a fair tonnage every minute. The tar sands are then transported along the spine of the reclaimer – the bridge, we call it – to the separators. From there –"

Brady interrupted: "Separators?"

"Sometimes the sands come in big, solid lumps as hard as

rock which could damage the conveyor belts. The separators are just vibrating screens which sort out the lumps."

"And without the separators the conveyor belts could be damaged?"

"Certainly."

"Put out of commission?"

"Probably. We don't know. It's never been allowed to happen yet."

"And then?"

"The tar sands go into the travelling hoppers you see there. They drop the stuff on to the conveyor belt, and off it goes to the processing plant. After that –"

"One minute." It was Dermott. "You have a fair amount of this conveyor belting?"

"A fair bit."

"How much exactly?"

Shore looked uncomfortable. "Sixteen miles." Dermott stared at him and Shore hurried on. "At the end of the conveyor system radial stackers direct it to what are called surge piles – just really storage dumps."

"Radial stackers?" said Brady. "What are they?"

"Elevated extensions of the conveyor belts. They can rotate through a certain arc to direct the tar sands to a suitable surge pile. They can also feed bins that take the sands underground to start the processes of chemical and physical separation of the bitumen. The first of those processes –"

"Jesus!" said Mackenzie incredulously.

"That about sums it up," Dermott said. "I have no wish to be rude, Mr Shore, but I don't want to hear about the extraction processes. I've already heard and seen all I want to."

"Good God Almighty!" exclaimed Mackenzie by way of variation.

Brady said: "What's the matter, gentlemen?"

51

Dermott picked his words carefully. "When Don and I were talking to Mr Shore and Mr Reynolds, the operations manager, last night, we thought we had reason to be concerned. I now realise we were wasting our time on trifles. But, by God, now I'm worried.

"Last night we had to face the fact – the ridiculous ease with which the perimeter can be penetrated and the almost equal ease with which subversives could be introduced on to the plant floor. In retrospect, those are but bagatelles. How many points did you pick up, Don?"

"Six."

"My count also. First off, the draglines. They look as impregnable as the Rock of Gibraltar: they are, in fact, pathetically vulnerable. A hundred tons of high explosive would hardly dent the Rock of Gibraltar; I could take out a dragline with two five-pound charges of wrap-round explosive placed where the boom is hinged to the machine house."

Brinckman, an intelligent and clearly competent person in his early thirties, spoke for the first time in fifteen minutes, then immediately wished he hadn't. He said: "Fine, if you could approach the dragline – but you can't. The area is lit by brilliant floodlamps."

"Jesus!" Mackenzie's limited repertoire was in use again.

"What do you mean, Mr Mackenzie?"

"What I mean is I would locate the breaker or switch or whatever that supplies the power to the floodlights and immobilise it by smashing it or by the brilliantly innovative device of turning it off. Or, I'd cut the power lines. Simpler still, with a five-second burst from a sub-machine gun I'd shoot them out. Assuming, of course, that they're not made of bullet-proof glass."

Dermott saved Brinckman the embarrassment of a long silence. "Five pounds of commercial Amatol would take out the bucketwheel for an indefinite period. A similar amount would take care of the reclaimer's bridge. Two pounds to buckle the separator plate. That's four ways. Getting at the radial stackers would be another excellent device – that would mean Sanmobil couldn't even get the tar sands stockpiled in the surge piles down below for processing. And then, best of all, is this little matter of sixteen unpatrolled miles of conveyor belting."

There was quiet in the bus until Dermott rumbled on. "Why bother sabotaging the separation plant when it's so much simpler and more effective to interrupt the flow of raw material? You can't very well carry out a processing operation if you've got nothing to process. It'd be childishly simple. Four draglines. Four bucketwheels. Four reclaimers' bridges. Four separators. Four radial stackers. Sixteen miles of conveyor, fourteen miles of unpatrolled perimeter, and eight men to cover. Situation's ludicrous. I'm afraid, Mr Brady, there's no way in the world we can stop our Anchorage friend from carrying out his threat."

Brady turned what appeared to be one cold, blue eye on the unfortunate Brinckman. "And what do you have to say?"

"What can I say except to agree? Even if I had ten times the number of men at my disposal, we still wouldn't be geared to meet a threat like this." He shrugged. "I'm sorry, I didn't even dream of anything like this."

"Nor did anyone else. Nothing to reproach yourself about. You security people thought you were in the oil business, not a war. What are your normal duties, anyway?"

"We're here to prevent three things – physical trouble among members of the work-force, petty pilfering, and drinking on the plant site. But so far we've had few instances of any of them."

Visibly, Brinckman's words struck a chord in Brady. "Ah,

yes. Trouble in moments of stress and all that." He turned in his seat. "Stella!"

"Yes, Dad." She opened a wicker basket, produced a flask and glass, poured a drink and handed it to her father.

"Daiquiri," he said. "We also have Scotch, gin, rum –"

"Sorry, Mr Brady," Shore said. "No. The company has very strict regulations –"

Brady gave him some terse suggestions as to what he could do with company regulations and turned to Brinckman again.

"So, in effect, you've been pretty superfluous up till now and , if anything, are going to be even more so in the future?"

"I'd agree with half of that. The fact that we've had little to do up to now doesn't mean we've been superfluous. Presence is important. You don't heave a half-brick through a jeweller's window if there's an interested cop standing by five feet away. As to the future, yes, I agree. I feel pretty helpless."

"If you were carrying out an attack somewhere, what would you go for?"

Brinckman was in no two minds. "The conveyor belting every time."

Brady looked at Dermott and Mackenzie. Both men nodded.

"Mr Shore?"

"Agreed." Shore was absentmindedly sipping some Scotch that had found its way into his hand. "Apart from the fact that there's so damn much of it, it's fragile. Six feet wide, but the steel cord belting is only an inch and a half thick. With a sledge-hammer and chisel I could wreck it myself." Shore looked and sounded tense. "Not many people are aware of the vast quantities of material that are processed here. To keep the plant operating at capacity and to make the project commercially viable, we need close on a quarter of a million tons of tar sands a day. As I said, the

54

biggest mining operation ever. Cut off the supplies, and the plant closes down in a few hours. That's a hundred and thirty thousand barrels of oil a day lost. Even Sanmobil couldn't stand this kind of loss indefinitely."

"How much did it cost to set up this plant?" Brady asked.

"Two billion, near enough."

"Two billion dollars. And a potential operating loss of a hundred and thirty thousand barrels of oil a day." Brady shook his head. "No-one's arguing about the brilliance of the men who dreamed up this idea. Same goes for the engineers who made it work. But there's another thing no-one would question – at least *I* would never question – and that is that those towering intellects had a huge blind spot. Why didn't the bosses foresee this? I know it's easy to be wise after the event, but, goddamn, you don't need much foresight to think of that. Oil is not just another business. Couldn't they have seen the giant potential for hate or crackpots – or blackmail? Couldn't they have foreseen that they'd built the biggest industrial hostage to fortune of all time?"

Shore gazed gloomily at his glass, gloomily drank its contents, and maintained a gloomy silence.

Dermott said: "Well, not quite."

"What do you mean 'not quite'?"

"Sure, it's an industrial hostage to fortune. But not the biggest of all time. That dubious distinction belongs without any question to the trans-Alaskan pipeline. Their capital outlay wasn't two billion: it was eight billion. They don't transport a hundred and thirty thousand barrels a day: they transport one million two hundred thousand. And they don't just have sixteen miles of conveyor belting to guard: they have eight hundred miles of pipeline."

Brady handed his glass back for a refill, digested this unpleasant thought, fortified himself and said: "Don't they have *any* means of protecting the damned thing?"

"To the extent that they can limit damage, certainly. They have magnificent communication and electronic control systems, with every imaginable fail-safe and back-up device, even to the extent of a satellite emergency control station." Dermott produced a paper from his pocket. "They have twelve pump stations, locally or remotely controlled. They have sixty-two remote gate valves, all radio-controlled from the pump station immediately to the north. Those gate valves can stop the flow of oil in either direction.

"There are eighty check valves to prevent the oil from flowing backwards and, well, all sorts of other weird valves that would only make sense to an engineer. Altogether they have a remote-control capability at well over a thousand points. In other words, they can isolate any section of the line at any time they want. Because it takes six minutes to shut down a big pump, some oil is bound to escape – up to fifty thousand barrels, it's estimated. That may seem a lot, but it's a drop in the bucket compared to what's in the pipeline. But there's no way the oil can keep on pumping out indefinitely."

"All very interesting." Brady sounded cool. "You can bet they try harder to protect the environment. You can also bet that crooks and extortioners don't give a damn about the environment one way or another. All they want is to interrupt the flow of oil. Can the line be protected?"

"Well, about this huge blind spot you mentioned –"

"What you're trying not to tell me is that the pipeline can be breached any place, any time."

"That's right."

Brady looked at Dermott. "You've thought about this problem?"

"Of course."

"And you, Donald?"

"Me, too."

"Well then, what have you come up with?"

"Nothing. That's why we sent for you. We thought *you* might come up with something."

Brady looked at him maliciously and resumed his pondering. By and by he said: "What happens if there's a break and the oil is stopped in the pipe? Does it gum up?"

"Eventually. But it takes time. The oil is hot when it comes out of the ground and it's still warm when it reaches Valdez. The pipeline is very heavily insulated, and the oil passing through the pipe generates friction heat. They reckon they might get it flowing again after a 21-day standstill. After that –" He spread his hands.

"No more oil-flow?"

"No."

"Not ever again?"

"I shouldn't think so. I don't really know. Nobody's talked to me about it. I don't think anyone really wants to talk about it."

No one did. Until Brady said: "Do you know what I wish?"

"I know," Dermott said. "You wish you were back in Houston."

The radio-phone rang. The driver listened briefly then turned to Shore.

"Operations manager's office. Will we return immediately. Mr Reynolds says it's urgent." The bus driver picked up speed.

Reynolds was waiting for them. He indicated a phone lying on his table and spoke to Brady. "Houston. For you."

Brady said "Hello". Then he made a gesture of irritation and turned to Dermott.

"Horseshit. Damn code. Take it, huh?" This was hardly reasonable of Brady, since it was he who had invented the code and insisted on using it for almost everything except "Hello" and "Goodbye". Dermott reached for a pad and pencil, took the phone and started writing. It took him about a minute to record the message and two more to decode it.

He said into the phone: "Is that all you have?" A pause. "When did you get this message, and when did this happen?" Another pause. "Fifteen minutes and two hours. Thank you." He turned to Brady, his face bleak. "The pipeline's been breached. Pump Station No. 4. Near Atigun Pass in the Brook Range. No hard details yet. Damage not severe, it seems, but enough to close down the line."

"No chance of an accident?"

"Explosives. They took out two gate valves."

There was a brief silence while Brady surveyed Dermott curiously.

"No need to look so goddamned grim, George. We were expecting something like this. It's not the end of the world."

"It is for two of the men on Pump Station Four. They've been murdered."

4

It was half-past two in the afternoon, Alaskan time, almost dark, but with good visibility, a ten-knot wind and a temperature of −4°F − 36° below − when the twin-jet touched down again on one of the Prudhoe Bay air-strips. Brady, Dermott and Mackenzie had moved quickly after receipt of the message from Houston. They had driven back to Fort McMurray, packed essentials, which in Brady's case consisted primarily of three flasks, said goodbye to Jean and Stella and driven straight to the airport. Brady was asleep when they entered Yukon airspace, and Mackenzie dozed off shortly afterwards. Only Dermott remained awake, trying to puzzle out why the enemy, in carrying out what they said would be − and, in fact proved to be − no more than a token demonstration, should have found it necessary to kill in the process.

As the jet came to a halt, a brightly-lit minibus pulled up alongside and slid open a front door. Brady, third out of the aircraft, was first into the bus. The others followed him in and the door was quickly closed. As the bus moved off the man who had ushered them aboard came and sat down beside them. Aged anywhere between forty and fifty, he was a broad, chunky man with a broad, chunky face. He looked tough but he also looked as if he could be humorous − although he had nothing worth smiling about at that moment.

"Mr Brady, Mr Dermott, Mr Mackenzie," he said, in the unmistakably, flat accent of one who had been born within commuting distance of Boston. "Welcome. Mr Finlayson sent me to meet you − as you can imagine he's right now

59

practically a prisoner in the master operations control centre. My name's Sam Bronowski."

Dermott said: "Security chief."

"For my sins." He smiled. "You'll be Mr Dermott, the man who's going to take over from me?"

Dermott looked at him. "Who the hell said that?"

"Mr Finlayson. Or words to that effect."

"I'm afraid Mr Finlayson must be slightly overwrought." Bronowski smiled again. "Well, now, that wouldn't surprise me either. He's been talking to London and I think he suffered some damage to his left ear."

Brady said: "We're not out to take over from anyone. That's not how we work. But unless we get co-operation – I mean total co-operation – we might as well have stayed home. For instance, Mr Dermott here wanted to talk to you right away. The chairman of your company himself had guaranteed me complete co-operation. Yet Finlayson refused point-blank to co-operate with Dermott and Mackenzie."

"I'd have come at once if I'd known," said Bronowski quickly. "Unlike Mr Finlayson, I've been a security man all my life, and I know who you are and the reputation you have. In a set-up like this I can do with all the expert help I can get. Go easy with him, will you? This isn't his line of country. He treats the pipeline as his favourite daughter. This is a new experience for him and he didn't know what to do. He wasn't stalling – just playing it safe until he'd consulted on the highest level."

"You don't need lessons in sticking up for your boss, do you?"

"I'm being fair to him. I hope you will be, too. You can imagine how he feels. Says that if he hadn't been so ornery those two men up at Pump Station Four might be alive now."

"That's plain daft," Mackenzie said. "I appreciate his

feelings, but this would have happened if there had been fifty Dermotts and fifty Mackenzies here."

"When," Brady asked, "are we going out there?"

"Mr Finlayson asked if you and your colleagues would come first to see him and Mr Black. The helicopter is ready to go any moment after that."

"Black?"

"General manager, Alaska."

"You been out at the station?"

"I was the man who found them. Rather, I was the first man on the scene after the attack. Along with my section chief, Tim Houston."

"You fly your own plane?"

"Yes. Not this time, though. That section of the Brooks Range is like the mountains on the moon. Helicopter. We've been making a continuous check on the pump stations and the remote gate valves since this damned threat came through, and we'd stayed at Station Five last night. We were just approaching Gate Four, a mile away, I'd reckon, when we saw this damned great explosion."

"*Saw* it?"

"You know, oil smoke and flames. You mean, did we *hear* anything? You never do in a helicopter. You don't have to – not when you see the roof take off into the air. So we put down and got out, me with a rifle, Tim with two pistols. Wasting our time. The bastards had gone. Being oilmen yourselves, you'll know it requires quite a group of men and a complex of buildings to provide the care and maintenance for a couple of 13,500 horsepower aircraft-type turbines, not to mention all the monitoring and communications they have to handle.

"It was the pump room itself that was on fire, not too badly, but badly enough for Tim and me not to go inside without fire extinguishers. We'd just started looking when we heard shouting come from a store room. It was locked.

naturally, but the key had been left in the lock. Poulson – he's the boss – came running out with his men. They had the extinguishers located and the fire out in three minutes. But it was too late for the two engineers inside – they'd come down the previous day from Prudhoe Bay to do a routine maintenance job on one of the turbines."

"They were dead?"

"Very." Bronowski's face registered no emotion. "They were brothers. Fine boys. Friends of mine; and Tim's."

"No possibility of accidental death? From the effects of the explosion?"

"Explosions don't shoot you. They were pretty badly charred, but charring doesn't hide a bullet-wound between the eyes."

"You searched the area?"

"Certainly. Conditions weren't ideal – it was dark, with a little snow falling. I thought I saw helicopter ski marks on a wind-blown stretch of rock. The others weren't so sure. On the remote off-chance I contacted Anchorage and asked them to alert every public and private airport and strip in the State. Also to have radio and TV stations ask the public to report hearing or sighting a helicopter in an unusual place. I haven't but one hope in ten thousand that the request will bring any results."

He grimaced. "Most people never realise how huge this State is. It's bigger than half Western Europe, but it's got a population of just over three hundred thousand, which is to say it's virtually uninhabited. Again, helicopters are an accepted fact of life in Alaska, and people pay no more attention to them than you would to a car in Texas. Third, we've still only got about three good hours of light, and the idea of carrying out an air search is laughable – anyway, we'd require fifty times the number of planes we have, and even then it would be sheer luck to find them.

"But, for the record, we did find out something unpleasant. In case anything should happen to the pump station, there's an emergency pipeline that can be switched in to bypass it. Our friends took care of that also. They blew up the control valve."

"So there's going to be a massive oil spillage?"

"No chance. The line is loaded with thousands of sensors all the way from Prudhoe Bay to Valdez, and any section of it can be closed down and isolated immediately. Even the repairs would normally present no problem. But neither metal nor men work too well in these abnormally low temperatures."

"Apparently that doesn't apply to saboteurs," Dermott said. "How many were there?"

"Poulson said two. Two others said three. The remainder weren't sure."

"Not a very observant lot, are they?"

"I wonder if that's fair, Mr Dermott. Poulson's a good man and he doesn't miss much."

"Did he see their faces?"

"No. That much is for certain."

"Masked?"

"No. Their fur collars were pulled high up and their hats low down so that only their eyes were visible. You can't tell the colour of a man's eyes in the darkness. Besides, our people had just been dragged from bed."

"But not the two engineers. They were working on the engines. How come at that very early hour?"

Bronowski spoke with restraint. "Because they had been up all night. Because they were going home to their families in Fairbanks for their week's leave. And because I had arranged to pick them up there shortly after that time."

"Did Poulson or any of his friends recognise the voices?"

"If they had, I'd have the owners behind bars by this time. Their collars were up to their eyes. Of course their voices

63

would have been muffled. You ask a lot of questions, Mr Dermott."

"Mr Dermott is a trained interrogator," Brady said cheerfully. "Trained him myself, as a matter of fact. What happened after that?"

"They were marched across to the food store and locked in there. We keep it locked because of bears. Unless bears are near starving, they aren't very partial to human beings, but they're partial indeed to all human goodies."

"Thank you, Mr Bronowski. One last question. Did Poulson or his men hear the fatal shots?"

"No. Both the men Poulson saw were carrying silenced guns. That's the great advantage of those modern educational pictures, Mr Dermott."

There was a pause in the questioning. Brady said: "Because I am an acute observer of character, George, I can tell something's eating you. What's on your mind?"

"It's only a thought. I'm wondering if the murderers are employees of the trans-Alaskan pipeline."

The silence was brief but marked. Then Bronowski said: "This beats everything. I speak as Dr Watson, you understand. I know that Sherlock Holmes could solve a crime without leaving his armchair, but I never knew of any cop or security man who could come up with the answer without at least visiting the scene of the crime."

Dermott said mildly: "I'm not claiming to have solved anything. I'm just putting forward a possibility."

Brady said: "What makes you think that?"

"In the first place, you pipeline people aren't just the biggest employer of labour around here: you're the only one. Where the hell else could the killers have come from? What else could they have been? Lonely trappers or prospectors on the North Slope of the Brooks Range in the depth of winter? They'd freeze to death the first day out. They wouldn't be prospectors, because the tundra is frozen solid, and beneath

64

that there's two thousand feet of solid permafrost. As for trappers, they'd be not only cold and lonely but very hungry indeed, because they wouldn't find any form of food north of Brooks Range until the late spring comes."

Brady grunted. "What you're saying in effect is that the pipeline is the sole means of life-support in those parts."

"It's a fact. Had this happened at Pump Station Seven or Eight, circumstances would have been quite different – those stations are only a hop, skip and jump from Fairbanks by car. But you don't take a car over the Brooks Range in the depth of winter. And you don't back-pack over the Range at this time of year, unless you're bent on quick suicide. So the question remains, how did they get there and away again?"

"Helicopter," Bronowski said. "Remember I said I thought I saw ski marks? Tim – Tim Houston – saw the marks too, although he was less sure. The others were frankly sceptical, but admitted the possibility. But I've been flying helicopters for as long as I can remember." Bronowski shook his head in exasperation. "God's sake, how else could they have got in and out?"

"I thought," Mackenzie said, "that those pump stations had limited range radar-scopes."

"They do." Bronowski shrugged. "But snow plays funny tricks on radar. Also, they may not have been looking, or maybe they had the set switched off, not expecting company in such bad weather."

Dermott said: "They were expecting you, surely."

"Not for another hour or so. We'd had deteriorating weather at No. 5, so we left ahead of schedule. Another thing – even if they had picked up an incoming helicopter, they'd automatically have assumed it was one of ours and would have had no reason to be suspicious."

"Be that as it may," said Dermott, "I'm convinced. It was an inside job. The killers are pipeline employees. The note announcing their intention of causing a slight spillage of oil seemed civil and civilised enough, with no hint of violence, but violence there has been. The saboteurs blundered, and so they had to kill."

"Blundered?" Mackenzie was a lap behind.

"Yes. Bronowski said the key had been left in the store room door. Don't forget, all the engineers locked inside *were* engineers. With the minimum of equipment they could have either turned the key in the lock or slipped a piece of paper, cardboard, linoleum, anything, under the bottom of the door, pushed the key out to fall on it and hauled the key inside. Me, I'd have thrown that key a mile away. But the killers didn't. Their intention was to bring the two pump-house engineers to the store room and usher them in to join their friends, and lock them in, too. But they didn't do that either. Why? Because one of the saboteurs said or did something that betrayed their identity to the two engineers. They were recognised by the engineers, who evidently knew them well enough to penetrate their disguises. The saboteurs had no option, so they killed them."

Brady said: "How's that for a hypothesis, Sam?"

Bronowski was pondering his reply when the minibus pulled up outside the main entrance to the administrative building. Brady, predictably, was the first out and scuttled – as far as a nearly spherical human being could be said to scuttle – to the welcoming shelter that lay behind the main door. The others followed more sedately.

John Finlayson rose as they entered his room. He extended his hand to Brady and said: "Delighted to meet you, sir." He nodded curtly towards Dermott, Mackenzie and Bronowski, then turned to a man seated to his right behind a table. "Mr Hamish Black, general manager, Alaska."

Mr Black didn't look like the general manager of anything, far less the manager of a tough and ruthless oil operation. The rolled umbrella and bowler hat were missing,

66

but even without them his lean, bony face, immaculately trimmed pencil moustache, thinning black hair parted with millimetric precision over the centre of his scalp and the eyes behind pince-nez made him the epitome of a top City of London accountant, which he was.

That such a man, who could hardly tell a nut from a bolt, should head up a huge industrial complex was not a new phenomenon. The tea-boy who had painstakingly fought his way up through the ranks to board-room level had become a man of no mean importance: it was Hamish Black, so adept at punching the keyboard of his pocket calculator, who called the industrial tune. It was rumoured that his income ran into six figures – sterling, not dollars. His employers, evidently, thought he was worth every penny of it.

He waited patiently while Finlayson made the introductions.

"I would not go as far as Mr Finlayson and say I'm delighted to meet you." Black's smile was as thin as his face. His flat, precise, controlled voice belonged to the City, to London's Wall Street, just as surely as did his appearance. "Under other circumstances, yes: under these, I can only say that I'm glad you, Mr Brady, and your colleagues are here. I assume Mr Bronowski has supplied you with details. How did you propose we proceed?"

"I don't know. Do we have a glass?"

The expression on Finlayson's face could have been interpreted as reluctant disapproval: Black, it seemed, didn't believe in using expressions. Brady poured his daiquiri, waved the flask at the others, who waved it on, and said: "The F.B.I. have been notified?"

Black nodded. "Reluctantly."

"Reluctantly?"

"There's a legal obligation to notify of any interruption of interstate commerce. Quite frankly, I don't see what they can achieve."

67

"They're out at the pump station now?"

"They haven't arrived here yet. They're waiting for some specialist Army Ordnance officers to accompany them – experts on bombs, explosives and the like."

"Waste of time. Among the people who built and run this line are as good – if not better – explosives experts than in any Army Ordnance Corps. The killers wouldn't have left a trace of explosives at Pump Station No. 4."

If a silence can be said to be cold, the ensuing silence was downright chilly. Finlayson said stonily: "Does that statement mean what I think it means?"

"I should imagine it does," said Brady. "Explain, George."

Dermott explained. When he had finished, Finlayson said: "Preposterous. Why should any of our pipeline employees want to do a thing like that? It doesn't make sense."

"It's never a pleasant thing to nurture a viper in your bosom," Brady said agreeably. "Mr Black?"

"Makes sense to me, if only because no other immediate explanation occurs. What do *you* think, Mr Brady?"

"Exactly what I was asking Mr Bronowski as we touched down."

"Yes. Well." Bronowski didn't seem any too comfortable. "I don't like it. An inside job is all too damn plausible. Point is, carry this line of thinking a little further, and the finger points at Tim Houston and myself as the two prime suspects." Bronowski paused. "Tim and I had a helicopter. We were in the right place at approximately the right time. We know of a dozen ways to sabotage the pipeline. It's no secret that we're both pretty experienced in the use of explosives, so taking out Station Four would have presented no problem for us." He paused. "But who's going to suspect the security chief and his number two?"

"Me, for one," said Brady. He sipped his drink

68

and sighed. "I'd have you clapped behind bars right now were it not for your impeccable record, lack of apparent motive, and the fact that it's incredible that you should have acted in such a clumsy fashion."

"Not clumsy, Mr Brady. The killers were stupid to the point of insanity, or badly frightened. The job certainly wasn't the work of professional hit men. Why shoot the two engineers? Why leave any evidence that murder had been done? Just knock them unconscious – a dozen ways that can be done without leaving a mark – then blow them to pieces along with the pump station. Act of God, and no hint of foul play."

"Amateurism is a grievesome thing, is it not?" Brady turned to Finlayson. "Could we have a line to Anchorage, please? Thank you. Give him the number, then take the call, George." Dermott did so and within four minutes had hung up, his part of the conversation having been limited mainly to monosyllables.

"Wouldn't you know it," Dermott said.

"No luck?" said Mackenzie.

"Too much. The Anchorage police have located not one but four hot phone boxes. Suspicious characters either inside them or lurking in the vicinity, and this at a most ungodly hour. All four of them, dammit, with a disproportionate number of high-denomination coins inside them. All four have been dismantled and taken along to the cop shop. But they haven't been fingerprinted yet, and it may be hours before the cops can check the prints against their files."

Black said with sardonic restraint: "The relevance of this call escapes me. It has something to do with Pump Station Four?"

"Maybe," said Brady. "Maybe not. All we know for certain is that Sanmobil – the people who have the tar sands concession north of Fort McMurray, in Alberta – have also received a threat against their oil production lines. Couched in almost identical forms with the threat you received, the only difference being that while yours arrived by mail, theirs came from a public phone booth in Anchorage. We're trying to trace which booth and, with any fingerprint luck, who the caller may have been."

Black thought briefly, then said: "Curious. A threat against Alaskan oil from Alberta, and one against Albertan oil from Alaska. Must tie up with Pump Station Four: the arm of coincidence isn't all that long ... and while you're sitting here, Mr Brady, some ill-intentioned person or persons may be planting an explosive device at some strategic point in Sanmobil's tar sands."

"The thought had not escaped me. However, surmise and speculation will serve no point until we turn up one or two hard facts. We hope that one may even result from a close inspection of Pump Station Four. Coming out there, Mr Black?"

"Good heavens, no, I'm very much a desk-bound citizen. But I shall await your return with interest."

"Return? I'm going no place. Those frozen wastes – not for me. My excellent representatives know what to look for. Besides, someone has to stay and run the command post. How far to the pump station, Mr Bronowski?"

"Helicopter miles? Hundred and forty, give or take."

"Splendid. That will leave us ample time for a belated lunch. Your commissary is still open, Mr Finlayson, I trust, and your wine cellar tolerable?"

"Sorry about that, Mr Brady." Finlayson made no effort to conceal the satisfaction in his voice. "Company regulations forbid alcohol."

"No need to distress yourself," Brady said urbanely. "Aboard my jet is the finest cellar north of the Arctic Circle."

70

5

Three generator-fed arc-lamps threw the half-demolished
pump-house and its shattered contents into harsh relief,
glaring white and Stygian blackness, with no intermediate
shading between. Snow drifted silently down through the
all-but-vanished roof, and a high wind blew a fine white
cloud through a gaping hole in the northern wall. Already
the combined effects of the two snows had softened and
blurred the outlines of the machinery, but not sufficiently to
conceal the fact that engines, motors, pumps and switchgear
had been either destroyed or severely damaged. Mercifully,
the snow had already covered the two mounds that lay side
by side before the mangled remains of a switchboard.
Dermott looked slowly around with a face again as bleak as
the scene that lay before him.

"Damage evenly spread," he said, "so it couldn't have
come from one central blast. Half-a-dozen charges, more
likely." He turned to Poulson, the charge-hand, a black-
bearded man with bitter eyes. "How many explosions did
you hear?"

"Just the one, I think. We really can't be sure. If there were
more after the first one, our eardrums were sure in no
condition to register them. But we're agreed that one was all
we heard."

"Triggered electrically, by radio or, if they used fulminate
of mercury, by sympathetic detonation. Experts, obviously." He looked at the two shapeless, snow-covered
mounds. "But not so expert in other ways. Why have those
two men been left here?"

"Orders."

71

"Whose orders?"

"Head Office. Not to be moved until the post-mortems have been carried out."

"Rubbish! You can't do a post-mortem on a frozen body." Dermott stooped, began to clear away the snow from the nearest of the mounds, then looked up in surprise as a heavy hand clamped on his left shoulder.

"You deaf or something, mister?" Poulson didn't sound truculent, just annoyed. "I'm in charge here."

"You were. Donald?"

"Sure." Mackenzie eased Poulson's hand away and said: "Let's go talk to the head officeman, Black, and hear what he has to say about obstructing murder investigations."

"That won't be necessary, Mr Mackenzie," Bronowski said. He nodded to Poulson. "John's upset. Wouldn't you be?"

Poulson hesitated briefly, turned and left the pump room. Dermott had most of the snow cleared away when he felt a light touch on his shoulder: it was Poulson again, proffering him, of all things, a long-handled clothes brush. Dermott took it, smiled his thanks and delicately brushed away the remaining snow.

The dreadfully charred skull of the dead man was barely recognisable as that of a human being, but the cause of the round hole above the eyeless left socket was unmistakable. With Mackenzie's help – the corpse was frozen solid – he lifted the body and peered at the back of the skull. The skin was unbroken.

"Bullet's lodged in the head," Dermott said. "Rifling marks on it should be of interest to the police ballistics department."

"There's that," Bronowski said. "After all, Alaska only covers just over half a million square miles. Optimism is not my long suit."

"Agreed." They lowered the body to the ground and

72

Dermott tried to unzip the shredded green parka, but it, too, was frozen. There was a slight crackling of ice as he eased the jacket away from the shirt beneath and peered into the gap between the two layers of clothing. He could see some documents, including a buff-coloured envelope, tucked away in the inside right pocket. By sliding his hand in flat he tried to extract them with his fore and middle fingers, but because he could achieve so little purchase, and because they seemed frozen – not only together but also to the side of the pocket – they proved impossible to move. Dermott straightened to an upright kneeling position, looked at the dead man thoughtfully, then up at Bronowski.

"Could we have the two bodies moved to some place where they can be thawed out a bit? I can't examine them in this state, nor by the same token, can the doctors carry out their post-mortems."

"John?" Bronowski looked at Poulson, who nodded, albeit with some reluctance.

"Another thing," Dermott said. "What's the quickest way of clearing away the snow here from the floor and machinery?"

"Canvas covers and a couple of hot air blowers. No time at all. Want me to fix it now? And the two men?"

"Please. Then there's a question or two I'd like to ask. In your living quarters, perhaps?"

"Straight across. Be with you in a few minutes."

Outside, on their way, Mackenzie said: "Your hound-dog instincts have been aroused. What gives?"

"Dead man back there. Index finger on his right hand is broken."

"That all? Wouldn't be surprised if half the bones in his body are broken."

"Could be. But this bone appears to have been broken in a rather peculiar fashion. Be able to tell better, later."

Bronowski and Poulson joined them round the table of

73

the comfortable kitchen living quarters. Poulson said: "Okay, fixed. Snow in the pump-room should be gone in fifteen minutes. About the two engineers – well, I wouldn't know."

"Considerably longer," Dermott said. "Thanks. Now, then. Bronowski, Mackenzie and myself think it likely that the murderers were employees of the trans-Alaskan pipeline. What would you think of that?"

Poulson glanced enquiringly at Bronowski, found no inspiration there, looked away and pondered. "It figures," he said at last. "The only living souls for ten thousand square miles around here – a hundred thousand as far as I know – are employed by the pipeline. More than that, while any mad bomber could have blown up the pump station, it took an oilman to know where to locate and destroy the bypass control valve."

"We also theorise that the engineers – what were their names, by the way?"

"Johnson and Johnson. Brothers."

"We think that the bombers gave themselves away in one fashion or another, that the Johnsons recognised them and had to be silenced for keeps. But you and your men didn't recognise them. That's for sure?"

"For sure." Poulson smiled without much humour. "If what you suppose is correct, it's just as well for us that we didn't. But then it's not surprising that we didn't. Don't forget that up here in Number Four we're no better than hermits living on a desert island. The only time we see anybody is when we go on leave every few weeks. Travelling maintenance engineers like the Johnsons – or, come to that, Mr Bronowski here – see ten times as many people as we do, and so are likely to recognise ten times as many people. Which makes your idea that it was an inside job all the more likely."

"You and your men are certain there wasn't the remotest

peculiarity about them, either in speech or dress, that struck a chord?"

"You're flogging a dead horse, Dermott."

"I suppose. There's a possibility that those saboteurs came by helicopter."

"Damned if I can see how else they could have come. Mr Bronowski here thought he saw skid marks. I wasn't sure one way or another. It was a bad night for being sure of anything: dark, with a strong wind and drifting snow. Circumstances like that, you can imagine almost anything."

"You didn't *hear* this helicopter approaching – or imagine you heard it?"

"We heard nothing. Don't forget we were all asleep and –"

"I thought you mounted a radar watch?"

"In a fashion. Any errant bleep triggers off an alarm. But we don't sit with our eyes glued to the screen night and day. Then, because of the extremely heavy insulation, it's difficult for any sound to penetrate from outside. The generator running next door doesn't help much either. Finally, of course, the wind was blowing – as it still is – almost directly from the north and would have carried away the sound of any craft approaching from the opposite direction. I know that a helicopter is one of the most rackety bits of machinery in existence but – even though we were wide awake then, we didn't hear Mr Bronowski's chopper coming in from the south. Sorry, that's all I can tell you."

"How long will it take to repair the pump-room?"

"A few days, a week. I'm not sure. We'll need new engines, switchgear, pipelines, a mobile crane and a bulldozer. All those we already have at Prudhoe except the engines, and I expect a Herc will fly those in this evening. Then a chopper or two can fly the stuff out here. The repair crews will be on the job in the morning."

"So a week before the oil starts flowing again?"

"No, no: tomorrow, with luck. The bypass control valve is not a major repair job; parts replacement mainly."

Dermott said: "You might look at all this as just a minor disruption?"

"Technically, yes. The ghosts of the Johnson brothers might see it differently. Want to look at the pump-room now? Most of the stuff should have melted by this time."

The snow in the pump-room had gone, and the atmosphere was warm and humid. Without the protective white covering, the scene was more repellent than before, the extent of the devastation more clearly and dishearteningly evident, and the stench of oil and charring more pungent and penetrating. Each with a powerful hand-torch to lighten the shadows cast by the arc-lamps, Dermott, Mackenzie and Bronowski embarked on a search of every square inch of the floors and walls.

After ten minutes Poulson said curiously: "What *are* you looking for?"

"I'll let you know when I find it," Dermott said. "Meantime I haven't a clue."

"In that case, can I join in the search?"

"Sure. Don't touch or turn anything over. The F.B.I. wouldn't like it."

Ten minutes later, Dermott straightened and switched off his torch. "That's it, then, gentlemen. If you've found no more than I have, among the four of us we've found nothing. Looks as if fire or blasts have wiped the platter clean. Let's have a look at the Johnson brothers. They should be in a fairly examinable state by now."

They were. Dermott moved first to the man he'd looked at in the pump-room. This time the zip on the green parka unfastened easily. The blast effect that had shredded the parka had not penetrated it, for the plaid shirt beneath bore

76

no signs of damage. Dermott removed some paper, cards and envelopes from the inside right pocket of the jacket, leafed through and replaced them. He then lifted both charred wrists, examined them and the hands in an apparently cursory fashion and lowered them again. He repeated the process with the other victim, then rose to his feet. Poulson bent a quizzical eye on him.

"That's the way a detective examines a murdered man?"

"I don't suppose it is. But then, I'm not a detective." He turned to Bronowski. "You all through?"

"If you are." Sam Bronowski led the way to the helicopter, Dermott and Mackenzie following through the thinly-driving snow that reduced visibility to a few yards. It was intensely cold.

"Clues," Mackenzie said into Dermott's ear, not from any wish for privacy but simply to make himself heard. "Man can't move around without tripping over them."

"None in the pump-room, that's sure. Place had been pretty comprehensively quartered before we ever got there. Almost certainly before the snow had started to cover anything."

"What do you mean?"

"The old fine tooth-comb is what I mean."

"Poulson and his men?"

"And/or. Who else?"

"Perhaps there was nothing to find?"

Dermott said – or rather shouted: "That dead man's forefinger had been deliberately broken. Bent in at forty-five degrees towards the thumb. Never seen anything like it before."

"Freak accident."

"'Odd' is better. Something else odd, too. When I searched him first there was a buff envelope in his inner pocket. I was unable to get it out."

"But you were when you unzipped it later?"

77

"No. It was gone."

"'And/or' at work, you think?"

"So it seems."

"All very curious," Mackenzie said.

* * *

Jim Brady was of the same opinion. After reporting the results of their investigation, Dermott and Mackenzie had retired with him to the room he'd been allocated for the night.

Brady said: "Why didn't you mention those things to Black and Finlayson? Those are hard facts – an oddly broken finger, a missing envelope?"

"Hard facts? There's only my word for it. I've no idea what was in the envelope anyway, and although I'd say the forefinger had been deliberately broken, I'm no osteologist."

"But no harm in mentioning those things, surely?"

"Bronowski and Houston were there too."

"You really don't trust anyone, do you, George?" Brady's tone was admiring, not reproachful.

"As you never fail to remind people, sir, you taught me yourself."

"True, true," Brady said complacently. "Very well, then, have them up. I'll do my Olympian act while you ply them with questions and strong drink."

Dermott spoke on the phone and within a minute Bronowski and Houston had knocked, entered and taken seats.

"Kind, gentlemen, kind." Brady was at his most avuncular. "Long day, I know, and you must be damnably tired. But we're babes in the wood up here. We're not only *short* of necessary information, we're totally devoid of it, and we believe you two gentlemen are those best equipped to supply us with that information. But I forget myself, gentlemen. I suggest a pre-inquisitional restorative."

Mackenzie said: "What Mr Brady means is a drink."

"That's what I said. You gentlemen like Scotch?"

"Off-duty, yes. But you know the company regulations, sir, and how strictly Mr Finlayson interprets those."

"Strict? I am iron-clad in the interpretation of my own regulations." The wave of Brady's arm was, indeed, Olympian. "You are off-duty. Off regular duty, anyhow. George, refreshments. Mr Dermott will ask the questions, alternating, I do not doubt, with Mr Mackenzie. You gentlemen, if you will be so kind, will fill in the gaps in our knowledge."

He took his daiquiri from Dermott, savoured it, laid down his glass, relaxed in his chair and steepled his hands under his chin. "I shall but listen and evaluate." Nobody was left with any doubt as to which was the most demanding task of the three. "Health, gentlemen."

Bronowski lifted his own glass, which he had accepted with no great show of reluctance. "And confusion to our enemies."

Dermott said: "That's precisely the point. The enemy aren't confused, we are. The taking out of Pump Station Four is only the opening skirmish in what promises to be bloody battle. They – the enemy – know where they're going to hit again. We have not the vaguest idea. But you must have – by the very nature of your job you must be more aware of the points most vulnerable to attack than anyone else between Prudhoe Bay and Valdez. Take off your security hats and put on those of the enemy. Where would *you* strike next?"

"Jesus!" Bronowski fortified himself with some of Brady's malt. "That's more than a sixty-four-dollar question. It's an 800-mile question – and every damned mile is virtually a sitting target."

"The boss is right," Tim Houston said. "If we sit here and

drink your whisky while pretending to help, we're only abusing your hospitality. There's nothing we or anyone else can do to help. A combat-ready division of the U.S. Army would be about as useful as a gaggle of girl guides. The task is impossible and the line indefensible."

Mackenzie said: "Well, George, at least we're operating on a bigger scale than with the tar-sands boys in Athabasca. There they said a battalion wouldn't be big enough to guard their installation. Now it's a division." Mackenzie turned to Bronowski. "Let's switch hats with the enemy. Where *wouldn't* you strike next?"

Bronowski said: "Well, I wouldn't strike at any of the pump stations again on the assumption that, until this matter is cleared up, they will be heavily guarded. I'd have been sorely tempted to go for Pump Station Ten at the Isabel Pass in the Alaska Range, or No. 12 at the Thompson Pass in the Chugach Mountains. All pump stations are vital of course, but some are more vital than others, and those are No. 10 and No. 12 — along with No. 4 here." He considered briefly. "Or maybe I *would* go for them . . . I mean, maybe you'd be so damned certain that I wouldn't hit again in the same place that you wouldn't much bother — "

Dermott held up his hand. "Start in on the double-guessing, and we're up all night. On with the hazards – the low priority ones, I mean."

"I wouldn't go for the two master operations control centres at Prudhoe Bay. They could be taken out easily enough and, sure, they'd stop all production from the wells immediately, but not for long. It's no secret that contingency plans for bypassing the centres are already in hand. Repairs wouldn't take all that long. In any event, security will be now tightened to the extent that the game wouldn't be worth the candle. So we can be pretty certain that there will be no attempt made to sabotage the oil supply before it enters the pipeline. Same goes for when it leaves the pipe at Valdez.

Maximum damage there could be inflicted at the oil movements control centre, where the pipeline controller can monitor and control the flow of oil all the way from Prudhoe to Valdez, and the terminal controller – he's in the same room, actually – controls practically everything that moves in the terminal itself. Both of those, in turn, are dependent on what's called the backbone supervisory system computer. Knock out any of those three and you're in dead trouble. But they're pretty secure as they are: from now on, they'll be virtually impregnable. Again, not worth it."

Dermott said: "How about the storage tanks?"

"Well, now. If one or two of them were attacked or ruptured – it would be impossible to get them all at once – the containment dykes would take care of the spillage. Fire would be another thing, but even then the snow would have a blanketing effect – we may only have an annual dusting of snow up here, but down there they have over three hundred inches. Anyway, the tank farms are the most open and easily guarded complex on the entire pipeline. There's no way you can really get at them without bombing the area: not very likely, one would think."

"What about the tanker terminals?"

"Again easily guarded. I hardly think they're likely to run to underwater demolition squads. Even if they did they couldn't do much damage, and that would be easily repaired."

"The tankers themselves?"

"Sink a dozen and there's always a thirteenth. No way you can interrupt the oil flow by hitting the tankers."

"The Valdez Narrows?"

"Block them?" Dermott nodded and Bronowski shook his head. "The Narrows aren't as narrow as they look on a small-scale chart. Three thousand feet – that's the minimum channel width – between the Middle Rock and the east

81

shore. You'd have to sink an awful lot of vessels to block the channel."

"So we cross off the unlikely targets. Where does that leave us?"

"It leaves us with eight hundred miles." Bronowski shifted.

"The air temperature is the over-riding factor," Houston said. "No saboteur worth his salt would consider wrecking anything except the pipeline itself. This time of the year any attack has to be in the open air."

"Why?"

"This is only early February, remember, and to all intents we're still in the depth of winter. As often as not the temperature is well on the wrong side of thirty below, and in these parts thirty below is the crucial figure. Rupture the pipeline at, say, thirty-five below, and it stays ruptured. Repair is virtually impossible. Men can work, although well below their norm, but unfortunately the metal they may try to repair or the machine tools they use to make the repairs won't co-operate with them. At extreme temperatures, profound molecular changes occur in metal and it becomes unworkable. Given the right – or wrong – conditions, a tap on an iron rod will shatter it like glass."

Brady said: "You mean, all I need is a hammer and a few taps on the pipeline –"

Houston was patient. "Not quite. What with the heat of the oil inside and the insulation lagging outside, the steel of the pipeline is always warm and malleable. It's the repair tools that would fracture."

Dermott said: "But surely it would be possible to erect canvas or tarpaulin covers over the fracture and bring the temperature up to workable levels by using hot-air blowers? You know, the way Poulson did at Station Four?"

"Of course. Which is why I wouldn't attack the pipeline

directly. I'd attack the structures that support the pipeline, those that are already frozen solid at air temperature and would require days, perhaps weeks, to bring up to a working temperature."

"Structures?"

"Indeed. The terrain between Prudhoe and Valdez is desperately uneven and traversed with innumerable watercourses which have to be forded or spanned in one way or another. There are over six hundred streams and rivers along the run. The 650-foot free-span suspension bridge over the Tazlina River would make a dolly of a target. Even better would be the 1,200-foot span – a similar type of construction – over the Tanana River. But one doesn't even have to operate on such a grandiose scale, and I, personally, would prefer not to." He looked at Bronowski. "Wouldn't you agree?"

"Completely. Operate on a much more moderate and undramatic scale but one equally effective. I'd go for the V.S.M.'s every time."

Dermott said: "V.S.M.'s?"

"Vertical support members. Roughly half the length of the pipeline is above ground and lies on a horizontal cradle or saddle supported by vertical metal posts. That makes for a fair number of targets – 78,000 of them, to be precise. They would be a snip to take out – wrap-round beehive plastic explosives which would need all of a minute to fix in position. Take out twenty of those, and the line would collapse under its own weight and the weight of the oil inside it. Take weeks to repair it."

"They could still use those hot-air canvas shelters."

"A hell of a lot of help that would be," Bronowski said, "if they couldn't bring up the cranes and crawler equipment to effect the repairs. Anyway, there are places where, at this time of year, it just couldn't be done. There is, for instance, one particularly vulnerable stretch which gave the designers

83

headaches, the builders sleepless nights and security nightmares. This steep and dangerous stretch is between Pump Station Five and the summit of Atigun Pass, which is between four and five thousand feet high."

Houston said: "4,775 feet."

"4,775 feet. In a run of a hundred miles from the pass the pipe comes down to 1,200 feet, which is quite a drop."

"With a corresponding amount of built-up pressure?"

"That's not the problem. In the event of a break in the line a special computer linkage between Four and Five will automatically shut down the pumps in Four and close every remote valve between the stations. The fail-safe procedures are highly sophisticated, and they work. At the very worst the spillage could be restricted to 50,000 barrels. But the point is, in winter the line couldn't be repaired."

Brady coughed apologetically and descended from his Olympian heights.

"So a break in this particular section, about now, could immobilise the line for weeks on end?"

"No question."

"Then forget it."

"Mr Brady?"

"The burdens I have to bear alone," Brady sighed. "Let me have men about me who can think. I begin to understand why I am what I am. I find it extraordinary that the construction company never carried out any tests to discover what happens to the viscosity of oil in low temperatures. Why didn't they seal off a couple of hundred feet of experimental pipe with oil inside it and see how long it would take before it gummed up to the extent that it would cease to flow?"

"Never occurred to them, I suppose," Bronowski said. "An eventuality that would never arise."

"It has arisen. An estimate of three weeks has been

bandied about. Based on scientific calculations, one assumes?"

Bronowski said: "I wouldn't know. Not my field. Maybe Mr Black or Mr Finlayson would know."

"Mr Black knows nothing about oil, and I doubt whether Mr Finlayson or any other professional oilman on the line has anything but the vaguest idea. Could be ten days. Could be thirty. You take my point, George?"

"Yes. Blackmail, threats, extortion, some positive and very material advantages to be gained. Interruption is one thing, cessation another. They require a lever, a bargaining counter. Close down the line completely, and the oil companies would laugh at their threats, for then they would have nothing to lose. The bargaining arm would have gone. The kidnapper can't very well hold a kidnapee for ransom if it's known that the kidnapee is dead."

"I question if I could have put it better myself," Brady said. He had about him an air of magnanimous self-satisfaction. "We are, clearly, not dealing with clowns. Our friends would have taken such imponderables into account and would err on the side of caution. You are with me, Mr Bronowski?"

"I am now. But when I was talking about hazards, I wasn't taking that side of it into account."

"I know you weren't. Nobody was. Well, I think that will do, gentlemen. We appear to have established two things. It is unlikely that any attack will be carried out on any major installation – that is Prudhoe, Valdez or the intervening twelve major pump stations. It is further unlikely that any attack will be carried out in regions so inaccessible that repairs may be impossible for weeks on end.

"So we're left with the likelihood that any further sabotage will take the form of attacks on accessible stretches of VSM's or the taking out of minor bridges – the possibility

85

of destroying the Tazlina or Tanana bridges is remote, as those could well take weeks to repair. We may not have come up with too much, but at least we have clarified matters and established some sort of system of priorities."

Not without difficulty Brady heaved himself to his feet to indicate that the interview was over. "Thank you, gentlemen, both for your time and information. I'll see you in the morning – at, of course, a reasonably Christian hour."

The door closed behind Bronowski and Houston. Brady asked: "Well, what did you make of that?"

Dermott said: "As you said, just a limitation of possibilities, which, unfortunately, still remain practically limitless. Three things I'd like to do. First, I'd like the F.B.I. or whoever to carry out a rigorous investigation into the pasts of Poulson and his pals at Pump Station Four."

"You have reason to suspect them?"

"Not really. But I've an odd feeling: something is wrong at Number Four. Don shares my feeling, but there's nothing we can put a finger on except that buff envelope that went missing from the dead engineer's pocket. Even with that I'm beginning to question whether my eyes or imagination were playing tricks on me: the lighting was damned harsh, and I could have got my colours wrong. No matter – as you'd be the first to agree, every pipeline employee is a suspect until his innocence is established."

"You bet. You said Poulson and Bronowski seemed on pretty cordial terms?"

"Bronowski is the sort of character who seems on pretty well cordial terms with everyone. If you're suggesting what I think you are I might mention that according to Finlayson there have been three security checks carried out on Bronowski."

"And passed with flying colours, no doubt. What does Finlayson know about security checks and how to evaluate them? Has he any guarantee that none of those three

86

professedly unbiased investigators was not, in fact, a bosom friend of Bronowski? Now, *I* have a very good and very discreet friend in New York. As you say yourself, every pipeline operator is as guilty as hell until proved otherwise."

"I didn't quite say that."

"Hair-splitting. The second thing?"

"I'd like a medical opinion, preferably that of a doctor with some osteopathic knowledge, on how the dead engineer's finger came to be broken."

"How can that help?"

"How should I know?" Dermott sounded almost irritable. "God knows, Jim, you've emphasised often enough never to overlook anything that seems odd."

"True, true," Brady said pacifically. "There was a third matter?"

"Let's find out how the fingerprint boys in Anchorage are getting on with that telephone booth affair. Three tiny things, I know, but it's all we have to go on."

"Four. There's also Bronowski. And now?"

The telephone rang. Brady picked it up, listened briefly, scowled and handed the phone over to Dermott. "For you." Dermott lifted an eyebrow. "It's that damnable code again."

Dermott gave him an old-fashioned look, put the phone to his ear, reached for a pad and started to make notes. After barely a minute he hung up and said: "And now? That was your last question, wasn't it?"

"What? Yes. So?"

"And now it's back to the old jet and heigh-ho for Canada."

Dermott gave Brady an encouraging smile. "Should be all right, sir. Still plenty of daiquiri in your airborne bar."

"What the devil is that meant to mean?"

"Just this, sir." Dermott's smile had gone. "You will recall our three brilliant minds sitting around in Sanmobil's office and coming to the unanimous conclusion that there were six points vulnerable to attack – the draglines, the bucketwheels, the reclaimers' bridges, the separator plates, the radial stackers and, above all, the conveyor belting? Some joker up there obviously didn't see it our way at all. He's taken out the main processing plant."

6

Four hours later the Brady Enterprises team stood shivering in Sanmobil's sabotaged processing plant at Athabasca. Brady himself was enveloped in his usual cocoon of coats and scarves, his temper not improved by the fact that the flight from Alaska had deprived him of dinner.

"How did it *happen?*" he repeated. "Here we have an easily-patrolled area, brilliantly lit, as you pointed out yourself, and staffed with 100 per cent – I beg your pardon, 98 per cent – loyal and patriotic Canadians." He peered through a large hole that had been blown in a cylindrical container. "How can such things be?"

"I don't think that's quite fair, Mr Brady." Bill Reynolds, the fair-haired and ruddy-faced operations manager, spoke up for his colleague Terry Brinckman, the security chief at whom Brady's remarks had been directed. "Terry had only eight men on duty last night – and that was his second shift of the day. In other words, he himself had been continuously on duty for fifteen hours when this incident occurred. You can see how hard he was trying."

Brady did not nod in assent. Reynolds went on:

"You remember we had all agreed on the priorities, the areas most liable to attack. Those were the places that Terry and his men were doing their best to protect – which didn't leave any men over for patrolling the plant itself. You will recall, Mr Brady, that you were in complete agreement. You also said Terry had nothing to reproach himself with. If we're going to apportion blame, let's not forget ourselves."

"Nobody's blaming anybody, Mr Reynolds. How extensive is the damage?"

"Enough. Terry and I figure that these guys let off three charges here – that's the gas oil hydrotreater – and the same number next door at the naphtha hydrotreater. In fact we've been extremely lucky – we could have had gas explosions and fuel fires. We had none. As it is, damage is comparatively slight. We should be on stream again in forty-eight hours."

"Meantime, everything is shut down?"

"Not the draglines. But the rest is. The radial stackers are full."

"One of the plant operatives, you think?"

Brinckman said: "I'm afraid we're sure. It's a big plant but it takes surprisingly few people to operate it, and everybody on a shift knows everybody else. A stranger would have been spotted at once. Besides, we *know* it was an inside job – six thirty-ounce explosive charges were taken from the blasting shed last night."

"Blasting shed?"

Reynolds said: "We use explosives to break up large chunks of tar sand that have become too tightly bound together. But we've only got small charges."

"Big enough, it would seem. The blasting shed is normally kept locked?"

"Double-locked."

"Somebody forced the door?"

"Nobody forced anything. That's why Brinckman told you we're sure it was an inside job. Somebody used keys."

"Who normally holds the keys?" Dermott asked.

Reynolds said: "There are three sets. I hold one, Brinckman has two."

"Why two?"

"One I keep permanently," Brinckman explained. "The other goes to the security charge-hand for the night-shift, who passes it on to the person in charge of the morning and afternoon shifts."

"Who are those other security shift charge-hands?"

90

Brinckman said: "My No. 2, Jorgensen – this is his shift, really – and Napier. I don't think that any of the three of us is much given to stealing explosives, Mr Dermott."

"Not unless you're certifiable. Now, it seems unlikely anyone would risk abstracting keys and having copies made. Not only would they be too likely to be missed, but there's also more than a fair chance that we could trace the key-cutter and so the thief."

"There could be illegal key-cutters."

"I still doubt the keys would have been taken. Much more likely someone took an impression: that would need seconds only. And that's where the illegal side would come in – no straight key-cutter would touch an impression. How easy would it be for anyone to get hold of the keys, even briefly?"

Brinckman said: "About Jorgensen's and Napier's I wouldn't know. I clip mine to my belt."

Mackenzie said: "Everybody's got to sleep."

"So?"

"You take your belt off then, don't you?"

"Sure." Brinckman shrugged. "And if you're going to ask me next if I'm a heavy sleeper, well, yes, I am. And if you're going to ask me if it would have been possible for anyone to sneak into my room while I was asleep, borrow my key for a couple of minutes and return it unseen, well, yes that would have been perfectly possible too."

"This," Brady said, "is not going to take us very far. Sticky-fingered characters with an affinity for keys are legion. Would there have been *any* security man in this area tonight?"

"Jorgensen would know," Brinckman said. "Shall I get him?"

"Won't he be out patrolling sixteen miles of conveyor belting or something?"

"He's in the canteen."

"But surely he's in charge, on duty?"

91

"In charge of what, Mr Brady? There are four men keeping an eye on the four draglines. The rest of the plant is closed down. We think it unlikely that this bomber will strike again tonight."

"Not much is unlikely."

"Bring him along to my office," Reynolds said. Brinckman left. "I think you'll find it warmer and more comfortable there, Mr Brady."

They followed Reynolds to the office block, through an external room where a bright-eyed and pretty young woman at the desk gave them a charming smile, and on into Reynolds's office where Brady began divesting himself of several outer layers of clothing even before Reynolds had the door closed. Reynolds took his chair behind the desk while Brady sunk wearily into the only armchair in the room.

Reynolds said: "Sorry to drag you all over the north-west like this. No sleep, no food, jet lags, all very upsetting. In the circumstances I feel entitled to bend company regulations. Come to think of it, I'm the only person in Sanmobil who can. A refreshment would be in order?"

"Ha!" Brady pondered. "Early in the morning. Not only no dinner but no breakfast either." A hopeful look crept into his eye. "Daiquiri?"

"But I thought you always –"

"We had an unfortunate experience over the Yukon," Dermott said. "We ran out."

Brady scowled. Reynolds smiled. "No daiquiris here. But a really excellent twelve-year-old malt." A few seconds later Brady lowered his half-tumbler and nodded appreciatively.

"A close second. Now you two" – this to Dermott and Mackenzie – "I've done all the work so far."

"Yes, sir." Not even the shadow of a smile touched Mackenzie's face. "Three questions, if I may. Who suggested checking up on the amount of explosives in the blasting shed?"

92

"Nobody. Terry Brinckman did it off his own bat. We have a meticulous checking system and an easy one. The tally sheet's kept up to date twice a day. We just count the numbers of each particular type of explosive, subtract that number from the latest entry on the tally sheet, and that's the number that's been issued that day. Or stolen, as the case may be."

"Well, that's certainly a mark in favour of your security chief."

"You have reservations about him?"

"Good heavens no. Why on earth should I? Number two – where do you hang up your keys at night?"

"I don't." He nodded towards a massive safe in a corner. "Kept there day and night."

"Ah! In that case I'll have to rephrase what was going to be my third question. You are the only person with a key to that safe?"

"There's one more key. Corinne has it."

"Ah. That lovely lassie in the outer office?"

"That, as you say, lovely lassie in the outer office is my secretary."

"And why does *she* have a key?"

"Various reasons. All big companies, as you must know, have their codes. We're no exception. Code books are kept there. Corinne's my coding expert. Also, I can't be here all the time. Under-managers, accountants, our legal people and the security chief all have access to the safe. I can assure you the safe contains items of vastly more importance than the keys to the blasting shed. Nothing has ever gone missing yet."

"People just walk in, help themselves and walk out?"

Reynolds lifted his eyebrows and looked hard at Mackenzie. "Not quite. We are security conscious to a degree. They have to sign in, show Corinne what they've taken and sign out again."

"A couple of keys in a trouser pocket?"

"Of course she doesn't search them. There has to be a certain amount of trust at executive levels."

"Yes. Could we have her in, do you think?"

Reynolds spoke into the box on his desk. Corinne entered looking good standing up, in her khaki cord Levi's and nicely disordered plaid shirt, a person with a smile for everyone. Reynolds said: "You know who those gentlemen are, Corinne?"

"Yes, sir. I think everybody does."

"I think Mr Mackenzie here would like to ask you some questions."

"Sir?"

"How long have you been with Mr Reynolds?"

"Just over two years."

"Before that?"

"I came straight from secretarial school."

"You have a pretty sensitive and responsible position here?"

She smiled again, but this time a little uncertainly, as if unsure where the questions were leading. "Mr Reynolds lists me as his confidential secretary."

"May I ask how old you are?"

"Twenty-two."

"You must be the youngest confidential secretary of any big corporation I've ever come across."

This time she caught her lip and glanced at Reynolds, who was leaning back in his chair, hands clasped lazily behind his neck, with the air of a man who was almost enjoying himself. He smiled and said: "Mr Mackenzie is an industrial sabotage investigator. He has a job to do and asking questions is part of that job. I know he's just made a statement, not asked a question, but it's one of those statements that expects comment."

She turned back to Mackenzie, with a swing of her long chestnut hair. "I suppose I've been pretty lucky at that."

She spoke with marked coolness and Mackenzie felt it. "None of my questions are directed against you, Corinne, okay? Now, you must know the executive level people pretty well?"

"I can hardly help it. They all come through me to get to Mr Reynolds."

"Including those who have business with that safe there?"

"Of course. I know them all well."

"All good friends, I take it?"

"Well." She smiled, but the smile had an edge to it. "Lots of them are much too senior to be my friends."

"But on good terms, shall we say?"

"Oh, yes." She smiled again. "I don't think I've made any enemies."

"Perish the thought!" This came from George Dermott, who took over the questioning on a brisker note. "Any of the people using the safe ever give you trouble? Like trying to take away what they shouldn't?"

"Not often, and then its only absentmindedness or because they haven't studied the classified list. And surely, Mr Dermott, if anyone wanted to get something past me they'd hide it in their clothing."

Dermott nodded. "That's true, Miss Delorme." The girl was inspecting his rough-and-ready good looks with a spark of humour in her eyes, as if amused by his blunt approach. He caught the expression and, in his turn, watched her for a reflective moment. "What do you think now?" he asked her. "Do you think anyone might have smuggled something past you out of the safe?"

She looked him in the eye. "They might," she said, "but I doubt it."

"Could I have a list of the people who used the safe in the past four or five days?"

"Certainly." She left and returned with a sheet which Dermott studied briefly.

95

"Good Lord! The safe appears to be the Mecca for half of Sanmobil. Twenty entries at least in the last four days." He looked up at the girl. "This is a carbon. May I keep it?"

"Of course."

"Thank you."

Corinne Delorme smiled at the room in general, but the blue eyes came back to Dermott before she went out.

"Charming indeed," said Brady.

"Plenty of spunk," Mackenzie said ruefully. "She built a whole generation gap between you and me, George." He frowned. "What gave you the idea her name was Delorme?"

"There was a plaque on her desk: 'Corinne Delorme', it said." Mackenzie shook his head. "Hawkeye Dermott," he said.

The other men laughed. Some of the tension that had grown in the room during the questioning of the girl fell away again.

"Well. Anything more I can do for you?" Reynolds asked.

Dermott said: "Yes, please. Could we have a list of the names of your security staff?"

Reynolds bent over the voice-box and spoke to Corinne. He had just finished when Brinckman arrived accompanied by a tall, red-haired man whom he introduced as Carl Jorgensen.

Dermott said: "You were in charge of the night security shift, I understand. Were you around the sabotage area at all tonight?"

"Several times."

"So often? I thought you would have been concentrating on what we regarded – mistakenly – as the more vulnerable areas."

"I went round them a couple of times but by jeep only. But I had this funny feeling that we might have been guarding the wrong places. Don't ask me why."

96

"Your funny feeling didn't turn out to be so funny after all. Anything off-beat, anything to arouse suspicion?"

"Nothing. I know everybody on the night shift and I know where they work. Nobody there that shouldn't have been there, nobody in any place that he hadn't any right to be."

"You've got a key to the blasting shed. Where do you keep it?"

"Terry Brinckman mentioned this. I have it only during my tour of duty and then I hand it over. I always carry it in the same button-down pocket on my shirt."

"Could anybody get at it?"

"Nobody except a professional pick-pocket, and even then I'd know."

The two security men left and Corinne came in with a sheet of paper. Reynolds said: "That was quick."

"Not really. They were typed out ages ago."

Brady said to the girl: "You must come and meet my daughter, Stella. I'm sure you'd get on. Both the same age. Stella is very like you, actually."

"Thank you, Mr Brady. I think I'd like that."

"I'll have her call you."

When she had gone, Dermott said: "What do you mean, like your daughter? I've never seen anyone less like Stella."

"Dancing eyes, my boy, dancing eyes. One must learn to probe beneath the surface." Brady heaved himself to his feet. "The years creep on. Breakfast and bed. I'm through detecting for the day. It's tougher than capping fires."

* * *

Dermott drove the rented car back to the hotel, Mackenzie sitting beside him. Brady took his ease across the entire width of the back seat. He said: "I'm afraid I wasn't quite levelling with Reynolds there. Breakfast, yes. But it'll be some hours before I – we – retire. I have come up with a plan." He paused.

Dermott said courteously: "We're listening."

"I think I'll do some listening first. Why do you think I employ you?"

"That's a fair question," Mackenzie said. "Why?"

"To investigate, to detect, to think, to plot, to scheme, to plan."

"All at once?" Mackenzie said.

Brady ignored him. "I don't want to come up with a proposal and then, if it goes wrong, have to spend the rest of my days listening to your carping reproaches. I'd like you two to come up with an idea and then if it's a lemon we can all share the blame. Incidentally, Donald, I take it you have your bug-box with you?"

"The electronic eavesdropping locator-detector?"

"That's what I said."

"Yes."

"Splendid. Now, George, let's have your reading of the situation."

"My reading of the situation is that for all the good we're doing we haven't a hope in hell of stopping the bad guys from doing exactly what they want and when they want. There is no way to forestall attacks on Sanmobil or the Alaska pipeline. They're calling the shots and we're the sitting ducks, if you'll pardon the mixing of the metaphors. They call the tune and we dance to it. They're active, we're passive. They're offensive, we're defensive. If we have any tactics, I'd say it's time we changed them."

"Go on," his leader urged him from behind.

"If that's meant to sound encouraging," Dermott said, "I don't know why. But how's this for a positive thought? Instead of letting them keep us off-balance, why don't we keep them off-balance? Instead of their harassing us, let us harass them."

"Go on, go on," the back seat exhorted.

"Let's attack them and put them on the defensive. Let *them* start worrying, instead of us." He paused. "I see things as through a glass darkly, but I say plant a light at the end of the tunnel. What we'll do is, we'll provoke them. Provoke a reaction. Provoke the hell out of them. We'll hang it on this one factor: our own pasts, our backgrounds, can be probed until the cows come home, and nothing will be turned up: but you can say *that* about how many people in a hundred?"

Dermott twisted his head briefly to locate a peculiar noise from the back of the car. Brady was actually rubbing his hands together. "Well, Donald, what's your reading of it?"

"Simple enough when you see it," Mackenzie said. "All you have to do is to antagonise anywhere between sixty and eighty people to hell and back again. Investigate them as openly as possible. Deploy maximum indiscretion."

Brady beamed. "What sixty to eighty people do we investigate?"

"In Alaska *all* the security agents. Here, the security agents again, plus everybody who's had access to Reynolds's safe in the past few days. Going to include Reynolds himself?"

"Good heavens, no."

Mackenzie said inconsequentially: "She *is* a lovely girl."

Brady looked aloof. Mackenzie asked him: "Do you really expect to find your panjandrum among that lot?"

"Panjandrum?"

"The prime mover. Mr Big. Messrs Big."

"Not for a moment. But if there's a rotten apple in the barrel, he may well find him for us."

Mackenzie said: "Right. So we get all their names and past histories. Later on – sooner rather than later – we'll have the lot fingerprinted. Sure, they're going to stand on their civic rights and yell blue murder, and that will please you no end – refusal to co-operate will point the finger of suspicion at the refusee, if that's the word I want. Then you feed the information to your investigators in Houston, Washington and New York: cost no object, urgency desperate. Not that you'll care a damn whether the investigators come up with anything or not. All that matters is that the suspects get to hear such enquiries are under way. That's all the provocation they'll need."

"What kind of reactions do we expect to provoke?" Dermott asked.

"Unpleasant ones, I should hope. For the villains, I mean."

"The first thing I'd do," Dermott told Brady, "is send your family back to Houston. Jean and Stella could really become a liability. The scheme might rebound on you. Can't you see the word coming through: lay off, Brady, or something unpleasant's going to happen to your family? These people are playing for high stakes. They've killed once, they won't hesitate to kill again. They can't be hung twice."

"Same thought occurred to me." Mackenzie turned to face the back seat. "Either get the girls right back home, or have the RCMP protect them."

"Hell – I *need* them!" Brady sat forward with indignation. "Number one, I have to be looked after. Number two, Stella's handling the Ekofisk business for me."

"Ekofisk?" Dermott almost turned backwards. "What's that?"

"Big fire in the North Sea, Norwegian half. Started after you'd come north. We have a team going in there today."

"Well, okay," Dermott gave way a little. "So you have to keep in touch. But why not work through the locals? That red-head of Reynolds's – Corinne. She could field calls for you."

"What happens when we go back to Alaska?"

"Use somebody up there. Finlayson's got a secretary — must have."

"No substitute for the personal touch," said Brady magisterially. He sank back in the seat as though the argument were over.

His two heavyweights turned forward again with an exchange of looks. Having been though all this a hundred times before, they knew that further pressure would be useless for the moment. Wherever he went, Brady maintained the fiction that his wife and daughter were part of his essential life-support system, and he kept them with him regardless of the expense. Or danger.

7

Not that Dermott and Mackenzie in the least minded having Jean and Stella around. Like mother, like daughter: whereas Jean was a strikingly handsome woman in her middle-forties, with that lovely, naturally blonde hair and intelligent grey eyes, Stella looked the spitting image of her mother, only younger, and even livelier, with, as her father was so fond of claiming, dancing eyes.

The men found Jean awaiting their return in the lounge bar of the Peter Pond Hotel. Tall and elegant, she advanced to meet them with her usual expression of tolerant, kindly amusement. This look, Dermott knew from experience, reflected her genuine feelings: an equable temperament was no small advantage for someone who had to spend her life humouring Jim Brady.

"Hi, honey!" He reached up slightly to kiss her on the forehead. "Where's Stella?"

"In your room. She's got some messages for you – been pretty busy on the phone."

"Excuse me, then, gentlemen. Maybe one of you would be so kind as to buy my wife a drink."

He waddled off along the corridor, while Dermott and Mackenzie settled comfortably into the warmth of the bar. In marked contrast to her husband, Jean scarcely drank alcohol at all, and she sipped carefully at a pineapple juice while the two men addressed themselves to the Scotch. Nor did she try to talk shop in Brady's absence: instead, she chatted pleasantly about Fort McMurray and its modest midwinter pleasures until her husband returned.

When he came back, Stella was with him, swinging along

with her easy, loose-hipped walk. Dermott – not normally given to flights of fancy – was suddenly struck by the absurd disparity between the two figures. Jesus, he thought to himself: a hippo and a gazelle. What a pair!

Scarcely had Brady subsided into an armchair, with an outsize glass of daiquiri in his podgy hand, than he made a slight sign to Dermott and Mackenzie, who muttered something and slipped off.

Brady seemed in buoyant form, and began to regale his family with an edited account of his movements around the far north. After a while Jean said doubtfully: "It doesn't seem to me you've *accomplished* very much."

Brady was unruffled. "Ninety per cent of our business is cerebral, my dear. When we move into action, what happens is merely the almost mechanical and inevitable culmination of all the invisible hard work that's gone on before." He tapped his head. "The wise general doesn't fling his troops into battle without reconnoitring beforehand. We've been reconnoitring."

Jean smiled. "Let us know when you've identified the enemy." Suddenly she became serious. "It's a nasty business, isn't it?"

"Murder always is, my dear."

"I don't like it, Jim. I don't like you being in it. Surely this is for the law. You've never come across murder before in your business."

"So I run away?"

She looked at his ample frame and laughed: "That's one thing you're not built for."

"Run?" Stella said, mock-scornfully. "Dad couldn't jog from here to the john!"

"Please!" Brady beamed. "I trust no such haste will be necessary."

"Where did Donald go?" Jean asked.

"Upstairs, doing a little job for me."

103

Mackenzie was at that moment moving slowly round Brady's apartment with a calibrated metal box in one hand, a portable antenna in the other, and a pair of earphones on his head. He moved purposefully, a man who knew what he was about. He soon found what he was looking for.

When he came back to the bar he headed straight for Brady's family encampment.

"Two," he reported.

"Two what, Uncle Donald?" Stella asked sweetly.

Mackenzie appealed to his boss. "When are you going to start training this incorrigibly nosey daughter of yours?"

"I've stopped. Failed. Mother's job, anyway." He jerked his head upwards. "Got them all, did you?"

"Guess so."

Dermott also reappeared to report.

"Ah, George," Brady greeted him. "How did it go?"

"Reynolds seems very co-operative. Unfortunately all records are stored at the head office in Edmonton. He says by the time they've been dug out and flown up here, it may be late this evening or even tomorrow morning."

"What records?" Stella asked.

"Affairs of state," Brady told her. "Well, can't be helped. Anything else?"

"Naturally enough he's got no fingerprinting equipment."

"Fix it after lunch."

"He says he'll fix it himself – the police chief's a pal of his, apparently. Thinks the chief might be a bit shirty about the delay in reporting the crime." He grinned across at Stella. "And don't ask 'what crime?'"

"No, sir, Mr Dermott, sir!" She wrinkled her upper lip in a fetching manner. "I *never* ask questions! I'm just permitted to fetch and carry, mend and clean."

Brady went on: "Reynolds can always claim that at first he thought it was an industrial accident."

"I understand the chief of police has 20-20 vision and intelligence to match."

"Well – Reynolds'll have to handle it as best he can. What about Prudhoe Bay?"

"An hour's hold. They'll page me."

"Fair enough." Brady shifted his attention to Stella. "We met an enchanting girl this morning – didn't we, George? Knock spots off you, any day. Wouldn't she, gentlemen?"

"Unquestionably," said Mackenzie.

Stella looked at Dermott. "Foul, aren't they?"

"Dead heat," said Dermott. "But she's very nice."

"The manager's secretary," Brady said. "Corinne Delorme. I thought maybe you'd like to meet her. She said she'd like to meet you. She must know all the night-clubs, discos and other iniquitous dens in Fort McMurray."

Stella said: "News for you, Dad. You've got to be talking about another town. I don't know what this place is like in summer, but whatever it is, it's a dead city in mid-winter. You might have warned us that this is an *Arctic* town."

"Lovely choice of phrase. Wonderful sense of geography. That's education for you," Brady said to no-one in particular. "Maybe you should have stayed in Houston."

Stella looked at her mother. "Did you hear what I just heard, Mummy?" she asked with a scornful shake of the head at her father which brought the pale blonde hair swinging round her face.

Jean smiled. "I heard. Sooner or later, my dear, you have to face up to the fact that your father is no more and no less than a fearful old hypocrite."

"But he dragged us up here, kicking and screaming against our will, and now ..." Remarkably, words failed her.

As much as it was possible for so rubicund a face to register an expression, Brady's was registering unhappiness. "Well, now you've found out you don't like it, maybe you'd

105

rather get back down to Houston." A note of wistfulness crept into his voice. "It'll be nearly seventy degrees back there now."

Silence descended. Brady looked at Dermott and Dermott looked at him. Jean Brady looked at both of them. "Something goes on that I don't understand," she said. Brady dropped his eyes, so she switched her attention to Dermott. "George?"

"Yes, ma'am?"

"George!" He looked at her. "And don't call me 'ma'am'."

"No, Jean." He sighed and spoke with some feeling. "The boss of Brady Enterprises is not only a fearful old hypocrite: he's a fearful old coward as well. What he wants, in the good old fashioned Western phrase, is that you should get out of town."

"Why? What on earth have we done?"

Dermott looked hopefully at Mackenzie, who said: "You've done nothing. He has – or is about to." Mackenzie shook his head at Dermott. "This is difficult," he said.

Dermott explained: "We've decided on a course of action to flush the ungodly into the open, make them show their hand. Don and I have this unpleasant feeling that their reaction may be directed against Brady Enterprises in general and its boss in particular. The reaction may be violent – these people don't play by any rules but their own. We don't think they'd go for Jim himself. It's well known that he can't be intimidated. But what's equally well known is what he thinks of his own family. If they got you or Stella, or both of you, they might figure they could force him to pull out."

Jean reached out to take Stella's hand. "But this must be nonsense," she said. "Drama. Things like that don't happen any more. Don, I appeal to you . . ." She looked anxiously at her daughter, gave her hand a little shake and released it.

Mackenzie was dogged. "Don't appeal to me, Jean. When they snip off your finger with the wedding ring on it, will you still be saying things like that don't happen any more?" She looked hurt. "Sorry if I sound brutal, but things like that have never stopped happening. It may not come to anything so bad: I'm looking on the blackest possible side. But that's the only sensible way to look. We've got to find a safe place for you and the girl. How can Jim operate at his best if you're on his mind?"

"He's right," muttered Brady. "Go pack your bags, please."

During Mackenzie's speech Stella had sat with her hands clasped together on her lap, like a schoolgirl, listening gravely. Now she said: "I can't do that, Dad."

"Why not?"

"Who's going to make your daiquiris for you?"

Her mother cut in sharply. "There's a little more to this than the damned daiquiris. If we left, who's going to be number one target?"

"Dad," said Stella flatly. She glowered at Dermott. "You know that, George."

"I do," he answered mildly. "But Donald and I are pretty good at looking after people."

"That would be just fine, wouldn't it?" She threw herself back in her chair, hazel eyes blazing. "All three of you shot or blown up or something."

"Getting upset isn't going to help," said Jean soothingly. "Logic will, though." She transferred her attention to Brady. "If we went, you'd still be worried stiff about us, and we'd be worried stiff about you. So where would that get us?"

Brady said nothing, and she went on: "But there's only one point that really matters. Not only will I not run away from my husband. I'll be damned if Jean Brady will run, period."

Stella said: "And *I'll* be damned if Stella Brady runs either. Who's gonna maintain communications, for one thing? You know how long I spent on the phone today – to England and all that? *Four hours.*" She stood up decisively. "Another drink, Dad?" She cocked an ear at him ostentatiously. "I'm sorry, I didn't hear that."

"Monstrous regiment of women, was what I said."

"Ah!" she smiled, collected the empty glasses and headed for the bar. Brady glared at Dermott and Mackenzie. "Hell of a lot of good you two are. Why didn't you back me up?" He sighed heavily and changed his tack. "Why don't we all get something to eat? Lunch, and after it I'll catch up on some sleep. What are you girls proposing to do this afternoon?"

Stella came back with full glasses. "We're going for a sleigh ride. Won't that be nice!"

"Good God! You mean *outside*?" Brady gloomily surveyed the few flakes drifting past the window. "Very nice for some, I'm sure, but not for the sane." He struggled to his feet. "The dining-room in two minutes, then. George, if you will." He took Dermott aside.

*   *   *

With a giant Caribou T-bone steak, a quarter of blueberry pie and some excellent California burgundy inside him, Brady watched his befurred wife and daughter go out through the main entrance and sighed with satisfaction at the feeling of physical well-being that enveloped him.

"Well, gentlemen, I really believe I might manage a brief snooze after all. Yourselves too?"

Dermott said: "Off and on. Donald and I thought we'd chivvy up Prudhoe Bay and Sanmobil and get those names and records through as soon as possible."

"Well, thank you, gentlemen. Very considerate. Do not

108

wake me up unless Armageddon is nigh. Aha! Here, not unexpectedly, return the ladies." He waited until his wife had reached the table. "Something up, then?"

"Something *is* up." Jean did not sound pleased. "There are two men on the driving bench of that sleigh. Why two?"

"My dear, I'm not the arbiter of local customs. Are you afraid they're homosexual?"

She lowered her voice. "They're both carrying guns. You can't see them, but you can, if you know what I mean."

Brady said: "Members of the Royal Canadian Mounted Police are entitled to bear arms at all times. Says so in their constitution."

Jean stared at him, snorted with resignation, turned and left. Jim Brady beamed in satisfaction. Mackenzie said airily: "They tell me there are some very handsome young constables in the R.C.M.P."

*   *   *

Apart from chatting with Ferguson, Brady's pilot, Dermott spent the afternoon alone in the lounge, consuming one cup of coffee after the other. About mid-afternoon Jean and Stella returned, rosy-cheeked and in high spirits. Stella, it appeared, had learned from their escorts of a place where the younger people congregated of an evening, and had called Corinne Delorme at work to invite her out. Whether they intended to invite their erstwhile escorts along, Stella did not say nor did Dermott enquire. Brady would have the place comprehensively checked out before he would let them near it. Shortly afterwards Dermott received a call from Alaska. It was Bronowski in Prudhoe Bay: John Finlayson he said, was out at Pump Station Four but was expected back soon; he, Bronowski, would immediately set about obtaining what Dermott wanted and would arrange for the services of a fingerprint expert from Anchorage.

At five o'clock Reynolds came through to say that the fingerprinting was well in hand. The records Dermott required were even then being delivered to Edmonton Airport and would be delivered straight from McMurray Airport to the hotel. At six-thirty Mackenzie appeared, looking refreshed but at the same time reproachful.

"You should have called me. I'd meant to come down a couple of hours ago."

"I'll sleep tonight," Dermott said. "That's four hours you owe me."

"Three and a half. I put a call through to Houston, explained what we had in mind, told them to alert Washington and New York, and emphasised the urgency."

"I trust your unofficial listener got it all down."

"He could hardly fail to," Mackenzie said. "There was a bug installed inside the base plate of the telephone."

"Well, that should be the final stirring-up of the hornets' nest. Let's hope the wrong people don't get stung. How's Jim?"

"Peered round his door on the way down. Looked like he'd died in his sleep."

At seven o'clock a call came through from Sanmobil. Dermott indicated to Mackenzie that he should listen in to the extension earphone slotted onto the back of the receiver.

"Mr Reynolds? Not more bad news, I hope."

"For me it is. I've been told to shut down the plant for a week."

"When?"

"Now. Well, a few minutes ago. And I'm to be contacted in forty-eight hours to see if I've complied."

"Was the message from Anchorage?"

"Where else?"

"Phone?"

"No. Telex."

"They sent an open message?"

"No. Code. Our own company code."

Dermott looked at Mackenzie. "Pretty sure of themselves, aren't they?"

Reynolds said: "What was that?"

"Talking to Donald Mackenzie. He's listening in. So they know that we know it's an inside job. They must be pretty sure of themselves. Who's got access to the code books?"

"Anybody who's got access to my safe."

"How many people does that make?"

"Twenty. Give or take."

"What do you intend to do?"

"Consult Edmonton. With their approval I intend to be on stream again inside forty-eight hours."

"I wish you luck." Dermott replaced the receiver and looked at Mackenzie. "Now what?"

"Do you think Armageddon is nigh enough to justify waking up the Boss?"

"Not yet. Nothing he, we or anybody can do. Infuriating. Let's try Anchorage. What's the betting they've had a similar threat to close down the pipeline?" He lifted the phone, asked for the number, listened briefly then hung up. "Hold, they say. One hour, two hours. They're not sure."

The telephone rang. Dermott picked it up. "Anchorage? No it can't be. I've just been told – ah, I see." He looked at Mackenzie. "Police." Mackenzie picked up the extension receiver. They both listened in silence, Dermott said: "Thank you. Thank you very much," and both hung up.

Mackenzie said: "Well, they seem pretty confident."

"They're certain. Perfect copies of the prints from the Anchorage phone boxes. But they can't match them up with any on their lists."

"It all helps," Mackenzie said gloomily.

"It's not all that bad. The Photostat is promised for tomorrow. Might just match up with some of the prints we hope to collect. The Alaskan ones, I mean."

111

"Of course?"

"Yes. It would be too easy to check up on anyone here who made a brief stopover in Anchorage."

Stella came into the lounge, all set for dancing in black sequined silk and coloured tights, and carrying her coat. Dermott said: "And where do you think you're going?"

Stella said: "I'm going out with Corinne. First a snack and then the bright lights and the light fantastic."

"You'll confine your dancing activities strictly to this hotel. You're not going any place."

When she had got through a diatribe, calling him a stuffed shirt and a spoil-sport, she added: "Mr Reynolds said it's all right."

"When did he say this?"

"We phoned about an hour ago."

"It's not up to Mr Reynolds to give you permission."

"But he knows Corinne is coming with me. She lives near here. You don't think he'd let his secretary walk into danger, do you?"

"*She* wouldn't be walking into danger. Nobody would be interested in her. But in you, yes."

Stella said: "You sound as if you're convinced something is going to happen to me."

"That's the way to make sure that nothing will happen to you – by taking precautions. See what your father says anyway."

"But how would *he* know what's safe and what isn't? How would he check up?"

"He'd go to the top: the chief of police, I'm certain."

Stella smiled brilliantly and said: "But we've talked already to him. Over the phone. He was with Mr Reynolds. He says it's perfectly okay." She smiled again, impishly. "Besides, we won't lack protection."

"Your friends of this afternoon?"

"John Carmody and Bill Jones."

112

"Well, I suppose that does make a difference. Ah, here comes Corinne." He beckoned her across, made the introductions and watched as they moved off. "Well, I suppose we worry too much." He glanced at the doorway. "When I look at that lot coming in, I hardly think we need worry at all."

"That lot" were a pretty formidable looking pair – big men in their late twenties or early thirties who looked eminently capable of taking care not only of themselves but of anyone who might be along with them. Dermott and Mackenzie rose and crossed to meet them.

Dermott said: "I could be wrong, but you wouldn't be two policemen disguised as civilians?"

"There we go," said the fair-haired man. "Can't be very good at undercover work if it's as obvious as that. I'm John Carmody. This is Bill Jones. You must be Mr Dermott and Mr Mackenzie. Miss Brady described you to us."

Mackenzie asked: "You gentlemen on overtime tonight?"

Carmody grinned. "Tonight? Two gallant volunteers. Labour of love. Doesn't look like being any great hardship."

"Watch them. Beautiful she may be, but Stella's a conniving young minx. One other thing: you know we have a feeling some bad actors might try to hurt her. Or take her out of circulation. Just a suspicion, but you never know."

"I think we might be able to take care of that."

"I'm sure you can. Most kind of you gentlemen. Very much appreciated, I can tell you. I know Mr Brady would like to thank you himself, but as he's in the land of dreams I'll do it on his behalf. The girls are through there. I hope you have a pleasant evening."

Dermott and Mackenzie returned to their table, where they talked in desultory fashion. Then the phone rang again. This time it was Alaska: Prudhoe Bay.

"Tim Houston here. Bad news, I'm afraid. Sam Bronowski is in the hospital. I found him lying unconscious on the floor of Finlayson's office. Appears to have been struck over the head with a heavy object. He was hit over the temple where the skull is thinnest. Doctor says there may be a fracture – he's just finishing some X-rays. He's certainly concussed."

"When did this happen?"

"Half hour ago. No more. But that's not all. John Finlayson is missing: he vanished soon after coming back from Pump Station Four. Searched everywhere. No trace of him. Not in any of the buildings. If he's outside on a night like this – well . . ." There was a grim pause. ". . . he won't be around for long. We've got a high wind and heavy drifting, and the temperature's between thirty and forty below. Every man in the place is out looking for him. Maybe he was attacked by the same person who attacked Bronowski. Maybe he wandered out dazed. Maybe he was forcibly removed – although I don't see how that could be possible with so many people around. Are you coming up?"

"Are the F.B.I. and the State police there?"

"Yes. But there's been another development."

"A message from Edmonton?"

"Yes."

"Telling you to close down the line?"

"How did you know?"

"They make similar demands, we've got one here. I'll talk to Mr Brady. If you don't hear, you'll know we're on our way." He replaced the receiver and said to Mackenzie: "Armageddon? Enough to wake Jim?"

"More than enough."

8

Ferguson, the pilot, was unhappy and with good reason. Throughout the flight he was in more or less continuous touch with the operations centre in Prudhoe Bay, and knew that the weather ahead was dangerous. The wind was gusting at 40 miles per hour: flying snow had cut ground visibility to a few feet, and the thickness of the drifting snow-blanket was estimated at sixty feet or even more – less than ideal circumstances for landing a fast jet in darkness.

Ferguson had every modern navigational and landing aid, but although he could make a hands-off touch-down if he had to, he preferred to see *terra firma* before he put his wheels down on it. One factor in Ferguson's favour was that he was a profound pessimist: his three passengers well knew that he was not given to endangering his own life, let alone those of other people on board, and would have turned back had the risks been too great.

Brady, who had been wakened from a deep sleep and was in a sour mood, spoke scarcely a word on the way north. Mackenzie and Dermott, aware that the flight might be their last opportunity for some time, spent most of the trip asleep.

The landing, with much advancing and retarding of the throttles, was a heavy, bouncing one, but nonetheless safely accomplished. Visibility was down to twenty feet, and Ferguson crept cautiously forward until he picked up the lights of a vehicle. When the cabin door was opened, freezing snow whirled in, and Brady lost no time in making his customary elephantine dash for the shelter of the waiting minibus. At the wheel was Tim Houston, lieutenant to the invalided Bronowski.

"Evening, Mr Brady." Houston wore no welcoming smile. "Filthy night. I won't ask if you had a good flight because I'm sure you didn't. Afraid you haven't had too much sleep since you came to the north-west."

"I'm exhausted." Brady didn't mention that he'd had six hours' sleep before leaving Fort McMurray. "What's the word about John Finlayson?"

"None. We've examined every building, every pump-house, every last shack within a mile of the operations centre. We thought there was a remote chance that he'd gone across to the ARCO centre, but they searched and found nothing."

"What's your feeling?"

"He's dead. He must be." Houston shook his head. "If he isn't – or wasn't – under cover, he couldn't have lasted a quarter of the time he's been missing. What makes that even more certain is that he didn't take his outdoor furs with him. Without furs? Ten minutes, if that."

"The F.B.I. or police come up with anything?"

"Zero. Conditions are bad, Mr Brady."

"I can see that." Brady spoke with feeling and shivered. "I suppose you'll have to wait for daylight before you can carry out a proper search?"

"Tomorrow will be too late. Even now it's too late. Anyway, even if he is around, the chances are we won't find him. We might not find him until warmer weather comes and the snow goes."

"Drifting, you mean?" This was Mackenzie.

"Yes. He could be in a gully or by the roadside – our roads are built five feet high on gravel – and he could be lying at the bottom of a ditch with not even a mound to show where he is." Houston gave a shrug.

"What a way to die," Mackenzie said.

116

"I'm accepting the fact that he is gone," Houston said, "and though it sounds callous, maybe, it's not such a bad way to go. Perhaps the easiest way to go. No suffering: you just go to sleep and never wake up again."

Dermott said: "You make it sound almost pleasant. How's Bronowski?"

"No fracture. Heavy contusions. Dr Blake reckons the concussion is only slight. He was stirring and seeming to make an effort to surface when I left the camp."

"No further progress in that direction?"

"Nothing. Very much doubt whether there will be either. Sam was the only person who could have told us anything or identified his assailant. It's a thousand to one that he was attacked from behind and never caught a glimpse of his attacker. If he had, the attacker would probably have silenced him for keeps. After you've killed two people, what's a third?"

"The same people, you reckon?"

Houston stared. "It's too much of a coincidence to be different people, Mr Brady!"

"I suppose. This telex from Edmonton?"

Houston scratched his head. "Told us to close down the line for a week. Says they're going to check in forty-eight hours."

"And in your own company code, you said?" Dermott asked him.

"They didn't give a damn about letting us see it was an inside job. Damned arrogance. And the telex was addressed to Mr Black. Only someone working on the pipeline would know that he was up here. He spends nearly all his time in Anchorage."

Dermott said: "How's Black taking this?"

"Difficult to say. Bit of a cold fish; not much given to showing his feelings. I know how I'd feel in his shoes. He's the general manager, Alaska, and the buck stops with him."

Houston was doing Black a degree less than justice. When they arrived at his office in the operations centre, he had a distinctly unhappy and *distrait* air about him. He said: "Good of you to come, Mr Brady. Must have been a highly unpleasant trip – and in the depths of a winter's night." He turned to a tall tanned man with iron-grey hair. This is Mr Morrison. FBI."

Morrison shook hands with all three. "Know of you, of course, Mr Brady. I'll bet you don't get too much of this sort of thing out in the Gulf States."

"Never. Don't get any of this damnable snow and cold either. Mr Houston here tells me that you're all up against a blank wall. Finlayson's just vanished."

Morrison said: "We were hoping that a fresh mind might be of use."

"I'm afraid your hopes are misplaced. I leave detection to the professionals. I'm merely, as are my colleagues here, a sabotage investigator, although in this case it's clear that sabotage and crimes of violence have a common ground. You've had Mr Finlayson's office fingerprinted, of course."

"From top to bottom. Hundreds of prints, and not one seems to be any use. No prints there that shouldn't have been there."

"You mean that the owners of those prints all had regular and legitimate access to the office?"

Morrison nodded. "Just that."

Brady scowled. "And since we're convinced that this character is someone working on the pipeline, any one of those fingerprints might be his."

Mackenzie asked the FBI man: "Any sign of the weapon used on Bronowski?"

"Nothing. Dr Blake believes the blow was administered by the butt of a gun."

Dermott asked: "Where's the doctor?"

118

"In the sick bay, with Bronowski, who's just recovered consciousness. He's still dazed and incoherent, but it seems he'll be okay."

"Can we see the two of them?"

"I don't know," Black said. "The doctor, certainly. I don't know whether he'll allow you to talk to Bronowski."

"He can't be all that bad if he's conscious," said Dermott. "It's a matter of urgency. He's the only person who *might* be able to give us a clue about what happened to Finlayson."

When they arrived in the sick bay, Bronowski was speaking coherently enough to Dr Blake. He was very pale; the right-hand side of his head had been shaved, and a huge plaster, stretching from the top of his skull to the lobe of the ear, covered the right temple. Dermott looked at the doctor, a tall, swarthy man with an almost cadaverous face and a hooked nose.

"How's the patient?"

"Coming on. The wound's not too bad. He's just been soundly stunned, which is apt to addle anyone's brains a bit. Headache for a couple of days."

"A couple of brief questions for Bronowski."

"Well, brief." Dr Blake nodded at Dermott's companions.

Dermott asked: "Did you see the guy who knocked you down?"

"See him?" Bronowski exclaimed. "Didn't even hear him. First thing I knew of anything was when I woke up in this bed here."

"Did you know Finlayson was missing?"

"No. How long's he been gone?"

"Some hours. Must have gone missing before you were clobbered. Did you see him at all? Speak to him?"

"I did. I was working on those reports you asked me to get for you. He asked about the conversation I had with you,

119

then left." Bronowski thought about it. "That was the last I saw of him." He looked at Black. "Those papers I was working on. Are they still on the table?"

"I saw them."

"Can you have them put back in the safe, please? They're confidential."

"I'll do that," Black said.

Dermott asked: "May I see you a minute, doctor?"

"You're seeing me now." The doctor looked quizzically at Dermott down his long nose.

Dermott smiled heavily: "Do you want me to discuss my chilblains and gout in public?"

In the consulting room Dr Blake said: "You look in pretty good shape to me."

"Advancing years, is all. Have you been up to Pump Station Four?"

"Ah, so it's that business! What stopped you discussing it out there?"

"Because I'm naturally cagey, distrustful and suspicious."

"I went up with Finlayson." Blake made a grimace at the memory. "Place was a ghastly mess. So were the two murdered men."

"They were all that," Dermott agreed. "Did you carry out an autopsy on them?"

There was a pause. "Have you the right to be asking me these questions?"

Dermott nodded. "I think so, Doctor. We're all interested in justice. I'm trying to find out who killed those two men. May be three, by now, if Finlayson stays missing."

"Very well," Blake said. "I carried out an autopsy. It was fairly perfunctory, I admit. When men have been shot through the forehead, it's pointless to try to establish the possibility that they died of heart failure instead. Although, mind you, from the mangled state of their bodies, it's clear

120

that the blast effect of the explosion would in itself have been enough to kill them."

"The bullets were still lodged in the head?"

"They were and are. A low-velocity pistol. I know they'll have to be recovered, but that's a job for the police surgeon, not for me."

"Did you search them?"

Blake lifted a saturnine eyebrow. "My dear fellow, I'm a doctor, not a detective. Why should I search them? I did see that one had some papers in an inside coat pocket, but I didn't examine them. That was all."

"No gun? No holster?"

"I can testify to that. I had to remove coat and shirt. Nothing of that nature."

"One last question," Dermott said. "Did you notice the index finger on the same man's right hand?"

"Fractured just below the knuckle bone? Odd sort of break in a way, but it could have resulted from a variety of causes. Don't forget the blast flung both of them heavily against some machinery."

"Thank you for your patience." Dermott made for the door, then turned. "The dead men are still at Pump Station Four?"

"No. We brought them back here. I understand their families want them buried in Anchorage, and that they'll be flown down there tomorrow."

*   *   *

Dermott looked round Finlayson's office and said to Black: "Anything been altered since Bronowski was discovered here?"

"You'd have to ask Mr Finlayson. At the time, I was across seeing my opposite number in ARCO and didn't get here for twenty minutes."

121

The F.B.I. man asked: "Some things have been touched, naturally. My men had to when they were carrying out their fingerprinting."

Mackenzie nodded to the buff folders on Finlayson's desk. "Are those the reports on the security men? The ones that Bronowski said he was studying when he was clobbered?"

Black looked at Houston, and the security man said: "Yes."

"There were fingerprints, too." Mackenzie raised an eyebrow.

"Those will be in the safe," Houston said.

"We'd like to see those and the records," Dermott said. "In fact, we'd like to see everything in that safe."

Black intervened. "But that's where all our company confidential information is kept."

"That's precisely why we'd like to examine it."

Black compressed his lips. "That's a very large order, Mr Dermott."

"If our hands are to be tied, we might as well go back to Houston. Or have you something to hide?"

"I consider that remark offensive."

"I don't." Brady had spoken from the depths of the only armchair in the room. "If you have something to hide, we'd like to know what it is. If you haven't, open up your safe. You may be the senior man in Alaska, but the people in London are the ones that matter, and they've promised me we would be afforded every co-operation. You are showing distinct signs of lack of co-operation. I must say that gives me food for thought."

Black's lips were very pale now. "That could be construed as a veiled threat, Mr Brady."

"Construe it any damned way you like. We've been through this up here once before, earlier. And John Finlayson has gone walk-about or somewhere even less attractive. Co-operate or we leave – and leave you with the task of explaining to London the reason for your secretiveness."

"I am not being secretive. In the best interests of the company –"

"The best interest of your company is to keep that oil flowing and head off these killers. If you don't let us examine that safe, we can only conclude that for some reason you choose to obstruct the best interest of your company." Brady poured himself a daiquiri as if to indicate that his part of the discussion was over.

Black surrendered: "Very well." The lips had now thinned almost to nothing. "Under protest and under, I may say, duress, I agree to what I regard as an outrageous request. The keys are in Mr Finlayson's desk. I will bid you goodnight."

"One moment." Dermott didn't sound any more friendly than Black. "Do you have records of *all* your employees on the pipeline?"

It was clear that Black was considering some further opposition, and then decided against it. "We do. But very concise. Couldn't call them reports, just brief notes of, mainly, previous jobs held."

"Where are they? Here?"

"No. Only reports on security personnel are kept here, and that's because Bronowski regards this as his base. The rest are kept in Anchorage."

"We'd like to see them. Perhaps you can arrange for them to be made available?"

"I can arrange it."

"I understand from Dr Blake that you have a flight to Anchorage tomorrow. Is it a big plane?"

"Too big," said Black the accountant. "A 737. Only one available tomorrow. Why?"

"One or more of us might want to hitch a lift," Dermott

123

answered. "We could, among other things, pick up those reports. Seats would be available?"

Black said: "Yes. No more questions, I trust?"

"One. You received this threatening telex message from Edmonton today, telling you to close down the line or else. What do you propose to do?"

"Carry on production, of course." Black tried to smile sardonically, but the moment was wrong. "Assuming, of course, that the criminals have been apprehended?"

"Where's the telex?"

"Bronowski had it. It may be on his person. Or in his desk."

"I'll find it," Dermott said.

"I don't think Bronowski would like you rummaging about his desk."

"He's not here, is he? Besides, he's a security man. He would understand." Dermott shook his head. "I don't think you ever will."

"No," Black said. "Goodnight." He turned on his heel and left. No-one said "goodnight" to him.

"Well, well." Brady exclaimed. "A friend for life in three minutes flat. Don't know how you do it, George. Pity he acts so suspiciously – otherwise he'd have made a splendid suspect."

"Badly ruffled feathers," Morrison said. "To put it in a restrained fashion, ruffling other people's feathers is his speciality. A martinet of the first order, they say, but an extraordinarily able man."

Dermott said: "Not, I gather, universally popular. Does he have friends?"

"Professional business contacts, that's all. Socially, nothing. If he has any friends, he hides them well." He tried to conceal a yawn. "My normal bedtime lies well behind me. In the F.B.I., we try to get to bed by ten p.m. Can I be of any assistance before I go?"

124

"Two things," Dermott said. "The maintenance crew at Pump Station Four. Fellow called Poulson in charge. Could you have their backgrounds investigated as rigorously as possible?"

"You have a reason for asking?" The F.B.I. man sounded hopeful.

"Nothing really. Just that they happened to be there when the sabotage occurred. I'm clutching at straws. We have damn little else to clutch at." Dermott smiled wryly.

"I think we can do that," Morrison said. "And the other?"

"Dr Blake tells me that the two dead engineers were brought back here today. Do you know where they were put?"

Morrison knew and told them, said his goodnights and left.

Brady said: "I think I shall go and rest lightly in my room. Notify me if the heavens fall in. But not after the first half hour or so. I take it you two are about to indulge your morbid curiosity in viewing the departed."

*　　*　　*

Dermott and Mackenzie looked down at the two murdered engineers. They had been covered in white sheets. No attempt had been made to clean them up since they last saw them at Pump Station Four. Perhaps it had been impossible. Perhaps no-one had had a strong enough stomach for the task. Mackenzie said: "I hope they're going to be sewn up in canvas or something before being taken to Anchorage tomorrow, or their relatives are going to have the screaming heebie-jeebies. Whatever you're looking for, George, look for it quick. I'm not enjoying myself."

Nor was Dermott. Not only was the sight revolting, but

125

the smell was nauseating. He lifted the hand of the man he'd briefly examined before and said: "How would you say that fore-finger got that way?"

Mackenzie bent, wrinkled his nose and said: "It sounds crazy, but it could have been broken by a pair of pliers. The trouble is that charring's obliterated any marks that might have been made on the skin."

Dermott went to a wash-basin, soaked his handkerchief and cleaned up the charred area as best he could. The black carbon came off surprisingly easily. It didn't leave the skin clean – the pitting was too deep for that – but clean enough to permit a closer examination.

"No pliers," Mackenzie said. "To break the bone, pliers would have had to close right into the flesh and would have been bound to leave saw-tooth marks. No saw-tooth marks, so no pliers. But I agree with you. I'm sure that bone was deliberately broken."

Dermott rubbed some carbon off the charred clothing and smeared it on the cleaned area so that it did not look as if it had been wiped. He opened the jacket and slid his hand into the inside pocket: it came out empty. Mackenzie said: "The papers and cards have taken wing and flown. With assistance, of course."

"Indeed. Could have been Poulson or one of his pals. Could have been Bronowski when he was out there yesterday. Could have been the kindly healer himself."

"Blake? He does look like a first cousin of Dracula," Mackenzie said.

Dermott raised the damp handkerchief again and started to clear the area round the bullet hole in the forehead. He peered closely at the wound and said to Mackenzie: "Can you see what I imagine I see?"

Mackenzie stooped low and peered closely. Still stooped, he said softly: "With the hawk eyes of my youth gone forever, I could do with a powerful magnifying glass." He straightened. "What I imagine I see is the brown scorch marks of burnt powder."

As before, Dermott smeared some carbon back on the cleaned area. "Funny – my imagination runs the same way. This guy was shot at point-blank range. The scenario reads that it was a very close thing indeed. The killer had a gun on this engineer and was probably searching him. What he didn't know was that the engineer not only had a gun of his own, but had it out. However it was, he must have seen it just in time and shot to kill – there could have been no time to indulge in any fancier gun-work. The engineer's gun-hand must have gone into muscular spasm – irreversible contraction; not unknown at the time of violent death. To free the gun, the killer had to wrench it so violently that he snapped the trigger finger. Don't you think that fits in with the peculiar angle at which the finger was broken?"

"I think you have it. It fits, anyway." Mackenzie frowned. "There's only one thing I see wrong with your scenario. Why should the killer take the gun in the first place? He had a gun of his own."

"Sure he had, but he couldn't use it any more," Dermott said. "More accurately, he couldn't afford to keep it any more. Having seen no exit holes at the back of the head he knew he had left two bullets in the region of two occiputs, and that the police could match up the bullets with the gun he was carrying. Which meant he would have to get rid of it. Which meant that he would be gunless, at least temporarily. So he took the engineer's gun. My guess is that he will have got rid of both guns by this time, and he's almost certainly got another weapon by now. In these United States – and don't forget Alaska is the United States – getting hold of a hand-gun is extremely simple."

Mackenzie said slowly: "It all fits. We may well be up against a professional killer."

127

"We may well be up against a psychopath."

Mackenzie shivered. "My Scottish Highland ancestry. Some ill-mannered lout has just walked all over my grave. Let's take counsel with the boss. Counsel and something else. If I know our worthy employer, he'll already have had half the contents of the jet's bar brought to his room."

"And you want his ideas?"

"I want some of those contents."

* * *

Mackenzie had exaggerated somewhat. Ferguson hadn't brought across more than a tenth of the plane's stock, but even that represented a goodly amount; Mackenzie had already had his first Scotch and was on his second. He looked at Brady, propped up in bed in a pair of shocking heliotrope pyjamas, which served only to accentuate his massive girth, and said: "Well, what do you make of George's theory?"

"I believe in the facts and I also believe in the theory, for the adequate reason that I see no alternative to it." Brady contemplated his finger-nails. "I also believe we're up against a trained, ruthless and intelligent killer. I don't doubt that he might be a psychotic on the loose. In fact there may be *two* psychopaths – an even more unpleasant prospect. The trouble is, George, I don't see how this advances us much. We don't know when this nut will hit again. What can we do to prevent it?"

"We can scare him," Dermott answered, "that's what we can do. I'll bet he's already worried by the fact that we're raking in fingerprints and records all over the shop. Let's try to worry him a little more. I'll go down to Anchorage tomorrow while you and Mackenzie stay here and do some work." Dermott sipped his Scotch. "It should be a change for at least one of you."

128

"I could be deeply wounded," Brady said, "but slings and arrows from an ungrateful staff are nothing new to me. What, precisely, do you have in mind?"

"Drastically narrowing the range of suspects is what I have in mind. All very simple, really. This is a close-knit community here in Prudhoe Bay. They more or less live out of each other's pockets. Everyone's movements must be known to at least a handful of other people, probably a great deal more. Check on everybody and find out who has a definite alibi for being here on the morning the engineers were being killed out in the mountains. If two or more people, say, can honestly tell you that X was here at the time of the crime, you can strike X off the suspects' list. At the end of the day we'll know how many suspects we have. Not even a handful, I bet. I wouldn't be surprised if there were none at all. Remember that Pump Station Four is a hundred and forty miles away, and the only feasible way of getting there is by helicopter. One would have to have the time and opportunity and the ability to fly a helicopter to get there, and there would be no hope of taking a chopper without someone noticing. I think you'll find it all very straightforward.

"Less straightforward is the next enquiry – who was in Anchorage on the day that the original phone message was sent from there to Sanmobil? There must have been quite a few. Don't forget they go on holiday every three or four weeks and, almost without exception, they go to Fairbanks or Anchorage. It will be more difficult to establish alibis: you won't find many people who have witnesses as to their whereabouts at six a.m. of a black winter morning in Alaska.

"In this case, though, we're more concerned about those who are not in the clear than those who are. I'll bring back a Photostat of the prints they've taken. We should be able to get the doubtfuls' fingerprints without too much trouble, and, with luck, match one set up with the phone booth's set.

I don't know how this sounds to you, but it seems quite straightforward to me."

"And to me," said Brady. "I think Don and I can manage that little chore without too much difficulty. Don't forget, though, that there's a fairly large community of people down at Valdez."

"As you're my boss," Dermott said, "I'll refrain from giving you a withering stare. Who in Valdez is going to fly a round trip of 1,300 miles during a winter night, stopping occasionally for fuel and to giving his identity away? And who's going to fly or helicopter the 1,600 miles round trip to clobber Bronowski and very possibly do away with Finlayson, especially as he would be immediately recognised as a stranger the moment he set foot in this area?"

Mackenzie said: "He has a point, you must admit. In fact, two points."

Dermott went on: "And don't tell me they could have come from one of the pumping stations. They don't have helicopters."

"I didn't say anything of the sort." Brady sounded aggrieved. "All right, we'll go along with the assumption that it's Prudhoe Bay or nothing. But what if we turn up zero?"

"Then it will be your turn to come up with the next bright idea."

"Hard day," Brady said. "You for bed?"

"Yes. I had intended to look at those records and prints tonight but the prints aren't going to be of any use to me until I return from Anchorage. Reports can wait, too. I'll just hunt up that Edmonton telex and take it down to the Anchorage police and see if they can help me." He stood up. "By the way: has it occurred to you that you yourself may be in danger tonight?"

"Me!" It was as if Dermott had suggested some unthinkable form of *lèse-majesté*. Then a look of vague apprehension crept into Brady's face.

"It may not be just your family who are at risk," Dermott persisted. "Why should these people bother about kidnapping when they could achieve their ends by putting a bullet in your back – which is not, if I may say so without offence, a very easy target to miss? How are you to know there isn't a homicidal maniac in the room next door to you?"

"Good God!" Brady drank deeply from his daiquiri. Then he sat back and smiled. "At last, action! Donald, get the Smith and Wesson from my case." He took the gun, thrust it deep under his pillow and said, almost hopefully: "Don't you think you two are at risk also?"

"Sure," Mackenzie said. "But not nearly as much as you. No Jim Brady, no Brady Enterprises. You're the legend. Without either of us, you could still function quite efficiently. This homicidal maniac doesn't strike me as the type who would go for a couple of lieutenants while the captain is around."

"Goodnight, then," Dermott said. "Don't forget to lock your door as soon as we're gone."

"Don't worry. You're armed, right?"

"Of course. But we don't think we'll be needing any weapons."

9

When Dermott woke up it was with such a heavy-headed feeling of exhaustion that he could have sworn he hadn't been to sleep at all. In fact, less than an hour had elapsed since he'd switched out the light, closed his eyes and dropped off. He did not wake up of his own volition. The overhead light was on and Morrison, looking as distraught as a senior F.B.I. agent is ever likely to look, was shaking him by the shoulder. Dermott eyed him blearily.

"Sorry about this," Morrison began. "But I thought you'd like to come along. In fact, I want you to."

Dermott peered at his watch and winced. "For God's sake, where?"

"We've found him."

Sleep, and all desire for it, dropped from Dermott like a cloak. "Finlayson?"

"Yes."

"Dead?"

"Yes."

"Murdered?"

"We don't know. You'll need warm clothing."

"Wake Mackenzie, will you?"

"Sure."

Morrison left. Dermott rose and dressed for the cruel temperatures outside. As he pulled on a quilted anorak his mind went back to his first meeting with Finlayson. He thought of the neatly-parted white hair, the grizzled Yukon beard, the hobo clothes. Had he been too hard on the man? No good worrying now. He pocketed a flashlight and moved into the passageway. Tim Houston was standing there. Dermott said: "So you know too?"

"I found him."

"How come?"

"Instinct, I guess." The bitterness in Houston's voice was unmistakable. "One of those finely-honed instincts that comes into operation about ten hours too late."

"Meaning that Finlayson could have been saved if this instinct of yours had been operational ten hours ago?"

"Maybe – but almost certainly not. John was murdered."

"Shot? Knifed? What?"

"Nothing like that. I didn't examine him. I knew that Mr Morrison and you wouldn't want me to touch him. I didn't have to examine him. He's outside, it's thirty below, and all he's wearing is a linen shirt and jeans. He's not even got shoes on. That makes it murder."

Dermott said nothing, so Houston continued. "Apart from the fact that he'd never have crossed the outside door-step voluntarily without his Arctic clothing, he'd never have been permitted to do so anyway. There are always people in the reception area, besides a person who mans the central telephone fulltime. By the same token, it would have been impossible for anyone to carry him out."

"Lugging corpses is conspicuous. So?"

"He wouldn't even have had to be a corpse. I think he was silenced in his own bedroom and bundled straight out the window. The cold would have finished him off. Here come your friends. I'll go get some more flashlights."

Outside, the cold was breathtaking. The temperature, as Houston had said, stood at thirty below. The forty-mile-per-hour gale brought the combination of temperature and chill-factor down to minus seventy. Even double-wrapped as a polar bear, without an exposed inch of flesh, the fact remains that one still has to breathe – and breathing in those conditions, until numbness intervenes, is a form of exquisite

133

and refined agony. In the initial stages it is impossible to tell whether one is inhaling glacial air or super-heated steam: a searing sensation dominates all else. The only way to survive for any length of time is to breathe pure oxygen from a suitably insulated tank – but those are not readily available in the Arctic.

Houston led them round the right-hand corner of the main building. After about ten yards he stopped, bent down and shone his flashlight between the supporting pilings. Other beams joined his.

A body lay face down, an insignificant heap already half-covered by the drifting snow. Dermott shouted: "You have sharp eyes, Houston. A lot of people would have missed this. Let's get him inside."

"Don't you want to examine him here, have a look around?"

"I do not. When this wind drops we'll come back and look for clues. In the meantime, I don't want to join Finlayson here."

"I agree," Morrison said. His teeth chattered audibly, and he was shaking with the cold.

Recovering the body from under the building provided the four men with no problem. Even if Finlayson had weighed twice as much, they would have had him out in seconds flat, such was their determination to regain shelter and warmth as soon as possible. As it was, Finlayson was slightly-built, and handling him was like handling a 150-pound log, so solidly frozen had he become. When they were clear of the pilings Dermott looked up at a brightly lit window above and yelled through the wind: "Whose room is that?"

Houston shouted: "His."

"Your theory fits, doesn't it?"

"It does."

When they brought Finlayson into the reception area,

134

there were perhaps half-a-dozen men sitting or standing around. For a moment nobody said anything. Then one man stepped forward and, with some diffidence, asked: "Shall I bring Dr Blake?"

Mackenzie shook his head, sadly. "I'm sure he's an excellent doctor, but no medical school has yet got round to offering a course on raising a man from the dead. Thanks all the same."

Dermott said: "Have we got an empty room where we can put him?" Houston looked at him and Dermott shook his head in self-reproach. "Okay. So my mind's gummed up with cold or lack of sleep or both. His own room, of course. Where can we find a rubber sheet?"

So they took Finlayson to his room and laid him on the rubber sheet on top of his bed. Dermott said: "Is there an individual thermostat control in here?"

"Sure," said Houston. "It's set on seventy-two."

"Turn it up."

"What for?"

"Dr Blake will want to do a post-mortem. You can't examine a person who's frozen solid. We're getting experienced at this sort of thing. Too experienced." Dermott turned to Mackenzie. "Houston thinks Finlayson was silenced in this room. Killed, knocked out, we don't know. He also thinks that our friends got rid of him by the simple expedient of opening the window and dumping him on to the snow-bank beneath."

Mackenzie crossed to the window, opened it, shivered at the icy blast of air that swept into the room, leaned out and peered down. Seconds later he had the window firmly closed again.

"Has to be that. We're directly above the spot where we found him. And it's in deep shadow down there." He looked at Houston. "Is there much traffic along there at night?"

135

"None. Nor during the day. No call for it. Track leads nowhere."

"So the killers left either by the front door or by this same window. They did the obvious thing – just stuffed him under the building, hoping the snow would have drifted over him before daylight came." Mackenzie sighed. "He couldn't by any chance have felt sick, opened the window for some fresh air, fell and crawled under the building?"

Dermott said: "You believe that's possible?"

"No. John Finlayson wouldn't get a *breath* of fresh air that way. He caught his death of it. Murder."

"Well, I think the boss should be told."

"He's sure going to be pleased, isn't he?"

*   *   *

Brady was furious. His black scowl accorded ill with his heliotrope pyjamas. He said: "Progress on all fronts. What do you two intend to do?"

Mackenzie said pacifically: "That's why we're here. We thought you might be able to give us a lead."

"A lead? How the hell can I give you a lead? I've been asleep." He corrected himself. "Well, for a few minutes, anyway. Sad about Finlayson. Fine man, by all accounts. What do you reckon, George?"

"One thing's for sure. The similarities between what happened here tonight and what occurred at Pump Station Four are too great to be a coincidence. As with the two engineers, so with Finlayson. They all saw or heard too much for their own health. They recognised a person or persons they knew well and who knew them, and those people were engaged in some things that couldn't be explained away. So they had to be silenced in the most final way."

Brady thought for a moment, and asked: "Is there a direct

connection between Bronowski being clobbered and Finlayson being killed?"

"I wouldn't bet on it," Dermott said. "Tie-up looks too obvious. You could argue that Bronowski escaped because he didn't catch his assailants red-handed in whatever they were doing, and that Finlayson died because he did. But that's too easy, too glib."

"What does Houston think?"

"He doesn't appear to have any more idea about it than we do."

"'Appear'." Brady seized on the word. "You mean he may know more than he's telling?"

"At the moment he's not saying or telling anything."

"But you don't trust him?"

"No. And while we're at it, I don't trust Bronowski."

"Hell, man, he's been savagely assaulted."

"Assaulted. Not savagely. I don't trust Dr Blake, either."

"Because he's unhelpful and unco-operative?"

"A good enough reason."

Brady became tactful. "Well, you do tend to ride a bit roughshod over people's feelings."

"To hell with their delicate sensibilities! We're dealing here with three cases of murder. Come to that, I don't trust Black either."

"You don't trust Black? General manager, Alaska?"

"He can be the King of Siam for all I care," Dermott said forcefully. "Some of the most successful businessmen in history number in their ranks the biggest swindlers ever. I'm not suggesting he *is* a swindler. All I say is that he's crafty, cagey, cold, and unco-operative. In short, I don't trust anyone."

"Look, friends. We're looking at this from the wrong angle," Brady suggested. "We're on the inside trying to look out. Maybe we should be on the outside trying to look in. Think of it this way. Who *wants* to hit the pipeline here and the tar sands of Athabasca? Do you see any significance in the fact that here they receive their instructions from Edmonton while in Alberta they come from Anchorage?"

"None." Dermott was positive. "May be just coincidence, at best a crude attempt to confuse us. Surely they can't be so naïve as to try to convey the impression that Canada is trying to interfere with America's oil supplies and vice versa. Idea's ludicrous. In these times of an acute oil shortage, what have two friendly neighbours to gain by cutting each other's throats?"

"Then who *has* to gain?"

Mackenzie spoke quietly.

"O.P.E.C.," he said.

Mackenzie was just as positive as Dermott had been. "If they could put a stranglehold on the two countries' supplies from the north, they stand to gain immensely in both profits and power. Both our governments have made it clear that they're prepared to go to any lengths to shake free once and for all from this crucifying dependence on O.P.E.C. oil. This wouldn't suit our foreign friends at all. They have us over a barrel – an oil barrel, if you will – and they want to keep it that way."

"Why now?" Jim Brady said. "Although I know as well as you do."

"They have tremendous leverage at the moment, and the last thing they'd ever want to do is to abdicate this position of almost dictatorial power. Decisions are being made now in both countries. Should North America become anywhere near self-sufficient in oil, our blackmailing friends would lose their power-base. They'd be forced to abandon their pretensions to playing an authoritative role in world affairs, and, perhaps worst of all for them, their profits would be reduced to such a trickle that they'd have to forgo their grandiose schemes for industrial and technological expansion, for hauling their countries into the middle of the late twentieth century, without any of the intermediate struggle or leasing and developmental process. When it comes to national survival, desperate men are prepared to go to desperate lengths."

Brady paced for some time, then said: "Do you really think the O.P.E.C. countries would take concerted action against us?"

"Hell, no. Half of them are barely on speaking terms with the other half, and you can't imagine relatively moderate countries like Saudi Arabia participating in any such combined operation. But you know as well as I do that among the O.P.E.C. rulers there are some certifiable loonies who would stop at nothing to achieve their own ends. And you won't have forgotten that some of those countries play host to the most ruthless terrorist trainers in the business."

Brady said: "What would you say to that, George?"

"It's a theory, and a perfectly tenable one. On the other hand, since coming here I haven't seen a single person who looks remotely like an Arabian or Middle Eastern terrorist."

"So what would your guess be?"

"As a *wild* guess, I would suspect our troubles are caused by good old-fashioned capitalistic free enterprise. And if that's the case, the potential sources of our troubles are legion. I'm afraid we won't solve this by looking at it from the outside: we'll have to look out from the inside."

"And the motive?"

"Blackmail, obviously."

"Cash?"

"Well, the only other bargaining counter is hostages. Nobody's holding any hostages. So what's left? They're now in the process of softening us up by proving they can carry out their threats when and as they wish."

"They won't be asking for pennies."·

"I shouldn't think so. To start with, the pipeline and Sanmobil have a combined investment of ten billion. For

139

every day that delivery is held up they'll be losing millions more. Most important of all, our two countries are desperate for oil. Whoever those people are, they have us not over but in a barrel. Naked. The ransom will be high. I should imagine it would be paid."

"Who'd pay it?" Mackenzie said.

"The oil companies. The governments. They've all got a stake in this."

Brady said: "And once the blackmailers have been paid, what's to prevent them repeating the process all over again?"

"Nothing that I can see."

"God, you're a Job's comforter."

"Let me comfort you some more, shall I? There could be a link-up between Don's theory and mine. *If* this is blackmail, and *if* the killers do collect, what's to prevent some of the O.P.E.C. countries approaching them and offering to double or triple their money if they destroy the supply lines for keeps – and get out? You've a big responsibility on your shoulders, Mr Brady."

"You, George are a rock of strength and compassion in times of trouble and stress." Brady sounded plaintive. "Well, if there are no constructive suggestions forthcoming, I suggest we all retire. There is thinking to be done and I must take counsel with myself. On such nights, the best company."

* * *

Dermott still felt unaccountably tired when the alarm clock dragged him up from the depths of a troubled sleep. It was just on eight in the morning. He rose reluctantly, showered, shaved, made his way to Finlayson's room, and was about to knock when the door was opened by Dr Blake. At that time of the morning the doctor's beaked nose, hollow cheeks and sunken eyes lent him a more cadaverous

140

look than ever – not the kind of physician's face, Dermott thought, to inspire hope and confidence.

"Ah, come in, Mr Dermott. I've finished with Finlayson. Was just about to send for his casket. He and the two engineers from Pump Station Four are being flown out at nine-thirty. I understand you're going with them."

"Yes. You have caskets?"

"Macabre, you think? Well, we do keep a few tucked away. Apart from natural illnesses, this is an accident-prone profession, and we have to be prepared. You can't very well whistle up an undertaker from Fairbanks or Anchorage at a moment's notice."

"I suppose not." Dermott nodded at the dead man. "Any luck in establishing the cause of death?"

"Well, normally it requires a full autopsy to discover whether a victim has been suffering from cerebrovascular disease or cardiac arrest. Fortunately – or unfortunately – it wasn't necessary in this case." Blake sounded grim. "What was before only a suspicion is now a certainty. What would be natural causes elsewhere are unnatural here. John Finlayson was murdered."

"How? Other than by exposure?"

"None of your usual methods. He was rendered unconscious and left to die in the cold. Clad as he was in those abnormally low temperatures, I'd say his heart must have stopped in under a minute."

"How was he knocked out?"

"Sand-bagged. In the classic spot, at the base of the neck. An expert. You can see the slight contusion and roughness there. A contusion can only be caused by blood still circulating, so he was clearly alive after the blow. The cold killed him."

"Where could the attacker have got sand in this God-forsaken frozen hole?"

Dr Blake smiled. Dermott wished he hadn't: the long

narrow teeth only accentuated the death's-head effect. "If you aren't too squeamish, you can smell what they used."

Dermott bent and rose almost immediately. "Salt."

Blake nodded. "Probably slightly dampened. Makes an even more effective cosh than sand."

"They teach you this in medical school?"

"I was on the forensic side once. If I make out and sign the death certificate, will you be kind enough to hand it in at Anchorage?"

"Of course."

*　　*　　*

Big, burly, high-coloured and irrepressibly cheerful, John Ffoulkes looked more like a prosperous farmer than a tough, competent senior police officer. He produced a bottle of whisky and two glasses and smiled at Dermott.

"In view of those ridiculous prohibition laws they have up at Prudhoe Bay, maybe we can make up here in Anchorage . . ."

"My chief would like your style. We don't do so badly there. Mr Brady claims to have the biggest portable bar north of the Arctic Circle. He has, too."

"Well, then, to help erase the memory of your flight. I gather you didn't enjoy it much?"

"Extreme turbulence, an absence of pretty stewardesses, and the knowledge that you're carrying three murdered men in the cargo hold doesn't make for a very relaxed flight."

Ffoulkes stopped smiling. "Ah, yes, the dead men. Not only a tragic affair but an extremely unpleasant one. I've had reports from my own State troopers and the F.B.I. I wonder if you could have anything to add to what they said?"

"I doubt it. Mr Morrison of the F.B.I. struck me as a highly competent officer."

142

"He's all that, and a close friend of mine. But tell me anyway, please."

Dermott's account was as succinct as it was comprehensive. At the end Ffoulkes said: "Tallies almost exactly with the other reports. But no hard facts?"

"Suspicions, yes. Hard facts, no."

"So the only lead you really have are the prints we got from that telephone booth?" Dermott nodded, and Ffoulkes brought out a buff folder from a desk drawer. "Here they are. Some are pretty smudged but a few are not too bad. Are you an expert?"

"I can read them with a powerful glass and a lot of luck. But an expert – no."

"I've got a first-class young lad here. Like to borrow him for a day or two?"

Dermott hesitated. "That's kind. But I don't want to tread on Mr Morrison's toes. He's got his own man up there."

"Not in the same class as our David Hendry. Mr Morrison won't object." He pressed an intercom button and gave an order.

David Hendry was fair-haired, smiling and seemed ridiculously young to be a police officer. After introductions, Ffoulkes said: "Lucky lad. How do you fancy a vacation in a winter wonderland?"

Hendry looked cautious. "Which wonderland, sir?"

"Prudhoe Bay."

"Oh, my God!"

"Good, glad you're happy. That's settled then. Pack your equipment and, of course, your clothes. Three parkas should be enough – worn on top of each other. When's your plane out, Mr Dermott?"

"Two hours."

"Report back in an hour, David." Hendry opened the door to leave, then stood to one side as a lean man, white-

143

bearded like an Old Testament prophet, bustled into the room.

"Apologies, John, apologies. Couldn't have caught me at a worse time or on a worse day. Two court cases, two suicides – people get more thoughtless every day."

"You have my sympathies, Charles – as I, one hopes, have yours. Dr Parker – Mr Dermott."

"Hah!" Parker looked at Dermott with an ill-concealed lack of enthusiasm. "You the fellow who's come to add to my burden of woes?"

"Through no wish of mine, doctor. Three burdens, to be precise."

"I'm afraid I can't do anything about them today, Mr Dermott. Snowed under, just snowed. Very likely I can't do anything about them tomorrow either. Most unprofessional."

"What is?"

"My two assistants. Going down with the flu at the busiest time of the year. This modern generation –"

"I daresay they couldn't help it."

"Namby-pambies. What happened to those three anyway?"

"Two we know for sure. They were in the close vicinity of an explosion. After that an oil fire broke out. Savagely scarred. The fumes alone would have finished them off."

"But they were already finished off. So. Blasted to death, burnt, asphyxiated. Doesn't leave very much for an old sawbones like me to do, does it?"

"Each of them has also a low-velocity bullet lodged somewhere near the back of his skull," Dermott said.

"Hah! So you want them out, is that it?"

"Not me, Dr Parker. The State police and the F.B.I. I'm no cop, just an oilfield sabotage investigator."

Parker looked sour. "I hope my efforts aren't as thoroughly wasted as usual."

144

Ffoulkes smiled. "What odds would you offer, Mr Dermott?"

"About a million to one that they'll be wasted. That gun has almost certainly been tossed out of a helicopter somewhere over the Brooks Range."

"I'll still have to ask you, Charles," said Ffoulkes.

Dr Parker was unimpressed. "What about this third man?"

"B.P./Sohio's field production manager in Prudhoe Bay, John Finlayson."

"Good lord! Know the man well. Suppose I should say 'knew', now."

"Yes." Dermott nodded to Ffoulkes's desk. "That's his death certificate."

Parker picked it up, screwed on a pince-nez and read through the report.

"Unusual," he said testily. "But it seems a straight-forward medical report to me. There's no autopsy required here." He peered at Dermott. "From your expression, you appear to disagree."

"I'm neither agreeing nor disagreeing. I'm just vaguely unhappy."

"Have you ever practised medicine, Mr Dermott?"

"No."

"And yet you presume to take issue with a colleague of mine?"

"You know him, then?"

"Never heard of him." Parker breathed deeply. "But, dammit, he's a physician."

"So was Dr Crippen."

"What the devil are you insinuating?"

"You read into my words what you choose," Dermott said flatly. "I'm insinuating nothing. I merely say that his examination was perfunctory and hurried, and that he may have missed something. You wouldn't claim a divine right of

145

infallibility for doctors?"

"I would not." His voice was still testy, but only a testy mutter now. "What is it you want?"

"A second opinion."

"That's a damned unusual request."

"It's a damned unusual murder."

Ffoulkes looked quizzically at Dermott and said: "I'll look in at Prudhoe Bay tomorrow. There's nothing like adding a touch of chaos to an existing state of confusion."

10

Dermott and David Hendry flew in from Anchorage to Prudhoe Bay in the leaden twilight of late afternoon to find the weather distinctly improved, with the wind down to ten knots, the top of the drifting snow-cloud not more than five feet above ground level, visibility in the plane's headlights almost back to normal, and the temperature at least twenty degrees higher than in the morning. In the administration building lounge the first recognisable face Dermott saw was that of Morrison of the F.B.I., who was sitting with a young, ginger-haired man incongruously dressed in grey flannels and blazer. Morrison looked up and smiled.

"Trust John Ffoulkes," he said. "No faith in the F.B.I." He gestured towards the ginger-haired young man. "Nick Turner. Ignore the way he dresses. He's been to Oxford. *My* fingerprint man. On your right, David Hendry, *your* fingerprint man."

Dermott said mildly: "John Ffoulkes just observed that two pairs of eyes were better than one. No developments?"

"Not one. You?"

"Largely a waste of time. Had a thought on the way up. Why don't we print John Finlayson's room?"

"No dice. We've done it."

"Clean as a whistle?"

"Close enough. Lots of unsatisfactory smudges which can only be Finlayson's, a couple belonging to a plumber who was there on his rounds, and one – would you believe it, just one – belonging to the bull cook, who must be a real whiz-kid with duster and polishing cloth."

"Bull cook?"

"Kind of house-keeper. Bed-maker and cleaner."

"Could some other industrious soul have been busy in there with a duster?"

Morrison produced two keys. "His room key and the master key. Had them in my pocket since Finlayson was taken out this morning."

"Here endeth the lesson." Dermott laid the buff folder on the low table before Morrison. "Prints from the Anchorage phone booth. Now, I must go and report to the boss."

Morrison said: "It should amuse the two young gentlemen here to compare your Anchorage prints with the ones in the office safe."

"You don't sound very optimistic," Dermott said.

The F.B.I. agent smiled. "By nature I've always been an optimist. But that was before I crossed the forty-ninth parallel."

*   *   *

Dermott found Brady and Mackenzie taking their ease in the only two chairs in Brady's room. He looked on them without favour.

"It's very pleasant and reassuring to see you two so comfortable and relaxed."

Brady said: "Rough afternoon, huh?" He waved a hand towards the serried row of bottles on the sideboard. "This'll restore your moral fibre."

Dermott helped himself and asked: "Any news from Athabasca? How are the family?"

"Fine, fine." Brady chuckled. "Stella passed on a lot more stuff from Norway. Apparently they've got that fire licked. No need to keep in touch any longer."

"That's good." Dermott sipped his Scotch. "What are the girls doing?"

"Right now, I guess, they're touring the Sanmobil plant,

courtesy of Bill Reynolds. Very hospitable lot, those Canadians."

"Who've they got to protect them?"

"Reynolds's own security man, Brinckman – the boss, you remember – and Jorgensen, his number two."

Dermott was unimpressed. "I'd rather they had those two young cops."

Brady snapped: "Your reason?"

"Three. First, they're a damned sight tougher, more competent than Brinckman's lot. Second, Brinckman, Jorgensen and Napier are prime suspects."

"Why prime?"

"For having the keys that opened the Sanmobil armoury door, for having given the keys to those who did. Third, they're security men."

Brady smiled blandly. "You're bushed, George. You're becoming paranoid about the security men of the great north-west."

"I hope you don't have reason to regret that remark."

Brady scowled but said nothing, so Dermott changed the subject. "How did the day go?"

"No progress. Along with Morrison we interviewed every man on the base. Every one had a cast-iron alibi for the night of the explosion in Pump Station Four. So it's all clear there."

"Except –" Dermott persisted.

"Who do you mean?"

"Bronowski and Houston."

Brady glowered at his chief operative and shook his head. "You're paranoid, George, I say it again. Shit, we *know* they were both out there. Bronowski's been hurt, and Houston didn't *have* to find Finlayson. If he *had* been crooked, it would have suited him far better to let the drifting snow obliterate every last trace of Finlayson. What do you say to that?"

"Three things. The fact that we know they were out at the pump station makes them *more* suspect, not less."

"Second guessing," growled Brady. "Hate second guessing."

"No doubt. But we've agreed that the bombers must be people working on the pipeline. We've eliminated everyone else, so it has to be them – does it not?"

Brady did not answer. Dermott went on: "The third thing is this: there must be some reason, albeit devious, why Bronowski was clobbered and Houston made the discovery. Look at it this way. What evidence do we have that Bronowski *was* assaulted? The only certain thing we know about him is that he's lying in the sick bay with an impressive bandage round his head. I don't think there's a damn thing wrong with Bronowski. I don't think anybody hit him. I suggest that if the bandage were removed, his temple would be un-blemished, except, perhaps, for an artistic touch of gentian blue."

Brady assumed the expression of a man praying for inner strength. "So, besides not trusting security men, you don't trust doctors, either?"

"Some I do. Some I don't. I've already told you that I'm leery of Blake."

"Got one single hard fact to back up your suspicions?"

"No."

"Okay, then." Brady didn't enlarge on this brief statement.

"We also rounded up the Prudhoe Bay members who were in Anchorage on the night of that telephone call," Mackenzie said. "Fourteen in all. They seemed a pretty harmless bunch to me. However, Morrison of the F.B.I. did call up the law in Anchorage, gave names and addresses and asked them to see if they could turn up anything."

"You printed those fourteen, right?"

"Yes. One of Morrison's assistants did. Some Ivy League kid."

"No objections offered?"

"None. They seemed eager to co-operate."

"Proves nothing. Anyway, I brought along the prints found on the phone booth. They're being checked now against the prints of the fourteen."

"That won't take long," Mackenzie said. "Give them a call, shall I?" He called, listened briefly, hung up and said to Dermott: "Cassandra."

"So." Brady looked positively lugubrious, no easy feat for a man without a line in his face. "Houston's finest have run into a brick wall."

"Let's not reproach ourselves too much," Dermott said. He looked less downcast than the other two. "Our business is investigating oil sabotage, not murder, which is the province of the F.B.I. and the Alaskan State police. They appear to have run into the same brick wall. Besides, we may have the lead into another line of investigation – John Finlayson's autopsy."

"Huh!" Brady gave a contemptuous lift of his hands. "That's over. It turned up nothing."

"The first one didn't. But the second one might."

Mackenzie said: "What! *Another* autopsy?"

"The first one was pretty superficial and perfunctory."

"Unprecedented." Brady shook his head. "Who the hell authorised this?"

"Nobody really. I did *ask* for it, but politely."

Brady cursed, whether because of Dermott's words or because he had spilled a goodly portion of a daiquiri over his immaculately trousered knee. He refilled his glass, breathed deeply and said: "Took your own goddamned good time in getting round to telling us, didn't you?"

"Everything in its own good time, Jim: just a matter of getting priorities right. It'll be a couple of days before we get the results of this autopsy. I really can't see why you are getting so steamed up."

"I can damn well tell you. Who the hell gave you the authorisation to make such a request without first getting permission from me?"

"Nobody did."

"You had time before you left here this morning to discuss the matter with me."

"Sure I had time, but I hadn't had the idea by then. I was half-way down to Anchorage before it occurred to me that there could be something far wrong. Do you imagine I'd talk to you in Prudhoe Bay over an open line?"

"You talk as if this place is an international hotbed of espionage," Brady came back to him sarcastically.

"It only requires one disaffected ear, and we might as well pack our bags and return to Houston. We already know how good those people are at covering their tracks."

"George." It was Mackenzie. "You've made your point. What triggered your suspicions?"

"Dr Blake. You know that as far as the murdered engineers at Pump Station Four and Bronowski's alleged accident were concerned, I already had reservations about Blake. I began to wonder if there was anything that could tie Blake in with Finlayson's death. I was the only person who saw the body between the completion of Blake's autopsy and the time the lid was screwed down on the coffin." Dermott stopped to sip.

"During that period Blake showed me marks on the back of the neck where, he said, Finlayson had been sand-bagged into unconsciousness. On the plane it occurred to me that I had never seen a bruise or contusion of that nature. There was no sign of discoloration, or of swelling. It seemed to me more than likely that the skin had been roughed up after death. Blake said Finlayson had been struck by a bag of damp salt. His neck smelled of salt all right, but it could have

152

been rubbed on during the night, after the body had been brought back up to the room. If he *had* been coshed, the vertebrae would have been depressed or broken."

Mackenzie said: "Obvious question – were they?"

"I don't know. They looked okay to me. But Dr Parker will know."

"Dr Parker?"

"Works with the Anchorage police in a forensic capacity. Struck me as a very bright old boy. My request wasn't too well received at first. Like yourselves, he regarded the concept of a second autopsy as unprecedented or unconstitutional or whatever. He read Blake's death certificate and seemed to think it perfectly in order."

"But you persuaded him to the contrary?"

"Not exactly. He promised nothing. But he seemed interested enough to do something."

Brady said: "You *are* a persuasive cuss, George."

Dermott paused reflectively. "It may be nothing, or it may be another straw in the wind – but Dr Parker has never heard of Dr Blake."

Brady resumed his favourite steeple-fingered pontificating attitude. "You're aware that Alaska is more than half the size of Western Europe?"

"I'm also aware that in Western Europe there must be the odd hundred million people. In Alaska, a few hundred thousand. I'd be surprised, if, outside the few hospitals, there are more than sixty or seventy doctors, and a veteran like Parker would be bound to know or know of them all."

Brady unsteepled his fingertips and said: "There is hope for you. An immediate investigation into Doctor Blake's antecedents would appear to be in order."

"Immediate," Mackenzie agreed. "Morrison's the man for that. Wouldn't it be interesting, too, to have a run-down on the man who appointed or recommended Blake to this post?"

153

"It would," Dermott said. "And it would certainly narrow the field a bit. I wonder. You remember just after we arrived here asking whether there were any ideas about the type of weapon used on Bronowski, and Morrison said – I think I quote him accurately – 'Dr Blake says he's no specialist in criminal acts of violence'?"

Brady nodded.

"So. This morning, when I was with him in Finlayson's room discussing the reasons for the man's death, he mentioned in an off-hand way that he used to be an expert in the forensic field. Obviously he said it to lend credence to his diagnosis. But it was a slip, all the same. One time or the other, he was lying."

Dermott looked at Brady and asked: "Your agents in New York who are investigating Bronowski's security firm there – they aren't, shall we say, exactly burning up the track. Give them a nudge?"

"Negative. You said yourself that an open line . . ."

"Who's talking about an open line? We do it through Houston, in your code."

"Huh! That damn code. You encode any message you like and authorise it in my name."

Mackenzie winked unobtrusively, but Dermott ignored him and began to spell out a message to the telephone operator. It said much for his mastery of a code which its inventor found insupportably burdensome that he encoded the words straight out of his head, without having to make a prior transcript.

He had barely finished when a knock on the door announced the arrival of Hamish Black. The pencil moustache on the Alaskan general manager was as immaculately trimmed as ever, the central parting of the hair still apparently drawn by ruler, the eyeglass so securely anchored that it looked as if it could have ridden out a hurricane. He still dressed in pure City accountant, first class. At that moment, however, there was a difference in his general demeanour: he looked like a first-class accountant who had just stumbled across proof of unmistakable and gross embezzlement in the books of his favourite client. Yet he maintained his cool – or cold.

"Good evening, gentlemen." He was a specialist in wintry smiles. "I hope I do not intrude, Mr Brady?"

"Come in, come in." Brady was affability itself, a sure sign that he didn't care too much for his visitor. "Make yourself at home." He glanced around the cramped confines of his room and at the only three already occupied chairs. "Well –"

"Thank you, I'll stand. I shall not detain you for long."

"A drink? One of my incomparable rum drinks? How about a cigar?"

"Thank you. I neither smoke nor drink." The minuscule twitch of the left-hand corner of his upper lip clearly indicated his opinion of those who did. "I have come here because in my capacity of general manager of Sohio/B.P. I felt it my duty to ask how much progress you have made in your investigations to date."

Dermott said: "What have we found out so far? Well –"

"Will you please be quiet, sir. I was addressing –"

"George!" Brady made a downward placatory movement of the hand towards a Dermott who was already half-way out of his seat. He looked coldly at Black. "We are not employees of yours, Mr Black. We are not even retained by you, but directly by your head office in London. I suggest that if you want to leave this room the way you entered it, you watch your language."

Black's lips had disappeared somewhere. "Sir! I am not accustomed –"

"Okay, okay. We all know that. You're obviously in a hostile mood. Our progress so far? Not much. Would there be anything else?"

Black was clearly taken aback. It is difficult for an old-time man-of-war to attack when the wind has been taken out of its sails.

"So you admit –"

"No admission. We're just making a statement. Can we be of further help?"

"Indeed you can. You can explain to me the justification for your staying on here. The firm can scarcely afford the fees you seem likely to charge, if it gets no advantage. You have achieved nothing, and seem unlikely to achieve anything. You investigate industrial sabotage, specifically oil-flow interruption. There is, I suggest, a considerable difference between the spilling of oil and the spilling of blood. One cannot but suspect but that you are out of your depth and that events are beyond your control. One further suspects that the investigation should be left to those qualified to investigate criminal matters – the F.B.I. and the Alaskan State police."

"We'd be interested to know what they've found out. Or don't you feel free to tell us?"

Black compressed his lips still tighter. Mackenzie said: "May I have a word, Mr Brady?"

"Certainly, Donald "

"Mr Black: Your attitude here is singularly reminiscent of the one you adopted when first we met you. Have you the power to make us leave?"

"Yes."

"Permanently?"

"No."

"Why not?"

"You know very well why not. London head office would reinstate you."

"Possibly with the qualification that if any such situation arose again it would be the general manager, Alaska, who would be required to leave."

"I couldn't really say."

"I can. Or didn't you know that Mr Brady is a close personal friend of the chairman of your company?"

From the way that Black touched his collar, it was clear that this was news to him. From the way Jim Brady experienced a sudden difficulty in swallowing a mouthful of daiquiri, it was clear that it was news to him also.

"To return to your earlier attitude, Mr Black," Mackenzie persisted. "On that occasion Mr Dermott said he thought you might have something to hide. Mr Brady suggested you were being unduly secretive and had – what was it again? – some undisclosed and possibly discreditable reason for choosing to obstruct the best interests of your company. Reasonable requests you regarded as being preposterous. Finally, as I recall, Mr Dermott said that you were either standing on your high horse as general manager, Alaska, and were above such petty annoyances, or that you were concealing something you didn't want us to know about."

Black was possibly a shade or two paler, but his pallor could well have been caused by anger. He reached for the door handle.

"This is intolerable! I refuse to be the subject of character assassination."

As he pulled open the door, Mackenzie said, reproachingly, "I think it's impolite to interrupt a man's speech."

Black's eyes matched well the icy conditions outside. "What does that mean?"

"Just that I would like to finish what I've been saying."

Black looked at his watch. "Make it short."

"I know you have a great deal to do, Mr Black." Two tiny spots of pink appeared on the pale cheekbones, for Mackenzie's tone had made it abundantly clear he didn't believe Black had anything to do. "So I'll keep it short. Your intransigence interests us. You have made it abundantly

157

clear that you would be happy to be rid of us. By your own admission you've acknowledged that we would be back very soon afterwards, perhaps even in a matter of days. The conclusion is that you want us out of the way even if for only a brief period. One wonders what you intend to do or have done during that short time?"

"I see. You leave me with no alternative other than to report your gross incompetence and insolence to my board of directors in London."

When the door had closed Dermott said: "Not a bad exit line. He'll do nothing of the kind, of course – not when he's had time to reflect on Mr Brady's close personal relationship with his board chairman." Dermott looked at Brady. "I didn't know –"

"Neither did I." Brady was positively jovial. He smacked one fat fist into the other podgy palm. "Tell me, Donald, how much of what you said did you mean?"

"Who's to know? Not me. I just don't like the bastard."

"Hardly the basis for a dispassionate judgment," Dermott said. "But a splendid demolition job, Donald. There are times when a man rises above himself." He paused for a moment, then looked at Brady. "Remember the last time we had a run-in with our friend, you said that it was a pity that he acted so suspiciously, otherwise he would have made a splendid suspect? Maybe we're outsmarting ourselves. It's barely possible that he should be a suspect. Maybe, in addition, he's outsmarting us. This won't have escaped you?"

Brady stopped being jovial. "Double-guessing again. How often do I have to tell you, George, I hate this god-damn double-guessing. General manager, Alaska. Jesus, George, *somebody*, by definition, has to be beyond suspicion."

* * *

158

In Dermott's cabin Mackenzie said: "Took you a long time to transmit that coded message to Houston. Your brief was merely to ask them to expedite the boss's earlier instructions. What the hell else did you say?"

"I asked them to find out if anybody had left Bronowski's security firm within six months before or after Bronowski's leaving."

"Maybe Brady's right. Maybe this security bit is getting to you. And even if Bronowski has hauled some of his old associates along with him, they may have changed their names."

"Hardly matters. Descriptions will be enough. And as for my being bitten by the bug, it's high time you and Jim were too. How would you try to account for the fact that the bastards in Alberta know the Alaskan company's code, while the villains in Alaska know the Albertan code, the private Sanmobil code?"

"Ever since the first identical messages were received at Prudhoe Bay and Sanmobil, we've known our Alaskan and Athabascan friends were in cahoots, nicely co-ordinating their efforts to keep us wrong-footed and ensuring that we were in A while we should have been in B, and vice versa. There's no doubt in my mind that both security corps have been infiltrated. Our only suspects on both sides are security people."

"So you think the overall co-ordinator must be a security man?"

"Not necessarily. But what I'm sure of is that pretty soon we're going to hear of some fresh calamity that has struck in Athabasca. The master puppeteer must be thinking it's time the puppets were dancing again."

"Co-ordination," Mackenzie said darkly.

"In this instance?"

"You heard what I said to Black. That he wants us out for a few days for some purpose. If he can't get rid of us in one way – by asking us to leave – then he'll do it in another by arranging a fresh Athabascan calamity."

Dermott sighed, drew a line under a list of names he had printed, and handed it over. "Names for investigation – let's hope – by our friend Morrison of the F.B.I. What d'you think of it?"

Mackenzie took the list and studied it. His eyebrows went up. "Make Morrison jump, for sure," he said.

"I don't care if he jumps over the moon, as long as he gets on with it when he comes down," said Dermott heavily. "We've got to get action somewhere." He was about to say something else when the telephone rang. He picked up the receiver to listen, and gradually his face went chalk white. He seemed not to notice when the glass in his left hand shattered, crushed by the pressure he had put on it, and a little rivulet of blood ran down his palm.

11

"What a *place*!" exclaimed Stella as she came back into Corinne's office. "Heavens – I had no idea it was so big. We seem to have driven about fifty miles."

"Well, it's quite a size, that's for sure." Corinne grinned, pleased that her guests had enjoyed themselves. "I hope *you* found it interesting too, Mrs Brady?"

"Incredible!" Jean eased off the hood of her parka and shook her hair loose. "Those draglines – I never saw anything like them. They're – they're sort of prehistoric monsters, burrowing into the bowels of the earth."

"That's right!" Stella's imagination had been fired no less. "Brontosauruses. Absolutely. Sure was kind of Mr Reynolds to fix our tour. *And* to ask us to supper."

"Don't mention it." Corinne tried out the deprecating smile she had been cultivating. "We all like having visitors – makes a change. You'll enjoy meeting Mary Reynolds, too. Now, let's see if the boss is ready to leave."

She buzzed the intercom and announced that the ladies were back. Over the loudspeaker they heard him say: "Fine – I'll be through in a minute."

"Be right with you," she said. "All set?" She tidied her desk, locked the drawers, put the keys in her handbag and pulled on a fetching, roly-poly combination suit of powder-blue quilted nylon, as well as a pair of blue fur-topped boots. A moment later Reynolds himself came through the connecting door, similarly muffled in navy blue and white.

"Evening, ladies," he said pleasantly. "Had a good tour, I hope. Not too dull?"

161

"Not at all!" Jean had no trouble sounding enthusiastic. "It was wonderful. Fascinating."

"Good." He turned to Corinne. "Where are our strong-arm boys, then?"

"Waiting for us in the lobby."

"Great. We'd better not leave them behind, or your father'll give us hell." He winked at Stella and ushered her through the door.

Terry Brinckman, Sanmobil's security chief, and his deputy Jorgensen were hovering in the entrance hall. As the party approached the two men opened the outside door and let in a blast of the Arctic evening. Out on the tarmac one of the firm's yellow-and-black chequered minibuses stood ready, with its engine running. Reynolds opened the passenger door, helped Jean and Stella into the front seat, nipped round the the driver's side and slammed the door, cursing the knifelike wind. Corinne hopped into the back seat between the two security men.

As they cruised down towards the main gates Reynolds called up the guard on his two-way radio and identified the vehicle, to save the man coming out into the cold. At the bus's approach the high weldmesh gates began to roll open, driven by electric motors. A few snowflakes drifted fast through the blaze of the arc-lamps that illuminated the perimeter fence. Reynolds gave a couple of toots on the horn to signal his thanks, and a moment later they were out in the open, with the headlight beams boring into the frozen darkness ahead.

The bus was warm and comfortable. The journey would take only twenty minutes. Yet Corinne somehow felt uneasy. Her boss had been on edge all day, and although she had maintained a sunny enough exterior, she wasn't looking forward to the evening: it could be sticky. Maybe they could get a bit of a concert or sing-song going – that would help. She leaned forward and asked Stella if she could play the guitar.

162

"Why, sure – if no-one else is listening."

"Ah, come on! I thought we could maybe have a sing-song."

"Course she can play," Jean said firmly. "Pick up any tune you care to sing."

"That's great." Corinne settled back between her two solid escorts. The bus had left the inhabited outskirts of the site and was winding through the low hills that separated the tar sands from Fort McMurray. Reynolds drove smoothly, without violent acceleration or braking, for the surface of the road was dusted with the ever-travelling snow, which flashed and glittered in the headlamp beams.

They had just passed a sharp corner which Brinckman said was known as Hangman's Turn when Reynolds *did* jam on his brakes. He cursed as the bus slewed to the left, then corrected the skid. Ahead, the road was blocked by a black truck which had also skidded sideways-on.

"Look out!" Corinne shouted. "There's someone on the road!"

The bus juddered to a halt a few yards short of the huddled figure lying face-down. The flying snow cleared for a few seconds to reveal another body, also on its front, but moving.

"Oh my God!" Jean cried from up front. "There's been an accident!"

"You ladies, sit tight," Reynolds ordered sharply. "Terry, go see what's happened."

Brinckman opened his door and got out. Corinne felt the blast of air hit her from the right. Then she saw another figure running, or rather staggering, towards them from the stranded vehicle. The man had his hands up, as if to shield his eyes from the minibus's lights. He was limping and lurching; she thought: he's been badly hurt.

Corinne felt Brinckman yank the first-aid box out from under the back seat. Next thing she knew, he was flat on his

163

side, his feet having gone from under him on the ice. He got up at once and advanced more cautiously, with his feet apart, apparently to the aid of the injured man.

What happened next was so fast that Corinne afterwards wondered a hundred times whether or not she had remembered it right. Everything seemed to go into a blur. One moment Brinckman was advancing to meet the crippled figure. Next second the cripple seemed suddenly to shake off his injuries: he stood upright and let fly an expertly-timed blow that felled Brinckman like a tree. The instant the man lowered his shielding hand, Corinne saw he was wearing a stocking mask.

Stella screamed: "Back up – quick!" Corinne also shouted something. But before any of them could move the attacker was at Reynolds's window. In a second he had wrenched it open and thrown in something that hissed.

Instinctively Corinne threw herself down flat on the floor in the back. From the front she heard stifled screams and ghastly tearing noises as people struggled for breath. Then the gas got her too, and she found herself fighting and choking as if for her life.

In spite of her distress she became aware that the people in front were being dragged out into the snow. She crouched flat on the floor, struggling to control her stinging throat and eyes. Then she heard a man shout: "Where's the other chick? We've only got two." In the next second she felt someone seize the hood of her combination suit and drag her bodily out onto the road.

Without knowing why, she pretended to be unconscious. Somehow it seemed safer. She felt herself sliding easily along the icy surface, being dragged like a sack of potatoes. Her backside skidded smoothly over the snow. As she was pulled round the front of the minibus, into the headlights, she noticed that the supposedly injured men had vanished. The bus's engine was still running, but the vehicle blocking the

164

road had started up as well. Suddenly she was hoisted and dumped in the open back of the truck.

For the first time she felt afraid – not of being kidnapped, but of freezing to death. In spite of her thick suit she was shivering already, and if they were going to be driven miles in an open truck, the cold would soon kill them all . . .

Her fears on that score proved groundless. After a rough, bumpy drive of only a few seconds the truck crunched to a halt. The noise of its motor was suddenly swamped by a far louder, heavier roar that burst out all round and over them. Corinne opened her eyes in terror and saw that they had pulled up beside a grey-white helicopter. Even as she looked up one of the rotor blades moved past her line of sight.

She felt she should scream or run – but would it do any good? Even a second's hesitation was too long. She felt herself grabbed by shoulders and ankles and swung aboard, again like an inert sack.

The noise was terrific. The engine-roar increased to a furious pitch, but through it she could hear a woman screaming and men yelling. She saw a bundle she recognised as Stella struggling frantically with one of the men in stocking masks, rolling across the bare steel. Another of the men slid the door in the side of the fuselage nearly shut, but he kept his head stuck out through the gap, bellowing at someone still on the ground.

The engine-note rose and fell, rose and fell, as though the pilot was having mechanical difficulty. Then it went up and stayed up – but only for a few seconds. Again it dropped. Corinne had never been in a helicopter before and did not know what to expect. She didn't know whether the pilot was going through his normal take-off routine, or whether he had some problem. What she did notice, however, was that the man who'd been shouting to his colleague on the ground had failed to close the door properly: it still stood a few inches ajar. A desperate idea flashed into her head: at the

165

moment of take-off, whenever it came, she would dart to the door, drag it open, and fling herself out.

Before she'd had time to evaluate the risks, she felt the floor tilt – they were off already. Then came a heavy bump. Down again, she thought. Next time they did lift. It was then or never.

She rolled over, flung herself at the door and hauled it back. She was hit by a stunningly cold wash of wind. Too late she realised that they were already off the ground. She was caught by the slipstream, whirled round and sucked out. She clutched wildly at the door-frame but her gloves slipped uselessly over the bare metal. At the edge of her consciousness she heard a man screaming: "You're crazy! You'll be killed!" Then she was falling through the snow-laden wind. She tumbled over in mid air and glimpsed a pair of headlights snaking through the night way below. That was the last thing she saw. The next couple of seconds would bring her nightmares for the rest of her life. Time stopped. She fell endlessly through the freezing sky, convinced that her body would be smashed to pieces any instant. She tried to scream, but could not. She tried to breathe, but could not. She tried to turn over, but could not alter her attitude in the slightest. She dropped helplessly, rigid with terror.

The impact was unbelievably gentle. Instead of smashing into iron-hard tundra, she landed in something soft and yielding. She hit it back-first, and went right on down through several feet of blessed cushioning. She was winded by the impact, but that was all. She lay on her back gasping and groaning for breath, but once she had got it back, she began to shake with relief. To her own amazement, she found she was laughing as well as crying. She had landed on her backside in a great big drift of snow.

*   *   *

Jay Shore was just about to leave his office at the Sanmobil plant when the telephone rang. He picked up the receiver and said "Yes?"

"Switchboard operator here," said a voice high with stress. "Got an emergency. Driver Pete Johnson is on the radio. Wants to talk to you immediately."

"I'll take it. Patch him through." Shore waited.

"Hullo? Hullo?" Johnson's voice crackled through, even more excited than the operator's. "Mr Shore, sir?"

"Speaking. Take it easy. What's the problem?"

"I'm on my way down to Fort McMurray, sir. Driving bus MB 3. Just come round a corner and found Bus MB 5 abandoned in the middle of the road."

"*Abandoned?*"

"That's right. Doors open, motor running, lights on. Point is, it's the bus Mr Reynolds took to go home in."

"Jesus! Where are you?"

"About a mile past Hangman's Turn. Mile towards Fort McMurray."

"Okay. I'll get someone right out there."

"Mr Shore?"

"What is it?"

"I just saw a chopper take off from near the road, and *somebody fell out of it.* And two of our security guys – Mr Brinckman and Mr Jorgensen – are lying in the road, like they've been hurt real bad."

"Damn!"

"Yeah, and there's a truck stuck in the snow by where the plane took off. It's trying to get back on the road, facing towards Fort McMurray."

"Keep away from it," Shore ordered. "Stay in your own vehicle. Back off a bit. But don't go near the truck. I'll get someone right down."

"Okay, Mr Shore, sir."

Shore banged down the receiver and snatched up another.

167

an outside line. He dialled and waited. He knew that Carmody and Jones, the two R.C.M.P. men assigned to protect the Brady family, were also due at the Reynolds's for supper, so he called directly there. Someone answered – Mrs Reynolds.

"Mary? Jay Shore speaking. Look – I'm afraid there's been some sort of a . . . mix-up. Bill and the ladies have got delayed. What's that? No – I hope not. Nothing to worry about. Have you the two constables there already? Great. Yes please. Either will do."

John Carmody came on the line.

"Emergency," said Shore quietly. "I think your party's been hijacked. Yes – I do." He explained all he knew in a couple of sentences. "What I want *you* to do is come right up the road to Hangman's Turn. You see anybody coming to meet you, stop him: it could be the grey truck we're after. O.K?"

"O.K. We're on our way."

"That's fine. Get moving."

*   *   *

Carmody drove. Jones rode shotgun, his .38 revolver ready in his hand. The Cherokee Jeep station wagon, in four-wheel drive, held the road better than a regular sedan, but even so they had to go carefully.

Carmody swore steadily as he nursed the wheel. "Goddam it to hell!" he kept muttering. "The first time we leave them, *this* happens. What in hell were the Sanmobil security guys doing, for Christ's sake?"

They drove on, snow whirling through the headlight-beams. Suddenly they saw lights coming the other way.

"Block the road!" Jones ordered. "Get sideways on."

"Better to keep head on – dazzle him. He can't get past, anyway."

168

Carmody stopped in the middle of the road and switched on the station wagon's flashers. The oncoming driver rounded a bend, saw them, braked and slewed violently from side to side before sliding to a halt.

Jones got out and moved towards the vehicle. He'd only gone three or four yards when a spurt of fire flashed from the driver's window, followed instantly by the crack of a gun. Jones spun sideways, clutching his left shoulder. The other driver slammed into gear and let out the clutch. For a second his tyres raced griplessly on the snow. Then he shot forward, cannoned into the Jeep, shunted it sideways enough for him to scrape past, and accelerated away in the direction of Fort McMurray.

Carmody tried to open his door but found it jammed: the bodywork was buckled all down that side. He bunked across to the other side and ran to the aid of his wounded colleague. Jones was conscious but bleeding badly from a wound in the top corner of his chest: a large, dark stain had spread out across the snow beneath his body.

Carmody thought fast. It was too cold to administer first aid to the wound. If he took off any of Jones's clothes, the man would die of exposure and shock. First priority was to get him somewhere warm, then to hospital. He ought to call up an ambulance.

"Come on, Bill," he said gently. "You gotta get up."

"O.K.," Jones muttered. "I'm O.K."

"On your feet, then." Carmody got him round the waist, avoiding his chest and shoulders, in case he made anything worse there, and hoisted him upright. Then he propelled him gently towards the Jeep and opened one of the back doors.

"In there," he said. "Front door's jammed."

He got the wounded man safely in, closed the door, climbed aboard himself and turned up the heater to maximum. Then he addressed himself to the radio. To his chagrin, he could get nothing out of it. The set was live, but

169

no signal came through. Something had been broken by the impact of the truck.

For a moment Carmody considered turning and giving chase. Then he realised the other driver had too much start on him: even with his four-wheel drive, he would never overtake him in the short distance between there and Fort McMurray. He was closer to the Sanmobil plant, in any case. Better get on and make contact with the bus driver who had first raised the alarm.

He set off as fast as he dared. Jones was ominously silent, not answering questions about how he felt. Carmody set his jaw and drove through the snow.

Five minutes later he came on the stranded minibus. Immediately he recognised the black-and-yellow chequered MB 5, which he had seen and ridden in many times before. Beyond it a line of vehicles had piled up, the drivers being kept at bay by Johnson, who had told them that the police were about to arrive, and that no-one must touch the bus until the cops had checked it out. The beaten-up security men were hunched in the seats of Johnson's bus, apparently comatose.

Carmody sized up the position in a moment. "Get it out the way," he ordered. "Let everybody else through."

They pushed the Reynolds bus to one side and waved the other vehicles past. Three back in the line was a Sanmobil truck with two storehands aboard – the only men Shore had been able to conscript immediately at that late hour. Over Johnson's bus radio Carmody called for police reinforcements and alerted the Sanmobil sick bay, warning them that three injured men were being brought in. Then he detailed one of the Sanmobil men to drive his own Jeep right on to the plant, with Jones still in it. Brinckman and Jorgensen, unsteady on their feet, also climbed aboard.

"Get back in the warm," Carmody told them. "I'll talk to

170

you guys later." As they drove off he turned to Johnson: "O.K., so what happened?"

"I just came on the bus in the middle of the road, like you saw it. The two security guys were lying in front of it, trying to get up. I got out to see what the matter was, and heard the racket of a helicopter engine, right close."

"Where was it?"

"Just over there. I'll show you."

He switched on a big flashlight and led the way over the frozen tundra. "Sounded like he had a problem with the motor – kept running it up and letting it die again. Then he *did* go: lifted off and headed thataway – north. Here – you can see the ski-marks."

In the torch-beam the imprint of long, heavy skis was still visible, though dusted over with the snow blown about by the rotor's down-draught.

"Any markings on the chopper, identification?" Carmody asked.

"Nothing – it was just like a big black shadow against the sky. Couldn't even tell the colour exactly but it looked off-white. Pair of small fins near the tail too."

"And then what happened? Where did the person fall?"

"A woman, it was: she screamed. Someplace over there." Johnson pointed. "Not too far."

"How high did she fall from?"

"Maybe a hundred feet. Maybe more."

"Must be dead. We'd better look, all the same. Oh my God! One of the Bradys killed."

They went up an incline into the teeth of the wind. On top of the slope the ground was rounded into smooth, gentle humps. The torch-beam, sweeping the snow, revealed nothing.

"Must have been around here," said Johnson doubtfully. "Can't have been much further, or I'd never have seen the body at all. Try over there a bit."

171

They cast a little to their left. Suddenly Carmody, who had been walking on hard-frozen tundra, sunk to his waist in snow. As he exclaimed and struggled to extricate himself from the drift, Johnson called: "Listen, I thought I heard something."

They waited, catching only the whine of the wind. Then Johnson heard the sound again – a cry that sounded faint yet close at hand.

"There it is!" he shouted. "Sure as hell, someone calling. This way!"

They tried to move eastwards, but both lunged into the deep snow again and realised that a rift in the ground ran in that direction.

They regained the hard edge of the invisible miniature valley and followed it another twenty steps. Then they heard the cry again, almost beneath them. This time they shouted back and got an answer. A few more steps brought them to the lip of a hole about a yard across that had been punched vertically downwards into the drift. Shining the light down it, they saw a bundle of powder-blue snow-suit.

"Hey! You! Mrs Brady? Stella?" Carmody called. "Are you hurt?"

"No," came the muffled answer. "I'm not Mrs Brady or Stella, and I'm not hurt. Just stuck."

"Who are you, then?"

"Corinne Delorme."

"Corinne! Heaven's sakes! John Carmody here. Hold on, and we'll get you right out of there." He sent Johnson running to the truck for a shovel and a rope, and in five minutes they had dug and hoisted the girl out. Considering she had been outdoors for more than half an hour, she was in remarkably good shape, mainly because the snow had insulated her and given her complete protection from the wind. But as soon as they got her into the warmth of the

172

truck-cab, reaction set in and she began to shudder uncontrollably.

Carmody's first impulse was to drive her to hospital, but then he changed his mind. Something – he could not quite tell what – made him favour a more devious approach. The guys in the helicopter must reckon she was dead: they must think they had another murder on their hands. It was a million-to-one that she had fallen into the drifted-up ravine rather than onto the ground: five yards to either side, and every bone in her body would have been broken. Something might be gained, Carmody thought, if the kidnappers did not realise anyone had survived; therefore he decided to move her away into safe-keeping, at any rate until Brady and his team returned.

"Know what I want you to do?" Carmody said to Johnson. "Drive Miss Delorme to the isolation unit on the plant. The *isolation* unit. When you reach the main gates, have her keep down out of sight, on the floor. I don't want anyone to know where she is. Any bother, say you're on a special run for Mr Shore, O.K.?"

Johnson nodded.

"You hear that, Corinne?" Carmody lifted up her chin. "He'll take you to a good place at Athabasca. Nice and warm and comfortable. Out of the way, too. I'll see you back there as soon as I can make it."

Shock and reaction had knocked the girl to pieces for the moment, and she could not answer.

"Go on, then," Carmody told Johnson. "Drive."

12

It was past midnight and still snowing heavily when Brady arrived back in Fort McMurray, but the lobby of the Peter Pond Hotel was as crowded and bustling with activity as if it had been just after noon. Brady sank wearily into a chair. The flight from Prudhoe Bay had been a grim one: between them Brady, Dermott and Mackenzie had uttered hardly a word.

A tall, lean man, dark-moustached and heavily tanned, approached. "Mr Brady? My name's Willoughby. Glad to make your acquaintance, sir, though not in these damnable circumstances."

"Ah – the police chief." Brady smiled without humour. "And rough for you, Mr Willoughby, to have this happen in your territory. I was sorry to hear that one of your men had been killed."

"I'm glad to say that report was premature. There was a great deal of confusion around here when we made that phone call to you. The man was shot through the left lung and certainly looked bad, but now the doctor says he has a more than even chance."

"That's something." Brady smiled wanly again.

Willoughby turned to two other men. "D'you know ...?"

"Those two gentlemen I've met," said Brady. "Mr Brinckman, Sanmobil security chief, and his deputy, Mr Jorgensen. Odd – for a couple of reportedly injured men, you look remarkably fit to me."

Brinckman said: "We don't exactly feel it. Like Mr Willoughby said, things got exaggerated in the heat of the moment. No broken bones, no knife or gun injuries, but they did knock us about a bit."

174

"Pete Johnson – the guy who raised the alarm – will vouch for that," said Willoughby. "When he got there, Jorgensen was lying on the road, out cold, and Brinckman was wandering round in a daze. He didn't know if it was last night or last month."

Brady turned to another man who had appeared at his side. "Evening, Mr Shore. Morning, rather. The Brady family seem to have disturbed a lot of people's sleep, I'm afraid."

"To hell with that." Shore was visibly upset. "I helped show Mrs Brady and your daughter round the plant yesterday. That this should happen to her. Just as bad, that this should happen to you when you and your family were virtually our guests and you were trying to help us. A black day and a black eye for Sanmobil."

"Maybe not all that black," said Dermott. "God knows, it must be a traumatic experience to be kidnapped, but I don't believe any of the four is in immediate danger. We're not dealing with political fanatics such as you get in Europe or the Mid East. We're up against hard-headed business men with no personal animosity against their victims: they almost certainly regard them as bargaining counters." He clasped and unclasped his big hands. "They're going to make demands, probably outrageous, for the return of the women, and if those demands are met, they'll honour the bargain. Professional kidnappers usually do. In their own twisted terms, it's sound business practice and plain commonsense."

Brady turned to Willoughby. "We haven't really heard what happened. I assume you haven't had time to make wide-ranging enquiries?"

"Afraid not."

"They've just vanished into thin air?"

"Thin air is right. Helicopter, as you heard. They could be a few hundred miles away in any direction by this time."

175

"Any chance of airfield radars having picked up their flight-path?"

"No, sir. It's a million to one that they were flying below radar level. Besides, there are more palm trees in Northern Alberta than there are radar stations. Down south, it's different. We've alerted the stations there to keep a watch, but nothing's been reported so far."

"Well –" Brady steepled his fingers, sinking back in his chair. "It might help if we could have a brief chronological account of what happened."

"That won't take long. Jay?"

Shore said: "Yes. I was the last person to see them, apart from these two" – he pointed at Brinckman and Jorgensen. "They left in one of Sanmobil's minibuses, with Bill Reynolds driving."

Mackenzie cut in: "Were there any phone calls before they left?"

"I wouldn't know. Why?"

"Let me ask another question." Mackenzie looked at Brinckman. "How did the kidnappers stop your bus?"

"They had a truck slewed across the road. Blocked it completely."

"It couldn't have been there long. There's a fair bit of traffic on that road, and drivers wouldn't take kindly to being held up. Was there, in fact, any other traffic at the time?"

"I don't think so. No."

Willoughby said: "Your point, Mr Mackenzie?"

"Plain as a pikestaff. The kidnappers were tipped off. They knew the precise time when Reynolds's bus left and when it could be expected at the interception point. Phone or short-wave radio – even a CB would have been enough. Two things are for sure: there was a tip-off, and it came from Sanmobil."

"Impossible!" Shore sounded shocked.

176

"Nothing else makes sense," said Brady. "Mackenzie's right."

"Good God!" Shore sounded outraged. "You make Sanmobil sound like a den of thieves."

"It's not a Sunday School," said Brady heavily.

Dermott turned back to Brinckman. "So Reynolds pulled up when he saw this truck across the road? Then?"

"It was all so quick. There were two men lying in the road. One was face-down and very still, as if he were hurt real bad. The other was moving – he'd both hands clutching at the small of his back and was rolling from side to side. He seemed to be in agony. Two other men came running towards us – well, hardly running, more staggering. One was limping badly, and he had an arm stuck inside his mackinaw jacket as if he was trying to support it. Both of them had a hand up in front of their faces, covering their eyes."

Dermott said: "Didn't that strike you as odd?"

"Not at all. It was dark, and we had our headlights on. It seemed natural they should shield their eyes from the glare."

There was a pause. Then Brinckman went on: "Well – this guy with the damaged arm – as I thought – came weaving up to my side of the bus. I grabbed the first-aid box and jumped out. I slipped on the ice, and by the time I had my balance I saw the man had dropped his hand and was wearing a stocking mask. Then I saw his left arm coming up. It was almost a blur, but I could see he had some kind of a sap in his hand. I had no time to react." He fingered his forehead gingerly. "That's all, I guess."

Dermott crossed to him and examined the contusion on the side of his forehead. "Nasty. Could have been worse, though. An inch or so further back and you'd likely have had a fractured temple. Looks as if your friend was using lead shot. A leather cosh wouldn't have done that."

Brinckman stared at him in an odd fashion. "Lead, you reckon?"

"I should think so." Dermott turned to Jorgensen. "I take it you hadn't much better luck?"

"At least I wasn't blackjacked. I just thought my jaw had been broken. The other guy was either a heavyweight champion, or he was clutching something heavy in his fist. I couldn't see. He jerked open Mr Reynolds's door, flung in some kind of smoke-bomb, then banged the door shut again."

"Tear gas," said Willoughby. "You can see his eyes are still inflamed."

"I got out," Jorgensen went on. "I waved my gun around, but it might have been a water pistol, the use it was. I was blind. Next thing I remember, Pete Johnson was trying to shake some sense into us."

"So, of course, you don't know how Reynolds and his passengers made out." Brady looked round. He was taking over. "Where's Carmody?"

"Down at the station," said Shore. "Still making his report. Pete Johnson's with him. They'll be here presently."

"Good." Brady turned back to Brinckman. "The man who attacked you – was he wearing gloves?"

"I'm not sure." Brinckman thought and then said: "Once he'd passed out of the beam of the headlights, he was in pretty deep shadow, and, as I said, it all happened so damn quickly. But I don't think so."

"Your man, Mr Jorgensen?"

"I could see his hand pretty clearly as he threw the tear-gas canister. No – no glove."

"Thank you, gentlemen. Mr Willoughby, a few questions if I may."

"Go ahead." Willoughby cleared his throat.

"This truck the kidnappers used – you say it was stolen?"

"That's right."

178

"It's been identified?"

"Belongs to a local garage proprietor. It was known he was off on a couple of days' hunting trip."

"At this time of year?"

"Your true enthusiast goes hunting any time. At all events, it was seen passing through the streets yesterday afternoon, and we assumed the owner was taking it along for his trip."

"Which argues a fairly intimate local knowledge?"

"Sure, but no help to us." Willoughby smoothed his dark moustache. "Fort McMurray's no longer a village."

"Have you fingerprinted the truck, inside and out?"

"Being done now. It's a long job – there are hundreds of prints."

"May we see them?"

"Of course. I'll have them Photostatted. But, with respect, Mr Brady, what do you hope to achieve that we, the police, can't?"

"You never know." Brady smiled enigmatically. "Mr Dermott here is an international expert in fingerprinting."

"I didn't know!" Willoughby smiled at Dermott, who smiled back. He hadn't known either.

Brady changed his tack. "Any chance of identifying the helicopter from the measurements of the ski-marks that Carmody took?"

Willoughby shook his head. "It was a good idea to record them, but no – the chances of identifying any one machine from its ski-prints are extremely remote, because there will almost certainly be dozens of its particular type around. This is helicopter country, Mr Brady, like Alaska. Here in Northern Alberta our communications are still very primitive. We have no divided highways – freeways – in this part of the world. In fact, north of Edmonton there only two paved roads that reach up north. Between them – nothing. Apart from ourselves, and Peace River and Fort

Chipewyan, there are no commercial airports in an area of 200,000 square miles."

"So," Brady nodded. "You use choppers."

"The preferred form of transport at all times. In winter, the only form."

"It's a good bet that an intensive air search wouldn't have a hope in hell of locating the getaway machine?"

"None. I've made a bit of a study of kidnapping, and I can answer you best by a comparison. The world's most kidnap-happy place is Sardinia. It's a kind of national pastime there. Whenever a millionaire is snatched, all the resources of the law and the Italian armed forces are brought into play. The Navy blockades harbours and virtually every fishing village on the coast. The Army sets up road-blocks, and specially-trained troops sweep the hills. The Air Force carries out exhaustive reconnaissance by plane and helicopter. In all the years these searches have been carried out, they've never yet located a single kidnapper's hideout. Alberta is twenty-seven times larger than Sardinia. Our resources are a fraction of theirs. Answer your question?"

"One begins to feel the first faint twinges of despair. But tell me, Mr Willoughby: if you had four kidnapped people on your hands, where would you hide them?"

"Edmonton or Calgary."

"But those are towns. Surely . . ."

"Cities, yes – and the population of each must be crowding half a million. The captives wouldn't be hidden – they'd be lost."

"Well." Brady pulled himself up in his chair. He looked weary. "Okay. I suppose we have to wait word from the kidnappers before we make a move. You two gentlemen –" he turned to Brinckman and Jorgensen – "I don't think we need keep you any longer. Thank you for your co-operation."

The two security men said their goodnights and left.

180

Brady hoisted himself to his feet. "No sign of Carmody yet? Let's go and make ourselves more comfortable while we wait for him. The desk will no doubt inform us when he arrives. This way, gentlemen."

*　　*　　*

Once in the privacy of his own room, armed with a fresh drink, Brady seemed suddenly to shake off his exhaustion.

"O.K., George," he said briskly. "You've been holding out on us. Why?"

"In what way?"

"Don't pussy-foot. You said you were more concerned about the demands the crooks are going to make than about my family. You love my family. Now what did you mean?"

"The first demand will be that you, Don and I take off for Houston. They must be convinced we're on the verge of a breakthrough.

"The second demand will be a ransom message. To keep things within reasonable bounds they can hardly ask for more than a couple of million dollars. But that would be peanuts compared with the stakes our friends are playing for.

"Third, the greater stakes. Obviously, they'll demand a fortune to cease their harassment of both Prudhoe Bay's and Sanmobil's oil supplies, and the increasing destruction of their equipment. That's where they hold all the aces: as we've seen, both systems are embarrassingly vulnerable to attack. For as long as the criminals' identity remains undiscovered, they can keep on destroying both systems piecemeal.

"Their price will be high. I imagine they'll base it on the development cost of the two systems – that's ten billion for starters – plus the daily revenue, which is the cost of over two million barrels a day. Five per cent of the total? Ten?

181

Depends what the market will bear. One thing's for sure: if they demand too much and price themselves out of the market, the oil companies are going to cut their losses and run, leaving the insurance companies to hold the baby – and it will surely be the most expensive baby in insurance history."

Brady said querulously: "Why didn't you bring this up downstairs?"

"I have an aversion to talking too much in crowded hotel foyers." Dermott leant towards Jay Shore. "Did your Edmonton office send the fingerprints we asked for?"

"I have them in the safe at home."

"Good." Dermott nodded approval; but Willoughby was curious: "What prints?"

Shore hesitated until he received an all-but-imperceptible nod from Dermott, and said: "Mr Brady and his men seem pretty well convinced that we have at Sanmobil one or more subversives actively aiding and abetting the men trying to destroy us. Mr Dermott particularly suspects our security staff and all those who have access to our safe."

Willoughby shot Dermott a cool, quizzical look. It was clear that he considered the matter one for the Canadian police and not for foreign amateurs. "Would you mind explaining why?" he asked coldly.

"They're the only suspects we have – especially the men in charge of the security shifts. Not only do they have access to the key of the armoury from which the explosives were stolen, they actually carry the damn thing around with them on duty. More, I have good reason to suspect the security staff on the Alaskan pipeline. Further, it appears more than likely that both security staffs are working hand-in-glove under the same boss or bosses. How else can you explain how some villains here know the Sohio/B.P. code, while the villains there know Sanmobil's?"

Willoughby said: "This is just conjecture . . ."

"Sure. But it's conjecture shading into probability. Isn't it a basic police philosophy to set up a theory and examine it from all sides before discarding it? Well, we've set up our theory, examined it from all sides, and don't feel like discarding it."

Willoughby frowned, then said: "You don't trust the security men?"

"Let me amplify that. The majority are straight, no doubt, but until I know for sure, they're all under suspicion."

"Including Brinckman and Jorgensen?"

"'Including' is not the word. 'Especially'."

"Jesus! You're talking crazy, Dermott. After what they went through?"

"Tell me what they went through."

"They told you already." Willoughby had become incredulous.

Dermott was unmoved. "I've only got their word for that – and I'm pretty sure in both cases that word's worthless."

"Carmody corroborated their story – or rather, Johnson did. Maybe you don't trust him either?"

"I'll decide that when I meet him. But the point is, Johnson *didn't* corroborate the story. All he said – correct me if I'm wrong – was that when he arrived on the scene he found Brinckman unconscious and Jorgensen staggering around. That's all he said. He had no more idea what went on before that than you or I do."

"Then how d'you account for their injuries?"

"Injuries?" Dermott smiled sarcastically. "Jorgensen didn't have a mark on him. Brinckman did, but if you'd been watching him, you'd have seen him jump when I told him he'd been struck by a lead-filled cosh. That didn't fit. There was something wrong with the scenario.

"I suggest both men were in perfectly good health until they saw the lights of Johnson's minibus approaching, whereupon Jorgensen, acting on instructions, tapped

183

Brinckman on the head just hard enough to lay him out briefly."

"What do you mean, 'under instructions'?" Willoughby demanded doggedly. "Whose?"

"That remains to be discovered. But you might like to know that these aren't the first peculiar injuries we've come across. A doctor in Prudhoe Bay, for one, has discovered that we have highly suspicious minds on this subject. Donald and I had to examine a murdered engineer whose finger had sustained a curious fracture. The good doctor explained it away to his own apparent satisfaction, but not to ours. He probably gave orders that if any other such – ah – marginal incidents happened, any security agents in the vicinity were to display proof of injuries sustained in the loyal execution of their duties – such as, in this case, their attempts to protect those whom they were supposed to be protecting."

Willoughby stared at him and muttered: "You have to be fantasising."

Dermott answered: "We'll see." But his reply was cut short by the sudden arrival of Carmody and Johnson. Both men looked pale and exhausted – a condition Brady sought to remedy by providing them with very large Scotches.

After a suitable pause for congratulation on his night's work, Carmody was taken through his account, step by step. The exercise proved disappointing until, when he came to describe the scene of the helicopter ski-marks, he suddenly became tongue-tied. He broke off in mid-sentence and stammered: "Say, Mr Brady, could I – er – could I talk with you *privately*?"

"Well!" Brady was somewhat taken aback. "By all means – but what purpose would it serve? These gentlemen enjoy my fullest confidence. Say what you want in their hearing."

"O.K., then. It's about the girl – Corinne . . ." Whereupon he told them the story of the rescue. Amazement

184

swiftly and thoroughly woke up his audience. They crowded forward, listening intently.

"Maybe I was wrong," Carmody ended up, "but I just figured that if news of her survival didn't get out, it might be a card up our sleeve."

"You figured correctly," Brady said.

"Where is she, then?" asked Dermott sharply.

"Right now she's in the isolation unit at the plant. She went a bit hysterical, with the reaction, but she's all right."

Dermott let out a whoosh of air and said "My, oh my!"

"A very original observation, George," Brady remarked wryly. "Do I detect a certain . . . pleasure on your part that the young lady is alive and well and in safe hands?"

"You do," said Dermott. Then he added quickly, as if feeling he had been over-enthusiastic: "And why not?"

"Point is, I took a statement from her," Carmody went on. "Want to hear it?"

"Certainly," Brady said. "Fire away."

The statement still existed only in Carmody's notebook, and so took some time to read. The beginning of it merely confirmed what had been established already – but then came a revelation. After the hold-up, the girl reported, "one man came staggering towards us along the road".

"*One* man?" snapped Dermott, half-rising out of his chair. "Did she say *one* man?"

"That's what she said." Carmody resumed his recitation, back-tracking a sentence to emphasise her account. "'I saw two men lying in the road, like they were hurt. One was dead still. The other could move a bit. Then one other man came limping back towards us. He had a hand up in front of his eyes. Mr Brinckman was sitting on my right. He jumped out and grabbed the first-aid box from under the seat. I think he slipped and fell over. Then he got up again. Then I saw the other man straighten up and hit him. He went down – Mr Brinckman, that is. The other man had a stocking mask on –

185

I could see that by now. He opened the door where Mr Reynolds was sitting and threw something into the bus . . .'"

"That's it!" cried Dermott, smiting his fist on the coffee-table. "We got them!"

Brady glowered at him. "Would you favour us slower brethren with an explanation?"

"The whole thing was a frame-up. They told us a load of garbage. They said *two* men came at them, to make it seem more realistic that they hadn't put up any resistance. Now it's obvious they didn't *try* to resist. They were part of the act. Jorgensen just sat there watching his partner get slugged."

"How come he wasn't much affected by the tear gas?" Brady asked.

"He was prepared for it, of course," Dermott replied instantly. "If you screw your eyes shut and hold your breath, tear gas has very little effect on you. Jorgensen only had to hold out for a couple of seconds before opening his own door and getting into the fresh air. Listen to what the girl said: there were no bodies left on the road when she was dragged away. Every damn one of them had got up, right as rain, to help get the captives aboard the chopper. It was only when they saw Johnson's headlights coming that Brinckman and Jorgensen resumed their artistic poses on the road."

Willoughby muttered a curse. "I believe you're right," he said slowly. "I really do. And we haven't a shred of hard evidence against them."

"No way you could dream up a charge and haul them in for preventive detention?" asked Dermott hopefully.

"None."

"I wish you could," said Dermott. "I'd sleep happier for the rest of the night. As it is, I don't intend to sleep at all. I've got a slight aversion to being murdered in bed."

Brady nearly choked on his drink. "And what the hell does that mean, mister?"

"Just that I think an attempt will soon be made to murder me. And Donald. And you."

Brady looked as though he might explode, but remained speechless. Dermott addressed him with some acerbity.

"Whenever you spoke down there in the foyer just now, you were tightening another screw in your own coffin-lid." He turned to Willoughby. "Could you spare a guard for Mr Shore's house tonight?"

"Of course; but why?"

"Simple. Mr Brady unfortunately made it clear that he wanted copies of fingerprints found on the stolen truck. Brinckman and Jorgensen know that we've asked your people for what could be damning prints from your Edmonton H.Q. They'll discover, if they haven't already, that the copies of their own prints which we took earlier are in the safe in Mr Shore's house."

"What good would it do them to get the copies?" Brady asked edgily. "The originals are at police H.Q. in Edmonton."

"How far d'you think this rot has spread?" said Dermott. "The originals may still be there, but they won't be much help once they've been through a shredding machine."

"Where's the problem?" asked Willoughby. "We just print 'em out again."

"On what grounds? Suspicion? Just one moderately competent lawyer, and the town would be looking for a new police chief. They'd refuse point-blank. What could you do then?"

"Point out to them – which is the case – that it's a condition of employment at Sanmobil."

"So you'd have mass resignations on your hands. Then what?"

Willoughby didn't answer. Mackenzie broke in: "You said I was the other grave-digger?"

"Yes. You said the kidnappers must have been tipped off

187

from Sanmobil as to when to expect Reynolds's bus. You were right, of course. But Brinckman and Jorgensen must have thought you meant it was they who gave the tip. They may even think we can trace the call to them, even though outgoing calls from the plant aren't normally tapped."

"Well, I'm sorry." Mackenzie shifted uneasily.

"Too bad. The damage has been done. And it wouldn't have helped to reproach you and Mr Brady in public."

The phone rang. Dermott, the nearest, picked it up, listened briefly and said: "One moment. I think the person you should talk to is Mr Shore. He's right here with us."

He handed the phone over and listened impassively to Shore's half of the conversation, which consisted almost entirely of muttered expletives. The phone rest settled as he replaced the receiver, so badly was his hand shaking. His face had gone white.

"They've shot Grigson," he gasped.

"Who's Grigson?" snapped Brady.

"Sanmobil's president. That's all."

13

The police doctor, a young man named Saunders, straightened and looked down at the unconscious man on the pile of blankets. "He'll be all right, eventually, but that's all I can do for him now. He needs the services of an orthopaedic surgeon."

"How long will it be before I can question him?" Brady asked.

"With the sedative I've given him, it'll be several hours before he comes round."

"Couldn't that damned sedative have waited a little?"

Dr Saunders looked at Brady with a marked lack of enthusiasm. "I hope, for your sake, you never have your shoulder and upper arm shattered, the bone structure completely fragmented. Mr Grigson was in agony. And even had he been conscious, I wouldn't have let you question him."

Brady muttered something about medical dictators, then looked at Shore and said testily: "What the hell was Grigson doing here anyway?"

"Dammit, Brady, he's more right to be here than you and I and the rest of us put together." Shore sounded shocked and angry. "Sanmobil is the dream-come-true of one man and one only, and he's lying there before you. Took him nine years to turn his dream into reality, and he had to fight all the way. He's the president. Do you understand that – the president?"

Mackenzie said pacifically: "When did he arrive?"

"Yesterday afternoon. Flew in from Europe."

Mackenzie nodded and looked round Reynolds's office. It

189

wasn't a small room, but it was fairly crowded. Apart from himself, Brady, Shore, Dr Saunders and the unconscious Grigson, there were Willoughby and two young men who had clearly been in the wars during the recent past. One had a bandaged forehead, the other an arm strapped from wrist to elbow. It was to this last person, Steve Dawson, that Mackenzie addressed himself.

"You were in charge of the night-shift?"

"Nominally. Tonight there *was* no night-shift. The plant's closed down."

"I know. So how many of you were here tonight – yourself apart?"

"Just six people." He glanced down at the wounded man. "Mr Grigson was asleep in his private room along the corridor there. Then there was Hazlitt – charge-hand of the night security shift – and four security guards deployed around the plant."

"Tell us what happened."

"Well – I was patrolling, reinforcing the security team, as I had nothing else to do. I saw a light come on here in Mr Reynolds's room. First I thought it must be Mr Grigson – he's a very active, restless person, and an erratic sleeper. Then I got to wondering what he could be doing, because he'd already spent a couple of hours with Mr Reynolds yesterday. So, quiet as I could, I came along the passage to Grigson's room.

"The door was closed, but not locked. I went in, and there he was asleep. I woke him, told him there were intruders in the plant, and asked to borrow a gun. I knew he had one, because he used to practise on a little private target range he'd set up here.

"He'd have none of it. He produced his automatic, but kept it himself. He said he'd had it for years and knew how to use it. I couldn't argue with him – after all, I'm only twenty-eight, and he's crowding seventy.

190

"Anyway, in here we found a man with the door of that safe open. He'd smashed Corinne's desk open with a fire-axe to get at the keys. He was wearing a stocking mask and examining a bunch of keys he had in his hand.

"Mr Grigson told him to turn around, real slow, and not to try anything, or he'd kill him. Then suddenly came two pistol shots, right close together, from behind, and Mr Grigson pitched headlong to the floor. He was wearing a white shirt, and blood from his right shoulder and arm was pumping through it. I could see he was hurt real bad.

"I dropped to my knees to help him. The man who'd fired the shots probably figured I was going for Mr Grigson's gun. Anyway, he fired at me too."

Dawson was breathing quickly, his distress evident. Brady poured him a Scotch and handed the glass over. "Take this."

Dawson's smile was wan. "I've never had a drink in my life, sir."

"Maybe you'll never have another," said Brady agreeably. "But you need this one, and we need your story."

Dawson drank, spluttered and coughed. He screwed up his eyes and drank some more. He clearly detested the stuff, but his system didn't, for almost immediately some colour began to return to his cheeks. He touched his bandaged forearm.

"Looks worse than it is. The bullet just grazed me, wrist all the way to elbow, but very superficial. Stung, more than anything. One of the masked men forced me to help lug Mr Grigson to the armoury. On the way out I picked up two first-aid kits – they didn't object. They pushed us into the armoury, locked the door and left.

"Then I took off Mr Grigson's shirt and staunched the wound as best I could. It took a lot of bandages – there was

191

so much blood coming. I thought he was going to bleed to death."

"He could have," Saunders said with certainty. "No question, your quick action saved his life."

"Glad I was some use." Dawson shuddered, looked at the doctor and went on; "Then I bandaged my own arm and had a go at the door, but there was no way I could get it open. I looked around and found a box full of detonators, each with a fuse attached. I struck one and dropped it out through one of the ventilation grilles. It went off with quite a bang. I must have let seven or eight of them off before Hazlitt came hammering on the door and asked what the hell was going on. I told him, and he ran off to fetch a duplicate key."

Dawson drank some more, spluttered, but less than before, and put his glass down. "I guess that's about all."

"And more than enough," said Brady with unaccustomed warmth. "A splendid job, son." He looked round the assembled group, then asked sharply; "Where's George?"

Until then no-one had noticed that Dermott was missing. Then Mackenzie said: "He slipped out with Carmody some time back. You want me to go find him?"

"Leave him be," said Brady. "I have little doubt our faithful bloodhound is pursuing some spoor of his own."

* * *

In fact the bloodhound was pursuing a fancy, not a line. He had taken Carmody aside and whispered in his ear that he urgently wanted to question the girl, Corinne. Where was she?

"In the isolation ward, like I said," Carmody replied. "But I doubt you'll find it on your own. It's way out by itself, near Dragline One. Want me to come with you?"

"Sure. That'd be real kind." Dermott swallowed his disappointment. He wanted to go alone. The instincts at

192

work inside him made him feel uncomfortable: nothing like this had happened to him in years. But he had better be realistic and accept the offer of guidance.

By then the wind had increased, as it often did late in the night, and was whistling across the flat, open site with a deadly chill. The noise made it almost impossible to talk in the open – not that anyone in his senses would remain in the open for more than the minimum time.

Carmody had been reunited with his damaged Cherokee. Shouting an excuse into the wind, he got in first at the passenger door and slid across behind the wheel. Dermott heaved his massive frame in close behind him and slammed the door.

Carmody drove steadily across an apparently unmarked plain. The film of drifting snow had obscured the road, and the flat ground all looked the same.

"How the hell do you know which way to go?" Dermott asked.

"Markers – there." Carmody pointed as a small stumpy, black-and-white post went past, with the number 323 stencilled on it in bold figures. "We're on Highway Three. In a minute we'll turn onto Highway Nine."

Altogether they drove for nearly ten minutes before lights showed up out of the darkness ahead. Dermott was amazed once again at the sheer size of the site: by then they were four or five miles from the administration buildings.

The lights grew to a blaze of several windows, and they pulled up outside a single long hut. As they went through the door the heat hit them like a hammer as did a smell of disinfectant. Dermott at once began to wrestle his way out of his outdoor clothes: he felt he would stifle if he kept them on for one more second.

They found Corinne propped up on a pile of pillows, looking pale but (to Dermott's eye) very sweet in a pair of pea-green pyjamas. Contrary to Carmody's predictions, she

193

was wide awake. She'd been asleep, she said, and had woken up thinking it was already morning.

"What time is it, anyway?" she asked.

"Four o'clock, near enough," Dermott answered. "How d'you feel?"

"Fantastic. Not even a bruise, as far as I can tell."

"That's wonderful. But my, were you lucky!" Dermott began asking routine questions, to which he didn't really want the answers. He wished to hell Carmody would go away someplace and leave him alone with the girl. What he would say to her if that happened, he didn't quite know: all the same it was what he wanted.

"You've given us a real good lead, you know," he said enthusiastically. "Can't say just what it was, but it may be the breakthrough we needed. Mr Brady's delighted . . ."

His voice tailed off as a heavy rumble suddenly shook the building. "Jesus!" he looked up sharply. "What was that?"

Carmody was gone already, out of the room and down the short passage. Dermott caught up with him at the outside door.

"Helicopter!" Carmody snapped. "Made a low pass right over the building. There he is, burning now." Way out in the blackness a red and a green light converged and then separated again as the aircraft swung round. As the two men stood watching a pair of car headlamps snapped on from a point about a hundred yards in front of them. The vehicle moved forward, turned and stopped, with its headlights steady on a patch of snow.

"It's a marker!" Carmody cried. "He's gonna land. Quick, get the girl out of here. They must have come for her."

"How in hell do they know she's here?" said Dermott.

"Don't worry about that. Let's get her away." Moving like a sprinter, Carmody slipped back into the building, bundled Corinne up in a cocoon of blankets and carried her

194

out to the Jeep, where he dumped her in the back seat. Dermott lumbered behind him, envying his speed, and hauled himself into the front.

Without putting on any lights Carmody started the engine and moved off into the inky night, heading out into the open behind the parked marker-vehicle. A couple of hundred yards beyond it he swung round and faced in the same direction as the lights, so that he and Dermott could watch what happened through the windshield.

They sat there with the heater going full blast.

"Warm enough?" asked Carmody over his shoulder.

"Plenty, thanks." Corinne sounded as though she was enjoying herself. "I've got enough blankets to keep an elephant warm."

Dermott wondered uneasily whether that was any sort of a joke at his expense, but his speculation was cut short by the arrival of the helicopter. Suddenly it was there, large and grey-white, riding down on a storm of snow into the headlight pool. The rotor flashed brilliantly in the silvery beams, and the snow flew outwards from the downdraught.

"That's the one!" said Carmody in a voice charged with excitement. "The getaway chopper. Description tallies perfectly with Johnson's: grey-white, no markings, small fins by the tail. That's our baby. Damn!"

As soon as the machine had landed, the car's headlights cut. The watchers sat blinded by the sudden darkness. They saw a flashlight bobbing about in the blackness, but nothing else.

"Boy, will they be mad when they find you've gone!" Carmody said happily.

"D'you think they're still in it?" Corinne asked. "The others, I mean?"

"Could be – easily. Depends where the chopper's been these past few hours. Must have been waiting on the ground someplace."

"Come on!" snapped Dermott. "Let's get out of here."

"Wait a minute," Carmody said easily. "I wanna see what they do. Any moment now they'll be at the building. There – I can see them now."

Two figures moved swiftly past the lighted windows. More light showed as the door opened and shut.

"Can't we ram the helicopter or something?" Corinne suggested. "Stop it taking off?"

"Too big," said Carmody immediately. "You notice the legs and skis? Higher than our roof. All we'd do would be to damage the landing gear, which wouldn't stop them getting off. Besides, if I know them, there's a couple of guys with guns guarding the thing, at least. Hey – what was that?"

"What?" Dermott looked at him.

"I heard something. Machinery. Sure I did." Carmody looked out past Dermott into the darkness. "Open your window a minute."

Dermott obeyed, and instantly the noise was far louder: a huge squealing and clanking, as of some giant engine.

"Jesus Christ!" Carmody shouted. "The dragline. It's right here beside us."

Dermott opened his door and got out. His eyes, accustomed to the dark, could just make out the gigantic outline towering above them. Suddenly the noise seemed terrific. "Good God!" Dermott yelled into the wind. "It's alive. It's *moving*!"

Instinctively he began to run towards the machine, or rather, round it, for already he was alongside. Beside him he could hear the whine of electric motors, the squeal of metal and the crunch of frosted dirt as the mighty shoe ground forward. The coldness of the wind seared his lungs and made his eyes stream briefly before they froze. In spite of the discomfort, he felt fired by excitement and by rage, for here was a final and outrageous act of sabotage taking place right on top of him. In a flash of intuition he saw what they

196

intended: to drive the monster machine over the edge of the pit which it had been excavating.

The facts and figures that had been flung at him came crowding into his head. Six and a half thousand tons. It could move at some 250 yards an hour. The pit was 150 feet deep. Although he was no engineer, he knew instinctively that if the monster went over the edge, it would never come out again.

He came round the front of it and got another shock. The edge of the pit, showing as a limitless black hole, was less than thirty yards away. Perhaps only twenty-five. That meant he had a tenth of an hour – six minutes – to get the damn thing stopped. He looked up desperately. The boom disappeared into the night, like an Eiffel Tower tilted over. Somehow he had to get into the cab and throw the right switches.

He ran back right under the thing, between the shoes. Somewhere there must be a ladder. At last he found it. But as he looked up towards the cab, far above him, he saw someone moving there in a faint glow of light. He hesitated, one foot on the steel ladder, wishing he had a gun and wondering whether he should go back for Carmody. That was the last thought that entered his head for a couple of minutes, for the blow caught him squarely on the back of the neck, and brilliant points of light seemed to shoot outwards through his head as he slumped to the ground.

* * *

He came round shaking from the cold and stuck in an awkward position. His hands were jammed, somehow – jammed behind him. He needed to straighten his arms and get them back into action. He strained to sort himself out and realised with a shock that his wrists were manacled together, *and manacled to something*.

He gave a grunt and heaved, whereupon a man spoke out of the dark behind him.

"Ah, Mr Dermott," said a voice he half-recognised but could not place. "Struggling will not help. You are anchored to a steel ring let into concrete. The ring is directly in the path of Dragline One, which, as you can see and hear, is now only a few feet from you. The controls have been preset and locked in position so that the middle of the right shoe will pass over you. Goodbye, Mr Dermott. You have less than two minutes to live."

Fear cleared Dermott's head. "Bastards!" he cried. "Sadistic bastards! Come back!" But even as he shouted, he knew it was useless. In the whistle of the wind and the monstrous grinding of the dragline, his voice was nothing and carried nowhere. He twisted round and discovered that he was tethered almost on the lip of the pit: the edge of the black abyss was no more than a yard away. In the opposite direction, the front of the dragline's shoe had ground remorselessly to within fifteen feet of him. The front of it was coming on like a tank. Above him, the steel tracery of the boom seemed to fill the sky with an angry black pattern.

Dermott stopped shouting and began to fight the manacles. At least there was some movement: he could feel that a length of chain had been passed through the shackle on the ground. He jerked it furiously back and forth in the faint hope that the chain would break, but all he achieved was to chafe his wrists viciously and expose them to the cold. He could feel the icy steel biting into his bare skin. Frostbite, he thought dully. But what did frostbite matter if he was going to be crushed like a beetle?

"Carmody!" he yelled desperately. "Help!" Where the hell had Carmody gone? Why didn't he come looking?

Dermott fought the chain again and flopped flat, gasping. The shoe was only twelve feet off, scrunching on inch by inch. The whine of the electric motors seemed to fill the night, as if hell had claimed him.

He threw his body feverishly to left and right, experimenting to see if he could get clear of the shoe's line of advance. Nothing he tried was the slightest good: the shoe was ten feet wide, and he was tethered right in the middle of its track. The monster had been set marching with hideous precision.

He lay still again, panting, beaten. Suddenly images began flashing through his mind, conjured up uninvoked by the extremity of his desperation. Once again he witnessed the final terrifying seconds of the car-crash that had killed his wife, the time when an explosion had blown him clean off a rig in the Gulf of Mexico, into the shark-infested sea . . .

All at once he became aware of a light flashing over him. Then someone was crouching, pulling at his arms. Then he heard a high, feminine cry.

"Corinne!"

"My God!" she cried. "What's happened? Oh, Jesus!" She leapt to her feet and began to run. "*Wait*!" she screamed over her shoulder.

Dermott saw her fall, get up again, and go like a greyhound, round the corner of the shoe, the flashlight swinging wildly in the blackness. He shouted something after her, but she was gone. *Wait*, she'd said. Wait! What a hell of a thing to say! How could he wait? The shoe was scarcely ten feet from him: one minute, give or take a few seconds.

He found his eyes were full of tears, though whether they were of fear or relief or gratitude or what, he couldn't tell. He was crying like a baby.

Seconds were passing. He began to count. He got to ten and couldn't go on. He had been overtaken by a horrific vision of the exact physical process of destruction that was about to annihilate him. He would feed his feet and legs to the monster first. Or could he? Could he listen and watch while his ankles, shins and knees were crunched and flattened on the tundra? No – he would have to get the end over quickly and give it his head. But what would *that* be like, for God's sake? To hear his skull crack and feel that unthinkable weight! Impossible! Never!

He roared again: "CARMODY!" As if by a miracle, his shout was answered. Headlights came boring up out of the night and swept across him as the vehicle turned. Dermott stared incredulously as the lights came on at speed, heading right for him and the front of the shoe. At the last moment the vehicle slowed, but not enough to stop. The driver deliberately slid it into the front of the shoe, using it as a last-ditch barrier to stop the monster's progress. There was a sharp crash and the tinkle of falling glass. Then the door of the Jeep opened and Corinne leapt out.

There was so little space left that Dermott had all but been run over. The Jeep's left-hand wheels were almost on him. The next thing he saw was the tyres being forced bodily sideways towards him by the irresistible pressure of the dragline's advance.

Corinne had the tail-gate of the Jeep open. She dragged out a steel box – the emergency equipment – and dumped it behind Dermott with a crash.

"Keep still!" she shouted above the noise. "No – come back a bit. There. Keep there! I've got the bolt shears."

Dermott leant backwards in the attitude she ordered, speechless with tension. He saw the wheels of the Jeep come sideways at him again. The back wheel was touching his feet already. The Jeep was being pushed like a toy. At that rate it was going to do more harm than good: it was merely acting as an extension of the shoe, and would crush him before the dragline itself reached him.

He felt Corinne struggling behind him. Suddenly she gave a desperate cry. "Oh my God! I can't do it. I'm not strong enough."

Dermott's voice returned. "What's happening?" he shouted.

"The cutters!" she sobbed. "The bolt shears are biting into the chain, but I can't get enough pressure on them. It's too bloody hard!"

"Put one end on the ground," he ordered calmly. "One handle on the ground. Then get your weight on the other."

He felt her try, but she slipped and went down with a crash. "Try again!" he yelled.

By then the noise of the dragline was overwhelming: its roaring and grinding filled the night. But suddenly a new sound: a sharp crack told him that the great steel treads of the shoe had hooked into some part of the Jeep's bodywork. Instead of being pushed back, the vehicle had been gripped and held down. Dermott stared incredulously as the Cherokee began collapsing like an eggshell. The remaining headlight was snuffed out. Cracking, snapping noises accompanied the collapse of the hood and front wheels.

Behind him Corinne gave a despairing scream. "I just can't do it. I've got half-way through, but that's all."

"Look for a hacksaw!" Dermott shouted. "In the emergency pack."

"Got one!" She began working again frantically.

For Dermott time seemed to have stopped. He saw that the Cherokee's engine block had at last offered the dragline a spot of serious resistance: only a spot, it was true, but a definite token. Ponderous as a dinosaur, the machine lifted one foot slowly into the air as it ground the little human vehicle beneath its steel sole. As if in a trance, Dermott saw the windshield shatter, the front of the roof crumple down, the passenger compartment flatten. Right in front of him a back wheel snapped off and was squashed flat onto the ground. If his arms had been free, he could have reached out and touched the front of the shoe – it was that close.

But his arms were *not* free.

"I can't!" Corinne screamed in desperation.

Dermott's head cleared, and he shouted: "Is there an axe?"

"A what?"

"An axe."

"Yes – here."

"Smash the chain with that. Aim for the link you've been working on."

"I might hit you."

"To hell with that. Belt it."

He felt the thump as she let drive. The chain snatched sharply at his wrists and nearly jerked his arms from their sockets. Suddenly he smelt the stink of gasoline: the tank had been crushed.

Clank! She brought the axe down, then again. When Dermott twisted to see how she was doing, the clawing thread of the shoe scraped down past his shoulder. The thing was touching him. He shrank away from the monstrous beast, and brought out his last, terrible idea.

"Chop my hands off!" he ordered, quite calmly.

"I can't!"

"Go on. It's them or me."

"*NO!*" She gave a piercing shriek and swung the axe down with every ounce of her behind it. Next second she was on her knees sobbing: "Oh my God, it's gone! It's gone!"

Dermott fought his instinct to leap up. He held himself down as she struggled with the severed link. The tread was bumping and bruising him now. In a few moments it would hook him under, as it had the car.

"For Christ's sake!" he shouted. "Hurry!"

Miraculously, his hands came free. He got his arms back to their normal position and twisted sideways. "Look out for the pit!" he yelled. He himself was on the very lip. Hardly had he rolled clear of the dragline when there was a huge *whumph* and a roar of dark-red flame shot sideways at

202

ground level. A chance spark had ignited the car's gasoline. By a fluke he had rolled into the wind, so that the fiery blast went the other way and left him unscathed. Corinne was there behind him, also intact.

The blaze made no difference to the monster's advance. The flames roared for a few seconds, then went out, and the dragline continued without faltering towards the brink.

Dermott felt weak with reaction – but not as weak as the girl. One moment she was standing behind him; the next, as Dermott struggled to find the words to express his gratitude to her, she had collapsed in a heap on the ground. He picked her up as tenderly as he knew how, laid her gingerly over his shoulder in a fireman's lift, and began carrying her towards the still-lighted windows of the isolation quarters. His eyes seemed to have gone blurred with the strain. Or was it just ice? He scrubbed them with his free hand and saw better. Out in the patch of white light ahead of him, the helicopter was preparing to take off, lights flashing, rotor spinning. Even as he watched, it lifted off and slanted away into the sky.

At once the car whose lights had provided the marker moved off and accelerated. Once again, Dermott realised, the villains had melted into the night. He knew he ought to feel disappointed: as it was, he could concentrate on nothing except getting back into the warmth of the hut and lying down.

He was very close to the building, going slow, when he saw someone pass across the lighted windows in front of him. Fear seized him. Maybe it was one of them. Was he going to be shot after making such an effort? Before he had time to put down his burden or alter course, a flashlight came on, searched briefly and found his face.

"Good God! Dermott!"

"Carmody! Where in hell have you been?"

"Trying to ditch the chopper. What about you?"

"Had a . . . had a bit of bother." Suddenly Dermott found

he could hardly talk. He was about to break down. "Take her, will you?" he croaked. "I've had it."

With an exclamation Carmody relieved him of his inert burden. "Quick," said the policeman. "Inside."

They laid Corinne on one bed and Dermott collapsed on to another with the manacles still dangling from his wrists. "Ring Shore!" he gasped. "Tell him for Christ's sake to switch off the power to Dragline One. Tell him and Brady to get up here like they never drove before."

* * *

They had turned on the floodlamps to illuminate the 150-foot depths of the pit below. They had also hammered in spikes ten yards back from the lip, and to these they had attached ropes so that the vertiginously-inclined or the less-than-sure-footed could cling to them as they peered over the edge.

Dragline One had ended up on its nose, tilted backwards towards the near-vertical face at an angle of thirty degrees. The massive casing appeared undamaged, as did the triangular arm over which the control cables passed. Even the boom, its enormous length stretched out horizontally across the uneven valley floor, seemed undamaged, at least from above.

Brady had prudently wrapped his belaying rope three times round his mighty girth. "Surprisingly little damage," he said. "Or so it looks. I suppose some of the electric motors were wrenched free from their beds."

"That'll be the least of our troubles." Jay Shore looked stricken, ashen-faced in the floodlights. The sight of the crippled monster had far more effect on him than on any of the others. "It's getting the damn thing out of there."

"Wouldn't it be easier to get a replacement?" asked Brady.

"Jesus! Do you know what a replacement would cost at today's prices? Forty million dollars. Probably more. And you don't order one up, just like that. If we could have one on our doorstep tomorrow, I'm sure Sanmobil would order it. But it can't be done that way. You can't transport a thing that size overland. Electric motors apart, the whole caboodle comes crated in tens of thousands of pieces, and it takes a team of skilled engineers months to assemble it."

"Cranes?" Brady suggested. He seemed fascinated by the sheer size of the problem. Or he was trying to be diverted, trying not to think of his missing wife and daughter.

Shore made a dismissive gesture with his gloved hands. "The biggest cranes in the world – a whole battery of them – couldn't lift the dragline an inch off the floor. We'll either have to dismantle it piece by piece and raise the bits up here for reassembly, or build a road from down there back up to the surface level and have it towed up on bogies – or, perhaps, under its own steam. The road would have to be a very gentle gradient, which would mean a length of over a mile, heavily metalled on massive foundations. Whatever we do, it'll cost millions." He swore at some considerable length. "And all this in just seven minutes' work!"

"Why in hell couldn't you *stop* it, when we phoned you?" asked Carmody.

"The bastards knew what they were doing," said Shore savagely. "They'd gone into the generator room, thrown the breaker that fed power to Dragline One, locked the door from the outside, left the key in the lock and smashed it so thoroughly that it'll need an oxy-acetylene torch to open it again. We just couldn't get in to shut down the power."

"They sure knew how to cause the maximum damage and disruption with the minimum of effort," said Brady. "I suggest, Mr Shore, there's no point in our remaining here a moment longer: all you're doing is twisting the knife deeper

205

into your wound. Let's all get back inside and ask George what happened."

"O.K. Let's go." Shore, who had supervised the construction of the dragline, working along with the contractors, Bucyrus-Erie, seemed strangely reluctant to leave the fallen giant. It was as if he were abandoning an old friend. Brady could appreciate how he felt. But he could also appreciate how he felt himself: he had become acutely conscious of the cold.

Shore took one last look at the dragline and turned back towards the heated haven of the minibus. "O.K.," he repeated automatically. "Let's go hear Dermott's story."

They drove the short distance back to the isolation block, where they found Dermott lying on a bed, already being questioned by Willoughby. Corinne was sitting on a chair in the corner of the small room, looking in better shape than the man she'd rescued.

"How is he?" Brady whispered to the nurse out in the corridor.

"His wrists look pretty bad: they got chewed up by the manacles, and frost-bitten as well. They're going to be real painful for the next few days. They'll mend, though."

"What about his general condition – exposure?"

"What are you *talking* about? He's got the constitution of an ox."

By the time Brady, Mackenzie and Carmody had filed into the room, the place was crammed full. Brady seemed much moved by the sight of his senior operative brought low, with hands and forearms heavily bandaged.

"Well, George," he began, clearing his throat heavily. "I am informed that you plan to survive."

"Sure do." Dermott grinned up at them. "But boy – I wouldn't want to go through *that* again."

"I got the story," Willoughby cut in, brisk and businesslike. He gave a quick précis of what had happened,

206

including the arrival and departure of the helicopter. "I'm sorry to say it, Mr Shore, but it seems the plant is riddled with corruption. Number one, somebody sabotaged the generator room, so that you couldn't turn the power off. Number two, somebody else set the controls of the dragline to take it over the edge. Number three, somebody else hit Dermott and manacled him to the steel ring. Number four, somebody else again informed the kidnappers that the girl had survived her fall out of the helicopter and was back in the isolation unit. That makes quite a lot of villains for one plant."

"Too right, it does," Shore said bitterly. "You don't think the chopper came back to do the dragline job – that somebody on board got out and set the controls?"

"Impossible. The dragline was moving before the chopper landed. Isn't that right, Mr Dermott?"

"Right. At least – no – not quite. But we saw men from the chopper go straight to the building here – and then we heard the dragline moving, right near us. The guys from the helicopter didn't have time to reach the dragline and set up the controls."

"What I'd like to know is whether your family, Mr Brady, were still on board the helicopter," Willoughby said.

"Yes, they were." Carmody startled them all with his sudden pronouncement. "And Mr Reynolds. He was with them."

"How d'you know?" Jim Brady asked. Dermott sat up abruptly.

"I *saw* them. That's what I was doing all the time you were involved with the dragline. I made a wide circle on foot and approached the helicopter from the back. There was a man armed with a machine pistol guarding the ladder, but I climbed up onto the skid-struts from the opposite side and got a look in through the cabin windows. They were all there – Mrs Brady, Stella, Mr Reynolds."

"How . . ." Brady faltered. "How did they look?"

"Fine – just fine. Quite calm, all of them. But they weren't quite as passive as they looked."

"What d'you mean?" Dermott asked quickly.

"One of them managed to drop this out of the door, or out of a window." From his breast pocket Carmody drew a brown leather bill-fold, which he handed to Brady. "Looks like one of yours – J.A.B., nicely embossed in gold."

"My God!" Brady took it. "That's Jean's. Her middle name's Anneliese. This was a birthday present. Anything in it?"

"Sure is. Take a look."

With his fingers trembling a little, Brady opened the bill-fold, unbuttoned a flap and drew out a small scrap of paper. "*Crowfoot Lake Met. Station,*" he read out loud. "Well I'm damned."

Dermott was elated. "I knew it! I knew it!" he kept saying. "I knew the bastards would over-reach themselves. Didn't I say they'd make a major mistake through over-confidence or desperation? Well, they've made it. Somebody couldn't resist the temptation to talk. Jean heard the name and wrote it down. Great, Jean!"

"Sheer luck I found it," said Carmody. "When the chopper took off it blew hell out of the snow and all-but buried the bill-fold. I was just having a quick look-round when I saw the corner sticking up out of a drift."

"We got it, anyway," said Dermott. "What are we waiting for?"

"Not so fast," Brady countered. "For one thing we don't know where Crowfoot Lake is."

"Oh yes we do," said Willoughby. "It's up beyond the Birch Mountains, seventy, eighty miles north. I know it well."

"How do we get there?" Dermott asked.

Willoughby looked at him reproachfully. "Helicopter. No other way."

"It's four o'clock in the morning, gentlemen," Brady said heavily. "An error to pursue further tonight. For one thing, we are all exhausted."

"And for another we don't have a helicopter," said Dermott.

"Precisely, George. I must say, your ordeal doesn't seem to have blunted your wits any."

"Thank you." Dermott lay back happily. "Maybe Mr Willoughby can help us in the morning – I mean, later this morning."

"Sure, sure." Willoughby stood up. "But everyone please be careful. We're up against professionals. Their performance has been pretty impressive to date. Nothing would please them better than to catch one of your gentlemen on your own, Mr Brady. Or you, for that matter." He turned to Corinne, only to find she had fallen asleep, sitting upright, in the corner. "O.K.," he said gently to Mackenzie. "Look after her. But whatever you do, all keep together."

"Like now," said Brady. "We'll all get in that bus together and drive back to town. Mr Carmody – it doesn't sound as though your vehicle's too serviceable. May I offer you a ride?"

"Flat as a pancake," said Carmody wryly. "Never saw anything to match it. Thank you."

They all piled in, with Shore driving. But before they even reached the administration block a radio message caught them.

"Mr Shore – urgent." It was Steve Dawson, charge-hand of the night-shift." We got another emergency."

"Oh *no*!" Shore groaned. "I'm coming. Be right there."

Dawson met them and led them straight into a room off the main corridor which held six beds and was obviously a dormitory. On one of the beds lay the body of a fair-haired young man whose sightless eyes gazed at the ceiling.

"Oh my God!" said Shore.

"Who is it?" Dermott snapped.

"David Crawford. The security man we were talking about."

"The one we suspected?"

"That's him. What happened?"

"Stabbed through the heart, from behind," said Saunders, the doctor, who was standing by the bed. "He's been dead some hours. We only just found him."

"How come?" Dermott demanded. "Isn't this the security men's dormitory?"

"One of two," said Saunders. "The other's larger. Normally both are occupied by off-duty shifts. But since the shut-down, the men have been living at home. Nobody had any cause to come in here tonight."

"Ruthless bastards," said Brady, very low. "Four dead and two critically injured so far. Well, Mr Willoughby You've got a murder investigation on your hands."

14

At 11.30 that same morning Brady and his team were the sole occupants of the hotel's dining-room. Outside, the wind had gone, the snow had been reduced to the occasional flurry, and the sun was making a valiant effort to shine through the drifting grey cloud. Inside, the mood was one of expectancy and suppressed excitement.

"One thing's for sure," said Brady firmly. "*You*'re not coming on this little jaunt."

"Oh yes I am," Dermott countered. "I most certainly am. You try leaving me behind."

"What can you *do*?" Brady was half-scornful, half-sympathetic. "You can't use a gun, knock anybody down, tie anybody up."

"All the same, I've got to be there." Dermott was grey from lack of sleep and the pain in his savaged wrists. He could use his hands for gentle tasks, but his fingers were stiff, and to ease the discomfort he kept both elbows propped on the table with his forearms sticking straight up. "I really need two slings," he muttered. "One for each arm."

"Why not stay here and look after your gallant saviour?" Mackenzie suggested slyly.

Dermott coloured perceptibly and grunted: "She's O.K., I guess."

"She's being guarded, sure," Mackenzie agreed. "But she might be even safer if she came with us. With the rot spreading as far as it has ..." He broke off and went back to eating as he saw Willoughby, the police chief, approaching across the room.

211

"Good morning, Chief," Brady beamed at him. "Get any sleep?"

"One hour." Willoughby tried to smile, but his heart wasn't in it. "Call of duty. Can't complain."

"News," Brady announced abruptly. "Take a seat." He handed a letter across the table. "Communication from our friends. Mailed yesterday in the local post office."

Willoughby read the first paragraph without alteration of expression. Then he looked slowly round the watching faces and said matter-of-factly: "One billion dollars." Suddenly his calm gave way. "One billion dollars!" he cried. "Jesus!" He qualified the word "dollars" several times. "The sonsabitches are crazy. Who's going to pay attention to this kind of drivel?"

"You think it's drivel?" Dermott asked. "I don't. Probably a rather optimistic estimate of what the market will stand, but not very, I would think."

"I can't believe it." Willoughby threw the letter down on the table. "A billion dollars! Even if they mean it, how could the money be transferred without being traced to the recipient?"

"Nothing simpler," said Mackenzie, forking a pancake. "You could lose Fort Knox in the labyrinth of Eurodollars and offshore funds."

Willoughby glared at him over the breakfast table. "You'd actually pay this blackmailing monster?"

"Not me," Mackenzie answered. "I couldn't. But somebody sure enough will."

"Who'd be so crazy?"

"There's no craziness involved," said Dermott patiently. "Just calculating, common business sense. The people who stand to lose most – our two governments, and the major oil companies who've invested in Alaska and Alberta. I don't know what the position is in Canada, but this is going to pose an intriguing problem in the States, because any

212

governmental operation in tandem with the oil companies requires Congressional approval – and as every schoolkid knows, Congress would cheerfully immolate the oil companies. Looks like it'll make a highly diverting spectacle."

Willoughby looked baffled.

"Read some more," Brady prompted. "The next paragraph is only a minor shock to the nervous system."

The policeman picked up the letter and started again. "So they want you out of Alaska and Alberta – specifically, south of the forty-ninth parallel."

"As predicted," said Brady.

"But no mention of any ransom?"

"Again, as we predicted." Brady sounded smug.

"You're not getting out, I take it."

"Oh no? I'm going to contact my pilot in a moment and have him file a flight plan for Los Angeles."

Willoughby stared at him. "I thought you wanted to go to Crowfoot Lake?"

"We do. But we don't want to advertise our destination to any ill-natured persons who may be listening-in. Therefore, we file a flight plan for L.A."

"O.K., I get it." Willoughby grinned. "What do you want *me* to do?"

"Well..." Brady became evasive. "First, we need a guarantee from you."

"You can't make deals with the police." Willoughby's tone suddenly hardened.

"Rubbish!" said Brady comfortably. "It's done all the time. Felons even make deals with judges in court."

"O.K. So what do you want?"

"What we *don't* want is a company of paratroopers. Sure, they could mop this lot up with their hands tied behind their backs, but they might mop up a few wrong people too. Softly, softly on this one. Finesse. Stealth. Secrecy. Our way or not at all."

"You making a point or something?"

"Tell me about Crowfoot Lake," said Brady.

"It's an ideal place for this sort of thing. Tucked right away in the hills. Big, covered helicopter shelter right by the station. A chopper would never be spotted from the air. I was up there a year back, investigating a reported murder which turned out to be death by misadventure. Couple of young city boys newly arrived at the weather station. Happens at the beginning of the hunting season every year, without fail: all the Dan'l Boones and Buffalo Bills dropping like flies all over the place."

"How big's the lake?" Dermott asked. "Can a plane land on it?"

"Well, you *can* land on it." Willoughby paused. "But I don't think it would do you much good. See here: the lake's only two miles long, so wherever you came down on it, the people in the Met. Station would be bound to hear you. I've got a better idea."

"We need one."

"Now, Mr Brady. I've got a request. I'm in a delicate position. I am the law around these parts, and I'm supposed to know what's going on. I'm also a blackmailer. In return for guaranteeing that I can get you to the Met. Station undetected, I'd like some degree of participation in your expedition. You can't operate without police authority, and I'm the authority. All cards very close to the chest, O.K. But I'd like an official watching brief – a presence."

"I know whose presence I'd like," Mackenzie said. Up till then he had been chewing steadily throughout the conversation, but a delicate patting of his big face with the napkin indicated that his meal was over. "I'd like Carmody." Willoughby said: "That's not a bad idea. I'll get him right away."

He went off to telephone, came back and said: "A couple of minutes."

214

"Fine." Brady turned to Mackenzie. "Don, tell Ferguson to go out to the airport and file a flight plan for Los Angeles. Tell him to expect people with provisions out there in just over an hour. Ask the kitchen to give us provisions for two or three days."

"Just food, Mr Brady?"

Brady loftily ignored the insinuation. "Ferguson is in charge of the commissariat. He'll know of any shortfalls. George, we'll need some hand compasses and, I guess, ammunition. Be generous with the ammunition."

Willoughby said: "Hand compasses we have in abundance. What guns?"

"Colt .38's."

"No problem."

Dermott said: "Well, thank you. Tell me, Mr Willoughby, you have a deputy chief?"

"Indeed. And a good one."

"Good enough to be left in sole charge here?"

"Sure. Why?"

"Why don't you come with us? Giving us the directions is all very well, but it's not the same as having you on the spot."

"Don't, Mr Dermott. You tempt me. You tempt me sorely." From the momentary gleam of anticipation in his eyes, it was clear that he spoke the truth. "Duty, alas, before pleasure. I have a murder investigation on my hands."

"You've just reported zero progress. There are short-cuts, Mr Willoughby. You wouldn't want us foreign amateurs to do the job for you, would you now?"

"I'm afraid I'm not quite at my best."

"You would be when we introduced you to Crawford's murderer. Where else would he be but at Crowfoot Lake?"

"Mr Dermott, forget my last remark. I'm back at my very best. Ah, here he is."

Carmody looked as large and formidable as ever.

Dermott said: "With Mr Willoughby's consent, a request to make on behalf of Mr Brady, Mr Mackenzie and myself. As alien civilians we can only request. Those kidnappers – you're aware they are multiple killers, desperate men. They'll shoot on sight and shoot to kill."

Carmody looked round in slight puzzlement but politely said nothing.

Dermott went on: "Mrs Brady, her daughter and Mr Reynolds: we know where they're being held."

Carmody, almost like a man in prayer, clasped his two hands lightly together and said, in a suitably churchlike whisper: "Boy, oh boy. Let's go get them."

Brady said: "Thank you. We appreciate it. One hour from now, O.K.?

Willoughby said: "I'll just nip back to the office and put in a call to Edmonton."

"Aha! I thought secrecy was the watchword?"

"It still is."

"Then may I ask?"

"You may not. A surprise. To be revealed at Crowfoot Lake. Or in the very close vicinity. You wouldn't rob me of my surprises?"

* * *

As the jet lifted off Brady looked across the aisle to where Carmody had just withdrawn a peculiar metallic device from its chamois-lined leather casing. It appeared to consist of a small telescope attached to a curving, semi-circular arm which in turn was bolted to a rectangular metal box. Brady said: "What do you have there, Mr Carmody?"

"John, please Mr Brady. Makes me feel less self-conscious. We cops are used to being called many things, but not 'Mister'. This? This is an infra-red telescopic night sight. These are the securing clamps. Fits on a rifle."

216

"You can see in the dark with that?"

"A little light helps. But total darkness is rare."

"You can see the enemy but he can't see you?"

"That's the idea behind it. Unsporting and unfair. Never give the bastards a break – especially, Mr Brady, if they're pointing guns at wives and daughters."

Brady turned to Willoughby who was in the window seat. "And what lethal armaments are *you* carrying?"

"Apart from the regulation revolver? Just this little number here." He reached down and picked up a zipped leather bag some eighteen inches by ten.

"Funny shape for a gun," Brady said, intrigued.

"Two pieces that screw together."

"It wouldn't be a sub-machine gun?"

"It would."

There was a short silence and then Brady said: "No chance you'll be carrying a few hand grenades on you?"

Carmody gave a deprecating shrug. "Only a few."

"Infra-red sights, sub-machine guns, grenades – aren't those illegal?"

"Could be." Carmody sounded vague. "I'm not sure they are at Crowfoot Lake. You'd have to ask Mr Willoughby about that."

The angle of climb had levelled off, and Brady nodded his thanks as Mackenzie brought him a daiquiri.

"Cruising altitude, Donald? No way could we possibly have reached that yet."

"Maybe this is high enough. You'd have to ask our police chief there." He nodded forward. Willoughby had gone up to the co-pilot's seat and was bent over a map with Ferguson. "Doing his navigator's bit, I see."

Some five minutes more passed before Willoughby rose and headed back to sit by Brady.

"How long, Mr Willoughby?"

"Seventy minutes."

"Seventy minutes! But I thought Crowfoot was only seventy miles away?"

"We filed a flight plan for Los Angeles, remember. Our first leg takes us through the radar control at Calgary. So, we're flying south. We're also flying low to lose the radar control at Fort McMurray. When we do, we'll circle to the west and then north. After ten minutes, north-east. We'll keep low. No danger of bumping into anything; it's pretty flat all the way." He spread out a chart. "Even the Birch Mountains here are really nothing of the sort. The highest peak is less than twenty-seven hundred feet. Really, it's just a low divide, a watershed: the streams on the west side flow west and north-west into the Peace and Birch rivers: the streams to the east flow east and south-east into the Athabasca river."

"Where's Crowfoot Lake?"

"Here, just on the west side of the divide."

"It doesn't have a name printed."

"Too small. Neither does Deerhorn – here – on the east side of the divide. That's where we're going. It's a lake, too, but it's always called just Deerhorn."

"How far from Deerhorn to Crowfoot?"

"Six miles. Maybe seven. Far enough, I hope. We go into Deerhorn low and we go into Deerhorn slow – as near stalling speed as possible. The chances of our being heard at that distance are remote. The only time we'll make any real noise is when we land. The only way a fast-landing jet like this can stop on a relatively short stretch of ice is to use reverse thrust on the engines. That makes quite a racket. But I'm pretty sure that the divide between the two lakes will act as a suitable baffle. I'm a little more concerned about the helicopter."

"Helicopter?" Brady said carefully.

"Yes. Left Edmonton about half an hour ago. Due in about an hour after us."

"You promised me –"

"And I keep my promise. No troops, no police, not even a peashooter. Just some Arctic gear I want. It's due to arrive just after dark."

"And without radar transmission or airfield landing lights, how's he going to find his way here?"

"A signal from us by radio beacon. He's only to follow his nose. What worries me slightly is the noise the helicopter will make in landing. It's the biggest you've ever seen, and the racket is corresponding."

"Of course." Brady showed his disquiet. "Our friends at Crowfoot Lake have their own helicopter. Won't they hop in and come over to investigate?"

"I hope not. I want them," Willoughby said grimly, "to stand trial, and they won't be able to if they're dead. If they come across, I'll have no option but to shoot them down."

"Fair enough." Brady seemed unperturbed at the thought. Then he added: "You can do that?"

"We came here equipped with weapons for the express purpose of doing just that."

"Ah! I was asking Carmody about some of his equipment and he mentioned this infra-red night sight. But I thought that was for shooting people."

"It can do that, too. Did he mention the fact that he's also got a rifle that can switch from single-shot to automatic at the touch of a switch? The combination of that, the night-spot and a squirrel-hunter's eye makes for a fairly lethal outcome. You know I have a sub-machine gun? He did? Did I also mention that it has a special large capacity magazine – the old circular drum type – and that every sixth shell is a tracer so that I can see how I'm doing?"

"No."

Willoughby smiled. "And of course we didn't mention my

own modest contribution – the jumping jacks. For use when we're not seeing too well what's going on up above. Just like fireworks, really – except that you get no fancy explosion of colour, just a blinding magnesium flare that drifts down slowly on a parachute. Lasts only ninety seconds, but if you can't accomplish what you want to in ninety seconds, you should have stayed at home in the first place."

"If I were a devout Christian I could almost weep for my adversaries."

"Don't."

"Who said I was a devout Christian?" Brady nodded to Carmody. "He really goes about killing people?"

"He *leans* on people."

"What, with sub-machine and high-powered rifles?"

"We'll use them if we have to"

Brady said dryly: "You surprise me. Those weapons are illegal, of course – for police use. Right?"

"That's the trouble with being in a remote northern town – you don't keep up as much as you might with all the notes, minutes and regulations that Edmonton issues every other day."

"Of course not."

Some time later, Brady winced as the jet engines went into reverse thrust. Even though reason told him that the decibel level was no higher than normal, his apprehensive frame of mind made him feel he was listening to a continuous thunderclap of sound. When they had landed, he said to Willoughby: "You could have heard that racket clear back in Fort McMurray."

"Wasn't all that bad." Willoughby seemed unconcerned. "Well, stretch the legs, a little fresh air. Coming?"

"What? Out in that mess?"

"What mess? It's not even snowing. And it's seven miles to Crowfoot Lake. A little exercise, a little acclimatisation. Remember what you told me back in Sanmobil? Inside the human frame there's no room for both cold and daiquiris. Let's put it to the test, shall we?"

"Hoist on your own petard," Dermott said behind him. Brady scowled, hauled himself upright and followed Willoughby to the fore end of the cabin. He looked at Ferguson and stopped.

"You look worried, boy. That was a perfect touchdown."

"Thank you. But I am, as you say, a little concerned. Aileron controls got a bit stiff as I came in to land. Nothing much, I daresay. Soon locate the trouble. First landing on ice, and maybe I was being a little oversensitive."

Brady followed Willoughby out and looked around. Deerhorn was a singularly bleak and unprepossessing place. Snow-dusted ice beneath their feet, flat, barren land, devoid of any form of vegetation, stretching away in featureless anonymity on three sides. To the north-east lay a range of low hills, sparsely covered with a scattering of stunted, snow-laden trees.

"Those are the Birch Mountains?"

"I told you. I don't think the person who named them knew much about mountains."

"And those are *birch* trees?"

Willoughby said: "He wasn't much of a botanist either. These are alders."

"And seven miles beyond –"

"Look out! Stand back!" Both men whirled round to see Ferguson racing down the boarding steps clutching in one hand a cylindrically-shaped object about ten inches long and three in diameter.

"Keep clear, keep clear!" He sprinted by them, covered another fifteen yards, arched his back while still running and, like a cricket bowler, over-armed the cylinder with a convulsive jerk of his body. The cylinder had travelled not more than three yards when it exploded.

The blast was powerful enough to knock both Brady and

Willoughby, even at a distance of almost twenty yards, off their feet. For several seconds they lay where they had fallen, then made their way unsteadily towards the prone figure of Ferguson. Even as they reached him they were joined by Dermott, Mackenzie and Carmody, who had been inside the plane.

Ferguson had fallen face-down on the ice. Gently, they turned him over. His face and body appeared unmarked. It was difficult to tell whether or not he was breathing.

"Into the plane with him," Brady said. "Warm blankets and heating pads from the Red Cross chest. His heart may have stopped. Anyone here know anything about heart massage?"

"We do," Carmody said. He picked up Ferguson and headed for the plane. "First-aid certificates."

Three minutes later Carmody, still kneeling in the aisle, sank back on his heels and smiled.

"Ticker's going like a watch," he said. "Bloody fast watch, mind you, but it's going."

"Good work," Brady said. "We leave him there?"

"Yes," Dermott said. "Even when he regains consciousness – no reason why he shouldn't, there's no sign of any head injury – he's still going to be in shock. Heat pads we have in plenty. That's all we can give him, and probably all he requires. Can someone tell us what the hell happened? He came running up the aisle shouting 'Stay where you are!' and clutching this damned thing in his hand. He was out through the door like a greyhound clearing his trap."

"I know what happened," Brady said. "He complained that the controls were a bit stiff when he came in to land. That was because whoever placed this charge made a sloppy job of it. The thing stayed in place while we were climbing or cruising at a steady altitude but slid forward and wedged itself against the ailerons when we started to descend. As we

222

left the plane he told me he was going to look for the cause of the stiffness." Brady pursed his lips. "He found it all right."

"He was lucky," said Dermott. "Had it been a metal-cased bomb, the casing would have turned into shrapnel when it exploded and the back-lash would have caught him. Not a mark on him. So, a plastic bomb. For plastic bombs, plastic fuses – chemicals, really. You have two acids separated by some synthetic plastic barrier. One of them eats through the barrier, and when the two different acids meet they detonate. When an acid eats its way through the plastic barrier it generates considerable heat. I'm sure Ferguson not only felt this heat but knew right away what it meant."

Brady looked sombre. "If we weren't such a devious bunch, we'd have been flying at 30,000 feet on the way up. Our last trip, gentlemen."

"Right," said Dermott. "Even flying low, like we did, we had the luck of the devil. The drawback of a chemical detonator is that it's almost impossible to get timing accuracy within ten or fifteen per cent. The timing could have gone off ten minutes earlier – and that would have been curtains for us. Our friends didn't want us out of this country: they wanted us out of this world. What better way to do it, neatly, cleanly and efficiently, than have your plane's tail fall off six miles up?"

*　　*　　*

The Sikorsky Sky-Crane landed in darkness just after three-thirty in the afternoon. It was, as Willoughby had promised, the biggest helicopter they had ever seen. The engines cut, the huge rotors idled to a standstill, and there was left only the sound of a generator whining somewhere inside the massive hull. Telescopic steps snaked down from an opened door and two men climbed nimbly down to the ice and approached the waiting group.

223

"Brown," the leading figure said. "Lieutenant Brown, Air Force, alleged skipper of this craft. This is Lieutenant Vos, co-pilot, also alleged. Which of you gentlemen are Mr Willoughby and Mr Brady?"

They shook hands and Brown turned to introduce a third person who had joined them. "Doctor Kenmore."

"How long can you stay?" Willoughby asked.

"As long as you wish."

"Very kind. You have some cargo for me?"

"We have. O.K. to unload now?"

"Please."

Brown shouted instructions. Brady said: "Two requests, Lieutenant?"

"You have but to ask."

"I wish we had some more of this civility in the United States Air Force," Brady said. He addressed Dr Kenmore. "My pilot's been hurt. Would you look at him?"

"Of course."

"Donald?" The two men left for the aircraft. "We have an excellent transmitter on our plane, Lieutenant, but unfortunately the pilot, who operates it, is out of action . . ."

"We've got an excellent transmitter and a first-class radio operator who's ready for action. James!"

A young man appeared at the head of the steps. "Take this gentleman to Bernie, will you?"

Bernie was a bespectacled young man seated by a huge RCA transceiver. Dermott introduced himself and said: "Could you get me some numbers do you think?"

"Local, sir? Albertan, I mean."

"Afraid not, Anchorage and New York."

"No problem. We can patch in through a radio link via our Edmonton H.Q." Bernie's professional confidence was reassuring in the extreme. "Numbers and names, sir?"

"I have them here." Dermott handed over a notebook. "I can actually speak to those people?"

224

"If they're home, sure."

"I may be gone for a few hours. If I am, and you get through, will you ask them to hold themselves available or let me know where I can reach them?"

"Of course."

Dermott rejoined the group outside. Two low-profiled vehicles were already on the ice. A third was being lowered. "What are those?" Dermott asked.

Willoughby said: "My surprise for Mr Brady. Snowmobiles."

"They're not snowmobiles," a black-haired slender youth said.

"Sorry." Willoughby turned to Dermott. "John Lowry, an expert on those machines. The Edmonton people sent him up to show us how to operate them."

"They're everything-mobiles," Lowry said. "Snow, roads, rough terrain, marshes, sand – you name it. Comparatively, the American and Canadian snowmobiles belong to the age of steam radio. Made by the firm of V.P.L.O. – initials only, the full name is unpronounceable – in Oulu, Finland. Called, naturally, the Finncat. Made of fibre-glass. Unlike the ordinary snowmobile, it has no skis up front. That motor-driven traction belt you see extends under the full length of the body."

"Where did they come from?"

"We got three to put through extended tests – you know, the old test-to-destruction bit. Those are the three."

Dermott said to Willoughby: "Nice to have friends."

"Not quite standard models," Lowry went on. "The front compartments are usually for stowage of gear. We've converted them into jump seats."

Brady said: "You mean I can ride in one of those right now?"

Dermott said, *sotto voce* to Willoughby: "Test to destruction is right."

225

Lowry said: "I should think so, sir."

"That's great, just great." Brady's tone was hushed and reverent. The prospect of trudging a fourteen-mile return journey through Albertan snows had held singularly little appeal for him.

"Driving is simple," Lowry said. "Changing the inclination of the traction belt changes the direction of travel: done by the handlebars. You have forward and reverse gears and, a very sophisticated touch, hydraulic disc brakes. It can also do forty miles an hour."

"Forty?" Dermott said. "It looks as if it would be hard pushed to touch five."

Lowry smiled. "Forty. Not on rough terrain, of course. Incidentally, these don't come cheap — four thousand dollars — but then the unique never does. I understand that you gentlemen are in a hurry. First three drivers up, please."

Dr Kenmore returned from the plane with Mackenzie while Willoughby and his two men were learning the controls of the Finncats. Kenmore said: "Concussion. Nothing very serious, not the blast, he must have hit his head on the ice — there's a beauty of a bruise just above his right ear. I'll have him brought across here — we have a heating and lighting generator running all the time when the motors are switched off."

Brady said: "Thank you, doctor. We appreciate it."

"Nothing. May one ask where you're off to in those toys?"

"Don't let young Lowry hear you. He'd have a fit," Dermott said.

Brady said: "Please understand we don't mean to be churlish. We'll tell you when we come back. How's your expertise on shotgun wounds and bones shattered by high-velocity bullets?"

"Not very extensive, I'm afraid." Kenmore's expression hadn't altered. "You plan to remedy that before the night is out?"

226

"I hope not." Brady's face was suddenly serious. "But it may come to that."

The six men left at four-thirty, exactly one hour after the Sikorsky had touched down. The helicopter's crew were there to see them go. Lieutenant Brown said: "Air Force personnel are not as stupid as they look. We know where you're going, naturally. Good fortune." He looked at the arsenal of weapons they carried, ready for action, shoulder-slung or in holsters. "Dr Kenmore may be in for a sleepless night."

The Finncats were everything that Lowry had promised, nimble, manoeuvrable, and possessed of remarkable traction. Two carried small but efficient headlamps which picked out a path through the straggling alders. It said much for the dogged willingness of the little two-cylinder engines that a heroically suffering Brady had only to get out twice – the Finncat on those occasions had refused to budge another inch – and walk a total of two hundred yards on the way to the gently-rounded convexity which marked the watershed of the Birch Mountains. Shortly before the little army reached this point they had switched off their headlights.

The descent was simple but just as slow as the ascent because, in the absence of lights, the half-seen alders had to be negotiated with care. The engines, no more than idling, were gratifyingly quiet. Willoughby called softly and the three Finncats came to a halt.

"Far enough," he said. "We can't be more than three hundred yards from the shore."

"O.K.," Dermott agreed. "How many crew at the Met. Station, Willoughby?"

"Just two. I shouldn't imagine that any harm has come to them. They have to keep sending their regular radio reports: any breakdown in those would have brought an official helicopter out here very quickly. So the reports must have continued to go out – under duress."

They made their way down to the lake's edge, keeping their voices low – sound travels as well over ice as it does over water. Tall reeds grew by the frozen shore. Carmody parted these, unshipped his infra-red night-sight, pressed his face against the rubber eye-piece and switched on.

The Crowfoot Lake meteorological station consisted of only two huts, one about three times the size of the other. The smaller one had a variety of poles, boxes and what appeared from that distance to be uncovered recording instruments on its roof. This smaller hut was dark; the larger, presumably the living quarters, showed two brightly-lit windows. Beyond this hut was parked a large, white-painted helicopter.

Jones passed the night-sight to Brady, who studied the station briefly, then handed the instrument on. The last man to use it, Dermott, took the sight from his eye and said: "As a target for tonight, I've seen worse. We go now?"

"We go now," Brady said. "And we don't treat them like human beings. No warnings. No fair play. No sportsman-ship. Shoot first, questions afterwards. People who plant time bombs in aircraft – or steal my Jean and Stella – know nothing of finer feelings – or the rules of civilised warfare."

Willoughby said: "Fair enough. But shoot to cripple, not to kill. I want those men to stand trial."

Brady said: "Of course, the conduct and termination of the trial would be greatly speeded if we had their confessions in advance."

"And how do you figure on getting those?" Dermott asked.

"Simple, George. It all depends upon how intrepid you're feeling this afternoon."

15

The wicked wind hissed through the clump of alders some twenty yards behind the meteorological station. The trees offered little in the way of cover, but it was the best and closest that the men could find. Luckily, the night was moonless: the buildings showed as black lumps in the snowy landscape.

Bulky as bears in their Arctic gear, the raiders silently watched another figure, flattened to the snow, inch his way up towards them, propelled only by elbows and toes. Arrived in the shelter of the trees, John Carmody rose to a kneeling position.

"They're there," he whispered. "Reynolds and the ladies. The ladies are handcuffed together, but they seem all right. Don't look as though they've been maltreated. There are five other men in there, smoking and drinking, but not drinking too much A little room leads off the big one. Could be there's someone asleep in there, but I don't think so. The door's ajar and the light's on. Any person who wanted to sleep would have switched the light off."

"Well done, boy," said Brady.

"Three other things, sir. At least three of the men are armed, although none actually had a gun in his hand. The whole group is sitting round the table listening to a radio. They're listening pretty hard, too – trying to catch something. That made me think there wouldn't be another of them in the small room: he'd have been out there listening too."

"Could be the two station operators are in there," said Dermott. "Tied up, I mean."

229

"I thought that too," said Carmody.

"I know what they're listening for," Brady whispered. "News of a certain jet having crashed in Alberta this afternoon. What was the third thing you saw?"

"All five men are wearing stocking masks."

Dermott said: "Which they wouldn't bother with if they intended to dispose of the hostages." His husky murmur dropped to a whisper. "Keep low. Keep quiet."

A rectangle of light had appeared at the side of the cabin. A figure walked through the opened doorway and headed towards the smaller building. Moments later lights came on there.

"One of them," Brady said. "Hardly likely to let one of the operators stroll across there and send off an S.O.S. Perfect. Come, George, this is where you earn your Congressional Medal of Honour or whatever."

Brady moved out, travelling quickly and silently, no trace of the comfort-loving fat man left. Arriving at the main cabin door, he looked over his shoulder to check the smaller cabin. The light was still on, the door still closed. Brady turned back to the cabin door, gripped the handle, opened the door and walked inside, .38 in hand, Dermott and Mackenzie at either elbow, with their guns levelled. Brady advanced on the four stocking-masked men sitting round the table. Several started up.

"Keep your hands on that table," he said. "If you're not entirely mad. We're just looking for an excuse to shoot you through the head. One of you turn that radio off – the good news you're waiting for has just arrived."

"Jim! Jim!" Jean Brady was on her feet. "You've come!"

"Of course." Brady's voice held a curious mixture of irritation and smug self-satisfaction. "You thought I wouldn't? Brady Enterprises always delivers." As his wife made to approach him, he raised his left hand. "Just a minute. Don't come too close. These are desperate men.

230

Mr Reynolds, Stella. Sorry we took so long about this but –"

"Dad!" Stella was on her feet, a desperate urgency in her voice. "Dad, a man –"

"Drop your guns." The deep voice came from the doorway. "Don't turn round or you're dead."

"Do what the man says." Brady set the example. Within a second the other two guns had clattered to the floor.

"Stay where you are," the same voice ordered. "Billy."

Billy didn't have to be told what to do. His search was quick but thorough. He stepped back and said: "Clean, boss."

"So." The door closed and a burly man appeared before them. Like the others, he was masked. "Sit on that bench there." He waited until they had done so, seated himself by the table and said: "Watch them." Three of his men produced pistols and covered the three seated men. He put away his gun.

"The ladies, I must say, seem very disappointed. They shouldn't, really."

Brady looked at them. "What he means is that things could be worse. If his plan had worked, we three would be dead. As it is, Ferguson is critically ill and two others seriously injured." He looked at the leader. "You placed that bomb in the plane?"

"I can't take all the credit. One of my men did." He lit a cigarette and stuck it through a hole in the stocking mask which had been cut out for that purpose. "So now I have Mr Jim Brady and his two invaluable associates. A full hand, one might say."

Brady said: "Designed to blow our tail off at 30,000 feet?"

"What else? It would be interesting to know how you're alive."

"*We're* alive. But one man's probably dying, and two are

231

seriously injured. God, man, what are you – a psychopathic killer?"

"Not psychopathic. Just a businessman. How come *you* didn't die?"

"Because we landed before the bomb went off." Brady sounded very tired. "We got a report from a forest ranger saying that an off-white helicopter had been seen in these parts. Nobody paid attention except us – we knew you had a white helicopter."

"How did you know that?"

"A lot of people saw it around the plant at Athabasca."

"No harm done." He waved a hand. "All the aces in the pack."

"Whoever placed that explosive charge in my plane made a lousy job of securing it," said Brady sarcastically.

"I can vouch for that. He was interrupted."

"The package moved forward and jammed the controls – the tail ailerons. The pilot had to land – it was on the way down that we caught a glimpse of your helicopter. We crash-landed on another lake. Pilot told us to get out. He tried to remove the charge, and the two others stayed with him. I guess they felt they had to – they were cops."

"We know that, too."

"So they were expendable. You had no compunction about murdering them, too?"

"Compunction is not a word in my vocabulary. Why did you come here?"

"For your helicopter, of course. We have to get those injured men to hospital."

"Why hold us up?"

"Don't be so stupid. We can't fly the damn thing."

The leader turned to one of the masked men. "Sorry about that, Lucky. A pleasure spared."

"And of course, you people killed Crawford."

232

"Crawford?" He turned to another of his men. "Fred, that lad you attended to –"

"Yeah. That was him."

"And you critically wounded Sanmobil's president, and a policeman?"

"Seems to have been an awful lot you didn't know."

"And it was you who blew up the plant and destroyed the dragline. A pity you had to kill and wound so many in the process."

"Look friend, we don't play kiddies' games. Too bad if someone gets in our way. This is a man's world, and we play for keeps."

Brady bowed his head in apparent acceptance, raised his hands to cross them behind his neck. His fingers touched.

What should have been the tinkling of shattered glass was lost in the crash of three shots that sounded almost as one. The masked men with the guns yelled out in agony and stared in shocked disbelief at their shattered shoulders. The door was kicked violently open and Carmody jumped in, machine pistol steady in his big hands. He moved a couple of steps forward. Willoughby ran into the cabin carrying a revolver.

Dermott said: "Your words. This is a man's world, and we play for keeps."

Carmody advanced on the masked leader and thrust the barrel of his machine pistol hard against the man's teeth. "Your gun. By the barrel. Do you know what is my one ambition in life right now?" The man, apparently, did. Carmody pocketed the pistol and turned to the remaining and unwounded member of the quintet, who had his gun on the table before Carmody could even speak to him.

Brady said: "Satisfactory, Mr Willoughby? The floor is yours."

"An Oscar, Mr Brady. They sang beautifully." He advanced to the table. "I think you all know who I am?"

233

Nobody spoke.

"You." He indicated the person who had so hastily placed his gun on the table. "Towels, cotton wool, bandages. Nobody's going to mind very much if your three friends bleed to death, but personally I would sooner see them die legally. After they've been tried, of course. Let's see your faces." He walked round ripping off masks. The first three faces apparently meant nothing to him. The fourth, belonging to the man he'd just appointed to first-aid duty, clearly did.

"Lucky Lorrigan," Willoughby said. "Erstwhile helicopter pilot, more recently a murderer on the run from Calgary. Severely wounded a couple of officers in your breakout, Lucky, didn't you? My, aren't they going to be pleased to see you again!"

He tore the mask from the leader's face. "Well, well, would you believe it? No less than Frederick Napier himself, second senior charge-hand in Sanmobil security. You've strayed a bit from home, haven't you, Freddie?

"All five of you are hereby taken into arrest and charged with murder, attempted murder, kidnapping and industrial sabotage. I don't have to remind you about your legal rights, silence, access to lawyers. You've heard it all before. Not that it will do any of you the slightest good. Not after the beautiful way Napier sang."

Brady said: "Would you say he was the best singer of the lot, Mr Willoughby?"

Willoughby stroked his chin. "A moot point, Mr Brady." He had no idea what Brady was talking about, but had learned to listen when he suggested something.

Brady said: "You really are extraordinarily naïve, Napier. I told you that Mr Willoughby and his officer were severely injured when our plane crash-landed, yet you seemed hardly surprised to see them here. Perhaps you're just stupid. Perhaps events have moved too fast for your limited intellect. Our plane, of course, did not crash-land. No forest ranger pilot spotted you. We never saw your helicopter on the way to our alleged crash-landing.

"Deerhorn, the lake just over the hill there, was our destination from the time we left Fort McMurray, because we knew exactly where you were. You sing like a lark, Napier. But Brinckman and Jorgensen sing like angels. They're going to turn State's evidence. Should get off with five years."

"Brinckman and Jorgensen!" Napier jumped to his feet then collapsed back in his chair with a whoosh of expelled air as the barrel of Carmody's machine pistol caught him in the solar plexus. He sat there gasping for breath. "Brinckman and Jorgensen," he wheezed, and had just started in on a résumé of their antecedents when Carmody's gun caught him lightly on the side of the head.

"Ladies present," Carmody said pleasantly.

"State's evidence!" Napier said huskily. "Five years! Good God, man, Brinckman's my boss. Jorgensen's his lieutenant. I'm only number three on the totem pole. Brinckman is the one who fixes everything, arranges everything, gives all the orders. I just do what I'm told. State's evidence! Five years! Brinckman!"

Willoughby said: "Would you swear to that in court?"

"Too damn right, I would! Treacherous bastard!" Napier stared into space, his mouth no more than a compressed white line.

Willoughby said: "And before all these witnesses, too."

Napier shifted his gaze from faraway places to Willoughby. His expression was one of total incomprehension.

"Mr Brady was quite right, Napier. You really are a rather simple person, but as a singer you just got raised to the rank of angel. Until this moment we didn't have a single solitary thing we could pin on either of them. Thanks to you, they'll join you behind bars tonight. It should be a fascinating get-together."

*　　*　　*

The big white helicopter touched down on Deerhorn at five forty-five in the afternoon. Lucky Lorrigan, with the muzzle of Carmody's pistol screwing into his ear, had flown the seven-minute hop in impeccable style. The two meteorological station operators had been freed and, when told why, had willingly sworn themselves to secrecy for the next twenty-four hours.

Brady was first off the plane, followed by Dermott and the wounded men. A curious reception committee from the Sikorsky, headed by Lieutenant Brown, was there to greet them.

Brown said: "That was fast work. Congratulations! No problems?"

"Routine exercise." Brady was a master of the throwaway phrase. "Some for Dr Kenmore, though. Three silly people got in the way of flying bullets."

Kenmore said: "I'll fix them up, Mr Brady."

"Thanks. But you look mighty young to me to be an orthopaedic surgeon."

"So it's like that?"

"Patch them up as best you can. Nobody's going to take your licence away from you if they peg out during the night."

"I understand." The young doctor's eyes widened as the women descended the steps. "Well, well."

"Brady Enterprises," Brady said with a smirk in his voice, "associate only with the best and the most beautiful. Well, Mr Lowry, we'll have to see about getting back those splendid machines of yours. And now, Lieutenant, if you will excuse me – a matter of some urgency."

He had taken some few steps towards his aircraft, when the lieutenant overtook him. "It got pretty cold in your plane, Mr Brady, so I took the liberty of transferring some essential supplies to our nice warm Sikorsky."

Brady turned ninety degrees without breaking stride and headed purposefully towards the Sky-Crane. He patted Lieutenant Brown on the arm. "A very promising future lies ahead of you."

Dermott said to Bernie, the Sikorsky radio operator: "Any luck?"

"Got through to all three, sir. Your New York number and one of your Anchorage numbers – a Mr Morrison – said they had no information for you yet and probably wouldn't have for the next twenty-four hours. Your other Anchorage number – a Dr Parker – asked if you would be kind enough to call him back now."

"Would you get him, please?"

"No bother." Bernie smiled. "And then you'd like some privacy?"

Brady had been reduced to the discomfort of sitting on a packing box – admittedly a large one – in the fore part of the Sikorsky's cavernous hold. He appeared not to be suffering too much. He was speaking to a fully conscious Ferguson.

"You've made it, son. You're damned lucky but not nearly as lucky as we are, thanks entirely to you. We'll discuss this – ah – later, in private. Sorry your eyes are still troubling you."

"Just a damned nuisance, Mr Brady. Otherwise, I could fly the plane with no trouble."

"You're not flying anything, anywhere," Kenmore said. "It may be two or three days before we can be sure that your eyesight is stabilised. I know a specialist in Edmonton."

"Thank you. How are our wounded heroes, by the way?"

237

"They'll live."

"Ah, well. We can't have everything."

* * *

Two and a half hours later Brady was again presiding over a cheerful company, but this time rather more comfortably ensconced in the best armchair in the Peter Pond Hotel. Doubtless inspired by the thought of the enormous fees he would extort, he was positively Maecenas-like in his hospitality. Reynolds had been joined by his wife. The atmosphere was festive; but Dermott and Mackenzie didn't seem very jovial. Dermott approached the beaming Brady – he wasn't beaming at anything in particular but was just sitting there, wife's hand in his left, daiquiri in his right – and said: "Donald and I would like to slip away for a bit, sir. Do you mind?"

"Of course not. Do you need me?"

"Minor matters, only."

"Go right ahead, George." The beam, which had faded slightly, lit up again. Brady would now have the field to himself, and it was possible that his retailing of recent events might vary slightly from the one he would have given if his two lieutenants had been present. He glanced at his watch. "Eight-thirty. Half an hour or so?"

"About that."

On their way out they stopped by Willoughby's chair. Dermott smiled at a rather misty-eyed Mrs Reynolds, then said to Willoughby: "Brinckman and Jorgensen?"

Willoughby smiled happily. "Are guests of the Canadian government. Heard fifteen minutes ago. Look, gentlemen, I don't know how to –"

"Wait." Mackenzie smiled. "We aren't through with you yet."

"Some more matters to be attended to?"

238

"Not in Alberta. But we have to cast a net again. Can we see you in the morning?"

"When?"

"Late. May we call you?"

Dermott and Mackenzie spent not half an hour but an hour and a half in Dermott's room, talking, planning, and, mostly, telephoning. When they returned to the lounge Brady greeted them effusively. He was totally unaware of how much time had elapsed. The number of the company had increased. Dermott and Mackenzie were introduced to a couple who turned out to be the mayor and his wife. Jay Shore had returned from the plant and they were introduced to *his* wife, too. They were introduced to a charming lady who turned out to be Mrs Willoughby. After that they were introduced to two other couples whose names they failed to catch. Jim Brady was spreading his wings that night.

Willoughby came up and spoke to them quietly. "Another item, although it's just another unnecessary nail in the coffin. We retrieved the prints from Shore's house and compared them to the ones in the kidnap truck. Two matching sets were found: Napier's and Lucky Lorrigan's."

At eleven o'clock, Dermott and Mackenzie approached Brady again. He was still in sparkling form: his tolerance for rum passed mortal understanding. Dermott said: "Mr Brady. We're bushed. We're off."

"Off? Bed? I'll be damned." He glanced at his watch. "The night's young." He made a grandiloquent gesture with his arm. "Look at *them*. Are *they* thinking of bed?" Jean gave Dermott a rueful smile which indicated that she was thinking of just that herself. "They're happy. They're enjoying themselves. Just look!"

Wearily they looked. No question, Brady had the right of it. They were enjoying themselves, not least young Carmody, who had discreetly withdrawn from the main body of the group to sit in a corner with Stella.

239

"We wish you luck. You want us to collapse dramatically in front of all your guests?"

"That's the trouble with you young people of today. No get-up-and-go." When the occasion arose Brady could conveniently forget that his associates and himself were of the same generation. "No stamina. Not fit." He seemed totally unaware of how preposterous he sounded, but they knew he wasn't.

"We'd like to talk to you in the morning."

"You would?" He eyed them both suspiciously. "When?"

"When you're fit, unlimited stamina, the lark singing."

"Damn it all, *when*?"

"Noon."

Brady relaxed. "In that case, why don't you stay?"

Dermott went and kissed Jean goodnight, Mackenzie did the same; they made the rounds with punctilious goodnights and left.

They got to bed just after one in the morning. The previous two hours had been spent on the telephone.

* * *

Dermott awoke at seven-thirty. By eight, he was showered, shaved, eating off his breakfast tray and busy on the telephone. At nine he was joined by Mackenzie. At ten they were both closeted with Willoughby. At noon, they joined Brady at his breakfast table and explained what they had in mind. Brady chewed through the last of his ham omelette, which had originally been the size of a soup-plate, then shook his head in a decisive fashion.

"It's out of the question. It's all over. O.K., there are a few stray threads in Alaska, but who am I to devote my time to that sort of small potatoes?"

"So it is in order if Donald and I resign?"

Fortunately for Brady he was neither eating nor drinking

240

at the moment, so he had nothing to choke over. "Resign? What the hell do you mean?"

"It's Donald's fault, really. Half Scots, you know. He hates to see good money being thrown away."

"Money being thrown away?" Momentarily, Brady looked almost appalled, but his recovery was swift. "What's this nonsense?"

"How much are you charging Sanmobil for our services?"

"Well, I'm not one to prey on the misfortunes of others. A half million I guess. Plus expenses, of course."

"In that case, I reckon Donald and I would rate a quarter of a million for picking up stray threads and small potatoes." Brady was silent, his eyes fixed on something beyond infinity. "With your name," Dermott persisted, "one can see no reason why the Prudhoe Bay oil companies shouldn't also come up with a half million. Plus, of course, expenses."

Brady brought his gaze back from outer space to the dining-room table. "It's not, as you may think, that I'm not at my best in the morning. It's just that I have so much on my mind. What time is this meeting tonight?"

16

The meeting was held that evening in the Sanmobil canteen, which was drably lit and decorated in dingy cream and pea-green. Nevertheless, the room had much to recommend it for such a gathering, not least the fact that it was large and warm and a place from which the public could easily be excluded.

The tables and chairs had been rearranged so that the men conducting the proceedings sat in a line – on stage, as it were – facing down the long room. The rest of the seats had been set out in two blocks, divided by a gangway.

In the middle of the top table sat Willoughby, acting as host in his own parish. On his right was Hamish Black, general manager of B.P./Sohio, Alaska, who had flown down from Prudhoe Bay to be present. On Willoughby's left sat Brady, overflowing a rickety wooden chair, and beside him were his two trusty henchmen.

Down on the floor, the home team was represented by Bill Reynolds, Jay Shore and a handful of others. On the Alaskan side there were eight men, among them Dr Blake, gaunt and cadaverous as ever; Ffoulkes, the Anchorage police chief; and Parker, the police forensic surgeon. Morrison of the F.B.I. had come on the same plane, and behind him sat four of his agents. At the back of the room were nearly thirty other men from Sanmobil brought in so that they could hear the full report of what had been happening. Finally, in an unobtrusive position at one side, John Carmody and a couple of fellow-policemen occupied a flat bench, with their backs against the wall; and sandwiched between them was

Corinne Delorme, looking small and wan and rather scared.

Willoughby stood up to open the proceedings.

"Good evening, ladies and gentlemen. As the senior representative of the law here in Alberta, and as your nominal host, I would like to thank all you people who've been good enough to come from places as far afield as Prudhoe Bay, Anchorage and even New York."

A murmur went round the room.

"That's right," Willoughby confirmed. "Two gentlemen at least have come all the way from New York. Now: the purpose of this meeting is to explain to the senior employees of Sanmobil and BP/Sohio just what's been going on these past few days, and, if possible, to clear up the few final questions to which we don't yet have the answers. I call on Mr Hamish Black, general manager of BP/Sohio, Alaska, to put you in the picture."

Black rose to his feet, all disapproval and severity. Yet when he began to speak, he seemed to acquire a stature and authority that thoroughly surprised Brady and his associates.

"I hardly need tell you," he began, "that both the Alaskan pipeline and the Sanmobil tar sands complex here at Athabasca have recently been subjected to deadly and intensive industrial sabotage. The action effectively closed down the flow of oil from both centres, and in the process of the sabotage at least four innocent people have been murdered, while several others have been gravely injured.

"We devoutly hope that the savage and brutal attacks are at an end. They certainly seem to be so in Alberta – and for this the sole credit goes to the investigation team of Brady Enterprises, headed by Mr Jim Brady himself and his two senior assistants, Mr Dermott and Mr Mackenzie."

With the ghost of a smile softening the line of his pencil

moustache, Black indicated the Brady team. To his acute discomfort, Brady found himself blushing for the first time in years. He ground his teeth and contrived to look sideways at Dermott without moving his head. The guy they'd treated like dirt was praising them!

"Unfortunately," Black went on, "no such happy conclusion has been reached in Alaska. Up there, we have no positive guarantee that the sabotage is at an end, for the simple reason that the individuals responsible for the criminal activity have not yet been brought to justice.

"Brady Enterprises have been as deeply involved in making enquiries in Alaska as they have here, and since they are the only people with an overall view of the present position, I should like to call upon Mr Brady himself to give us a report."

Brady heaved himself upright and cleared his throat.

"Thank you, Mr Black. Ladies and gentlemen, I promise to be as brief as possible, and to waste none of your time. First I will ask for a word from Mr John Young, who is director of City Services, a Federally-backed investigative agency in New York. One of its functions is to oversee and regulate the conduct of private detective and investigative agencies in the State of New York. Mr Young?"

In the front row of the Sanmobil team seats a lean, bald-headed man with thick-rimmed glasses rose to his feet. He looked at the papers in his hand and smiled at Brady, and turning to face the body of the hall, he began.

"City Services was asked by Brady Enterprises – this was with governmental consent – to investigate the background of a private security agency owned and run by one Samuel Bronowski, who later became head of security on the Alaskan pipeline.

"Apart from the fact that an unusually large percentage of valuables entrusted to the firm's safekeeping had been missing – for readily explainable reasons – we found no

244

evidence of any outright misconduct. But I was further asked to find out the names and identities of any of Bronowski's associates who left the firm at about the same time as he did – that is to say, within six months either side of his departure date. We came up with ten names – not a particularly high wastage rate in such an agency – but Brady Enterprises were particularly interested in four of them." Here Young consulted the notes in his right hand. "Their names are Houston, Brinckman, Jorgensen, and Napier."

Young sat down and Brady rose again to thank him. "Well," he continued, "for those of you who do not already know, three of the four just mentioned are already in gaol, charged with various crimes from murder downwards. The other man, and Bronowski, you can now see for your-selves."

He made a small sign to Willoughby, who nodded to one of his uniformed men at the door. Next moment the door opened, to admit Bronowski and Houston, manacled together. They were hustled to seats in the front row of the Alaska-side stalls. Bronowski still sported his impressive head-bandage, and beneath it, his broad, strong face was sullen.

"So." Brady purred. "I promised we would not waste time. We have established that at least two security agents from the pipeline and three from Sanmobil were old acquaintances, that they were acting in concert, organised widespread sabotage, exchanged codes and were responsible for murder. We have also established that Bronowski was the undisputed leader. These facts have been put on record by many witnesses, who will testify in court. But let us move on, I would like to call on Dr Parker."

"Yes, well." Parker paused reflectively. "I act in a forensic capacity for the police at Anchorage. Mr Dermott brought down three corpses from Prudhoe Bay. I examined one of them – an engineer who had been murdered in Pump Station

245

No. 4. He had sustained a most unusual injury to his right index finger. I understand that Dr Blake here attributed this to the force of the explosion which destroyed the pump station. I have to disagree. The finger was deliberately broken – there is no other way it could have happened. Mr Dermott?"

Dermott stood up. "Mr Mackenzie and I have a theory. It's our belief that this dead engineer was carrying a pistol when he was held up by the people who had planted the explosives. We further believe that he recognised his assailants, and they, knowing this, killed him before he could use his gun in self-defence. We also believe that his dead finger locked over the trigger-grip. That would be possible, doctor?"

"Indeed – quite possible."

"We surmise the criminals had to break the man's forefinger to get the gun away. A dead man found with a gun in his hand would have raised serious doubts as to whether the explosion had been a genuine accident.

"Further, papers seen in his coat pocket were later missing. Neither my colleagues nor I know what those papers were. We can only assume that he had accumulated incriminating evidence against someone – which would account for the fact that he was carrying a gun."

Dermott paused. Then he said: "I would like to ask Mr Brady to discuss the vital question of who is ultimately responsible for this spate of crime."

Brady hoisted himself upright again. "Mr Carmody – would you be so kind as to stand by Bronowski? I am aware that he is handcuffed, but I'm also convinced he's a man of violence. Dr Parker?"

Dr Parker rose leisurely and walked across to Bronowski. Carmody was already there. The doctor said to him: "Get behind him and hold his arms."

Carmody did so. Bronowski yelped with pain as Parker

246

reached forward and ripped away the bandage that covered his forehead and temple. The doctor peered closely at the temple, touched it, then straightened.

"This is a delicate area of the head," he said. "A blow such as he is alleged to have received would have left a bruise for at least a fortnight. Probably longer. As you can see, there is no such bruise, no sign of any contusion. In other words," he said, pausing for effect, "he was never struck."

Brady said: "Things look rather black for you, Dr Blake."

"They're going to look a damn sight blacker," Parker said. He had resumed his place. "Mr Dermott, in Anchorage, made what I then regarded as an extremely strange request. I no longer regard it as such. Despite the fact that you, Dr Blake, had carried out an autopsy on John Finlayson, Mr Dermott asked me to carry out another. Unheard of. But, as it turns out, justified.

"Your certificate said that Finlayson had been struck on the occiput with some form of loaded salt-bag. As in the case of Bronowski, there was no sign of any contusion. The skin had been somewhat abraded, which could have occurred before or after death. What is important is that one of my younger associates discovered traces of ethyl oxide in the blood. It is difficult to conceal such trace elements. On closer examination, we discovered a tiny blue puncture just under the rib cage. Further investigation proved beyond any doubt that a needle or probe had been inserted through this puncture and pierced the heart. Death would have been pretty well instantaneous. In other words, Finlayson had been anaesthetised, then murdered. I do not think there is one medical authority in either of our countries who would dispute my findings."

Brady said: "Comment, Dr Blake?"

He appeared to have none.

The F.B.I.'s Morrison said: "I have. He's not a doctor. He was trained in an English university and flung out in his fourth year for reasons as yet undisclosed but which I'm sure we can readily ascertain. No doubt he learnt enough in that time to use a needle or probe."

Brady said: "Comment, Blake?"

Again he had none.

"I do not know, but I'm pretty sure that this is what happened," Dermott said. "Finlayson came across Bronowski and Houston tampering with the fingerprint card index. I suggest that Bronowski was removing his own prints from the file. I suggest he was substituting some other prints for his own. Whose, I do not know, but that again we can ascertain. The next suggestion is straightforward and obvious. The prints on that Anchorage telephone box were Bronowski's. We have only to take his prints to confirm."

Brady said: "Comment, Bronowski?"

Silence.

"Well." Brady looked round the room. "Guilty as hell. That almost wraps it up." He stood up, as if to end the meeting. "But not quite. None of the accused has the intelligence or knowledge to master-mind an operation of this nature. This required a highly specialised degree of knowledge. Someone who had the inside track."

Willoughby asked: "We have an idea of this person's identity?"

"I know who he is. But I think I'll let Mr Morrison and the F.B.I. take over here. My colleagues and I had our suspicions as to the identity of the mastermind behind the killings and sabotage both here and in Alaska, but it was Mr Morrison who got the proof."

"I got the proof," Morrison said, "but that was only because my nose was pointed in the right direction. Bronowski claimed to have owned – and maintains he still owns – an investigative agency in New York. This is untrue. As Mr Young discovered in the course of his investigations,

Bronowski only acted in the capacity of a front man, a figure-head. The real source of power, the owner, was someone else. Right, Bronowski?"

Bronowski scowled, clamped his lips, and kept his counsel.

"No matter. At least you don't deny it. Mr Young, accompanied by New York detectives and armed with a search warrant, examined the firm's private correspondence. The firm had been so naïve as to file away, instead of destroying, fatally damaging and incriminating evidence. This evidence not only revealed the identity of the true owner: it also revealed the astonishing fact that this same individual owned no fewer than four other protection or investigative agencies in the city of New York." Morrison glanced to one side. "Mr Willoughby?"

Willoughby nodded and looked aside. Carmody nodded, rose and walked leisurely to the back of the room.

"This owner," Morrison went on, "was an absentee landlord, but only during the past couple of years. Before that he was on the New York stock exchange and an investment counsellor on Wall Street. He wasn't too successful: not really a financial man at all, though he liked money. More like a bull in a china shop: too extroverted.

"The landlord's most recent absence was caused by the fact that he had become busy elsewhere. He was busy in Athabasca, at an inconvenient distance from Wall Street. He was, in fact, working for Sanmobil. He was busy being Sanmobil's operations manager."

"Don't move. Keep quite still." Carmody leant over Reynolds's shoulder and relieved him of a silenced automatic which he had begun to slide out of a shoulder-holster. "You could cause yourself an injury. What's a law-abiding citizen like you doing carrying a hand-gun?"

Gasps of surprise broke out all round the room. Almost everybody stood up to get a better view. Reynolds's face, normally so rubicund, had gone grey. He sat as if paralysed while Carmody slipped manacles on him.

"This is in no way a trial," Brady announced. "So I do not propose to question him. Nor will I adumbrate the factors that made him turn the way he did – save to say that his main grievance appears to have been that he had been passed over for promotion. He found his way ahead blocked: he conceived the idea that outsiders were always brought into the firm to occupy senior positions. You may think his reaction a little excessive."

Brady stopped. He had, at this point, intended to have a dig at Black, by mentioning the oil companies' practice of installing accountants in senior management positions. As things had turned out, however, he decided against it, and merely asked Black to sum up.

This Black did, in a surprisingly warm and human manner. Again he praised Brady Enterprises effusively, and he ended by reassuring everyone present that the campaign of terror and destruction was over. The meeting was closed. Police officers escorted Reynolds, Blake, Bronowski and Houston away to the cells, and in small groups and very slowly everyone else began to leave the hall.

Brady, feeling unwontedly nervous, sidled up to Black.

"My apologies," he muttered. "Must offer you my sincere apologies. My associates were infernally rude to you that time in the course of their ... ah ... investigations ... no cause for it."

"My dear fellow – not at all," said Black magnanimously. "I daresay it was my fault anyway. I hardly realised what deep trouble we were in. I thought your investigations were superfluous. Now I know different."

"I'd like to apologise, too, sir," muttered Dermott, stiff with embarrassment. "Trouble was – if I may say so – you seemed so unco-operative."

"It was the *cost* that frightened me. Don't forget, I'm an

accountant by training." To the amazement of the Brady team, Black actually laughed. They laughed too, from sheer release of tension – and the next second, Black caught them neatly on the rebound.

"Well now, Mr Brady," he said briskly. "As to the question of your fee ..."

"Oh ... now!" Brady spluttered, caught right off-balance. "I assumed all along I would negotiate that with your London office."

"No need, I'm glad to say." Black was all breezy sunshine. "London has empowered me to deal directly with you. Our chairman felt that despite your close friendship, or perhaps because of it – I should settle this up."

"That's ... well ... NO! I mean, I ... I never discuss fees myself." Brady sounded lame, and knew it. But he pulled himself together fast. "I have to consult *my* accountant, even if you don't."

"Forty love, and Black to serve," muttered Dermott as they moved away. He was about to go for his coat when, down one side of the room, he spotted Corinne Delorme still sitting on a bench, as if in a trance.

"Come on, honey," he said gently. "Time to go."

"I just can't believe it," she said. "It's not possible."

"Well – it happened. Are you upset?"

"Not really – no. I didn't care that much about him. It's just that I kind of got used to believing what he said."

"I know, one does. But you saw how devious he was. Anyone who has himself kidnapped to add verisimilitude to the proceedings – anyone who does that is hardly straightforward."

"I guess that's right. Those murders, too. Oh God, it's awful."

"It *was* awful. But it's over. Coming?"

"I suppose so." She stood up, and Dermott helped her into her coat.

"You and I were the two luckiest people in the whole damn business," he said. "We both ought to be dead. Without you I would be."

Suddenly her blank eyes lit up and she smiled.

Dermott smiled back. "What are you going to do now you've got no boss to work for?"

"I don't know. Find another job first."

"Not many good jobs in Fort McMurray. Why not come south and work for me?"

"For *you*?" Her eyes widened. "I hadn't thought of that."

"Think of it now. Shall we go?"

"O.K."

"I'd offer you my arm, if it wasn't still so damned sore."

"And I might even take it." She looked upward and snuggled close against him as they went out through the door.

The sight seemed to occasion the most immense merriment in Brady and his one remaining associate. They rolled in their seats like clowns, giving vent to noisy explosions.

"Stay me with flagons, Donald," cried Brady, as he recovered. "I am seriously in need of liquid refreshment. For unless my investigative powers are dwindling, we have a romance on our hands."

Ice Station Zebra

To Lachlan, Michael and Alistair

U.S.S. *Dolphin*

1. Rudder	11. Radio Room (port)
2. Stern Room	12. Control Room
3. Nucleonics Room	13. Captain's Cabin
4. Manœuvring Room	(port; Sickbay
5. Engine Room	(starboard)
6. Machinery space	14. Wardroom
7. Passage over reactor	15. Inertial Navigation
8. Reactor Room	Room
9. Sail	16. Electronics Room
10. Bridge	17. Crew's Quarters

18. Galley
19. Medical Store
20. Disposal chute
21. Periscope (retracted)
22. Torpedo Storage
Room
23. Collision Space
24. Torpedo Room
25. Torpedo Tubes
26. Bow Caps

ICE STATION ZEBRA

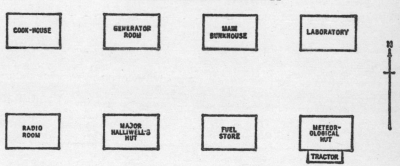

1

Commander James D. Swanson of the United States Navy was short, plump and crowding forty. He had jet black hair topping a pink cherubic face, and with the deep permanent creases of laughter lines radiating from his eyes and curving round his mouth he was a dead ringer for the cheerful, happy-go-lucky extrovert who is the life and soul of the party where the guests park their brains along with their hats and coats. That, anyway, was how he struck me at first glance but on the reasonable assumption that I might very likely find some other qualities in the man picked to command the latest and most powerful nuclear submarine afloat I took a second and closer look at him and this time I saw what I should have seen the first time if the dank grey fog and winter dusk settling down over the Firth of Clyde hadn't made seeing so difficult. His eyes. Whatever his eyes were they weren't those of the gladhanding wisecracking *bon vivant*. They were the coolest, clearest grey eyes I'd ever seen, eyes that he used as a dentist might his probe, a surgeon his lancet or a scientist his electronic microscope. Measuring eyes. They measured first me and then the paper he held in his hand but gave no clue at all as to the conclusions arrived at on the basis of measurements made.

"I'm sorry, Dr. Carpenter." The south-of-the-Mason-Dixon-line voice was quiet and courteous, but without any genuine regret that I could detect, as he folded the telegram back into its envelope and handed it to me. "I can accept neither this telegram as sufficient authorisation nor yourself as a passenger. Nothing personal, you know that; but I have my orders."

"Not sufficient authorisation?" I pulled the telegram from its cover and pointed to the signature. "Who do you think this is—the resident window-cleaner at the Admiralty?"

It wasn't funny, and as I looked at him in the failing light I thought maybe I'd overestimated the depth of the laughter lines in the face. He said precisely: "Admiral Hewson

259

is commander of the Nato Eastern Division. On Nato exercises I come under his command. At all other times I am responsible only to Washington. This is one of those other times. I'm sorry. And I must point out, Dr. Carpenter, that you could have arranged for anyone in London to send this telegram. It's not even on a naval message form."

He didn't miss much, that was a fact, but he was being suspicious about nothing. I said: "You could call him up by radio-telephone, Commander."

"So I could," he agreed. "And it would make no difference. Only accredited American nationals are allowed aboard this vessel—and the authority must come from Washington."

"From the Director of Underseas Warfare or Commander Atlantic submarines?" He nodded, slowly, speculatively, and I went on : "Please radio them and ask them to contact Admiral Hewson. Time is very short, Commander." I might have added that it was beginning to snow and that I was getting colder by the minute, but I refrained.

He thought for a moment, nodded, turned and walked a few feet to a portable dockside telephone that was connected by a looping wire to the long dark shape lying at our feet. He spoke briefly, keeping his voice low, and hung up. He barely had time to rejoin me when three duffel-coated figures came hurrying up an adjacent gangway, turned in our direction and stopped when they reached us. The tallest of the three tall men, a lean rangy character with wheat-coloured hair and the definite look of a man who ought to have had a horse between his legs, stood slightly in advance of the other two. Commander Swanson gestured towards him.

"Lieutenant Hansen, my executive officer. He'll look after you till I get back." The commander certainly knew how to choose his words.

"I don't need looking after," I said mildly. "I'm all grown up now and I hardly ever feel lonely."

"I shall be as quick as I can, Dr. Carpenter," Swanson said. He hurried off down the gangway and I gazed thoughtfully after him. I put out of my mind any idea I might have had about the Commander U.S. Atlantic Submarines picking his captains from the benches in Central Park. I had tried to effect an entrance aboard Swanson's ship and if such an

260

entrance was unauthorised he didn't want me taking off till he'd found out why. Hansen and his two men, I guessed, would be the three biggest sailors on the ship.

The ship. I stared down at the great black shape lying almost at my feet. This was my first sight of a nuclear-engined submarine, and the *Dolphin* was like no submarine that I had ever seen. She was about the same length as a World War II long-range ocean-going submarine but there all resemblance ceased. Her diameter was at least twice that of any conventional submarine. Instead of having the vaguely boat-shaped lines of her predecessors, the *Dolphin* was almost perfectly cylindrical in design : instead of the usual V-shaped bows, her fore end was completely semi-spherical. There was no deck, as such : the rounded sheer of sides and bows rose smoothly to the top of the hull then fell as smoothly away again, leaving only a very narrow fore-and-aft working space so dangerously treacherous in its slippery convexity that it was permanently railed off in harbour. About a hundred feet back from the bows the slender yet massive conning-tower reared over twenty feet above the deck, for all the world like the great dorsal fin of some monstrous shark : half-way up the sides of the conning-tower and thrust out stubbily at right angles were the swept-back auxiliary diving planes of the submarine. I tried to see what lay farther aft but the fog and the thickening snow swirling down from the north of Loch Long defeated me. Anyway, I was losing interest. I'd only a thin raincoat over my clothes and I could feel my skin start to gooseflesh under the chill fingers of that winter wind.

"Nobody said anything about us having to freeze to death," I said to Hansen. "That naval canteen there. Would your principles prevent you from accepting a cup of coffee from Dr. Carpenter, that well-known espionage agent?"

He grinned and said : "In the matter of coffee, friend, I have no principles. Especially to-night. Someone should have warned us about those Scottish winters." He not only looked like a cowboy, he talked like one : I was an expert on cowboys as I was sometimes too tired to rise to switch off the TV set. "Rawlings, go tell the captain that we are sheltering from the elements."

While Rawlings went to the dockside phone Hansen

led the way to the nearby neon-lit canteen. He let me precede him through the door then made for the counter while the other sailor, a red-complexioned character about the size and shape of a polar bear, nudged me gently into an angled bench seat in one corner of the room. They weren't taking too many chances with me. Hansen came and sat on the other side of me, and when Rawlings returned he sat squarely in front of me across the table.

"As neat a job of corralling as I've seen for a long time," I said approvingly. "You've got nasty suspicious minds, haven't you?"

"You wrong us," Hansen said sadly. "We're just three friendly sociable guys carrying out our orders. It's Commander Swanson who has the nasty suspicious mind, isn't that so, Rawlings?"

"Yes, indeed, Lieutenant," Rawlings said gravely. "Very security-minded, the captain is."

I tried again. "Isn't this very inconvenient for you?" I asked. "I mean, I should have thought that every man would have been urgently required aboard if you're due to sail in less than two hours' time."

"You just keep on talking, Doc," Hansen said encouragingly. There was nothing encouraging about his cold blue Arctic eyes, "I'm a right good listener."

"Looking forward to your trip up to the ice-pack?" I inquired pleasantly.

They operated on the same wavelength, all right. They didn't even look at one another. In perfect unison they all hitched themselves a couple of inches closer to me, and there was nothing imperceptible about the way they did it either. Hansen waited, smiling in a pleasantly relaxed fashion until the waitress had deposited four steaming mugs of coffee on the table, then said in the same encouraging tone: "Come again, friend. Nothing we like to hear better than top classified information being bandied about in canteens. How the hell do *you* know where we're going?"

I reached up my hand beneath my coat lapel and it stayed there, my right wrist locked in Hansen's right hand.

"We're not suspicious or anything," he said apologetically. "It's just that we submariners are very nervous on account of the dangerous life we lead. Also, we've a very fine library of films aboard the *Dolphin* and every time a character in one of those films reaches up under his coat it's always for the same reason and that's not just because he's checking to see if his wallet's still there."

I took his wrist with my free hand, pulled his arm away and pushed it down on the table. I'm not saying it was easy, the U.S. Navy clearly fed its submariners on a high protein diet, but I managed it without bursting a blood-vessel. I pulled a folded newspaper out from under my coat and laid it down. "You wanted to know how the hell I knew where you were going," I said. "I can read, that's why. That's a Glasgow evening paper I picked up in Renfrew Airport half an hour ago."

Hansen rubbed his wrist thoughtfully, then grinned. "What did you get your doctorate in, Doc? Weight-lifting? About that paper—how could you have got it in Renfrew half an hour ago?"

"I flew down here. Helicopter."

"A whirlybird, eh? I heard one arriving a few minutes ago. But that was one of ours."

"It had U.S. Navy written all over it in four-foot letters," I conceded, "and the pilot spent all his time chewing gum and praying out loud for a quick return to California."

"Did you tell the skipper this?" Hansen demanded.

"He didn't give me the chance to tell him anything."

"He's got a lot on his mind and far too much to see to," Hansen said. He unfolded the paper and looked at the front page. He didn't have far to look to find what he wanted : the two-inch banner headlines were spread over seven columns.

"Well, would you look at this." Lieutenant Hansen made no attempt to conceal his irritation and chagrin. "Here we are, pussy-footing around in this God-forsaken dump, sticking-plaster all over our mouths, sworn to eternal secrecy about mission and destination and then what? I pick up this blasted Limey newspaper and here are all the top-secret details plastered right across the front page."

"You are kidding, Lieutenant," said the man with the red face and the general aspect of a polar bear. His voice seemed to come from his boots.

263

" I am not kidding, Zabrinski," Hansen said coldly, "as you would appreciate if you had ever learned to read. 'Nuclear submarine to the rescue,' it says. 'Dramatic dash to the North Pole.' God help us, the North Pole. And a picture of the *Dolphin*. And of the skipper. Good lord, there's even a picture of me."

Rawlings reached out a hairy paw and twisted the paper to have a better look at the blurred and smudged representation of the man before him. "So there is. Not very flattering, is it, Lieutenant? But a speaking likeness, mind you, a speaking likeness. The photographer has caught the essentials perfectly."

" You are utterly ignorant of the first principles of photography," Hansen said witheringly. " Listen to this lot. 'The following joint statement was issued simultaneously a few minutes before noon (G.M.T.) to-day in both London and Washington : "In view of the critical condition of the survivors of Drift Ice Station Zebra and the failure either to rescue or contact them by conventional means, the United States Navy has willingly agreed that the United States nuclear submarine *Dolphin* be dispatched with all speed to try to effect contact with the survivors."

" ' The *Dolphin* returned to its base in the Holy Loch, Scotland, at dawn this morning after carrying out extensive exercises with the Nato naval forces in the Eastern Atlantic. It is hoped that the *Dolphin* (Commander James D. Swanson, U.S.N., commanding) will sail at approximately 7 p.m. (G.M.T.) this evening.

" ' The laconic understatement of this communique heralds the beginning of a desperate and dangerous rescue attempt which must be without parallel in the history of the sea or the Arctic. It is now sixty hours——' "

" 'Desperate,' you said, Lieutenant?" Rawlings frowned heavily. " 'Dangerous,' you said? The captain will be asking for volunteers?"

" No need. I told the captain that I'd already checked with all eighty-eight enlisted men and that they'd volunteered to a man."

" You never checked with me."

" I must have missed you out. Now kindly clam up, your executive officer is talking. 'It is now sixty hours since the world was electrified to learn of the disaster which had struck Drift Ice Station Zebra, the only British meteorological station in the Arctic, when an English-speaking ham radio operator in Bodo, Norway picked up the faint S O S from the top of the world.

" ' A further message, picked up less than twenty-four hours ago by the British trawler *Morning Star* in the Barents Sea makes it clear that the position of the survivors of the fuel oil fire that destroyed most of Drift Ice Station Zebra in the early hours of Tuesday morning is desperate in the extreme. With their oil fuel reserves completely destroyed and their food stores all but wiped out, it is feared that those still living cannot long be expected to survive in the twenty-below temperatures—fifty degrees of frost—at present being experienced in that area.

" ' It is not known whether all the prefabricated huts, in which the expedition members lived, have been destroyed.

" ' Drift Ice Station Zebra, which was established only in the late summer of this year, is at present in an estimated position of 85° 40' N. 21° 30' E., which is only about three hundred miles from the North Pole. Its position cannot be known with certainty because of the clockwise drift of the polar ice-pack.

" ' For the past thirty hours long-range supersonic bombers of the American, British and Russian air forces have been scouring the polar ice-pack searching for Station Zebra. Because of the uncertainty about the Drift Station's actual position, the complete absence of daylight in the Arctic at this time of year and the extremely bad weather conditions they were unable to locate the station and forced to return.' "

" They didn't have to locate it," Rawlings objected. " Not visually. With the instruments those bombers have nowadays they could home in on a humming-bird a hundred miles away. The radio operator at the Drift Station had only to keep on sending and they could have used that as a beacon."

" Maybe the radio operator is dead," Hansen said heavily. " Maybe his radio has packed up on him. Maybe the fuel that was destroyed was essential for running the radio. All depends what source of power he used."

" Diesel-electric generator," I said. " He had a standby battery of Nife cells. Maybe he's conserving the batteries.

265

using them only for emergencies. There's also a hand-cranked generator, but its range is pretty limited."

"How do you know that?" Hansen asked quietly. "About the type of power used?"

"I must have read it somewhere."

"You must have read it somewhere." He looked at me without expression, then turned back to his paper. "'A report from Moscow,'" he read on, "'states that the atomic-engined *Dvina*, the world's most powerful ice-breaker, sailed from Murmansk some twenty hours ago and is proceeding at high speed towards the Arctic pack. Experts are not hopeful about the outcome for at this late period of the year the ice-pack had already thickened and compacted into a solid mass which will almost certainly defy the efforts of any vessel, even those of the *Dvina*, to smash its way through.

"'The use of the submarine *Dolphin* appears to offer the only slender hope of life for the apparently doomed survivors of Station Zebra. The odds against success must be regarded as heavy in the extreme. Not only will the *Dolphin* have to travel several hundred miles continuously submerged under the polar ice-cap, but the possibilities of its being able to break through the ice-cap at any given place or to locate the survivors are very remote. But undoubtedly if any ship in the world can do it it is the *Dolphin*, the pride of the United States Navy's nuclear submarine fleet.'"

Hansen broke off and read on silently for a minute. Then he said: "That's about all. A story giving all the known details of the *Dolphin*. That, and a lot of ridiculous rubbish about the enlisted men in the *Dolphin*'s crew being the *élite* of the cream of the U.S. Navy."

Rawlings looked wounded. Zabrinski, the polar bear with the red face, grinned, fished out a pack of cigarettes and passed them around. Then he became serious again and said: "What are those crazy guys doing up there at the top of the world anyway?"

"Meteorological, lunkhead," Rawlings informed him. "Didn't you hear the lieutenant say so? A big word, mind you," he conceded generously, "but he made a pretty fair stab at it. Weather station to you, Zabrinski."

"I still say they're crazy guys," Zabrinski rumbled. "Why do they do it, Lieutenant?"

266

" I suggest you ask Dr. Carpenter about it," Hansen said dryly. He stared through the plate-glass windows at the snow whirling greyly through the gathering darkness, his eyes bleak and remote, as if he were already visualising the doomed men drifting to their death in the frozen immensity of the polar ice-cap. " I think he knows a great deal more about it than I do."

" I know a little," I admitted. " There's nothing mysterious or sinister about what I know. Meteorologists now regard the Arctic and the Antarctic as the two great weather factories of the world, the areas primarily responsible for the weather that affects the rest of the hemisphere. We already know a fair amount about Antarctic conditions, but practically nothing about the Arctic. So we pick a suitable ice-floe, fill it with huts crammed with technicians and all sorts of instruments and let them drift around the top of the world for six months or so. Your own people have already set up two or three of those stations. The Russians have set up at least ten, to the best of my knowledge, most of them in the East Siberian Sea."

" How do they establish those camps, Doc?" Rawlings asked.

" Different ways. Your people prefer to establish them in winter-time, when the pack freezes up enough for plane landings to be made. Someone flies out from, usually, Point Barrow in Alaska and searches around the polar pack till they find a suitable ice-floe—even when the ice is compacted and frozen together into one solid mass an expert can tell which pieces are going to remain as good-sized floes when the thaw comes and the break-in begins. Then they fly out all huts, equipment, stores and men by ski-plane and gradually build the place up.

" The Russians prefer to use a ship in summer-time. They generally use the *Lenin,* a nuclear-engined ice-breaker. It just batters its way into the summer pack, dumps everything and everybody on the ice and takes off before the big freeze-up starts. We used the same technique for Drift Ice Station Zebra—our one and only ice station. The Russians lent us the *Lenin*—all countries are only too willing to co-operate on meteorological research as everyone benefits by it—and took us pretty deep into the ice-pack north of Franz Josef

267

Land. Zebra has already moved a good bit from its original position—the polar ice-cap, just sitting on top of the Arctic Ocean, can't quite manage to keep up with the west-east spin of the earth so that it has a slow westward movement in relation to the earth's crust. At the present moment it's about four hundred miles due north of Spitzbergen."

"They're still crazy," Zabrinski said. He was silent for a moment then looked speculatively at me. "You in the Limey navy, Doc?"

"You must forgive Zabrinski's manners, Dr. Carpenter," Rawlings said coldly. "But he's denied the advantages that the rest of us take for granted. I understand he was born in the Bronx."

"No offence," Zabrinski said equably. "Royal Navy, I meant. Are you, Doc?"

"Attached to it, you might say."

"Loosely, no doubt," Rawlings nodded. "Why so keen on an Arctic holiday, Doc? Mighty cool up there, I can tell you."

"Because the men on Drift Station Zebra are going to be badly in need of medical aid. If there are any survivors, that is."

"We got our own medico on board and he's no slouch with a stethoscope, or so I've heard from several who have survived his treatment. A well-spoken-of quack."

"Doctor, you ill-mannered lout," Zabrinski said severely.

"That's what I meant," Rawlings apologised. "It's not often that I get the chance to talk to an educated man like myself, and it just kinda slipped out. The point is, the *Dolphin*'s already all buttoned up on the medical side."

"I'm sure it is." I smiled. "But any survivors we might find are going to be suffering from advanced exposure, frostbite and probably gangrene. The treatment of those is rather a speciality of mine."

"Is it now?" Rawlings surveyed the depths of his coffee cup. "I wonder how a man gets to be a specialist in those things?"

Hansen stirred and withdrew his gaze from the darkly-white world beyond the canteen windows.

"Dr. Carpenter is not on trial for his life," he said mildly. "The counsel for the prosecution will kindly pack it in."

They packed it in. This air of easy familiarity between officer and men, the easy camaraderie, the mutually tolerant disparagement with the deceptively misleading overtones of knock-about comedy, was something very rare in my experience but not unique. I'd seen it before, in first-line R.A.F. bomber crews, a relationship found only among a close-knit, close-living group of superbly trained experts each of whom is keenly aware of their complete interdependence. The casually informal and familiar attitude was a token not of the lack of discipline but of the complete reverse: it was the token of a very high degree of self-discipline, of the regard one man held for another not only as a highly-skilled technician in his own field but also as a human being. It was clear, too, that a list of unwritten rules governed their conduct. Off-hand and frequently completely lacking in outward respect though Rawlings and Zabrinski were in their attitude towards Lieutenant Hansen, there was an invisible line of propriety over which it was inconceivable that they would ever step: for Hansen's part, he scrupulously avoided any use of his authority when making disparaging remarks at the expense of the two enlisted men. It was also clear, as now, who was boss.

Rawlings and Zabrinski stopped questioning me and had just embarked upon an enthusiastic discussion of the demerits of the Holy Loch in particular and Scotland in general as a submarine base when a jeep swept past the canteen windows, the snow whirling whitely, thickly, through the swathe of the headlights. Rawlings jumped to his feet in mid-sentence, then subsided slowly and thoughtfully into his chair.

" The plot," he announced, " thickens."

" You saw who it was?" Hansen asked.

" I did indeed. Andy Bandy, no less."

" I didn't hear that, Rawlings," Hansen said coldly.

" Vice-Admiral John Garvie, United States Navy, sir."

" Andy Bandy, eh?" Hansen said pensively. He grinned at me. " Admiral Garvie, Officer Commanding U.S. Naval Forces in Nato. Now this is very interesting, I submit. I wonder what he's doing here."

" World War III has just broken out," Rawlings announced. " It's just about time for the Admiral's first martini of the day and no lesser crisis——"

" He didn't by any chance fly down with you in that chopper from Renfrew this afternoon?" Hansen interrupted shrewdly.

" No."

" Know him, by any chance?"

" Never even heard of him until now."

" Curiouser and curiouser," Hansen murmured.

A few minutes passed in desultory talk—the minds of Hansen and his two men were obviously very much on the reason for the arrival of Admiral Garvie—and then a snow-filled gust of chilled air swept into the canteen as the door opened and a blue-coated sailor came in and crossed to our table.

" The captain's compliments, Lieutenant. Would you bring Dr. Carpenter to his cabin, please?"

Hansen nodded, rose to his feet and led the way outside. The snow was beginning to lie now, the darkness was coming down fast and the wind from the north was bitingly chill. Hansen made for the nearest gangway, halted at its head as he saw seamen and dockyard workers, insubstantial and spectral figures in the swirling flood-lit snow, carefully easing a slung torpedo down the for'ard hatch, turned and headed towards the after gangway. We clambered down and at the foot Hansen said: " Watch your step, Doc. It's a mite slippery hereabouts."

It was all that, but with the thought of the ice-cold waters of the Holy Loch waiting for me if I put a foot wrong I made no mistake. We passed through the hooped canvas shelter covering the after hatch and dropped down a steep metal ladder into a warm, scrupulously clean and gleaming engine-room packed with a baffling complexity of grey-painted machinery and instrument panels, its every corner brightly illuminated with shadowless fluorescent lighting.

" Not going to blindfold me, Lieutenant?" I asked.

" No need." He grinned. " If you're on the up and up, it's not necessary. If you're not on the up and up it's still not necessary, for you can't talk about what you've seen— not to anyone that matters—if you're going to spend the next few years staring out from behind a set of prison bars."

I saw his point. I followed him for'ard, our feet soundless on the black rubber decking past the tops of a couple of huge

270

machines readily identifiable as turbo-generator sets for producing electricity. More heavy banks of instruments, a door, then a thirty-foot-long very narrow passageway. As we passed along its length I was conscious of a heavy vibrating hum from beneath my feet. The *Dolphin*'s nuclear reactor had to be somewhere. This would be it, here. Directly beneath us. There were circular hatches on the passageway deck and those could only be covers for the heavily-leaded glass windows, inspection ports which would provide the nearest and only approach to the nuclear furnace far below.

The end of the passage, another heavily-clipped door, and then we were into what was obviously the control centre of the *Dolphin*. To the left was a partitioned-off radio room, to the right a battery of machines and dialled panels of incomprehensible purpose, straight ahead a big chart table. Beyond that again, in the centre were massive mast housings and, still farther on, the periscope stand with its twin periscopes. The whole control room was twice the size of any I'd ever seen in a conventional submarine but, even so, every square inch of bulkhead space seemed to be taken up by one type or another of highly-complicated looking machines or instrument banks : even the deckhead was almost invisible, lost to sight above thickly twisted festoons of wires, cables and pipes of a score of different kinds.

The for'ard port side of the control room was for all the world like a replica of the flight-deck of a modern multi-engined jet airliner. There were two separate yoke aircraft-type control columns, facing on to banks of hooded calibrated dials. Behind the yokes were two padded leather chairs, each chair, I could see, fitted with safety-belts to hold the helmsman in place. I wondered vaguely what type of violent manœuvres the *Dolphin* might be capable of when such safety-belts were obviously considered essential to strap the helmsman down.

Opposite the control platform, on the other side of the passageway leading forward from the control room, was a second partitioned-off room. There was no indication what this might be and I wasn't given time to wonder. Hansen hurried down the passage, stopped at the first door on his left, and knocked. The door opened and Commander Swanson appeared.

271

"Ah, there you are. Sorry you've been kept waiting, Dr. Carpenter. We're sailing at six-thirty, John "—this to Hansen. "You can have everything buttoned up by then?"

"Depends how quickly the loading of the torpedoes goes, Captain."

"We're taking only six aboard."

Hansen lifted an eyebrow, made no comment. He said: "Loading them into the tubes?"

"In the racks. They have to be worked on."

"No spares?"

"No spares."

Hansen nodded and left. Swanson led me into his cabin and closed the door behind him.

Commander Swanson's cabin was bigger than a telephone booth, I'll say that for it, but not all that much bigger to shout about. A built-in bunk, a folding washbasin, a small writing-bureau and chair, a folding camp-stool, a locker, some calibrated repeater instrument dials above the bunk and that was it. If you'd tried to perform the twist in there you'd have fractured yourself in a dozen places without ever moving your feet from the centre of the floor.

"Dr. Carpenter," Swanson said, "I'd like you to meet Admiral Garvie, Commander U.S. Nato Naval Forces."

Admiral Garvie put down the glass he was holding in his hand, rose from the only chair and stretched out his hand. As he stood with his feet together, the far from negligible clearance between his knees made it easy to understand the latter part of his "Andy Bandy" nickname: like Hansen, he'd have been at home on the range. He was a tall florid-faced man with white hair, white eyebrows and a twinkle in the blue eyes below: he had that certain indefinable something about him common to all senior naval officers the world over, irrespective of race or nationality.

"Glad to meet you, Dr. Carpenter. Sorry for the—um—lukewarm reception you received, but Commander Swanson was perfectly within his rights in acting as he did. His men have looked after you?"

"They permitted me to buy them a cup of coffee in the canteen."

He smiled. "Opportunists all, those nuclear men. I feel

272

that the good name of American hospitality is in danger. Whisky, Dr. Carpenter?"

" I thought American naval ships were dry, sir."

" So they are, my boy, so they are. Except for a little medicinal alcohol, of course. My personal supply." He produced a hip-flask about the size of a canteen, reached for a convenient tooth-glass. " Before venturing into the remoter fastnesses of the Highlands of Scotland the prudent man takes the necessary precautions. I have to make an apology to you, Dr. Carpenter. I saw your Admiral Hewson in London last night and had intended to be here this morning to persuade Commander Swanson here to take you aboard. But I was delayed."

" Persuade, sir?"

" Persuade." He sighed. " Our nuclear submarine captains, Dr. Carpenter, are a touchy and difficult bunch. From the proprietary attitude they adopt towards their submarines you'd think that each one of them was a majority shareholder in the Electric Boat Company of Groton, where most of those boats are built." He raised his glass. " Success to the commander and yourself. I hope you manage to find those poor devils. But I don't give you one chance in a thousand."

" I think we'll find them, sir. Or Commander Swanson will."

" What makes you so sure?" He added slowly, " Hunch?"

" You could call it that."

He laid down his glass and his eyes were no longer twinkling. " Admiral Hewson was most evasive about you, I must say. Who are you, Carpenter? *What* are you?"

" Surely he told you, Admiral? Just a doctor attached to the navy to carry out——"

" A naval doctor?"

" Well, not exactly. I——"

" A civilian, is it?"

I nodded, and the admiral and Swanson exchanged looks which they were at no pains at all to conceal from me. If they were happy at the prospect of having aboard America's latest and most secret submarine a man who was not only a foreigner but a civilian to boot, they were hiding it well. Admiral Garvie said : " Well, go on."

273

"That's all. I carry out environmental health studies for the services. How men react to extremes of environmental conditions, such as in the Arctic or the tropics, how they react to conditions of weightlessness in simulated space flights or to extremes of pressure when having to escape from submarines. Mainly——"

"Submarines." Admiral Garvie pounced on the word. "You have been to sea in submarines, Dr. Carpenter. Really sailed in them, I mean?"

"I had to. We found that simulated tank escapes were no substitute for the real thing."

The admiral and Swanson looked unhappier than ever. A foreigner—bad. A foreign civilian—worse. But a foreign civilian with at least a working knowledge of submarines— terrible. I didn't have to be beaten over the head to see their point of view. I would have felt just as unhappy in their shoes.

"What's your interest in Drift Ice Station Zebra, Dr. Carpenter?" Admiral Garvie asked bluntly.

"The Admiralty asked me to go there, sir."

"So I gather, so I gather," Garvie said wearily. "Admiral Hewson made that quite plain to me already. Why *you*, Carpenter?"

"I have some knowledge of the Arctic, sir. I'm supposed to be an expert on the medical treatment of men subjected to prolonged exposure, frostbite and gangrene. I might be able to save lives or limbs that your own doctor aboard might not."

"I could have half a dozen such experts here in a few hours," Garvie said evenly. "Regular serving officers of the United States Navy, at that. That's not enough, Carpenter."

This was becoming difficult. I tried again. I said: "I know Drift Station Zebra. I helped select the site. I helped establish the camp. The commandant, a Major Halliwell, has been my closest friend for many years." The last was only half the truth but I felt that this was neither the time nor the place for over-elaboration.

"Well, well," Garvie said thoughtfully. "And you still claim you're just an ordinary doctor?"

"My duties are flexible, sir."

"I'll say they are. Well, then, Carpenter, if you're just a

274

common-or-garden sawbones, how do you explain this?"
He picked a signal form from the table and handed it to me.
" This has just arrived in reply to Commander Swanson's
radioed query to Washington about you."

I looked at the signal. It read : " Dr. Neil Carpenter's
bonafides beyond question. He may be taken into your fullest,
repeat fullest confidence. He is to be extended every facility
and all aid short of actually endangering the safety of your
submarine and the lives of your crew." It was signed by
the Director of Naval Operations.

" Very civil of the Director of Naval Operations, I must
say." I handed back the signal. " With a character reference
like this, what are you worrying about. That ought to
satisfy anyone."

" It doesn't satisfy me," Garvie said heavily. " The ultimate
responsibility for the safety of the *Dolphin* is mine. This
signal more or less gives you *carte blanche* to behave as you
like, to ask Commander Swanson to act in ways that might be
contrary to his better judgment. I can't have that."

" Does it matter what you can or can't have? You have
your orders. Why don't you obey them?"

He didn't hit me. He didn't even bat an eyelid. He
wasn't activated by pique about the fact that he wasn't
privy to the reason for the seeming mystery of my presence
there, he was genuinely concerned about the safety of the
submarine. He said : " If I think it more important that
the *Dolphin* should remain on an active war footing rather
than to go haring off on a wild-goose chase to the Arctic,
or if I think you constitute a danger to the submarine, I can
countermand the D.N.O.'s orders. I'm the C.-in-C. on the
spot. And I'm not satisfied."

This was damnably awkward. He meant every word he
said and he didn't look the type who would give a hoot
for the consequences if he believed himself to be in the
right. I looked at both men, looked at them slowly and
speculatively, the unmistakable gaze, I hoped, of a man
who was weighing others in the balance : what I was really
doing was thinking up a suitable story that would satisfy
both. After I had given enough time to my weighing-up—
and my thinking—I dropped my voice a few decibels and
said : " Is that door soundproof?"

275

"More or less," Swanson said. He'd lowered his own voice to match mine.

"I won't insult either of you by swearing you to secrecy or any such rubbish," I said quietly. "I want to put on record the fact that what I am about to tell you I am telling you under duress, under Admiral Garvie's threat to refuse me transport if I don't comply with his wishes."

"There will be no repercussions," Garvie said.

"How do you know? Not that it matters now. Well, gentlemen, the facts are these. Drift Ice Station Zebra is officially classed as an Air Ministry meteorological station. Well, it belongs to the Air Ministry all right, but there's not more than a couple of qualified meteorologists among its entire personnel."

Admiral Garvie refilled the toothglass and passed it to me without a word, without a flicker of change in his expression. The old boy certainly knew how to play it cool.

"What you will find there," I went on, "are some of the most highly skilled men in the world in the fields of radar, radio, infra-red and electronic computers, operating the most advanced instruments ever used in those fields. We know now, never mind how, the count-down succession of signals the Russians use in the last minute before launching a missile. There's a huge dish aerial in Zebra that can pick up and amplify any such signals within seconds of it beginning. Then long-range radar and infra-red home in on that bearing and within three minutes of the rocket's lift-off they have its height, speed and course pin-pointed to an infinitesimal degree of error. The computers do this, of course. One minute later the information is in the hands of all the anti-missile stations between Alaska and Greenland. One minute more and solid fuel infra-red homing anti-missile rockets are on their way; then the enemy missiles will be intercepted and harmlessly destroyed while still high over the Arctic regions. If you look at a map you will see that in its present position Drift Ice Station Zebra is sitting practically on Russia's missile doorstep. It's hundreds of miles in advance of the present DEW line—the distant early warning system. Anyway, it renders the DEW line obsolete."

"I'm only the office boy around those parts," Garvie said quietly. "I've never heard of any of this before."

I wasn't surprised. I'd never heard any of it myself either, not until I'd just thought it up a moment ago. Commander Swanson's reactions, if and when we ever got to Drift Station Zebra, were going to be very interesting. But I'd cross that bridge when I came to it. At present, my only concern was to get there.

"Outside the Drift Station itself," I said, "I doubt if a dozen people in the world know what goes on there. But now you know. And you can appreciate how vitally important it is to the free world that this base be maintained in being. If anything has happened to it we want to find out just as quick as possible *what* has happened so that we can get it operating again."

"I still maintain that you're not an ordinary doctor," Garvie smiled. "Commander Swanson, how soon can you get under way?"

"Finish loading the torpedoes, move alongside the *Hunley*, load some final food stores, pick up extra Arctic clothing and that's it, sir."

"Just like that? You said you wanted to make a slow-time dive out in the loch to check the planes and adjust the underwater trim—those missing torpedoes up front are going to make a difference you know."

"That's before I heard Dr. Carpenter. Now I want to get up there just as fast as he does, sir. I'll see if immediate trim checks are necessary: if not, we can carry them out at sea."

"It's your boat," Garvie acknowledged. "Where are you going to accommodate Dr. Carpenter, by the way?"

"There's space for a cot in the Exec's and Engineer's cabin." He smiled at me. "I've already had your suitcase put in there."

"Did you have much trouble with the lock?" I inquired.

He had the grace to colour slightly. "It's the first time I've ever seen a combination lock on a suitcase," he admitted. "It was that, more than anything else—and the fact that we couldn't open it—that made the admiral and myself so suspicious. I've still one or two things to discuss with the admiral, so I'll take you to your quarters now. Dinner will be at eight to-night."

"I'd rather skip dinner, thanks."

277

"No one ever gets seasick on the *Dolphin*, I can assure you," Swanson smiled.

"I'd appreciate the chance to sleep instead. I've had no sleep for almost three days and I've been travelling non-stop for the past fifty hours. I'm just tired, that's all."

"That's a fair amount of travelling." Swanson smiled. He seemed almost always to be smiling, and I supposed vaguely that there would be some people foolish enough to take that smile always at its face value. "Where were you fifty hours ago, Doctor?"

"In the Antarctic."

Admiral Garvie gave me a very old-fashioned look indeed, but he let it go at that.

11

When I awoke I was still heavy with sleep, the heaviness of a man who has slept for a long time. My watch said nine-thirty, and I knew it must be the next morning, not the same evening : I had been asleep for fifteen hours.

The cabin was quite dark. I rose, fumbled for the light switch, found it and looked around. Neither Hansen nor the engineer officer was there : they must have come in after I had gone to sleep and left before I woke. I looked around some more, and then I listened. I was suddenly conscious of the almost complete quiet, the stillness, the entire lack of any perceptible motion. I might have been in the bedroom of my own house. What had gone wrong? What hold-up had occurred? Why in God's name weren't we under way? I'd have sworn the previous night that Commander Swanson had been just as conscious of the urgency as I had been.

I had a quick wash in the folding Pullman-type basin, passed up the need for a shave, pulled on shirt, trousers and shoes and went outside. A few feet away a door opened to starboard off the passage. I went along and walked in. The officers' wardroom, without a doubt, with one of them still at breakfast, slowly munching his way through a huge plateful of steak, eggs and French fries, glancing at a magazine in a leisurely fashion and giving every im-

278

pression of a man enjoying life to the luxurious full. He was about my own age, big, inclined to fat—a common condition, I was to find, among the entire crew who ate so well and exercised so little—with close-cropped black hair already greying at the temples and a cheerful intelligent face. He caught sight of me, rose and stretched out a hand.

" Dr. Carpenter, it must be. Welcome to the wardroom. I'm Benson. Take a seat, take a seat."

I said something, appropriate but quick, then asked: " What's wrong? What's been the hold-up? Why aren't we under way?"

" That's the trouble with the world to-day," Benson said mournfully. " Rush, rush, rush. And where does all the hurry get them? I'll tell you——"

" Excuse me. I must see the captain." I turned to leave but he laid a hand on my arm.

" Relax, Dr. Carpenter. We *are* at sea. Take a seat."

" At sea? On the level? I don't feel a thing."

" You never do when you're three hundred feet down. Maybe four hundred. I don't," he said expansively, " concern myself with those trifles. I leave them to the mechanics."

" Mechanics?"

" The captain, engineer officer, people like those." He waved a hand in a generously vague gesture to indicate the largeness of the concept he understood by the term " mechanics ". " Hungry?"

" We've cleared the Clyde?"

" Unless the Clyde extends to well beyond the north of Scotland, the answer to that is, yes, we have."

" Come again?"

He grinned. " At the last check we were well into the Norwegian Sea, about the latitude of Bergen."

" This is still only Tuesday morning?" I don't know if I looked stupid : I certainly felt it.

" It's still only Tuesday morning." He laughed. " And if you can work out from that what kind of speed we have been making in the last fifteen hours we'd all be obliged if you'd keep it to yourself." He leaned back in his seat and lifted his voice. " Henry!"

A steward, white-jacketed, appeared from what I took to be the pantry. He was a tall thin character with a dark complexion and the long lugubrious face of a dyspeptic spaniel. He looked at Benson and said in a meaningful voice: " *Another* plate of French fries, Doc?"

" You know very well that I never have more than one helping of that carbohydrated rubbish," Benson said with dignity. " Not, at least, for breakfast. Henry, this is Dr. Carpenter."

" Howdy," Henry said agreeably.

" Breakfast, Henry," Benson said. " And, remember, Dr. Carpenter is a Britisher. We don't want him leaving with a low opinion of the chow served up in the United States Navy."

" If anyone aboard this ship has a low opinion of the food," Henry said darkly, " they hide it pretty well. Breakfast. The works. Right away."

" Not the works, for heaven's sake," I said. " There are some things we decadent Britishers can't face up to first thing in the morning. One of them is French fries."

He nodded approvingly and left. I said: " Dr. Benson, I gather."

" Resident medical officer aboard the *Dolphin*, no less," he admitted. " The one who's had his professional competence called into question by having a competing practitioner called in."

" I'm along for the ride. I assure you I'm not competing with anyone."

" I know you're not," he said quickly. Too quickly. Quickly enough so that I could see Swanson's hand in this, could see him telling his officers to lay off quizzing Carpenter too much. I wondered again what Swanson was going to say when and if we ever arrived at the Drift Station and he found out just how fluent a liar I was. Benson went on, smiling: " There's no call for even one medico aboard this boat, far less two."

" You're not overworked?" From the leisurely way he was going about his breakfast it seemed unlikely.

" Overworked! I've sickbay call once a day and no one ever turns up—except the morning after we arrive in port with a long cruise behind us and then there are liable to be a few sore heads around. My main job, and what is supposed to be my speciality, is checking on radiation and atmosphere pollution of one kind or another—in the olden submarine days the atmosphere used to get pretty foul after only a few hours submerged but we have to stay down for months, if necessary." He grinned. "Neither job is very exacting. We issue each member of the crew with a dosimeter and periodically check a film badge for radiation dosage—which is invariably less than you'd get sitting on the beach on a moderately warm day.

"The atmospheric problem is even easier. Carbon dioxide and carbon monoxide are the only things we have to worry about. We have a scrubbing machine that absorbs the breathed-out carbon dioxide from the atmosphere and pumps it out into the sea. Carbon monoxide—which we could more or less eliminate if we forbade cigarette smoking, only we don't want a mutiny on our hands when we're three hundred feet down—is burned to dioxide by a special heater and then scrubbed as usual. And even that hardly worries me, I've a very competent engineman who keeps those machines in tip-top condition." He sighed. "I've a surgery here that will delight your heart, Dr. Carpenter. Operating table, dentist's chair, the lot, and the biggest crisis I've had yet is a cigarette burn between the fingers sustained by a cook who fell asleep during one of the lectures."

"Lectures?"

"I've got to do something if I'm not to go round the bend. I spend a couple of hours a day keeping up with all the latest medical literature but what good is that if you don't get a chance to practise it? So I lecture. I read up about places we're going to visit and everyone listens to those talks. I give lectures on general health and hygiene and some of them listen to those. I give lectures on the perils of over-eating and under-exercise and no one listens to those. I don't listen to them myself. It was during one of those that the cook got burned. That's why our friend Henry, the steward, adopts his superior and critical attitude towards the eating habits of those who should obviously be watching their habits. He eats as much as any two men aboard but owing to some metabolic defect he remains as thin as a rake. Claims it's all due to dieting."

"It all sounds a bit less rigorous than the life of the average G.P."

281

" It is, it is." He brightened. " But I've got one job—
a hobby to me—that the average G.P. can't have. The ice-
machine. I've made myself an expert on that."

" What does Henry think about it?"

" What? Henry?" He laughed. " Not that kind of ice-
machine. I'll show you later."

Henry brought food and I'd have liked the *maîtres d'hôtel*
of some allegedly five-star hotels in London to be there to
see what a breakfast should be like. When I'd finished and
told Benson that I didn't see that his lectures on the dangers
of overweight were going to get him very far, he said :
" Commander Swanson said you might like to see over the
ship. I'm at your complete disposal."

" Very kind of you both. But first I'd like to shave, dress
and have a word with the captain."

" Shave if you like. No one insists on it. As for dress,
shirt and pants are the rig of the day here. And the captain
told me to tell you that he'd let you know immediately anything came through that could possibly be of any interest
to you."

So I shaved and then had Benson take me on a conducted
tour of this city under the sea : the *Dolphin,* I had to admit
made any British submarine I'd ever seen look like a relic
from the Ice Age.

To begin with, the sheer size of the vessel was staggering
So big had the hull to be to accommodate the huge nuclear
reactor that it had internal accommodation equivalent to that
of a 3,000-ton surface ship, with three decks instead of
the usual one and lower hold found in the conventional
submarine. The size, combined with the clever use of
pastel paints for all accommodation spaces, working spaces
and passageways, gave an overwhelming impression of light-
ness, airiness and above all, spaciousness.

He took me first, inevitably, to his sickbay. It was at once
the smallest and most comprehensively equipped surgery I'd
ever seen, whether a man wanted a major operation or just
a tooth filled, he could have himself accommodated there.
Neither clinical nor utilitarian, however, was the motif Benson
had adopted for the decoration of the one bulkhead in his
surgery completely free from surgical or medical equipment of
any kind—a series of film stills in colour featuring every

282

cartoon character I'd ever seen, from Popeye to Pinnochio, with, as a two-foot square centrepiece, an immaculately cravatted Yogi Bear industriously sawing off from the top of a wooden signpost the first word of a legend which read " Don't feed the bears." From deck to deckhead, the bulkhead was covered with them.

" Makes a change from the usual pin-ups," I observed.

" I get inundated with those, too," Benson said regretfully. " Film librarian, you know. Can't use them, supposed to be bad for discipline. However. Lightens the morgue-like atmosphere, what? Cheers up the sick and suffering, I like to think —and distracts their attention while I turn up page 217 in the old textbook to find out what's the matter with them."

From the surgery we passed through the wardroom and officers' quarters and dropped down a deck to the crew's living quarters. Benson took me through the gleaming tiled washrooms, the immaculate bunk-room, then into the crew's mess hall.

" The heart of the ship," he announced. " Not the nuclear reactor, as the uninformed maintain, but here. Just look at it.. Hifi, juke box, record player, coffee machine, ice-cream machine, movie theatre, library and the home of all the card-sharps on the ship. What chance has a nuclear reactor against this lot? The old-time submariners would turn in their graves if they could see this : compared to the prehistoric conditions they lived in we must seem completely spoiled and ruined. Maybe we are, then again maybe we're not : the old boys never had to stay submerged for months at a time. This is also where I send them to sleep with my lectures on the evils of overeating." He raised his voice for the benefit of seven or eight men who were sitting about the tables, drinking coffee, smoking and reading. " You can observe for yourself, Dr. Carpenter, the effects of my lectures in dieting and keeping fit. Did you ever see a bunch of more out-of-condition fat-bellied slobs in your life?"

The men grinned cheerfully. They were obviously well used to this sort of thing : Benson was exaggerating and they knew it. Each of them looked as if he knew what to do with a knife and fork when he got them in his hands, but that was about as far as it went. All had a curious similarity, big men and small men, the same characteristic as I'd seen

283

in Zabrinski and Rawlings—an air of calmly relaxed competence, a cheerful imperturbability, that marked them out as being the men apart that they undoubtedly were.

Benson conscientiously introduced me to everyone, telling me exactly what their function aboard ship was and in turn informing them that I was a Royal Navy doctor along for an acclimatisation trip. Swanson would have told him to say this, it was near enough the truth and would stop speculation on the reason for my presence there.

Benson turned into a small compartment leading off the mess hall. " The air purification room. This is Engineman Harrison. How's our box of tricks, Harrison?"

" Just fine, Doc, just fine. CO reading steady on thirty parts a million." He entered some figures up in a log book, Benson signed it with a flourish, exchanged a few more remarks and left.

" Half my day's toil done with one stroke of the pen," he observed. " I take it you're not interested in inspecting sacks of wheat, sides of beef, bags of potatoes and about a hundred different varieties of canned goods."

" Not particularly. Why?"

" The entire for'ard half of the deck beneath our feet— a storage hold, really—is given up mainly to that. Seems an awful lot, I know, but then a hundred men can get through an awful lot of food in three months, which is the minimum time we must be prepared to stay at sea if the need arises. We'll pass up the inspection of the stores, the sight of all that food just makes me feel I'm fighting a losing battle all the time, and have a look where the food's cooked."

He led the way for'ard into the galley, a small square room all tiles and glittering stainless steel. A tall, burly, white-coated cook turned at our entrance and grinned at Benson. " Come to sample to-day's lunch, Doc?"

" I have not," Benson said coldly. " Dr. Carpenter, the chief cook and my arch-enemy, Sam MacGuire. What form does the excess of calories take that you are proposing to thrust down the throats of the crew to-day?"

" No thrusting required," said MacGuire happily. " Cream soup, sirloin of beef, no less, roast potatoes and as much apple pie as a man can cope with. All good nourishing food."

Benson shuddered. He made to leave the galley, stopped and pointed at a heavy bronze ten-inch tube that stood about four feet above the deck of the galley. It had a heavy hinged lid and screwed clamps to keep the lid in position. " This might interest you, Dr. Carpenter. Guess what?"

" A pressure cooker?"

" Looks like it, doesn't it? This is our garbage disposal unit. In the old days when a submarine had to surface every few hours garbage disposal was no problem, you just tipped the stuff over the side. But when you spend weeks on end cruising at three hundred feet you can't just walk up to the upper deck and tip the waste over the side : garbage disposal becomes quite a problem. This tube goes right down to the bottom of the *Dolphin*. There's a heavy watertight door at the lower end corresponding to this one, with interlocking controls which made it impossible for both doors to be open at the same time—it would be curtains for the *Dolphin* if they were. Sam here, or one of his henchmen, sticks the garbage into nylon mesh or polythene bags, weighs them with bricks——"

" Bricks, you said?"

" Bricks. Sam, how many bricks aboard this ship?"

" Just over a thousand at the latest count, Doc."

" Regular builder's yard, aren't we?" Benson grinned. " Those bricks are to ensure that the garbage bags sink to the bottom of the sea and not float to the surface—even in peacetime we don't want to give our position away to anyone. In go three or four bags, the top door is clamped shut and the bags pumped out under pressure. Then the outer door is closed again. Simple."

" Yes." For some reason or other this odd contraption had a curious fascination for me. Days later I was to remember my inexplicable interest in it and wonder whether, after all, I wasn't becoming psychic with advancing years.

" It's not worth all that attention," Benson said good-humouredly. " Just an up-to-date version of the old rubbish chute. Come on, a long way to go yet."

He led the way from the galley to a heavy steel door set in a transverse bulkhead. Eight massive clips to release, then replace after we had passed through the doorway.

" The for'ard torpedo storage room." Benson's voice was

285

lowered, for at least half of the sixteen or so bunks that lined the bulkheads or were jammed up close to the torpedoes and racks were occupied and every man occupying them was sound asleep. "Only six torpedoes as you can see. Normally there's stowage for twelve plus another six constantly kept loaded in the torpedo tubes. But those six are all we have just now. We had a malfunction in two of our torpedoes of the newest and more or less untested radio-controlled type —during the Nato exercises just ended—and Admiral Garvie ordered the lot removed for inspection when we got back to the Holy Loch. The *Hunley*, that's our depot ship, carries experts for working on those things. However, they were no sooner taken off yesterday morning than this Drift Station operation came our way and Commander Swanson insisted on having at least six of them put back on straight away." Benson grinned. "If there's one thing a submarine skipper hates it's putting to sea without his torpedoes. He feels he might just as well stay at home."

"Those torpedoes are still not operational?"

"I don't know whether they are or not. Our sleeping warriors here will do their best to find out when they come to."

"Why aren't they working on them now?"

"Because before our return to the Clyde they were working on them for nearly sixty hours non-stop trying to find out the cause of the malfunction—and if it existed in the other torpedoes. I told the skipper that if he wanted to blow up the *Dolphin* as good a way as any was to let those torpedo-men keep on working—they were starting to stagger around like zombies and a zombie is the last person you want to have working on the highly-complicated innards of a torpedo. So he pulled them off."

He walked the length of the gleaming torpedoes and halted before another steel door in a cross bulkhead. He opened this, and beyond, four feet away, was another such heavy door set in another such bulkhead. The sills were about eighteen inches above deck level.

"You don't take many chances in building these boats, do you?" I asked. "It's like breaking into the Bank of England."

"Being a nuclear sub doesn't mean that we're not as

286

vulnerable to underwater hazards as the older ships," Benson said. "We are. Ships have been lost before because the collision bulkhead gave way. The hull of the *Dolphin* can withstand terrific pressures, but a relatively minor tap from a sharp-edged object can rip us wide like an electric can-opener. The biggest danger is surface collision which nearly always happens at the bows. So, to make doubly sure in the event of a bows collision, we have those double collision bulkheads—the first submarine ever to have them. Makes fore and aft movement here a bit difficult but you've no idea how much more soundly we all sleep at night."

He closed the after door behind him and opened the for'ard one: we found ourselves in the for'ard torpedo room, a narrow cramped compartment barely long enough to permit torpedoes to be loaded or withdrawn from their tubes. Those tubes, with their heavy-hinged rear doors, were arranged close together in two vertical banks of three. Overhead were the loading rails with heavy chain tackles attached. And that was all. No bunks in here and I didn't wonder: I wouldn't have liked to be the one to sleep for'ard of those collision bulkheads.

We began to work our way aft and had reached the mess hall when a sailor came up and said that the captain wanted to see me. I followed him up the wide central stairway into the control room, Dr. Benson a few paces behind to show that he wasn't being too inquisitive. Commander Swanson was waiting for me by the door of the radio room.

"Morning, Doctor. Slept well?"

"Fifteen hours. What do you think? And breakfasted even better. What's up, Commander." Something was up, that was for sure: for once, Commander Swanson wasn't smiling.

"Message coming through about Drift Station Zebra. Has to be decoded first but that should take minutes only." Decoding or not, it seemed to me that Swanson already had a fair idea of the content of that message.

"When did we surface?" I asked. A submarine loses radio contact as soon as it submerges.

"Not since we left the Clyde. We are close on three hundred feet down right now."

287

"This is a *radio* message that's coming through?"

"What else? Times have changed. We still have to surface to transmit but we can receive down to our maximum depth. Somewhere in Connecticut is the worlds largest radio transmitter using an extremely low frequency which can contact us at this depth far more easily than any other radio station can contact a surface ship. While we're waiting, come and meet the drivers."

He introduced me to some of his control centre crew—as with Benson it seemed to be a matter of complete indifference to him whether it was officer or enlisted man—finally stopped by an officer sitting just aft of the periscope stand, a youngster who looked as if he should still be in high school. "Will Raeburn," Swanson said. "Normally we pay no attention to him but after we move under the ice he becomes the most important man on the ship. Our navigation officer. Are we lost, Will?"

"We're just there, Captain." He pointed to a tiny pin-point of light on the Norwegian Sea chart spread out below the glass on the plotting-table. "Gyro and sins are checking to a hair."

"Sins?" I said.

"You may well look surprised, Dr. Carpenter," Swanson said. "Lieutenant Raeburn here is far too young to have any sins. He is referring to S.I.N.S.—Ship's Inertial Navigational System—a device once used for guiding intercontinental missiles and now adapted for submarine use, specifically nuclear submarines. No point in my elaborating, Will's ready to talk your head off about it if he manages to corner you." He glanced at the chart position. "Are we getting along quickly enough to suit you, Doctor?"

"I still don't believe it," I said.

"We cleared the Holy Loch a bit earlier than I expected, before seven," Swanson admitted. "I had intended to carry out some slow-time dives to adjust trim—but it wasn't necessary. Even the lack of twelve torpedoes up in the nose didn't make her as stern-heavy as I'd expected. She's so damned big that a few tons more or less here or there doesn't seem to make any difference to her. So we just came haring on up——"

He broke off to accept a signal sheet from a sailor, and

288

read through it slowly, taking his time about it. Then he jerked his head, walked to a quiet corner of the control centre and faced me as I came up to him. He still wasn't smiling.

" I'm sorry," he said. " Major Halliwell, the commandant of the Drift Station—you said last night he was a very close friend of yours?"

I felt my mouth begin to go dry. I nodded, took the message from him. It read : " A further radio message, very broken and difficult to decipher, was received 0945 Greenwich Mean Time from Drift Ice Station Zebra by the British trawler *Morning Star,* the vessel that picked up the previous broadcast. Message stated that Major Halliwell, Officer Commanding, and three others unnamed critically injured or dead, no indication who or how many of the four are dead. Others, number again unknown, suffering severely from burns and exposure. Some message about food and fuel, atmospheric conditions and weakness in transmission made it quite indecipherable. Understood from very garbled signal that survivors in one hut, unable to move because of weather. Word ' icestorm ' clearly picked up. Apparently details of wind speed and temperature but unable to make out.

" *Morning Star* several times attempted contact Drift Station Zebra immediately afterwards. No acknowledgment.

" *Morning Star,* at request of British Admiralty, has abandoned fishing grounds and is moving closer in to Barrier to act as listening post. Message ends."

I folded the paper and handed it back to Swanson. He said again : " Sorry about this, Carpenter."

" Critically injured or dead," I said. " In a burnt-out station on the ice-cap in winter, what's the difference?" My voice fell upon my ears as the voice of another man, a voice flat and lifeless, a voice empty of all emotion. " Johnny Halliwell and three of his men. Johnny Halliwell. Not the kind of man you would meet often, Commander. A remarkable man. Left school at fifteen when his parents died to devote himself to the support of a brother eight years younger than himself. He slaved, he scraped, he sacrificed, he devoted many of the best years of his life to doing everything for his young brother, including putting him through a six-year University course. Not till then did he think of himself, not till then did he get married. He leaves a lovely wife and three marvellous kids. Two nieces and a nephew not yet six months old."

"Two nieces——" He broke off and stared at me. "Good God, your brother? *Your* brother?" He didn't, for the moment seem to find anything peculiar in the difference of surname.

I nodded silently. Young Lieutenant Raeburn approached us, an odd expression of anxiety on his face, but Swanson abruptly waved him away without seeming even to glance in his direction. He shook his head slowly and was still shaking it when I said abruptly: "He's tough. He may be one of the survivors. He may live. We must get Drift Station Zebra's position. We *must* get it."

"Maybe they haven't got it themselves," Swanson said. You could see he was grateful for something to talk about. "It *is* a drifting station, remember. The weather being what it is, it may have been days since they got their last fixes—and for all we know their sextants, chronometers and radio direction finders have been lost in the fire."

"They must know what their latest fix was, even although it was a week ago. They must have a fairly accurate idea of the speed and direction of their drift. They'll be able to provide approximate data. The *Morning Star* must be told to keep transmitting non-stop with a continuous request for their position. If you surface now, can you contact the *Morning Star*?"

"I doubt it. The trawler must be the best part of a thousand miles north of us. His receiver wouldn't be big enough to pull us in—which is another way of saying that our transmitter is too small."

"The B.B.C. have plenty of transmitters that are big enough. So have the Admiralty. Please ask one or other to contact the *Morning Star* and ask it to make a continuous send for Zebra's position."

"They could do that themselves direct."

"Sure they could. But they couldn't hear the reply. The *Morning Star* can—if there's any reply. And she's getting closer to them all the time."

"We'll surface now," Swanson nodded. He turned away from the chart table we'd been standing beside and headed for the diving stand. As he passed the plotting table he said to the navigator: "What was it you wanted, Will?"

Lieutenant Raeburn turned his back on me and lowered his voice, but my hearing has always been a little abnormal. He whispered: "Did you see his face, Captain? I thought he was going to haul off and clobber you one."

"I thought the same thing myself," Swanson murmured. "For a moment. But I think I just happened to be in his line of vision, that's all."

I went forward to my cabin and lay down in the cot.

III

"There it is, then," said Swanson. "That's the Barrier."

The *Dolphin*, heading due north, her great cylindrical bulk at one moment completely submerged, the next showing clear as she rolled heavily through the steep quartering seas, was making less than three knots through the water, the great nuclear-powered engines providing just enough thrust to the big twin eight-foot propellers to provide steerage way and no more: thirty feet below where we stood on the bridge the finest sonar equipment in the world was ceaselessly probing the waters all around us but even so Swanson was taking no chances on the effects of collision with a drifting ice-block. The noonday Arctic sky was so overcast that the light was no better than that of late dusk. The bridge thermometer showed the sea temperature as 28° F., the air temperature as −16° F. The gale-force wind from the north-east was snatching the tops off the rolling steel-grey waves and subjecting the steep-walled sides of the great conning-tower—sail, the crew called it—to the ceaseless battering of a bullet-driven spray that turned to solid ice even as it struck. The cold was intense.

Shivering uncontrollably, wrapped in heavy duffel-coat and oilskins and huddled against the illusory shelter of the canvas wind-dodger, I followed the line of Swanson's pointing arm: even above the high thin shrill whine of the wind and the drum-fire of the flying spray against the sail, I could hear the violent chattering of his teeth. Less than two miles

291

away a long, thin, greyish-white line, at that distance apparently smooth and regular, seemed to stretch the entire width of the northern horizon. I'd seen it before and it wasn't much to look at but it was a sight a man never got used to, not because of itself but because of what it represented, the beginning of the polar ice-cap that covered the top of the world, at this time of year a solid compacted mass of ice that stretched clear from where we lay right across to Alaska on the other side of the world. And we had to go under that mass. We had to go under it to find men hundreds of miles away, men who might be already dying, men who might be already dead. Who probably were dead. Men, dying or dead, whom we had to seek out by guess and by God in that great wasteland of ice stretching out endlessly before us, for we did not know where they were.

The relayed radio message we had received just forty-nine hours previously had been the last. Since then, there had been only silence. The trawler *Morning Star* had been sending almost continuously in the intervening two days, trying to raise Drift Station Zebra, but out of that bleak desert of ice to the north had come nothing but silence. No word, no signal, no faintest whisper of sound had come out of that desolation.

Eighteen hours previously the Russian atomic-engined *Dvina* had reached the Barrier and had started on an all-out and desperate attempt to smash its way into the heart of the ice-cap. In this early stage of winter the ice was neither so thick nor so compacted as it would be at the time of its maximum density, in March, and the very heavily armoured and powerfully engined *Dvina* was reputed to be able to break through ice up to a thickness of eighteen feet : given fair conditions, the *Dvina* was widely believed to be capable of battering its way to the North Pole. But the conditions of the rafted ice had proved abnormal to a degree and the attempt a hopeless one. The *Dvina* had managed to crash its way over forty miles into the ice-cap before being permanently stopped by a thick wall of rafter ice over twenty feet in height and probably more than a hundred deep. The *Dvina,* according to reports, had sustained heavy damage to its bows and was still in the process of extricating itself, with the greatest difficulty, from the pack. A very gallant effort that had achieved nothing except an improvement in East-West relations to an extent undreamed of for many years.

Nor had the Russian efforts stopped there. Both they and the Americans had made several flights over the area with front-line long-range bombers. Through the deep overcast and driving ice- and snow-filled winds those planes had criss-crossed the suspected area a hundred times, searching with their fantastically accurate radar. But not one single radar sighting had been reported. Various reasons had been put forward to explain the failure, especially the failure of the Strategic Air Command's B52 bomber whose radar was known to be easily capable of picking out a hut against contrasting background from ten thousand feet and in pitch darkness. It had been suggested that the huts were no longer there: that the radar's eye was unable to distinguish between an ice-sheathed hut and the thousands of ice-hummocks which dot the polar cap in winter; and that they had been searching in the wrong area in the first place. The most probable explanation was that the radar waves had been blurred and deflated by the dense clouds of ice-spicules blowing over the area. Whatever the reason, Drift Ice Station Zebra remained as silent as if no life had ever been there, as lost as if it had never existed.

"There's no percentage in staying up here and getting frozen to death." Commander Swanson's voice was a half-shout, it had to be to make him heard. "If we're going under that ice, we might as well go now." He turned his back to the wind and stared out to the west where a big broad-beamed trawler was rolling heavily and sluggishly in the seas less than a quarter of a mile away. The *Morning Star*, which had closed right up to the edge of the ice-pack over the last two days, listening, waiting, and all in vain, was about to return to Hull : her fuel reserves were running low.

"Make a signal," Swanson said to the seaman by his side. " 'We are about to dive and proceed under the ice. We do not expect to emerge for minimum four days, are prepared to remain maximum fourteen.' " He turned to me and said : "If we can't find them in that time . . ." and left the sentence unfinished.

293

I nodded, and he went on: "'Many thanks for your splendid co-operation. Good luck and a safe trip home.'" As the signalman's lamp started chattering out its message, he said wonderingly: "Do those fishermen trawl up in the Arctic the entire winter?"

"They do."

"The whole winter. Fifteen minutes and I'm about dead. Just a bunch of decadent Limeys, that's what they are." A lamp aboard the *Morning Star* flickered for some seconds and Swanson said: "What reply?"

"'Mind your heads under that ice. Good luck and good-bye.'"

"Everybody below," Swanson said. As the signalman began to strip the canvas dodger I dropped down a ladder into a small compartment beneath, wriggled through a hatch and down a second ladder to the pressure hull of the submarine, another hatch, a third ladder and then I was on the control deck of the *Dolphin*. Swanson and the signalman followed, then last of all Hansen, who had to close the two heavy watertight doors above.

Commander Swanson's diving technique would have proved a vast disappointment to those brought up on a diet of movie submarines. No frenzied activity, no tense steely-eyed men hovering over controls, no Tannoy calls of "Dive, dive, dive," no blaring of klaxons. Swanson reached down a steel-spring microphone, said quietly: "This is the captain. We are about to move under the ice. Diving now," hung up and said: "Three hundred feet."

The chief electronics technician leisurely checked the rows of lights indicating all hatches, surface openings and valves closed to the sea. The disc lights were out: the slot lights burned brightly. Just as leisurely he re-checked them, glanced at Swanson and said: "Straight line shut, sir." Swanson nodded. Air hissed loudly out of the ballast tanks, and that was it. We were on our way. It was about as wildly exciting as watching a man push a wheelbarrow. And there was something oddly reassuring about it all.

Ten minutes later Swanson came up to me. In the past two days I'd come to know Commander Swanson fairly well, like him a lot and respect him tremendously. The crew had complete and implicit faith in him. I was beginning

294

to have the same thing. He was a kindly genial man with a vast knowledge of every aspect of submarining, a remarkable eye for detail, an even more remarkably acute mind and an imperturbability that remained absolute under all conditions. Hansen, his executive officer and clearly no respecter of persons, had said flatly that Swanson was the best submarine officer in the Navy. I hoped he was right, that was the kind of man I wanted around in conditions like those.

"We're about to move under the ice now, Dr. Carpenter," he said. "How do you feel about it?"

"I'd feel better if I could see where we were going."

"We can see," he said. "We've the best eyes in the world aboard the *Dolphin*. We've got eyes that look down, around, ahead and straight up. Our downward eye is the fathometer or echo-sounder that tells us just how deep the water below our keel is—and as we have about five thousand feet of water below our keel at this particular spot we're hardly likely to bump into underwater projections and its use right now is purely a formality. But no responsible navigation officer would ever think of switching it off. We have two sonar eyes for looking around and ahead, one sweeping the ship, another searching out a fifteen-degree path on either side of the bow. Sees everything, hears everything. You drop a spanner on a warship twenty miles away and we know all about it. Fact. Again it seems purely a formality. The sonar is searching for underwater ice stalactites forced down by the pressure of rafted ice above, but in five trips under the ice and two to the Pole I've never seen underwater stalactites or ridges deeper than 200 feet, and we're at 300 feet now. But we still keep them on."

"You might bump into a whale?" I suggested.

"We might bump into another submarine." He wasn't smiling. "And that would be the end of both of us. What with the Russian and our own nuclear submarines busy crisscrossing to and fro across the top of the world the underside of the polar ice-cap is getting more like Times Square every day."

"But surely the chances——"

"What are the chances of mid-air collision to the only two aircraft occupying ten thousand square miles of sky? On paper, they don't exist. There have been three such collisions ms year already. So we keep the sonar pinging. But the really important eye, when you're under the ice, is the one that looks up. Come and have a squint at it."

He led the way to the after starboard end of the control room where Dr. Benson and another man were busy studying a glassed-in eye-level machine which outwardly consisted of a seven-inch-wide moving ribbon of paper and an inked stylus that was tracing a narrow straight black line along it. Benson was engrossed in adjusting some of the calibrated controls.

" The surface fathometer," Swanson said. " Better known as the ice-machine. It's not really Dr. Benson's machine at all, we have two trained operators aboard, but as we see no way of separating him from it without actually court-martialling him, we take the easy way out and let him be." Benson grinned, but his eye didn't leave the line traced by the stylus. " Same principle as the echo-sounding machine, it just bounces an echo back from the ice—when there is any. That thin black line you see means open water above. When we move under the ice the stylus has an added vertical motion which not only indicates the presence of ice but also gives us its thickness."

" Ingenious," I said.

" It's more than that. Under the ice it can be life or death for the *Dolphin*. It certainly means life or death for Drift Station Zebra. If we ever get its position we can't get at it until we break through the ice and this is the only machine that can tell us where the ice is thinnest."

" No open water at this time of year? No leads?"

" Polynyas, we call them. None. Mind you, the ice-pack is never static, not even in winter, and surface pressure changes can very occasionally tear the ice apart and expose open water. With air temperatures such as you get in winter you can guess how long the open water stays in a liquid condition. There's a skin of ice on it in five minutes, an inch in an hour and a foot inside two days. If we get to one of those frozen over polynyas inside, say, three days, we've a fair chance of breaking through."

" With the conning-tower?"

" That's it. The sail. All new nuclear subs have specially

strengthened sails designed for one purpose only—breaking through Arctic ice. Even so we have to go pretty gently as the shock, of course, is transmitted to the pressure hull."

I thought about this a bit then said: "What happens to the pressure hull if you come up too fast—as I understand may happen with a sudden change in salinity and sea temperature—and you find out at the last minute that you've drifted away from the indicated area of thin ice and have ten solid feet of the stuff above you?"

"That's it," he said. "Like you say, it's the last minute. Don't even think about such things, far less talk about them: I can't afford to have nightmares on this job." I looked at him closely, but he wasn't smiling any more. He lowered his voice. "I don't honestly think that there is one member of the crew of the *Dolphin* who doesn't get a little bit scared when we move in under the ice. I know I do. I think this is the finest ship in the world, Dr. Carpenter, but there are still a hundred things that can go wrong with it and if anything happens to the reactor or the steam turbines or the electrical generators—then we're already in our coffin and the lid screwed down. The ice-pack above is the coffin lid. In the open sea most of those things don't matter a damn—we just surface or go to snorkel depth and proceed on our diesels. But for diesels you need air—and there's no air under the ice-pack. So if anything happens we either find a polynya to surface in, one chance in ten thousand at this time of year, before our standby battery packs up or—well, that's it."

"This is all very encouraging," I said.

"Isn't it?" He smiled, none too soon for me. "It'll never happen. What's the worthy Benson making all the racket about?"

"Here it is," Benson called. "The first drift-block. And another. And another! Come and have a look, Doctor."

I had a look. The stylus, making a faint soft hissing sound, was no longer tracing out a continuously horizontal line but was moving rapidly up and down across the paper, tracing out the outline of the block of ice passing astern above us. Another thin straight line, more agitated vertical movements of the stylus, and again another block of ice had gone.

297

Even as I watched the number of thin horizontal lines became fewer and fewer and shorter and shorter until eventually they disappeared altogether.

" That's it, then," Swanson nodded. " We'll take her deep now, real deep, and open up all the stops."

When Commander Swanson had said he was going to hurry, he'd meant every word of it. In the early hours of the following morning I was awakened from a deep sleep by a heavy hand on my shoulder. I opened my eyes, blinked against the glare of the overhead light then saw Lieutenant Hansen.

" Sorry about the beauty sleep, Doc," he said cheerfully. " But this is it."

" This is what?" I said irritably.

" 85° 35′ north, 21° 20′ east—the last estimated position of Drift Station Zebra. At least, the last estimated position with estimated correction for polar drift."

" Already?" I glanced at my watch, not believing it. " We're there already?"

" We have not," Hansen said modestly, " been idling The skipper suggests you come along and watch us at work."

" I'll be right with you." When and if the *Dolphin* managed to break through the ice and began to try her one in a million chance of contacting Drift Station Zebra, I wanted to be there.

We left Hansen's cabin and had almost reached the control room when I lurched, staggered and would have fallen but for a quick grab at a handrail that ran along one side of the passageway. I hung on grimly as the *Dolphin* banked violently sideways and round like a fighter plane in a tight turn. No submarine in my experience had ever been able to begin to behave even remotely in that fashion. I understood now the reasons for the safety belts on the diving control seats.

" What the hell's up?" I said to Hansen. " Avoiding some underwater obstruction ahead?"

" Must be a possible polynya. Some place where the ice is thin, anyway. As soon as we spot a possible like that we come around like a chicken chasing its own tail just so we don't

298

miss it. It makes us very popular with the crew, especially when they're drinking coffee or soup."

We passed into the control room. Commander Swanson, flanked by the navigator and another man, was bent over the plotting table, examining something intently. Farther aft a man at the surface fathometer was reading out ice thickness figures in a quiet unemotional voice. Commander Swanson looked up from the chart.

"Morning, Doctor. John, I think we may have something here."

Hansen crossed to the plot and peered at it. There didn't seem to be much to peer at—a tiny pin-point of light shining through the glass top of the plot and a squared sheet of chart paper marked by a most unseamanlike series of wavering black lines traced out by a man with a pencil following the track of the tiny moving light. There were three red crosses superimposed on the paper, two very close together, and just as Hansen was examining the paper the crewman manning the ice-machine—Dr. Benson's enthusiasm for his toy did not, it appeared, extend to the middle of the night—called out "Mark!" Immediately the black pencil was exchanged for a red and a fourth cross made.

"'Think' and 'may' are just about right, Captain," Hansen said. "It looks awfully narrow to me."

"It looks the same way to me, too," Swanson admitted. "But it's the first break in the heavy ice that we've had in an hour, almost. And the farther north we go, the poorer our chances. Let's give it a go. Speed?"

"One knot," Raeburn said.

"All back one-third," Swanson said. No sharp imperatives, not ever, in the way Swanson gave his orders, more a quiet and conversational suggestion, but there was no mistaking the speed with which one of the crewmen strapped into the diving-stand bucket seat leaned forward to telegraph the order to the engine-room. "Left full rudder."

Swanson bent over to check the plot, closely watching the tiny pin-point of light and tracing pencil move back towards the approximate centre of the elongated quadrangle formed by the four red crosses. "All stop," he went on. "Rudder amidships." A pause then: "All ahead one-third. So. All stop."

299

speed zero," Raeburn said.

" 120 feet," Swanson said to the diving officer. " But gently, gently."

A strong steady hum echoed in the control centre. I asked Hansen : " Blowing ballast?"

He shook his head. " Just pumping the stuff out. Gives a far more precise control of rising speed and makes it easier to keep the sub on an even keel. Bringing a stopped sub up on a dead even keel is no trick for beginners. Conventional subs never try this sort of thing."

The pumps stopped. There came the sound of water flooding back into the tanks as the diving officer slowed up the rate of ascent. The sound faded.

" Secure flooding," the diving officer said. " Steady on 120 feet."

" Up periscope," Swanson said to the crewman by his side. An overhead lever was engaged and we could hear the hiss of high-pressure oil as the hydraulic piston began to lift the starboard periscope off its seating. The gleaming cylinder rose slowly against the pressure of the water outside until finally the foot of the periscope cleared its well. Swanson opened the hinged handgrips and peered through the eyepiece.

" What does he expect to see in the middle of the night at this depth?" I asked Hansen.

" Never can tell. It's rarely completely dark, as you know Maybe a moon, maybe only stars—but even starlight will show as a faint glow through the ice—if the ice is thin enough."

" What's the thickness of the ice above, in this rectangle?"

" The sixty-four thousand dollar question," Hansen admitted, " and the answer is that we don't know. To keep that ice-machine to a reasonable size the graph scale has to be very small. Anything between four and forty inches. Four inches we go through like the icing on a wedding cake : forty inches and we get a very sore head indeed." He nodded across to Swanson. " Doesn't look so good. That grip he's twisting is to tilt the periscope lens upwards and that button is for focusing. Means he's having trouble in finding anything."

Swanson straightened. " Black as the earl of hell's waist-

300

coat," he said conversationally. " Switch on hull and sail floodlights."

He stooped and looked again. For a few seconds only. " Pea-soup. Thick and yellow and strong. Can't see a thing. Let's have the camera, shall we?"

I looked at Hansen, who nodded to a white screen that had just been unshuttered on the opposite bulkhead. " All mod cons, Doc. Closed circuit TV. Camera is deck mounted under toughened glass and can be remotely controlled to look up or round."

"You could do with a new camera, couldn't you?" The TV screen was grey, fuzzy, featureless.

" Best that money can buy," Hansen said. " It's the water. Under certain conditions of temperature and salinity it becomes almost completely opaque when floodlit. Like driving into a heavy fog with your headlights full on."

" Floodlights off," Swanson said. The screen became quite blank. " Floodlights on." The same drifting misty grey as before. Swanson sighed and turned to Hansen. " Well, John?"

" If I were paid for imagining things," Hansen said carefully, " I could imagine I see the top of the sail in that left corner. Pretty murky out there, Captain. Heigh-ho for the old blind man's buff, is that it?"

" Russian roulette, I prefer to call it." Swanson had the clear unworried face of a man contemplating a Sunday afternoon in a deck-chair. " Are we holding position?"

" I don't know." Raeburn looked up from the plot. " It's difficult to be sure."

" Sanders?" This to the man at the ice-machine.

" Thin ice, sir. Still thin ice."

" Keep calling. Down periscope." He folded the handles up and turned to the diving officer. " Take her up like we were carrying a crate of eggs atop the sail and didn't want to crack even one of them."

The pumps started again. I looked around the control room. Swanson excepted, everyone was quiet and still and keyed-up. Raeburn's face was beaded with sweat and Sanders's voice was too calm and impersonal by half as he kept repeating: " Thin ice, thin ice," in a low monotone. You could reach out and touch the tension in the air. I said quietly to Hansen:

301

" Nobody seems very happy. There's still a hundred feet to go."

" There's forty feet," Hansen said shortly. " Readings are taken from keel level and there's sixty feet between the keel and the top of the sail. Forty feet minus the thickness of the ice—and maybe a razor-sharp or needle-pointed stalactite sticking down ready to skewer the *Dolphin* through the middle You know what that means?"

" That it's time I started getting worried too?"

Hansen smiled, but he wasn't feeling like smiling. Neither was I, not any more.

" Ninety feet," the diving officer said.

" Thin ice, thin ice," Sanders intoned.

" Switch off the deck flood, leave the sail flood on," Swanson said. " And keep that camera moving. Sonar?"

" All clear," the sonar operator reported. " All clear all round." A pause, then : " No, hold it, hold it ! Contact dead astern ! "

" How close?" Swanson asked quickly.

" Too close to say. Very close."

" She's jumping !" the diving officer called out sharply. " 80, 75." The *Dolphin* had hit a layer of colder water or extra salinity.

" Heavy ice, heavy ice !" Sanders called out urgently.

" Flood emergency !" Swanson ordered—and this time it was an order.

I felt the sudden build-up of air pressure as the diving officer vented the negative tank and tons of sea-water poured into the emergency diving tank, but it was too late. With a shuddering jarring smash that sent us staggering the *Dolphin* crashed violently into the ice above, glass tinkled, lights went out and the submarine started falling like a stone.

" Blow negative to the mark !" the diving officer called. High pressure air came boiling into the negative tank—at our rate of falling we would have been flattened by the sea-pressure before the pumps could even have begun to cope with the huge extra ballast load we had taken aboard in seconds. Two hundred feet, two hundred and fifty and we were still falling. Nobody spoke, everybody just stood or sat in a frozen position staring at the diving stand. It

302

required no gift for telepathy to know the thought in every mind. It was obvious that the *Dolphin* had been struck aft by some underwater pressure ridge at the same instant as the sail had hit the heavy ice above : if the *Dolphin* had been holed aft this descent wasn't going to stop until the pressure of a million tons of water had crushed and flattened the hull and in a flicker of time snuffed out the life of every man inside it.

" Three hundred feet," the diving officer called out. " Three fifty—and she's slowing ! She's slowing."

The *Dolphin* was still falling, sluggishly passing the four-hundred-foot mark, when Rawlings appeared in the control room, tool-kit in one hand, a crate of assorted lamps in the other.

" It's unnatural," he said. He appeared to be addressing the shattered lamp above the plot which he had immediately begun to repair. " Contrary to the laws of nature, I've always maintained. Mankind was never meant to probe beneath the depths of the ocean. Mark my words, those new-fangled inventions will come to a bad end."

" So will you, if you don't keep quiet," Commander Swanson said acidly. But there was no reprimand in his face, he appreciated as well as any of us the therapeutic breath of fresh air that Rawlings had brought into that tension-laden atmosphere. " Holding?" he went on to the diving officer.

The diving officer raised a finger and grinned. Swanson nodded, swung the coiled-spring microphone in front of him. " Captain here," he said calmly. " Sorry about that bump. Report damage at once."

A green light flashed in the panel of a box beside him. Swanson touched a switch and a loudspeaker in the deck-head crackled.

" Manœuvring room here." The manœuvring room was in the after end of the upper level engine-room, towards the stern. " Hit was directly above us here. We could do with a box of candles and some of the dials and gauges are out of kilter. But we still got a roof over our heads."

" Thank you, Lieutenant. You can cope?"

" Sure we can."

Swanson pressed another switch. " Stern room?"

303

" We still attached to the ship?" a cautious voice inquired.

" You're still attached to the ship," Swanson assured him.
" Anything to report?"

" Only that there's going to be an awful lot of dirty laundry
by the time we get back to Scotland. The washing-machine's
had a kind of fit."

Swanson smiled and switched off. His face was untroubled,
he must have had a special sweat-absorbing mechanism on
his face, I felt I could have done with a bath towel. He
said to Hansen : " That was bad luck. A combination of
a current where a current had no right to be, a temperature
inversion where a temperature inversion had no right to be,
and a pressure ridge where we least expected it. Not to mention the damned opacity of the water. What's required is a
few circuits until we know this polynya like the backs of
our hands, a small offset to allow for drift and a little pre-
cautionary flooding as we approach the ninety-foot mark."

" Yes, sir. That's what's required. Point is, what are we
going to do?"

" Just that. Take her up and try again."

I had my pride so I refrained from mopping my brow.
They took her up and tried again. At 200 feet and for
fifteen minutes Swanson juggled propellers and rudder till
he had the outline of the frozen polynya above as accurately
limned on the plot as he could ever expect to have it.
Then he positioned the *Dolphin* just outside one of the
boundary lines and gave an order for a slow ascent.

" One twenty feet," the diving officer said. " One hundred
ten."

" Heavy ice," Sanders intoned. " Still heavy ice."

Sluggishly the *Dolphin* continued to rise. Next time in
the control room, I promised myself, I wouldn't forget that
bath towel. Swanson said : " If we've overestimated the
speed of the drift, there's going to be another bump I'm
afraid." He turned to Rawlings who was still busily repairing lights. " If I were you, I'd suspend operations for the
present. You may have to start all over again in a moment
and we don't carry all that number of spares aboard."

" One hundred feet," the diving officer said. He didn't
sound as unhappy as his face looked.

" The water's clearing," Hansen said suddenly. " Look."

304

The water had cleared, not dramatically so, but enough. We could see the top corner of the sail clearly outlined on the TV screen. And then, suddenly, we could see something else again, heavy ugly ridged ice not a dozen feet above the sail.

Water flooding into the tanks. The diving officer didn't have to be told what to do, we'd gone up like an express lift the first time we'd hit a different water layer and once like that was enough in the life of any submarine.

"Ninety feet," he reported. "Still rising." More water flooded in, then the sound died away. "She's holding. Just under ninety feet."

"Keep her there." Swanson stared at the TV screen. "We're drifting clear and into the polynya—I hope."

"Me too," Hansen said. "There can't be more than a couple of feet between the top of the sail and that damned ugly stuff."

"There isn't much room," Swanson acknowledged. "Sanders?"

"Just a moment, sir. The graph looks kinda funny—no, we're clear." He couldn't keep the excitement out of his voice. "Thin ice!"

I looked at the screen. He was right. I could see the vertical edge of a wall of ice move slowly across the screen, exposing clear water above.

"Gently, now, gently," Swanson said. "And keep the camera on the ice wall at the side, then straight up, turn about."

The pumps began to throb again. The ice wall, less than ten yards away, began to drift slowly down past us.

"Eighty-five feet," the diving officer reported. "Eighty."

"No hurry," Swanson said. "We're sheltered from that drift by now."

"Seventy-five feet." The pumps stopped, and water began to flood into the tanks. "Seventy." The *Dolphin* was almost stopped now, drifting upwards as gently as thistledown. The camera switched upwards, and we could see the top corner of the sail clearly outlined with a smooth ceiling of ice floating down to meet it. More water gurgled into the tanks, the top of the sail met the ice with a barely perceptible bump and the *Dolphin* came to rest.

"Beautifully done," Swanson said warmly to the diving officer. "Let's try give that ice a nudge. Are we slewing?"

"Bearing constant."

Swanson nodded. The pumps hummed, pouring out water, lightening ship, steadily increasing positive buoyancy. The ice stayed where it was. More time passed, more water pumped out, and still nothing happened. I said softly to Hansen: "Why doesn't he blow the main ballast? You'd get a few hundred tons of positive buoyancy in next to no time and even if that ice is forty inches thick it couldn't survive all that pressure at a concentrated point."

"Neither could the *Dolphin*," Hansen said grimly. "With a suddenly induced big positive buoyancy like that, once she broke through she'd go up like a cork from a champagne bottle. The pressure hull might take it, I don't know, but sure as little apples the rudder would be squashed flat as a piece of tin. Do you want to spend what little's left of your life travelling in steadily decreasing circles under the polar ice-cap?"

I didn't want to spend what little was left of my life in travelling in steadily decreasing circles under the ice-cap so I kept quiet. I watched Swanson as he walked across to the diving stand and studied the banked dials in silence for some seconds. I was beginning to become a little apprehensive about what Swanson would do next: I was beginning to realise, and not slowly either, that he was a lad who didn't give up very easily.

"That's enough of that lot," he said to the diving officer. "If we go through now with all this pressure behind us we'll be airborne. This ice is even thicker than we thought. We've tried the long steady' shove and it hasn't worked. A sharp tap is obviously what is needed. Flood her down, but gently, to eighty feet or so, a good sharp whiff of air into the ballast tanks and we'll give our well-known imitation of a bull at a gate."

Whoever had installed the 240-ton air-conditioning unit in the *Dolphin* should have been prosecuted, it just wasn't working any more. The air was very hot and stuffy—what little there was of it, that was. I looked around cautiously and saw that everyone else appeared to be suffering from this same shortage of air, all except Swanson, who seemed to

306

carry his own built-in oxygen cylinder around with him. I hoped Swanson was keeping in mind the fact that the *Dolphin* had cost 120 million dollars to build. Hansen's narrowed eyes held a definite core of worry and even the usually imperturbable Rawlings was rubbing a bristly blue chin with a hand the size and shape of a shovel. In the deep silence after Swanson had finished speaking the scraping noise sounded unusually loud, then was lost in the noise of water flooding into the tanks.

We stared at the screen. Water continued to pour into the tanks until we could see a gap appear between the top of the sail and the ice. The pumps started up, slowly, to control the speed of descent. On the screen, the cone of light thrown on to the underside of the ice by the flood-lamp grew fainter and larger as we dropped, then remained stationary, neither moving nor growing in size. We had stopped.

"Now," said Swanson. "Before that current gets us again."

There came the hissing roar of compressed air under high pressure entering the ballast tanks. The *Dolphin* started to move sluggishly upwards while we watched the cone of light on the ice slowly narrow and brighten.

"More air," Swanson said.

We were rising faster now, closing the gap to the ice all too quickly for my liking. Fifteen feet, twelve feet, ten feet.

"More air," Swanson said.

I braced myself, one hand on the plot, the other on an overhead grab bar. On the screen, the ice was rushing down to meet us. Suddenly the picture quivered and danced, the *Dolphin* shuddered, jarred and echoed hollowly along its length, more lights went out, the picture came back on the screen, the sail was still lodged below the ice, then the *Dolphin* trembled and lurched and the deck pressed against our feet like an ascending elevator. The sail on the TV vanished, nothing but opaque white taking its place. The diving officer, his voice high with strain that had not yet found relief, called out. "Forty feet, forty feet." We had broken through.

"There you are now," Swanson said mildly. "All it needed was a little perseverance." I looked at the short plump

307

figure, the round good-humoured face, and wondered for the hundredth time why the nerveless iron men of this world so very seldom look the part.

I let my pride have a holiday. I took my handkerchief from my pocket, wiped my face and said to Swanson: " Does this sort of thing go on all the time?"

" Fortunately, perhaps, no." He smiled. He turned to the diving officer. " We've got our foothold on this rock. Let's make sure we have a good belay."

For a few seconds more compressed air was bled into the tanks, then the diving officer said: " No chance of her dropping down now, Captain."

" Up periscope."

Again the long gleaming silver tube hissed up from its well. Swanson didn't even bother folding down the hinged handles. He peered briefly into the eyepiece, then straightened.

" Down periscope."

" Pretty cold up top?" Hansen asked.

Swanson nodded. " Water on the lens must have frozen solid as soon as it hit that air. Can't see a thing." He turned to the diving officer. " Steady at forty?"

" Guaranteed. And all the buoyancy we'll ever want."

" Fair enough." Swanson looked at the quartermaster who was shrugging his way into a heavy sheepskin coat. " A little fresh air, Ellis, don't you think?"

" Right away, sir." Ellis buttoned his coat and added: " Might take some time."

" I don't think so," Swanson said. " You may find the bridge and hatchways jammed with broken ice but I doubt it. My guess is that that ice is so thick that it will have fractured into very large sections and fallen outside clear of the bridge."

I felt my ears pop with the sudden pressure change as the hatch swung up and open and snapped back against its standing latch. Another more distant sound as the second hatch-cover locked open and then we heard Ellis on the voice-tube.

" All clear up top."

" Raise the antennæ," Swanson said. " John, have them

start transmitting and keep transmitting until their fingers fall off. Here we are and here we stay—until we raise Drift Ice Station Zebra."

" If there's anyone left alive there," I said.

" There's that, of course," Swanson said. He couldn't look at me. " There's always that."

IV

This, I thought, death's dreadful conception of a dreadful world, must have been what had chilled the hearts and souls of our far-off Nordic ancestors when life's last tide slowly ebbed and they had tortured their failing minds with fearful imaginings of a bleak and bitter hell of eternal cold. But it had been all right for the old boys, all they had to do was to imagine it, we had to experience the reality of it and I had no doubt at all in my mind as to which was the easier. The latter-day Eastern conception of hell was more comfortable altogether, at least a man could keep reasonably warm there.

One thing sure, nobody could keep reasonably warm where Rawlings and I were, standing a half-hour watch on the bridge of the *Dolphin* and slowly freezing solid. It had been my own fault entirely that our teeth were chattering like frenzied castanets. Half an hour after the radio room had started transmitting on Drift Ice Station Zebra's wavelength and all without the slightest whisper by way of reply or acknowledgment, I had suggested to Commander Swanson that Zebra might possibly be able to hear us without having sufficient power to send a reply but that they might just conceivably let us have an acknowledgment some other way I'd pointed out that Drift Stations habitually carried rockets— the only way to guide home any lost members of the party if radio communication broke down—and radio-sondes and rockoons. The sondes were radio-carrying balloons which could rise to a height of twenty miles to gather weather information : the rockoons, radio rockets fired from balloons, could rise even higher. On a moonlit night such as this, those balloons, if released, would be visible at least twenty miles away: if flares were attached to them, at twice that distance. Swanson had seen my point, called for volunteers for the first watch and in the circumstances I hadn't had much option. Rawlings had offered to accompany me.

It was a landscape—if such a bleak, barren and featureless desolation could be called a landscape—from another and ancient world, weird and strange and oddly frightening. There were no clouds in the sky, but there were no stars either: this I could not understand. Low on the southern horizon a milky misty moon shed its mysterious light over the dark lifelessness of the polar ice-cap. Dark, not white. One would have expected moonlit ice to shine and sparkle and glitter with the light of a million crystal chandeliers—but it was dark. The moon was so low in the sky that the dominating colour on the ice-cap came from the blackness of the long shadows cast by the fantastically ridged and hummocked ice: and where the moon did strike directly the ice had been so scoured and abraded by the assaults of a thousand ice-storms that it had lost almost all its ability to reflect light of any kind.

This ridged and hummocked ice-cap had a strange quality of elusiveness, of impermanence, of evanescence: one moment there, definitively hard and harsh and repellent in its coldly contrasting blacks and whites, the next, ghost-like, blurring, coalescing and finally vanishing like a shimmering mirage fading and dying in some ice-bound desert. But this was no trick of the eye or imagination, it was the result of a ground-level ice-storm that rose and swirled and subsided at the dictates of an icy wind that was never less than strong and sometimes gusted up to gale force, a wind that drove before it a swirling rushing fog of billions of needle-pointed ice-spicules. For the most part, standing as we were on the bridge twenty feet above the level of the ice—the rest of the *Dolphin* might never have existed as far as the eye could tell—we were above this billowing ground-swell of ice particles; but occasionally the wind gusted strongly, the spicules lifted, drummed demonaically against the already ice-sheathed starboard side of the sail, drove against the few exposed inches of our skin with all the painfully stinging impact of a sand-blaster held at arm's length; but unlike a sand-blaster, the pain-filled shock of those spear-tipped spicules was only momentary, each wasp-like sting carried with it its own ice-cold anæsthetic and all surface sensation was quickly lost. Then the wind would drop, the furious rattling on the sail would fade and in the momentary contrast of near-silence we could hear the stealthy rustling as of a million rats advancing as the ice-spicules brushed their blind way across the iron-hard surface of the polar cap. The bridge thermometer stood at $-21°$ F. $-53°$ of frost. If I were a promoter interested in developing a summer holiday resort, I thought, I wouldn't pay very much attention to this place.

Rawlings and I stamped our feet, flailed our arms across our chests, shivered non-stop, took what little shelter we could from the canvas windbreak, rubbed our goggles constantly to keep them clear, and never once, except when the ice-spicules drove into our faces, stopped examining every quarter of the horizon. Somewhere out there on those frozen wastes was a lost and dying group of men whose lives might depend upon so little a thing as the momentary misting up of one of our goggles. We stared out over those shifting ice-sands until our eyes ached. But that was all we had for it, just aching eyes. We saw nothing, nothing at all. The ice-cap remained empty of all signs of life. Dead.

When our relief came Rawlings and I got below with all the speed our frozen and stiffened limbs would allow. I found Commander Swanson sitting on a canvas stool outside the radio room. I stripped off outer clothes, face coverings and goggles, took a steaming mug of coffee that had appeared from nowhere and tried not to hop around too much as the blood came pounding back into arms and legs.

"How did you cut yourself like that?" Swanson asked, concern in his voice. "You've a half-inch streak of blood right across your forehead."

"Flying ice, it just looks bad." I felt tired and pretty low. "We're wasting our time transmitting. If the men on Drift Station Zebra were without any shelter it's no wonder all signals ceased long ago. Without food and shelter no one could last more than a few hours in that lot. Neither Rawlings nor I is a wilting hothouse flower but after half an hour up there we've both just about had it."

"I don't know," Swanson said thoughtfully. "Look at

Amundsen. Look at Scott, at Peary. They *walked* all the way to the Poles."

" A different breed of men, Captain. Either that or the sun shone for them. All I know is that half an hour is too long to be up there. Fifteen minutes is enough for anyone."

" Fifteen minutes it shall be." He looked at me, face carefully empty of all expression. " You haven't much hope?"

" If they're without shelter, I've none."

" You told me they had an emergency power pack of Nife cells for powering their transmitter," he murmured. " You also said those batteries will retain their charge indefinitely, years if necessary, irrespective of the weather conditions under which they are stored. They must have been using that battery a few days ago when they sent out their first S O S. It wouldn't be finished already."

His point was so obvious that I didn't answer. The battery wasn't finished: the men were.

" I agree with you," he went on quietly. " We're wasting our time. Maybe we should just pack up and go home. If we can't raise them, we'll never find them."

" Maybe not. But you're forgetting your directive from Washington, Commander."

" How do you mean?"

" Remember? I'm to be extended every facility and all aid short of actually endangering the safety of the submarine and the lives of the crew. At the present moment we're doing neither. If we fail to raise them I'm prepared for a twenty-mile sweep on foot round this spot in the hope of locating them. If that fails we could move to another polynya and repeat the search. The search area isn't all that big, there's a fair chance, but a chance, that we might locate the station eventually. I'm prepared to stay up here all winter till we do find them."

" You don't call that endangering the lives of my men? Making extended searches of the ice-cap, on foot, in midwinter?"

" Nobody said anything about endangering the lives of your men."

" You mean—you mean you'd go it alone." Swanson

stared down at the deck and shook his head. " I don't know what to think. I don't know whether to say you're crazy or whether to say I'm beginning to understand why they— whoever ' they ' may be—picked you for the job, Dr. Carpenter." He sighed, then regarded me thoughtfully. " One moment you say there's no hope, the next that you're prepared to spend the winter here, searching. If you don't mind my saying so, Doctor, it just doesn't make sense."

" Stiff-necked pride," I said. " I don't like throwing my hand in on a job before I've even started it. I don't know what the attitude of the United States Navy is on that sort of thing."

He gave me another speculative glance, I could see he believed me the way a fly believes the spider on the web who has just offered him safe accommodation for the night. He smiled. He said : " The United States Navy doesn't take offence all that easily, Dr. Carpenter. I suggest you catch a couple of hours' sleep while you can. You'll need it all if you're going to start walking towards the North Pole."

" How about yourself? You haven't been to bed at all to-night."

" I think I'll wait a bit." He nodded towards the door of the radio room. " Just in case anything comes through."

" What are they sending? Just the call sign?"

" Plus request for position and a rocket, if they have either. I'll let you know immediately anything comes through. Good night, Dr. Carpenter. Or rather, good morning."

I rose heavily and made my way to Hansen's cabin.

The atmosphere round the 8 a.m. breakfast table in the ward-room was less than festive. Apart from the officer on deck and the engineer lieutenant on watch, all the *Dolphin*'s officers were there, some just risen from their bunks, some just heading for them, none of them talking in anything more than monosyllables. Even the ebullient Dr. Benson was remote and withdrawn. It seemed pointless to ask whether any contact had been established with Drift Station Zebra, it was painfully obvious that it hadn't. And that after almost five hours' continuous sending. The sense of des-

313

pondency and defeat, the unspoken knowledge that time had run out for the survivors of Drift Station Zebra hung heavy over the wardroom.

No one hurried over his meal—there was nothing to hurry for—but by and by they rose one by one and drifted off, Dr. Benson to his sick-bay call, the young torpedo officer, Lieutenant Mills, to supervise the efforts of his men who had been working twelve hours a day for the past two days to iron out the faults in the suspect torpedoes, a third to relieve Hansen, who had the watch, and three others to their bunks. That left only Swanson, Raeburn and myself. Swanson, I knew, hadn't been to bed at all the previous night, but for all that he had the rested clear-eyed look of a man with eight solid hours behind him.

The steward, Henry, had just brought in a fresh pot of coffee when we heard the sound of running footsteps in the passageway outside and the quartermaster burst into the wardroom. He didn't quite manage to take the door off its hinges, but that was only because the Electric Boat Company put good solid hinges on the doors of their submarines.

"We got it made!" he shouted, and then perhaps recollecting that enlisted men were expected to conduct themselves with rather more decorum in the wardroom, went on : " We've raised them, Captain, we've raised them !"

"What!" Swanson could move twice as fast as his comfortable figure suggested and he was already half-out of his chair.

"We are in radio contact with Drift Ice Station Zebra, sir," Ellis said formally.

Commander Swanson got to the radio room first, but only because he had a head start on Raeburn and myself. Two operators were on watch, both leaning forward towards their transmitters, one with his head bent low, the other with his cocked to one side, as if those attitudes of concentrated listening helped them to isolate and amplify the slightest sounds coming through the earphones clamped to their heads. One of them was scribbling away mechanically on a signal pad. DSY, he was writing down, DSY repeated over and over again. DSY. The answering call-sign of Drift Station Zebra. He stopped writing as he caught sight of Swanson out of the corner of one eye.

"We've got 'em, Captain, no question. Signal very weak and intermittent but——"

"Never mind the signal!" It was Raeburn who made this interruption without any by-your-leave from Swanson. He tried, and failed, to keep the rising note of excitement out of his voice and he looked more than ever like a youngster playing hookey from high school. "The bearing? Have you got their bearing? That's all that matters."

The other operator swivelled in his seat and I recognised my erstwhile guard, Zabrinski. He fixed Raeburn with a sad and reproachful eye.

"Course we got their bearing, Lieutenant. First thing we did. O-forty-five, give or take a whisker. North-east, that is."

"Thank you, Zabrinski," Swanson said dryly. "O-forty-five is north-east. The navigating officer and I wouldn't have known. Position?"

Zabrinski shrugged and turned to his watchmate, a man with a red face, leather neck and a shining polished dome where his hair ought to have been. "What's the word, Curly?"

"Nothing. Just nothing." Curly looked at Swanson. "Twenty times I've asked for his position. No good. All he does is send out his call-sign. I don't think he's hearing us at all, he doesn't even know we're listening, he just keeps sending his call-sign over and over again. Maybe he hasn't switched his aerial in to ' receive '."

"It isn't possible," Swanson said.

"It is with this guy," Zabrinski said. "At first Curly and I thought that it was the signal that was weak, then we thought it was the operator who was weak or sick, but we were wrong, he's just a ham-handed amateur."

"You can tell?" Swanson asked.

"You can always tell. You can——" He broke off, stiffened and touched his watchmate's arm.

Curly nodded. "I got it," he said matter-of-factly. "Position unknown, the man says."

Nobody said anything, not just then. It didn't seem important that he couldn't give us his position, all that mattered was that we were in direct contact. Raeburn turned and ran forward across the control room. I could hear him speak rapidly on the bridge telephone. Swanson turned to me.

" Those balloons you spoke of earlier. The ones on Zebra. Are they free or captive?"

" Both."

" How do the captive ones work?"

" A free-running winch, nylon cord marked off in hundreds and thousands of feet."

" We'll ask them to send a captive balloon up to 5,000 feet," Swanson decided. " With flares. If they're within thirty or forty miles we ought to see it, and if we get its elevation and make an allowance for the effect of wind on it, we should get a fair estimate of distance . . . What is it, Brown?" This to the man Zabrinski called " Curly."

" They're sending again," Curly said. " Very broken, fades a lot. ' God's sake, hurry.' Just like that, twice over. ' God's sake hurry.' "

" Send this," Swanson said. He dictated a brief message about the balloons. " And send it real slow."

Curly nodded and began to transmit. Raeburn came running back into the radio room.

" The moon's not down yet," he said quickly to Swanson. " Still a degree or two above the horizon. I'm taking a sextant up top and taking a moon-sight. Ask them to do the same. That'll give us the latitude difference and if we know they're o-forty-five of us we can pin them down to a mile."

" It's worth trying," Swanson said. He dictated another message to Brown. Brown transmitted the second message immediately after the first. We waited for the answer. For all of ten minutes we waited. I looked at the men in the radio room, they all had the same remote withdrawn look of men who are there only physically, men whose minds are many miles away. They were all at the same place and I was too, wherever Drift Ice Station Zebra was.

Brown started writing again, not for long. His voice this time was still matter-of-fact, but with overtones of emptiness. He said : " ' All balloons burnt. No moon.' "

" No moon." Raeburn couldn't hide the bitterness, the sharpness of his disappointment. " Damn! Must be pretty heavy overcast up there. Or a bad storm."

" No," I said. " You don't get local weather variations

like that on the ice-cap. The conditions will be the same over 50,000 square miles. The moon is down. For them, the moon is down. Their latest estimated position must have been pure guesswork, and bad guesswork at that. They must be at least a hundred miles farther north and east than we had thought."

"Ask them if they have any rockets," Swanson said to Brown.

"You can try," I said. "It'll be a waste of time. If they are as far off as I think, their rockets would never get above our horizon. Even if they did, we wouldn't see them."

"It's always a chance, isn't it?" Swanson asked.

"Beginning to lose contact, sir," Brown reported. "Something there about food but it faded right out."

"Tell them if they have any rockets to fire them at once," Swanson said. "Quickly, now, before you lose contact."

Four times in all Brown sent the message before he managed to pick up a reply. Then he said: "Message reads: 'Two minutes.' Either this guy is pretty far through or his transmitter batteries are. That's all. 'Two minutes,' he said."

Swanson nodded wordlessly and left the room. I followed. We picked up coats and binoculars and clambered up to the bridge. After the warmth and comfort of the control room, the cold seemed glacial, the flying ice-spicules more lancet-like than ever. Swanson uncapped the gyro-repeater compass, gave us the line of o-forty-five, told the two men who had been keeping watch what to look for and where.

A minute passed, two minutes, five. My eyes began to ache from staring into the ice-filled dark, the exposed part of my face had gone completely numb and I knew that when I removed those binoculars I was going to take a fair bit of skin with them.

A phone bell rang. Swanson lowered his glasses, leaving two peeled and bloody rings round his eyes—he seemed unaware of it, the pain wouldn't come until later—and picked up the receiver. He listened briefly, hung up.

"Radio room," he said. "Let's get below. All of us. The rockets were fired three minutes ago."

We went below. Swanson caught sight of his face reflected in a glass gauge and shook his head. "They must have shelter," he said quietly. "They must. Some hut left. Or

317

they would have been gone long ago." He went into the radio room. " Still in contact?"

"Yeah." Zabrinski spoke. " Off and on. It's a funny thing. When a dicey contact like this starts to fade it usually gets lost and stays lost. But this guy keeps coming back. Funny."

" Maybe he hasn't even got batteries left," I said. " Maybe all they have is a hand-cranked generator. Maybe there's no one left with the strength to crank it for more than a few moments at a time."

" Maybe," Zabrinski agreed. " Tell the captain that last message, Curly."

" ' Can't late many tours,' " Brown said. " That's how the message came through. ' Can't late many tours.' I think it should have read ' Can't last many hours.' Don't see what else it can have been."

Swanson looked at me briefly, glanced away again. I hadn't told anyone else that the commandant of the base was my brother and I knew he hadn't told anyone either. He said to Brown : " Give them a time-check. Ask them to send their call-signs five minutes every hour on the hour. Tell them we'll contact them again within six hours at most, maybe only four. Zabrinski, how accurate was that bearing?"

" Dead accurate, Captain. I've had plenty of re-checks. O-forty-five exactly."

Swanson moved out into the control centre. " Drift Station Zebra can't see the moon. If we take Dr. Carpenter's word for it that weather conditions are pretty much the same all over, that's because the moon is below their horizon. With the elevation we have of the moon, and knowing their bearing, what's Zebra's minimum distance from us?"

" A hundred miles, as Dr. Carpenter said," Raeburn confirmed after a short calculation. " At least that."

" So. We leave here and take a course o-forty. Not enough to take us very far from their general direction but it will give us enough offset to take a good cross-bearing eventually. We will go exactly a hundred miles and try for another polynya. Call the executive officer, secure for diving." He smiled at me. " With two cross-bearings and an accurately measured base-line, we can pin them down to a hundred yards."

318

" How do you intend to measure a hundred miles under the ice? Accurately, I mean?"

" Our inertia navigation computer does it for me. It's very accurate, you wouldn't believe just how accurate. I can dive the *Dolphin* off the eastern coast of the United States and surface again in the Eastern Mediterranean within five hundred yards of where I expect to be. Over a hundred miles I don't expect to be twenty yards out."

Radio aerials were lowered, hatches screwed down and within five minutes the *Dolphin* had dropped down from her hole in the ice and was on her way. The two helmsmen at the diving stand sat idly smoking, doing nothing : the steering controls were in automatic interlock with the inertial navigation system which steered the ship with a degree of accuracy and sensitivity impossible to human hands. For the first time I could feel a heavy jarring vibration rumbling throughout the length of the ship : " can't last many hours " the message had said : the *Dolphin* was under full power.

I didn't leave the control room that morning. I spent most of the time peering over the shoulder of Dr. Benson who had passed his usual five minutes in the sick-bay waiting for the patients who never turned up and then had hurried to his seat by the ice-machine. The readings on that machine meant living or dying to the Zebra survivors. We had to find another polynya to surface in to get a cross-bearing : no cross-bearing, no hope. I wondered for the hundredth time how many of the survivors of the fire were still alive. From the quiet desperation of the few garbled messages that Brown and Zabrinski had managed to pick up I couldn't see that there would be many.

The pattern traced out by the hissing stylus on the chart was hardly an encouraging sight. Most of the time it showed the ice overhead to be of a thickness of ten feet or more. Several times the stylus dipped to show thicknesses of thirty to forty feet, and once it dipped down almost clear of the paper, showing a tremendous inverted ridge of at least 150 feet in depth. I tried to imagine what kind of fantastic pressures created by piled-up log-jams of rafted ice on the surface must have been necessary to force ice down to such a depth : but I just didn't have the imagination to cope with that sort of thing.

319

Only twice in the first eighty miles did the stylus trace out the thin black line that meant thin ice overhead. The first of those polynas might have accommodated a small rowing boat, but it would certainly never have looked at the *Dolphin*: the other had hardly been any bigger.

Shortly before noon the hull vibration died away as Swanson gave the order for a cutback to a slow cruising speed. He said to Benson: " How does it look?"

" Terrible. Heavy ice all the way."

" Well, we can't expect a polynya to fall into our laps straight away," Swanson said reasonably, " We're almost there. We'll make a grid search. Five miles east, five miles west, a quarter-mile farther to the north each time."

The search began. An hour passed, two, then three. Raeburn and his assistant hardly ever raised their heads from the plotting table where they were meticulously tracing every movement the *Dolphin* was making in its criss-cross search under the sea. Four o'clock in the afternoon. The normal background buzz of conversation, the occasional small talk from various groups in the control centre, died away completely. Benson's occasional " Heavy ice, still heavy ice," growing steadily quieter and more dispirited, served only to emphasise and deepen the heavy brooding silence that had fallen. Only a case-hardened undertaker could have felt perfectly at home in that atmosphere. At the moment, undertakers were the last people I wanted to think about.

Five o'clock in the afternoon. People weren't looking at each other any more, far less talking. Heavy ice, still heavy ice. Defeat, despair, hung heavy in the air. Heavy ice, still heavy ice. Even Swanson had stopped smiling, I wondered if he had in his mind's eye what I now constantly had in mine, the picture of a haggard, emaciated, bearded man with his face all but destroyed with frostbite, a frozen, starving, dying man draining away the last few ounces of his exhausted strength as he cranked the handle of his generator and tapped out his call-sign with lifeless fingers, his head bowed as he strained to listen above the howl of the ice-storm for the promise of aid that never came. Or maybe there was no one tapping out a call-sign any more. They were no ordinary men who had been sent to man

320

Drift Ice Station Zebra but there comes a time when even the toughest, the bravest, the most enduring will abandon all hope and lie down to die. Perhaps he had already lain down to die. Heavy ice, still heavy ice.

At half past five Commander Swanson walked across to the ice-machine and peered over Benson's shoulder. He said: "What's the average thickness of that stuff above?"

"Twelve to fifteen feet," Benson said. His voice was low and tired. "Nearer fifteen, I would say."

Swanson picked up a phone. "Lieutenant Mills? Captain here. What is the state of readiness of those torpedoes you're working on? . . . Four? . . . Ready to go? . . . Good. Stand by to load. I'm giving this search another thirty minutes, then it's up to you. Yet, that is correct. We shall attempt to blow a hole through the ice." He replaced the phone.

Hansen said thoughtfully: "Fifteen feet of ice is a helluva lot of ice. And that ice will have a tamping effect and will direct 90 per cent of the explosive force down the way. You think we *can* blow a hole through fifteen feet of ice, Captain?"

"I've no idea," Swanson admitted. "How can anyone know until we try it?"

"Nobody ever tried to do this before? I asked.

"No. Not in the U.S. Navy, anyway. The Russians may have tried it, I wouldn't know. They don't," he added dryly, "keep us very well informed on those matters."

"Aren't the underwater shock waves liable to damage the *Dolphin*?" I asked. I didn't care for the idea at all, and that was a fact.

"If they do, the Electric Boat Company can expect a pretty strong letter of complaint. We shall explode the warhead electronically about 1,000 yards after it leaves the ship— it has to travel eight hundred yards anyway before a safety device unlocks and permits the warhead to be armed. We shall be bows-on to the detonation and with a hull designed to withstand the pressures this one is, the shock effects should be negligible."

"Very heavy ice," Benson intoned. "Thirty feet, forty feet, fifty feet. Very, very heavy ice."

321

"Just too bad if your torpedo ended up under a pile like the stuff above us just now," I said. "I doubt if it would even chip off the bottom layer."

"We'll take care that doesn't happen. We'll just find a suitably large layer of ice of normal thickness, kind of back off a thousand yards and then let go."

"Thin ice!" Benson's voice wasn't a shout, it was a bellow. "Thin ice. No, by God, clear water! Clear water! Lovely clear, clear water!"

My immediate reaction was that either the ice-machine or Benson's brain had blown a fuse. But the officer at the diving panel had no such doubts for I had to grab and hang on hard as the *Dolphin* heeled over violently to port and came curving round, engines slowing, in a tight circle to bring her back to the spot where Benson had called out. Swanson watched the plot, spoke quietly and the big bronze propellers reversed and bit into the water to bring the *Dolphin* to a stop.

"How's it looking now, Doc?" Swanson called out.

"Clear, clear water," Benson said reverently. "I got a good picture of it. It's pretty narrow, but wide enough to hold us. It's long, with a sharp left-hand dog-leg, for it followed us round through the first forty-five degrees of our curve."

"One fifty feet," Swanson said.

The pumps hummed. The *Dolphin* drifted gently upwards like an airship rising from the ground. Briefly, water flooded back into the tanks. The *Dolphin* hung motionless.

"Up periscope," Swanson said.

The periscope hissed up slowly into the raised position. Swanson glanced briefly through the eyepiece, then beckoned me. "Take a look," he beamed. "As lovely a sight as you'll ever see."

I took a look. If you'd made a picture of what could be seen above and framed it you couldn't have sold the result even if you added Picasso's name to it: but I could see what he meant. Solid black masses on either side with a scarcely lighter strip of dark jungle green running between them on a line with the fore-and-aft direction of the ship. An open lead in the polar pack.

Three minutes later we were lying on the surface of the

Arctic Ocean, just under two hundred and fifty miles from the Pole.

The rafted, twisted ice-pack reared up into contorted ridges almost fifty feet in height, towering twenty feet above the top of the sail, so close you could almost reach out and touch the nearest ridge. Three or four of those broken and fantastically hummocked icehills we could see stretching off to the west and then the light of the floodlamp failed and we could see no more. Beyond that there was only blackness.

To the east we could see nothing at all. To have stared out to the east with opened eyes would have been to be blinded for life in a very few seconds : even goggles became clouded and scarred after the briefest exposure. Close in to the *Dolphin's* side you could, with bent head and hooded eyes, catch, for a fleeting part of a second, a glimpse of black water, already freezing over : but it was more imagined than seen.

The wind, shrieking and wailing across the bridge and through raised antennæ, showed at consistently over 60 m.p.h. on the bridge anemometer. The ice-storm was no longer the gusting, swirling fog of that morning but a driving wall of stiletto-tipped spears, near-lethal in its ferocity, high speed ice-spicule lances that would have skewered their way through the thickest cardboard or shattered in a second a glass held in your hand. Over and above the ululating threnody of the wind we could hear an almost constant grinding, crashing and deep-throated booming as millions of tons of racked and tortured ice, under the influence of the gale and some mighty pressure centre, heaven knew how many hundreds of miles away, reared and twisted and tore and cracked, one moment forming another rafted ridge as a layer of ice, perhaps ten feet thick, screeched and roared and clambered on to the shoulders of another and then another, the next rending apart in indescribably violent cacophony to open up a new lead, black wind-torn water that started to skim over with ice almost as soon as it was formed.

"Are we both mad? Let's get below." Swanson cupped his hands to my ear and had to shout, but even so I could hardly hear him above that hellish bedlam of sound.

323

We clambered down into the comparatively sudden stillness of the control room. Swanson untied his parka hood
and pulled off scarf and goggles that had completely masked
his face. He looked at me and shook his head wonderingly.

"And some people talk about the white silence of the
Arctic. My God, a boilermaker's shop is like a library
reading-room compared to that lot." He shook his head
again. "We stuck our noses out a few times above the
ice-pack last year, but we never saw anything like this.
Or heard it. Winter-time, too. Cold, sure, damned cold,
and windy, but never so bad that we couldn't take a brief
stroll on the ice, and I used to wonder about those stories
of explorers being stuck in their tents for days on end,
unable to move. But I know now why Captain Scott died."

"It is pretty nasty," I admitted. "How safe are we here,
Commander?"

"That's anybody's guess," Swanson shrugged. "The wind's
got us jammed hard against the west wall of this polynya and
there's maybe fifty yards of open water to starboard. For the
moment we're safe. But you can hear and see that pack is on
the move, and not slowly either. The lead we're in was
torn open less than an hour ago. How long? Depends on
the configuration of the ice, but those polynyas can close up
damned quickly at times, and while the hull of the *Dolphin*
can take a fair old pressure, it can't take a million tons
of ice leaning against it. Maybe we can stay here for hours,
maybe only for minutes. Whichever it is, as soon as that
east wall comes within ten feet of the starboard side we're
dropping down out of it. You know what happens when
a ship gets caught in the ice."

"I know. They get squeezed flat, are carried round the
top of the world for a few years then one day are released
and drop to the bottom, two miles straight down. The
United States Government wouldn't like it, Commander."

"The prospects of further promotion for Commander
Swanson would be poor," Swanson admitted. "I think——"

"Hey!" The shout came from the radio room. "Hey,
c'm here."

"I rather think Zabrinski must be wanting me," Swanson
murmured. He moved off with his usual deceptive speed and

I followed him into the radio room. Zabrinski was sitting half-turned in his chair, an ear-to-ear beam on his face, the earphones extended in his left hand. Swanson took them, listened briefly, then nodded.

"DSY," he said softly. "DSY, Dr. Carpenter. We have them. Got the bearing? Good." He turned to the doorway, saw the quartermaster. "Ellis, ask the navigating officer to come along as soon as possible."

"We'll pick 'em all up yet, Captain," Zabrinski said jovially. The smile on the big man's face, I could see now, didn't extend as far as his eyes. "They must be a pretty tough bunch of boys out there."

"Very tough, Zabrinski," Swanson said absently. His eyes were remote and I knew he was listening to the metallic cannonading of the ice-spicules, a billion tiny pneumatic chisels drumming away continuously against the outer hull of the submarine, a sound loud enough to make low speech impossible. "Very tough. Are you in two-way contact?"

Zabrinski shook his head and turned away. He'd stopped smiling. Raeburn came in, was handed a sheet of paper and left for his plotting table. We went with him. After a minute or two he looked up, and said: "If anyone fancies a Sunday afternoon's walk, this is it."

"So close?" Swanson asked.

"So very close. Five miles due east, give or take half a mile. Pretty fair old bloodhounds, aren't we?"

"We're just lucky," Swanson said shortly. He walked back to the radio room. "Talking to them yet?"

"We've lost them altogether."

"Completely?"

"We only had 'em a minute, Captain. Just that. Then they faded. Got weaker and weaker. I think Doc Carpenter here is right, they're using a hand-cranked generator." He paused, then said idly: "I've a six-year-old-daughter who could crank one of those machines for five minutes without turning a hair."

Swanson looked at me, then turned away without a word. I followed him to the unoccupied diving stand. From the bridge access hatch we could hear the howl of the storm, the grinding ice with its boom and scream that spanned the

325

entire register of hearing. Swanson said: Zabrinski put it very well . . . I wonder how long this damnable storm is going to last?"

"Too long. I have a medical kit in my cabin, a fifty-ounce flask of medicinal alcohol and cold-weather clothes. Could you supply me with a thirty-pound pack of emergency rations, high protein high-calorie concentrates, Benson will know what I mean."

"Do you mean what I think you mean?" Swanson said slowly. "Or am I just going round the bend?"

"What's this about going round the bend?" Hansen had just come through the doorway leading to the for'ard passageway, and the grin on his face was clear enough indication that though he'd caught Swanson's last words he'd caught neither the intonation nor the expression on Swanson's face. "Very serious state of affairs, going round the bend. I'll have to assume command and put you in irons, Captain. Something about it in regulations, I dare say."

"Dr. Carpenter is proposing to sling a bag of provisions on his back and proceed to Drift Station Zebra on foot."

"You've picked them up again?" Just for the moment Hansen had forgotten me. "You really got them? And a cross-bearing?"

"Just this minute. We've hit it almost on the nose. Five miles, young Raeburn says."

"My God! Five miles. Only five miles!" Then the elation vanished from voice and face as if an internal switch had been touched. "In weather like this it might as well be five hundred. Even old Amundsen couldn't have moved ten yards through this stuff."

"Dr. Carpenter evidently thinks he can improve on Amundsen's standard's," Swanson said dryly. "He's talking about walking there."

Hansen looked at me for a long and considering moment, then turned back to Swanson. "I think maybe it's Doc Carpenter we should be clapping in the old irons."

"I think maybe it is," Swanson said.

"Look," I said. "There are men out there on Drift Station Zebra. Maybe not many, not now, but there are some. One, anyway. Men a long way past being sick. Dying men. To a dying man it takes only the very smallest thing to spell out the difference between life and death. I'm a doctor, I know. The smallest thing. An ounce of alcohol, a few ounces of food, a hot drink, some medicine. Then they'll live. Without those little things they will surely die. They're entitled to what smallest aid they can get, and I'm entitled to take whatever risks I care to see they get it. I'm not asking anyone else to go, all I'm asking is that you implement the terms of your orders from Washington to give me all possible assistance without endangering the *Dolphin* or its crew. Threatening to stop me is not my idea of giving assistance. And I'm not asking you to endanger your submarine or the lives of your men."

Swanson gazed at the floor. I wondered what he was thinking of : the best way to stop me, his orders from Washington, or the fact that he was the only man who knew that the commandant on Zebra was my brother. He said nothing.

"You must stop him, Captain," Hansen said urgently. "Any other man you saw putting a pistol to his head or a razor to his throat, you'd stop that man. This is the same. He's out of his mind, he's wanting to commit suicide." He tapped the bulkhead beside him. "Good God, Doc, why do you think we have the sonar operators in here on duty even when we're stopped. So that they can tell us when the ice wall on the far side of the polynya starts to close in on us, that's why. And *that's* because it's impossible for any man to last thirty seconds on the bridge or see an inch against the ice-storm up there. Just take a quick twenty-second trip up there, up on the bridge, and you'll change your mind fast enough, I guarantee."

"We've just come down from the bridge," Swanson said matter-of-factly.

"And he still wants to go? It's like I say, he's crazy."

"We could drop down now," Swanson said. "We have the position. Perhaps we can find a polynya within a mile, half a mile of Zebra. That would be a different proposition altogether."

"Perhaps you could find a needle in a haystack," I said. "It took you six hours to find this one, and even at that we were lucky. And don't talk about torpedoes, the ice in this area is rafted anything up to a hundred feet in depth. Pretty

327

much all over. You'd be as well trying to blast your way through with a .22. Might be twelve hours, might be days before we could break through again. I can get there in two-three hours."

" *If* you don't freeze to death in the first hundred yards," Hansen said. " *If* you don't fall down a ridge and break your leg. *If* you don't get blinded in a few minutes. *If* you don't fall into a newly-opened polynya that you can't see, where you'll either drown or, if you manage to get out, freeze solid in thirty seconds. And even if you do survive all those things, I'd be grateful if you'd explain to me exactly how you propose to find your way blind to a place five miles away. You can't carry a damn' great gyro weighing about half a ton on your back, and a magnetic compass is useless in those latitudes. The magnetic north pole is a good bit *south* of where we are now and a long way to the west. Even if you *did* get some sort of bearing from it, in the darkness and the ice-storm you could still miss the camp—or what's left of it—by only a hundred yards and never know it. And even if by one chance in a million you do manage to find your way there, how on earth do you ever expect to find your way back again. Leave a paper-trail? A five-mile ball of twine. Crazy is hardly the word for it."

" I may break a leg, drown or freeze," I conceded. " I'll take my chance on that. Finding my way there and back is no great trick. You have a radio bearing on Zebra and know exactly where it lies. You can take a radio bearing on any transmitter. All I have to do is to tote a receiver-transmitter radio along with me, keep in touch with you and you can keep me on the same bearing as Zebra. It's easy."

" It would be," Hansen said, " except for one little thing. We don't have any such radio."

" I have a twenty-mile walkie-talkie in my case," I said.

" Coincidence, coincidence," Hansen murmured. " Just happened to bring it along, no doubt. I'll bet you have all sorts of funny things in that case of yours, haven't you, Doc?"

" What Dr. Carpenter has in his case is really no business of ours," Swanson said in mild reproof. He hadn't thought so earlier. " What does concern us is his intention to do away with himself. You really can't expect us to consent to this ridiculous proposal, Dr. Carpenter."

" No one's asking you to consent to anything," I said. " Your consent is not required. All I'm asking you to do is to stand to one side. And to arrange for that food provision pack for me. If you won't, I'll have to manage without."

I left and went to my cabin. Hansen's cabin, rather. But even although it wasn't my cabin that didn't stop me from turning the key in the lock as soon as I had passed through the door.

Working on the likely supposition that if Hansen did come along soon he wasn't going to be very pleased to find the door of his own cabin locked against him, I wasted no time. I spun the combination lock on the case and opened the lid. At least three-quarters of the available space was taken up by Arctic survival clothing, the very best that money could buy. It hadn't been my money that had bought it.

I stripped off the outer clothes I was wearing, pulled on long open-mesh underwear, woollen shirt and cord breeches, then a triple-knit wool parka lined with pure silk. The parka wasn't quite standard, it had a curiously shaped suède-lined pocket below and slightly to the front of the left armpit, and a differently shaped suède-lined pocket on the right-hand side. I dug swiftly to the bottom of my case and brought up three separate items. The first of these, a nine-millimetre Mannlicher-Schoenauer automatic, fitted into the left-hand pocket as securely and snugly as if the pocket had been specially designed for it, which indeed it had : the other items, spare magazine clips, fitted as neatly into the right-hand pocket.

The rest of the dressing didn't take long. Two pairs of heavy-knit woollen socks, felt undershoes and then the furs— caribou for the outer parka and trousers, wolverine for the hood, sealskin for the boots and reindeer for the gloves, which were pulled on over other layers of silk gloves and woollen mittens. Maybe a polar bear would have had a slight edge over me when it came to being equipped to survive an Arctic blizzard, but there wouldn't have been much in it.

329

I hung snow-mask and goggles round my neck, stuck a rubberised waterproofed torch into the inside pocket of the fur parka, unearthed my walkie-talkie and closed the case. I set the combination again. There was no need to set the combination any more, not now that I had the Mannlicher-Schoenauer under my arm, but it would give Swanson something to do while I was away. I shoved my medicine case and a steel flask of alcohol in a rucksack and unlocked the door.

Swanson was exactly where I'd left him in the control room. So was Hansen. So were two others who had not been there when I had left, Rawlings and Zabrinski. Hansen, Rawlings, and Zabrinski, the three biggest men in the ship. The last time I'd seen them together was when Swanson had whistled them up from the *Dolphin* in the Holy Loch to see to it that I didn't do anything he didn't want me to do. Maybe Commander Swanson had a one-track mind. Hansen, Rawlings, and Zabrinski. They looked bigger than ever.

I said to Swanson: "Do I get those iron rations or not?"

"One last formal statement," Swanson said. His first thoughts, as I came waddling into the control centre, must have been that a grizzly bear was loose inside his submarine, but he hadn't batted an eyelid. "For the record. Your intentions are suicidal, your chances are non-existent. I cannot give my consent."

"All right, your statement is on record, witnesses and all. The iron rations."

"I cannot give my consent because of a fresh and dangerous development. One of our electronic technicians was carrying out a routine calibration test on the ice-machine just now and an overload coil didn't function. Electric motor burnt out. No spares, it will have to be rewired. You realise what that means. If we're forced to drop down I can't find my way to the top again. Then it's curtains for everybody—everybody left above the ice, that is."

I didn't blame him for trying, but I was vaguely disappointed in him: he'd had time to think up a better one than that. I said: "The iron rations, Commander. Do I get them?"

"You mean to go through with this? After what I've said?"

"Oh, for God's sake. I'll do without the food."

330

"My executive officer, Torpedoman Rawlings and Radioman Zabrinski," Swanson said formally, "don't like this."

"I can't help what they like or don't like."

"They feel they can't let you go through with it," he
persisted.

They were more than big. They were huge. I could get
past them the way a lamb gets past a starving lion. I had
a gun all right but with that one-piece parka I was wearing
I'd practically have to undress myself to get at it and
Hansen, in that Holy Loch canteen, had shown just how
quickly he could react when he saw anyone making a suspicious move. And even if I did get my gun out, what
then? Men like Hansen, like Rawlings and Zabrinski, didn't
scare. I couldn't bluff them with a gun. And I couldn't use
the gun. Not against men who were just doing their duty.

"They *won't* let you go through with it," Swanson went
on, "unless, that is, you will permit them to accompany you,
which they have volunteered to do."

"Volunteered," Rawlings sniffed. "You, you, and you."

"I don't want them," I said.

"Gracious, ain't he?" Rawlings asked of no one in particular. "You might at least have said thanks, Doc."

"You are putting the lives of your men in danger, Commander Swanson. You know what your orders said."

"Yes. I also know that in Arctic travels, as in mountain-
eering and exploring, a party has always double the chances
of the individual. I also know that if it became known that
we had permitted a civilian doctor to set off on his own
for Drift Station Zebra while we were all too scared to
stir from our nice warm sub, the name of the United States
Navy would become pretty muddy."

"What do your men think of your making them risk their
lives to save the good name of the submarine service?"

"You heard the captain," Rawlings said. "We're volunteers. Look at Zabrinski there, anyone can see that he is
a man cast in a heroic mould."

"Have you thought of what happens," I said, "if the
ice closes in when we're away and the captain has to take
the ship down?"

"Don't even talk of it," Zabrinski urged. "I'm not all
that heroic."

I gave up. I'd no option but to give up. Besides, like Zabrinski, I wasn't all that heroic and I suddenly realised that I would be very glad indeed to have those three men along with me.

V

Lieutenant Hansen was the first man to give up. Or perhaps " give up " is wrong, the meaning of the words was quite unknown and the thought totally alien to Hansen, it would be more accurate to say that he was the first of us to show any glimmerings of common sense. He caught my arm, brought his head close to mine, pulled down his snow mask and shouted : " No farther, Doc. We must stop."

" The next ridge," I yelled back. I didn't know whether he'd heard me or not, as soon as he'd spoken he'd pulled his mask back up into position again to protect the momentarily exposed skin against the horizontally driving ice-storm, but he seemed to understand for he eased his grip on the rope round my waist and let me move ahead again. For the past two and a half hours Hansen, Rawlings and I had each taken his turn at being the lead man on the end of the rope, while the other three held on to it some ten yards behind, the idea being not that the lead man should guide the others but that the others should save the life of the lead man, should the need arise. And the need already had arisen, just once, Hansen, slipped and scrambling on all-fours across a fractured and upward sloping raft of ice, had reached gropingly forward with his arms into the blindness of the night and the storm and found nothing there. He had fallen eight vertical feet before the rope had brought him up with a vicious jerk that had been almost as painful for Rawlings and myself, who had taken the brunt of the shock, as it had been for Hansen. For nearly two minutes he'd dangled above the wind-torn black water of a freshly opened lead before we'd managed to drag him back to safety. It had been a close thing, far too close a thing, for in far sub-zero temperatures with a gale-force wind blowing, even a few seconds' submersion in water makes the certainty of death absolute, the process of dissolution as swift as it is irreversible. In those conditions the clothes of a man pulled from the water become a frozen and impenetrable suit of armour inside seconds, an armour that can neither be removed nor chipped away. Petrified inside this ice-shroud, a man just simply and quickly freezes to death—in the unlikely event, that is, of his heart having withstood the thermal shock of the body surface being exposed to an almost instantaneous hundred degree drop in temperature.

So now I stepped forward very cautiously, very warily indeed, feeling the ice ahead of me with a probe we'd devised after Hansen's near accident—a chopped-off five foot length of rope which we'd dipped into the water of the lead then exposed to the air until it had become as rigid as a bar of steel. At times I walked, at times I stumbled, at times, when a brief lull in the gale-force wind, as sudden as it was unexpected, would catch me off balance I'd just fall forward and continue on hands and knees, for it was quite as easy that way. It was during one of those periods when I was shuffling blindly forward on all-fours that I realised that the wind had, for the time being, lost nearly all of its violence and that I was no longer being bombarded by that horizontally driving hail of flying ice-spicules. Moments later my probe made contact with some solid obstacle in my path: the vertical wall of a rafted ice ridge. I crawled thankfully into its shelter, raised my goggles and pulled out and switched on my torch as the others came blindly up to where I lay.

Blindly. With arms outstretched they pawed at the air before them like sightless men, which for the past two and a half hours was exactly what they had been. For all the service our goggles had given us we might as well have stuck our heads in gunny sacks before leaving the *Dolphin*. I looked at Hansen, the first of the three to come up. Goggles, snow-mask, hood, clothing—the entire front part of his body from top to toe was deeply and solidly encrusted in a thick and glittering layer of compacted ice, except for some narrow cracks caused by joint movements of legs and arms. As he drew close to me I could hear him splintering and crackling a good five feet away. Long ice-feathers streamed back from his head, shoulders and elbows; as an extra-terrestrial monster from one of the chillier planets, such as Pluto, he'd have been a sensation in any horror movie. I suppose I looked much the same.

We huddled close together in the shelter of the wall. Only four feet above our heads the ice-storm swept by in a glittering grey-white river. Rawlings, sitting on my left, pushed up his goggles, looked down at his ice-sheathed furs and started to beat himself with his fist across the chest to break up the covering. I reached out a hand and caught his arm.

" Leave it alone," I said.

" Leave it alone?" Rawlings's voice was muffled by his snow-mask, but not so muffled that I couldn't hear the chattering of his teeth. " This damn' suit of armour weighs a ton. I'm out of training for this kind of weight-lifting, Doc."

" Leave it alone. If it weren't for that ice, you'd have frozen to death by this time : it's insulating you from that wind and the ice-storm. Let's see the rest of your face. And your hands."

I checked him and the two others for frost-bite, while Hansen checked me. We were still lucky. Blue and mottled and shaking with the cold, but no frost-bite. The furs of the other three might not have been quite as fancy as mine, but they were very adequate indeed. Nuclear subs always got the best of everything, and Arctic clothing was no exception. But although they weren't freezing to death I could see from their faces and hear from their breathing that they were pretty far gone in exhaustion. Thrusting into the power of that ice-storm was like wading upstream against the current of a river of molasses : that was energy-sapping enough, but the fact that we had to spend most of our time clambering over, slipping on, sliding and falling across fractured ice or making detours round impassable ridges while being weighed down with forty pound packs on our back and heaven only knew how many additional pounds of ice coating our furs in front had turned our trudge across that contorted treacherous ice into a dark and frozen nightmare.

" The point of no return, I think," Hansen said. His breathing, like Rawlings's, was very quick, very shallow, almost gasping. " We can't take much more of this, Doc."

" You ought to listen to Dr. Benson's lectures a bit more."

334

I said reprovingly. All this ice-cream and apple pie and lolling around in your bunks is no training for this sort of thing."

"Yeah?" He peered at me. "How do *you* feel?"

"A mite tired," I admitted. "Nothing much to speak of." Nothing much to speak of, my legs felt as if they were falling off, that was all, but the goad of pride was always a useful one to have to hand. I slipped off my rucksack and brought out the medicinal alcohol. "I suggest fifteen minutes' break. Any more and we'll just start stiffening up completely. Meantime, a little drop of what we fancy will help keep the old blood corpuscles trudging around."

"I thought medical opinion was against alcohol in low temperatures," Hansen said doubtfully. "Something about opening the pores."

"Name me any form of human activity," I said, "and I'll find you a group of doctors against it. Spoilsports. Besides, this isn't alcohol, it's very fine Scotch whisky."

"You should have said so in the first place. Pass it over. Not too much for Rawlings and Zabrinski, they're not used to the stuff. Any word, Zabrinski?"

Zabrinski, with the walkie-talkie's aerial up and one earphone tucked in below the hood of his parka, was talking into the microphone through cupped hands. As the radio expert, Zabrinski had been the obvious man to handle the walkie-talkie and I'd given it to him before leaving the submarine. This was also the reason why Zabrinski wasn't at any time given the position of lead man in our trudge across the pack ice. A heavy fall or immersion in water would have finished the radio he was carrying slung on his back: and if the radio were finished then so would we be, for without the radio not only had we no hope of finding Drift Station Zebra, we wouldn't have a chance in a thousand of ever finding our way back to the *Dolphin* again. Zabrinski was built on the size and scale of a medium-sized gorilla and was about as durable; but we couldn't have treated him more tenderly had he been made of Dresden china.

"It's difficult," Zabrinski said. "Radio's O.K., but this ice-storm causes such damn' distortion and squeaking—no, wait a minute, though, wait a minute."

He bent his head over the microphone, shielding it from the sound of the storm, and spoke again through cupped hands. "Zabrinski here . . . Zabrinski. Yeah, we're all kinda tuckered out, but Doc here seems to think we'll make it. . . . Hang on, I'll ask him."

He turned to me. "How far do you reckon we've come, they want to know."

"Four miles." I shrugged. "Three and a half, four and a half. You guess it."

Zabrinski spoke again, looked interrogatively at Hansen and myself, saw our headshakes and signed off. He said: "Navigating officer says we're four-five degrees north of where we should be and that we'll have to cut south if we don't want to miss Zebra by a few hundred yards."

It could have been worse. Over an hour had passed since we'd received the last bearing position from the *Dolphin* and, between radio calls, our only means of navigating had been by judging the strength and direction of the wind in our faces. When a man's face is completely covered and largely numb it's not a very sensitive instrument for gauging wind direction—and for all we knew the wind might be either backing or veering. It could have been a lot worse and I said so to Hansen.

"It could be worse," he agreed heavily. "We could be travelling in circles or we could be dead. Barring that, I don't see how it could be worse." He gulped down the whisky, coughed, handed the flask top back to me. "Things look brighter now. You honestly think we can make it?"

"A little luck, that's all. You think maybe our packs are too heavy? That we should abandon some of it here?" The last thing I wanted to do was to abandon any of the supplies we had along with us: eighty pounds of food, a stove, thirty pounds of compressed fuel tablets, 100 ounces of alcohol, a tent, and a very comprehensive medical kit; but if it was to be abandoned I wanted the suggestion to be left to them, and I was sure they wouldn't make it.

"We're abandoning nothing," Hansen said. Either the rest or the whisky had done him good, his voice was stronger, his teeth hardly chattering at all.

"Let the thought die stillborn," Zabrinski said. When first I'd seen him in Scotland he had reminded me of a polar bear and now out here on the ice-cap, huge and crouched in his ice-whitened furs, the resemblance was redoubled. He had the physique of a bear, too, and seemed completely tireless; he was in far better shape than any of us. "This weight on my bowed shoulders is like a bad leg: an old friend that gives me pain, but I wouldn't be without it."

"You?" I asked Rawlings.

"I am conserving my energy," Rawlings announced. "I expect to have to carry Zabrinski later on."

We pulled the starred, abraded and now thoroughly useless snow-goggles over our eyes again, hoisted ourselves stiffly to our feet and moved off to the south to find the end of and round the high ridge that here blocked our path. It was by far the longest and most continuous ridge we'd encountered yet, but we didn't mind, we required to make a good offing to get us back on course and not only were we doing just that but we were doing it in comparative shelter and saving our strength by so doing. After perhaps four hundred yards the ice wall ended so abruptly, leading to so sudden and unexpected an exposure to the whistling fury of the ice-storm that I was bowled completely off my feet. An express train couldn't have done it any better. I hung on to the rope with one hand, clawed and scrambled my way back on to my feet with the help of the other, shouted a warning to the others, and then we were fairly into the wind again, holding it directly in our faces and leaning far forward to keep our balance.

We covered the next mile in less than half an hour. The going was easier now, much easier than it had been, although we still had to make small detours round rafted, compacted and broken ice: on the debit side, we were all of us, Zabrinski excepted, pretty far gone in exhaustion, stumbling and falling far more often than was warranted by the terrain and the strength of the ice-gale: for myself, my leaden dragging legs felt as if they were on fire, each step now sent a shooting pain stabbing from ankle clear to the top of the thigh. For all that, I think I could have kept going longer than any of them, even Zabrinski, for I had the motivation, the driving force that would have kept me going hours after my legs would have told me that it was impossible to carry on a step farther. Major John Halliwell.

My elder, my only brother. Alive or dead. Was he alive or was he dead, this one man in the world to whom I owed everything I had or had become? Was he dying, at that very moment when I was thinking of him, was he dying? His wife, Mary, and his three children who spoilt and ruined their bachelor uncle as I spoilt and ruined them : whatever way it lay they would have to know and only I could tell them. Alive or dead? My legs weren't mine, the stabbing fire that tortured them belonged to some other man, not to me. I had to know, I had to know, and if I had to find out by covering whatever miles lay between me and Drift Ice Station Zebra on my hands and knees, then I would do just that. I would find out. And over and above the tearing anxiety as to what had happened to my brother there was yet another powerful motivation, a motivation that the world would regard as of infinitely more importance than the life or death of the commandant of the station. As infinitely more important than the living or dying of the score of men who manned that desolate polar outpost. Or so the world would say.

The demented drumming of the spicules on my mask and ice-sheathed furs suddenly eased, the gale wind fell away and I found myself standing in the grateful shelter of an ice-ridge even higher than the last one we'd used for shelter. I waited for the others to come up, asked Zabrinski to make a position check with the *Dolphin* and doled out some more of the medicinal alcohol. More of it than on the last occasion. We were in more need of it. Both Hansen and Rawlings were in a very distressed condition, their breath whistling in and out of their lungs in the rapid, rasping, shallow panting of a long-distance runner in the last tortured moments of his final exhaustion. I became gradually aware that the speed of my own breathing matched theirs almost exactly, it required a concentrated effort of will-power to hold my breath even for the few seconds necessary to gulp down my drink. I wondered vaguely if perhaps Hansen hadn't had the right of it, maybe the alcohol wasn't good for us. But it certainly tasted as if it were.

Zabrinski was already talking through cupped hands into the microphone. After a minute or so he pulled the earphones out from under his parka and buttoned up the walkie-

338

talkie set. He said : " We're either good or lucky or both. The *Dolphin* says we're exactly on the course we ought to be on." He drained the glass I handed him and sighed in satisfaction. " Well, that's the good part of the news. Here comes the bad part. The sides of the polynya the *Dolphin* is lying in are beginning to close together. They're closing pretty fast. The captain estimates he'll have to get out of it in two hours. Two at the most." He paused, then finished slowly : " And the ice-machine is still on the blink."

" The ice-machine," I said stupidly. Well, anyway, I felt stupid, I don't know how I sounded. " Is the ice——?"

" It sure is, brother," Zabrinski said. He sounded tired. " But you didn't believe the skipper, did you, Dr. Carpenter? You were too clever for that."

" Well, that's a help," Hansen said heavily. " That makes everything just perfectly splendid. The *Dolphin* drops down, the ice closes up, and there we are, the *Dolphin* below, us on top and the whole of the polar ice-cap between us. They'll almost certainly never manage to find us again, even if they do fix the ice-machine. Shall we just lie down and die now or shall we first stagger around in circles for a couple of hours and then lie down and die?"

" It's tragic," Rawlings said gloomily. " Not the personal aspect of it, I mean the loss to the United States Navy. I think I may fairly say, Lieutenant, that we are—or were —three promising young men. Well, you and me, anyway. I think Zabrinski there had reached the limit of his poten- tialities. He reached them a long time ago."

Rawlings got all this out between chattering teeth and still painful gasps of air. Rawlings, I reflected, was very much the sort of person I would like to have by my side when things began to get awkward, and it looked as if things were going to become very awkward indeed. He and Zabrinski had, as I'd found out, established themselves as the home- spun if slightly heavy-handed humorists on the *Dolphin*; for reasons known only to themselves both men habitually concealed intelligence of a high order and advanced educa- tion under a cloak of genial buffoonery.

" Two hours yet," I said. " With this wind at our back we can be back in the sub in well under an hour. We'd be practically blown back there."

"And the men on Drift Station Zebra?" Zabrinski asked.

"We'd have done our best. Just one of those things."

"We are profoundly shocked, Dr. Carpenter," Rawlings said. The tone of genial buffoonery was less noticeable than usual.

"Deeply dismayed," Zabrinski added, "by the very idea." The words were light, but the lack of warmth in the voice had nothing to do with the bitter wind.

"The only dismaying thing around here is the level of intelligence of certain simple-minded sailors," Hansen said with some asperity. He went on, and I wondered at the conviction in his voice: "Sure, Dr. Carpenter thinks we should go back. That doesn't include him. Dr. Carpenter wouldn't turn back now for all the gold in Fort Knox." He pushed himself wearily to his feet. "Can't be much more than half a mile to go now. Let's get it over with."

In the backwash of light from my torch I saw Rawlings and Zabrinski glance at each other, saw them shrug their shoulders at the same moment. Then they, too, were on their feet and we were on our way again.

Three minutes later Zabrinski broke his ankle.

It happened in an absurdly simple fashion, but for all its simplicity it was a wonder that nothing of the same sort had happened to any of us in the previous three hours. After starting off again, instead of losing our bearing by working to the south and north until we had rounded the end of the ice ridge blocking our path, we elected to go over it. The ridge was all of ten feet high but by boosting and pulling each other we reached the top without much difficulty. I felt my way forward cautiously, using the ice-probe—the torch was useless in that ice-storm and my goggles completely opaque. After twenty feet crawling across the gently downward sloping surface I reached the far side of the ridge and stretched down with the probe.

"Five feet," I called to the others as they came up. "It's only five feet." I swung over the edge, dropped down and waited for the others to follow. Hansen came first, then Rawlings, both sliding down easily beside me. What happened to Zabrinski was impossible to see, he either misjudged his distance from the edge or a sudden easing of the wind made him lose his footing. Whatever the cause, I heard

340

him call out, the words whipped away and lost by the wind, as he jumped down beside us. He seemed to land squarely and lightly enough on his feet, then cried out sharply and fell heavily to the ground.

I turned my back to the ice-storm, raised the useless snow-goggles and pulled out my torch. Zabrinski was half-sitting, half-lying on the ice, propped up on his right elbow and cursing steadily and fluently and, as far as I could tell because of the muffling effect of his snow-mask, without once repeating himself. His right heel was jammed in a four-inch crack in the ice, one of the thousands of such fractures and fissures that criss-crossed the pressure areas of the pack : his right leg was bent over at an angle to the outside, an angle normally impossible for any leg to assume. I didn't need to have a medical diploma hung around my neck to tell that the ankle was gone : either that or the lowermost part of the tibia, for the ankle was so heavily encased in a stout boot with lace binding that most of the strain must have fallen on the shin bone. I hoped it wasn't a compound fracture, but it was an unreasonable hope : at that acute angle the snapped bone could hardly have failed to pierce the skin. Compound or not, it made no immediate difference, I'd no intention of examining it : a few minutes' exposure of the lower part of his leg in those temperatures was as good a way as any of ensuring that Zabrinski went through the rest of his life with one foot missing.

We lifted his massive bulk, eased the useless foot out of the crack in the ice and lowered him gently to a sitting position. I unslung the medical kit from my back, knelt beside him and asked : " Does it hurt badly?"

" No, it's numb, I hardly feel a thing." He swore disgustedly. " What a crazy thing to do. A little crack like that. How stupid can a man get?"

" You wouldn't believe me if I told you," Rawlings said acidly. He shook his head. " I prophesied this, I prophesied this. I said it would end up with me carrying this gorilla here."

I had splints to the injured leg and taped them as tightly as possible over the boot and the furs, trying not to think of the depth of trouble we were in now. Two major blows in one. Not only had we lost the indispensable services

341

of the strongest man in our party, we now had an extra 220 lbs.—at least—of weight, of dead-weight, to carry along with us. Not to mention his 40-lb. pack. Zabrinski might almost have read my thoughts.

"You'll have to leave me here, Lieutenant," he said to Hansen. His teeth were rattling, with shock and cold. "We must be almost there now. You can pick me up on the way back."

"Don't talk rubbish," Hansen said shortly. "You know damn' well we'd never find you again."

"Exactly," Rawlings said. His teeth were like Zabrinski's, stuttering away irregularly like an asthmatic machine-gun. He knelt on the ice to support the injured man's bulk. "No medals for morons. It says so in the ship's articles."

"But you'll never get to Zebra," Zabrinski protested. "If you have to carry me——"

"You heard what I said," Hansen interrupted. "We're not leaving you."

"The lieutenant is perfectly correct," Rawlings agreed. "You aren't the hero type, Zabrinski. You haven't the face for it, for one thing. Now clam up while I get some of this gear off your back."

I finished tightening the splints and pulled mittens and fur gloves back on my silk-clad but already frozen hands. We shared out Zabrinski's load among the three of us, pulled goggles and snow-masks back into position, hoisted Zabrinski to his one sound leg, turned into the wind and went on our way again. It would be truer to say that we staggered on our way again.

But now, at last and when we most needed it, luck was with us. The ice-cap stretched away beneath our feet level and smooth as the surface of a frozen river. No ridges, no hummocks, no crevasses, not even the tiny cracks one of which had crippled Zabrinski. Just billiard flat unbroken ice and not even slippery, for its surface had been scoured and abraded by the flying ice-storm.

Each of us took turns at being lead man, the other two supporting a Zabrinski who hopped along in uncomplaining silence on one foot. After maybe three hundred yards of this smooth ice, Hansen, who was in the lead at the moment, stopped so suddenly and unexpectedly that we bumped into him.

" We're there!" he yelled above the wind. " We've made it. We're there! Can't you smell it?"

" Smell what?"

" Burnt fuel oil. Burnt rubber. Don't you get it?"

I pulled down my snow-mask, cupped my hands to my face and sniffed cautiously. One sniff was enough. I hitched up my mask again, pulled Zabrinski's arm more tightly across my shoulder and followed on after Hansen.

The smooth ice ended in another few feet. The ice sloped up sharply to a level plateau and it took the three of us all of what pitifully little strength remained to drag Zabrinski up after us. The acrid smell of burning seemed to grow more powerful with every step we took. I moved forward, away from the others, my back to the storm, goggles down and sweeping the ice with semicircular movements of my torch. The smell was strong enough now to make my nostrils wrinkle under the mask. It seemed to be coming from directly ahead. I turned round into the wind, protectively cupped hand over my eyes, and as I did my torch struck something hard and solid and metallic. I lifted my torch and vaguely through the driving ice I could just make out the ghostly hooped steel skeleton, ice-coated on the windward side, fire-charred on the leeward side, of what had once been a nissen-shaped hut.

We had found Drift Ice Station Zebra.

I waited for the others to come up, guided them past the gaunt and burnt-out structure, then told them to turn backs to wind and lift their goggles. For maybe ten seconds we surveyed the ruin in the light of my torch. No one said anything. Then we turned round into the wind again.

Drift Station Zebra had consisted of eight separate huts, four in each of two parallel rows, thirty feet between the two rows, twenty feet between each two huts in the rows— this to minimise the hazard of fire spreading from hut to hut. But the hazard hadn't been minimised enough. No one could be blamed for that. No one, except in the wildest flights of nightmarish imagination, could have envisaged what must indeed have happened—exploding tanks and thousands of gallons of blazing oil being driven through the night by a gale-force wind. And, by a double inescapable irony, fire, without which human life on the polar ice-cap cannot survive, is there the most dreaded enemy of all: for although the entire ice-cap consists of water, frozen water, there is nothing that can melt that water and so put out the fire. Except fire itself. I wondered vaguely what had happened to the giant chemical fire-extinguishers housed in every hut.

Eight huts, four in each row. The first two on either side were completely gutted. No trace remained of the walls, which had been of two layers of weather-proofed bonded ply that had enclosed the insulation of shredded glass-fibre and kapok: on all of them even the aluminium-sheeted roofs had disappeared. In one of the huts we could see charged and blackened generator machinery, ice-coated on the windward side, bent and twisted and melted almost out of recognition: one could only wonder at the furnace ferocity of the heat responsible.

The fifth hut—the third on the right-hand side—was a gutted replica of the other four, the framing even more savagely twisted by the heat. We were just turning away from this, supporting Zabrinski and too sick at heart even to speak to each other, when Rawlings called out something unintelligible. I leaned closer to him and pulled back my parka hood.

" A light!" he shouted. "A light. Look, Doc—across there!"

And a light there was, a long narrow strangely white vertical strip of light from the hut opposite the charred wreck by which we stood. Leaning sideways into the storm we dragged Zabrinski across the intervening gap. For the first time my torch showed something that was more than a bare framework of steel. This was a hut. A blackened, scorched and twisted hut with a roughly nailed-on sheet of plywood where its solitary window had been, but nevertheless a hut. The light was coming from a door standing just ajar at the sheltered end. I laid my hand on the door, the one unscorched thing I'd seen so far in Drift Station Zebra. The hinges creaked like a rusty gate in a cemetery at midnight and the door gave beneath my hand. We passed inside.

344

Suspended from a hook in the centre of the ceiling a hissing Coleman lamp threw its garish light, amplified by the glittering aluminium ceiling, over every corner and detail of that eighteen by ten hut. A thick but transparent layer of ice sheathed the aluminium roof except for a three-foot circle directly above the lamp, and the ice spread from the ceiling down the plywood walls all the way to the door. The wooden floor, too, was covered with ice, except where the bodies of the men lay. There may have been ice under them as well. I couldn't tell.

My first thought, conviction rather, and one that struck at me with a heart-sapping sense of defeat, with a chill that even the polar storm outside had been unable to achieve, was that we had arrived too late. I had seen many dead men in my life, I knew what dead men looked like, and now I was looking at just that many more. Shapeless, huddled, lifeless forms lying under a shapeless mass of blankets, mackinaws, duffels and furs, I wouldn't have bet a cent on my chances of finding one heart-beat among the lot of them. Lying packed closely together in a rough semicircle at the end of the room remote from the door, they were utterly still, as unmoving as men would be if they had been lying that way for a frozen eternity. Apart from the hissing of the pressure-lamp there was no sound inside the hut other than the metallic drumfire of the ice-spicules against the ice-sheathed eastern wall of the hut.

Zabrinski was eased down into a sitting position against a wall. Rawlings unslung the heavy load he was carrying on his back, unwrapped the stove, pulled off his mittens and started fumbling around for the fuel tablets. Hansen pulled the door to behind him, slipped the buckles of his ruck-sack and wearily let his load of tinned food drop to the floor of the shack.

For some reason, the voice of the storm outside and the hissing of the Coleman inside served only to heighten the deathly stillness in the hut, and the unexpected metallic clatter of the falling cans made me jump. It made one of the dead men jump, too. The man nearest to me by the left-hand wall suddenly moved, rolled over and sat up, bloodshot faded eyes staring out unbelievingly from a frost-bitten, haggard and cruelly burnt face, the burns patchily covered by a long dark stubble of beard. For long seconds he looked at us unblinkingly, then, some obscure feeling of pride making him ignore the offer of my outstretched arm, he pushed himself shakily and with obvious pain to his feet. Then the cracked and peeling lips broke into a grin.

"You've been a bleedin' long time getting here." The voice was hoarse and weak and cockney as the Bow Bells themselves. "My name's Kinnaird. Radio operator."

"Whisky?" I asked.

He grinned again, tried to lick his cracked lips, and nodded. The stiff tot of whisky went down his throat like a man in a barrel going over the Niagara Falls, one moment there, the next gone for ever. He bent over, coughing harshly until the tears came to his eyes, but when he straightened life was coming back into those same lack-lustre eyes and colour touching the pale emaciated cheeks.

"If you go through life saying 'Hallo' in this fashion, mate," he observed, "then you'll never lack for friends." He bent and shook the shoulder of the man beside whom he had been lying. "C'mon, Jolly, old boy, where's your bleedin' manners. We got company."

It took quite a few shakes to get Jolly, old boy, awake, but when he did come to he was completely conscious and on his feet with remarkable speed in the one case and with re-markable nimbleness in the other. He was a short, chubby character with china-blue eyes, and although he was as much in need of a shave as Kinnaird, there was still colour in his face and the round good-humoured face was far from emaciated : but frost-bite had made a bad mess of both mouth and nose. The china-blue eyes, flecked with red and momentarily wide in surprise, crinkled into a grin of welcome. Jolly, old boy, I guess, would always adjust fast to circumstances.

"Visitors, eh?" His deep voice held a rich Irish brogue. "And damned glad we are to see you, too. Do the honours, Jeff."

"We haven't introduced ourselves," I said. "I'm Dr. Carpenter and this——"

"Regular meeting of the B.M.A., old boy," Jolly said. I was to find out later that he used the phrase "old boy" in every second or third sentence, a mannerism which went strangely with his Irish accent.

"Dr. Jolly?"

"The same. Resident medical officer, old boy."

"I see. This is Lieutenant Hansen of the United States Navy submarine *Dolphin*——"

"Submarine?" Jolly and Kinnard stared at each other, then at us. "You said 'submarine,' old top?"

"Explanations can wait. Torpedoman Rawlings. Radioman Zabrinski." I glanced down at the huddled men on the floor, some of them already stirring at the sound of voices, one or two propping themselves up on their elbows. "How are they?"

"Two or three pretty bad burn cases," Jolly said. "Two or three far gone with cold and exhaustion, but not so far gone that food and warmth wouldn't have them right as rain in a few days. I made them all huddle together like this for mutual warmth."

I counted them. Including Jolly and Kinnaird, there were twelve all told. I said: "Where are the others?"

"The others?" Kinnaird looked at me in momentary surprise, then his face went bleak and cold. He pointed a thumb over his shoulder. "In the next hut, mate."

"Why?"

"Why?" He rubbed a weary forearm across bloodshot eyes. "Because we don't fancy sleeping with a roomful of corpses, that's why."

"Because you don't——" I broke off and stared down at the men at my feet. Seven of them were awake now, three of them propped on elbows, four still lying down, all seven registering various degrees of dazed bewilderment: the three who were still asleep—or unconscious—had their faces covered by blankets. I said slowly. "There were nineteen of you."

"Nineteen of us," Kinnaird echoed emptily. "The others —well, they never had a chance."

I said nothing. I looked carefully at the faces of the conscious men, hoping to find among them the one face I wanted to see, hoping perhaps that I had not immediately recognised it because frost-bite or hunger or burns had made it temporarily unrecognisable. I looked very carefully indeed and I knew that I had never seen any of those faces before.

347

I moved over to the first of the three still sleeping figures and lifted the blanket covering the face. The face of a stranger. I let the blanket drop. Jolly said in puzzlement: "What's wrong? What do you want?"

I didn't answer him. I picked my way round recumbent men, all staring uncomprehendingly at me, and lifted the blanket from the face of the second sleeping man. Again I let the blanket drop and I could feel my mouth go dry, the slow heavy pounding of my heart. I crossed to the third man, then stood there hesitating, knowing I must find out, dreading what I must find. Then I stooped quickly and lifted the blanket. A man with a heavily bandaged face. A man with a broken nose and a thick blond beard. A man I had never seen in my life before. Gently I spread the blanket back over his face and straightened up. Rawlings, I saw, already had the solid-fuel stove going.

"That should bring the temperature up to close to freezing," I said to Dr. Jolly. "We've plenty of fuel. We've also brought food, alcohol, a complete medical kit. If you and Kinnaird want to start in on those things now I'll give you a hand in a minute. Lieutenant, that was a polynya, that smooth stretch we crossed just before we got here? A frozen lead?"

"Couldn't be anything else." Hansen was looking at me peculiarly, a wondering expression on his face. "These people are obviously in no fit state to travel a couple of hundred yards, far less four or five miles. Besides, the skipper said he was going to be squeezed down pretty soon. So we whistle up the Dolphin and have them surface at the back door?"

"Can he find that polynya—without the ice-machine, I mean?"

"Nothing simpler. I'll take Zabrinski's radio, move a measured two hundred yards to the north, send a bearing signal, move two hundred yards to the south and do the same. They'll have our range to a yard. Take a couple of hundred yards off that and the Dolphin will find itself smack in the middle of the polynya."

"But still under it. I wonder how thick that ice is. You had an open lead to the west of the camp some time ago, Dr. Jolly. How long ago?"

348

" A month. Maybe five weeks. I can't be sure."

" How thick?" I asked Hansen.

" Five feet, maybe six. Couldn't possibly break through it. But the captain's always had a hankering to have a go with his torpedoes." He turned to Zabrinski. " Still fit to operate that radio of yours?"

I left them to it. I'd hardly been aware of what I'd been saying, anyway. I felt sick and old and empty and sad, and deathly tired. I had my answer now. I'd come 12,000 miles to find it, I'd have gone a million to avoid it. But the inescapable fact was there and now nothing could ever change it. Mary, my sister-in-law and her three wonderful children—she would never see her husband again, they would never see their father again. My brother was dead and no one was ever going to see him again. Except me. I was going to see him now.

I went out, closing the door behind me, moved round the corner of the hut and lowered my head against the storm. Ten seconds later I reached the door of the last hut in the line. I used the torch to locate the handle, twisted it, pushed and passed inside.

Once it had been a laboratory : Now it was a charnel house, a house of the dead. The laboratory equipment had all been pushed roughly to one side and the cleared floor space covered with the bodies of dead men. I knew they were dead men, but only because Kinnaird had told me so : hideously charred and blackened and grotesquely misshapen as they were, those carbonised and contorted lumps of matter could have been any form of life or indeed no form of life at all. The stench of incinerated flesh and burnt diesel fuel was dreadful. I wondered which of the men in the other hut had had the courage, the iron resolution, to bring those grisly burdens, the shockingly disfigured remains of their former comrades into this hut. They must have had strong stomachs.

Death must have been swift, swift for all of them. Theirs had not been the death of men trapped by fire, it had been the death of men who had themselves been on fire. Caught, drenched, saturated by a gale-borne sea of burning oil, they must have spent the last few seconds of life as incandescently blazing human torches before dying in insane screaming agony. They must have died as terribly as men can ever die.

Something about one of the bodies close to me caught my attention. I stooped and focused the torch beam on what had once been a right hand, now no more than a blackened claw with the bone showing through. So powerful had been that heat that it had warped, but not melted, the curiously shaped gold ring on the third finger. I recognised that ring, I had been with my sister-in-law when she had bought it.

I was conscious of no grief, no pain, no revulsion. Perhaps, I thought dully, those would come later when the initial shock had worn off. But I didn't think so. This wasn't the man I remembered so well, the brother to whom I owed everything, a debt that could never now be repaid. This charred mass of matter before me was a stranger, so utterly different from the man who lived on in my memory, so changed beyond all possibility of recognition that my numbed mind in my exhausted body just could not begin to bridge the gap.

As I stood there, staring down, something ever so slightly off-beat about the way the body lay caught my professional attention. I stooped low, very low, and remained bent over for what seemed a long time. I straightened, slowly, and as I did I heard the door behind me open. I whirled round and saw that it was Lieutenant Hansen. He pulled down his snow-mask, lifted up his goggles, looked at me and then at the man at my feet. I could see shock draining expression and colour from his face. Then he looked up at me.

" So you lost out, Doc?" I could hardly hear the husky whisper above the voice of the storm. "God, I'm sorry."

" What do you mean?"

" Your brother?" He nodded at the man at my feet.

" Commander Swanson told you?"

" Yeah. Just before we left. That's why we came." His gaze moved in horrified fascination over the floor of the hut, and his face was grey, like old parchment. " A minute, Doc, just a minute." He turned and hurried through the doorway.

When he came back he looked better, but not much. He

said : " Commander Swanson said that that was why he had to let you go."

" Who else knows?"

" Skipper and myself. No one else."

" Keep it that way, will you? As a favour to me."

" If you say so, Doc." There was curiosity in his face now, and puzzlement, but horror was still the dominant expression. " My God, have you ever seen anything like it?"

" Let's get back to the others," I said. " We're doing nobody any good by staying here."

He nodded without speaking. Together we made our way back to the other hut. Apart from Dr. Jolly and Kinnaird, three other men were on their feet now, Captain Folsom, an extraordinarily tall thin man with savagely burnt face and hands who was second in command of the base, Hewson, a dark-eyed taciturn character, a tractor driver and engineer who had been responsible for the diesel generators, and a cheerful Yorkshireman, Naseby, the camp cook. Jolly, who had opened my medical kit and was applying fresh bandages to the arms of the men still lying down, introduced them, then turned back to his job. He didn't seem to need my help, not for the moment, anyway. I heard Hansen say to Zabrinski : " In contact with the *Dolphin*?"

" Well, no." Zabrinski stopped sending his call-sign and shifted slightly to ease his broken ankle. " I don't quite know how to put this, Lieutenant, but the fact is that this little ol' set here seems to have blown a fuse."

" Well, now," Hansen said heavily. " That *is* clever of you, Zabrinski. You mean you can't raise them?"

" I can hear them, they can't hear me." He shrugged, apologetically. " Me and my clumsy feet, I guess. It wasn't just only my ankle that went when I took that tumble out there."

" Well, can't you repair the damn' thing?"

" I don't think so, Lieutenant."

" Damn it, you're supposed to be a radioman."

" That's so," Zabrinski acknowledged reasonably. " But I'm not a magician. And with a couple of numbed and frozen hands, no tools, an old-type set without a printed circuit and the code signs in Japanese—well, even Marconi would have called it a day."

351

" *Can* it be repaired?" Hansen insisted.

" It's a transistor set. No valves to smash. I expect it could be repaired. But it might take hours, Lieutenant— I'd even have to fake up a set of tools first."

" Well, fake them. Anything you like. Only get that thing working."

Zabrinski said nothing. He held out the headphones to Hansen. Hansen looked at Zabrinski, then at the phones, took them without a word and listened briefly. Then he shrugged, handed back the phones and said : " Well, I guess there *is* no hurry to repair that radio."

" Yeah," Zabrinski said. " Awkward, you might say, Lieutenant."

" What's awkward," I asked.

" Looks as if *we're* going to be next on the list for a rescue party," Hansen said heavily. " They're sending a more or less continuous signal : ' Ice closing rapidly, return at once.' "

" I was against this madness from the very beginning," Rawlings intoned from the floor. He stared down at the already melting lumps of frozen tinned soup and stirred it moodily with a fork. " A gallant attempt, men, but fore-doomed to failure."

" Keep your filthy fingers out of that soup and kindly clam up," Hansen said coldly. He turned suddenly to Kinnaird. " How about *your* radio set. Of course, that's it. We have fit men here to crank your generator and——"

" I'm sorry." Kinnaird smiled the way a ghost might smile. " It's not a hand-powered generator, that was destroyed, it's a battery set. The batteries are finished. Completely finished."

" A battery set, you said?" Zabrinski looked at him in mild surprise. " Then what caused all the power fluctuations when you were transmitting?"

" We kept changing over the nickel cadmium cells to try to make the most of what little power was left in them : we'd only fifteen left altogether, most of them were lost in the fire. That caused the power fluctuations. But even Nife cells don't last for ever. They're finished, mate. The combined power left in those cells would light a pencil torch."

Zabrinski didn't say anything. No one said anything. The ice-spicules drummed incessantly against the east wall, the Coleman hissed, the solid-fuel stove purred softly : but the sole effect of those three sounds was to make the silence inside seem that little bit more absolute. No one looked at his neighbours, everyone stared down at the floor with the fixed and steadfast gaze of an entomologist hunting for traces of woodworm. Any newspaper printing a picture taken at that instant wouldn't have found it any too easy to convince its readers that the men on Drift Ice Station Zebra had been rescued just ten minutes previously, and rescued from certain death at that. The readers would have pointed out that one might have expected a little more jubilation in the atmosphere, a touch, perhaps, of lighthearted relief, and they wouldn't have been far wrong at that, there wasn't very much gaiety around.

After the silence had gone on just that little too long I said to Hansen : "Well, that's it, then. We don't have to hire any electronic computer to work this one out. Someone's got to get back to the *Dolphin* and get back there now. I'm nominating myself."

"No!" Hansen said violently, then more quietly : "Sorry, friend, but the skipper's orders didn't include giving permission to anyone to commit suicide. You're staying here."

"So I stay here," I nodded. This wasn't the time to tell him I didn't need his permission for anything, far less was it the time to start flourishing the Mannlicher-Schoenauer. "So we all stay here. And then we all die here. Quietly, without any fighting, without any fuss, we just lie down and die here. I suppose you reckon that comes under the heading of inspiring leadership. Amundsen would have loved that." It wasn't fair, but then I wasn't feeling fair-minded at the moment.

"Nobody's going any place," Hansen said. "I'm not my brother's keeper, Doc, but for all that I'll be damned if I let you kill yourself. You're not fit, none of us is fit to make the return trip to the *Dolphin*—not after what we've just been through. That's one thing. The next thing is that without a transmitter from which the *Dolphin* can pick up our directional bearings, we could never hope to find the *Dolphin* again. The third thing is that the closing ice will

353

probably have forced the *Dolphin* to drop down before anyone could get half-way there. And the last thing is that if we failed to find the *Dolphin* either because we missed her or because she was gone, we could never make our way back to Zebra again : we wouldn't have the strength and we would have nothing to guide us back anyway."

"The odd's offered aren't all that attractive," I admitted. "What odds are you offering on the ice-machine being repaired?"

Hansen shook his head, said nothing. Rawlings started stirring his soup again, carefully not looking up, he didn't want to meet the anxious eyes, the desperate eyes, in that circle of haggard and frost-bitten faces any more than I did. But he looked up as Captain Folsom pushed himself away from the support of a wall and took a couple of unsteady steps towards us. It didn't require any stethoscope to see that Folsom was in a pretty bad way.

"I am afraid that we don't understand," he said. His voice was slurred and indistinct, the puffed and twisted lips had been immobilised by the savage charring of his face: I wondered bleakly how many months of pain would elapse, how many visits to the surgeon's table, before Folsom could show that face to the world again. In the very remote event, that was, of our ever getting him to hospital. "Would you please explain? What is the difficulty?"

"Simply this," I said. "The *Dolphin* has an ice fathometer, a device for measuring the thickness of the overhead ice. Normally, even if Commander Swanson—the captain of the *Dolphin*—didn't hear from us, we could expect him on our doorstep in a matter of hours. He has the position of this Drift Station pinned down pretty closely. All he would have to do is to drop down, come under us here, start a grid search with his ice fathometer and it would be only minutes before he would locate the relatively thin ice out in that lead there. But things aren't normal. The ice-machine has broken down and if it stays that way he'll never find that lead. That's why I want to go back there. Now. Before Swanson's forced to dive by the closing ice."

"Don't see it, old boy," Jolly said. "How's that going to help? Can *you* fix this ice what-you-may-call-it."

"I don't have to. Commander Swanson knows his distance

354

from this camp give or take a hundred yards. All I have to do is to tell him to cover the distance less quarter of a mile and loose off a torpedo. That ought——"

"Torpedo?" Jolly asked. "Torpedo? To break through the ice from beneath?"

"That's it. It's never been tried before. I suppose there's no reason why it shouldn't work if the ice is thin enough and it won't be all that thick in the lead out there. I don't really know."

"They'll be sending planes, you know, Doc," Zabrinski said quietly. "We started transmitting the news as soon as we broke through and everybody will know by now that Zebra has been found—at least, they'll know exactly where it is. They'll have the big bombers up here in a few hours."

"Doing what?" I asked. "Sculling around uselessly in the darkness up above? Even if they do have the exact position, they still won't be able to see what's left of this station because of the darkness and the ice-storm. Perhaps they can with radar, it's unlikely, but even if they do, what then? Drop supplies? Maybe. But they won't dare drop supplies directly on us for fear of killing us. They'd have to drop them some distance off—and even a quarter-mile would be too far away for any chance we'd ever have of finding stuff in those conditions. As for landing—even if weather conditions were perfect, no plane big enough to have the range to fly here could ever hope to land on the ice-cap. You know that."

"What's your middle name, Doc?" Rawlings asked dolefully. "Jeremiah?"

"The greatest good of the greatest number," I said. "The old yardstick, but there's never been a better one. If we just hole up here without making any attempt to help ourselves and the ice-machine remains useless, then we're all dead. All sixteen of us. If I make it there safely, then we're all alive. Even if I don't, the ice-machine may be fixed and there would only be one lost then." I started pulling on my mittens. "One is less than sixteen."

"We might as well make it two," Hansen sighed and began to pull on his own gloves. I was hardly surprised, when he'd last spoken he'd talked at first of "you" having no chance and finished by saying that "we" had none and

355

it hadn't required any psychiatrist to follow his quick shift in mental orientation : whatever men like Hansen were hand-picked for, it wasn't for any predilection for shifting the load to others' shoulders when the going became sticky.

I didn't waste time arguing with him.

Rawlings got to his feet.

"One skilled volunteer for the soup-stirring," he requested. "Those two wouldn't get as far as the door there without my holding their hands. I shall probably get a medal for this. What's the highest decoration awarded in peace-time, Lieutenant?"

"There are no medals given for soup-stirring, Rawlings," Hansen said, "which is what you are going to keep on doing. You're staying right here."

"Uh-uh." Rawlings shook his head. "Prepare yourself to deal with your first mutiny, Lieutenant. I'm coming with you. I can't lose. If we get to the *Dolphin* you'll be too damned glad and happy to have made it to dream of reporting me, apart from being a fair-minded man who will have to admit that our safe arrival back at the ship will be entirely due to Torpedoman Rawlings." He grinned. "And if we don't make it—well, you can't very well report it, can you, Lieutenant?"

Hansen walked across to him. He said quietly : "You know that there's more than an even chance that we won't reach the *Dolphin*. That would leave twelve pretty sick men here, not to mention Zabrinski with a broken ankle, and with no one to look after them. They must have one fit man to look after them. You couldn't be that selfish, now, could you, Rawlings? Look after them, will you? As a favour to me?"

Rawlings looked at him for long seconds, then squatted down and started stirring the soup again.

"As a favour to me, you mean," he said bitterly. "O.K., I'll stay. As a favour to me. Also to prevent Zabrinski tripping over his legs again and breaking another ankle." He stirred the soup viciously. Well, what are you waiting for? The skipper may be making up his mind to dive any minute."

He had a point. We brushed off protests and attempts to stop us made by Captain Folsom and Dr. Jolly and were ready to leave in thirty seconds. Hansen was through the door first. I turned and looked at the sick and emaciated and injured survivors of Drift Station Zebra. Folsom, Jolly, Kinnaird, Hewson, Naseby and seven others. Twelve men altogether. They couldn't all be in cahoots together, so it had to be a single man, maybe two, acting in concert. I wondered who those men might be, those men I would have to kill, that person or persons who had murdered my brother and six other men on Drift Ice Station Zebra.

I pulled the door to behind me and followed Hansen out into the dreadful night.

VI

We had been tired, more than tired, even before we had set out. We had been leaden-legged, bone-weary, no more than a short hand-span from total exhaustion. But for all that we flitted through the howling darkness of that night like two great white ghosts across the dimly seen whiteness of a nightmare lunar landscape. We were no longer bowed under the weight of heavy packs. Our backs were to that gale-force wind so that for every laborious plodding step we had made on our way to Zebra, we now covered five, with so little a fraction of our earlier toil that at first it seemed all but effortless. We had no trouble in seeing where we were going, no fear of falling into an open lead or of crippling ourselves against some unexpected obstacle, for with our useless goggles removed and powerful torch beams dancing erratically ahead of us as we jog-trotted along, visibility was seldom less than five yards, more often near to ten. Those were the physical aids that helped us on our way but even more sharply powerful as a spur to our aching legs was that keen and ever-growing fear that dominated our minds to the exclusion of all else, the fear that Commander Swanson had already been compelled to drop down and that we would be left to die in that shrieking wasteland : with our lacking both shelter and food, the old man with the scythe would not be keeping us waiting too long.

We ran, but we did not run too fast, for to have done

that would have been to have the old man tapping us on the shoulder in very short order indeed. In far sub-zero temperatures, there is one thing that the Eskimo avoids as he would the plague—over-exertion, in those latitudes more deadly, even, than the plague itself. Too much physical effort while wearing heavy furs inevitably results in sweat, and when the effort ceases, as eventually cease it must, the sweat freezes on the skin: the only way to destroy that film of ice is by further exertion, producing even more sweat, the beginnings of a vicious and steadily narrowing circle that can have only one end. So though we ran it was only at a gentle jog-trot, hardly more than a fast walk: we took every possible precaution against overheating.

After half an hour, perhaps a little more, I called for a brief halt in the shelter of a steep ice-wall. Twice in the past two minutes Hansen had stumbled and fallen where there hadn't appeared to be any reason to stumble and fall: and I had noticed that my own legs were more unsteady than the terrain warranted.

" How are you making out?" I asked.

" Pretty bushed, Doc." He sounded it, too, his breathing quick and rasping and shallow. "But don't write me off yet. How far do you reckon we've come?"

" Three miles, near enough." I patted the ice-wall behind us. "When we've had a couple of minutes I think we should try climbing this. Looks like a pretty tallish hummock to me."

" To try to get into the clear above the ice-storm?" I nodded my head and he shook his. "Won't do you any good, Doc. This ice-storm must be at least twenty feet thick, and even if you do get above it the *Dolphin* will still be below it. She's only got the top of her sail clear above the ice."

" I've been thinking," I said. "We've been so lost in our own woes and sorrows that we have forgotten about Commander Swanson. I think we have been guilty of under-estimating him pretty badly."

" It's likely enough. Right now I'm having a full-time job worrying about Lieutenant Hansen. What's on your mind?"

" Just this. The chances are better than fifty-fifty that Swanson believes we are on the way back to the *Dolphin*.

After all, he's been ordering us to return for quite some time; and if he thinks we didn't get the order because something has happened to us or to the radio, he'll still figure that we will be returning."

" Not necessarily. Radio or not, we might still be pushing on for Drift Station Zebra."

" No. Definitely not. He'll be expecting us to be smart enough to figure it the way he would; and smart enough to see that that is the way he *would* figure it. He would know that if our radio broke down before we got to Zebra that it would be suicidal for us to try to find it without radio bearing—but that it *wouldn't* be suicidal for us to try to make it back to the *Dolphin,* for he would be hoping that we would have sufficient savvy to guess that he would put a lamp in the window to guide the lost sheep home."

" My God, Doc, I believe you've got it! Of course he would, of course he would. Lordy, lordy, what am I using for brains?" He straightened and turned to face the ice-wall.

Pushing and pulling, we made it together to the top. The summit of the rafted ice hummock was less than twenty feet above the level of the ice-pack and not quite high enough. We were still below the surface of that gale-driven river of ice-spicules. Occasionally, for a brief moment of time, the wind force would ease fractionally and let us have a brief glimpse of the clear sky above but only occasionally and for a fraction of a second. And if there was anything to be seen in that time, we couldn't see it.

" There'll be other hummocks," I shouted in Hansen's ear. " Higher hummocks." He nodded without answering. I couldn't see the expression on his face but I didn't have to see it. The same thought was in both our minds : we could see nothing because there was nothing to see. Commander Swanson hadn't put a lamp in the window, for the window was gone, the *Dolphin* forced to dive to avoid being crushed by the ice.

Five times in the next twenty minutes we climbed hummocks, and five times we climbed down, each time more dejected, more defeated. By now I was pretty far gone, moving in a pain-filled nightmare: Hansen was in even worse case, lurching and staggering around like a drunken

359

man. As a doctor, I knew well of the hidden and un-suspected resources that an exhausted man can call on in times of desperate emergency; but I knew, too, that those resources are not limitless and that we were pretty close to the end. And when that end came we would just lie down in the lee of an ice-wall and wait for the old man to come along: he wouldn't keep us waiting long.

Our sixth hummock all but defeated us. It wasn't that it was hard to climb, it was well ridged with foot and hand holds in plenty, but the sheer physical effort of climbing came very close to defeating us. And then I dimly began to realise that part of the effort was due to the fact that this was by far the highest hummock we had found yet. Some colossal pressures had concentrated on this one spot, rafting and log-jamming the ice-pack until it had risen a clear thirty feet above the general level: the giant underwater ridge beneath must have stretched down close on two hundred feet towards the black floor of the Arctic.

Eight feet below the summit our heads were in the clear: on the summit itself, holding on to each other for mutual support against the gale, we could look down on the ice-storm whirling by just beneath our feet: a fantastic sight, a great grey-white sea of undulating turbulence, a giant rushing river that stretched from horizon to horizon. Like so much else in the high Arctic the scene had an eerie and terrifying strangeness about it, a mindless desolation that belonged not to earth but to some alien and long-dead planet.

We scanned the horizon to the west until our eyes ached. Nothing. Nothing at all. Just that endless desolation. From due north to due south, through 180°, we searched the surface of that great river; and still we saw nothing. Three minutes passed. Still nothing. I began to feel the ice running in my blood.

On the remote off-chance that we might already have by-passed the *Dolphin* to the north or south, I turned and peered towards the east. It wasn't easy, for that far sub-zero gale of wind brought tears to the eyes in an instant of time; but at least it wasn't impossible, we no longer had to contend with the needle-pointed lances of the ice-spicules. I made another slow 180° sweep of the eastern horizon, and again, and again. Then I caught Hansen's arm.

"Look there," I said. "To the north-east. Maybe quarter of a mile away, maybe half a mile. Can you see anything?"

For several seconds Hansen squinted along the direction of my outstretched hand, then shook his head. " I see nothing. What do you think you see?"

" I don't know. I'm not sure. I can imagine I see a very faint touch of luminescence on the surface of the ice-storm there, maybe just a fraction of a shade whiter than the rest."

For a full half-minute Hansen stared out through cupped hands. Finally he said : " It's no good. I don't see it. But then my eyes have been acting up on me for the past half-hour. But I can't even *imagine* I see anything."

I turned away to give my streaming eyes a rest from that icy wind and then looked again. "Damn it," I said, " I can't be sure that there is anything there; but I can't be sure that there isn't, either."

"What do you fancy it would be?" Hansen's voice was dispirited, with overtones of hopelessness. " A light?"

" A searchlight shining vertically upwards. A searchlight that's not able to penetrate that ice-storm."

"You're kidding yourself, Doc," Hansen said wearily. " The wish father to the thought. Besides, that would mean that we had already passed the *Dolphin*. It's not possible."

" It's not impossible. Ever since we started climbing those damned ice-hummocks I've lost track of time and space. It *could* be "

" Do you still see it?" The voice was empty, uninterested, he didn't believe me and he was just making words.

" Maybe my eyes are acting up, too," I admitted. " But, damn it, I'm still not sure that I'm not right."

" Come on, Doc, let's go."

" Go where?"

" I don't know." His teeth chattered so uncontrollably in that intense cold that I could scarcely follow his words. " I guess it doesn't matter very much where——"

With breath-taking abruptness, almost in the centre of my imagined patch of luminescence and not more than four hundred yards away, a swiftly climbing rocket burst through

361

the rushing river of ice-spicules and climbed high into the clear sky trailing behind it a fiery tale of glowing red sparks. Five hundred feet it climbed, perhaps six hundred, then burst into a brilliantly incandescent shower of crimson stars, stars that fell lazily back to earth again, streaming away to the west on the wings of the gale and dying as they went, till the sky was colder and emptier than ever before.

" You still say it doesn't matter very much where we go?" I asked Hansen. " Or maybe you didn't see that little lot?"

" What I just saw," he said reverently, " was the prettiest ol' sight that Ma Hansen's little boy ever did see—or ever will see." He thumped me on the back, so hard that I had to grab him to keep my balance. " We got it made, Doc!" he shouted. " We got it made. Suddenly I have the strength of ten. Home sweet home, here we come."

Ten minutes later we were home.

" God this is wonderful," Hansen sighed. He stared in happy bemusement from the captain to me to the glass in his hand to the water dripping from the melting ice on his furs on to the corticene decking of the captain's tiny cabin. " The warmth, the light, the comfort and home sweet home. I never thought I'd see any of it again. When that rocket went up, Skipper, I was just looking around to pick a place to lay me down and die. And don't think I'm joking, for I'm not."

" And Dr. Carpenter?" Swanson smiled.

" Defective mental equipment somewhere," Hansen said. " He doesn't seem to know how to set about giving up. I think he's just mule-headed. You get them like that."

Hansen's slightly off-beat, slightly irrational talk had nothing to do with the overwhelming relief and relaxation that comes after moments of great stress and tension. Hansen was too tough for that. I knew that and I knew that Swanson knew it also. We'd been back for almost twenty minutes now, we'd told our story, the pressure was off, a happy ending for all seemed in sight and normalcy was again almost the order of the day. But when the strain is off and conditions are back to normal a man has time to start thinking about things again. I knew only too well what was in Hansen's mind's eye, that charred and huddled shapelessness that had once been my brother. He didn't want me to talk about him, and for that I didn't blame him; he didn't want me even to think about him, although he must have known that that was impossible. The kindest men nearly always are like that, hard and tough and cynical on the outside, men who have been too kind and showed it.

"However it was," Swanson smiled, "you can consider yourselves two of the luckiest men alive. That rocket you saw was the third last we had, it's been a regular fourth of July for the past hour or so. And you reckon Rawlings, Zabrinski and the survivors on *Zebra* are safe for the present?"

"Nothing to worry about for the next couple of days," Hansen nodded. "They'll be O.K. Cold, mind you, and a good half of them desperately in need of hospital treatment, but they'll survive."

"Fine. Well, this is how it is. This lead here stopped closing in about half an hour ago, but it doesn't matter now, we can drop down any time and still hold our position. What does matter is that we have located the fault in the ice-machine. It's a damnably tricky and complicated job and I expect it will take several hours yet to fix. But I think we'll wait until it is fixed before we try anything. I'm not too keen on this idea of making a dead reckoning approach to this lead near *Zebra* then loosing off a shot in the dark. Since there's no desperate hurry, I'd rather wait till we got the ice fathometer operating again, make an accurate survey of this lead then fire a torpedo up through the middle. If the ice is only four or five feet thick there, we shouldn't have much trouble blowing a hole through."

"That would be best," Hansen agreed. He finished off his medicinal alcohol—an excellent bourbon—rose stiffly to his feet and stretched. "Well, back to the old treadmill again. How many torpedoes in working order?"

"Four, at the last count."

"I may as well go help young Mills load them up now. If that's O.K. by you, Skipper."

"It is not O.K. by me," Swanson said mildly, "and if you'll take a quick gander at that mirror there you'll understand why. You're not fit to load a slug into an airgun far less a torpedo into its tube. You haven't just been on a Sunday

363

afternoon stroll, you know. A few hours sleep, John, then we'll see."

Hansen didn't argue. I couldn't imagine anyone arguing with Commander Swanson. He made for the door. " Coming, Doc?"

" In a moment. Sleep well."

" Yeah. Thanks." He touched me lightly on the shoulder and smiled through bloodshot and exhausted eyes. " Thanks for everything. Good-night, all."

When he was gone Swanson said : " It was pretty wicked out there to-night?"

" I wouldn't recommend it for an old ladies' home Sunday afternoon outing."

" Lieutenant Hansen seems to imagine he's under some kind of debt to you," he went on inconsequentially.

" Imagination, as you say. They don't come any better than Hansen. You're damned lucky to have him as an exec."

" I know that." He hesitated, then said quietly : " I promise you, I won't mention this again—but, well, I'm most damnably sorry, Doctor."

I looked at him and nodded slowly. I knew he meant it, I knew he had to say it, but there's not much you can say in turn to anything like that. I said : " Six others died with him, Commander."

He hesitated again. " Do we—do we take the dead back to Britain with us?"

" Could I have another drop of that excellent bourbon, Commander. Been a very heavy run on your medicinal alcohol in the past few hours, I'm afraid." I waited till he had filled my glass then went on : " We don't take them back with us. They're not dead men, they're just unrecognisable and unidentifiable lumps of charred matter. Let them stay here."

His relief was unmistakable and he was aware of it for he went on hurriedly, for something to say : " All this equipment for locating and tracking the Russian missiles. Destroyed?"

" I didn't check." He'd find out for himself soon enough that there had been no such equipment. How he'd react to that discovery in light of the cock-and-bull story I'd spun to himself and Admiral Garvie in the Holy Loch I couldn't

364

even begin to guess. At the moment I didn't even care. It didn't seem important, nothing seemed important, not any more. All at once I felt tired, not sleepy, just deathly tired, so I pushed myself stiffly to my feet, said good-night and left.

Hansen was in his bunk when I got back to his cabin, his furs lying where he had dropped them. I checked that he was no longer awake, slipped off my own furs, hung them up and replaced the Mannlicher-Schoenauer in my case. I lay down in my cot to sleep, but sleep wouldn't come. Exhausted though I was, I had never felt less like sleep in my life.

I was too restless and unsettled for sleep, too many problems coming all at once were causing a first-class log-jam in my mind. I got up, pulled on shirt and denim pants, and made my way to the control room. I spent the better part of what remained of the night there, pacing up and down, watching two technicians repairing the vastly complicated innards of the ice-machine, reading the messages of congratulation which were still coming in, talking desultorily to the officer on deck and drinking endless cups of coffee. It passed the night for me and although I hadn't closed an eye I felt fresh and almost relaxed by the time morning came.

At the wardroom breakfast table that morning everyone seemed quietly cheerful. They knew they had done a good job, the whole world was telling them they had done a magnificent job, and you could see that they all regarded that job as being as good as over. No one appeared to doubt Swanson's ability to blow a hole through the ice. If it hadn't been for the presence of the ghost at the feast, myself, they would have been positively jovial.

"We'll pass up the extra cups of coffee this morning, gentlemen," Swanson said. "Drift Station Zebra is still waiting for us and even although I'm assured everyone there will survive, they must be feeling damned cold and miserable for all that. The ice-machine has been in operation for almost an hour now, at least we hope it has. We'll drop down right away and test it and after we've loaded the torpedoes —two should do it, I fancy—we'll blow our way up into this lead at Zebra."

Twenty minutes later the Dolphin was back where she belonged, 150 feet below the surface of the sea—or the ice-cap. After ten minutes' manœuvring, with a close check being kept on the plotting table to maintain our position relative to Drift Station Zebra, it was clear that the ice-machine was behaving perfectly normally again, tracing out the inverted ridges and valleys in the ice with its usual magical accuracy. Commander Swanson nodded his satisfaction.

"That's it, then." He nodded to Hansen and Mills, the torpedo officer. "You can go ahead now. Maybe you'd like to accompany them, Dr. Carpenter. Or is loading torpedoes old hat to you?"

"Never seen it," I said truthfully. "Thanks, I'd like to go along." Swanson was as considerate towards men as he was towards his beloved *Dolphin* which was why every man in the ship swore by him. He knew, or suspected that, apart from the shock I felt at my brother's death, I was worried stiff about other things: he would have heard, although he hadn't mentioned it to me and hadn't even asked me how I had slept, that I'd spent the night prowling aimlessly and restlessly above the control room: he knew I would be grateful for any distraction, for anything that would relieve my mind, however temporarily, of whatever it was that was troubling it. I wondered just how much that extraordinarily keen brain knew or guessed. But that was an unprofitable line of thought so I put it out of my mind and went along with Hansen and Mills. Mills was another like Raeburn, the navigation officer, he looked to me more like a college undergraduate than the highly competent officer he was, but I supposed it was just another sign that I was growing old.

Hansen crossed to a panel by the diving console and studied a group of lights. The night's sleep had done Hansen a great deal of good and, apart from the abraded skin on his forehead and round the cheekbones where the ice-spicules of last night had done their work, he was again his normal cheerfully-cynical relaxed self, fresh and rested and fit. He waved his hand at the panel.

"The torpedo safety light, Dr. Carpenter. Each green light represents a closed torpedo tube door. Six doors that open to the sea—bow caps, we call them—six rear doors

366

for loading the torpedoes. Only twelve lights but we study them very, very carefully—just to make sure that all the lights are green. For if any of them were red—any of the top six, that is, which represent the sea doors—well, that wouldn't be so good, would it?" He looked at Mills. "All green?"

"All green," Mills echoed.

We moved for'ard along the wardroom passage, and dropped down the wide companionway into the crew's mess. From there we moved into the for'ard torpedo storage room. Last time I'd been there, on the morning after our departure from the Clyde, nine or ten men had been sleeping in their bunks; now all the bunks were empty. Five men were waiting for us: four ratings and a Petty Officer Bowen whom Hansen, no stickler for protocol, addressed as Charlie.

"You will see now," Hansen observed to me, "why officers are more highly paid than enlisted men, and deservedly so. While Charlie and his gallant men skulk here behind two sets of collision bulkheads, we must go and test the safety of the tubes. Regulations. Still, a cool head, and an iron nerve: we do it gladly for our men."

Bowen grinned and unclipped the first collision bulkhead door. We stepped over the eighteen-inch sill, leaving the five men behind, and waited until the door had been clipped up again before opening the for'ard collision bulkhead door and stepping over the second sill into the cramped torpedo room. This time the door was swung wide open and hooked back on a heavy standing catch.

"All laid down in the book of rules," Hansen said. "the only time the two doors can be opened at the same time is when we're actually loading the torpedoes." He checked the position of metal handles at the rear of the tubes, reached up, swung down a steel-spring microphone and flicked a switch. "Ready to test tubes. All manual levers shut. All lights showing green?"

"All lights still green." The answering voice from the overhead squawk box was hollow, metallic, queerly impersonal.

"You already checked," I said mildly.

"So we check again. Same old book of rules." He grinned. "Besides, my grandpa died at ninety-seven and I aim

367

to beat his record. Take no chances and you run no risk. What are they to be, George?"

"Three and four." I could see the brass plaques on the circular rear doors of the tubes, 2, 4 and 6 on the port side, 1, 3 and 5 on the starboard. Lieutenant Mills was proposing to use the central tubes on each side.

Mills unhooked a rubber torch from the bulkhead and approached number 3 first. Hansen said: "Still no chances. First of all George opens the test cock in the rear door which will show if there is any water at all in the tubes. Shouldn't be, but sometimes a little gets past the bow caps. If the test cock shows nothing, then he opens the door and shines his torch up to examine the bow cap and see that there is no obstruction in the tube. How's it, George?"

"O.K., number three." Three times Mills lifted the test cock handle and no trace of water appeared. "Opening the door now."

He hauled on the big lever at the rear, pulled it clear and swung back the heavy circular door. He shone his torch up the gleaming inside length of the tube, then straightened. "Clean as a whistle and dry as a bone."

"That's not the way he was taught to report it," Hansen said sorrowfully. "I don't know what the young officers are coming to these days. Right, George, number four."

Mills grinned, secured the rear door on number 3 and crossed to number 4. He lifted the test cock handle and said: "Oh-oh."

"What is it?" Hansen asked.

"Water," Mills said tersely.

"Is there much? Let's see?"

"Just a trickle."

"Is that bad?" I asked.

"It happens," Hansen said briefly. He joggled the handle up and down and another spoonful of water appeared. "You can get a slightly imperfect bow-cap and if you go deep enough to build up sufficient outside pressure you can get a trickle of water coming in. Probably what has happened in this case. If the bow-cap was open, friend, at this depth the water would come out of that spout like a bullet. But no chances, no chances." He reached for

368

the microphone again. "Number four bow-cap still green? We have a little water here."

"Still green."

Hansen looked down at Mills. "How's it coming?"

"Not so much now."

"Control centre," Hansen said into the microphone. "Check the trim chit, just to make sure."

There was a pause, then the box crackled again.

"Captain here. All tubes showing 'Empty.' Signed by Lieutenant Hansen and the foreman engineer."

"Thank you, sir." Hansen switched off and grinned. "Lieutenant Hansen's word is good enough for me any day. How's it now?"

"Stopped."

"Open her up."

Mills tugged the heavy lever. It moved an inch or two, then stuck. "Uncommon stiff," he commented.

"You torpedomen never heard of anything called lubricating oil?" Hansen demanded. "Weight, George, weight."

Mills applied more weight. The lever moved another couple of inches. Mills scowled, shifted his feet to get maximum purchase and heaved just as Hansen shouted: "No! Stop! For God's sake, stop!"

He was too late. He was a lifetime too late. The lever snapped clear, the heavy circular rear door smashed open as violently as if it had been struck by some gigantic battering ram and a roaring torrent of water burst into the for'ard torpedo room. The sheer size, the enormous column of water was staggering. It was like a giant hosepipe, like one of the outlet pipes of the Boulder Dam. It caught up Lieutenant Mills, already badly injured by the flailing sweep of that heavy door and swept him back across the torpedo room to smash heavily against the after bulkhead; for a moment he half-stood there, pinned by the power of that huge jet, then slid down limply to the deck.

"Blow all main ballast!" Hansen shouted into the microphone. He was hanging on to a rear torpedo door to keep from being carried away and even above the thunderous roar of the waters his voice carried clearly. "Emergency. Blow all main ballast. Number four tube open to the sea.

369

Blow all main ballast!" He released his grip, staggered across the deck trying to keep his balance in the madly swirling already foot-deep waters. "Get out of here, for God's sake."

He should have saved his energy and breath. I was already on my way out of there. I had Mills under the arms and was trying to drag him over the high sill of the for'ard collision bulkhead and I was making just no headway at all. The proper trim of a submarine is a delicate thing at the best of times and even after these few seconds the nose of the *Dolphin,* heavy with the tons of water that had already poured in, was beginning to cant sharply downwards: trying to Drag Mills and at the same time keep my balance on that sloping deck with knee-high water boiling around me was more than I could do; but suddenly Hansen had Mills by the feet and I stumbled off-balance, tripped over the high sill and fell backwards into the confined space between the two collision bulkheads, dragging Mills after me.

Hansen was still on the other side of the bulkhead. I could hear him cursing steadily, monotonously and as if he meant it as he struggled to unhook the heavy door from its standing catch. Because of the steep downward pitch of the *Dolphin's* deck he had to lean all his weight against the massive steel door to free the catch, and with his insecure footing among the swirling waters on that sloping slippery deck he was obviously having the devil's own time trying to release it. I let Mills lie, jumped over the sill, flung my shoulder against the door and with the suddenly added pressure the latch clicked free. The heavy door at once swung half-shut, carrying us along with it and knocking us both off our feet into the battering-ram path of that torrent still gushing from number 4 tube. Coughing and spluttering we scrambled upright again, crossed the sill and, hanging on to a clip handle apiece, tried to drag the door shut.

Twice we tried and twice we failed. The water boiled in through the tube and its level was now almost lipping the top of the sill. With every second that passed the downward angle of the *Dolphin* increased and with every extra degree of steepness the task of pulling that door uphill against the steadily increasing gravity became more and more difficult.

The water began to spill over the sill on to our feet.

Hansen grinned at me. At least, I thought for a moment he was grinning, but the white teeth were clamped tightly together and there was no amusement at all in his eyes. He shouted above the roar of the water: "It's now or never."

A well-taken point. It was indeed now or never. At a signal from Hansen we flung our combined weights on to those clip-handles each with one hand to a clip while the other braced against the bulkhead to give maximum purchase. We got the door to within four inches. It swung open. We tried again. Still four inches and I knew that all our strength had gone into that one.

"Can you hold it for a moment?" I shouted.

He nodded. I shifted both hands to the lower corner clip, dropped to the deck, braced my feet against the sill and straightened both legs in one convulsive jerk. The door crashed shut, Hansen jammed his clip home, I did the same with mine and we were safe. For the moment we were safe.

I left Hansen to secure the remaining clips and started knocking the clips off the after collision bulkhead door. I'd only got as far as the first one when the others started falling off by themselves. Petty Officer Bowen and his men, on the other side of that door, needed no telling that we wanted out of there just as fast as possible. The door was pulled open and my ear drums popped with the abrupt fall in air pressure. I could hear the steady echoing roar of air blasting into the ballast tanks under high pressure. I hoisted Mills by the shoulders, strong competent hands lifted him out and over the sill and a couple of seconds later Hansen and I were beside him.

"In God's name!" Petty Officer Bowen said to Hansen. "What's gone wrong?"

"Number four tube open to the sea."

"Jesus!"

"Clip up that door," Hansen ordered. "But good." He left at a dead run, clawing his way up the sharply sloping deck of the torpedo storage room. I took a look at Lieutenant Mills—one short look was all I needed—and followed after Hansen. Only I didn't run. Running wasn't going to help anybody now.

371

The roar of compressed air filled the ship, the ballast tanks were rapidly emptying, but still the *Dolphin* continued on its deadly dive, arrowing down for the dark depths of the Arctic: not even the massive compressed-air banks of the submarine could hope to cope so soon with the effects of the scores of tons of sea-water that had already flooded into the for'ard torpedo room: I wondered bleakly if they would ever be able to cope at all. As I walked along the wardroom passage, using the hand-rail to haul myself up that crazily canted deck, I could feel the entire submarine shudder beneath my feet. No doubt about what that was, Swanson had the great turbines turning over at maximum revolutions, the big bronze propellers threshing madly in reverse, trying to bite deep into the water to slow up the diving submarine.

You can smell fear. You can smell it and you can see it and I could do both as I hauled my way into the control centre of the *Dolphin* that morning. Not one man as much as flickered an eye in my direction as I passed by the sonar room. They had no eyes for me. They had no eyes for anybody: tense, strained, immobile, with hunted faces, they had eyes for one thing only—the plummetting needle on the depth gauge.

The needle was passing the six-hundred-feet mark. Six hundred feet. No conventional submarine I'd ever been on could have operated at this depth. Could have survived at this depth. Six hundred and fifty. I thought of the fantastic outside pressure that represented and I felt far from happy. Someone else was feeling far from happy also, the young seaman manning the inboard diving seat. His fists were clenched till the knuckles showed, a muscle was jumping in his cheek, a nerve twitching in his neck and he had the look on his face of a man who sees the bony finger of death beckoning.

Seven hundred feet. Seven hundred and fifty. Eight hundred. I'd never heard of a submarine that had reached that depth and lived. Neither, apparently, had Commander Swanson.

"We have just set up a new mark, men," he said. His voice was calm and relaxed and although he was far too intelligent a man not to be afraid, no trace of it showed in tone or manner. "Lowest recorded dive ever, as far as I am aware. Speed of descent?"

"No change."

"It will change soon. The torpedo room must be about full now—apart from the pocket of air compressed under high pressure." He gazed at the dial and tapped his teeth thoughtfully with a thumb-nail—this, for Swanson, was probably the equivalent of going into hysterics. "Blow the diesel tanks: blow the fresh-water tanks." Imperturbable though he sounded, Swanson was close to desperation for this was the counsel of despair: thousands of miles from home and supplies, yet jettisoning all the diesel and drinking water, the lack of either of which could make all the difference between life and death. But, at that moment, it didn't matter: all that mattered was lightening ship.

"Main ballast tanks empty," the diving officer reported. His voice was hoarse and strained.

Swanson nodded, said nothing. The volume of the sound of the compressed air had dropped at least seventy-five per cent and the suddenly comparative silence was sinister, terrifying, as if it meant that the *Dolphin* was giving up the fight. Now we had only the slender reserves of the fresh water and diesel to save us: at the rate at which the *Dolphin* was still diving I didn't see how it could.

Hansen was standing beside me. I noticed blood dripping from his left hand to the deck and when I looked more closely I could see that two of his fingers were broken. It must have happened in the torpedo room. At the moment, it didn't seem important. It certainly didn't seem important to Hansen. He was entirely oblivious of it.

The pressure gauge fell farther and still farther. I knew now that nothing could save the *Dolphin*. A bell rang. Swanson swung down a microphone and pressed a button.

"Engine-room here," a metallic voice came through. "We must slow down. Main bearings beginning to smoke, she'll seize up any moment."

"Maintain revolutions." Swanson swung back the microphone. The youngster at the diving console, the one with the jumping cheek muscles and the nervous twitch, started to mumble, "Oh, dear God, oh, dear God," over and over again, softly at first, then the voice climbing up the scale

373

to hysteria. Swanson moved two paces, touched him on the shoulder. "Do you mind, laddie? I can hardly hear myself think." The mumblings stopped and the boy sat quite still, his face carved from grey granite, the nerve in his neck going like a trip-hammer.

"How much more of this will she take?" I asked casually. At least, I meant it to sound casual but it came out like the croak of an asthmatic bullfrog.

"I'm afraid we're moving into the realms of the unknown," Swanson admitted calmly. "One thousand feet plus. If that dial is right, we passed the theoretical implosion point—where the hull should have collapsed—fifty feet ago. At the present moment she's being subjected to well over a million tons of pressure." Swanson's repose, his glacial calm, was staggering, they must have scoured the whole of America to find a man like that. If ever there was the right man in the right place at the right time it was Commander Swanson in the control room of a runaway submarine diving to depths hundreds of feet below what any submarine had ever experienced before.

"She's slowing," Hansen whispered.

"She's slowing," Swanson nodded.

She wasn't slowing half fast enough for me. It was impossible that the pressure hull could hold out any longer. I wondered vaguely what the end would be like, then put the thought from my mind, I would never know anything about it, anyway. At that depth the pressure must have been about twenty tons to the square foot, we'd been squashed as flat as flounders before our senses could even begin to record what was happening to us.

The engine-room call-up bell rang again. The voice this time was imploring, desperate. We must ease up, Captain. Switch gear is turning red hot. We can see it glowing."

"Wait till it's white hot, then you can complain about it," Swanson said curtly. If the engines were going to break down they were going to break down; but until they did he'd tear the life out of them in an attempt to save the *Dolphin*. Another bell rang.

"Control room?" The voice was harsh, high-pitched. "Crew's mess deck here. Water is beginning to come in." For the first time, every eye in the control room turned

374

away from the depth gauge and fixed itself on that loud-speaker. The hull was giving at last under the fantastic pressure, the crushing weight. One little hole, one tiny threadlike crack as a starting point and the pressure hull would rip and tear and flatten like a toy under a steam-hammer. A quick glance at the strained, shocked faces showed this same thought in every mind.

"Where?" Swanson demanded.

"Starboard bulkhead."

"How much?"

"A pint or two, just trickling down the bulkhead. And it's getting worse. It's getting worse all the time. For God's sake, Captain, what are we going to do?"

"What are you going to do?" Swanson echoed. "Mop the damn' stuff up, of course. You don't want to live in a dirty ship, do you?" He hung up.

"She's stopped. She's stopped." Four words and a prayer. I'd been wrong about every eye being on the loudspeaker, one pair of eyes had never left the depth gauge, the pair belonging to the youngster at the console.

"She's stopped," the diving officer confirmed. His voice had a shake in it.

No one spoke. The blood continued to drip unheeded from Hansen's crushed fingers. I thought that I detected, for the first time, a faint sheen of sweat on Swanson's brow, but I couldn't be sure. The deck still shuddered beneath our feet as the giant engines strove to lift the *Dolphin* out of those deadly depths, the compressed air still hissed into the diesel and fresh-water tanks. I could no longer see the depth gauge, the diving officer had drawn himself up so close to it that he obscured most of it from me.

Ninety seconds passed, ninety seconds that didn't seem any longer than a leap year, ninety interminable seconds while we waited for the sea to burst in to our hull and take us for its own, then the diving officer said: "Ten feet. *Up.*"

"Are you sure?" Swanson asked.

"A year's pay."

"We're not out of the wood yet," Swanson said mildly. "The hull can still go—it should have gone a damn' long time ago. Another hundred feet—that means a couple of tons less pressure to the square foot—and I think we'll have a chance. At least a fifty-fifty chance. And after that the chances will improve with every foot we ascend; and as we ascend the highly compressed air in the torpedo room will expand, driving out water and so lightening ship."

" Still rising," the diving officer said. " Still rising. Speed of ascent changed."

Swanson walked across to the diving stand and studied the slow movement of the depth gauge dial. " How much fresh water left?"

" Thirty per cent."

" Secure blowing fresh-water ballast. Engines all back two-thirds."

The roar of compressed air fell away and the deck vibration eased almost to nothing as the engine revolutions fell from emergency power to two-third full speed.

" Speed of ascent unchanged," the diving officer reported. " One hundred feet up."

" Secure blowing diesel." The roar of compressed air stopped completely. " All back one-third."

" Still rising. Still rising."

Swanson took a silk handkerchief from his pocket and wiped his face and neck. "I was a little worried there," he said to no one in particular, " and I don't much care who knows it." He reached for a microphone and I could hear his voice booming faintly throughout the ship.

"Captain here. All right, you can all start breathing again. Everything is under control, we're on our way up. As a point of interest we're still over three hundred feet deeper than the lowest previous submarine dive ever recorded."

I felt as if I had just been through the rollers of a giant mangle. We all looked as if we'd just been through the rollers of a giant mangle. A voice said: " I've never smoked in my life, but I'm starting now. Someone give me a cigarette." Hansen said: " When we get back to the States do you know what I'm going to do?"

" Yes," Swanson said. " You're going to scrape together your last cent, go up to Groton and throw the biggest, the most expensive party ever for the men who built this boat. You're too late, Lieutenant, I thought of it first." He

376

checked abruptly and said sharply: "What's happened to your hand?"

Hansen lifted his left hand and stared at it in surprise. "I never even knew I'd been scratched. Must have happened with that damn' door in the torpedo room. There's a medical supply box there, Doc. Would you fix this."

"You did a damn' fine job there, John," Swanson said warmly. "Getting that door closed, I mean. Couldn't have been easy."

"It wasn't. All pats on the back to our friend here," Hansen said. "He got it closed, not me. And if we hadn't got it closed——"

"Or if I'd let you load the torpedoes when you came back last night," Swanson said grimly. "When we were sitting on the surface and the hatches wide open. We'd have been eight thousand feet down now and very, very dead."

Hansen suddenly snatched his hand away. "My God!" he said remorsefully. "I'd forgotten. Never mind this damned hand of mine. George Mills, the torpedo officer. He caught a pretty bad smack. You'd better see him first. Or Doc Benson."

I took his hand back. "No hurry for either of us. Your fingers first. Mills isn't feeling a thing."

"Good lord!" Astonishment showed in Hansen's face, maybe shock at my callousness. "When he recovers consciousness——"

"He'll never recover consciousness again," I said. "Lieutenant Mills is dead."

"What!" Swanson's fingers bit deeply, painfully into my arm. "'Dead,' did you say?"

"That column of water from number four tube came in like an express train," I said tiredly. "Flung him right back against the after bulkhead and smashed in the occiput —the back of his head—like an eggshell. Death must have been instantaneous."

"Young George Mills," Swanson whispered. His face had gone very pale. "Poor young beggar. His first trip on the *Dolphin*. And now—just like that. Killed."

"Murdered," I said.

"What!' If Commander Swanson didn't watch out with his fingers he'd have my upper arm all black and blue. "What was that you said?"

" 'Murdered,' I said. 'Murdered,' I meant."

Swanson stared at me for a long moment, his face empty of expression, but the eyes strained and tired and suddenly somehow old. He wheeled, walked across to the diving officer, spoke a few words to him and returned. "Come on," he said abruptly. "You can fix up the lieutenant's hand in my cabin."

VII

"You realise the seriousness of what you are saying?" Swanson asked. "You are making a grave accusation——"

"Come off it," I said rudely. "This is not a court of law and I'm not accusing anyone. All I say is that murder has been done. Whoever left that bow-cap door open is directly responsible for the death of Lieutenant Mills."

"What do you mean 'left the door open'? Who says anyone left the door open? It could have been due to natural causes. And even if—I can't see it—that door had been left open, you can't accuse a man of murder because of carelessness or forgetfulness or because——"

"Commander Swanson," I said. "I'll go on record as saying that you are probably the best naval officer I have ever met. But being best at that doesn't mean that you're best at everything. There are noticeable gaps in your education, Commander, especially in the appreciation of the finer points of skulduggery. You require an especially low and devious type of mind for that and I'm afraid that you just haven't got it. Doors left open by natural causes, you say. What natural causes?"

"We've hit the ice a few hefty smacks," Swanson said slowly. "That could have jarred it open. Or when we poked through the ice last night a piece of ice, a stalactite, say, could have——"

"Your tubes are recessed, aren't they. Mighty oddly-shaped stalactite that would go down then bend in at a right angle

378

to reach the door—and even then it would only shut it more tightly."

"The doors are tested every time we're in harbour," Commander Swanson persisted quietly. "They're also opened when we open tubes to carry out surface trimming tests in dock. Any dockyard has pieces of waste, rope and other rubbish floating around that could easily have jammed a door open."

"The safety lights showed the doors shut."

"They could have been opened just a crack, not enough to disengage the safety contact."

"Open a crack! Why do you think Mills is dead? If you've ever seen the jet of water that hits the turbine blades in a hydro-electric plant, then you'll know how that water came in. A crack? My God! How are those doors operated?"

"Two ways. Remote control, hydraulic, just press a button: then there are manually-operated levers in the torpedo room itself."

I turned to Hansen. He was sitting on the bunk beside me, his face pale as I splinted his broken fingers. I said: "Those hand-operated levers. Were they in the shut position?"

"You heard me say so in there. Of course they were. First thing we always check."

"Somebody doesn't like you," I said to Swanson. "Or somebody doesn't like the *Dolphin*. Or somebody knew that the *Dolphin* was going searching for the Zebra survivors and they didn't like that either. So they sabotaged the ship. You will remember you were rather surprised you didn't have to correct the *Dolphin*'s trim? It had been your intention to carry out a slow-time dive to check the underwater trim because you thought that would have been affected by the fact that you had no torpedoes in the for'ard tubes. But surprise, surprise. She didn't need any correction."

"I'm listening," Swanson said quietly. He was with me now. He was with me all the way. He cocked an eyebrow as we heard water flooding back into the tanks. The repeater gauge showed 200 feet, Swanson must have ordered his diving officer to level off at that depth. The *Dolphin* was still canted nose downwards at an angle of about 25°.

"She didn't need any correcting because some of her tubes were already full of water. For all I know maybe

379

number three tube, the one we tested and found O.K. is the only one that is *not* full of water. Our clever little pal left the doors open, disconnected the hand-operated levers so that they appeared to be in the shut position when they were actually open and crossed over a few wires in a junction box so that the open position showed green while the closed showed red. A man who knew what he was about could have done it in a few minutes. Two men who knew what they were about could have done it in no time at all. I'll lay anything you like that when you're eventually in a position to check you'll find the levers disconnected, the wires crossed and the inlets of the test-cocks blocked with sealing-wax, quick-drying paint or even chewing-gum so that when the test-cocks were opened nothing would show and you would assume the tubes to be empty."

" There was a trickle from the test-cock in number four tube," Hansen objected.

" Low-grade chewing-gum."

" The murderous swine," Swanson said calmly. His restraint was far more effective than the most thunderous denunciations could ever have been. " He could have murdered us all. But for the grace of God and the Groton boatyard shipwrights he would have murdered us all."

" He didn't mean to," I said. " He didn't mean to kill anyone. You had intended to carry out a slow-time dive to check trim in the Holy Loch before you left that evening. You told me so yourself. Did you announce it to the crew, post it up in daily orders or something like that?"

" Both."

" So. Our pal knew. He also knew that you carried out those checks when the boat is still awash or just under the surface. When you checked the tubes to see if they were O.K., water would come in, too much water to permit the rear doors to be shut again, but not under such high pressure that you wouldn't have time and to spare to close the for'ard collision bulkhead door and make a leisurely retreat in good order. What would have happened? Not much. At the worst you would have settled down slowly to the bottom and stayed there. Not deep enough to worry the *Dolphin*. In a submarine of even ten years ago it might have been fatal for all, because of the limited air supply. Not to-day when your air purifying machines can let you stay down for months at a time. You just float up your emergency indicator buoy and telephone, tell your story, sit around and drink coffee till a naval diver comes down and replaces the bow cap, pump out the torpedo room and surface again. Our unknown pal—or pals—didn't mean to kill anyone. But they did mean to delay you. And they would have delayed you. We know now that you could have got to the surface under your own steam, but even so your top brass would have insisted that you go into dock for a day or two to check that everything was O.K."

"Why should anyone want to delay us?" Swanson asked. I thought he had an unnecessarily speculative look in his eyes, but it was hard to be sure, Commander Swanson's face showed exactly what Commander Swanson wanted it to show and no more.

"My God, do you think I know the answer to that one?" I said irritably.

"No. No, I don't think so." He could have been more emphatic about it. "Tell me, Dr. Carpenter, do you suspect some member of the *Dolphin*'s crew to be responsible?"

"Do you really need an answer to that one?"

"I suppose not," he sighed. "Going to the bottom of the Arctic Ocean is not a very attractive way of committing suicide, and if any member of the crew had jinxed things he'd damn' soon have unjinxed them as soon as he realised that we weren't going to carry out trim checks in shallow water. Which leaves only the civilian dockyard workers in Scotland— and every one of them has been checked and rechecked and given a top-grade security clearance."

"Which means nothing. There are plushy Moscow hotels and British and American prisons full of people who had top-grade security clearances . . . What are you going to do now, Commander. About the *Dolphin*, I mean?"

"I've been thinking about it. In the normal course of events the thing to do would be to close the bow-cap of number four and pump out the torpedo room, then go in and close the rear door of number four. But the bow-cap door won't close. Within a second of John's telling us that number four was open to the sea the diving officer hit the hydraulic button—the one that closes it by remote control. You saw for yourself that not! ing happened. It must be jammed."

" You bet your life it's jammed," I said grimly. " A sledge-hammer might do some good but pressing buttons won't."

" I could go back to that lead we've just left, surface again and send a diver under the ice to investigate and see what he can do, but I'm not going to ask any man to risk his life doing that. I could retreat to the open sea, surface and fix it there, but not only would it be a damned slow and uncomfortable trip with the *Dolphin* canted at this angle, it might take us days before we got back here again. And some of the Drift Station Zebra men are pretty far through. It might be too late."

" Well, then," I said. " You have the man to hand, Commander. I told you when I first met you that environmental health studies were my speciality, especially in the field of pressure extremes when escaping from submarines. I've done an awful lot of simulated sub escapes, Commander. I do know a fair amount about pressures, how to cope with them and how I react to them myself."

" How do you react to them, Dr. Carpenter?"

" A high tolerance. They don't worry me much."

" What do you have in mind?"

" You know damn' well what I have in mind," I said impatiently. " Drill a hole in the door of the after collision bulkhead, screw in a high-pressure hose, open the door, shove someone in the narrow space between the two collision bulkheads and turn up the hose until the pressure between the collision bulkheads equals that in the torpedo room. You have the clips eased off the for'ard collision door. When the pressures are equalised it opens at a touch, you walk inside, close number four rear door and walk away again. That's what you had in mind wasn't it?"

" More or less," he admitted. " Except that *you* are no part of it. Every man on this ship has made simulated escapes. They all know the effects of pressure. And most of them are a great deal younger than you."

" Suit yourself," I said. " But age has little to do with the ability to stand stresses. You didn't pick a teen-ager as the first American to orbit the earth, did you? As for simulated escapes, making a free ascent up a hundred-foot tank is a different matter altogether from going inside an iron box, waiting for the slow build-up of pressure, working under that pressure, then waiting for the slow process of decompression. I've seen young men, big, tough, very, very fit young men break up completely under those circumstances and almost go crazy trying to get out. The combination of physiological and psychological factors involved is pretty fierce."

" I think," Swanson said slowly, " that I'd sooner have you —what do the English say, batting on a sticky wicket—than almost any man I know. But there's a point you've overlooked. What would the Admiral Commanding Atlantic Submarines say to me if he knew I'd let a civilian go instead of one of my own men?"

" If you *don't* let me go, I know what he'll say. He'll say: " We must reduce Commander Swanson to lieutenant, j-g., because he had on board the *Dolphin* an acknowledged expert in this speciality and refused, out of stiff-necked pride, to use him, thereby endangering the lives of his crew and the safety of his ship.' "

Swanson smiled a pretty bleak smile, but with the desperately narrow escape we had just had, the predicament we were still in and the fact that his torpedo officer was lying dead not so many feet away, I hardly expected him to break into gales of laughter. He looked at Hansen: " What do you say, John?"

" I've seen more incompetent characters that Dr. Carpenter," Hansen said. " Also, he gets about as nervous and panic-stricken as a bag of Portland cement."

" He has qualifications you do not look to find in the average medical man," Swanson agreed. " I shall be glad to accept your offer. One of my men will go with you. That way the dictates of common sense and honour are both satisfied."

It wasn't all that pleasant, not by quite a way, but it wasn't all that terribly bad either. It went off exactly as it could have been predicted it would go off. Swanson cautiously eased the *Dolphin* up until her stern was just a few feet beneath the ice: this reduced the pressure in the torpedo room to a minimum, but even at that the bows were still about a hundred feet down.

A hole was drilled in the after collision bulkhead door and an armoured high-pressure hose screwed into position. Dressed in porous rubber suits and equipped with an aqualung apiece, a young torpedoman by the name of Murphy and I went inside and stood in the gap between the two collision bulkheads. High-powered air hissed into the confined space. Slowly the pressure rose: twenty, thirty, forty, fifty pounds to the square inch. I could feel the pressure on lungs and ears, the pain behind the eyes, the slight wooziness that comes from the poisonous effect of breathing pure oxygen under such pressure. But I was used to it, I knew it wasn't going to kill me: I wondered if young Murphy knew that. This was the stage where the combined physical and mental effects became too much for most people, but if Murphy was scared or panicky or suffering from bodily distress he hid it well. Swanson would have picked his best man and to be the best man in a company like that Murphy had to be something very special.

We eased off the clips on the for'ard bulkhead door, knocked them off cautiously as the pressures equalised. The water in the torpedo room was about two feet above the level of the sill and as the door came ajar the water boiled whitely through into the collision space while compressed air hissed out from behind us to equalise the lowering pressure of the air in the torpedo room. For about ten seconds we had to hang on grimly to hold the door and maintain our balance while water and air fought and jostled in a seething maelstrom to find their own natural levels. The door opened wide. The water level now extended from about thirty inches up on the collision bulkhead to the for'ard deckhead of the torpedo room. We crossed the sill, switched on our waterproof torches and ducked under.

The temperature of that water was about 28° F.—four below freezing. Those porous rubber suits were specially designed to cope with icy waters but even so I gasped with the shock of it—as well as one can gasp when breathing pure oxygen under heavy pressure. But we didn't linger, for the longer we remained there the longer we would have to spend

384

decompressing afterwards. We half-walked, half-swum towards the fore end of the compartment, located the rear door on number 4 tube and closed it, but not before I had a quick look at the inside of the pressure cock. The door itself seemed undamaged: the body of the unfortunate Lieutenant Mills had absorbed its swinging impact and prevented it from being wrenched off its hinges. It didn't seem distorted in any way, and fitted snugly into place. We forced its retaining lever back into place and left.

Back in the collision compartment we gave the prearranged taps on the door. Almost at once we heard the subdued hum of a motor as the high-speed extraction pumps in the torpedo room got to work, forcing the water out through the hull. Slowly the water level dropped and as it dropped the air pressure as slowly decreased. Degree by degree the *Dolphin* began to come back on even keel. When the water was finally below the level of the for'ard sill we gave another signal and the remaining over-pressure air was slowly bled out through the hose.

A few minutes later, as I was stripping off the rubber suit, Swanson asked: "Any trouble?"

"None. You picked a good man in Murphy."

"The best. Many thanks, Doctor." He lowered his voice. "You wouldn't by any chance——"

"You know damned well I would," I said. "I did. Not sealing-wax, not chewing-gum, not paint. Glue, Commander Swanson. That's how they blocked the test-cock inlet. The old-fashioned animal hide stuff that comes out of a tube. Ideal for the job."

"I see," he said, and walked away.

The *Dolphin* shuddered along its entire length as the torpedo hissed out of its tube—number 3 tube, the only one in the submarine Swanson could safely rely upon.

"Count it down," Swanson said to Hansen. "Tell me when we should hit, tell me when we should hear it hit."

Hansen looked at the stop-watch in his bandaged hand and nodded. The seconds passed slowly. I could see Hansen's lips move silently. Then he said: "We should be hitting—now," and two or three seconds later: "We should be hearing —now."

Whoever had been responsible for the settings and time calculations on that torpedo had known what he was about. Just on Hansen's second "now" we felt as much as heard the clanging vibration along the *Dolphin*'s hull as the shock-waves from the exploding war-head reached us. The deck shook briefly beneath our feet but the impact was nowhere nearly as powerful as I had expected. I was relieved. I didn't have to be a clairvoyant to know that everyone was relieved. No submarine had ever before been in the vicinity of a torpedo detonating under the ice-pack: no one had known to what extent the tamping effect of overhead ice might have increased the pressure and destructive effect of the lateral shock-waves.

"Nicely," Swanson murmured. "Very nicely done indeed. Both ahead one-third. I hope that bang had considerably more effect on the ice than it had on our ship." He said to Benson at the ice-machine: "Let us know as soon as we reach the lead, will you?"

He moved to the plotting table. Raeburn looked up and said: "Five hundred yards gone, five hundred to go."

"All stop," Swanson said. The slight vibration of the engine died away. "We'll just mosey along very carefully indeed. That explosion may have sent blocks of ice weighing a few tons apiece pretty far down into the sea. I don't want to be doing any speed at all if we meet any of them on the way up."

"Three hundred yards to go," Raeburn said.

"All clear. All clear all round," the sonar room reported.

"Still thick ice," Benson intoned. "Ah! That's it. We're under the lead. Thin ice. Well, five or six feet."

"Two hundred yards," Raeburn said. "It checks."

We drifted slowly onwards. At Swanson's orders the propellers kicked over once or twice then stopped again.

"Fifty yards," Raeburn said. "Near enough."

"Ice reading?"

"No change? Five feet, about."

"Speed?"

"One knot."

"Position?"

"One thousand yards exactly. Passing directly under target area."

" And nothing on the ice-machine. Nothing at all?"

" Not a thing." Benson shrugged and looked at Swanson.
The captain walked across and watched the inked stylus
draw its swiftly etched vertical lines on the paper.

" Peculiar, to say the least of it," Swanson murmured.
" Seven hundred pounds of very high-grade amatol in that lot.
Must be uncommonly tough ice in those parts. Again to
say the least of it. We'll go up to ninety feet and make a
few passes under the area. Floodlights on, TV on."

So we went up to ninety feet and made a few passes and
nothing came of it. The water was completely opaque, the
floods and camera useless. The ice-machine stubbornly
registered four to six feet—it was impossible to be more
accurate—all the time.

" Well, that seems to be it," Hansen said. " We back off and
have another go?"

" Well, I don't know," Swanson said pensively. " What
say we just try to shoulder our way up?"

" Shoulder our way up?" Hansen wasn't with him : neither
was I. " What kind of shoulder is going to heave five
feet of ice to one side?"

" I'm not sure. The thing is, we've been working from
unproved assumptions and that's always a dangerous basis.
We've been assuming that if the torpedo didn't blow the
ice to smithereens it would at least blow a hole in it. Maybe
it doesn't happen that way at all. Maybe there's just a big
upward pressure of water distributed over a fair area that
heaves the ice up and breaks it into pretty big chunks that
just settle back into the water again in their original position
in the pattern of a dried-up mud hole with tiny cracks all
round the isolated sections. But with cracks all round.
Narrow cracks, but there. Cracks so narrow that the ice-
machine couldn't begin to register them even at the slow
speed we were doing." He turned to Raeburn. " What's our
position?"

" Still in the centre of the target area, sir."

" Take her up till we touch the ice," Swanson said.

He didn't have to add any cautions about gentleness. The
diving officer took her up like floating thistledown until we
felt a gentle bump.

" Hold her there," Swanson said. He peered at the TV

screen but the water was so opaque that all definition vanished half-way up the sail. He nodded to the diving officer. " Kick her up—hard."

Compressed air roared into the ballast tanks. Seconds passed without anything happening then all at once the *Dolphin* shuddered as something very heavy and very solid seemed to strike the hull. A moment's pause, another solid shock then we could see the edge of a giant segment of ice sliding down the face of the TV screen.

" Well, now, I believe I might have had a point there," Swanson remarked. " We seem to have hit a crack between two chunks of ice almost exactly in the middle. Depth?"

" Forty-five."

" Fifteen feet showing. And I don't think we can expect to lift the hundreds of tons of ice lying over the rest of the hull. Plenty of positive buoyancy?"

" All we'll ever want."

" Then we'll call it a day at that. Right, Quartermaster, away you go up top and tell us what the weather is like."

I didn't wait to hear what the weather was like. I was interested enough in it, but I was even more interested in ensuring that Hansen didn't come along to his cabin in time to find me putting on the Mannlicher-Schoenauer along with my furs. But this time I stuck it not in its special holster but in the outside pocket of my caribou trousers. I thought it might come in handier there.

It was exactly noon when I clambered over the edge of the bridge and used a dangling rope to slide down a great rafted chunk of ice that slanted up almost to the top of the sail. The sky had about as much light in it as a late twilight in winter when the sky is heavy with grey cloud. The air was as bitter as ever, but the weather had improved for all that. The wind was down now, backed round to the north-east, seldom gusting at more than twenty m.p.h., the ice-spicules rising no more than two or three feet above the ice-cap. Nothing to tear your eyes out. To be able to see where you were going on that damned ice-cap made a very pleasant change.

There were eleven of us altogether—Commander Swanson himself, Dr. Benson, eight enlisted men and myself. Four of the men were carrying stretchers with them.

Even seven hundred pounds of the highest grade conventional explosive on the market hadn't managed to do very
much damage to the ice in that lead. Over an area of seventy
yards square or thereabouts the ice had fractured into large
fragments curiously uniform in size and roughly hexagonal
in shape but fallen back so neatly into position that you
couldn't have put a hand down most of the cracks between
the adjacent fragments of ice: many of the cracks, indeed,
were already beginning to bind together. A poor enough
performance for a torpedo war-head—until you remembered
that though most of its disruptive power must have been
directed downwards it had still managed to lift and fracture
a chunk of ice-cap weighing maybe 5,000 tons. Looked at in
that way, it didn't seem such a puny effort after all. Maybe
we'd been pretty lucky to achieve what we had.

We walked across to the eastern edge of the lead, scrambled
up on to the ice-pack proper and turned round to get our
bearings, to line up on the unwavering white finger of the
searchlight that reached straight up into the gloom of the
sky. No chance of getting lost this time. While the wind
stayed quiet and the spicules stayed down you could see
that lamp in the window ten miles away.

We didn't even need to take any bearings. A few steps
away and up from the edge of the lead and we could see
it at once. Drift Station Zebra. Three huts, one of them
badly charred, five blackened skeletons of what had once
been huts. Desolation.

"So that's it," Swanson said in my ear. "Or what's left
of it. "I've come a long way to see this."

"You nearly went a damned sight longer and never saw it,"
I said. "To the floor of the Arctic, I mean. Pretty, isn't it?"

Swanson shook his head slowly, moved on. There were
only a hundred yards to go. I led the way to the nearest
intact hut, opened the door and passed inside.

The hut was about thirty degrees warmer than the last
time I had been there, but still bitterly cold. Only Zabrinski
and Rawlings were awake. The hut smelt of burnt fuel,
disinfectant, iodine, morphine and a peculiar aroma arising
from a particularly repulsive looking hash that Rawlings was
industriously churning around in a dixie over the low stove.

"Ah, there you are." Rawlings said conversationally. He

might have been hailing a neighbour who'd phoned a minute previously to see if he could come across to borrow the lawnmower rather than greeting men he'd been fairly certain he'd never see again. " The time is perfect—just about to ring the dinner bell, Captain. Care for some Maryland chicken —I think."

" Not just at the moment, thank you," Swanson said politely. " Sorry about the ankle, Zabrinski. How is it?"

" Just fine, Captain, just fine. In a plaster cast." He thrust out a foot, stiffly. " The Doc here—Dr. Jolly—fixed me up real nice. Had much trouble last night?" This was for me.

" Dr. Carpenter had a great deal of trouble last night," Swanson said. " And we've had a considerable amount since. But later. Bring that stretcher in here. You first, Zabrinski. As for you, Rawlings, you can stop making like Escoffier. The *Dolphin*'s less than a couple of hundred yards from here. We'll have you all aboard in half an hour."

I heard a shuffling noise behind me. Dr. Jolly was on his feet, helping Captain Folsom to his. Folsom looked even weaker than he had done yesterday: his face, bandaged though it was, certainly looked worse.

" Captain Folsom," I introduced him. " Dr. Jolly. This is Commander Swanson, captain of the *Dolphin*. Dr. Benson."

" *Doctor* Benson, you said, old boy?" Jolly lifted an eyebrow. " My word, the pill-rolling competition's getting a little fierce in these parts. And Commander. By jove, but we're glad to see you fellows." The combination of the rich Irish brogue and the English slang of the twenties fell more oddly than ever on my ear, he reminded me of educated Singhalese I'd met with their precise, lilting, standard southern English interlarded with the catch-phrases of forty years ago. Topping, old bean, simply too ripping for words.

" I can understand that," Swanson smiled. He looked around the huddled unmoving men on the floor, men who might have been living or dead but for the immediate and smoky condensation from their shallow breathing, and his smile faded. He said to Captain Folsom: " I cannot tell you how sorry I am. This has been a dreadful thing."

Folsom stirred and said something but we couldn't make out what it was. Although his shockingly burnt face had

390

been bandaged since I'd seen him last it didn't seem to have done him any good: he was talking inside his mouth all right but the ravaged cheek and mouth had become so paralysed that his speech didn't emerge as any recognisable language. The good side of his face, the left, was twisted and furrowed and the eye above almost completely shut. This had nothing to do with any sympathetic neuro-muscular reaction caused by the wickedly charred right cheek. The man was in agony. I said to Jolly: "No morphine left?" I'd left him, I'd thought, with more than enough of it.

"Nothing left," he said tiredly. "I used the lot. The lot."

"Dr. Jolly worked all through the night," Zabrinski said quietly. "Eight hours. Rawlings and himself and Kinnaird. They never stopped once."

Benson had his medical kit open. Jolly saw it and smiled, a smile of relief, a smile of exhaustion. He was in far worse case than he'd been the previous evening. He hadn't had all that much in him when he'd started. But he'd worked. He'd worked a solid eight hours. He'd even fixed up Zabrinski's ankle. A good doctor. Conscientious, Hippocratic, anyway. He was entitled to relax. Now that there were other doctors here, he'd relax. But not before.

He began to ease Folsom into a sitting position and I helped him. He slid down himself, his back to the wall. "Sorry, and all that, you know," he said. His bearded frostbitten face twisted into the semblance of a grin. "A poor host."

"You can leave everything to us now, Dr. Jolly," Swanson said quietly. "You've got all the help that's going. One thing. All those men fit to be moved?"

"I don't know." Jolly rubbed an arm across bloodshot, smudged eyes. "I don't know. One or two of them slipped pretty far back last night. It's the cold. Those two. Pneumonia, I think. Something an injured man could fight off in a few days back home can be fatal here. It's the cold," he repeated. "Uses up ninety per cent of his energy not in fighting illness and infection but just generating enough heat to stay alive."

"Take it easy," Swanson said. "Maybe we'd better change our minds about that half-hour to get you all aboard. Who's

391

first for the ambulance, Dr. Benson?" Not Dr. Carpenter. Dr. Benson. Well, Benson was his own ship's doctor. But pointed, all the same. A regrettable coolness, as sudden in its onset as it was marked in degree, had appeared in his attitude towards me, and I didn't have to be beaten over the head with a heavy club to guess at the reason for the abrupt change.

"Zabrinski, Dr. Jolly, Captain Folsom and this man here," Benson said promptly.

"Kinnaird, radio operator," Kinnaird identified himself. "We never thought you'd make it, mate." This to me. He dragged himself somehow to his feet and stood there swaying. "I can walk."

"Don't argue," Swanson said curtly. "Rawlings stop stirring that filthy mush and get to your feet. Go with them. How long would it take you to run a cable from the boat, fix up a couple of big electric heaters in here, some lights?"

"Alone?"

"All the help you want, man."

"Fifteen minutes. I could rig a phone, sir."

"That would be useful. When the stretcher bearers come back bring blankets, sheets, hot water. Wrap the water containers in the blankets. Anything else, Dr. Benson?"

"Not now, sir."

"That's it then. Away you go."

Rawlings lifted the spoon from the pot, tasted it, smacked his lips in appreciation and shook his head sadly. "It's a crying shame," he said mournfully. "It really is." He went out in the wake of the stretcher bearers.

Of the eight men left lying on the floor, four were conscious. Hewson the tractor-driver, Naseby the cook, and two others who introduced themselves as Harrington. Twins. They'd even been burnt and frost-bitten in the same places. The other four were either sleeping or in coma. Benson and I started looking them over, Benson much more carefully than myself, very busy with thermometer and stethoscope. Looking for signs of pneumonia. I didn't think he'd have to look very far. Commander Swanson looked speculatively around the cabin, occasionally throwing a very odd look in my direction, occasionally flailing his arms across his chest to keep the circulation going. He had to. He didn't have the fancy furs I had and in spite of the solid-fuel stove the place was like an ice-box.

The first man I looked at was lying on his side in the far right-hand corner of the room. He had half-open eyes, just showing the lower arcs of his pupils, sunken temples, marble-white forehead and the only part of his face that wasn't bandaged was as cold as the marble in a winter graveyard. I said: "Who is this?"

"Grant. John Grant." Hewson, the dark quiet tractor-driver answered me. "Radio operator. Kinnaird's side-kick. How's it with him?"

"He's dead. He's been dead quite some time."

"Dead?" Swanson said sharply. "You sure?" I gave him my aloof professional look and said nothing. He went on to Benson: "Anybody too ill to be moved?"

"Those two here, I think," Benson said. He wasn't noticing the series of peculiar looks Swanson was letting me have, so he handed me his stethoscope. After a minute I straightened and nodded.

"Third-degree burns," Benson said to Swanson. "What we can see of them, that is. Both high temperatures, both very fast, very weak and erratic pulses, both with lung fluids."

"They'd have a better chance inside the *Dolphin*," Swanson said.

"You'll kill them getting there," I said. "Even if you could wrap them up warmly enough to take them back to the ship, hauling them up to the top of the sail and then lowering them vertically through those hatchways would finish them off."

"We can't stay out in that lead indefinitely," Swanson said. "I'll take the responsibility for moving them."

"Sorry, Captain." Benson shook his head gravely. "I agree with Dr. Carpenter."

Swanson shrugged and said nothing. Moments later the stretcher bearers were back, followed soon after by Rawlings and three other enlisted men carrying cables, heaters, lamps and a telephone. It took only a few minutes to button the heaters and lamps on to the cable. Rawlings cranked the call-up generator of his field-phone and spoke briefly into the mouthpiece. Bright lights came on and the heaters started to crackle and after a few seconds glow.

393

Hewson, Naseby and the Harrington twins left by stretcher. When they'd gone I unhooked the Coleman lamp. " You won't be needing this now," I said. " I won't be long."

" Where are you going?" Swanson's voice was quiet.

" I won't be long," I repeated. " Just looking around."

He hesitated, then stood to one side. I went out, moved round a corner of the hut and stopped. I heard the whirr of the call-up bell, a voice on the telephone. It was only a murmur to me, I couldn't make out what was being said. But I'd expected this.

The Coleman storm lantern flickered and faded in the wind, but didn't go out. Stray ice-spicules struck against the glass, but it didn't crack or break, it must have been one of those specially toughened glasses immune to a couple of hundred degrees' temperature range between the inside and the outside.

I made my way diagonally across to the only hut left on the south side. No trace of burning, charring or even smoke-blackening on the outside walls. The fuel store must have been the one next to it, on the same side and to the west, straight downwind : that almost certainly must have been its position to account for the destruction of all the other huts, and the grotesquely buckled shape of its remaining girders made this strong probability a certainty. Here had been the heart of the fire.

Hard against the side of the undamaged hut was a lean-to shed, solidly built. Six feet high, six wide, eight long. The door opened easily. Wooden floor, gleaming aluminium for the sides and ceiling, big black heaters bolted to the inside and outside walls. Wires led from those and it was no job for an Einstein to guess that they led—or had led— to the now destroyed generator house. This lean-to shed would have been warm night and day. The squat low-slung tractor that took up nearly all the floor space inside would have started any time at the touch of a switch. It wouldn't start at the turn of a switch now, it would take three or four blow-torches and the same number of strong men even to turn the engine over once. I closed the door and went into the main hut.

It was packed with metal tables, benches, machinery and every modern device for the automatic recording and interpretation of every conceivable observed detail of the Arctic weather. I didn't know what the functions of most of the instruments were and I didn't care. This was the meteorological office and that was enough for me. I examined the hut carefully but quickly and there didn't seem to be anything odd or out of place that I could see. In one corner, perched on an empty wooden packing-case, was a portable radio transmitter with listening phones—transceivers, they called them nowadays. Near it, in a box of heavy oiled wood, were fifteen Nife cells connected up in series. Hanging from a hook on the wall was a two-volt test lamp. I touched its bare leads to the outside terminals of the battery formed by the cells. Had those cells left in them even a fraction of their original power that test lamp should have burnt out in a white flash. It didn't even begin to glow. I tore a piece of flex from a nearby lamp and touched its ends to the terminals. Not even the minutest spark. Kinnaird hadn't been lying when he had said that his battery had been completely dead. But, then, I hadn't for a moment thought he'd been lying.

I made my way to the last hut—the hut that held the charred remnants of the seven men who had died in the fire. The stench of charred flesh and burnt diesel seemed stronger, more nauseating than ever. I stood in the doorway and the last thing I wanted to do was to approach even an inch closer. I peeled off fur and woollen mittens, set the lamp on a table, pulled out my torch and knelt by the first dead man.

Ten minutes passed and all I wanted was out of there. There are some things that doctors, even hardened pathologists, will go a long way to avoid. Bodies that have been too long in the sea is one : bodies that have been in the immediate vicinity of under-water explosion is another; and men who have literally been burned alive is another. I was beginning to feel more than slightly sick; but I wasn't going to leave there until I was finished.

The door creaked open. I turned and watched Commander Swanson come in. He'd been a long time, I'd expected him before then. Lieutenant Hansen, his damaged left hand wrapped in some thick woollen material, came in after him. That was what the phone call had been about, the Commander calling up reinforcements. Swanson switched off his torch, pushed up his snow-goggles and pulled down his mask. His eyes narrowed at the scene before him, his nostrils wrinkled in involuntary disgust, and the colour drained swiftly from his ruddy cheeks. Both Hansen and I had told him what to expect, but he hadn't been prepared for this : not often can the imagination encompass the reality. For a moment I thought he was going to be sick, but then I saw a slight tinge of colour touch the cheekbones and I knew he wasn't.

" Dr. Carpenter," he said in a voice in which the unsteady huskiness seemed only to emphasise the stilted formality, " I wish you to return at once to the ship where you will remain confined to your quarters. I would prefer you went voluntarily, accompanied by Lieutenant Hansen here. I wish no trouble. I trust you don't either. If you do, we can accommodate you. Rawlings and Murphy are waiting outside that door."

" Those are fighting words, Commander," I said, " and very unfriendly. Rawlings and Murphy are going to get uncommon cold out there." I put my right hand in my caribou pants pocket—the one with the gun in it—and surveyed him unhurriedly. " Have you had a brainstorm?"

Swanson looked at Hansen and nodded in the direction of the door. Hansen half-turned, then stopped as I said : " Very high-handed, aren't we? I'm not worth an explanation, is that it?"

Hansen looked uncomfortable. He didn't like any part of this. I suspected Swanson didn't either, but he was going to do what he had to do and let his feelings look elsewhere.

" Unless you're a great deal less intelligent than I believe —and I credit you with a high intelligence—you know exactly what the explanation is. When you came aboard the *Dolphin* in the Holy Loch both Admiral Garvie and myself were highly suspicious of you. You spun us a story about being an expert in Arctic conditions and of having helped set up this station here. When we wouldn't accept that as sufficient authority or reason to take you along with us you told a highly convincing tale about this being an advanced missile-warning outpost and even although it was peculiar that Admiral Garvie had never heard of it, we accepted it. The huge dish aerial you spoke of, the radar masts, the electronic computers—what's happened to them, Dr. Carpenter? A bit insubstantial, weren't they? Like all figments of the imagination."

I looked at him, considering, and let him go on.

"There never were any of those things, were there? You're up to the neck in something very murky indeed, my friend. What it is I don't know nor, for the moment, do I care. All I care for is the safety of the ship, the welfare of the crew and bringing the Zebra survivors safely back home and I'm taking no chances at all."

"The wishes of the British Admiralty, the orders from your own Director of Underseas Warfare—those mean nothing to you?"

"I'm beginning to have very strong reservations about the way those orders were obtained," Swanson said grimly. "You're altogether too mysterious for my liking, Dr. Carpenter—as well as being a fluent liar."

"Those are harsh, harsh words, Commander."

"The truth not infrequently sounds that way. Will you please come?"

"Sorry. I'm not through here yet."

"I see. John, will you——"

"I can give you an explanation. I see I have to. Won't you listen?"

"A third fairy-story?" A headshake. "No."

"And I'm not ready to leave. Impasse."

Swanson looked at Hansen, who turned to go. I said: "Well, if you're too stiff-necked to listen to me, call up the bloodhounds. Isn't it just luck, now, that we have three fully-qualified doctors here?"

"What do you mean?"

"I mean this." Guns have different characteristics in appearance. Some look relatively harmless, some ugly, some business-like, some wicked-looking. The Mannlicher-Schoenauer in my hand just looked plain downright wicked. Very wicked indeed. The white light from the Coleman glittered off the blued metal, menacing and sinister. It was a great gun to terrify people with.

"You wouldn't use it," Swanson said flatly.

"I'm through talking. I'm through asking for a hearing. Bring on the bailiffs, friend."

397

" You're bluffing, mister," Hansen said savagely. " You don't dare."

" There's too much at stake for me not to dare. Find out now. Don't be a coward. Don't hide behind your enlisted men's backs. Don't order them to get themselves shot." I snapped off the safety-catch. " Come and take it from me yourself."

" Stay right where you are, John," Swanson said sharply. " He means it. I suppose you have a whole armoury in that combination-lock suitcase of yours," he said bitterly.

" That's it. Automatic carbines, six-inch naval guns, the lot. But for a small-size situation a small-size gun. Do I get my hearing?"

" You get your hearing."

" Send Rawlings and Murphy away. I don't want anyone else to know anything about this. Anyway, they're probably freezing to death."

Swanson nodded. Hansen went to the door, opened it, spoke briefly and returned. I laid the gun on the table, picked up my torch and moved some paces away. I said : " Come and have a look at this."

They came. Both of them passed by the table with the gun lying there and didn't even look at it. I stopped before one of the grotesquely misshapen charred lumps lying on the floor. Swanson came close and stared down. His face had lost whatever little colour it had regained. He made a queer noise in his throat.

" That ring, that gold ring——" he began, then stopped short.

" I wasn't lying about that."

" No. No you weren't. I—I don't know what to say. I'm most damnably——"

" It doesn't matter," I said roughly. " Look here. At the back. I'm afraid I had to remove some of the carbon."

" The neck," Swanson whispered. " It's broken."

" Is that what you think?"

" Something heavy, I don't know, a beam from one of the huts, must have fallen——"

" You've just seen one of those huts. They have no beams. There's an inch and half of the vertebræ missing. If anything sufficiently heavy to smash off an inch and a half

398

of the backbone had struck him, the broken piece would be imbedded in his neck. It's not. It was blown out. He was shot from the front, through the base of the throat. The bullet went out the back of the neck. A soft-nosed bullet—you can tell by the size of the exit hole—from a powerful gun, something like a .38 Colt or Luger or Mauser."

"Good God above!" For the first time, Swanson was badly shaken. He stared at the thing on the floor, then at me. "Murdered. You mean he was murdered."

"Who would have done this?" Hansen said hoarsely. "Who, man, who? And in God's name, why?"

"I don't know who did it."

Swanson looked at me, his eyes strange. "You just found this out?"

"I found out last night."

"You found out last night." The words were slow, far-spaced, a distinct hiatus between each two. "And all the time since, aboard the ship, you never said—you never showed—my God, Carpenter, you're inhuman."

"Sure," I said. "See that gun there. It makes a loud bang and when I use it to kill the man who did this I won't even blink. I'm inhuman, all right."

"I was speaking out of turn. Sorry." Swanson was making a visible effort to bring himself under normal control. He looked at the Mannlicher-Schoenauer, then at me, then back at the gun. "Private revenge is out, Carpenter. No one is going to take the law into his own hands."

"Don't make me laugh out loud. A morgue isn't a fit place for it. Besides, I'm not through showing you things yet. There's more. Something that I've just found out now. Not last night." I pointed to another huddled black shape on the ground. "Care to have a look at this man here?"

"I'd rather not," Swanson said steadily. "Suppose you tell us?"

"You can see from where you are. The head. I've cleaned it up. Small hole in the front, in the middle of the face and slightly to the right: larger exit hole at the back of the top of the head. Same gun. Same man behind the gun."

Neither man said anything. They were too sick, too shocked to say anything.

"Queer path the bullet took," I went on. "Ranged

399

sharply upwards. As if the man who fired the shot had been lying or sitting down while his victim stood above him."

"Yes." Swanson didn't seem to have heard me. "Murder. Two murders. This is a job for the authorities, for the police."

"Sure," I said. "For the police. Let's just ring the sergeant at the local station and ask him if he would mind stepping this way for a few minutes."

"It's not a job for us," Swanson persisted. "As captain of an American naval vessel with a duty to discharge I am primarily interested in bringing my ship and the Zebra survivors back to Scotland again."

"Without endangering the ship?" I asked. "With a murderer aboard the possibility of endangering the ship does not arise?"

"We don't know he is—or will be—aboard."

"You don't even begin to believe that yourself. You know he will be. You know as well as I do why this fire broke out and you know damn' well that it was no accident. If there was any accidental element about it it was just the size and extent of the fire. The killer may have miscalculated that. But both time and weather conditions were against him: I don't think he had very much option. The only possible way in which he could obliterate all traces of his crime was to have a fire of sufficient proportions to obliterate those traces. He would have got off with it too, if I hadn't been here, if I hadn't been convinced before we left port that something was very far wrong indeed. But he would take very good care that he wouldn't obliterate himself in the process. Like it or not, Commander, you're going to have a killer aboard your ship."

"But all of those men have been burned, some very severely——"

"What the hell did you expect? That the unknown X would go about without a mark on him, without as much as a cigarette burn, proclaiming to the world that he had been the one who had been throwing matches about and had then thoughtfully stood to one side? Local colour. He *had* to get himself burnt."

"It doesn't follow," Hansen said. "He wasn't to know that anyone was going to get suspicious and start investigating."

" You'll be well advised to join your captain in keeping out of the detecting racket," I said shortly. " The men behind this are top-flight experts with far-reaching contacts —part of a criminal octopus with tentacles so long that it can even reach out and sabotage your ship in the Holy Loch. Why they did that, I don't know. What matters is that top-flight operators like those *never* take chances. They always operate on the assumption that they *may* be found out. They take every possible precaution against every possible eventuality. Besides, when the fire was at its height—we don't know the story of that, yet—the killer would have had to pitch in and rescue those trapped. It would have seemed damned odd if he hadn't. And so he got burnt."

" My God." Swanson's teeth were beginning to chatter with the cold but he didn't seem to notice it. "What a hellish set-up."

" Isn't it? I dare say there's nothing in your navy regulations to cover this lot."

" But what—what are we going to do?"

" We call the cops. That's me."

" What do you mean?"

" What I say. I have more authority, more official backing, more scope, more power and more freedom of action than any cop you ever saw. You must believe me. What I say is true."

" I'm beginning to believe it *is* true," Swanson said in slow thoughtfulness. " I've been wondering more and more about you in the past twenty-four hours. I've kept telling myself I was wrong, even ten minutes before I kept telling myself. You're a policeman? Or detective?"

" Naval officer. Intelligence. I have credentials in my suit-case which I am empowered to show in an emergency." It didn't seem the time to tell him just how wide a selection of credentials I did have. " This is the emergency."

" But—but you are a doctor."

" Sure I am. A navy doctor—on the side. My speciality is investigating sabotage in the U.K. armed forces. The cover-up of research doctor is the ideal one. My duties are deliberately vague and I have the power to poke and pry into all sorts of corners and situations and talk to all sorts of people on the grounds of being an investigating psychologist that would be impossible for the average serving officer."

There was a long silence, then Swanson said bitterly : " You might have told us before this."

" I might have broadcast it all over your Tannoy system. Why the hell should I? I don't want to trip over blundering amateurs every step I take. Ask any cop. The biggest menace of his life is the self-appointed Sherlock. Besides, I couldn't trust you, and before you start getting all hot and bothered about that I might add that I don't mean you'd deliberately give me away or anything like that but that you may inadvertently give me away. Now I've no option but to tell you what I can and chance the consequences. Why couldn't you just have accepted that directive from your Director of Naval Operations and acted accordingly?"

" Directive?" Hansen looked at Swanson. " What directive?"

" Orders from Washington to give Dr. Carpenter here *carte blanche* for practically everything. Be reasonable, Carpenter. I don't like operating in the dark and I'm naturally suspicious. You came aboard in highly questionable circumstances. You knew too damn' much about submarines. You were as evasive as hell. You had this sabotage theory all cut and dried. Damn it, man, of course I had reservations. Wouldn't you have had, in my place?"

" I suppose so. I don't know. Me, I obey orders."

" Uh-huh. And your orders in this case?"

" Meaning what exactly is all this about," I sighed. " It would have to come to this. You must be told now— and you'll understand why your Director of Naval Operations was so anxious that you give me every help possible."

" We can believe this one?" Swanson asked.

" You can believe this one. The story I spun back in the Holy Loch wasn't all malarkey—I just dressed it up a bit to make sure you'd take me along. They did indeed have a very special item of equipment here—an electronic marvel that was used for monitoring the count-down of Soviet missiles and pin-pointing their locations. This machine was kept in one of the huts now destroyed—the second from the west in the south now. Night and day a giant captive radio-sonde balloon reached thirty thousand feet up into the sky—but it had no radio attached. It was just a huge aerial. Incidentally, I should think that is the reason why the oil fuel appears to have been flung over so large an area— an explosion caused by the bursting of the hydrogen cylinders used to inflate the balloons. They were stored in the fuel hut."

" Did everybody in Zebra know about this monitoring machine?"

" No. Most of them thought it a device for investigating cosmic rays. Only four people knew what it really was— my brother and the three others who all slept in the hut that housed this machine. Now the hut is destroyed. The free world's most advanced listening-post. You wonder why your D.N.O. was so anxious?"

" Four men?" Swanson looked at me, a faint speculation still in his eye. "Which four men, Dr. Carpenter?"

" Do you have to ask? Four of the seven men you see lying here, Commander."

He stared down at the floor then looked quickly away. He said : " You mentioned that you were convinced even before we left port that something was far wrong. Why?"

" My brother had a top-secret code. We had messages sent by himself—he was an expert radio operator. One said that there had been two separate attempts to wreck the monitor. He didn't go into details. Another said that he had been attacked and left unconscious when making a mid-night check and found someone bleeding off the gas from the hydrogen cylinders—without the radio-sonde aerial the monitor would have been useless. He was lucky, he was out only for a few minutes, as long again and he would have frozen to death. In the circumstances did you expect me to believe that the fire was unconnected with the attempts to sabotage the monitor?"

" But how would anyone *know* what it was?" Hansen objected. " Apart from your brother and the other three men, that is?" Like Swanson, he glanced at the floor and, like Swanson looked as hurriedly away. " For my money this is the work of a psycho. A madman. A coldly calculating criminal would—well, he wouldn't go in for wholesale murder like this. But a psycho would."

" Three hours ago," I said, " before you loaded the torpedo

403

into number three tube you checked the manually controlled levers and the warning lights for the tube bow-caps. In the one case you found that the levers had been disconnected in the open position: in the other you found that the wires had been crossed in a junction-box. Do you think that was the work of a psycho? Another psycho?"

He said nothing. Swanson said: "What can I do to help, Dr. Carpenter?"

"What are you willing to do, Commander?"

"I will not hand over command of the *Dolphin*." He smiled, but he wasn't feeling like smiling. "Short of that, I—and the crew of the *Dolphin*—are at your complete disposal. You name it, Doctor, that's all."

"This time you believe my story?"

"This time I believe your story."

I was pleased about that, I almost believed it myself.

VIII

The hut where we'd found all the Zebra survivors huddled together was almost deserted when we got back to it—only Dr. Benson and the two very sick men remained. The hut seemed bigger now, somehow, bigger and colder, and very shabby and untidy like the remnants of a church rummage sale where the housewives have trained for a couple of months before moving up to battle stations. Pieces of clothing, bedding, frayed and shredded blankets, gloves, plates, cutlery and dozens of odds and ends of personal possessions lay scattered all over the floor. The sick men had been too sick— and too glad to be on their way—to worry overmuch about taking too many of their various knick-knacks out of there. All they had wanted out of there was themselves. I didn't blame them.

The two unconscious men had their scarred and frost-bitten faces towards us. They were either sleeping or in a coma. But I took no chances. I beckoned Benson and he came and stood with us in the shelter of the west wall.

I told Benson what I'd told the commander and Hansen. He had to know. As the man who would be in the most constant and closest contact with the sick men, he had to know. I suppose he must have been pretty astonished and shaken, but he didn't show it. Doctors' faces behave as doctors tell them to, when they come across a patient in a pretty critical state of health they don't beat their breasts and break into loud lamentations, as this tends to discourage the patient. This now made three men from the *Dolphin*'s crew who knew what the score was—well, half the score, anyway. Three was enough. I only hoped it wasn't too much.

Thereafter Swanson did the talking: Benson would take it better from him than he would from me. Swanson said: " Where were you thinking of putting the sick men we've sent back aboard?"

" In the most comfortable places I can find. Officers' quarters, crew's quarters, scattered all over so that no one is upset too much. Spread the load, so to speak." He paused. " I didn't know of the latest—um—development at the time. Things are rather different now."

" They are. Half of them in the wardroom, the other half in the crew's mess—no, the crew's quarters. No reason why they shouldn't be fixed up comfortably. If they wonder at this, you can say it's for ease of medical treatment and that they can all be under constant medical watch, like heart patients in a ward. Get Dr. Jolly behind you in this, he seems a co-operative type. And I've no doubt he'll support you in your next move—that all patients are to be stripped, bathed and provided with clean pyjamas. If they're too ill to move, bed-bath. Dr. Carpenter here tells me that prevention of infection is of paramount importance in cases of severe burn injuries."

" And their clothes?"

" You catch on more quickly than I did," Swanson grunted. " All their clothes to be taken away and labelled. All contents to be removed and labelled. The clothes, for anyone's information, are to be disinfected and laundered."

" It might help if I am permitted to know just what we are looking for," Benson suggested.

Swanson looked at me.

" God knows," I said. " Anything and everything. One thing certain—you won't find a gun. Be especially careful in labelling gloves—when we get back to Britain we'll have the experts test them for nitrates from the gun used."

"If anyone has brought aboard anything bigger than a postage stamp I'll find it," Benson promised.

"Are you sure?" I asked. "Even if you brought it aboard yourself?"

"Eh? Me? What the devil are you suggesting?"

"I'm suggesting that something may have been shoved inside your medical kit, even your pockets, when you weren't looking."

"Good lord." He dug feverishly into his pockets. "The idea never occurred to me."

"You haven't the right type of nasty suspicious mind," Swanson said dryly. "Off you go. You too, John."

They left, and Swanson and I went inside. Once I'd checked that the two men really were unconscious, we went to work. It must have been many years since Swanson had policed a deck or parade-ground, far less doubled as scavenger, but he took to it in the manner born. He was assiduous, painstaking, and missed nothing. Neither did I. We cleared a corner of the hut and brought across there every single article that was either lying on the floor or attached to the still ice-covered walls. Nothing was missed. It was either shaken, turned over, opened or emptied according to what it was. Fifteen minutes and we were all through. If there was anything bigger than a matchstick to be found in that room then we would have found it. But we found nothing. Then we scattered everything back over the floor again until the hut looked more or less as it had been before our search. If either of the two unconscious men came to I didn't want him knowing that we had been looking for anything.

"We're no great shakes in the detecting business," Swanson said. He looked slightly discouraged.

"We can't find what isn't there to be found. And it doesn't help that we don't know what we're looking for. Let's try for the gun now. May be anywhere, he may even have thrown it away on the ice-cap, though I think that unlikely. A killer never likes to lose his means of killing —and he couldn't have been sure that he wouldn't require it again. There aren't so very many places to search. He wouldn't have left it here, for this is the main bunk-house and in constant use. That leaves only the met. office and the lab. where the dead are lying."

"He could have hidden it among the ruins of one of the burnt-out huts," Swanson objected.

"Not a chance. Our friend has been here for some months now, and he must know exactly the effect those ice-storms have. The spicules silt up against any object that lies in their path. The metal frameworks at the bases of the destroyed buildings are still in position, and the floors of the huts—or where the wooden floors used to be—are covered with solid ice to a depth of from four to six inches. He would have been as well to bury his gun in quick-setting concrete."

We started on the meteorological hut. We looked in every shelf, every box, every cupboard and had just started ripping the backs off the metal cabinets that housed the meteorological equipment when Swanson said abruptly: "I have an idea. Back in a couple of minutes."

He was better than his word. He was back in a minute flat, carrying in his hands four objects that glittered wetly in the lamplight and smelled strongly of petrol. A gun—a Luger automatic—the haft and broken-off blade of a knife and two rubber-wrapped packages which turned out to be spare magazines for the Luger. He said: "I guess this was what you were looking for."

"Where did you find them?"

"The tractor. In the petrol tank."

"What made you think of looking there?"

"Just luck. I got to thinking about your remark that the guy who had used this gun might want to use it again. But if he was to hide it anywhere where it was exposed to the weather it might have become jammed up with ice. Even if it didn't, he might have figured that the metal would contract so that the shells wouldn't fit or that the firing mechanism and lubricating oil would freeze solid. Only two things don't freeze solid in these sub-zero temperatures —alcohol and petrol. You can't hide a gun in a bottle of gin."

"It wouldn't have worked," I said. "Metal would still contract—the petrol is as cold as the surrounding air."

407

" Maybe he didn't know that. Or if he did, maybe he just thought it was a good place to hide it, quick and handy." He looked consideringly at me as I broke the butt and looked at the empty magazine, then said sharply : " You're smearing that gun a little, aren't you?"

" Fingerprints? Not after being in petrol. He was probably wearing gloves anyway."

" So why did you want it?"

" Serial number. May be able to trace it. It's even possible that the killer had a police permit for it. It's happened before, believe it or not. And you must remember that the killer believed there would be no suspicion of foul play, far less that a search would be carried out for the gun.

" Anyway, this knife explains the gun. Firing guns is a noisy business and I'm surprised—I was surprised—that the killer risked it. He might have waked the whole camp. But he had to take the risk because he'd gone and snapped off the business end of this little sticker here. This is a very slender blade, the kind of blade it's very easy to snap unless you know exactly what you're doing, especially when extreme cold makes the metal brittle. He probably struck a rib or broke the blade trying to haul it out—a knife slides in easily enough but it can jam against cartilage or bone when you try to remove it."

" You mean—you mean the killer murdered a *third* man?" Swanson asked carefully. " With this knife?"

" The third man but the first victim," I nodded. " The missing half of the blade will be stuck inside someone's chest. But I'm not going to look for it—it would be pointless and take far too long."

" I'm not sure that I don't agree with Hansen," Swanson said slowly. " I know it's impossible to explain away the sabotage on the boat—but, my God, this looks like the work of a maniac. All this—all this senseless killing."

" All this killing," I agreed. " But not senseless—not from the point of view of the killer. No, don't ask me, I don't know what his point of view was—or is. I know—you know—why he started the fire : what we don't know is why he killed those men in the first place."

Swanson shook his head, then said : " Let's get back to the other hut. I'll phone for someone to keep a watch

408

over those sick men. I don't know about you, but I'm frozen stiff. And you had no sleep last night."

"I'll watch them meantime," I said. "For an hour or so. And I've some thinking to do, some very hard thinking."

"You haven't much to go on, have you?"

"That's what makes it so hard."

I'd said to Swanson that I didn't have much to go on, a less than accurate statement, for I didn't have anything to go on at all. So I didn't waste any time thinking. Instead I took a lantern and went once again to the lab. where the dead men lay. I was cold and tired and alone, and the darkness was falling and I didn't very much fancy going there. Nobody would have fancied going there, a place of dreadful death which any sane person would have avoided like the plague. And that was why I was going there, not because I wasn't sane, but because it was a place that no man would ever voluntarily visit—unless he had an extremely powerful motivation, such as the intention of picking up some essential thing he had hidden there in the near certainty that no one else would ever go near the place. It sounded complicated, even to me. I was very tired. I made a fuzzy mental note to ask around, when I got back to the *Dolphin*, to find out who had suggested shifting the dead men in there.

The walls of the lab. were lined with shelves and cupboards containing jars and bottles and retorts and test-tubes and such-like chemical junk, but I didn't give them more than a glance. I went to the corner of the hut where the dead men lay most closely together, shone my torch along the side of the room and found what I was looking for in a matter of seconds—a floorboard standing slightly proud of its neighbours. Two of the blackened contorted lumps that had once been men lay across that board. I moved them just far enough, not liking the job at all, then lifted one end of the loose floorboard.

It looked as if someone had had it in mind to start up a supermarket. In the six-inch space between the floor and the base of the hut were stacked dozens of neatly arranged cans—soup, beef, fruit, vegetables, a fine varied diet with all the proteins and vitamins a man could want. Someone had had no intention of going hungry. There was even a small pressure-stove and a couple of gallons of kerosene to thaw out the cans. And to one side, lying flat, two rows of gleaming Nife cells—there must have been about forty in all.

I replaced the board, left the lab. and went across to the meteorological hut again. I spent over an hour there, unbuttoning the backs of metal cabinets and peering into their innards, but I found nothing. Not what I had hoped to find, that was. But I did come across one very peculiar item, a small green metal box six inches by four by two, with a circular control that was both switch and tuner, and two glassed-in dials with neither figures nor marking on them. At the side of the box was a brass-rimmed hole.

I turned the switch and one of the dials glowed green, a magic-eye tuning device with the fans spread well apart. The other dial stayed dead. I twiddled the tuner control but nothing happened. Both the magic eye and the second dial required something to activate them—something like a pre-set radio signal. The hole in the side would accommodate the plug of any standard telephone receiver. Not many people would have known what this was, but I'd seen one before—a transistorised homing device for locating the direction of a radio signal, such as emitted by the " Sarah " device on American space capsules which enables searchers to locate it once it has landed in the sea.

What legitimate purpose could be served by such a device in Drift Ice Station Zebra? When I'd told Swanson and Hansen of the existence of a console for monitoring rocket-firing signals from Siberia, that much of my story, anyway, had been true. But that had called for a giant aerial stretching far up into the sky : this comparative toy couldn't have ranged a twentieth of the distance to Siberia.

I had another look at the portable radio transmitter and the now exhausted Nife batteries that served them. The dialling counter was still tuned into the waveband which the *Dolphin* had picked up the distress signals. There was nothing for me there. I looked more closely at the nickel-cadmium cells and saw that they were joined to one another and to the radio set by wire-cored rubber leads with very powerfully spring-loaded saw-tooth clips on the terminals : those last ensured perfect electrical contact as well as being very convenient to use. I undid two of the clips, brought a torch-beam to bear and peered closely at the terminals. The indentations made by the sharpened steel saw-teeth were faint but unmistakable.

I made my way back to the laboratory hut, lifted the loose floorboard again and shone the torch on the Nife cells lying there. At least half of the cells had the same characteristic markings. Cells that looked fresh and unused, yet they had those same markings and if anything was certain it was that those cells had been brand-new and unmarked when Drift Ice Station Zebra had been first set up. A few of the cells were tucked so far away under adjacent floorboards that I had to stretch my hand far in to reach them. I pulled out two and in the space behind I seemed to see something dark and dull and metallic.

It was too dark to distinguish clearly what the object was but after I'd levered up another two floorboards I could see without any trouble at all. It was a cylinder about thirty inches long and six in diameter with brass stopcock and mounted pressure gauge registering " full " : close beside it was a package about eighteen inches square and four thick, stencilled with the words " RADIO-SONDE BALLOONS ". Hydrogen, batteries, balloons, corned beef and mulligatawny soup. A catholic enough assortment of stores by any standards; but there wouldn't have been anything haphazard about the choice of that assortment.

When I made it back to the bunkhouse, the two patients were still breathing. That was about all I could say for myself, too, I was shaking with the cold and even clamping my teeth together couldn't keep them from chattering. I thawed out under the big electric heaters until I was only half-frozen, picked up my torch and moved out again into the wind and the cold and the dark. I was a sucker for punishment, that was for sure.

In the next twenty minutes I made a dozen complete circuits of the camp, moving a few yards farther out with each circuit. I must have walked over a mile altogether and that was all I had for it, just the walk and a slight touch of frostbite high up on the cheekbones, the only part of my face, other than the eyes, exposed to that bitter cold. I knew I had frost-bite for the skin had suddenly ceased to feel

411

cold any more and was quite dead to the touch. Enough was enough and I had a hunch that I was wasting my time anyway. I headed back to the camp.

I passed between the meteorological hut and the lab. and was just level with the eastern end of the bunkhouse when I sensed as much as saw something odd out of the corner of my eye. I steadied the torch-beam on the east wall and peered closely at the sheath of ice that had been deposited there over the days by the ice-storm. Most of the encrustation was of a homogeneous greyish-white, very smooth and polished, but it wasn't all grey-white: it was speckled here and there with dozens of black flecks of odd shapes and sizes, none of them more than an inch square. I tried to touch them but they were deeply imbedded in and showing through the gleaming ice. I went to examine the east wall of the meteorological hut, but it was quite innocent of any such black flecking. So was the east wall of the lab.

A short search inside the meteorological hut turned up a hammer and screw-driver. I chipped away a section of the black-flecked ice, brought it into the bunkhouse and laid it on the floor in front of one of the big electrical heaters. Ten minutes later I had a small pool of water and, lying in it, the sodden remains of what had once been fragments of burnt paper. This was very curious indeed. It meant that there were scores of pieces of burnt paper imbedded in the east wall of the bunkhouse. Just there: nowhere else. The explanation, of course, could be completely innocuous: or not, as the case might be.

I had another look at the two unconscious men. They were warm enough and comfortable enough but that was about all you could say for them. I couldn't see them as fit enough to be moved inside the next twenty-four hours. I lifted the phone and asked for someone to relieve me and when two seamen arrived, I made my way back to the *Dolphin*.

There was an unusual atmosphere aboard ship that afternoon, quiet and dull and almost funereal. It was hardly to be wondered at. As far as the crew of the *Dolphin* had been concerned, the men manning Drift Ice Station Zebra had been just so many ciphers, not even names, just unknowns. But now the burnt, frost-bitten, emaciated survivors had come

412

aboard ship, sick and suffering men each with a life and individuality of his own, and the sight of those wasted men still mourning the deaths of their eight comrades had suddenly brought home to every man on the submarine the full horror of what had happened on Zebra. And, of course less than seven hours had elapsed since their own torpedo officer, Lieutenant Mills, had been killed. Now, even although the mission had been successful, there seemed little enough reason for celebration. Down in the crew's mess the hi-fi and the juke-box were stilled. The ship was like a tomb.

I found Hansen in his cabin. He was sitting on the edge of his pullman bunk, still wearing his fur trousers, his face bleak and hard and cold. He watched me in silence as I stripped off my parka, undid the empty holster tied round my chest, hung it up and stuck inside it the automatic I'd pulled from my caribou pants. Then he said suddenly: " I wouldn't take them off, Doc. Not if you want to come with us, that is." He looked at his own furs and his mouth was bitter. " Hardly the rig of the day for a funeral, is it?"

" You mean——"

" Skipper's in his cabin. Boning up on the burial service. George Mills and that assistant radio operator—Grant, wasn't it—who died out there to-day. A double funeral. Out on the ice. There's some men there already, chipping a place with crowbars and sledges at the base of a hummock."

" I saw no one."

" Port side. To the west."

" I thought Swanson would have taken young Hills back to the States. Or Scotland."

" Too far. And there's the psychological angle. You could hardly dent the morale of this bunch we have aboard here far less shoot it to pieces, but carrying a dead man as a shipmate is an unhappy thing. He's had permission from Washington . . ." He broke off uncertainly, looked quietly up at me and then away again. I didn't have any need of telepathy to know what was in his mind.

" The seven men on Zebra?" I shook my head. " No, no funeral service for them. How could you? I'll pay my respects some other way."

His eyes flickered up at the Mannlicher-Schoenauer hanging

413

in its holster, then away again. He said in a quiet savage voice: "Goddam his black murderous soul. That devil's aboard here, Carpenter. Here. On our ship." He smacked a bunched fist hard against the palm of his other hand. "Have you no idea what's behind this, Doc? No idea who's responsible?"

"If I had, I wouldn't be standing here. Any idea how Benson is getting along with the sick and injured?"

"He's all through. I've just left him."

I nodded, reached up for the automatic and stuck it in the pocket of my caribou pants. Hansen said quietly: "Even aboard here?"

"Especially aboard here." I left him and went along to the surgery. Benson was sitting at his table, his back to his art gallery of technicolour cartoons, making entries in a book. He looked up as I closed the door behind me.

"Find anything?" I asked.

"Nothing that I would regard as interesting. Hansen did most of the sorting. You may find something." He pointed to neatly folded piles of clothing on the deck, several small attache-cases and a few polythene bags, each labelled. "Look for yourself. How about the two men left out on Zebra?"

"Holding their own. I think they'll be O.K., but it's too early to say yet." I squatted on the floor, went carefully through all the pockets in the clothes and found, as I had expected, nothing. Hansen wasn't the man to miss anything. I felt every square inch of the lining areas and came up with the same results. I went through the small cases and the polythene bags, small items of clothing and personal gear, shaving kits, letters, photographs, two or three cameras. I broke open the cameras and they were all empty. I said to Benson: "Dr. Jolly brought his medical case aboard with him?"

"Wouldn't even trust one of your own colleagues, would you?"

"No."

"Neither would I." He smiled with his mouth only. "You're an evil influence. I went through every item in it. Not a thing. I even measured the thickness of the bottom of the case. Nothing there."

"Good enough for me. How are the patients?"

"Nine of them," Benson said. "The psychological effect of knowing that they're safe has done them more good than any medication ever could." He consulted cards on his desk. "Captain Folsom is the worst. No danger, of course, but his facial burns are pretty savage. We've arranged to have a plastic surgeon standing by in Glasgow when we return. The Harrington twins, both met. officers, are rather less badly burnt, but very weak, from both cold and hunger. Food, warmth and rest will have them on their feet in a couple of days again. Hassard, another met. officer, and Jeremy, a lab. technician, moderate burns, moderate frost-bite, fittest of the lot otherwise—it's queer how different people react so differently to hunger and cold. The other four—Kinnaird, the senior radio operator, Dr. Jolly, Naseby, the cook, and Hewson, the tractor-driver and man who was in charge of the generator—are much of a muchness : they're suffering most severely of all from frost-bite, especially Kinnaird, all with moderate burns, weak, of course, but recovering fast. Only Folsom and the Harrington twins have consented to become bed-patients. The rest we've provided with rigouts of one sort or another. They're all lying down, of course, but they won't be lying down long. All of them are young, tough, and basically very fit—they don't pick children or old men to man places like Drift Station Zebra."

A knock came to the door and Swanson's head appeared. He said, "Hallo, back again," to me then turned to Benson. "A small problem of medical discipline here, Doctor." He stood aside to let us see Naseby, the Zebra cook, standing close behind him, dressed in a U.S. Navy's petty officer's uniform. "It seems that your patients have heard about the funeral service. They want to go along—those who are able, that is—to pay their last respects to their colleagues. I understand and sympathise, of course, but their state of health——"

"I would advise against it, sir," Benson said. "Strongly."

"You can advise what you like, mate," a voice came from behind Naseby. It was Kinnaird, the cockney radio operator, also clad in blue. "No offence. Don't want to be rude or ungrateful. But I'm going. Jimmy Grant was my mate."

"I know how you feel," Benson said. "I also know how

415

I feel about it—your condition, I mean. You're in no fit state to do anything except lie down. You're making things very difficult for me."

" I'm the captain of this ship," Swanson put in mildly. " I can forbid it, you know. I can say ' No,' and make it stick."

" And you are making things difficult for us, sir," Kinnaird said. " I don't reckon it would advance the cause of Anglo-American unity very much if we started hauling off at our rescuers an hour or two after they'd saved us from certain death." He smiled faintly. " Besides, look at what it might do to our wounds and burns."

Swanson cocked an eyebrow at me. " Well, they're your countrymen."

" Dr. Benson is perfectly correct," I said. " But it's not worth a civil war. If they could survive five or six days on that damned ice-cap, I don't suppose a few minutes more is going to finish them off."

" Well, if it does," Swanson said heavily, " we'll blame you."

If I ever had any doubt about it I didn't have then, not after ten minutes out in the open. The Arctic ice-cap was no place for a funeral; but I couldn't have imagined a more promising set-up for a funeral director who wanted to drum up some trade. After the warmth of the *Dolphin* the cold seemed intense and within five minutes we were all shivering violently. The darkness was as nearly absolute as it ever becomes on the ice-cap, the wind was lifting again and thin flurries of snow came gusting through the night. The solitary floodlamp served only to emphasise the ghostly unreality of it all, the huddled circle of mourners with bent heads, the two shapeless canvas-wrapped forms lying huddled at the base of an ice-hummock, Commander Swanson bent over his book, the wind and the snow snatching the half-heard mumble from his lips as he hurried through the burial service. I caught barely one word in ten of the committal and then it was all over, no meaningless rifle salutes, no empty blowing of bugles, just the service and the silence and the dark shapes of stumbling men hurriedly placing fragments of broken ice over the canvas-sheeted forms. And

416

within twenty-four hours the eternally drifting spicules and blowing snow would have sealed them for ever in their icy tomb, and there they might remain for ever, drifting in endless circles about the North Pole; or some day, perhaps a thousand years from then, an ice-lead might open up and drop them down to the uncaring floor of the Arctic, their bodies as perfectly preserved as if they had died only that day. It was a macabre thought.

Heads bent against the snow and ice, we hurried back to the shelter of the *Dolphin*. From the ice-cap to the top of the sail it was a climb of over twenty feet up the almost vertically inclined huge slabs of ice that the submarine had pushed upwards and sideways as she had forced her way through. Hand-lines had been rigged from the top of the sail but even then it was a fairly tricky climb. It was a set-up where with the icy slope, the frozen slippery ropes, the darkness and the blinding effect of the snow and ice, an accident could all too easily happen. And happen it did.

I was about six feet up, giving a hand to Jeremy, the lab. technician from Zebra whose burnt hands made it almost impossible for him to climb alone, when I heard a muffled cry above me. I glanced up and had a darkly-blurred impression of someone teetering on top of the sail, fighting for his balance, then jerked Jeremy violently towards me to save him from being swept away as that same someone lost his footing, toppled over backwards and hurtled down past us on to the ice below. I winced at the sound of the impact, two sounds, rather, a heavy muffled thud followed immediately by a sharper, crisper crack. First the body, then the head. I half imagined that I heard another sound afterwards, but couldn't be sure. I handed Jeremy over to the care of some-one else and slithered down an ice-coated rope, not looking forward very much to what I must see. The fall had been the equivalent of a twenty-foot drop on to a concrete floor.

Hansen had got there before me and was shining his torch down not on to one prostrate figure as I had expected, but two. Benson and Jolly, both of them out cold.

I said to Hansen: "Did you see what happened?"

"No. Happened too quickly. All I know is that it was Benson that did the falling and Jolly that did the cushioning. Jolly was beside me only a few seconds before the fall."

" If that's the case then Jolly probably saved your doctor's life. We'll need to strap them in stretchers and haul them up and inside. We can't leave them out here."

" Stretchers? Well, yes, if you say so. But they might come round any minute."

" One of them might. But one of them is not going to come round for a long time. You heard that crack when a head hit the ice, it was like someone being clouted over the head with a fence-post. And I don't know which it is yet."

Hansen left. I stooped over Benson and eased back the hood of the duffel-coat he was wearing. A fence-post was just about right. The side of his head, an inch above the right ear, was a blood-smeared mess, a three-inch long gash in the purpling flesh with the blood already coagulating in the bitter cold. Two inches farther forward and he'd have been a dead man, the thin bone behind the temple would have shattered under such an impact. For Benson's sake, I hoped the rest of his skull was pretty thick. No question but that this had been the sharp crack I'd heard.

Benson's breathing was very shallow, the movement of his chest barely discernible. Jolly's, on the other hand, was fairly deep and regular. I pulled back his anorak hood, probed carefully over his head and encountered a slight puffiness far back, near the top on the left-hand side. The inference seemed obvious. I hadn't been imagining things when I thought I had heard a second sound after the sharp crack caused by Benson's head striking against the ice. Jolly must have been in the way of the falling Benson, not directly enough beneath him to break his fall in any way but directly enough to be knocked backwards on to the ice and clout the back of his head as he fell.

It took ten minutes to have them strapped in stretchers, taken inside and placed in a couple of temporary cots in the sick-bay. With Swanson waiting anxiously I attended to Benson first, though there was little enough I could do, and had just started on Jolly when his eyes flickered and he slowly came back to consciousness, groaning a bit and trying to hold the back of his head. He made to sit up in his cot but I restrained him.

418

"Oh, lord, my head." Several times he squeezed his eyes tightly shut, opened them wide, focused with difficulty on the bulkhead riotous with the colour of Benson's cartoon characters, then looked away as if he didn't believe it. "Oh, my word, that must have been a dilly. Who did it, old boy?"

"Did what?" Swanson asked.

"Walloped me on the old bean. Who? Eh?"

"You mean to say you don't remember?"

"Remember?" Jolly said irritably. "How the devil should I . . ." He broke off as his eye caught sight of Benson in the adjacent cot, a huddled figure under the blankets with only the back of his head and a big gauze pack covering his wound showing. "Of course, of course. Yes, that's it. He fell on top of me, didn't he?"

"He certainly did," I said. "Did you try to catch him?"

"Catch him? No, I didn't try to catch him. I didn't try to get out of the way either. It was all over in half a second. I just don't remember a thing about it." He groaned a bit more then looked across at Benson. "Came a pretty nasty cropper, eh? Must have done."

"Looks like it. He's very severely concussed. There's X-ray equipment here and I'll have a look at his head shortly. Damned hard luck on you too, Jolly."

"I'll get over it," he grunted. He pushed off my hand and sat up. "Can I help you?"

"You may not," Swanson said quietly. "Early supper then twelve hours solid for you and the eight others, Doctor, and those are *my* doctor's orders. You'll find supper waiting in the wardroom now."

"Aye, aye, sir." Jolly gave a ghost of a smile and pushed himself groggily to his feet. "That bit about the twelve hours sounds good to me."

After a minute or two, when he was steady enough on his feet, he left. Swanson said: "What now?"

"You might inquire around to see who was nearest or near to Benson when he slipped climbing over the edge of the bridge. But discreetly. It might do no harm if at the same time you hinted around that maybe Benson had just taken a turn."

419

" What are *you* hinting at?" Swanson asked slowly.

" Did he fall or was he pushed? that's what I'm hinting at."

" Did he fall or . . ." He broke off then went on warily : " Why should anyone want to push Dr. Benson?"

" Why should anyone want to kill seven—eight, now—men in Drift Ice Station Zebra?"

" You have a point," Swanson acknowledged quietly. He left.

Making X-ray pictures wasn't very much in my line but apparently it hadn't been very much in Dr. Benson's line either for he'd written down, for his own benefit and guidance, a detailed list of instructions for the taking and development of X-ray pictures. I wondered how he would have felt if he had known that the first beneficiary of his meticulous thoroughness was to be himself. The two finished negatives I came up with wouldn't have caused any furore in the Royal Photographic Society, but they were enough for my wants.

By and by Commander Swanson returned, closing the door behind him. I said : " Ten gets one that you got nothing."

" You won't die a poor man," he nodded. " Nothing is what it is. So Chief Torpedoman Patterson tells me, and you know what he's like."

I knew what he was like. Patterson was the man responsible for all discipline and organisation among the enlisted men and Swanson had said to me that he regarded Patterson, and not himself, as the most indispensable man on the ship.

" Patterson was the man who reached the bridge immediately before Benson," Swanson said. " He said he heard Benson cry out, swung round and saw him already beginning to topple backwards. He didn't recognise who it was at the time, it was too dark and snowy for that. He said he had the impression that Benson had already had one hand and one knee on the bridge coaming when he fell backwards."

" A funny position in which to start falling backwards," I said. " Most of his body weight must already have been inboard. And even if he did topple outwards he would

420

surely still have had plenty of time to grab the coaming with both hands."

"Maybe he did take a turn," Swanson suggested. "And don't forget that the coaming is glass-slippery with its smooth coating of ice."

"As soon as Benson disappeared Patterson ran to the side to see what had happened to him?"

"He did," Swanson said wearily. "And he said there wasn't a person within ten feet of the top of the bridge when Benson fell."

"And who *was* ten feet below?"

"He couldn't tell. Don't forget how black it was out there on the ice-cap and that the moment Patterson had dropped into the brightly lit bridge he'd lost whatever night-sight he'd built up. Besides, he didn't wait for more than a glance. He was off for a stretcher even before you or Hansen got to Benson. Patterson is not the sort of man who has to be told what to do."

"So it's a dead end there?"

"A dead end."

I nodded, crossed to a cupboard and brought back the two X-rays, still wet, held in their metal clips. I held them up to the light for Swanson's inspection.

"Benson?" he asked, and when I nodded peered at them more closely and finally said : "That line there—a fracture?"

"A fracture. And not a hair-line one either, as you can see. He really caught a wallop."

"How bad is it? How long before he comes out of this coma—he *is* in a coma?"

"He's all that. How long? If I were a lad fresh out of medical school I'd let you have a pretty confident estimate. If I were a top-flight brain surgeon I'd say anything from half an hour to a year or two, because people who really know what they are talking about are only too aware that we know next to nothing about the brain. Being neither, I'd guess at two or three days—and my guess could be hopelessly wrong. There may be cerebral bleeding. I don't know. I don't think so. Blood-pressure, respiration and temperature shows no evidence of organic damage. And now you know as much about it as I do."

421

" Your colleagues wouldn't like that." Swanson smiled faintly. " This cheerful confession of ignorance does nothing to enhance the mystique of your profession. How about your other patients—the two men still out in Zebra?"

" I'll see them after supper. Maybe they'll be fit enough to be brought here to-morrow. Meanwhile, I'd like to ask a favour of you. Could you lend me the services of your Torpedoman Rawlings? And would you have any objections to his being taken into our confidence?"

" Rawlings? I don't know why you want him, but why Rawlings? The officers and petty officers aboard this ship are the pick of the United States Navy. Why not one of them? Besides, I'm not sure that I like the idea of passing on to an enlisted man secrets denied to my officers."

" They're strictly non-naval secrets. The question of hierarchy doesn't enter into it. Rawlings is the man I want. He's got a quick mind, quick reflexes, and a dead-pan give-away-nothing expression that is invaluable in a game like this. Besides, in the event—the unlikely event, I hope—of the killer suspecting that we're on to him, he wouldn't look for any danger from one of your enlisted men because he'd be certain that we wouldn't let them in on it."

" What do you want him for?"

" To keep a night guard on Benson here."

" On Benson?" A fractional narrowing of the eyes, that could have been as imagined as real, was the only change in Swanson's impassive face. " So you don't think it was an accident, do you?"

" I don't honestly know. But I'm like yourself when you carry out a hundred and one different checks, most of which you know to be unnecessary, before you take your ship to sea—I'm taking no chances. If it wasn't an accident—then someone might have an interest in doing a really permanent job next time."

" But how can Benson represent a danger to anyone?" Swanson argued. " I'll wager anything you like, Carpenter, that Benson doesn't—or didn't—know a thing about them that could point a finger at anyone. If he did, he'd have told me straight away. He was like that."

" Maybe he saw or heard something the significance of which he didn't then realise. Maybe the killer is frightened

422

that if Benson has time enough to think about it the significance will dawn on him. Or maybe it's all a figment of my overheated imagination: maybe he just fell. But I'd still like to have Rawlings."

"You shall have him." Swanson rose to his feet and smiled. "I don't want you quoting that Washington directive at me again."

Two minutes later Rawlings arrived. He was dressed in a light brown shirt and overall pants, obviously his own conception of what constituted the well-dressed submariner's uniform, and for the first time in our acquaintance he didn't smile a greeting. He didn't even glance at Benson on his cot. His face was still and composed, without any expression.

"You sent for me, sir?" "Sir," not "Doc."

"Take a seat, Rawlings." He sat, and as he did I noticed the heavy bulge in the twelve-inch thigh pocket on the side of his overall pants. I nodded and said: "What have you got there? Doesn't do much for the cut of your natty suiting, does it?"

He didn't smile. He said. "I always carry one or two tools around with me. That's what the pocket is for."

"Let's see this particular tool," I said.

He hesitated briefly, shrugged and, not without some difficulty, pulled a heavy gleaming drop-forged steel pipe-wrench from the pocket. I hefted it in my hand.

"I'm surprised at you, Rawlings," I said. "What do you think the average human skull is made of—concrete? One little tap with this thing and you're up on a murder or manslaughter charge." I picked up a roll of bandage. "Ten yards of this wrapped round the business end will automatically reduce the charge to one of assault and battery."

"I don't know what you're talking about," he said mechanically.

"I'm talking about the fact that when Commander Swanson, Lieutenant Hansen and I were inside the laboratory this afternoon and you and Murphy were outside, you must have kind of leaned your ear against the door and heard more than was good for you. You know there's something far wrong and though you don't know what your motto is 'be prepared'. Hence the cosh. Correct?"

423

" Correct."

" Does Murphy know?"

" No."

" I'm a naval intelligence officer. Washington know all about me. Want the captain to vouch for me?"

" Well, no." The first faint signs of a grin. " I heard you pull a gun on the skipper, but you're still walking about loose. You must be in the clear."

" You heard me threaten the captain and Lieutenant Hansen with a gun. But then you were sent away. You heard nothing after that?"

" Nothing."

" Three men have been murdered on Zebra. Two shot, one knifed. Their bodies were burned to conceal traces of the crime. Four others died in the fire. The killer is aboard this ship."

Rawlings said nothing. His eyes were wide, his face pale and shocked. I told him everything I'd told Swanson and Hansen and emphasised that he was to keep it all to himself. Then I finished : " Dr. Benson here has been seriously hurt. A deliberate attempt for God knows what reason, may have been made on his life. We don't know. But if it was a deliberate attempt, then it's failed—so far."

Rawlings had brought himself under control. He said, his voice as empty of expression as his face : " Our little pal might come calling again?"

" He may. No member of the crew except the captain, the executive officer or I will come here. Anyone else—well, you can start asking him questions when he recovers consciousness."

" You recommended ten yards of this bandage, Doc?"

" It should be enough. And only a gentle tap, for God's sake. Above and behind the ear. You might sit behind that curtain there where no one can see you."

" I'm feeling lonesome to-night," Rawlings murmured. He broke open the bandage, started winding it around the head of the wrench and glanced at the cartoon-decorated bulkhead beside him. " Even old Yogi Bear ain't no fit companion for me to-night. I hope I have some other company calling."

I left him there. I felt vaguely sorry for anyone who should come calling, killer or not. I felt, too, that I had

424

taken every possible precaution. But when I left Rawlings there guarding Benson I did make one little mistake. Just one. I left him guarding the wrong man.

The second accident of the day happened so quickly, so easily, so inevitably that it might almost have been just that—an accident.

At supper that evening I suggested that, with Commander Swanson's permission, I'd have a surgery at nine next morning; because of enforced neglect most of the burn wounds were suppurating fairly badly, requiring constant cleaning and changing of coverings: I also thought it about time that an X-ray inspection be made of Zabrinski's broken ankle. Medical supplies in the sick-bay were running short. Where did Benson keep his main supplies? Swanson told me and detailed Henry, the steward, to show me where it was.

About ten that night, after I'd returned from seeing the two men out on Zebra, Henry led me through the now deserted control room and down the ladder which led to the inertial navigation room and the electronics space, which abutted on it. He undid the strong-back clamp on the square heavy steel hatch in a corner of the electronics room and with an assist from me—the hatch must have weighed about 150 pounds—swung it up and back until the hatch clicked home on its standing latch.

Three rungs on the inside of the hatch-cover led on to the vertical steel ladder that reached down to the deck below. Henry went down first, snapping on the light as he went, and I followed.

The medical storage room, though tiny, was equipped on the same superbly lavish scale as was everything else on the *Dolphin*. Benson, as thoroughly meticulous in this as he had been in his outlining of X-ray procedure, had everything neatly and logically labelled so that it took me less than three minutes to find everything I wanted. I went up the ladder first, stopped near the top, stretched down and took the bag of supplies from Henry, swung it up on the deck above, then reached up quickly with my free hand to grab the middle of the three rungs welded on the lower side of the hatch cover to haul myself up on to the deck of the electronics space. But I didn't haul myself up. What happened was that I hauled the hatch cover down. The retaining latch had become disengaged, and the 150-pound dead weight of that massive cover was swinging down on top of me before I could even begin to realise what was happening.

I fell half-sideways, half-backwards, pulling the hatch cover with me. My head struck against the hatch coaming. Desperately I ducked my head forward—if it had been crushed between the coaming and the falling cover the two sides of my skull would just about have met in the middle—and tried to snatch my left arm back inside. I was more or less successful with my head—I had it clear of the coaming and was ducking so quickly that the impact of the cover was no more than enough to give me a slight headache afterwards; but my left arm was a different matter altogether. I almost got it clear—but only almost. If my left hand and wrist had been strapped to a steel block and a gorilla had had a go at it with a sledge-hammer, the effect couldn't have been more agonising. For a moment or two I hung there, trapped, dangling by my left wrist, then the weight of my body tore the mangled wrist and hand through the gap and I crashed down to the deck beneath. Then the gorilla seemed to have another go with the sledge-hammer and consciousness went.

"I won't beat about the bush, old lad," Jolly said. "No point in it with a fellow pill-roller. Your wrist is a mess—I had to dig half your watch out of it. The middle and little fingers are broken, the middle in two places. But the permanent damage, I'm afraid, is to the back of your hand— the little and ring finger tendons have been sliced."

"What does that mean?" Swanson asked.

"It means that in his left hand he'll have to get by with two fingers and a thumb for the rest of his life," Jolly said bluntly.

Swanson swore softly and turned to Henry. "How in God's name could you have been so damnably careless? An experienced submariner like you? You know perfectly well that you are required to make a visual check every time a hatch cover engages in a standing latch. Why didn't you?"

426

" I didn't need to, sir." Henry was looking more dyspeptic and forlorn than ever. " I heard it click and I gave a tug. It was fixed, all right. I can swear to it, sir."

" How could it have been fixed? Look at Dr. Carpenter's hand. Just a hair-line engagement and the slightest extra pressure—my God, why can't you people obey regulations?"

Henry stared at the deck in silence. Jolly, who was understandably looking about as washed-out as I felt, packed away the tools of his trade, advised me to take a couple of days off, gave me a handful of pills to take, said a weary good-night and climbed up the ladder leading from the electronics space, where he had been fixing my hand. Swanson said to Henry: " You can go now, Baker." It was the first time I'd ever heard anyone address Henry by his surname, a sufficient enough token of what Swanson regarded as the enormity of his crime. " I'll decide what to do about this in the morning."

" I don't know about the morning," I said after Henry was gone. " Maybe the next morning. Or the one after that. Then you can apologise to him. You and me both. That cover was locked on its standing latch. *I* checked it visually, Commander Swanson."

Swanson gave me his cool impassive look. After a moment he said quietly : " Are you suggesting what I think you are suggesting?"

" Someone took a risk," I said. " Not all that much of a risk, though—most people are asleep now and the control room was deserted at the moment that mattered. Some one in the wardroom to-night heard me ask your permission to go down to the medical store and heard you giving your okay. Shortly after that nearly everyone turned in. One man didn't —he kept awake and hung around patiently until I came back from the Drift Station. He followed us down below— he was lucky, Lieutenant Sims, your officer on deck, was taking star-sights up on the bridge and the control room was empty— and he unhooked the latch but left the hatch cover in a standing position. There was a slight element of gambling as to whether I would come up first, but not all that much, it would have been a matter of elementary courtesy, he would have thought, for Henry to see me up first. Anyway, he won his gamble, slight though it was. After that our

427

unknown friend wasn't quite so lucky—I think he expected the damage to be a bit more permanent."

"I'll get inquiries under way immediately," Swanson said. "Whoever was responsible, someone must have seen him. Someone must have heard him leaving his cot——"

"Don't waste your time, Commander. We're up against a highly intelligent character who doesn't overlook the obvious. Not only that but word of your inquiries is bound to get around and you'd scare him under cover where I'd never get at him."

"Then I'll just keep the whole damned lot under lock and key until we get back to Scotland," Swanson said grimly. "*That* way there'll be no more trouble."

"That way we'll *never* find out who the murderer of my brother and the six—seven now—others are. Whoever it is has to be given sufficient rope to trip himself up."

"Good lord, man, we can't just sit back and let things be done to us." A hint of testiness in the commander's voice and I couldn't blame him. "What do we—what do *you* propose to do now?"

"Start at the beginning. To-morrow morning we'll hold a court of inquiry among the survivors. Let's find out all we can about that fire. Just an innocent above-board fact-finding inquiry—for the Ministry of Supply, let us say. I've an idea we might turn up something very interesting indeed."

"You think so?" Swanson shook his head. "I don't believe it. I don't believe it for a moment. Look what's happened to you. It's obvious, man, that someone knows or suspects that you're on to them. They'll take damned good care to give nothing away."

"You think that's why I was clouted to-night?"

"What other reason could there be?"

"Was that why Benson was hurt?"

"We don't know that he was. Deliberately, I mean. May have been pure coincidence."

"Maybe it was," I agreed. "And again maybe it wasn't. My guess, for what it's worth, is that the accident or accidents have nothing at all to do with any suspicions the killer may have that we're on to him. Anyway, let's see what to-morrow brings."

It was midnight when I got back to my cabin. The engineer officer was on watch and Hansen was asleep so I didn't put on any light lest I disturb him. I didn't undress, just removed my shoes, lay down on the cot and pulled a cover over me.

I didn't sleep. I couldn't sleep. My left arm from the elbow downwards still felt as if it were caught in a bear-trap. Twice I pulled from my pocket the pain-killers and sleeping-tablets that Jolly had given me and twice I put them away.

Instead I just lay there and thought and the first and most obvious conclusion I came up with was that there was someone aboard the *Dolphin* who didn't care any too much for the members of the medical profession. Then I got to wondering why the profession was so unpopular and after half an hour of beating my weary brain-cells around I got silently to my feet and made my way on stockinged soles to the sick-bay.

I passed inside and closed the door softly behind me. A red night-light burnt dully in one corner of the bay, just enough to let me see the huddled form of Benson lying on a cot. I switched on the overhead light, blinked in the sudden fierce wash of light and looked at the curtain at the other end of the bay. Nothing stirred behind it. I said : " Just kind of take your itching fingers away from that pipe-wrench, Rawlings. It's me, Carpenter."

The curtain was pulled to one side and Rawlings appeared, the pipe-wrench, with its bandage-wrapped head, dangling from one hand. He had a disappointed look on his face.

" I was expecting someone else," he said reproachfully. " I was kinda hoping—my God, Doc, what's happened to your arm?"

" Well may you ask, Rawlings. Our little pal had a go at me to-night. I think he wanted me out of the way. Whether he wanted me out of the way permanently or not I don't know, but he near as a toucher succeeded." I told him what had happened, then asked him : " Is there any man aboard you can trust absolutely?" I knew the answer before I had asked the question.

" Zabrinski," he said unhesitatingly.

429

" Do you think you could pussy-foot along to wherever it is that he's sleeping and bring him here without waking up anyone?"

He didn't answer my questions. He said : " He can't walk, Doc, you know that."

" Carry him. You're big enough."

He grinned and left. He was back with Zabrinski inside three minutes. Three-quarters of an hour later, after telling Rawlings he could call off his watch, I was back in my cabin.

Hansen was still asleep. He didn't wake even when I switched on a side light. Slowly, clumsily, painfully, I dressed myself in my furs, unlocked my case and drew out the Luger, the two rubber-covered magazines and the broken knife which Commander Swanson had found in the tractor's petrol tank. I put those in my pocket and left. As I passed through the control room I told the officer on deck that I was going out to check on the two patients still left out in the camp. As I had pulled a fur mitten over my injured hand he didn't raise any eyebrows, doctors were a law to themselves and I was just the good healer *en route* to give aid and comfort to the sick.

I did have a good look at the two sick men, both of whom seemed to me to be picking up steadily, then said " goodnight " to the two *Dolphin* crewmen who were watching over them. But I didn't go straight back to the ship. First I went to the tractor shed and replaced the gun, magazines and broken knife in the tractor tank. Then I went back to the ship.

IX

" I'm sorry to have to bother you with all these questions," I said pleasantly. " But that's the way it is with all government departments. A thousand questions in quadruplicate and each of them more pointlessly irritating than the rest. But I have this job to do and the report to be radioed off as soon as possible and I would appreciate all the information

430

and co-operation you can give me. First off, has anyone any idea at all how this damnable fire started?"

I hoped I sounded like a Ministry of Supply official which was what I'd told them I was—making a Ministry of Supply report. I'd further told them, just to nip any eyebrow-raising in the bud, that it was the Ministry of Supply's policy to send a doctor to report on any accident where loss of life was involved. Maybe this was the case. I didn't know and I didn't care.

"Well, I was the first to discover the fire, I think," Naseby, the Zebra cook, said hesitantly. His Yorkshire accent was very pronounced. He was still no picture of health and strength but for all that he was a hundred per cent improved on the man I had seen yesterday. Like the other eight survivors of Drift Ice Station Zebra who were present in the wardroom that morning, a long night's warm sleep and good food had brought about a remarkable change for the better. More accurately, like seven others. Captain Folsom's face had been so hideously burnt that it was difficult to say what progress he was making although he had certainly had a good enough breakfast, almost entirely liquid, less than half an hour previously.

"It must have been about two o'clock in the morning," Naseby went on. "Well, near enough two. The place was already on fire. Burning like a torch, it was. I——"

"What place?" I interrupted. "Where were you sleeping?"

"In the cookhouse. That was also our dining-hall. Farthest west hut in the north row."

"You slept there alone?"

"No. Hewson, here, and Flanders and Bryce slept there also. Flanders and Bryce, they're—they were—lab. technicians. Hewson and I slept at the very back of the hut, then there were two big cupboards, one each side, that held all our food stores, then Flanders and Bryce slept in the dining-hall itself, by a corner of the galley."

"They were nearest the door?"

"That's right. I got up, coughing and choking with smoke, very groggy, and I could see flames already starting to eat through the east wall of the hut. I shook Hewson then ran

431

for the fire extinguisher—it was kept by the door. It wouldn't work. Jammed solid with the cold, I suppose. I don't know. I ran back in again. I was blind by this time, you never saw smoke like it in your life. I shook Flanders and Bryce and shouted at them to get out then I bumped into Hewson and told him to run and wake Captain Folsom here."

I looked at Hewson. " You woke Captain Folsom?"

" I went to wake him. But not straight away. The whole camp was blazing like the biggest Fifth of November bonfire you ever saw and flames twenty feet high were sweeping down the lane between the two rows of huts. The air was full of flying oil, a lot of it burning. I had to make a long swing to the north to get clear of the oil and the flames."

" The wind was from the east?"

" Not quite. Not that night. South-east, I would say. East-south-east would be more like it, rather. Anyway, I gave a very wide berth to the generator house—that was the one next the dining-hall in the north row—and reached the main bunkhouse. That was the one you found us in."

" Then you woke Captain Folsom?"

" He was already gone. Shortly after I'd left the dining-hall the fuel drums in the fuel storage hut—that was the one directly south of the main bunkhouse—started exploding. Like bloody great bombs going off they were, the noise they made. They would have waked the dead. Anyway, they woke Captain Folsom. He and Jeremy here "—he nodded at a man sitting across the table from him—" had taken the fire extinguisher from the bunkhouse and tried to get close to Major Halliwell's hut."

" That was the one directly west of the fuel store?"

" That's right. It was an inferno. Captain Folsom's extinguisher worked well enough but he couldn't get close enough to do any good. There was so much flying oil in the air that even the extinguisher foam seemed to burn."

" Hold on a minute," I said. " To get back to my original question. How did the fire start?"

" We've discussed that a hundred times among ourselves," Dr. Jolly said wearily. " The truth is, old boy, we haven't a clue. We know *where* it started all right: match the huts destroyed against the wind direction that night and it could only have been in the fuel store. But how? It's anybody's guess. I don't see that it matters a great deal now."

"I disagree. It matters very much. If we could find out how it started we might prevent another such tragedy later on. That's why I'm here. Hewson, you were in charge of the fuel store and generator hut. Have you no opinion on this?"

"None. It *must* have been electrical, but how I can't guess. It's possible that there was a leakage from one of the fuel drums and that oil vapour was present in the air. There were two black heaters in the fuel store, designed to keep the temperature up to zero Fahrenheit, so that the oil would always flow freely. Arcing across the make and break of the thermostats might have ignited the gas. But it's only a wild guess, of course."

"No possibility of any smouldering rags or cigarette ends being the cause?"

Hewson's face turned a dusky red.

"Look, mister, I know my job. Burning rags, cigarette ends—I know how to keep a bloody fuel store——"

"Keep your shirt on," I interrupted. "No offence. I'm only doing *my* job." I turned back to Naseby. "After you'd sent Hewson here to rouse up Captain Folsom, what then?"

"I ran across to the radio room—that's the hut due south of the cookhouse and west of Major Halliwell's——"

"But those two lab. technicians—Flanders and Bryce, wasn't it—surely you checked they were awake and out of it before you left the dining-hall?"

"God help me, I didn't." Naseby stared down at the deck, his shoulders hunched, his face bleak. "They're dead. It's my fault they're dead. But you don't know what it was like inside that dining-hall. Flames were breaking through the east wall, the place was full of choking smoke and oil, I couldn't see, I could hardly breathe. I shook them both and shouted at them to get out. I shook them hard and I certainly shouted loud enough."

"I can bear him out on that," Hewson said quietly. "I was right beside him at the time."

"I didn't wait," Naseby went on. "I wasn't thinking of saving my own skin. I thought Flanders and Bryce were

433

all right and that they would be out the door on my heels. I wanted to warn the others. It wasn't—it wasn't until minutes later that I realised that there was no sign of them. And then—well, then it was too late."

"You ran across to the radio room. That's where you slept, Kinnaird, wasn't it?"

"That's where I slept, yes." His mouth twisted. "Me and my mate Grant, the boy that died yesterday. And Dr. Jolly slept in the partitioned-off east end of the hut. That's where he had his surgery and the little cubby-hole where he carried out his tests on ice samples."

"So your end would have started to go on fire first?" I said to Jolly.

"Must have done," he agreed. "Quite frankly, old chap, my recollection of the whole thing is just like a dream— a nightmare, rather. I was almost asphyxiated in my sleep, I think. First thing I remember was young Grant bending over me, shaking me and shouting. Can't recall what he was shouting but it must have been that the hut was on fire. I don't know what I said or did, probably nothing, for the next thing I clearly remember was being hit on both sides of the face, and not too gently either. But, by jove, it worked! I got to my feet and he dragged me out of my office into the radio room. I owe my life to young Grant. I'd just enough sense left to grab the emergency medical kit that I always kept packed."

"What woke Grant?"

"Naseby, here, woke him," Kinnaird said. "He woke us both, shouting and hammering on the door. If it hadn't been for him Dr. Jolly and I would both have been goners, the air inside that place was like poison gas and I'm sure if Naseby hadn't shouted on us we would never have woken up. I told Grant to waken the doctor while I tried to get the outside door open."

"It was locked?"

"The damned thing was jammed. That was nothing un- usual at night. During the day when the heaters were going full blast to keep the huts at a decent working temperature the ice around the doors tended to melt : at night, when we got into our sleeping-bags, we turned our heaters down and the melted ice froze hard round the door openings, sealing

434

it solid. That happened most nights in most of the huts —usually had to break our way out in the morning. But I can tell you that I didn't take too long to burst it open that night."

" And then?"

" I ran out," Kinnaird said. " I couldn't see a thing for black smoke and flying oil. I ran maybe twenty yards to the south to get some idea of what was happening. The whole camp seemed to be on fire. When you're woken up like that at two in the morning, half-blinded, half-asleep and groggy with fumes your mind isn't at its best, but thank God I'd enough left of my mind to realise that an S O S radio message was the one thing that was going to save our lives. So I went back inside the radio hut."

" We all owe our lives to Kinnaird." Speaking for the first time was Jeremy, a burly red-haired Canadian who had been chief technician on the base. " And if I'd been a bit quicker with my hands we'd have all been dead."

" Oh, for Christ's sake, mate, shut up," Kinnaird growled.

" I won't shut up," Jeremy said soberly. " Besides, Dr. Carpenter wants a full report. I was first out of the main bunkhouse after Captain Folsom here. As Hewson said, we tried the extinguisher on Major Halliwell's hut. It was hopeless from the beginning but we had to do it—after all, we knew there were four men trapped in there. But, like I say, it was a waste of time. Captain Folsom shouted that he was going to get another extinguisher and told me to see how things were in the radio room.

" The place was ablaze from end to end. As I came round as close as I could to the door at the west end I saw Naseby here bending over Dr. Jolly, who'd keeled over as soon as he had come out into the fresh air. He shouted to me to give him a hand to drag Dr. Jolly clear and I was just about to when Kinnaird, here, came running up. I saw he was heading straight for the door of the radio room." He smiled without humour. " I thought he had gone off his rocker. I jumped in front of him, to stop him. He shouted at me to get out of the way. I told him not to be crazy and he yelled at me—you had to yell to make yourself heard above the roar of the flames—that he had to get the portable radio out, that all the oil was

435

gone and the generator and the cookhouse with all the food were burning up. He knocked me down and the next I saw was him disappearing through that door. Smoke and flames were pouring through the doorway. I don't know how he ever got out alive."

"Was that how you got your face and hands so badly burnt?" Commander Swanson asked quietly. He was standing in a far corner of the wardroom, having taken no part in the discussion up till now, but missing nothing all the same. That was why I had asked him to be present: just because he was a man who missed nothing.

"I reckon so, sir."

"I fancy that should earn a trip to Buckingham Palace," Swanson murmured.

"The hell with Buckingham Palace," Kinnaird said violently. "How about my mate, eh? How about young Jimmy Grant? Can he make the trip to Buckingham Palace? Not now he can't, the poor bastard. Do you know what he was doing? He was still *inside* the radio room when I went back in, sitting at the main transmitter, sending out an S O S on our regular frequency. His clothes were on fire. I dragged him off his seat and shouted to him to grab some Nife cells and get out. I caught up the portable transmitter and a nearby box of Nife cells and ran through the door. I thought Grant was on my heels but I couldn't hear anything, what with the roar of flames and the bursting of fuel drums the racket was deafening. Unless you'd been there you just can't begin to imagine what it was like. I ran far enough clear to put the radio and cells in a safe place. Then I went back. I asked Naseby, who was still trying to bring Dr. Jolly round, if Jimmy Grant had come out. He said he hadn't. I started to run for the door again—and, well, that's all I remember."

"I clobbered him," Jeremy said with gloomy satisfaction. "From behind. I had to."

"I could have killed you when I came round," Kinnaird said morosely. "But I guess you saved my life at that."

"I certainly did, brother." Jeremy grimaced. "That was my big contribution that night. Hitting people. After Naseby, here, had brought Dr. Jolly round he suddenly

436

started shouting: "Where's Flanders and Bryce, where's Flanders and Bryce?' Those were the two who had been sleeping with Hewson and himself in the cookhouse. A few others had come down from the main bunkhouse by that time and the best part of a minute had elapsed before we realised that Flanders and Bryce weren't among them. Naseby, here, started back for the cookhouse at a dead run. He was making for the doorway, only there was no doorway left, just a solid curtain of fire where the doorway used to be. I swung at him as he passed and he fell and hit his head on the ice." He looked at Naseby. "Sorry again, Johnny, but you were quite crazy at the moment."

Naseby rubbed his jaw and grinned wearily. "I can still feel it. And God knows you were right."

"Then Captain Folsom arrived, along with Dick Foster, who also slept in the main bunkhouse," Jeremy went on. "Captain Folsom said he'd tried every other extinguisher on the base and that all of them were frozen solid. He'd heard about Grant being trapped inside the radio room and he and Foster were carrying a blanket apiece, soaked with water. I tried to stop them but Captain Folsom ordered me to stand aside." Jeremy smiled faintly. "When Captain Folsom orders people to stand aside—well, they do just that.

"He and Foster threw the wet blankets over their heads and ran inside. Captain Folsom was out in a few seconds, carrying Grant. I've never seen anything like it, they were burning like human torches. I don't know what happened to Foster, but he never came out. By that time the roofs of both Major Halliwell's hut and the cookhouse had fallen in. Nobody could get anywhere near either of those buildings. Besides, it was far too late by then, Major Halliwell and the three others inside the major's hut and Flanders and Bryce inside the cookhouse must already have been dead. Dr. Jolly, here, doesn't think they would have suffered very much—asphyxiation would have got them, like enough, before the flames did."

"Well," I said slowly, "that's as clear a picture of what must have been a very confusing and terrifying experience as we're ever likely to get. It wasn't possible to get anywhere near Major Halliwell's hut?"

" You couldn't have gone within fifteen feet of it and hoped to live," Naseby said simply.

" And what happened afterwards?"

" I took charge, old boy," Jolly said. " Wasn't much to take charge of, though, and what little there was to be done could be done only by myself—fixing up the injured, I mean. I made 'em all wait out there on the ice-cap until the flames had died down a bit and there didn't seem to be any more likelihood of further fuel drums bursting then we all made our way to the bunkhouse where I did the best I could for the injured men. Kinnaird here, despite pretty bad burns, proved himself a first-class assistant doctor. We bedded down the worst of them. Young Grant was in a shocking condition—'fraid there never really was very much hope for him. And—well, that was about all there was to it."

" You had no food for the next few days and nights?"

" Nothing at all, old boy. No heat either, except for the standby Coleman lamps that were in the three remaining huts. We managed to melt a little water from the ice, that was all. By my orders everyone remained lying down and wrapped up in what was available in order to conserve energy and warmth."

" Bit rough on you," I said to Kinnaird. " Having to lose any hard-earned warmth you had every couple of hours in order to make those S O S broadcasts."

" Not only me," Kinnaird said. " I'm no keener on frost-bite than anyone else. Dr. Jolly insisted that everyone who could should take turn about at sending out the S O S's. Wasn't hard. There was a pre-set mechanical call-up and all anyone had to do was to send this and listen in on the earphones. If any message came through I was across to the met. office in a flash. It was actually Hewson, here, who contacted the ham operator in Bodo and Jeremy who got through to that trawler in the Barents Sea. I carried on from there, of course. Apart from them there were Dr. Jolly and Naseby, here, to give a hand, so it wasn't so bad. Hassard, too, took a turn after the first day—he'd been more or less blinded on the night of the fire."

" You remained in charge throughout, Dr. Jolly?" I asked.

438

"Bless my soul, no. Captain Folsom, here, was in a pretty shocked condition for the first twenty-four hours, but when he'd recovered from that he took over. I'm only a pill-roller, old boy. As a leader of men and a dashing man of action—well, no, quite frankly, old top, I don't see myself in that light at all."

"You did damned well, all the same." I looked round the company. "That most of you won't be scarred for life is due entirely to the quick and highly-efficient treatment Dr. Jolly gave you under almost impossible circumstances. Well, that's all. Must be a pretty painful experience for all of you, having to relive that night again. I can't see that we can ever hope to find out how the fire started, just one of those chance in a million accidents, what the insurance companies call an act of God. I'm certain, Hewson, that no shadow of negligence attaches to you and that your theory on the outbreak of fire is probably correct. Anyway, although we've paid a hellishly high cost, we've learnt a lesson—never again to site a main fuel store within a hundred yards of the camp."

The meeting broke up. Jolly bustled off to the sick-bay, not quite managing to conceal his relish at being the only medical officer aboard who wasn't *hors de combat*. He had a busy couple of hours ahead of him—changing bandages on burns, checking Benson, X-raying Zabrinski's broken ankle and resetting the plaster.

I went to my cabin, unlocked my case, took out a small wallet, relocked my case and went to Swanson's cabin. I noticed that he wasn't smiling quite so often now as when I'd first met him in Scotland. He looked up as I came in answer to his call and said without preamble: "If those two men still out in the camp are in any way fit to be moved I want them both aboard at once. The sooner we're back in Scotland and have some law in on this the happier I'll be. I warned you that this investigation of yours would turn up nothing. Lord knows how short a time it will be before someone else gets clobbered. God's sake, Carpenter, we have a murderer running loose."

"Three things," I said. "Nobody's going to get clobbered any more, that's almost for certain. Secondly, the law, as you call it, wouldn't be allowed to touch it. And in the third

439

place, the meeting this morning was of some use. It eliminated three potential suspects."

" I must have missed something that you didn't."

" Not that. I knew something that you didn't. I knew that under the floor of the laboratory were about forty Nife cells in excellent condition—but cells that had been used."

" The hell you did," he said softly. " Sort of forgot to tell me, didn't you?"

" In this line of business I never tell anyone anything unless I think he can help me by having that knowledge."

" You must win an awful lot of friends and influence an awful lot of people," Swanson said dryly.

" It gets embarrassing. Now, who could have used cells? Only those who left the bunkhouse from time to time to send out the S O S's. That cuts out Captain Folsom and the Harrington twins—there's no question of any of the three of them having left the bunkhouse at any time. They weren't fit to. So that leaves Hewson, Naseby, Dr. Jolly, Jeremy, Hassard and Kinnaird. Take your choice. One of them is a murderer."

" Why did they want those extra cells?" Swanson asked. " And if they had those extra cells why did they risk their lives by relying on those dying cells that they did use. Does it make sense to you?"

" There's sense in everything," I said. If you want evasion, Carpenter has it. I brought out my wallet, spread cards before him. He picked them up, studied them and returned them to my wallet.

" So now we have it," he said calmly. " Took quite a while to get round to it, didn't you? The truth, I mean. Officer of M.I.6. Counter-espionage. Government agent, eh? Well, I won't make any song and dance about it, Carpenter, I've known since yesterday what you must be : you couldn't be anything else." He looked at me in calm speculation. " You fellows never disclose your identity unless you have to." He left the logical question unspoken.

" Three reasons why I'm telling you. You're entitled to some measure of my confidence. I want you on my side. And because of what I'm about to tell you, you'd have known anyway. Have you ever heard of the Perkin-Elmer Roti satellite missile tracker camera?"

440

"Quite a mouthful," he murmured. " No."

"Heard of Samos? Samos III?"

"Satellite and Missile Observation System?" He nodded. " I have. And what conceivable connection could that have with a ruthless killer running amok on Drift Station Zebra?"

So I told him what connection it could have. A connection that was not only conceivable, not only possible, not only probable, but absolutely certain. Swanson listened very carefully, very attentively, not interrupting even once and at the end of it he leaned back in his chair and nodded. " You have the right of it, no doubt about that. The question is, who? I just can't wait to see this fiend under close arrest and armed guard."

" You'd clap him in irons straight away?"

"Good God!" He stared at me. " Wouldn't you?"

" I don't know. Yes, I do. I'd leave him be. I think our friend is just a link in a very long chain and if we give him enough rope he'll not only hang himself, he'll lead us to the other members of the chain. Besides, I'm not all that sure that there *is* only one murderer : killers have been known to have accomplices before now, Commander."

" Two of them? You think there may be two killers aboard my ship?" He pursed his lips and squeezed his chin with a thoughtful hand, Swanson's nearest permissible approach to a state of violent agitation. Then he shook his head definitely. " There may only be one. If that is so, and I knew who he was, I'd arrest him at once. Don't forget, Carpenter, we've hundreds of miles to go under the ice before we're out into the open sea. We can't watch all six of them all the time and there are a hundred and one things that a man with even only a little knowledge of submarines could do that would put us all in mortal danger. Things that wouldn't matter were we clear of the ice, things that would be fatal under it."

" Aren't you rather overlooking the fact that if the killer did us in he'd also be doing himself in?"

" I don't necessarily share your belief in his sanity. All killers are a little crazy. No matter how excellent their reasons for killing, the very fact that they do kill makes them a rogue human being, an abnormal. You can't judge them by normal standards."

441

He was only half-right, but unfortunately that half might apply in this case. Most murderers kill in a state of extreme emotional once-in-a-lifetime stress and never kill again. But our friend in this case had every appearance of being a stranger to emotional stress of any kind—and, besides, he'd killed a great deal more than once.

"Well," I said doubtfully. "Perhaps. Yes, I think I do agree with you." I refrained from specifying our common ground for agreement. "Who's your candidate for the high jump, Commander?"

"I'm damned if I know. I listened to every word that was said this morning. I watched the face of each man who spoke—and the faces of the ones who weren't speaking. I've been thinking nonstop about it since and I'm still damned if I have a clue. How about Kinnaird?"

"He's the obvious suspect, isn't he? But only because he's a skilled radio operator. I could train a man in a couple of days to send and receive in morse. Slow, clumsy, he wouldn't know a thing about the instrument he was using, but he could still do it. Any of them may easily have been competent enough to operate a radio. The fact that Kinnaird is a skilled operator may even be a point in his favour."

"Nife cells were removed from the radio cabin and taken to the laboratory," Swanson pointed out. "Kinnaird had the easiest access to them. Apart from Dr. Jolly who had his office and sleeping quarters in the same hut."

"So that would point a finger at Kinnaird or Jolly?"

"Well, wouldn't it?"

"Certainly. Especially if you will agree that the presence of those tinned foods under the lab. floor also points a finger at Hewson and Naseby, both of whom slept in the cookhouse where the food was stored, and that the presence of the radio-sonde balloon and the hydrogen in the lab. also points a finger at Jeremy and Hassard, one a met. officer and the other a technician who would have had the easiest access to those items."

"That's right, confuse things," Swanson said irritably. "As if they weren't confused enough already."

"I'm not confusing things. All I'm saying is that if you admit a certain possibility for a certain reason then you must admit similar possibilities for similar reasons. Besides, there

442

are points in Kinnaird's favour. He risked his life to go back into the radio room to bring out the portable transmitter. He risked almost certain suicide when he tried to go in the second time to bring out his assistant, Grant, and probably would have died if Jeremy hadn't clobbered him. Look what happened to that man Foster who went in there immediately afterwards with a wet blanket over his head—*he* never came out.

"Again, would Kinnaird have mentioned the Nife cells if he had any guilt complex about them? But he did. That, incidentally, might have been why Grant, the assistant radio operator, collapsed in there and later died—Kinnaird had told him to bring out the other Nife cells and he was overcome because he stayed there too long looking for things that had already been removed from the hut. And there's one final point : we have Naseby's word for it that the door of the radio room was jammed, presumably by ice. Had Kinnaird been playing with matches a few moments previously, that door wouldn't have had time to freeze up."

"If you let Kinnaird out," Swanson said slowly, "you more or less have to let Dr. Jolly out too." He smiled. "I don't see a member of your profession running round filling people full of holes, Dr. Carpenter. Repairing holes is their line of business, not making them. Hippocrates wouldn't have liked it."

"I'm not letting Kinnaird out," I said. "But I'm not going off half-cocked and pinning a murder rap on him either. As for the ethics of my profession—would you like a list of the good healers who have decorated the dock in the Old Bailey? True, we have nothing on Jolly. His part in the proceedings that night seems to have consisted in staggering out from the radio room, falling flat on his face and staying there till pretty near the end of the fire. That, of course, has no bearing upon whatever part he might have taken in the proceedings prior to the fire. Though against that possibility there's the fact of the jammed door, the fact that Kinnaird or Grant would have been almost bound to notice if he had been up to something—Jolly's bunk was at the back of the radio room and he would have had to pass Kinnaird and Grant to get out, not forgetting that he would also have to stop to pick up the Nife cells. And there is one more

443

point in his favour—an apparent point, that is. I still don't think that Benson's fall was an accident and if it was no accident it is difficult to see how Jolly could have arranged it while he was at the foot of the sail and Benson at the top and it's even more difficult to see why he should have stood at the foot of the sail and let Benson fall on top of him."

"You're putting up a very good defence case for both Jolly and Kinnaird," Swanson murmured.

"No. I'm only saying what a defence lawyer would say."

"Hewson," Swanson said slowly. "Or Naseby, the cook. Or Hewson *and* Naseby. Don't you think it damned funny that those two, who were sleeping at the back or east side of the cookhouse, which was the first part of the hut to catch fire, should have managed to escape while the other two—Flanders and Bryce, wasn't it—who slept in the middle should have suffocated in there? Naseby said he shouted at them and shook them violently. Maybe he could have shouted and shaken all night without result. Maybe they were already unconscious—or dead. Maybe they had seen Naseby or Hewson or both removing food supplies and had been silenced. Or maybe they had been silenced *before* anything had been removed. And don't forget the gun. It was hidden in the petrol tank of the tractor, a pretty damn' funny place for a man to hide anything. But nothing funny about the idea occurring to Hewson, was there? He was the tractor-driver. And he seems to have taken his time about getting around to warn Captain Folsom. He said he had to make a wide circuit to avoid the flames but apparently Naseby didn't find it so bad when he went to the radio room. Another thing, a pretty telling point, I think, he said that when he was on the way to the bunkhouse the oil drums in the fuel store started exploding. If they only started exploding then how come all the huts—the five that were eventually destroyed, that is—were already uncontrollably on fire. They were uncontrollably on fire because they were saturated by flying oil so the first explosions, must have come a long time before then. And, apart from warning Folsom— who had already been warned—Hewson doesn't seem to have done very much after the fire started."

444

"You'd make a pretty good prosecuting counsel yourself, Commander. But wouldn't you think there is just too *much* superficially against Hewson? That a clever man wouldn't have allowed so much superficial evidence to accumulate against him? You would have thought that, at least, he would have indulged in a little fire-fighting heroics to call attention to himself?"

"No. You're overlooking the fact that he would never have had reason to expect that there would be any investigation into the causes of the fire? That the situation would never arise where he—or anyone else, for that matter—would have to justify their actions and behaviour if accusations were to be levelled against them?"

"I've said it before and I say it again. People like that *never* take a chance. They always act on the assumption that they *may* be found out."

"How could they be found out?" Swanson protested. "How could they possibly expect to have suspicion aroused?"

"You don't think it possible that they suspect that we are on to them?"

"No, I don't."

"That wasn't what you were saying last night after that hatch fell on me," I pointed out. "You said it was obvious that someone was on to me."

"Thank the lord that all I have to do is the nice uncomplicated job of running a nuclear submarine," Swanson said heavily. "The truth is, I don't know what to think any more. How about this cook fellow—Naseby?"

"You think he was in cahoots with Hewson?"

"If we accept the premise that the men in the cookhouse who were not in on this business had to be silenced, and Naseby wasn't, then he must have been, mustn't he? But, dammit, how then about his attempt to rescue Flanders and Bryce?"

"May just have been a calculated risk. He saw how Jeremy flattened Kinnaird when he tried to go back into the radio-room a second time and perhaps calculated that Jeremy would oblige again if he tried a similar but fake rescue act."

"Maybe Kinnaird's second attempt was also fake," Swan-

445

son said. "After all, Jeremy had already tried to stop him once."

"Maybe it was," I agreed. "But Naseby. If he's your man, why should he have said that the radio room door was jammed with ice, and that he had to burst it open. That gives Kinnaird and Jolly an out—and a murderer wouldn't do anything to put any other potential suspect in the clear."

"It's hopeless," Swanson said calmly. "I say let's put the whole damn' crowd of them under lock and key."

"That would be clever," I said. "Yes, let's do just that. That way we'll never find out who the murderer is. Anyway, before you start giving up, remember it's even more complicated than that. Remember you're passing up the two most obvious suspects of all—Jeremy and Hassard, two tough, intelligent birds who, if they were the killers, were clever enough to see that *nothing* pointed the finger against them. Unless, of course, there might have been something about Flanders and Bryce that Jeremy didn't want anyone to see, so he stopped Naseby from going back into the cookhouse. Or not."

Swanson almost glared at me. Watching his submarine plummetting out of control beyond the 1000-feet mark was something that rated maybe the lift of an eyebrow; but this was something else again. He said: "Very well, then, we'll let the killer run loose and wreck the *Dolphin* at his leisure. I must have very considerable confidence in you, Dr. Carpenter. I feel sure my confidence will not be misplaced. Tell me one last thing. I assume you are a highly skilled investigator. But I was puzzled by one omission in your questioning. A vital question, I should have thought."

"Who suggested moving the corpses into the lab. knowing that by doing so he would be making his hiding-place for the cached material a hundred per cent foolproof?"

"I apologise." He smiled faintly. "You had your reasons, of course."

"Of course. You're not sure whether or not the killer is on to the fact that we are on to him. I'm sure. I know he's not. But had I asked that question, he'd have known immediately that there could be only one reason for my asking it. Then he would have known I was on to him.

446

Anyway, it's my guess that Captain Folsom gave the order, but the original suggestion, carefully camouflaged so that Folsom may no longer be able to pin it down, would have come from another quarter."

Had it been a few months earlier with the summer Arctic sun riding in the sky, it would have been a brilliant day. As it was, there was no sun not in that latitude and so late in the year, but for all that the weather was about as perfect as it was possible for it to be. Thirty-six hours —the time that had elapsed since Hansen and I had made that savage trip back to the *Dolphin*—had brought about a change that seemed pretty close to miraculous. The knifing east wind had died, completely. That flying sea of ice-spicules was no more. The temperature had risen at least twenty degrees and the visibility was as perfect as visibility on the winter ice-pack ever is.

Swanson, sharing Benson's viewpoint on the crew's over-sedentary mode of existence and taking advantage of the fine weather, had advised everyone not engaged in actual watch-keeping to take advantage of the opportunity offered to stretch their legs in the fresh air. It said much for Swanson's powers of persuasion that by eleven that morning the *Dolphin* was practically deserted; and of course the crew, to whom Drift Ice Station Zebra was only so many words, were understandably curious to see the place, even the shell of the place, that had brought them to the top of the world.

I took my place at the end of the small queue being treated by Dr. Jolly. It was close on noon before he got round to me. He was making light of his own burns and frost-bite and was in tremendous form, bustling happily about the sick-bay as if it had been his own private domain for years.

"Well," I said, "the pill-rolling competition wasn't so fierce after all, was it? I'm damned glad there was a third doctor around. How are things on the medical front?"

"Coming along not too badly, old boy," he said cheerfully. "Benson's picking up very nicely, pulse, respiration, blood-pressure close to normal, level of unconsciousness very slight now, I should say. Captain Folsom's still in considerable pain, but no actual danger, of course. The rest have improved a hundred per cent, little thanks to the medical fraternity: excellent food, warm beds and the knowledge that they're safe have done them more good than anything we could ever do. Anyway, it's done me a lot of good, by jove!"

"And then," I agreed. "All your friends except Folsom and the Harrington twins have followed most of the crew on to the ice and I'll wager that if you had suggested to them forty-eight hours ago that they'd willingly go out there again in so short a time, they'd have called for a strait-jacket."

"The physical and mental recuperative power of homo sapiens," Jolly said jovially. "Beyond belief at times, old lad, beyond belief. Now, let's have a look at that broken wing of yours."

So he had a look, and because I was a colleague and therefore inured to human suffering he didn't spend any too much time in molly-coddling me, but by hanging on to the arm of my chair and the shreds of my professional pride I kept the roof from falling in on me. When he was finished he said: "Well, that's the lot, except for Brownell and Bolton, the two lads out on the ice."

"I'll come with you," I said. "Commander Swanson is waiting pretty anxiously to hear what we have to say. He wants to get away from here as soon as possible."

"Me, too," Jolly said fervently. "But what's the commander so anxious about?"

"Ice. You never know the hour or minute it starts to close in. Want to spend the next year or two up here?"

Jolly grinned, thought over it for a bit, then stopped grinning. He said apprehensively: "How long are we going to be under this damned ice? Before we reach the open sea, I mean?"

"Twenty-four hours, Swanson says. Don't look so worried, Jolly. Believe me, it's far safer under this stuff than among it."

With a very unconvinced look on his face Jolly picked up his medical kit and led the way from the sick-bay. Swanson was waiting for us in the control room. We climbed up the hatches, dropped down over the side and walked over to the Drift Station.

Most of the crew had already made their way out there We passed numbers of them on the way back and most of them looked grim or sick or both and didn't even glance up as we passed. I didn't have to guess why they looked as they did, they'd been opening doors that they should have left closed.

With the sharp rise in outside temperature and the effect of the big electric heaters having been burning there for twenty-four hours the bunkhouse hut was now, if anything, overheated, with the last traces of ice long vanished from walls and ceiling. One of the men, Brownell, had recovered consciousness and was sitting up, supported, and drinking soup provided by one of the two men who had been keeping watch over him.

"Well," I said to Swanson, "here's one ready to go."

"No doubt about that," Jolly said briskly. He bent over the other, Bolton, for some seconds, then straightened and shook his head. "A very sick man, Commander, very sick. I wouldn't care to take the responsibility of moving him.

"I might be forced to take the responsibility myself," Swanson said bluntly. "Let's have another opinion on this." His tone and words, I thought, could have been more diplomatic and conciliatory; but if there were a couple of murderers aboard the *Dolphin* there was a thirty-three and a third per cent chance that Jolly was one of them and Swanson wasn't forgetting it for a moment.

I gave Jolly an apologetic half-shrug, bent over Bolton and examined him as best I could with only one hand available for the task. I straightened and said : " Jolly's right. He is pretty sick. But I think he might just stand the transfer to the ship."

" ' Might just ' is not quite the normally accepted basis for deciding the treatment of a patient," Jolly objected.

" I know it's not. But the circumstances are hardly normal either."

" I'll take the responsibility," Swanson said. "Dr. Jolly, I'd be most grateful if you would supervise the transport of those two men back to the ship. I'll let you have as many men as you want straight away."

449

Jolly protested some more, then gave in with good grace. He supervised the transfer, and very competent he was about it too. I remained out there a little longer, watching Rawlings and some others dismantling heaters and lights and rolling up cables and, after the last of them was gone and I was alone, I made my way round to the tractor shed.

The broken haft of the knife was still in the tank of the tractor. But not the gun and not the two magazines. Those were gone. And whoever had taken them it hadn't been Dr. Jolly, he hadn't been out of my sight for two consecutive seconds between the time he'd left the *Dolphin* and the time of his return to it.

At three o'clock that afternoon we dropped down below the ice and headed south for the open sea.

X

The afternoon and evening passed quickly and pleasantly enough. Closing our hatches and dropping down from our hardly won foothold in that lead had had a symbolic significance at least as important as the actual fact of leaving itself. The thick ceiling of ice closing over the hull of the *Dolphin* was a curtain being drawn across the eye of the mind. We had severed all physical connection with Drift Ice Station Zebra, a home of the dead that might continue to circle slowly about the Pole for mindless centuries to come; and with the severance had come an abrupt diminution of the horror and the shock which had hung pall-like over the ship and its crew for the past twenty-four hours. A dark door had swung to behind us and we had turned our backs on it. Mission accomplished, duty done, we were heading for home again and the sudden upsurge of relief and happiness among the crew to be on their way again, their high anticipation of port and leave, was an almost tangible thing. The mood of the ship was close to that of lighthearted gaiety. But there was no gaiety in my mind, and no peace: I was leaving too much behind. Nor could there be any peace in the minds of Swanson and Hansen, of Rawlings and

450

Zabrinski : they knew we were carrying a killer aboard, a killer who had killed many times. Dr. Benson knew also, but for the moment Dr. Benson did not count : he still had not regained consciousness and I held the very unprofessional hope that he wouldn't for some time to come. In the twilight world of emergence from coma a man can start babbling and say all too much.

Some of the Zebra survivors had asked if they could see around the ship and Swanson agreed. In light of what I had told him in his cabin that morning, he must have agreed very reluctantly indeed, but no trace of this reluctance showed in his calmly smiling face. To have refused their request would have been rather a churlish gesture, for all the secrets of the *Dolphin* were completely hidden from the eye of the layman. But it wasn't good manners that made Swanson give his consent : refusing a reasonable request could have been responsible for making someone very suspicious indeed.

Hansen took them around the ship and I accompanied them, less for the exercise or interest involved than for the opportunity it gave me to keep a very close eye indeed on their reactions to their tour. We made a complete circuit of the ship, missing out only the reactor room, which no one could visit, anyway, and the inertial navigation-room which had been barred to me also. As we moved around I watched them all, and especially two of them, as closely as it is possible to watch anyone without making him aware of your observation, and I learned precisely what I had expected to learn—nothing. I'd been crazy even to hope I'd learn anything, our pal with the gun was wearing a mask that had been forged into shape and riveted into position. But I'd had to do it, anyway : playing in this senior league I couldn't pass up the one chance in a million.

Supper over, I helped Jolly as best I could with his evening surgery. Whatever else Jolly was, he was a damn' good doctor. Quickly and efficiently he checked and where necessary rebandaged the walking cases, examined and treated Benson and Folsom then asked me to come right aft with him to the nucleonics laboratory in the stern room which had been cleared of deck gear to accommodate the four other

451

bed patients, the Harrington twins, Brownell and Bolton. The sick-bay itself had only two cots for invalids and Benson and Folsom had those.

Bolton, despite Jolly's dire predictions, hadn't suffered a relapse because of his transfer from the hut to the ship—which had been due largely to Jolly's extremely skilful and careful handling of the patient and the stretcher into which he had been lashed. Bolton, in fact, was conscious now and complaining of severe pain in his badly burned right forearm. Jolly removed the burn covering and Bolton's arm was a mess all right, no skin left worth speaking of, showing an angry violent red between areas of suppuration. Different doctors have different ideas as to the treatment of burns: Jolly favoured a salve-coated aluminium foil which he smoothed across the entire burn area then lightly bandaged in place. He then gave him a pain-killing injection and some sleeping tablets, and briskly informed the enlisted man who was keeping watch that he was to be informed immediately of any change or deterioration in Bolton's condition. A brief inspection of the three others, a changed bandage here and there and he was through for the night.

So was I. For two nights now I had had practically no sleep—what little had been left for me the previous night had been ruined by the pain in my left hand. I was exhausted. When I got to my cabin, Hansen was already asleep and the engineer officer gone.

I didn't need any of Jolly's sleeping pills that night.

I awoke at two o'clock. I was sleep-drugged, still exhausted and felt as if I had been in bed about five minutes. But I awoke in an instant and in that instant I was fully awake.

Only a dead man wouldn't have stirred. The racket issuing from the squawk box just above Hansen's bunk was appalling: a high-pitched, shrieking, atonic whistle, two-toned and altering pitch every half-second, it drilled stiletto-like against my cringing ear-drums. A banshee in its death agonies could never have hoped to compete with that lot.

Hansen already had his feet on the deck and was pulling on clothes and shoes in desperate haste. I had never thought

452

to see that slow-speaking laconic Texan in such a tearing hurry, but I was seeing it now.

"What in hell's name is the matter?" I demanded. I had to shout to make myself heard above, the shrieking of the alarm whistle.

"Fire!" His face was shocked and grim. "The ship's on fire. And under this goddamned ice!"

Still buttoning his shirt, he hurdled my cot, crashed the door back on its hinges and was gone.

The atonic screeching of the whistle stopped abruptly and the silence fell like a blow. Then I was conscious of something more than silence—I was conscious of a complete lack of vibration throughout the ship. The great engines had stopped. And then I was conscious of something else again: feathery fingers of ice brushing up and down my spine. Why had the engines stopped? What could make a nuclear engine stop so quickly and what happened once it did? My God, I thought, maybe the fire is coming from the reactor room itself. I'd looked into the heart of the uranium atomic pile through a heavily leaded glass inspection port and seen the indescribable unearthly radiance of it, a nightmarish coalescence of green and violet and blue, the new "dreadful light" of mankind. What happened when this dreadful light ran amok? I didn't know, but I suspected I didn't want to be around when it happened.

I dressed slowly, not hurrying. My damaged hand didn't help me much but that wasn't why I took my time. Maybe the ship was on fire, maybe the nuclear power plant had gone out of kilter. But if Swanson's superbly trained crew couldn't cope with every emergency that could conceivably arise then matters weren't going to be improved any by Carpenter running around in circles shouting: "Where's the fire?"

Three minutes after Hansen had gone I walked along to the control room and peered in: if I was going to be in the way then this was as far as I was going to go. Dark acrid smoke billowed past me and a voice—Swanson's—said sharply: "Inside and close that door."

I pulled the door to and looked around the control room. At least, I tried to. It wasn't easy. My eyes were already streaming as if someone had thrown a bag of pepper into them and what little sight was left them didn't help

453

me much. The room was filled with black evil-smelling smoke, denser by far and more throat-catching than the worst London fog. Visibility was no more than a few feet, but what little I could see showed me men still at their stations. Some were gasping, some were half-choking, some were cursing softly, all had badly watering eyes, but there was no trace of panic.

"You'd have been better on the other side of that door," Swanson said dryly. "Sorry to have barked at you, Doctor, but we want to limit the spread of the smoke as much as possible."

"Where's the fire?"

"In the engine-room." Swanson could have been sitting on his front porch at home discussing the weather. "Where in the engine-room we don't know. It's pretty bad. At least, the smoke is. The extent of the fire we don't know, because we can't locate it. Engineer officer says it's impossible to see your hand in front of your face."

"The engines," I said. "They've stopped. Has anything gone wrong?"

He rubbed his eyes with a handkerchief, spoke to a man who was pulling on a heavy rubber suit and a smoke-mask, then turned back to me.

"We're not going to be vaporised, if that's what you mean." I could have sworn he was smiling. "The atomic pile can only fail safe no matter what happens. If anything goes wrong the uranium rods slam down in very quick time indeed—a fraction under a one-thousandth of a second—stopping the whole reaction. In this case, though, we shut it off ourselves. The men in the manœuvring-room could no longer see either the reactor dials or the governor for the control rods. No option but to shut it down. The engine-room crew have been forced to abandon the engine and manœuvring-rooms and take shelter in the stern room."

Well, that was something at least. We weren't going to be blown to pieces, ignobly vaporised on the altar of nuclear advancement: good old-fashioned suffocation, that was to be our lot. "So what do we do?" I asked.

"What we should do is surface immediately. With four-teen feet of ice overhead that's not easy. Excuse me, will you?"

He spoke to the now completely masked and suited man

454

who was carrying a small dialled box in his hands. They walked together past the navigator's chart desk and ice-machine to the heavy door opening on the passage that led to the engine-room over the top of the reactor compartment. They unclipped the door, pushed it open. A dense blinding cloud of dark smoke rolled into the room as the masked man stepped quickly into the passageway and swung the door to behind him. Swanson clamped the door shut, walked, temporarily blinded, back to the control position and fumbled down a roof microphone.

"Captain speaking." His voice echoed emptily through the control centre. "The fire is located in the engine-room. We do not know yet whether it is electrical, chemical or fuel oil: the source of the fire has not been pin-pointed. Acting on the principle of being prepared for the worst, we are now testing for a radiation leak." So that was what the masked man had been carrying, a Geiger counter. "If that proves negative, we shall try for a steam leak; and if that is negative we shall carry out an intensive search to locate the fire. It will not be easy as I'm told visibility is almost zero. We have already shut down all electrical circuits in the engine-room, lighting included, to prevent an explosion in the event of atomised fuel being present in the atmosphere. We have closed the oxygen intake valves and isolated the engine-room from the air-cleaning system in the hope that the fire will consume all available oxygen and burn itself out.

"All smoking is prohibited until further notice. Heaters, fans, and all electrical circuits other than communication lines to be switched off—and that includes the juke-box and the ice-cream machine. All lamps to be switched off except those absolutely essential. All movements is to be restricted to a minimum. I shall keep you informed of any progress we may make."

I became aware of someone standing by my side. It was Dr. Jolly, his normally jovial face puckered and woebegone, the tears flowing down his face. Plaintively he said to me: "This *is* a bit thick, old boy, what? I'm not sure that I'm so happy now about being rescued. And all those prohibitions—no smoking, no power to be used, no moving around —do those mean what I take them to mean?"

455

"I'm afraid they do indeed." It was Swanson who answered Jolly's question for him. "This, I'm afraid, is every nuclear submarine captain's nightmare come true—fire under the ice. At one stroke we're not only reduced to the level of a conventional submarine—we're two stages worse. In the first place, a conventional submarine wouldn't be under the ice, anyway. In the second place, it has huge banks of storage batteries, and even if it were beneath the ice it would have sufficient reserve power to steam far enough south to get clear of the ice. Our reserve battery is so small that it wouldn't take us a fraction of the way."

"Yes, yes," Jolly nodded. "But this no smoking, no moving——"

"That same very small battery, I'm afraid, is the only source left to us for power for the air-purifying machines, for lighting, ventilation, heating—I'm afraid the *Dolphin* is going to get very cold in a short time—so we have to curtail its expenditure of energy on those things. So no smoking, minimum movement—the less carbon dioxide breathed into the atmosphere the better. But the real reason for conserving electric energy is that we need it to power the heaters, pumps and motors that have to be used to start up the reactor again. If that battery exhausts itself before we get the reactor going—well, I don't have to draw a diagram."

"You're not very encouraging, are you, Commander?" Jolly complained.

"No, not very. I don't see any reason to be," Swanson said dryly.

"I'll bet you'd trade in your pension for a nice open lead above us just now," I said.

"I'd trade in the pension of every flag officer in the United States Navy," he said matter-of-factly. "If we could find a polynya I'd surface, open the engine-room hatch to let most of the contaminated air escape, start up our diesel—it takes its air direct from the engine-room—and have the rest of the smoke sucked out in nothing flat. As it is, that diesel is about as much use to me as a grand piano."

"And the compasses?" I asked.

"That's another interesting thought," Swanson agreed. "If the power output from our reserve battery falls below a certain level, our three Sperry gyro-compass systems and the

N6A—that's the inertial guidance machine—just pack up. After that we're lost, completely. Our magnetic compass is quite useless in these latitudes—it just walks in circles."

"So we would go around and around in circles, too," Jolly said thoughtfully. "For ever and ever under the jolly old ice-cap, what? By jove, Commander, I'm really beginning to wish we'd stayed up at Zebra."

"We're not dead yet, Doctor . . . Yes, John?" This to Hansen, who had just come up.

"Sanders, sir. On the ice-machine. Can he have a smoke mask. His eyes are watering pretty badly."

"Give him anything you like in the ship," Swanson said, "just so long as he can keep his eyes clear to read that graph. And double the watch on the ice-machine. If there's a lead up there only the size of a hair, I'm going for it. Immediate report if the ice thickness falls below, say, eight or nine feet."

"Torpedoes?" Hansen asked. "There hasn't been ice thin enough for that in three hours. And at the speed we're drifting there won't be for three months. I'll go keep the watch myself. I'm not much good for anything else, this hand of mine being the way it is."

"Thank you. First you might tell Engineman Harrison to turn off the CO_2 scrubber and monoxide burners. Must save every amp of power we have. Besides, it will do this pampered bunch of ours the world of good to sample a little of what the old-time submariners had to experience when they were forced to stay below maybe twenty hours at a time."

"That's going to be pretty rough on our really sick men," I said. "Benson and Folsom in the sick-bay, the Harrington twins, Brownell and Bolton in the nucleonics lab, right aft. They've got enough to contend with without foul air as well."

"I know," Swanson admitted. "I'm damnably sorry about it. Later on, when—and if—the air gets really bad, we'll start up the air-purifying systems again but blank off every place except the lab. and sick-bay." He broke off and turned round as a fresh wave of dark smoke rolled in from the suddenly opened after door. The man with the smoke mask was back from the engine-room and even with my eyes streaming in that smoke-filled acrid atmosphere I could see he was in a

457

pretty bad way. Swanson and two others rushed to meet him, two of them catching him as he staggered into the control room, the third quickly swinging the heavy door shut against the darkly-evil clouds of smoke.

Swanson pulled off the man's smoke mask. It was Murphy, the man who had accompanied me when we'd closed the torpedo tube door. People like Murphy and Rawlings, I thought, always got picked for jobs like this.

His face was white and he was gasping for air, his eyes upturned in his head. He was hardly more than half-conscious, but even that foul atmosphere in the control centre must have seemed to him like the purest mountain air compared to what he had just been breathing for within thirty seconds his head had begun to clear and he was able to grin up painfully from where he'd been lowered into a chair.

" Sorry, Captain," he gasped. " This smoke-mask was never meant to cope with the stuff that's in the engine-room. Pretty hellish in there, I tell you." He grinned again. " Good news, Captain. No radiation leak."

" Where's the Geiger counter?" Swanson asked quietly.

" It's had it, I'm afraid, sir. I couldn't see where I was going in there, honest, sir, you can't see three inches in front of your face. I tripped and damn' near fell down into the machinery space. The counter did fall down. But I'd a clear check before then. Nothing at all." He reached up to his shoulder and unclipped his film badge. " This'll show, sir."

" Have that developed immediately. That was very well done, Murphy," he said warmly. " Now nip for'ard to the mess room. You'll find some really clear air there."

The film badge was developed and brought back in minutes. Swanson took it, glanced at it briefly, smiled and let out his breath in a long slow whistle of relief. " Murphy was right. No radiation leak. Thank God for that, anyway. If there had been—well, that was that, I'm afraid."

" The for'ard door of the control room opened, a man passed through, and the door was as quickly closed. I guessed who it was before I could see him properly.

" Permission from Chief Torpedoman Patterson to approach you, sir," Rawlings said with brisk formality: " We've

458

just seen Murphy, pretty groggy he is, and both the Chief and I think that youngsters like that shouldn't be——"

"Am I to understand that you are volunteering to go next, Rawlings?" Swanson asked. The screws of responsibility and tension were turned hard down on him, but I could see that it cost him some effort to keep his face straight.

"Well, not exactly volunteering, sir. But—well, who else is there?"

"The torpedo department aboard his ship," Swanson observed acidly, "always did have a phenomenally high opinion of itself."

"Let him try an underwater oxygen set," I said. "Those smoke-masks seem to have their limitations."

"A steam leak, Captain?" Rawlings asked. "That what you want me to check on?"

"Well, you seemed to have been nominated, voted for and elected by yourself," Swanson said. "Yes, a steam leak."

"That the suit Murphy was wearing?" Rawlings pointed to the clothes on the desk.

"Yes. Why?"

"You'd have thought there would be some signs of moisture or condensation if there had been a steam leak, sir."

"Maybe. Maybe soot and smoke particles are holding the condensing steam in suspension. Maybe it was hot enough in there to dry off any moisture that did reach his suit. Maybe a lot of things. Don't stay too long in there."

"Just as long as it takes me to get things fixed up," Rawlings said confidently. He turned to Hansen and grinned. "You baulked me once back out there on the ice-cap, Lieutenant, but sure as little apples I'm going to get that little old medal this time. Bring undying credit on the whole ship, I will."

"If Torpedoman Rawlings will ease up with his ravings for a moment," Hansen said, "I have a suggestion to make, Captain. I know he won't be able to take off his mask inside there but if he would give a call-up signal on the engine telephone or ring through on the engine answering telegraph every four or five minutes we'd know he was O.K. If he doesn't, someone can go in after him."

Swanson nodded. Rawlings pulled on suit and oxygen

459

apparatus and left. That made it the third time the door leading to the engine compartment had been opened in a few minutes and each time fresh clouds of that black and biting smoke had come rolling in. Conditions were now very bad inside the control room, but someone had issued a supply of goggles all round and a few were wearing smoke-masks.

A phone rang. Hansen answered, spoke briefly and hung up.

"That was Jack Cartwright, Skipper." Lieutenant Cartwright was the main propulsion officer, who'd been on watch in the manœuvring-room and had been forced to retreat to the stern room. "Seems he was overcome by the fumes and was carried back into the stern room. Says he's O.K. now and could we send smoke-masks or breathing apparatus for himself and one of his men—they can't get at the ones in the engine-room. I told him yes."

"I'd certainly feel a lot happier if Jack Cartwright was in there investigating in person," Swanson admitted. "Send a man, will you?"

"I thought I'd take them myself. Someone else can double on the ice-machine."

Swanson glanced at Hansen's injured hand, hesitated then nodded. "Right. But straight through the engine-room and straight back."

Hansen was on his way inside a minute. Five minutes later he was back again. He stripped off his breathing equipment. His face was pale and covered in sweat.

"There's fire in the engine-room, all right," he said grimly. "Hotter than the hinges of hell. No trace of sparks or flames but that doesn't mean a thing, the smoke in there is so thick that you couldn't see a blast furnace a couple of feet away."

"See Rawlings?" Swanson asked.

"No. Has he not rung through?"

"Twice, but——" He broke off as the engine-room telegraph rang. "So. He's still O.K. How about the stern room, John?"

"Damn' sight worse than it is here. The sick men aft there are in a pretty bad way, especially Bolton. Seems the smoke got in before they could get the door shut."

460

"Tell Harrison to start up his air scrubbers. But for the lab. only. Blank off the rest of the ship."

Fifteen minutes passed, fifteen minutes during which the engine-room telegraph rang three times, fifteen minutes during which the air became thicker and fouler and steadily less breathable, fifteen minutes during which a completely equipped fire-fighting team was assembled in the control centre, then another billowing cloud of black smoke announced the opening of the after door.

It was Rawlings. He was very weak and had to be helped out of his breathing equipment and his suit. His face was white and streaming sweat, his hair and clothes so saturated with sweat that he might easily have come straight from an immersion in the sea. But he was grinning triumphantly.

"No steam leak, Captain, that's for certain." It took him three breaths to get that out. "But fire down below in the machinery space. Sparks flying all over the shop. Some flame, not much. I located it, sir. Starboard high-pressure turbine. The lagging's on fire."

"You'll get that medal, Rawlings," Swanson said, "even if I have to make the damn' thing myself." He turned to the waiting firemen. "You heard. Starboard turbine. Four at a time, fifteen minutes maximum. Lieutenant Raeburn, the first party. Knives, claw-hammers, pliers, crow-bars, CO_2. Saturate the lagging first then rip it off. Watch out for flash flames when you're pulling it off. I don't have to warn you about the steam pipes. Now on your way."

They left. I said to Swanson : "Doesn't sound so much. How long will it take. Ten minutes, quarter of an hour?"

He looked at me sombrely. "A minimum of three or four hours—if we're lucky. It's hell's own maze down in the machinery space there. Valves, tubes, condensers and miles of that damned steam piping that would burn your hands off if you touched it. Working conditions even normally are so cramped as to be almost impossible. Then there's that huge turbine housing with this thick insulation lagging wrapped all round it—and the engineers who fitted it meant it to stay there for keeps. Before they start they have to douse the fire with the CO_2 extinguishers and even that won't help much. Every time they rip off a piece of charred insulation the oil-soaked stuff below will burst into flames again as soon

461

as it comes into contact with the oxygen in the atmosphere."

" Oil-soaked?"

" That's where the whole trouble must lie," Swanson exclaimed. "Wherever you have moving machinery you must have oil for lubrication. There's no shortage of machinery down in the machine space—and no shortage of oil either. And just as certain materials are strongly hygroscopic so that damned insulation has a remarkable affinity for oil. Where there's any around, whether in its normal fluid condition or in fine suspension in the atmosphere that lagging attracts it as a magnet does iron filings. And it's as absorbent as blotting-paper."

" But what could have caused the fire?"

" Spontaneous combustion. There have been cases before. We've run over 50,000 miles in this ship now and in that time I suppose the lagging has become thoroughly saturated. We've been going at top speed ever since we left Zebra and the excess heat generated has set the damn thing off . . . John, no word from Cartwright yet?"

" Nothing."

" He must have been in there for the best part of twenty minutes now."

" Maybe. But he was just beginning to put his suit on— himself and Ringman—when I left. That's not to say they went into the engine-room straight away. I'll call the stern room." He did, spoke then hung up, his face grave. " Stern room says that they have been gone twenty-five minutes. Shall I investigate, sir?"

" You stay right here. I'm not——"

He broke off as the after door opened with a crash and two men came staggering out—rather, one staggering, the other supporting him. The door was heaved shut and the men's masks removed. One man I recognised as an enlisted man who had accompanied Raeburn : the other was Cartwright, the main propulsion officer.

" Lieutenant Raeburn sent me out with the lieutenant here," the enlisted man said. " He's not so good, I think, Captain."

It was a pretty fair diagnosis. He wasn't so good and that was a fact. He was barely conscious but none the less fighting grimly to hang on to what few shreds of consciousness were left him.

462

"Ringman," he jerked out. "Five minutes—five minutes ago. We were going back——"

"Ringman," Swanson prompted with a gentle insistence. "What about Ringman?"

"He fell. Down into the machinery space. I—I went after him, tried to lift him up the ladder. He screamed. God, he screamed. I—he——"

He slumped in his chair, was caught before he fell to the floor. I said: "Ringman. Either a major fracture or internal injuries."

"Damn!" Swanson swore softly. "Damn and blast it all. A fracture. Down there. John, have Cartwright carried through to the crew's mess. A fracture!"

"Please have a mask and suit ready for me," Jolly said briskly. "I'll fetch Dr. Benson's emergency kit from the sick-bay."

"You?" Swanson shook his head. "Damned decent, Jolly. I appreciate it but I can't let you——"

"Just for once, old boy, the hell with your navy regulations," Jolly said politely. "The main thing to remember, Commander, is that I'm aboard this ship too. Let us remember that we all—um—sink or swim together. No joke intended."

"But you don't know how to operate those sets——"

"I can learn, can't I?" Jolly said with some asperity. He turned and left.

Swanson looked at me. He was wearing goggles, but they couldn't hide the concern in his face. He said, curiously hesitant: "Do you think——"

"Of course Jolly's right. You've no option. If Benson were fit you know very well you'd have him down there in jig-time. Besides, Jolly is a damned fine doctor."

"You haven't been down there, Carpenter. It's a metal jungle. There isn't room to splint a broken finger far less——"

"I don't think Dr. Jolly will try to fix or splint anything. He'll just give Ringman a jab that will lay him out so that he can be brought up here without screaming in agony all the way."

Swanson nodded, pursed his lips and walked away to

463

examine the ice fathometer. I said to Hansen: "It's pretty bad, isn't it?"

"You can say that again, friend. It's worse than bad. Normally, there should be enough air in the submarine to last us maybe sixteen hours. But well over half the air in the ship, from here right aft is already practically unbreathable. What we have left can't possibly last us more than a few hours. Skipper's boxed in on three sides. If he doesn't start the air purifiers up the men working down in the machinery space are going to have the devil of a job doing anything. Working in near-zero visibility with breathing apparatus on you're practically as good as blind—the floods will make hardly any difference. If he does start up the purifiers in the engine-room, the fresh oxygen will cause the fire to spread. And, when he starts them up, of course, that means less and less power to get the reactor working again."

"That's very comforting," I said. "How long will it take you to restart the reactor?"

"At least an hour. That's after the fire has been put out and everything checked for safety. At least an hour."

"And Swanson reckoned three or four hours to put the fire out. Say five, all told. It's a long time. Why doesn't he use some of his reserve power cruising around to find a lead?"

"An even bigger gamble than staying put and trying to put out the fire. I'm with the skipper. Let's fight the devil we know rather than dice with the one we don't."

Medical case in hand, Jolly came coughing and spluttering his way back into the control centre and started pulling on suit and breathing apparatus. Hansen gave him instructions on how to operate it and Jolly seemed to get the idea pretty quickly. Brown, the enlisted man who'd helped Cartwright into the control centre, was detailed to accompany him. Jolly had no idea of the location of the ladder leading down from the upper engine-room to the machinery space.

"Be as quick as you can," Swanson said. "Remember, Jolly, you're not trained for this sort of thing. I'll expect you back inside ten minutes."

They were back in exactly four minutes. They didn't have an unconscious Ringman with them either. The only unconscious figure was that of Dr. Jolly, whom Brown half-carried, half-dragged over the sill into the control room.

"Can't say for sure what happened," Brown gasped. He was trembling from the effort he had just made, Jolly must have out-weighed him by at least thirty pounds. "We'd just got into the engine-room and shut the door. I was leading and suddenly Dr. Jolly fell against me—I reckon he must have tripped over something. He knocked me down. When I got to my feet he was lying there behind me. I put the torch on him. Out cold, he was. His mask had been torn loose. I put it on as best I could and pulled him out."

"My word," Hansen said reflectively. "The medical profession on the *Dolphin is* having a rough time." He gloomily surveyed the prone figure of Dr. Jolly as it was carried away towards the after door and relatively fresh air. "All three sawbones out of commission now. That's very handy, isn't it, Skipper?"

Swanson didn't answer. I said to him: "The injection for Ringman. Would you know what to give, how to give it and where?"

"No."

"Would any of your crew?"

"I'm in no position to argue, Dr. Carpenter."

I opened Jolly's medical kit, hunted among the bottles on the lid rack until I found what I wanted, dipped a hypodermic and injected it in my left forearm, just where the bandage ended. "Pain-killer," I said. "I'm just a softy. But I want to be able to use the forefinger and thumb of that hand." I glanced across at Rawlings, as recovered as anyone could get in that foul atmosphere, and said: "How are you feeling now?"

"Just resting lightly." He rose from his chair and picked up his breathing equipment. "Have no fears, Doc. With Torpedoman First-class Rawlings by your side——"

"We have plenty of fresh men still available aft, Dr. Carpenter," Swanson said.

"No. Rawlings. It's for his own sake. Maybe he'll get two medals now for this night's work."

Rawlings grinned and pulled the mask over his head. Two minutes later we were inside the engine-room.

It was stiflingly hot in there, and visibility, even with powerful torches shining, didn't exceed eighteen inches, but for the rest it wasn't too bad. The breathing apparatus functioned well enough and I was conscious of no discomfort. At first, that was.

Rawlings took my arm and guided me to the head of a ladder that reached down to the deck of the machinery space. I heard the penetrating hiss of a fire-extinguisher and peered around to locate its source.

A pity they had no submarines in the Middle Ages, I thought, the sight of that little lot down there would have given Dante an extra fillip when he'd started in on his *Inferno*. Over on the starboard side two very powerful floodlamps had been slung above the huge turbine: the visibility they gave varied from three to six feet, according to the changing amount of smoke given off by the charred and smouldering insulation. At the moment, one patch of the insulation was deeply covered in a layer of white foam —carbon dioxide released under pressure immediately freezes anything with which it comes in contact. As the man with the extinguisher stepped back, three others moved forward in the swirling gloom and started hacking and tearing away at the insulation. As soon as a sizeable strip was dragged loose the exposed lagging below immediately burst into flames reaching the height of a man's head, throwing into sharp relief weird masked figures leaping backwards to avoid being scorched by the flames. And then the man with the CO_2 would approach again, press his trigger, the blaze would shrink down, flicker and die, and a coat of creamy-white foam would bloom where the fire had been. Then the entire process would be repeated all over again. The whole scene with the repetitively stylised movements of the partici- pants highlit against a smoky oil-veined background of flicker- ing crimson was somehow weirdly suggestive of the priests of a long-dead and alien culture offering up some burnt sacrifice on their bloodstained pagan altar.

It also made me see Swanson's point: at the painfully but necessarily slow rate at which those men were making progress, four hours would be excellent par for the course. I tried not to think what the air inside the *Dolphin* would be like in four hours' time.

The man with the extinguisher—it was Raeburn—caught sight of us, came across and led me through a tangled maze of steam pipes and condensers to where Ringman was lying. He was on his back, very still, but conscious: I could see the movement of the whites of his eyes behind his goggles. I bent down till my mask was touching his.

"Your leg?" I shouted.

He nodded.

"Left?"

He nodded again, reached out gingerly and touched a spot halfway down the shin-bone. I opened the medical case, pulled out scissors, pinched the clothes on his upper arm between finger and thumb and cut a piece of the material away. The hypodermic came next and within two minutes he was asleep. With Rawlings's help I laid splints against his leg and bandaged them roughly in place. Two of the fire-fighters stopped work long enough to help us drag him up the ladder and then Rawlings and I took him through the passage above the reactor room. I became aware that my breathing was now distressed, my legs shaking and my whole body bathed in sweat.

Once in the control centre I took off my mask and immediately began to cough and sneeze uncontrollably, tears streaming down my cheeks. Even in the few minutes we had been gone the air in the control room had deteriorated to a frightening extent.

Swanson said: "Thank you, Doctor. What's it like in there?"

"Quite bad. Not intolerable, but not nice. Ten minutes is long enough for your fire-fighters at one time."

"Fire-fighters I have in plenty. Ten minutes it shall be."

A couple of burly enlisted men carried Ringman through to the sick-bay. Rawlings had been ordered for'ard for rest and recuperation in the comparatively fresh air of the mess-room, but elected to stop off at the sick-bay with me. He'd glanced at my bandaged left hand and said: "Three hands are better than one, even although two of them do happen to belong to Rawlings."

Benson was restless and occasionally murmuring, but still below the level of consciousness. Captain Folsom was asleep, deeply so, which I found surprising until Rawlings told me

467

that there were no alarm boxes in the sick-bay and that the door was completely soundproofed.

We laid Ringman down on the examination table and Rawlings slit up his left trouser leg with a pair of heavy surgical scissors. It wasn't as bad as I had feared it would be, a clean fracture of the tibia, not compound : with Rawlings doing most of the work we soon had his leg fixed up. I didn't try to put his leg in traction, when Jolly, with his two good hands, had completely recovered he'd be able to make a better job of it than I could.

We'd just finished when a telephone rang. Rawlings lifted it quickly before Folsom could wake, spoke briefly and hung up.

"Control room," he said. I knew from the wooden expression on his face that whatever news he had for me, it wasn't good. "It was for you. Bolton, the sick man in the nucleonics lab., the one you brought back from Zebra yesterday afternoon. He's gone. About two minutes ago." He shook his head despairingly. "My God, another death."

"No," I said. "Another murder."

XI

The *Dolphin* was an ice-cold tomb. At half past six that morning, four and a half hours after the outbreak of the fire, there was still only one dead man inside the ship, Bolton. But as I looked with bloodshot and inflamed eyes at the men sitting or lying about the control room—no one was standing any more—I knew that within an hour, two at the most, Bolton would be having company. By ten o'clock, at the latest, under those conditions, the *Dolphin* would be no more than a steel coffin with no life left inside her.

As a ship, the *Dolphin* was already dead. All the sounds we associated with a living vessel, the murmurous pulsation of great engines, the high-pitched whine of generators, the deep hum of the air-conditioning unit, the unmistakable transmission from the sonar, the clickety-clack from the radio room, the soft hiss of air, the brassy jingle from the juke-box, the whirring fans, the rattle of pots from the galley, the movement of men, the talking of men—all those were gone. All those vital sounds, the heart-beats of a living vessel, were gone; but in their place was not silence but something worse than silence, something that bespoke not living but dying, the frighteningly rapid, hoarse, gasping breathing of lung-tortured men fighting for air and for life.

Fighting for air. That was the irony of it. Fighting for air while there were still many days' supply of oxygen in the giant tanks. There were some breathing sets aboard, similar to the British Built-in Breathing System which takes a direct oxy-nitrogen mixture from tanks, but only a few, and all members of the crew had had a turn at those, but only for two minutes at a time. For the rest, for the more than ninety per cent without those systems, there was only the panting straining agony that leads eventually to death. Some portable closed-circuit sets were still left, but those were reserved exclusively for the fire-fighters.

Oxygen was occasionally bled from the tanks directly into the living spaces and it just didn't do any good at all; the only effect it seemed to have was to make breathing even more cruelly difficult by heightening the atmospheric pressure. All the oxygen in the world was going to be of little avail as long as the level of carbon dioxide given off by our anguished breathing mounted steadily with the passing of each minute. Normally, the air in the *Dolphin* was cleaned and circulated throughout the ship every two minutes, but the giant 200-ton air-conditioner responsible for this was a glutton for the electric power that drove it; and the electricians' estimate was that the reserve of power in the stand-by battery, which alone could reactivate the nuclear power-plant, was already dangerously low. So the concentration of carbon dioxide increased steadily towards lethal levels and there was nothing we could do about it.

Increasing, too, in what passed now for air, were the Freon fumes from the refrigerating machinery and the hydrogen fumes from the batteries. Worse still, the smoke was now so thick that visibility, even in the for'ard parts of the ship, was down to a few feet, but that smoke had to remain also, there was no power to operate the electrostatic precipitators and even when those had been briefly tried they had proved totally inadequate to cope with the concentration of billions

469

of carbon particles held in suspension in the air. Each time the door to the engine-room was opened—and that was progressively oftener as the strength of the fire-fighters ebbed—fresh clouds of that evil acrid smoke rolled through the submarine. The fire in the engine-room had stopped burning over two hours previously; but now what remained of the redly-smouldering insulation round the starboard high-pressure turbine gave off far more smoke and fumes than flames could ever have done.

But the greatest enemy of all lay in the mounting count of carbone monoxide, that deadly, insidious, colourless, taste-less, odourless gas with its murderous affinity for the red blood cells—five hundred times that of oxygen. On board the *Dolphin* the normal permissible tolerance of carbon monoxide in the air was thirty parts in a million. Now the reading was somewhere between four and five hundred parts in a million. When it reached a thousand parts, none of us would have more than minutes to live.

And then there was the cold. As Commander Swanson had grimly prophesied, the *Dolphin,* with the steam pipes cooled down and all heaters switched off, had chilled down to the sub-freezing temperature of the sea outside, and was ice-cold. In terms of absolute cold, it was nothing—a mere two degrees below zero on the centigrade scale. But in terms of cold as it reacted on the human body it was very cold indeed. Most of the crew were without warm clothing of any kind—in normal operating conditions the temperature inside the *Dolphin* was maintained at a steady 22° C. regardless of the temperature outside—they were both forbidden to move around and lacked the energy to move around to counteract the effects of the cold, and what little energy was left in their rapidly weakening bodies was so wholly occupied in forcing their labouring chest muscles to gulp in more and ever more of that foul and steadily worsening air that they had none at all left to generate sufficient animal heat to ward off that dank and bitter cold. You could actually *hear* men shivering, could listen to their violently shaking limbs knock-ing and rat-tat-tatting helplessly against bulkheads and deck, could hear the chattering of their teeth, the sound of some of them, far gone in weakness, whimpering softly with the cold: but always the dominant sound was that harsh

470

strangled moaning, a rasping and frightening sound, as men sought to suck air down into starving lungs.

With the exception of Hansen and myself—both of whom were virtually one-handed—and the sick patients, every man in the *Dolphin* had taken his turn that night in descending into the machinery space and fighting that red demon that threatened to slap us all. The number in each fire-fighting group had been increased from four to eight and the time spent down there shortened to three or four minutes, so that efforts could be concentrated and more energy expended in a given length of time; but because of the increasingly Stygian darkness in the machinery space, the ever-thickening coils of oily black smoke, and the wickedly cramped and confined space in which the men had to work, progress had been frustratingly, maddeningly slow; and entered into it now, of course, was the factor of that dreadful weakness that now assailed us all, so that men with the strength only of little children were tugging and tearing at the smouldering insulation in desperate near-futility and seemingly making no progress at all.

I'd been down again in the machinery space, just once, at 5.30 a.m. to attend to Jolly who had himself slipped, fallen and laid himself out while helping an injured crewman up the ladder, and I knew I would never forget what I had seen there, dark and spectral figures in a dark and spectral and swirling world, lurching and staggering around like zombies in some half-forgotten nightmare, swaying and stumbling and falling to the deck or down into the bilges now deep-covered in great snowdrifts of carbon dioxide foam and huge smoking blackened chunks of torn-off lagging. Men on the rack, men in the last stages of exhaustion. One little spark of fire, one little spark of an element as old as time itself and all the brilliant technological progress of the twentieth century was set at nothing, the frontiers of man's striving translated in a moment from the nuclear age to the dark unknown of pre-history.

Every dark hour brings forth its man and there was no doubt in the minds of the crew of the *Dolphin* that that dark night had produced its own here. Dr. Jolly. He had made a swift recovery from the effects of his first disastrous entry into the engine-room that night, appearing back in the control

471

centre only seconds after I had finished setting Ringman's broken leg. He had taken the news of Bolton's death pretty badly, but never either by word or direct look did he indicate to either Swanson or myself that the fault lay with us for insisting against his better judgment on bringing on board the ship a man whose life had been hanging in the balance even under the best of conditions. I think Swanson was pretty grateful for that and might even have got around to apologising to Jolly had not a fire-fighter come through from the engine-room and told us that one of his team had slipped and either twisted or broken an ankle—the second of many minor accidents and injuries that were to happen down in the machinery space that night. Jolly had reached for the nearest closed-circuit breathing apparatus before we could try to stop him and was gone in a minute.

We eventually lost count of the number of trips he made down there that night. Fifteen at least, perhaps many more, by the time six o'clock had come my mind was beginning to get pretty fuzzy round the edges. He'd certainly no lack of customers for his medical skill. Paradoxically enough, the two main types of injury that night were diametrically opposite in nature: burning and freezing, burning from the red-hot lagging—and, earlier, the steam pipes—and freezing from a carelessly directed jet of carbon dioxide against exposed areas of face or hands. Jolly never failed to answer a call, not even after the time he'd given his own head a pretty nasty crack. He would complain bitterly to the captain, old boy, for rescuing him from the relative safety and comfort of Drift Ice Station Zebra, crack some dry joke, pull on his mask and leave. A dozen speeches to Congress or Parliament couldn't have done what Jolly did that night in cementing Anglo-American friendship.

About 6.45 a.m. Chief Torpedoman Patterson came into the control centre. I suppose he walked through the doorway, but that was only assumption, from where I sat on the deck between Swanson and Hansen you couldn't see half-way to the door; but when he came up to Swanson he was crawling on his hands and knees, head swaying from side to side, whooping painfully, his respiration rate at least fifty to the minute. He was wearing no mask of any kind and was shivering constantly.

472

" We must do something, Captain," he said hoarsely. He spoke as much when inhaling as when exhaling, when your breathing is sufficiently distressed one is as easy as the other. " We've got seven men passed out now between the for'ard torpedo room and the crew's mess. They're pretty sick men, Captain."

" Thank you, Chief." Swanson, also without a mask, was in as bad a way as Patterson, his chest heaving, his breath hoarsely rasping, tears and sweat rolling down the greyness of his face. " We will be as quick as possible."

" More oxygen," I said. " Bleed more oxygen into the ship."

" Oxygen? More oxygen?" He shook his head. " The pressure is too high as it is."

" Pressure won't kill them." I was dimly aware through my cold and misery and burning chest and eyes that my voice sounded just as strange as did those of Swanson and Patterson. " Carbon monoxide will kill them. Carbon monoxide is what is killing them now. It's the relative proportion of CO_2 to oxygen that matters. It's too high, it's far too high. That's what's going to finish us all off."

" More oxygen," Swanson ordered. " Even the unnecessary acknowledgment of my words would have cost too much. " More oxygen."

Valves were turned and oxygen hissed into the control room and, I know, into the crew spaces. I could feel my ears pop as the pressure swiftly built up, but that was all I could feel. I certainly couldn't feel any improvement in my breathing, a feeling that was borne out when Patterson, noticeably weaker this time, crawled back and croaked out the bad news that he now had a dozen unconscious men on his hands.

I went for'ard with Patterson and a closed-circuit oxygen apparatus—one of the few unexhausted sets left—and clamped it for a minute or so on to the face of each unconscious man in turn, but I knew it was but a temporary palliative, the oxygen revived them but within a few minutes of the mask being removed most of them slipped back into unconsciousness again. I made my way back to the control room, a dark dungeon of huddled men nearly all lying down, most of them barely conscious. I was barely conscious myself. I wondered

473

vaguely if they felt as I did, if the fire from the lungs had now spread to the remainder of the body, if they could see the first slight changes in colour in their hands and faces, the deadly blush of purple, the first unmistakable signs of a man beginning to die from carbon monoxide poisoning. Jolly, I noticed, still hadn't returned from the engine-room : he was keeping himself permanently on hand, it seemed, to help those men who were in ever increasingly greater danger of hurting themselves and their comrades, as their weakness increased, as their level of care and attention and concentration slid down towards zero.

Swanson was where I'd left him, propped on the deck against the plotting table. He smiled faintly as I sunk down beside himself and Hansen.

" How are they, Doctor?" he whispered. A whisper, but a rock-steady whisper. The man's monolithic calm had never cracked and I realised dimly that here was a man who could never crack; you do find people like that, once in a million or once in a lifetime. Swanson was such a man.

" Far gone," I said. As a medical report it maybe lacked a thought in detail but it contained the gist of what I wanted to say and it saved me energy. "You will have your first deaths from carbon monoxide poisoning within the hour."

" So soon?" The surprise was in his red, swollen streaming eyes as well as in his voice. "Not so soon, Doctor. It's hardly—well, it's hardly started to take effect."

" So soon," I said. " Carbon monoxide poisoning is very rapidly progressive. Five dead within the hour. Within two hours fifty. At least fifty."

" You take the choice out of my hands," he murmured. " For which I am grateful. John, where is our main propulsion officer. His hour has come."

" I'll get him." Hansen hauled himself wearily to his feet, an old man making his last struggle to rise from his deathbed, and at that moment the engine-room door opened and blackened exhausted men staggered into the control room. Waiting men filed out to take their place. Swanson said to one of the men who had just entered : " Is that you, Will?"

" Yes, sir." Lieutenant Raeburn, the navigating officer, pulled off his mask and began to cough, rackingly, painfully Swanson waited until he had quieted a little.

474

" How are things down there, Will?"

" We've stopped making smoke, Skipper." Raeburn wiped his streaming face, swayed dizzily and lowered himself groggily to the floor. " I think we've drowned out the lagging completely."

" How long to get the rest of it off?"

" God knows. Normally, ten minutes. The way we are— an hour. Maybe longer."

" Thank you. Ah!" He smiled faintly as Hansen and Cartwright appeared out of the smoke-filled gloom. " Our main propulsion officer. Mr. Cartwright, I would be glad if you would put the kettle on to boil. What's the record for activating the plant, getting steam up and spinning the turbo-generators?"

" I couldn't say, Skipper." Red-eyed, coughing, smoke-blackened and obviously in considerable pain, Cartwright nevertheless straightened his shoulders and smiled slowly. " But you may consider it broken."

He left. Swanson heaved himself to his feet with obvious weakness—except for two brief inspection trips to the engine-room he had not once worn any breathing apparatus during those interminable and pain-filled hours. He called for power on the broadcast circuit, unhooked a microphone and spoke in a calm clear strong voice: it was an amazing exhibition in self-control, the triumph of a mind over agonised lungs still starving for air.

" This is your captain speaking," he said. " The fire in the engine-room is out. We are already reactivating our power plant. Open all watertight doors throughout the ship. They are to remain open until further orders. You may regard the worst of our troubles as lying behind us. Thank you for all you have done." He hooked up the microphone, and turned to Hansen. " The worst *is* behind, John—if we have enough power left to reactivate the plant."

" Surely the worst is still to come," I said. " It'll take you how long, three-quarters of an hour, maybe an hour to get your turbine generators going and your air-purifying equipment working again. How long do you think it will take your air cleaners to make any noticeable effect on this poisonous air?"

" Half an hour. At least that. Perhaps more."

" There you are, then." My mind was so woolly and doped now that I had difficulty in finding words to frame my thoughts, and I wasn't even sure that my thoughts were worth thinking. "An hour and a half at least—and you said the worst was over. The worst hasn't even begun." I shook my head, trying to remember what it was that I had been been going to say next, then remembered. " In an hour and a half one out of every four of your men will be gone."

Swanson smiled. He actually, incredibly, smiled. He said : " As Sherlock used to say to Moriarty, I think not, Doctor. Nobody's going to die of monoxide poisoning. In fifteen minutes' time we'll have fresh breathable air throughout the ship."

Hansen glanced at me just as I glanced at him. The strain had been too much, the old man had gone off his rocker. Swanson caught our interchange of looks and laughed, the laugh changing abruptly to a bout of convulsive coughing as he inhaled too much of that poisoned smoke-laden atmosphere. He coughed for a long time then gradually quietened down.

" Serves me right," he gasped. " Your faces . . . Why do you think I ordered the watertight doors opened, Doctor?"

" No idea."

" John?"

Hansen shook his head. Swanson looked at him quizzically and said : " Speak to the engine-room. Tell them to light up the diesel."

" Yes, sir," Hansen said woodenly. He made no move.

" Lieutenant Hansen is wondering whether he should fetch a strait-jacket," Swanson said. " Lieutenant Hansen knows that a diesel engine is never *never* lit up when a submarine is submerged—unless with a snorkel which is useless under ice—for a diesel not only uses air straight from the engine-room atmosphere, it gulps it down in great draughts and would soon clear away all the air in the ship. Which is what I want. We bleed compressed air under fairly high pressure into the forepart of the ship. Nice clean fresh air. We light up the diesel in the after part—it will run rough at first because of the low concentration of oxygen in this poisonous muck—but it will run. It will suck up much of this filthy air, exhausting its gases over the side, and as it does it will lower the atmospheric pressure aft and

476

the fresh air will make its way through from for'ard. To have done this before now would have been suicidal, the fresh air would only have fed the flames until the fire was out of control. But we can do it now. We can run it for a few minutes only, of course, but a few minutes will be ample. You are with me, Lieutenant Hansen?"

Hansen was with him all right, but he didn't answer. He had already left.

Three minutes passed, then we heard, through the now open passageway above the reactor room, the erratic sound of a diesel starting, fading, coughing, then catching again— we learned later that the engineers had had to bleed off several ether bottles in the vicinity of the air intake to get the engine to catch. For a minute or two it ran roughly and erratically and seemed to be making no impression at all on that poisonous air: then, imperceptibly, almost, at first, then with an increasing degree of definition, we could see the smoke in the control room, illuminated by the single lamp still left burning there, begin to drift and eddy towards the reactor passage. Smoke began to stir and eddy in the corners of the control room as the diesel sucked the fumes aft, and more smoke-laden air, a shade lighter in colour, began to move in from the wardroom passageway, pulled in by the decreasing pressure in the control room, pushed in by the gradual build-up of fresh air in the forepart of the submarine as compressed air was bled into the living spaces.

A few more minutes made the miracle. The diesel thudded away in the engine-room, running more sweetly and strongly as air with a higher concentration of oxygen reached its intake, and the smoke in the control room drained steadily away to be replaced by a thin greyish mist from the forepart of the ship that was hardly deserving of the name of smoke at all. And that mist carried with it air, an air with fresh life-giving oxygen, an air with a proportion of carbon dioxide and carbon monoxide that was now almost negligible. Or so it seemed to us.

The effect upon the crew was just within the limits of credibility. It was as if a wizard had passed through the length of the ship and touched them with the wand of life. Unconscious men, men for whom death had been less than half an hour away, began to stir, some to open their eyes:

477

sick, exhausted, nauseated and pain-racked men who had been lying or sitting on the decks in attitudes of huddled despair sat up straight or stood, their faces breaking into expressions of almost comical wonderment and disbelief as they drew great draughts down into their aching lungs and found that it was not poisonous gases they were inhaling but fresh breathable air: men who had made up their minds for death began to wonder how they could ever have thought that way. As air went, I suppose, it was pretty substandard stuff and the Factory Acts would have had something to say about it; but, for us, no pine-clad mountain air ever tasted half so sweet.

Swanson kept a careful eye on the gauges recording the air pressure in the submarine. Gradually it sunk down to the fifteen pounds at which the atmosphere was normally kept, then below it; he ordered the compressed air to be released under higher pressure and then when the atmospheric pressure was back to normal ordered the diesel stopped and the compressed air shut off.

"Commander Swanson," I said. "If you ever want to make admiral you can apply to me for a reference any time."

"Thank you." He smiled. "We have been very lucky." Sure we had been lucky, the way men who sailed with Swanson would always be lucky.

We could hear now the sounds of pumps and motors as Cartwright started in on the slow process of bringing the nuclear power plant to life again. Everyone knew that it was touch and go whether there would be enough life left in the batteries for that, but, curiously, no one seemed to doubt that Cartwright would succeed; we had been through too much to entertain even the thought of failure now.

Nor did we fail. At exactly eight o'clock that morning Cartwright phoned to say that he had steam on the turbine blades and that the *Dolphin* was a going proposition again. I was glad to hear it.

For three hours we cruised along at slow speed while the air-conditioning plant worked under maximum pressure to bring the air inside the *Dolphin* back to normal. After that Swanson slowly stepped up our speed until we had reached about fifty per cent of normal cruising speed, which was

478

as fast as the propulsion officer deemed it safe to go. For a variety of technical reasons it was impractical for the *Dolphin* to operate without all turbines in commission, so we were reduced to the speed of the slowest and, without lagging on it, Cartwright didn't want to push the starboard high-pressure turbine above a fraction of its power. This way, it would take us much longer to clear the ice-pack and reach the open sea but the captain, in a broadcast, said that if the limit of the ice-pack was where it had been when we'd first moved under it—and there was no reason to think it should have shifted more than a few miles—we should be moving out into the open sea about four o'clock the following morning.

By four o'clock of that afternoon, members of the crew, working in relays, had managed to clear away from the machinery space all the debris and foam that had accumulated during the long night. After that, Swanson reduced all watches to the barest skeletons required to run the ship so that as many men as possible might sleep as long as possible. Now that the exultation of victory was over, now that the almost intolerable relief of knowing that they were not after all to find their gasping end in a cold iron tomb under the ice-cap had begun to fade, the inevitable reaction, when it did come, was correspondingly severe. A long and sleepless night behind them; hours of cruelly back-breaking toil in the metal jungle of the machinery space; that lifetime of tearing tension when they had not known whether they were going to live or die but had believed they were going to die: the poisonous fumes that had laid them all on the rack: all of those combined had taken cruel toll of their reserves of physical and mental energy and the crew of the *Dolphin* were now sleep-ridden and exhausted as they had never been. When they lay down to sleep they slept at once, like dead men.

I didn't sleep. Not then, not at four o'clock. I couldn't sleep. I had too much to think about, like how it had been primarily my fault, through mistake, miscalculation or sheer pig-headedness, that the *Dolphin* and her crew had been brought to such desperate straits: like what Commander Swanson was going to say when he found out how much I'd kept from him, how little I'd told him. Still, if I had kept him in the dark so long, I couldn't see that there

479

would be much harm in it if I kept him in the dark just that little time longer. It would be time enough in the morning to tell him all I knew. His reactions would be interesting, to say the least. He might be striking some medals for Rawlings, but I had the feeling that he wouldn't be striking any for me. Not after I'd told him what I'd have to.

Rawlings. That was the man I wanted now. I went to see him, told him what I had in mind and asked him if he would mind sacrificing a few hours' sleep during the night. As always, Rawlings was co-operation itself.

Later that evening I had a look at one or two of the patients. Jolly, exhausted by his Herculean efforts of the previous night, was fathoms deep in slumber, so Swanson had asked if I would deputise for him. So I did, but I didn't try very hard. With only one exception they were sound asleep and none of them was in so urgent need of medical attention that there would have been any justification for waking him up. The sole exception was Dr. Benson, who had recovered consciousness late that afternoon. He was obviously on the mend but complained that his head felt like a pumpkin with someone at work on it with a riveting gun so I fed him some pills and that was the extent of the treatment. I asked him if he had any idea as to what had been the cause of his fall from the top of the sail, but he was either too woozy to remember or just didn't know. Not that it mattered now. I already knew the answer.

I slept for nine hours after that, which was pretty selfish of me considering that I had asked Rawlings to keep awake half the night; but then I hadn't had much option about that, for Rawlings was in the position to perform for me an essential task that I couldn't perform for myself.

Some time during the night we passed out from under the ice-cap into the open Arctic Ocean again.

I awoke shortly after seven, washed, shaved and dressed as carefully as I could with one hand out of commission, for I believe a judge owes it to his public to be decently turned out when he goes to conduct a trial, then breakfasted well in the wardroom. Shortly before nine o'clock I walked into the control room. Hansen had the watch. I went up to him and

480

said quietly; so that I couldn't be overheard: "Where is Commander Swanson?"

"In his cabin."

"I'd like to speak to him and yourself. Privately."

Hansen looked at me speculatively, nodded, handed over the watch to the navigator and led the way to Swanson's cabin. We knocked, went in and closed the door behind us. I didn't waste any time in preamble.

"I know who the killer is," I said. "I've no proof but I'm going to get it now. I would like you to be on hand. If you can spare the time."

They'd used up all their emotional responses and reactions during the previous thirty hours so they didn't throw up their hands or do startled double-takes or make any of the other standard signs of incredulousness. Instead Swanson just looked thoughtfully at Hansen, rose from his table, folded the chart he'd been studying and said dryly: "I think we might spare the time, Dr. Carpenter. I have never met a murderer." His tone was impersonal, even light, but the clear grey eyes had gone very cold indeed. "It will be quite an experience to meet a man with eight deaths on his conscience."

"You can count yourself lucky that it is only eight," I said. "He almost brought it up to the hundred mark yesterday morning."

This time I did get them. Swanson stared at me, then said softly: "What do you mean?"

"Our pal with the gun also carries a box of matches around with him," I said. "He was busy with them in the engine-room in the early hours of yesterday morning."

"Somebody *deliberately* tried to set the ship on fire?" Hansen looked at me in open disbelief. "I don't buy that, Doc."

"I buy it," Swanson said. "I buy anything Dr. Carpenter says. We're dealing with a madman, Doctor. Only a madman would risk losing his life along with the lives of a hundred others."

"He miscalculated," I said mildly. "Come along."

They were waiting for us in the wardroom as I'd arranged, eleven of them in all—Rawlings, Zabrinski, Captain Folsom,

481

Dr. Jolly, the two Harrington twins, who were now just barely well enough to be out of bed, Naseby, Hewson, Hassard, Kinnaird and Jeremy. Most of them were seated round the wardroom table except for Rawlings, who opened the door for us, and Zabrinski, his foot still in the cast, who was sitting in a chair in one corner of the room, studying an issue of the *Dolphin Daze*, the submarine's own mimeographed newspaper. Some of them made to get to their feet as we came in but Swanson waved them down. They sat, silently, all except Dr. Jolly who boomed out a cheerful: "Good morning, Captain. Well, well, this is an intriguing summons. Most intriguing. What is it you want to see us about, Captain?"

I cleared my throat. "You must forgive a small deception. It is I who wants to see you, not the captain."

"You?" Jolly pursed his lips and looked at me speculatively. "I don't get it, old boy. Why you?"

"I have been guilty of another small deception. I am not, as I gave you to understand, attached to the Ministry of Supply. I am an agent of the British Government. An officer of M.I.6, counter-espionage."

Well, I got my reaction, all right. They just sat there, mouths wide open like newly-landed fish, staring at me. It was Jolly, always a fast adjuster, who recovered first.

"Counter-espionage, by jove! Counter-espionage! Spies and cloaks and daggers and beautiful blondes tucked away in the wardrobes—or wardroom, should I say. But why—but why are you *here*? What do you—well, what *can* you want to see us about, Dr. Carpenter?"

"A small matter of murder," I said.

"Murder!" Captain Folsom spoke for the first time since coming aboard ship, the voice issuing from that savagely burnt face no more than a strangled croak. "Murder?"

"Two of the men lying up there now in the Drift Station lab. were dead *before* the fire. They had been shot through the head. A third had been knifed. I would call that murder, wouldn't you?"

Jolly groped for the table and lowered himself shakily into his seat. The rest of them looked as if they were very glad that they were already sitting down.

"It seems so superfluous to add," I said, adding it all the same, "that the murderer is in this room now."

482

You wouldn't have thought it, not to look at them. You could see at a glance that none of those high-minded citizens could possibly be a killer. They were as innocent as life's young morning, the whole lot of them, pure and white as the driven snow.

XII

It would be an understatement to say that I had the attention of the company. Maybe had I been a two-headed visitor from outer space, or had been about to announce the result of a multi-million pound sweepstake in which they held the only tickets, or was holding straws for them to pick to decide who should go before the firing squad—maybe then they might have given me an even more exclusive degree of concentration. But I doubt it. It wouldn't have been possible.

"If you'll bear with me," I began, "first of all I'd like to give you a little lecture in camera optics—and don't ask me what the hell that has to do with murder, it's got everything to do with it, as you'll find out soon enough.

"Film emulsion and lens quality being equal, the clarity of detail in any photograph depends upon the focal length of the lens—that is, the distance between the lens and the film. As recently as fifteen years ago the maximum focal length of any camera outside an observatory was about fifty inches. Those were used in reconnaissance planes in the later stages of the Second World War. A small suitcase lying on the ground would show up on a photograph taken from a height of ten miles, which was pretty good for those days.

But the American Army and Air Force wanted bigger and better aerial cameras, and the only way this could be done was by increasing the focal length of the lens. There was obviously a superficial limit to this length because the Americans wanted this camera to fit into a plane—or an orbiting satellite—and if you wanted a camera with a focal length of, say, 250 inches, it was obviously going to be quite impossible to install a twenty-foot camera pointing vertically downwards in a plane or small satellite. But scientists came up with a new type of camera using the folded lens principle, where the light, instead of coming down a long straight barrel, is bounced round a series of angled mirrored corners, which permits the focal length to be increased greatly without having to enlarge the camera itself. By 1950 they'd developed a hundred-inch focal length lens. It was quite an improvement on the World War II cameras which could barely pick up a suitcase at ten miles—this one could pick up a cigarette packet at ten miles. Then, ten years later, came what they called the Perkin-Elmer Roti satellite missile tracker, with a focal length of five hundred inches—equivalent to a barrel type camera forty feet long: this one could pick up a cube of sugar at ten miles."

I looked inquiringly around the audience for signs of inattention. There were no signs of inattention. No lecturer ever had a keener audience that I had there.

"Three years later," I went on, "another American firm had developed this missile tracker into a fantastic camera that could be mounted in even a small-size satellite. Three years' non-stop work to create this camera—but they reckoned it worth it. We don't know the focal length, it's never been revealed: we do know that, given the right atmospheric conditions, a white saucer on a dark surface will show up clearly from 300 miles up in space. This on a relatively tiny negative capable of almost infinite enlargement—for the scientists have also come up with a completely new film emulsion, still super-secret and a hundred times as sensitive as the finest films available on the commercial market to-day.

"This was to be fitted to the two-ton satellite the Americans called Samos III—Samos for Satellite and 'Missile Observation System. It never was. This, the only camera of its kind in the world, vanished, hi-jacked in broad daylight and, as we later learned, dismantled, flown from New York to Havana by a Polish jet-liner which had cleared for Miami and so avoided customs inspection.

"Four months ago this camera was launched in a Soviet satellite on a polar orbit, crossing the American middle west seven times a day. Those satellites can stay up indefinitely, but in just three days, with perfect weather conditions, the

Soviets had all the pictures they ever wanted—pictures of every American missile launching base west of the Mississippi. Every time this camera took a picture of a small section of the United States another smaller camera in the satellite, pointing vertically upwards, took a fix on the stars. Then it was only a matter of checking map co-ordinates and they could have a Soviet inter-continental ballistic missile ranged in on every launching-pad in America. But first they had to have the pictures.

" Radio transmission is no good, there's far too much quality and detail lost in the process—and you must remember this was a relatively tiny negative in the first place. So they had to have the actual films. There are two ways of doing this—bring the satellite back to earth or have it eject a capsule with the films. The Americans, with their Discoverer tests, have perfected the art of using planes to snatch falling capsules from the sky. The Russians haven't, although we do know they have a technique for ejecting capsules should a satellite run amok. So they had to bring the satellite down. They planned to bring it down some two hundred miles east of the Caspian. But something went wrong. Precisely what we don't know, but our experts say that it could only have been due to the fact that the retro-rockets on one side of the capsule failed to fire when given the radio signal to do so. You are beginning to understand, gentlemen?"

" We are beginning to understand indeed." It was Jeremy who spoke, his voice very soft. " The satellite took up a different orbit."

" That's what happened. The rockets firing on one side didn't slow her up any that mattered, they just knocked her far off course. A new and wobbly orbit that passed through Alaska, south over the Pacific, across Grahamland in Antarctica and directly south of South America, up over Africa and Western Europe, then round the North Pole in a shallow curve, maybe two hundred miles distant from it at the nearest point.

" Now, the only way the Russians could get the films was by ejecting the capsule, for with retro-rockets firing on one side only they knew that even if they did manage to slow up the satellite sufficiently for it to leave orbit, they

485

had no idea where it would go. But the damnably awkward part of it from the Russian's viewpoint was that nowhere in its orbit of the earth did the satellite pass over the Soviet Union or any sphere of Communist influence whatsoever. Worse, ninety per cent of its travel was over open sea and if they brought it down there they would never see their films again as the capsule is so heavily coated with aluminium and Pyroceram to withstand the heat of re-entry into the atmosphere that it was much heavier than water. And as I said, they had never developed the American know-how of snatching falling capsules out of the air—and you will appreciate that they couldn't very well ask the Americans to do the job for them.

" So they decided to bring it down in the only safe place open to them—either the polar ice-cap in the north or the Antarctic in the south. You will remember, Captain, that I told you that I had just returned from the Antarctic. The Russians have a couple of geophysical stations there and, up until a few days ago, we thought that there was a fifty-fifty chance that the capsule might be brought down there. But we were wrong. Their nearest station in the Antarctic was 300 miles from the path of orbit—and no field parties were stirring from home."

" So they decided to bring it down in the vicinity of Drift Ice Station Zebra?" Jolly asked quietly. It was a sign of his perturbation that he didn't even call me " old boy."

" Drift Ice Station Zebra wasn't even in existence at the time the satellite went haywire, although all preparations were complete. We had arranged for Canada to lend us a St. Lawrence ice-breaker to set up the station but the Russians in a burst of friendly goodwill and international co-operation offered us the atomic-powered *Lenin*, the finest ice-breaker in the world. They wanted to make good and sure that Zebra was set up and set up in good time. It was. The east-west drift of the ice-cap was unusually slow this year and almost eight weeks elapsed after the setting up of the station until it was directly beneath the flight trapectory of the satellite.

" You *knew* what the Russians had in mind?" Hansen asked.

" We knew. But the Russians had no idea whatsoever that we were on to them. They had no idea that one of the pieces

486

ot equipment which was landed at Zebra was a satellite monitor which would tell Major Halliwell when the satellite received the radio signal to eject the capsule." I looked slowly round the Zebra survivors. " I'll wager none of you knew that. But Major Halliwell did—and the three other men who slept in his hut where this machine was located.

" What we did not know was the identity of the member of Zebra's company that had been suborned by the Russians. We were certain someone *must* have been but had no idea who it was. Every one of you had first-class security clearances. But someone was suborned—and that someone, when he arrived back in Britain, would have been a wealthy man for the rest of his days. In addition to leaving what was in effect an enemy agent planted in Zebra, the Soviets also left a portable monitor—an electronic device for tuning in on a particular radio signal which would be activated inside the capsule at the moment of its ejection from the satellite A capsule can be so accurately ejected 300 miles up that it will land within a mile of its target, but the ice-cap is pretty rough territory and dark most of the time, so this monitor would enable our friend to locate the capsule which would keep on emitting its signal for at least, I suppose, twenty-four hours after landing. Our friend took the monitor and went out looking for the capsule. He found it, released it from its drogue and brought it back to the station. You are still with me, gentlemen? Especially one particular gentleman?"

" I think we are all with you, Dr. Carpenter," Commander Swanson said softly. " Every last one of us."

"Fine. Well, unfortunately, Major Halliwell and his three companions also knew that the satellite had ejected its capsule—don't forget that they were monitoring this satellite twenty-four hours a day. They knew that someone was going to go looking for it pretty soon, but who that someone would be they had no idea. Anyway, Major Halliwell posted one of his men to keep watch. It was a wild night, bitterly cold, with a gale blowing an ice-storm before it, but he kept a pretty good watch all the same. He either bumped into our friend returning with the capsule or, more probably, saw a light in a cabin, investigated, found our friend stripping the film from the capsule and, instead of going quietly

487

away and reporting to Major Halliwell, he went in and challenged this man. If that was the way of it, it was a bad mistake, the last he ever made. He got a knife between the ribs." I gazed at all the Zebra survivors in turn. "I wonder which one of you did it? Whoever it was, he wasn't very expert. He broke off the blade inside the chest. I found it there." I was looking at Swanson and he didn't bat an eyelid. He knew I hadn't found the blade there: he had found the haft in the petrol tank. But there was time enough to tell them that.

"When the man he had posted didn't turn up, Major Halliwell got worried. It must have been something like that. I don't know and it doesn't matter. Our friend with the broken knife was on the alert now, he knew someone was on to him—it must have come as a pretty severe shock, he'd thought himself completely unsuspected—and when the second man the Major sent turned up he was ready for him He had to kill him—for the first man was lying dead in his cabin. Apart from his broken knife he'd also a gun. He used it.

"Both those men had come from Halliwell's cabin, the killer knew that Halliwell must have sent them and that he and the other man still in the major's cabin would be around in double quick time if the second watcher didn't report back immediately. He decided not to wait for that —he'd burnt his boats anyway. He took his gun, went into Major Halliwell's cabin and shot him and the other man as they lay on their beds. I know that because the bullets in their heads entered low from the front and emerged high at the back—the angle the bullets would natur-ally take if the killer was standing at the foot of their beds and fired at them as they were lying down. I suppose this is as good a time as any to say that my name is not really Carpenter. It's Halliwell. Major Halliwell was my elder brother."

"Good God!" Dr. Jolly whispered. "Good God above!"

"One thing the killer knew it was essential to do right away—to conceal the traces of his crime. There was only one way—burn the bodies out of all recognition. So he dragged a couple of drums of oil out of the fuel store, poured them against the walls of Major Halliwell's hut—

he'd already pulled in there the first two men he'd killed —and set fire to it. For good measure he also set fire to the fuel store. A thorough type, my friends, a man who never did anything by halves."

The men seated around the wardroom table were dazed and shocked, uncomprehending and incredulous. But they were only incredulous because the enormity of the whole thing was beyond them. But not beyond them all.

"I'm a man with a curious turn of mind," I went on. "I wondered why sick, burnt, exhausted men had wasted their time and their little strength in shifting the dead men into the lab. Because someone had suggested that it might be a good thing to do, the decent thing to do. The real reason, of course, was to discourage anyone from going there. I looked under the floor-boards and what did I find? Forty Nife cells in first-class condition, stores of food, a radio-sonde balloon and a hydrogen cylinder for inflating the balloon. I had expected to find the Nife cells—Kinnaird, here, has told us that there were a good many reserves, but Nife cells won't be destroyed in a fire. Buckled and bent a bit, but not destroyed. I hadn't expected to find the other items of equipment, but they made everything clear.

"The killer had had bad luck on two counts—being found out and with the weather. The weather really put the crimp on all his plans. The idea was that when conditions were favourable he'd send the films up into the sky attached to a radio-sonde balloon which could be swept up by a Russian plane: snatching a falling capsule out of the sky it very tricky indeed; snaring a stationary balloon is dead easy. The relatively unused Nife cells our friend used for keeping in radio touch with his pals to let them know when the weather had cleared and when he was going to send the balloon up. There is no privacy on the air-waves, so he used a special code; when he no longer had any need for it he destroyed the code by the only safe method of destruction in the Arctic—fire. I found scores of pieces of charred paper embedded in the walls of one of the huts where the wind had carried them from the met. office after our friend had thrown the ashes away.

"The killer also made sure that only those few worn-out Nife cells were used to send the SOS's and to contact the *Dolphin*. By losing contact with us so frequently, and by sending such a blurred transmission, he tried to delay our arrival here so as to give the weather a chance to clear up and let him fly off his balloon. Incidentally you may have heard radio reports—it was in all the British newspapers— that Russian as well as American and British planes scoured this area immediately after the fire. The British and Americans were looking for Zebra: the Russians were looking for a radio-sonde balloon. So was the ice-breaker *Dvina* when it tried to smash its way through here a few days ago. But there have been no more Russian planes: our friend radioed *his* friends to say that there was no hope of the weather clearing, that the *Dolphin* had arrived and that they would have to take the films back with them on the submarine."

"One moment, Dr. Carpenter," Swanson interrupted in a careful sort of voice. "Are you saying that those films are aboard this ship now?"

"I'll be very much surprised if they aren't, Commander. The other attempt to delay us, of course, was by making a direct attack on the *Dolphin* itself. When it became known that the *Dolphin* was to make an attempt to reach Zebra, orders went through to Scotland to cripple the ship. Red Clydeside is no more red than any other maritime centre in Britain, but you'll find Communists in practically every ship-yard in the country—and, more often than not, their mates don't know who they are. There was no intention, of course, of causing any fatal accident—and, as far as whoever was responsible for leaving the tube doors open was concerned, there was no reason why there should be. International espionage in peacetime shuns violence—which is why our friend here is going to be very unpopular with his masters. Like Britain or America, they'll adopt any legitimate or illegitimate tactic to gain their espionage end—but they stop short of murder, just as we do. Murder was no part of the Soviet plan."

"Who is it, Dr. Carpenter?" Jeremy said very quietly. "For God's sake, who is it? There's nine of us here and —do you *know* who it is?"

"I know. And only six, not nine, can be under suspicion. The ones who kept radio watches after the disaster. Captain Folsom and the two Harringtons here were completely immobilised. We have the word of all of you for that. So that, Jeremy, just leaves yourself Kinnaird, Dr. Jolly, Hassard, Naseby and Hewson. Murder for gain, and high treason. There's only one answer for that. The trial will be over the day it begins : three weeks later it will all be over. You're a very clever man, my friend. You're more than that, you're brilliant. But I'm afraid it's the end of the road for you, Dr. Jolly."

They didn't get it. For long seconds they didn't get it. They were too shocked, too stunned. They'd heard my words all right, but the meaning hadn't registered immediately. But it was beginning to register now for like marionettes under the guidance of a master puppeteer they all slowly turned their heads and stared at Jolly. Jolly himself rose slowly to his feet and took two paces towards me, his eyes wide, his face shocked, his mouth working.

" Me?" His voice was low and hoarse and unbelieving. " *Me*? Are you—are you mad, Dr. Carpenter? In the name of God, man——"

I hit him. I don't know why I hit him, a crimson haze seemed to blur my vision, and Jolly was staggering back to crash on the deck, holding both hands to smashed lips and nose, before I could realise what I had done. I think if I had had a knife or a gun in my hand then, I would have killed him. I would have killed him the way I would have killed a fer-de-lance, a black widow spider or any other such dark and evil and deadly thing, without thought or compunction or mercy. Gradually the haze cleared from my eyes. No one had stirred. No one had stirred an inch. Jolly pushed himself painfully to his knees and then his feet and collapsed heavily in his seat by the table. He was holding a blood-soaked handkerchief to his face. There was utter silence in the room.

" My brother, Jolly," I said. " My brother and all the dead men on Zebra. Do you know what I hope?" I said. " I hope that something goes wrong with the hangman's rope and that you take a long, long time to die."

He took the handkerchief from his mouth.

" You're crazy man," he whispered between smashed and already puffing lips. " You don't know what you are saying."

491

" The jury at the Old Bailey will be the best judge of that I've been on to you now, Jolly, for almost exactly sixty hours."

" What did you say?" Swanson demanded. " You've known for sixty hours!"

" I knew I'd have to face your wrath some time or other, Commander," I said. Unaccountably, I was beginning to feel very tired, weary and heart-sick of the whole business. " But if you had known who he was you'd have locked him up straightaway. You said so in so many words. I wanted to see where the trail led to in Britain, who his associates and contacts would be. I had splendid visions of smashing a whole spy ring. But I'm afraid the trail is cold. It ends right here. Please hear me out.

" Tell me, did no one think it strange that when Jolly came staggering out of his hut when it caught fire that he should have collapsed and remained that way? Jolly claimed that he had been asphyxiated. Well, he wasn't asphyxiated inside the hut because he managed to come out under his own steam. Then he collapsed. Curious. Fresh air invariably revives people. But not Jolly. He's a special breed. He wanted to make it clear to everyone that he had nothing to do with the fire. Just to drive home the point, he has repeatedly emphasised that he is not a man of action. If he isn't, then I've never met one."

" You can hardly call that proof of guilt," Swanson interrupted.

" I'm not adducing evidence," I said wearily. " I'm merely introducing pointers. Pointer number two. You, Naseby, felt pretty bad about your failure to wake up your two friends, Flanders and Bryce. You could have shaken them for an hour and not woken them up. Jolly, here, used either ether or chloroform to lay them out. This was after he had killed Major Halliwell and the three others; but before he started getting busy with matches. He realised that if he burnt the place down there might be a long, long wait before rescue came and he was going to make damned certain that he wasn't going to go hungry. If the rest of you had died from starvation—well, that was just your bad luck. But Flanders and Bryce lay between him and the food. Didn't it strike you as very strange, Naseby, that your shouting and shaking had no effect. The only reason could be that they had been drugged—and only one man had access to drugs. Also, you said that both Hewson and yourself felt pretty groggy. No wonder. It was a pretty small hut and the chloroform or ether fumes had reached and affected Hewson and yourself—normally you'd have smelt it on waking up, but the stink of burning diesel obliterates every other smell. Again, I know this is not proof of any kind.

" Third pointer. I asked Captain Folsom this morning who had given the orders for the dead men to be put in the lab. He said he had. But, he remembered, it was Jolly's suggestion to him. Something learnedly medical about helping the morale of the survivors by putting the charred corpses out of sight.

" Fourth pointer. Jolly said that *how* the fire started was unimportant. A crude attempt to side-track me. Jolly knew as well as I did that it was all-important. I suppose, by the way, Jolly, that you deliberately jammed all the fire-extinguishers you could before you started the fire. About that fire, Commander. Remember you were a bit suspicious of Hewson, here, because he said the fuel drums hadn't started exploding until he was on his way to the main bunkhouse. He was telling the truth. There were no fewer than four drums in the fuel stores that didn't explode—the ones Jolly, here, used to pour against the huts to start the fire. How am I doing, Dr. Jolly?"

" It's all a nightmare," he said very quietly. " It's a nightmare. Before God, I know nothing of any of this."

" Pointer number five. For some reason that is unclear to me Jolly wanted to delay the *Dolphin* on its return trip. He could best do this, he reckoned, if Bolton and Brownell, the two very sick men still left out on the station could be judged to be too sick to be transferred to the *Dolphin*. The snag was, there were two other doctors around who might say that they *were* fit to be transferred. So he tried, with a fair measure of success, to eliminate us.

" First Benson. Didn't it strike you as strange, Commander, that the request for the survivors to be allowed to attend the funeral of Grant and Lieutenant Mills should have come from Naseby in the first place, then Kinnaird? Jolly, as the senior man of the party with Captain Folsom, here, temporarily unfit, was the obvious man to make the approach—but he didn't want to go calling too much attention to himself. Doubtless by dropping hints, he engineered it so that someone else should do it for him. Now Jolly had noticed how glass-smooth and slippery the ice-banked sides of the sail were and he made a point of seeing that Benson went up the rope immediately ahead of him. You must remember it was almost pitch dark—just light enough for Jolly to make out the vague outline of Benson's head from the wash of light from the bridge as it cleared the top of the rail A swift outward tug on the rope and Benson overbalanced. It seemed that he had fallen on top of Jolly. But only seemed. The loud sharp crack I heard a fraction of a second after Benson's body struck was not caused by his head hitting the ice—it was caused by Jolly, here, trying to kick his head off. Did you hurt your toes much, Jolly?"

"You're mad," he said mechanically. "This is utter nonsense. Even if it wasn't nonsense, you couldn't prove a word of it."

"We'll see. Jolly claimed that Benson fell on top of him. He even flung himself on the ice and cracked his head to give some verisimilitude to his story—our pal never misses any of the angles. I felt the slight bump on his head. But he wasn't laid out. He was faking. He recovered just that little bit too quickly and easily when he got back to the sick-bay. And it was then that he made his first mistake, the mistake that put me on to him—and should have put me on guard for an attack against myself. You were there, Commander."

"I've missed everything else," Swanson said bitterly. "Do you want me to spoil a hundred per cent record?"

"When Jolly came to he saw Benson lying there. All he could see of him was a blanket and a big gauze pack covering the back of his head. As far as Jolly was concerned, it could have been anybody—it had been pitch dark when the accident occurred. But what did he say? I remember his exact words. He said: 'Of course, of course. Yes, that's it. He fell on top of me, didn't he?' *He never thought to ask who it was*—the natural, the inevitable question in the circumstances. But Jolly didn't have to ask. He knew."

494

" He knew." Swanson stared at Jolly with cold bleak eyes and there was no doubt in his mind now about Jolly. " You have it to rights, Dr. Carpenter. He knew."

" And then he had a go at me. Can't prove a thing, of course. But he was there when I asked you where the medical store was, and he no doubt nipped down smartly behind Henry and myself and loosened the latch on the hatch-cover. But he didn't achieve quite the same high degree of success this time. Even so, when we went out to the station next morning he still tried to stop Brownell and Bolton from being transferred back to the ship by saying Bolton was too ill. But you overruled him."

" I was right about Bolton," Jolly said. He seemed strangely quiet now. " Bolton died."

" He died," I agreed. " He died because you murdered him and for Bolton alone I can make certain you hang. For a reason I still don't know, Jolly was still determined to stop this ship. Delay it, anyway. I think he wanted only an hour or two's delay. So he proposed to start a small fire, nothing much, just enough to cause a small scare and have the reactor shut down temporarily. As the site of his fire he chose the machinery space—the one place in the ship where he could casually let something drop and where it would lie hidden, for hours if need be, among the maze of pipes down there. In the sick-bay he concocted some type of delayed action chemical fuse which would give off plenty of smoke but very little flame—there are a dozen combinations of acids and chemicals that can bring this about and our friend will be a highly-trained expert well versed in all of them. Now all Jolly wanted was an excuse to pass through the engine-room when it would be nice and quiet and virtually deserted. In the middle of the night. He fixed this too. He can fix anything. He is a very, very clever man indeed is our pal here; he's also an utterly ruthless fiend.

" Late on the evening of the night before the fire the good healer here made a round of his patients. I went with him. One of the men he treated was Bolton in the nucleonics lab.—and, of course, to get to the nucleonics lab. you have to pass through the engine-room. There was an enlisted man watching over the patients and Jolly left special word that he was to be called at any hour if Bolton became any worse. He was called. I checked with the engine-room staff after the fire. The engineer officer was on watch and two others were in the manœuvring-room but an engine-man carrying out a routine lubrication job saw him passing through the engine-room about 1.30 a.m. in answer to a call from the man watching over the patients. He took the opportunity to drop his little chemical fuse as he was passing by the machinery space. What he didn't know was that his little toy lodged on or near the oil-saturated lagging on the housing of the starboard turbo-generator and that when it went off it would generate sufficient heat to set the lagging on fire."

Swanson looked at Jolly, bleakly and for a long time, then turned to me and shook his head. "I can't wear that, Dr. Carpenter. This phone call because a patient just happens to turn sick. Jolly is not the man to leave *anything* to chance."

"He isn't," I agreed. "He didn't. Up in the refrigerator in the sick-bay I have an exhibit for the Old Bailey. A sheet of aluminium foil liberally covered with Jolly's fingerprints. Smeared on this foil is the remains of a salve. That foil was what Jolly had bandaged on to Bolton's burnt forearm that night, just after he had given him pain-killing shots—Bolton was suffering very badly. But before Jolly put the salve on the foil he spread on something else first—a layer of sodium chloride—common or garden household salt. Jolly knew that the drugs he had given Bolton would keep him under for three or four hours; he also knew that by the time Bolton had regained consciousness body heat would have thinned the salve and brought the salt into contact with the raw flesh on the forearm. Bolton, he knew, when he came out from the effects of the drugs, would come out screaming in agony. Can you imagine what it must have been like: the whole forearm a mass of raw flesh—and covered with salt? When he died soon after, he died from shock. Our good healer here—a lovable little lad, isn't he?

"Well, that's Jolly. Incidentally, you can discount most of the gallant doctor's heroism during the fire—although he was understandably as anxious as any of us that we survive.

496

The first time he went into the engine-room it was too damned hot and uncomfortable for his liking so he just lay down on the floor and let someone carry him for'ard to where the fresh air was. Later——"

" He'd his mask off," Hansen objected.

" He took it off. *You* can hold your breath for ten or fifteen seconds—don't you think Jolly can too? Later on, when he was performing his heroics in the engine-room it was because conditions there were better, conditions outside were worse—and because by going into the engine-room he was entitled to a closed-circuit breathing set. Jolly got more clean air last night than any of us. He doesn't mind if he causes someone to die screaming his head off in agony— but he himself isn't going to suffer the slightest degree of hard- ship. Not if he can help it. Isn't that so, Jolly?"

He didn't answer.

" Where are the films, Jolly?"

" I don't know what you are talking about," he said in a quiet toneless voice. " Before God, my hands are clean."

" How about your fingerprints on that foil with the salt on it?"

" Any doctor can make a mistake."

" My God! Mistake! Where are they, Jolly—the films?"

" For God's sake leave me alone," he said tiredly.

" Have it your own way." I looked at Swanson. " Got some nice secure place where you can lock this character up?"

" I certainly have," Swanson said grimly. " I'll conduct him there in person."

" No one's conducting anyone anywhere," Kinnaird said. He was looking at me and I didn't care very much for the way he was looking at me. I didn't care very much either for what he held in his hand, a very nasty-looking Luger. It was cradled in his fist as if it had grown there and it was pointing straight between my eyes.

"Clever, clever counter-espionage, Carpenter," Dr. Jolly murmured. "How swiftly the fortunes of war change, old boy. But you shouldn't be surprised really. You haven't found out anything that actually matters, but surely you should have found out enough to realise that you are operating out of your class. Please don't try anything foolish. Kinnaird is one of the finest pistol shots I have ever known—and you will observe how strategically he's placed so that everyone in the room is covered."

He delicately patted his still-bleeding mouth with a handkerchief, rose, went behind me and ran his hands quickly down my clothes.

"My word," he said. "Not even carrying a gun. You really are unprepared, Carpenter. Turn round, will you, so that your back is to Kinnaird's gun?"

I turned round. He smiled pleasantly then hit me twice across the face with all his strength, first with the back of his right hand and then with the back of the left. I staggered, but didn't fall down. I could taste the salt of blood.

"Can't even call it regrettable loss of temper," Jolly said with satisfaction. "Did it deliberately and with malice aforethought. Enjoyed it, too."

"So Kinnaird was the killer," I said slowly, thickly. "He was the man with the gun?"

"Wouldn't want to take all the credit, mate," Kinnaird said modestly. "Let's say we sorted them out fifty-fifty."

"_You_ were the one who went out with the monitor to find the capsule," I nodded. "That's why you got your face so badly frost-bitten."

"Got lost," Kinnaird admitted. "Thought I'd never find the damned station again."

"Jolly and Kinnaird," Jeremy said wonderingly. "Jolly and Kinnaird. Your own mates. You two filthy murderous——"

"Be quiet," Jolly ordered. "Kinnaird, don't bother answering questions. Unlike Carpenter here, I take no pleasure

498

in outlining my *modus operandi* and explaining at length how clever I've been. As you observed, Carpenter, I'm a man of action. Commander Swanson, get on that phone there, call up your control room, order your ship to surface and steam north."

"You're becoming too ambitious, Jolly," Swanson said calmly. "You can't hi-jack a submarine."

"Kinnaird," Jolly said. "Point your gun at Hansen's stomach. When I reach the count of five, pull the trigger. One, two, three——"

Swanson half-raised a hand in acknowledgment of defeat, crossed to the wall-phone, gave the necessary orders, hung up and came back to stand beside me. He looked at me without either respect or admiration. I looked round all the other people in the room. Jolly, Hansen and Rawlings standing, Zabrinski sitting on a chair by himself with the now disregarded copy of the *Dolphin Daze* on his knees, all the others sitting round the table, Kinnaird well clear of them, the gun very steady in his hand. So very steady. No one seemed to be contemplating any heroics. For the most part everyone was too shocked, too dazed, to think of anything.

"Hi-jacking a nuclear submarine is an intriguing prospect —and no doubt would be a highly profitable one, Commander Swanson," Jolly said. "But I know my limitations. No, old top, we shall simply be leaving you. Not very many miles from here is a naval vessel with a helicopter on its after deck. In a little while, Commander, you will send a wireless message on a certain frequency giving our position : the helicopter will pick us up. And even if your crippled engine would stand the strain I wouldn't advise you to come chasing after that ship with ideas about torpedoing it or anything of that dramatic ilk. Apart from the fact that you wouldn't like to be responsible for triggering off a nuclear war, you couldn't catch it, anyway. You won't even be able to see the ship, Commander—and if you did it wouldn't matter, anyway. It has no nationality markings."

"Where are the films?" I asked.

"They're already aboard that naval vessel."

"They're *what*?" Swanson demanded. "How in hell's name can they be?"

"Sorry and all that, old boy. I repeat that unlike Carpenter,

499

here, I don't go around shooting off my mouth. A professional, my dear captain, *never* gives information about his methods."

"So you get off with it," I said bitterly. My mouth felt thick and swollen.

"Don't see what's to stop us. Crimes don't always come home to roost, you know."

"Eight men murdered," I said wonderingly. "Eight men. You can stand there and cheerfully admit that you are responsible for the deaths of eight men."

"Cheerfully?" he said consideringly. "No, not cheerfully. I'm a professional, and a professional never kills unnecessarily. But this time it was necessary. That's all."

"That's the second time you've used the word 'professional'," I said slowly. "I was wrong on one theory. You weren't just suborned after the Zebra team had been picked. You've been at this game a long time—you're too good not to have been."

"Fifteen years, old lad," Jolly said calmly. "Kinnaird and I—we were the best team in Britain. Our usefulness in that country, unfortunately, is over. I should imagine that our—um—exceptional talents can be employed elsewhere."

"You admit to all those murders?" I asked.

He looked at me in sudden cold speculation. "A damned funny question, Carpenter. Of course. I've told you. Why?"

"And do you, Kinnaird?"

He looked at me in bleak suspicion. "Why ask?"

"You answer my question and I'll answer yours." At the corner of my range of vision I could see Jolly looking at me with narrowed eyes. He was very sensitive to atmosphere, he knew there was something off-key.

"You know damn' well what I did, mate," Kinnaird said coldly.

"So there we have it. In the presence of no less than twelve witnesses, you both confess to murder. You shouldn't have done that, you know. I'll answer your question, Kinnaird. I wanted to have an oral confession from you because, apart from the sheet of aluminium foil and something I'll mention in a minute, we have no actual proof at all against either of you. But now we have your confessions. Your great talents are not going to be used in any other sphere, I'm afraid.

500

You'll never see that helicopter or that naval vessel. You'll both die jerking on the end of a rope."

"What rubbish is this?" Jolly asked contemptuously. But there was worry under the contempt. "What last-minute despairing bluff are you trying to pull, Carpenter?"

I ignored his question. I said: "I've been on to Kinnaird, here, for some sixty hours also, Jolly. But I had to play it this way. Without letting you gain what appeared to be the upper hand you would never have admitted to the crimes. But now you have."

"Don't fall for it, old boy," Jolly said to Kinnaird. "It's just some desperate bluff. He never had any idea that you were in on this."

"When I knew you were one of the killers," I said to Jolly, "I was almost certain Kinnaird had to be another. You shared the same cabin and unless Kinnaird had been sapped or drugged he had to be in on it. He was neither. He was in on it. That door wasn't jammed when Naseby ran round to the radio room to warn you—the two of you were leaning all your weight against it to give the impression that it had been closed for hours and that ice had formed.

"By the same token, young Grant, the assistant radio operator, was in cahoots with you—or he wasn't. If he wasn't, he would have to be silenced. He wasn't. So you silenced him. After I'd caught on to the two of you I had a good look at Grant. I went out and dug him up from where we'd buried him. Rawlings and I. I found a great big bruise at the base of his neck. He surprised you in something, or he woke when you knifed or shot one of Major Halliwell's men, and you laid him out. You didn't bother killing him, you were about to set the hut on fire and incinerate him, so killing would have been pointless. But you didn't reckon on Captain Folsom, here, going in and bringing him out—alive.

"That was most damnably awkward for you, wasn't it, Jolly? He was unconscious but when and if he recovered consciousness he could blow the whole works on you. But you couldn't get at him to finish him off, could you? The bunkhouse was full of people, most of them suffering so severely that sleep was impossible for them. When we arrived on the scene you got desperate. Grant was showing signs of regaining consciousness. You took a chance, but not all that much of a chance. Remember how surprised I was to find that you had used up all my morphine? Well, I *was* surprised then. But not now. I know now where it went. You gave him an injection of morphine—and you made damn' sure the hypodermic had a lethal dose. Am I correct?"

"You're cleverer than I thought you were," he said calmly. "Maybe I have misjudged you a little. But it still makes no difference, old boy."

"I wonder. If I'd known about Kinnaird so long why do you think I allowed a situation to develop where you could apparently turn the tables?"

"Apparently is not the word you want. And the answer to your question is easy. You didn't know Kinnaird *had* a gun."

"No?" I looked at Kinnaird. "Are you sure that thing works?"

"Don't come that old stuff with me, mate," Kinnaird said in contempt.

"I just wondered," I said mildly. "I thought perhaps the petrol in the tractor's tank might have removed all the lubricating oil."

Jolly came close to me, his face tight and cold. "You *knew* about this? What goes on, Carpenter?"

"It was actually Commander Swanson, here, who found the gun in the tank," I said. "You had to leave it there because you knew you'd all be getting a good clean-up and medical examination when we got you on board and it would have been bound to be discovered. But a murderer—a professional, Jolly—will never part with his gun unless he is compelled to. I knew if you got the slightest chance you would go back for it. So I put it back in the tank."

"The hell you did!" Swanson was as nearly angry as I'd ever seen him. "Forget to tell me, didn't you?"

"I must have done. That was after I'd cottoned on to you, Jolly. I wasn't *absolutely* sure you had a partner, but I knew if you had it must be Kinnaird. So I put the gun back there in the middle of the night and I made good and certain that you, Jolly, didn't get the chance to go anywhere near the tractor shed at any time. But the gun vanished that following morning when everyone was out sampling the fresh

502

air. So then I knew you had an accomplice. But the real reason for planting that gun, of course, is that without it you'd never have talked. But now you have talked and it's all finished. Put up that gun, Kinnaird."

"I'm afraid your bluff's run out, mate." The gun was pointing directly at my face.

"Your last chance, Kinnaird. Please pay attention to what I am saying. Put up that gun or you will be requiring the services of a doctor within twenty seconds."

He said something, short and unprintable. I said: "It's on your own head. Rawlings, you know what to do."

Every head turned towards Rawlings who was standing leaning negligently against a bulkhead, his hands crossed lightly in front of him. Kinnaird looked too, the Luger following the direction of his eyes. A gun barked, the sharp flat crack of a Mannlicher-Schoenauer, Kinnaird screamed and his gun spun from his smashed hand. Zabrinski, holding my automatic in one hand and his copy of the *Dolphin Daze* —now with a neat charred hole through the middle—in the other, regarded his handiwork admiringly then turned to me. "Was that how you wanted it done, Doc?"

"That was exactly how I wanted it done, Zabrinski. Thank you very much. A first-class job."

"A first-class job," Rawlings sniffed. He retrieved the fallen Luger and pointed it in Jolly's general direction. "At four feet even Zabrinski couldn't miss." He dug into a pocket, pulled out a roll of bandage and tossed it to Jolly. "We kinda thought we might be having to use this so we came prepared. Dr. Carpenter said your pal here would be requiring the services of a doctor. He is. You're a doctor. Get busy."

"Do it yourself," Jolly snarled. No "old boy," no "old top." The *bonhomie* was gone and gone for ever.

Rawlings looked at Swanson and said woodenly: "Permission to hit Dr. Jolly over the head with this little old gun, sir?"

"Permission granted," Swanson said grimly. But no further persuasion was necessary. Jolly cursed and started ripping the cover off the bandage.

For almost a minute there was silence in the room while we watched Jolly carry out a rough, ready and far from gentle

repair job on Kinnaird's hand. Then Swanson said slowly :
" I still don't understand how in the devil Jolly got rid of the
film."

" It was easy. Ten minutes thinking and you'd get it.
They waited until we had cleared the ice-cap then they took
the films, shoved them in a waterproof bag, attached a yellow
dye marker to the bag then pumped it out through the
garbage disposal unit in the galley. Remember, they'd
been on a tour of the ship and seen it—although the suggestion was probably radioed them by a naval expert. I had
Rawlings posted on watch in the early hours of this morning
and he saw Kinnaird go into the galley about half past four.
Maybe he just wanted a ham sandwich, I don't know. But
Rawlings says he had the bag and marker with him when
he sneaked in and empty hands when he came out. The
bag would float to the surface and the marker stain thousands of square yards of water. The naval ship up top
would have worked out our shortest route from Zebra
to Scotland and would be within a few miles of our point of
exit from the ice-pack. It could probably have located it
without the helicopter : but the chopper made it dead
certain.

" Incidentally, I was being rather less than accurate when
I said I didn't know the reason for Jolly's attempts to delay
us. I knew all along. He'd been told that the ship couldn't
reach our exit point until such and such a time and that
it was vital to delay us until then. Jolly, here, even had
the effrontery to check with me what time we would be emerg-
ing from the ice-pack."

Jolly looked up from Kinnaird's hand and his face was
twisted in a mask of malevolence.

" You win, Carpenter. So you win. All along the line.
But you lost out in the only thing that really mattered.
They got the films—the films showing the location, as you
said, of nearly every missile base in America. And that was
all that mattered. Ten million pounds couldn't buy that
information. But we got it." He bared his teeth in a savage
smile. " We may have lost out, Carpenter, but we're professionals. We did our job."

" They got the films, all right," I acknowledged. " And
I'd give a year's salary to see the faces of the men who

504

develop them. Listen carefully, Jolly. Your main reason in trying to cripple Benson and myself was not so much that you could have the say-so on Bolton's health and so delay us : your main reason, your over-riding reason, was that you wanted to be the only doctor on the ship so that it could only be you who would carry out the X-ray on Zabrinski's ankle here and remove the plaster cast. Literally everything hinged on that : basically, nothing else mattered. That was why you took such a desperate chance in crippling me when you heard me say I intended to X-ray Zabrinski's ankle the following morning. That was the one move you made that lacked the hall-mark of class—of a professional —but then I think you were close to panic. You were lucky.

"Anyway, you removed the plaster cast two mornings ago and also the films which you had hidden there in oilskin paper when you'd fixed the plaster on to Zabrinski's leg the first night we arrived in Zebra. A perfect hiding-place. You could always, of course, have wrapped them in bandages covering survivors' burns, but that would be too dicey. The cast was brilliant.

"Unfortunately for you and your friends I had removed the original plaster during the previous night, extracted the films from the oiled paper and replaced them with others. That, incidentally, is the second piece of evidence I have on you. There are two perfect sets of prints on the leaders of the satellite films—yours and Kinnaird's. Along with the salt-covered aluminium foil and the confession freely made in front of witnesses that guarantees you both the eight o'clock walk to the gallows. The gallows and failure, Jolly You weren't even a professional. Your friends will never see those films."

Mouthing soundless words through smashed lips, his face masked in madness and completely oblivious to the two guns, Jolly flung himself at me. He had taken two steps and two only when Rawlings's gun caught him, not lightly, on the side of the head. He crashed to the floor as if the Brooklyn bridge had fallen in on top of him. Rawlings surveyed him dispassionately.

"Never did a day's work that gave me profounder satisfaction," he said conversationally. "Except, perhaps, those

505

pictures I took with Dr. Benson's camera to give Dr. Carpenter, here, some negatives to shove inside that oiled paper."

"Pictures of what?" Swanson asked curiously.

Rawlings grinned happily. "All those pin-ups in Doc Benson's sick-bay. Yogi Bear, Donald Duck, Pluto, Popeye, Snow-white and the seven dwarfs—you name it, I got it. The lot. Each a guaranteed work of art—and in glorious Technicolor." He smiled a beatific smile. "Like Doc Carpenter, here, I'd give a year's pay to see their faces when they get around to developing those negatives."

THE END

Partisans

To Avdo and Inge

ONE

The chill night wind off the Tiber was from the north and carried with it the smell of snow from the distant Apennines. The sky was clear and full of stars and there was light enough to see the swirling of the dust-devils in the darkened streets and the paper, cardboard and assorted detritus that blew about every which way. The darkened, filthy streets were not the result of the electrical and sanitation departments of the Eternal City, as was their peacetime wont, staging one of their interminable strikes, for this was not peacetime: events in the Mediterranean theatre had reached a delicate stage where Rome no longer cared to advertise its whereabouts by switching on the street lights: the sanitation department, for the most part, was some way off to the south fighting a war it didn't particularly care about.

Petersen stopped outside a shop doorway – the nature of its business was impossible to tell for the windows were neatly masked in regulation blackout paper – and glanced up and down the Via Bergola. It appeared to be deserted as were most streets in the city at that time of night. He produced a hooded torch and a large bunch of peculiarly shaped keys and let himself in with a speed, ease and dexterity which spoke well for whoever had trained him in such matters. He took up position behind the opened door, removed the hood from the torch, pocketed the keys, replaced them with a silenced Mauser and waited.

He had to wait for almost two minutes, which, in the

circumstances, can be a very long time, but Petersen didn't seem to mind. Two stealthy footsteps, then there appeared beyond the edge of the door the dimly seen silhouette of a man whose only identifiable features were a peaked cap and a hand clasping a gun in so purposeful a grip that even in the half-light the faint sheen of the knuckles could be seen.

The figure took two further stealthy steps into the shop then halted abruptly as the torch clicked on and the silencer of the Mauser rammed none too gently into the base of his neck.

'Drop that gun. Clasp your hands behind your neck, take three steps forward and don't turn round.'

The intruder did as told. Petersen closed the shop door, located the light switch and clicked it on. They appeared to be in what was, or should have been, a jeweller's shop, for the owner, a màn with little faith in the occupying forces, his fellow-countrymen or both, had prudently and totally cleared all his display cabinets.

'Now you can turn round,' Petersen said.

The man turned. The set expression on the youthful face was tough and truculent, but he couldn't do much about his eyes or the apprehension reflected in them.

'I will shoot you,' Petersen said conversationally, 'if you are carrying another gun and don't tell me.'

'I have no other gun.'

'Give me your papers.' The youngster compressed his lips, said nothing and made no move. Petersen sighed.

'Surely you recognize a silencer? I can just as easily take the papers off your body. Nobody will know a thing. What's more to the point, neither will you.'

The youngster reached inside his tunic and handed over a wallet. Petersen flicked it open.

'Hans Wintermann,' he read. 'Born August 24, 1924. Just nineteen. *And* a lieutenant. You must be a bright young man.' Petersen folded and pocketed the wallet. 'You've been following me around tonight. And most of yesterday. And the evening before that. I find such persistence tedious, especially when it's so obvious. Why do you follow me?'

'You have my name, rank, regiment –'

Petersen waved him to silence. 'Spare me. Well, I'm left with no option.'

'You're going to shoot me?' The truculence had left the youngster's face.

'Don't be stupid.'

The Hotel Splendide was anything but: but its dingy anonymity suited Petersen well enough. Peering through the cracked and stained glass of the front door he noted, with mild surprise, that the concierge, fat, unshaven and well stricken in years, was, for once, not asleep or, at least, wide enough awake to be able to tilt a bottle to his head. Petersen circled to the rear of the hotel, climbed the fire escape, let himself in to the third-floor passage, moved along this, turned into a left-hand corridor and let himself into his room with a skeleton key. He quickly checked cupboards and drawers, seemed satisfied, shrugged into a heavy coat, left and took up position on the fire escape. Despite the added protection of the coat his exposed position was considerably colder than it had been in the comparative shelter of the streets below and he hoped he would not have to wait too long.

The wait was even shorter than he had expected. Less than five minutes had passed when a German officer strode briskly along the corridor, turned left, knocked on a door, knocked again, this time peremptorily, rattled the handle then re-appeared, frowning heavily. There came the creaking and clanking of the ancient elevator, a silence, more creaking and clanking, then the officer again hove into sight this time with the concierge, who had a key in his hand.

When ten minutes had passed with no sign of either man

Petersen went inside, eased his way along the passage and peered round the corner to his left. Halfway along the corridor stood the concierge, obviously on guard. Just as obviously, he was an experienced campaigner prepared for any contingency for, as Petersen watched, he produced a hip flask from his pocket and was still savouring the contents, his eyes closed in bliss, when Petersen clapped him heartily on the shoulder.

'You keep a good watch, my friend.'

The concierge coughed, choked, spluttered and tried to speak but his larynx wasn't having any of it. Petersen looked past him and through the doorway.

'And good evening to you, Colonel Lunz. Everything is in order, I trust?'

'Ah, good evening.' Lunz was almost a look-alike for Petersen himself, medium height, broad shoulders, aquiline features, grey eyes and thin black hair: an older version, admittedly, but nevertheless the resemblance was startling. He didn't seem in any way put out. 'I've just this moment arrived and —'

'Ah, ah, Colonel.' Petersen wagged a finger. 'Officers, whatever their nationality, are officers and gentlemen the world over. Gentlemen don't tell lies. You've been here for exactly eleven minutes. I've timed you.' He turned to the still red-faced and gasping concierge who was making valiant efforts to communicate with them and clapped him encouragingly on the back. 'You were trying to say something?'

'You were out.' The convulsions were easing. 'I mean, you were in, but I saw you go out. Eleven minutes, you said? I didn't see — I mean, your key —'

'You were drunk at the time,' Petersen said kindly. He bent, sniffed and wrinkled his nose. 'You still are. Be off. Send us a bottle of brandy. Not that fearful rot-gut you drink: the French cognac you keep for the Gestapo. And two

514

glasses – *clean* glasses.' He turned to Lunz. 'You will, of course, join me, my dear Colonel?'

'Naturally.' The Colonel was a hard man to knock off balance. He watched Petersen calmly as he took off his coat and threw it on the bed, lifted an eyebrow and said: 'A sudden chill snap outside, yes?'

'Rome? January? No time to take chances with one's health. It's no joke hanging about those fire escapes, I can tell you.'

'So that's where you were. I should have exercised more care, perhaps.'

'No perhaps about your choice of lookout.'

'True.' The Colonel brought out a briar pipe and began to fill it. 'I hadn't much choice.'

'You sadden me, Colonel, you really do. You obtain my key, which is illegal. You post a guard so that you won't be discovered breaking the law yet again. You ransack my belongings –'.

'Ransack?'

'Carefully examine. I don't know what kind of incriminating evidence you were expecting to find.'

'None, really. You don't strike me as the kind of man who would leave –'

'And you had me watched earlier tonight. You must have done, otherwise you wouldn't have known that I had been out earlier without a coat. Saddens? It shocks. Where is this mutual trust that should exist between allies?'

'Allies?' He struck a match. 'I hadn't thought about it very much in that way.' Judging by his expression, he still wasn't thinking very much about it in that way.

'And more evidence of mutual trust.' Petersen handed over the wallet he had taken from the young lieutenant, together with a revolver. 'I'm sure you know him. He was waving his gun around in a very dangerous fashion.'

'Ah!' Lunz looked up from the papers. 'The impetuous

515

young Lieutenant Wintermann. You were right to take this gun from him, he might have done himself an injury. From what I know of you I assume he's not resting at the bottom of the Tiber?'

'I don't treat allies that way. He's locked up in a jeweller's shop.'

'Of course.' Lunz spoke as if he had expected nothing else. 'Locked up. But surely he can —'

'Not the way I tied him up. You not only sadden me, Colonel, you insult me. Why didn't you give him a red flag to wave or a drum to beat? Something that would really attract my attention.'

Lunz sighed. 'Young Hans is well enough in a tank but subtlety is not really his métier. I did not, by the way, insult you. Following you was entirely his own idea. I knew what he was up to, of course, but I didn't try to stop him. For hardly won experience a sore head is little enough to pay.'

'He hasn't even got that. An ally, you see.'

'Pity. It might have reinforced the lesson.' He broke off as a knock came to the door and the concierge entered bearing brandy and glasses. Petersen poured and lifted his glass.

'To Operation Weiss.'

'*Prosit.*' Lunz sipped appreciatively. 'Not all Gestapo officers are barbarians. Operation Weiss? So you know? You're not supposed to.' Lunz didn't seem at all put out.

'I know lots of things that I'm not supposed to.'

'You surprise me.' Lunz's tone was dry. He sipped some more brandy. 'Excellent, excellent. Yes, you do have a penchant for picking up unconsidered — and classified — trifles. Which leads to your repeated use of the world "ally". Which leads, in turn, to what you possibly regard as our undue interest in you.'

'You don't trust me?'

'You'll have to improve on that injured tone of yours. Certainly we trust you. Your record — and it is a formidable

516

one – speaks for itself. What we – and especially myself – find difficult to understand is why such a man with such a record aligns himself with – well, I'm afraid I have to say it – with a quisling. I do not hurt your feelings?'

'You'd have to find them first. I would remind you that it was your Führer who forced our departed Prince Regent to sign this treaty with you and the Japanese two years ago. I assume he's the quisling you're talking about. Weak, certainly, vacillating, perhaps cowardly and no man of action. You can't blame a man for those things: nature's done its worst and there's nothing we can do about nature. But no quisling – he did what he thought was best for Yugoslavia. He wanted to spare it the horrors of war. "*Bolje grob nego rob*". You know what that means?'

Lunz shook his head. 'The intricacies of your language –'

'"Better death than slavery". That's what the Yugoslav crowds shouted when they learned that Prince Paul had acceded to the Tripartite Pact. That's what they shouted when he was deposed and the pact denounced. What the people didn't understand was that there was no "*nego*", no "than". It was to be death *and* slavery as they found out when the Führer, in one of his splendid rages, obliterated Belgrade and crushed the army. I was one of those who were crushed. Well, nearly.'

'If I might have some more of that excellent cognac.' Lunz helped himself. 'You don't seem greatly moved by your recollections.'

'Who can live with all his yesterdays?'

'Nor by the fact that you find yourself in the unfortunate position of having to fight your own countrymen.'

'Instead of joining them and fighting you? War makes for strange bed-fellows, Colonel. Take yourselves and the Japanese, for instance. Hardly entitles you to a holier-than-thou attitude.'

'A point. But at least we're not fighting our own people.'

517

'Not yet. I wouldn't bank on it. God knows, you've done it enough in the past. In any event, moralizing is pointless. I'm a loyalist, a Royalist, and when – and if ever – this damned war is over I want to see the monarchy restored. A man's got to live for something and if that's what I choose to live for, then that's my business and no-one else's.'

'All to hell our own way,' Lunz said agreeably. 'It's just that I have some difficulty in visualizing you as a Serbian Royalist.'

'What does a Serbian Royalist look like? Come to that, what does a Serbian look like?'

Lunz thought then said: 'A confession, Petersen. I haven't the slightest idea.'

'It's my name,' Petersen said kindly. 'And my background. There are Petersens all over. There's a village up in the Italian Alps where every second surname starts with "Mac". The remnants, so I'm told, of some Scottish regiment that got cut off in one of those interminable medieval wars. My great-great-great grandfather or whatever, was a soldier of fortune, which sounds a lot more romantic than the term "mercenary" they use today. Like a thousand others he arrived here and forgot to go home again.'

'Where was home? I mean, Scandinavian, Anglo-Saxon, what?'

'Genealogy bores me and, not only don't I care, I don't know either. Ask any Yugoslav what his ancestors five times removed were and he almost certainly wouldn't know.'

Lunz nodded. 'You Slavic people *do* have rather a chequered history. And then, of course, just to complicate matters, you graduated from Sandhurst.'

'Dozens of foreign countries have had their officers graduate from there. In my case, what more natural? My father was, after all, the military attaché in London. If he'd been the naval attaché in Berlin I'd probably have ended up in Kiel or Mürwik.'

518

'Nothing wrong with Sandhurst. I've been there, as a visitor only. But a bit on the conservative side as far as the courses offered are concerned.'

'You mean?'

'Nothing on guerrilla warfare. Nothing on espionage and counter-espionage. Nothing on code and cypher breaking. I understand you're a specialist on all three.'

'I'm self-educated in some things.'

'I'm sure you are.' Lunz was silent for some seconds, savouring his brandy, then said: 'Whatever became of your father?'

'I don't know. You may even know more than I do. Just disappeared. Thousands have done so since the spring of '41. Disappeared, I mean.'

'He was like you? A Royalist? A Četnik?' Petersen nodded. 'And very senior. Senior officers don't just disappear. He fell foul of the Partisans, perhaps?'

'Perhaps. Anything is possible. Again, I don't know.' Petersen smiled. 'If you're trying to suggest I'm carrying on a vendetta because of a blood feud, you'd better try again. Wrong country, wrong century. Anyway, you didn't come here to pry into my motives or my past.'

'And now *you* insult *me*. I wouldn't waste my time. You'd tell me just as much as you wanted me to know and no more.'

'And you didn't come here to carry out a search of my belongings – that was just a combination of opportunity and professional curiosity. You came here to give me something. An envelope with instructions for our commander. Another assault on what it pleases you to call Titoland.'

'You're pretty sure of yourself.'

'I'm not pretty sure. I'm certain. The Partisans have radio transceivers. British. They have skilled radio operators, both their own and British. And they have skilled code-crackers. You don't dare send secret and important messages any more by radio. So you need a reliable message boy. There's no other reason why I'm in Rome.'

'Frankly, I can't think of any other, which saves any explanation on my part.' Lunz produced and handed over an envelope.

'This is in code?'

'Naturally.'

'Why "naturally"? In *our* code?'

'So I believe.'

'Stupid. Who do you think devised that code?'

'I don't think. I know. You did.'

'It's still stupid. Why don't you give me the message verbally? I've a good memory for this sort of thing. And there's more. I may be intercepted, and then two things may happen. Either I succeed in destroying it, in which case the message is useless. Or the Partisans take it intact and decipher it in nothing flat.' Petersen tapped his head. 'A clear case for a psychiatrist.'

Lunz took some more brandy and cleared his throat. 'You know, of course, of Colonel General Alexander von Löhr?'

'The German Commander in Chief for south-eastern Europe. Of course. Never met him personally.'

֗ 'Perhaps it is as well that you never do. I don't think General von Löhr would react too favourably to the suggestion that he is in need of psychiatric treatment. Nor does he take too kindly to subordinate officers – and, despite your nationality, you can take it that he very definitely regards you as subordinate – who question far less disobey his orders. And those are his orders.'

'Two psychiatrists. One for von Löhr, one for the person who appointed him to his command. That would be the Führer, of course.'

Colonel Lunz said mildly: 'I do try to observe the essential civilities. It's not normally too difficult. But bear in mind that I am a German Regimental Commander.'

520

'I don't forget it and no offence was intended. Protests are useless. I have my orders. I assume that this time I will not be going in by plane?'

'You are remarkably well informed.'

'Not really. Some of your colleagues are remarkably garrulous in places where not only have they no right to be garrulous but have no right to be in the first place. In this case I am not well informed, but I can think, unlike – well, never mind. You'd have to notify my friends if you were sending in a plane and that message could be just as easily intercepted and deciphered as any other. You don't know how crazy those Partisans could be. They wouldn't hesitate to send a suicide commando behind our lines and shoot down the plane when it's still at an altitude of fifty or a hundred metres, which is an excellent way of ensuring that no-one gets out of that plane alive.' Petersen tapped the envelope. 'That way the message never gets delivered. So I go by boat. When?'

'Tomorrow night.'

'Where?'

'A little fishing village near Termoli.'

'What kind of boat?'

'You do ask a lot of questions.'

'It's my neck.' Petersen shrugged his indifference. 'If your travel arrangements don't suit me, I'll make my own.'

'It wouldn't be the first time you'd borrowed shall we say, a boat from your – ah – allies?'

'Only in the best interests of all.'

'Of course. An Italian torpedo boat.'

'You can hear one of those things twenty kilometres away.'

'So? You'll be landing near Ploče. That's in Italian hands, as you know. And even if you could be heard fifty kilometres away, what's the difference? The Partisans have no radar, no planes, no navy, nothing that could stop you.'

'So the Adriatic is your pond. The torpedo boat it is.'

521

'Thank you. I forgot to mention that you'll be having some company on the trip across.'

'You didn't forget. You just saved it for last.' Petersen refilled their glasses and looked consideringly at Lunz. 'I'm not sure that I care for this. You know I like to travel alone.'

'I know you *never* travel alone.'

'Ah! George and Alex. You know them, then?'

'They're hardly invisible. They attract attention – they have that look about them.'

'What look?'

'Hired killers.'

'You're half right. They're different. My insurance policy – they watch my back. I'm not complaining, but people are always spying on me.'

'An occupational hazard.' Lunz's airily dismissive gesture showed what he thought of occupational hazards. 'I would be grateful if you would allow those two people I have in mind to accompany you. More, I would regard it as a personal favour if you would escort them to their destination.'

'What destination?'

'Same as yours.'

'Who are they?'

'Two radio operator recruits for your Ćetniks. Carrying with them, I may say, the very latest in transceiver equipment.'

'That's not enough, and you know it. Names, background.'

'Sarina and Michael. Trained – highly trained, I might say – by the British in Alexandria. With the sole intent of doing what they are about to do – joining your friends. Let us say that we intercepted them en route.'

'What else? Male and female, no?'

'Yes.'

'No.'

522

'No what?'

'I'm a fairly busy person. I don't like being encumbered and I've no intention of acting as a shipborne chaperon.'

'Brother and sister.'

'Ah.' Petersen said. 'Fellow citizens?'

'Of course.'

'Then why can't they find their own way home?'

'Because they haven't been home for three years. Educated in Cairo.' Again the wave of a hand. 'Troubled times in your country, my friend. Germans here, Italians there, Ustaša, Četniks, Partisans everywhere. All very confusing. You know your way around your country in these difficult times. Better than any, I'm told.'

'I don't get lost much.' Petersen stood. 'I'd have to see them first, of course.'

'I would have expected nothing else.' Lunz drained his glass, rose and glanced at his watch. 'I'll be back in forty minutes.'

George answered Petersen's knock. Despite Lunz's unflattering description George didn't look a bit like a killer, hired or otherwise: genial buffoons, or those who look like them, never do. With a pudgy, jovial face crowned by a tangled thatch of grey-black hair, George, on the wrong side of fifty, was immense – immensely fat, that was: the studded belt strung tightly around what used to be his waist served only to emphasize rather than conceal his gargantuan paunch. He closed the door behind Petersen and crossed to the left-hand wall: like many very heavy men, as is so often seen in the case of overweight dancers, he was quick and light on his feet. He removed from the plaster a rubber suction cap with a central spike which was attached by a wire to a transformer and thence to a single earphone.

'Your friend seems to be a very pleasant man.' George sounded genuinely regretful. 'Pity we have to be on opposite

523

sides.' He looked at the envelope Petersen had brought. 'Aha! Operational orders, no?'

'Yes. Hotfoot, you might say, from the presence of Colonel General von Löhr himself.' Petersen turned to the recumbent figure on one of the two narrow beds. 'Alex?'

Alex rose. Unlike George, he had no welcoming smile but that meant nothing, for Alex never smiled. He was of a height with George but there any resemblance ended. His weight was about half George's as were his years: he was thin-faced, swarthy and had black watchful eyes which rarely blinked. Wordlessly, for his taciturnity was almost on a par with the stillness of his face, he took the envelope, dug into a knapsack, brought out a small butane burner and an almost equally small kettle, and began to make steam. Two or three minutes later Petersen extracted two sheets of paper from the opened envelope and studied the contents carefully. When he had finished he looked up and regarded the two men thoughtfully.

'This *will* be of great interest to a great number of people. It may be the depths of winter but things look like becoming very hot in the Bosnian hills in the very near future.'

George said: 'Code?'

'Yes. Simple. I made sure of that when I made it up. If the Germans never meant business before, they certainly mean it now. Seven divisions, no less. Four German, under General Lütters, whom we know, and three Italian under General Gloria, whom we also know. Supported by the Ustaša and, of course, the Četniks. Somewhere between ninety thousand and a hundred thousand troops.'

George shook his head. 'So many?'

'According to this. It's common knowledge of course that the Partisans are stationed in and around Bihać. The Germans are to attack from the north and east, the Italians from south and west. The battle plan, God knows, is simple enough. The Partisans are to be totally encircled and then

524

wiped out to a man. Simple, but comprehensive. And just to make certain, both the Italians and Germans are bringing in squadrons of bomber and fighter planes.'

'And the Partisans haven't got a single plane.'

'Even worse for them they don't have anti-aircraft guns. Well, a handful, but they should be in a museum.' Petersen replaced the sheets and re-sealed the envelope. 'I have to go out in fifteen minutes. Colonel Lunz is coming to take me to meet a couple of people I don't particularly want to meet, two radio operator Četnik recruits who have to have their hands held until we get to Montenegro or wherever.'

'Or so Colonel Lunz says.' Suspicion was one of the few expressions that Alex ever permitted himself.

'Or so he says. Which is why I want you two to go out as well. Not with me, of course – behind me.'

'A little night air will do us good. These hotel rooms get very stuffy.' George was hardly exaggerating, his penchant for beer was equalled only by his marked weakness for evil-smelling, black cigars. 'Car or foot?'

'I don't know yet. You have your car.'

'Either way, tailing in a blackout is difficult. Chances are, we'd be spotted.'

'So? You've been spotted a long time ago. Even if Lunz or one of his men does pick you up it's most unlikely that he'll have you followed. What he can do, you can do.'

'Pick up *our* tail, you mean. What do you want us to do?'

'You'll see where I'm taken. When I leave find out what you can about those two radio operators.'

'A few details might help. It would be nice to know who we're looking for.'

'Probably mid-twenties, brother and sister, Sarina and Michael. That's all I know. No breaking down of doors, George. Discretion, that's what's called for. Tact. Diplomacy.'

'Our specialities. We use our Carabinieri cards?'

'Naturally.'

When Colonel Lunz had said that the two young radio operator recruits were brother and sister, that much, Petersen reflected, had been true. Despite fairly marked differences in bulk and colouring, they were unmistakably twins. He was very tanned, no doubt from all his years in Cairo, with black hair and hazel eyes: she had the flawless peach-coloured complexion of one who had no difficulties in ignoring the Egyptian sunshine, close-cropped auburn hair and the same hazel eyes as her brother. He was stocky and broad: she was neither, but just how slender or well proportioned she might have been it was impossible to guess as, like her brother, she was clad in shapeless khaki-coloured fatigues. Side by side on a couch, where they had seated themselves after the introductions, they were trying to look relaxed and casual, but their overly expressionless faces served only to accentuate their wary apprehensiveness.

Petersen leaned back in his arm-chair and looked appreciatively around the large living-room. 'My word. This is nice. Comfort? No. Luxury. You two young people do yourselves well, don't you?'

'Colonel Lunz arranged it for us,' Michael said.

'Inevitably. Favouritism. My spartan quarters –'

'Are of your own choosing,' Lunz said mildly. 'It is difficult to arrange accommodation for a person who is in town for three days before he lets anyone know that he's here.'

'You have a point. Not, mind you, that this place is perfect in all respects. Take, for instance, the matter of cocktail cabinets.'

'Neither my brother nor I drink.' Sarina's voice was low-pitched and quiet. Petersen noticed that the slender interlaced hands were ivory-knuckled.

526

'Admirable.' Petersen picked up a briefcase he had brought with him, extracted a brandy bottle and two glasses and poured for Lunz and himself. 'Your health. I hear you wish to join the good Colonel in Montenegro. You must, then, be Royalists. You can prove that?'

Michael said: 'Do we have to prove it? I mean, don't you trust us, believe us?'

'You'll have to learn and learn quickly – and by that I mean now – to adopt a different tone and attitude.' Petersen was no longer genial and smiling. 'Apart from a handful of people – and I mean a handful – I haven't trusted in or believed anyone for many years. Can you prove you're a Royalist?'

'We can when we get there.' Sarina looked at Petersen's unchanged expression and gave a helpless little shrug. 'And I know King Peter. At least, I did.'

'As King Peter is in London and London at the moment isn't taking any calls from the Wehrmacht, that would be rather difficult to prove from here. And don't tell me you can prove it when we get to Montenegro for that would be too late.'

Michael and Sarina looked at each other, momentarily at a loss for words, then Sarina said hesitatingly: 'We don't understand. When you say it would be too late –'

'Too late for me if my back is full of holes. Bullet wounds, stab wounds, that sort of thing.'

She stared at him, colour staining her cheeks, then said in a whisper: 'You must be mad. Why on earth should we –'

'I don't know and I'm not mad. It's just by liking to live a little longer that I manage to live a little longer.' Petersen looked at them for several silent moments, then sighed. 'So you want to come to Yugoslavia with me?'

'Not really.' Her hands were still clenched and now the brown eyes were hostile. 'Not after what you've just said.' She looked at her brother, then at Lunz, then back at Petersen. 'Do we have any options?'

'Certainly. Any amount. Ask Colonel Lunz.'

527

'Colonel?'

'Not any amount. Very few and I wouldn't recommend any of them. The whole point of the exercise is that you both get there intact and if you go by any other means the chances of your doing just that are remote: if you try it on your own the chances don't exist. With Major Petersen you have safe conduct and guaranteed delivery – alive, that is.'

Michael said, doubt in his voice: 'You have a great deal of confidence in Major Petersen.'

'I do. So does Major Petersen. He has every right to, I may add. It's not just that he knows the country in a way neither of you ever will. He moves as he pleases through any territory whether it's held by friend or enemy. But what's really important is that the fields of operations out there are in a state of constant flux. An area held by the Četniks today can be held by the Partisans tomorrow. You'd be like lambs in the fold when the wolves come down from the hills.'

For the first time the girl smiled slightly. 'And the Major is another wolf?'

'More like a sabre-toothed tiger. And he's got two others who keep him constant company. Not, mind you, that I've ever heard of sabre-toothed tigers meeting up with wolves but you take my point, I hope.'

They didn't say whether they took his point or not. Petersen looked at them both in turn and said: 'Those fatigues you're wearing – they're British?'

They both nodded.

'You have spares?'

Again they nodded in unison.

'Winter clothing? Heavy boots?'

'Well, no.' Michael looked his embarrassment. 'We didn't think we would need them.'

'You didn't think you would need them.' Petersen briefly contemplated the ceiling then returned his gaze to the uncomfortable pair on the couch. 'You're going up the mountains, maybe two thousand metres, in the depths of winter, not to a garden party in high summer.'

Lunz said hastily: 'I shouldn't have much trouble in arranging for these things by morning.'

'Thank you, Colonel.' Petersen pointed to two fairly large, canvas-wrapped packages on the floor. 'Your radios, I take it. British?'

'Yes,' Michael said. 'Latest models. Very tough.'

'Spares?'

'Lots. All we'll ever need, the experts say.'

'The experts have clearly never fallen down a ravine with a radio strapped to their backs. You're British-trained, of course.'

'No. American.'

'In Cairo?'

'Cairo is full of them. This was a staff sergeant in the US Marines. An expert in some new codes. He taught quite a few Britishers at the same time.'

'Seems fair enough. Well, a little cooperation and we should get along just fine.'

'Cooperation?' Michael seemed puzzled.

'Yes. If I have to give some instructions now and again I expect them to be followed.'

'Instructions?' Michael looked at his sister. 'Nobody said anything –'

'I'm saying something now. I must express myself more clearly. Orders will be implicitly obeyed. If not, I'll leave you behind in Italy, jettison you in the Adriatic or just simply abandon you in Yugoslavia. I will not jeopardize my mission for a couple of disobedient children who won't do as they're told.'

'Children!' Michael actually clenched his fists. 'You have no right to –'

'He has every right to.' Lunz's interruption was sharp. 'Major Petersen was talking about garden parties. He should have been talking about kindergartens. You're young, ignorant and arrogant and are correspondingly dangerous on all three counts. Whether you've been sworn in or not, you're now members of the Royal Yugoslav Army. Other rankers, such as you, take orders from officers.'

They made no reply, not even when Petersen again regarded the ceiling and said: 'And we all know the penalty for the wartime disobedience of orders.'

In Lunz's staff car Petersen sighed and said: 'I'm afraid I didn't quite achieve the degree of rapport back there that I might have. They were in a rather unhappy frame of mind when we left.'

'They'll get over it. Young, as I said. Spoilt, into the bargain. Aristocrats, I'm told, even some royal blood. Von Karajan or something like that. Odd name for a Yugoslav.'

'Not really. Almost certainly from Slovenia and the descendants of Austrians.'

'Be that as it may, they come from a family that's clearly not accustomed to taking orders and even less accustomed to being talked to the way you did.'

'I daresay they'll learn very quickly.'

'I daresay they will.'

Half an hour after returning to his room, Petersen was joined by George and Alex. George said, 'Well, at least we know their name.'

'So do I. Von Karajan. What else?'

George was in no way put out. 'The reception clerk, very old but sharp, told us he'd no idea where they'd arrived from – they'd been brought there by Colonel Lunz. He gave us their room number – no hesitation – but said that if we wanted to see them he'd have to announce us, ask permission and then escort us. Then we asked him if either of the rooms next to the number he had given us was vacant and when he told us those were their bedrooms we left.'

'You took your time about getting back.'

'We are accustomed to your injustices. We went round to the back of the hotel, climbed a fire escape and made our way along a narrow ledge. A very narrow ledge. No joke, I can tell you, especially for an old man like me. Perilous, dizzying heights –'

'Yes, yes.' Petersen was patient. The von Karajans had been staying on the first floor. 'Then?'

'There was a small balcony outside their room. Net curtains on their French windows.'

'You could see clearly?'

'And hear clearly. Young man was sending a radio message.'

'Interesting. Hardly surprising, though. Morse?'

'Plain language.'

'What was he saying?'

'I have no idea. Could have been Chinese for all I knew. Certainly no European language I've ever heard. A very short message. So we came back.'

'Anyone see you on the fire escape, ledge or balcony?'

George tried to look wounded. 'My dear Peter –'

Petersen stopped him with an upraised hand. Not many people called him "Peter" – which was his first name – but, then, not many people had been pre-war students of George's in Belgrade University where George had been the vastly respected Professor of Occidental Languages. George was known – not reputed, but known – to be fluent in at least a dozen languages and to have a working knowledge of a considerable number more.

'Forgive me, forgive me.' Petersen surveyed George's vast bulk. 'You're practically invisible anyway. So tomorrow morning, or perhaps even within minutes, Colonel Lunz will know that you and Alex have been around asking questions – he would have expected nothing less of me – but he won't

531

know that young Michael von Karajan has been seen and heard to be sending radio messages soon after our departure. I do wonder about the nature of that message.'

George pondered briefly then said: 'Alex and I could find out on the boat tomorrow night.'

Petersen shook his head. 'I promised Colonel Lunz that we would deliver them intact.'

'What's Colonel Lunz to us or your promise to him?'

'*We* want them delivered intact too.'

George tapped his head. 'The burden of too many years.'

'Not at all, George. Professorial absent-mindedness.'

TWO

The Wehrmacht did not believe in limousines or luxury coaches for the transportation of its allies: Petersen and his companions crossed Italy that following day in the back of a vintage truck that gave the impression of being well enough equipped with tyres of solid rubber but sadly deficient in any form of springing. The vibration was of the teeth-jarring order and the rattling so loud and continuous as to make conversation virtually impossible. The hooped canvas covering was open at the back, and at the highest point in the Apennines the temperature dropped below freezing point. It was, in some ways, a memorable journey but not for its creature comforts.

The stench of the diesel fumes would normally have been overpowering enough but on that particular day faded into relative insignificance compared to the aroma, if that was the word, given off by George's black cigars. Out of deference to his fellow-travellers' sensibilities he had seated himself at the very rear of the truck and on the rare occasion when he wasn't smoking, kept himself busy and contented enough with the contents of a crate of beer that lay at his feet. He seemed immune to the cold and probably was: nature had provided him with an awesome insulation.

The von Karajans, clad in their newly acquired winter clothing, sat at the front of the left-hand unpadded wooden bench. Withdrawn and silent they appeared no happier than when Petersen had left them the previous night: this could

533

have been an understandable reaction to their current sufferings but more probably, Petersen thought, their injured feelings had not yet had time to mend. Matters were not helped by the presence of Alex, whose totally withdrawn silence and dark, bitter and brooding countenance could be all too easily misinterpreted as balefulness: the von Karajans were not to know that Alex regarded his parents, whom he held in vast respect and affection, with exactly the same expression.

They stopped for a midday meal in a tiny village in the neighbourhood of Corfinio after having safely, if at times more or less miraculously, negotiated the hazardous hair-pin switch-backs of the Apennine spine. They had left Rome at seven o'clock that morning and it had taken over five hours to cover a hundred miles. Considering the incredibly dilapidated state of both the highway and the ancient Wehrmacht truck – unmarked as such and of Italian make – an average of almost twenty miles an hour was positively creditable. Not without difficulty for, with the exception of George, the passengers' limbs were stiff and almost frozen, they climbed down over the tail-board and looked around them through the thinly falling snow.

There was miserably little to see. The hamlet – if it could even be called that, it didn't as much as have a name – consisted of a handful of stone cottages, a post office store and a very small inn. Nearby Corfinio, if hardly ranking as a metropolis, could have afforded considerably more in the way of comfort and amenities: but Colonel Lunz, apart from a professional near-mania for secrecy, shared with his senior Wehrmacht fellow-officers the common if unfair belief that all his Italian allies were renegades, traitors and spies until proved otherwise.

In the inn itself, the genial host was far from being that. He seemed diffident, almost nervous, a markedly unusual trait in mountain innkeepers. A noticeably clumsy waiter, civil and helpful in his own way, volunteered only the fact that he was called Luigi but thereafter was totally uncommunicative. The inn itself was well enough, both warmed and illuminated by a pine log fire in an open hearth that gave off almost as much in the way of sparks as it did heat. The food was simple but plentiful, and wine and beer, into which George made his customary inroads, appeared regularly on the table without having to be asked for. Socially, however, the meal was a disaster.

Silence makes an uncomfortable table companion. At a distant and small corner table, the truckdriver and his companion – really an armed guard who travelled with a Schmeisser under his seat and a Luger concealed about his person – talked almost continuously in low voices; but of the five at Petersen's table, three seemed afflicted with an almost permanent palsy of the tongue. Alex, remote and withdrawn, seemed, as·was his wont, to be contemplating a bleak and hopeless future: the von Karajans who, by their own admission, had had no breakfast, barely picked at their food, had time and opportunity to talk, but rarely ventured a word except when directly addressed: Petersen, relaxed as ever, restricted himself to pleasantries and civilities but otherwise showed no signs of wishing to alleviate the conversational awkwardness or, indeed, to be aware of it: George, on the other hand, seemed to be acutely aware of it and did his talkative best to dispel it, even to the point of garrulity.

His conversational gambit took the form of questions directed exclusively at the von Karajans. It did not take him long to elicit the fact that they were, as Petersen had guessed, Slovenians of Austrian ancestry. They had been to primary school in Ljubljana, secondary school in Zagreb and thence to Cairo University.

'Cairo!' George tried to make his eyebrows disappear into his hairline. 'Cairo! What on earth induced you to go to that cultural backwater?'

535

'It was our parents' wish,' Michael said. He tried to be cold and distant but he only succeeded in sounding defensive.

'Cairo!' George repeated. He shook his head in slow disbelief. 'And what, may one ask, did you study there?'

'You ask a lot of questions,' Michael said.

'Interest,' George explained. 'A paternal interest. And, of course, a concern for the hapless youth of our unfortunate and disunited country.'

For the first time Sarina smiled, a very faint smile, it was true, but enough to give some indication of what she could do if she tried. 'I don't think such things would really interest you, Mr – ah –'

'Just call me George. How do you know what would interest me? All things interest me.'

'Economics and politics.'

'Good God!' George clapped a hand to his forehead. As a classical actor he would have starved: as a ham actor he was a nonpareil. 'Good heavens, girl, you go to Egypt to learn matters of such importance? Didn't they even teach you enough to make you realize that theirs is the poorest country in the Middle East, that their economy is not only a shambles but is in a state of total collapse and that they owe countless millions, sterling, dollars, any currency you care to name, to practically any country you care to name. So much for their economy. As for politics, they're no more than a political football for any country that wants to play soccer on their arid and useless desert sands.'

George stopped briefly, perhaps to admire the eloquence of his own oratory, perhaps to await a response. None was forthcoming so he got back to his head-shaking.

'And what, one wonders, did your parents have against our premier institute of learning. I refer, of course, to the University of Belgrade.' He paused, as if in reflection. 'One admits that Oxford and Cambridge have their points. So, for that matter, does Heidelberg, the Sorbonne, Padua and one or two lesser educational centres. But, no, Belgrade iş best.'

Again the faint smile from Sarina. 'You seem to know a great deal about universities, Mr – ah – George.'

George didn't smirk. Instead, he achieved the near impossible – he spoke with a lofty diffidence. 'I have been fortunate enough, for most of my adult life, to be associated with academics, among them some of the most eminent.' The von Karajans looked at each other for a long moment but said nothing: it was unnecessary for them to say that, in their opinion, any such association must have been on a strictly janitorial level. They probably assumed that he had learned his mode of speech when cleaning out common rooms or, it may have been, while waiting on high table. George gave no indication that he had noticed anything untoward, but, then, he never did.

'Well,' George said in his best judicial tones, 'far be it from me to visit the sins of the fathers upon their sons or, come to that, those of mothers upon their daughters.' Abruptly, he switched the subject. 'You are Royalists, of course.'

'Why "of course"?' Michael's voice was sharp.

George sighed. 'I would have hoped that that institute of lower learning on the Nile hadn't driven all the native sense out of your head. If you weren't a Royalist you wouldn't be coming with us. Besides, Major Petersen told me.'

Sarina looked briefly at Petersen. 'This is the way you treat confidences?'

'I wasn't aware it was a confidence.' Petersen gestured with an indifferent hand. 'It was too unimportant to rate as a confidence. In any event, George is my confidant.'

Sarina looked at him uncertainly, then lowered her eyes: the rebuke could have been real, implied or just imagined. George said: 'I'm just puzzled, you see. You're Royalists. Your parents, one must assume, are the same. It's not unusual for the royal family and those close to them to send their children abroad to be educated. But not to Cairo. To

537

Northern Europe. Specifically, to England. The ties between the Yugoslav and British royal families are very close – especially the blood ties. What place did King Peter choose for his enforced exile? London, where he is now. The Prince Regent, Prince Paul, is in the care of the British.'

'They say in Cairo that he's a prisoner of the British.' Michael didn't seem particularly concerned about what they said in Cairo.

'Rubbish. He's in protective custody in Kenya. He's free to come and go. He makes regular withdrawals from a bank in London. Coutts, it's called – it also happens to be the bank of the British royal family. Prince Paul's closest friend in Europe – and his brother-in-law – is the Duke of Kent: well, he was until the Duke was killed in a flying-boat accident last year. And it's common knowledge that very soon he's going to South Africa, whose General Smuts is a particularly close friend of the British.'

'Ah, yes,' Michael said. 'You said you're puzzled. I'm puzzled too. This General Smuts has two South African divisions in North Africa fighting alongside the Eighth Army, no?'

'Yes.'

'Against the Germans?'

George showed an unusual trace of irritation. 'Who else would they be fighting?'

'So our royal family's friends in North Africa are fighting the Germans. We're Royalists, and we're fighting with the Germans, not against them. I mean it's all rather confusing.'

'I'm sure *you're* not confused.' Again Sarina's little smile. Petersen was beginning to wonder whether he would have to revise his first impression of her. 'Are you, George?'

'No confusion.' George waved a dismissive hand. 'Simply a temporary measure of convenience and expediency. We are fighting *with* the Germans, true, but we are not fighting *for* them. We are fighting for ourselves. When the Germans have served their purpose it will be time for them to be gone.' George refilled his beer mug, drained half the contents and sighed either in satisfaction or sorrow. 'We are consistently underestimated, a major part, as the rest of Europe sees it, of the insoluble Balkan problem. To me, there is no problem just a goal.' He raised his glass again. 'Yugoslavia.'

'Nobody's going to argue with that,' Petersen said. He looked at the girl. 'Speaking – as George has been doing at some length – of royalty, you mentioned last night you knew King Peter. How well?'

'He was Prince Peter then. Not well at all. Once or twice on formal occasions.'

'That's about how it was for me. I don't suppose we've exchanged more than a couple of dozen words. Bright lad, pleasant, should make a good king. Pity about his limp.'

'His what?'

'You know, his left foot.'

'Oh, that. Yes. I've wondered –'

'He doesn't talk about it. All sorts of sinister stories about how he was injured. All ridiculous. A simple hunting accident.' Petersen smiled. 'I shouldn't imagine there's much of a diplomatic future for a courtier who mistakes his future sovereign for a wild boar.' He lifted his eyes and right arm at the same time: the innkeeper came hurrying towards him. 'The bill, if you please.'

'The bill?' Momentarily the innkeeper gave the impression of being surprised, even taken aback. 'Ah, the bill. Of course. The bill. At once.' He hurried off.

Petersen looked at the von Karajans. 'Sorry you didn't have a better appetite – you know, stoked the furnaces for the last part of the trip. Still, it's downhill now all the way and we're heading for the Adriatic and a maritime climate. Should be getting steadily warmer.'

'Oh, no, it won't.' It was the first time Alex had spoken since they had entered the inn and, predictably, it was in tones of dark certainty. 'It's almost an hour since we came in here and the wind has got stronger. Much stronger. Listen and you can hear it.' They listened. They heard it, a deep, low-pitched, ululating moaning that boded no good at all. Alex shook his head gravely. 'An east-north-easter. All the way from Siberia. It's going to be very cold.' His voice sounded full of gloomy satisfaction but it meant nothing, it was the only way he knew how to talk. 'And when the sun goes down, it's going to be very *very* cold.'

'Job's comforter,' Petersen said. He looked at the bill the innkeeper had brought, handed over some notes, waved away the proffered change and said: 'Do you think we could buy some blankets from you?'

'Blankets?' The innkeeper frowned in some puzzlement: it was, after all, an unusual request.

'Blankets. We've a long way to go, there's no heating in our transport and the afternoon and evening are going to be very cold.'

'There will be no problem.' The innkeeper disappeared and was back literally within a minute with an armful of heavy coloured woollen blankets which he deposited on a nearby empty table. 'Those will be sufficient?'

'More than sufficient. Most kind of you.' Petersen produced money. 'How much, please?'

'Blankets?' The innkeeper lifted his hands in protest. 'I am not a shopkeeper. I do not charge for blankets.'

'But you must. I insist. Blankets cost money.'

'Please.' The truckdriver had left his table and approached them. 'I shall be passing back this way tomorrow. I shall bring them with me.'

Petersen thanked them and so it was arranged. Alex, followed by the von Karajans, helped the innkeeper carry the blankets out to the truck. Petersen and George lingered briefly in the porch, closing both the inner and outer doors.

'You really are the most fearful liar, George,' Petersen said

540

admiringly. 'Cunning. Devious. I've said it before, I don't think I'd care to be interrogated by you. You ask a question and whether people say yes, no or nothing at all you still get your answer.'

'When you've spent twenty-five of the best years of your life dealing with dim-witted students –' George shrugged as if there were no more to say.

'I'm not a dim-witted student but I still wouldn't care for it. You have formed an opinion about our young friends?'

'I have.'

'So have I. I've also formed another opinion about them and that is that while Michael is no intellectual giant, the girl could bear watching. I think she could be clever.'

'I've often observed this with brother and sister, especially when they're twins. I share your opinion. Lovely and clever.'

Petersen smiled. 'A dangerous combination?'

'Not if she's nice. I've no reason to think she's not nice.'

'You're just middle-aged and susceptible. The innkeeper?'

'Apprehensive and unhappy. He doesn't look like a man who should be apprehensive and unhappy, he looks a big tough character who would be perfectly at home throwing big tough drunks out of his inn. Also, he seemed caught off-balance when you offered to pay for the meal. One got the unmistakable impression that there are some travellers who do not pay for their meals. Also his refusal to accept money for the blankets was out of character. Out of character for an Italian, I mean, for I've never known of an Italian who wasn't ready, eager rather, to make a deal on some basis or other. Peter, my friend, wouldn't even you be slightly nervous if you worked for, or were forced to work for the German SS?'

'Colonel Lunz casts a long shadow. The waiter?'

'The Gestapo have fallen in my estimation. When they send in an espionage agent in the guise of a waiter they should at least give him some training in the rudiments of table-waiting. I felt positively embarrassed for him.' George paused, then went on: 'You were talking about King Peter a few minutes ago.'

'You introduced that subject.'

'That's irrelevant and don't hedge. As a departmental head in the university I was regarded – and rightly – as being a man of culture. Prince Paul was nothing if not a man of culture although his interests lay more in the world of art than in philology. Never mind. We met quite a few times, either in the university or at royal functions in the city. More to the point, I saw Prince Peter – as he was then – two or three times. He didn't have a limp in those days.'

'He still doesn't.'

George looked at him then nodded slowly. 'And you called me devious.'

Petersen opened the outer door and clapped him on the shoulder. 'We live in devious times, George.'

The second half of the trip was an improvement on the first but just marginally. Cocooned, as they were, to the ears in heavy blankets, the von Karajans were no longer subject to involuntary bouts of shivering and teeth-chattering but otherwise looked no happier and were no more communicative than they had been in the morning, which meant that they were both totally miserable and silent. They didn't even speak when George, shouting to make himself heard above the fearful mechanical din, offered them brandy to relieve their sufferings. Sarina shuddered and Michael shook his head. They may have been wise for what George was offering them was no French cognac but his own near-lethal form of slivovitz, his native plum brandy.

Some twelve kilometres from Pescara they bore right off

the Route 5 near Chieti, reaching the Adriatic coast road at Francavilla as a premature dusk was falling – premature, because of gathering banks of dark grey cloud which Alex, inevitably, said could only presage heavy snow. The coastal road, Route 16 was an improvement over the Apennines road – it could hardly have failed to be otherwise – and the relatively comfortable though still cacophonous ride to Termoli took no more than two hours. Wartime Termoli, on a winter's night, was no place to inspire a rhapsody in the heart of the poet or composer: the only feelings it could reasonably expect to give rise to were gloom and depression. It was grey, bleak, bare, grimy and seemingly uninhabited except for a very few half-heartedly blacked-out premises which were presumably cafés or taverns. The port area itself, however, was an improvement on Rome: here was no blackout, just a dimout which probably didn't vary appreciably from the normal. As the truck stopped along a wharf-side there was more than enough light from the shaded yellow overhead lamps to distinguish the lines of the craft alongside the wharf, their transport to Yugoslavia.

That it was a motor torpedo boat was beyond question. Its vintage was uncertain. What was certain was that it had been in the wars. It had sustained considerable, though not incapacitating, damage to both hull and superstructure. No attempt had been made at repair: no-one had even thought it worthwhile to repaint the numerous dents and scars that pockmarked its side. It carried no torpedoes, for the sufficient reason that the torpedo tubes had been removed; nor had it depth-charges, for even the depth-charge racks had been removed. The only armament, if such it could be called, that it carried was a pair of insignificant little guns, single-barrelled, one mounted for'ard of the bridge, the other on the poop. They looked suspiciously like Hotchkiss repeaters, one of the most notoriously inaccurate weapons ever to find its mistaken way into naval service.

A tall man in a vaguely naval uniform was standing on the wharf-side at the head of the MTB's gangway. He wore a peaked badgeless naval cap which shaded his face but could not conceal his marked stoop and splendid snow-white Buffalo Bill beard. He raised his hand in half-greeting, half-salute as Petersen, the others following close behind, approached him.

'Good evening. My name is Pietro. You must be the Major we are expecting.'

'Good evening and yes.'

'And four companions, one a lady. Good. You are welcome aboard. I will send someone for your luggage. In the meantime, it is the commanding officer's wish that you see him as soon as you arrive.'

They followed him below and into a compartment that could have been the captain's cabin, a chart-room, an officers' mess-room and was probably all three: space is at a premium on MTBs. The captain was seated at his desk, writing, as Pietro entered without benefit of knocking. He swung round in his swivel-chair which was firmly bolted to the deck as Pietro stood to one side and said: 'Your latest guests, Carlos. The Major and the four friends we were promised.'

'Come in, come in, come in. Thank you, Pietro. Send that young ruffian along, will you?'

'When he's finished loading the luggage?'

'That'll do.' Pietro left. The captain was a broad-shouldered young man with thick curling black hair, a deep tan, very white teeth, a warm smile and warm brown eyes. He said: 'I'm Lieutenant Giancarlo Tremino. Call me Carlos. Nearly everyone else does. No discipline left in the Navy.' He shook his head and indicated his white polo neck jersey and grey flannel trousers. 'Why wear uniform? No-one pays any attention to it anyway.' He extended his hand – his left hand – to Petersen. 'Major, you are very welcome. I cannot

544

offer you Queen Mary type accommodation – peacetime accommodation, that is – but we have a very few small cabins, washing and toilet facilities, lots of wine and can guarantee safe transit to Ploče. The guarantee is based on the fact that we have been to the Dalmatian coast many times and haven't been sunk yet. Always a first time, of course, but I prefer to dwell on happier things.'

'You are very kind,' Petersen said. 'If it's to be first name terms, then mine is Peter.' He introduced the other four, each by their first name. Carlos acknowledged each introduction with a handshake and smile but made no attempt to rise. He was quick to explain this seeming discourtesy and quite unembarrassed about doing so.

'I apologize for remaining seated. I'm not really ill-mannered or lazy or averse to physical exertion.' He moved his right arm and, for the first time, brought his glove-sheathed right hand into view. He bent and tapped his right hand against his right leg, about halfway between knee and ankle. The unmistakable sound of hollow metal meeting hollow metal made the onlookers wince. He straightened and tapped the tips of his left fingers against the back of his right glove. The sound was against unmistakable although different – flesh meeting metal. 'Those metal appliances take some getting used to.' Carlos was almost apologetic. 'Unnecessary movement – well, any movement – causes discomfort and who likes discomfort? I am not the noblest Roman of them all.'

Sarina gnawed her lower lip. Michael tried to look as if he weren't shocked but was. The other three, with eighteen months of vicious and bitter warfare in the Yugoslav mountains behind them, predictably showed no reaction. Petersen said: 'Right hand, right leg. That's quite a handicap.'

'Just the right foot really – blown off at the ankle. Handicap? Have you heard of the English fighter pilot who got both legs destroyed? Did he shout for a bath-chair? He shouted to get back into the cockpit of his Spitfire or whatever. He did, too. Handicap!'

'I know of him. Most people do. How did you come by those two – um – trifling scratches?'

'Perfidious Albion,' Carlos said cheerfully. 'Nasty, horrible British. Never trust them. To think they used to be my best friends before the war – sailed with them in the Adriatic and the Channel, raced against them at Cowes – well, never mind. We were in the Aegean going, as the lawyers say, about our lawful occasions and bothering no-one. Dawn, lots of heavy mist about when suddenly, less than two kilometres away, this great big British warship appeared through a gap in the mist.'

Carlos paused, perhaps for effect, and Petersen said mildly: 'It was my understanding that the British never risked their capital ships north of Crete.'

'Size, like beauty, is in the eye of the beholder. It was, in fact, a very small frigate, but to us, you understand, it looked like a battleship. We weren't ready for them but they were ready for us – they had their guns already trained on us. No fault of ours – we had four men, not counting myself, on lookout: they must have had radar, we had none. Their first two shells struck the water only a few metres from our port side and exploded on contact: didn't do our hull much good, I can tell you. Two other light shells, about a kilo each, I should think – pom-poms, the British call them – scored direct hits. One penetrated the engine-room and put an engine out of action – I regret to say it's still out of action but we can get by without it – and the other came into the wheelhouse.'

'A kilo of explosives going off in a confined space is not very nice,' Petersen said. 'You were not alone?'

'Two others. They were not as lucky as I was. Then I had more luck – we ran into a fog bank.' Carlos shrugged. 'That's all. The past is past.'

A knock came at the door. A very young sailor entered, stood at attention, saluted and said: 'You sent for me, Captain.'

'Indeed. We have guests, Pietro. Tired, thirsty guests.'

'Right away, Captain.' The boy saluted and left.

Petersen said: 'What's all this you were saying about no discipline?'

Carlos smiled: 'Give him time. He's been with us for only a month.'

George looked puzzled. 'He is a truant from school, no?'

'He's older than he looks. Well, at least three months older.'

'Quite an age span you have aboard,' Petersen said. 'The elder Pietro. He can't be a day under seventy.'

'He's a great number of days over seventy.' Carlos laughed. The world seemed to be a source of constant amusement to him. 'A so-called captain with only two out of four functioning limbs. A beardless youth. An old age pensioner. What a crew. Just wait till you see the rest of them.'

Petersen said: 'The past is past, you say. Accepted. One may ask a question about the present?' Carlos nodded. 'Why haven't you been retired, invalided out of the Navy or at very least given some sort of shore job? Why are you still on active service?'

'Active service?' Carlos laughed again. 'Highly inactive service. The moment we run into anything resembling action I hand in my commission. You saw the two light guns we have mounted fore and aft? It was just pride that made me keep them there. They'll never be used for either attack or defence for the perfectly adequate reason that neither works. This is a very undemanding assignment and I do have one modest qualification for it. I was born and brought up in Pescara where my father had a yacht – more than one. I spent my boyhood and the ridiculously long university vacations sailing. Around the Mediterranean and Europe for part of the time but mainly off the Yugoslav coast. The Adriatic coast of Italy is dull and uninteresting, with not an island worth mentioning between Bari and Venice: the thousand and one Dalmatian islands are a paradise for the cruising yachtsman. I know them better than I know the streets of Pescara or Termoli. The Admiralty finds this useful.'

'On a black night?' Petersen said. 'No lighthouses, no lit buoys, no land-based navigational aids?'

'If I required those I wouldn't be much use to the Admiralty, would I? Ah! Help is at hand.'

It took young Pietro an heroic effort not to stagger under the weight of his burden, a vertically-sided, flat-bottomed wicker basket holding the far from humble nucleus of a small but well-stocked bar. In addition to spirits, wines and liqueurs, Pietro had even gone to the length of providing a soda syphon and a small ice-bucket.

'Pietro hasn't yet graduated to bar-tender and I've no intention of leaving this chair,' Carlos said. 'Help yourselves, please. Thank you, Pietro. Ask our two passengers to join us at their convenience.' The boy saluted and left. 'Two other Yugoslav-bound passengers. I don't know their business as I don't know yours. You don't know theirs and they don't know yours. Ships that pass in the night. But such ships exchange recognition signals. Courtesy of the high seas.'

Petersen gestured at the basket from which George was already helping the von Karajans to orange juice. 'Another courtesy of the high seas. Lessens the rigours of total war, I must say.'

'My feeling exactly. No thanks, I may say, to our Admiralty who are as stingy as Admiralties the world over. Some of the supplies come from my father's wine cellars – they would have your three-star sommeliers in raptures, I can tell you – some are gifts from foreign friends.'

'Kruškovac.' George touched a bottle. 'Grappa. Pelinkovac. Stara Šljivovica. Two excellent vintages from the Neretva delta. Your foreign friends. All from Yugoslavia. Our hospitable and considerate young friend, Pietro. Clairvoyant? He thinks we go to Yugoslavia? Or has he been informed?'

'Suspicion, one would suppose, is part of your stock-in-trade. I don't know what Pietro thinks. I don't even know if he *can* think. He hasn't been informed. He knows.' Carlos sighed. 'The romance and glamour of the cloak-and-dagger, sealed-orders missions are not, I'm afraid, for us. Search Termoli and you might find a person who is deaf, dumb and blind, although I much doubt it. If you did, he or she would be the only person in Termoli who doesn't know that the *Colombo* – that's the name of this crippled greyhound – plies a regular and so far highly dependable ferry-service to the Yugoslav coast. If it's any consolation, I'm the only person who knows *where* we're going. Unless, of course, one of you has talked.' He poured himself a small scotch. 'Your health, gentlemen. And yours, young lady.'

'We don't talk much about such things, but about other things I'm afraid I talk too much.' George sounded sad but at once refuted himself. 'University, eh? Some kind of marine school?'

'Some kind of medical school.'

'Medical school.' With the air of a man treating himself for shock George poured some more grappa. 'Don't tell me you're a doctor.'

'I'm not telling you anything. But I have a paper that says so.'

Petersen waved a hand. 'Then why this?'

'Well you might ask.' Momentarily, Carlos sounded as sad as George had done. 'The Italian Navy. Any navy. Take a highly skilled mechanic, obvious material for an equally highly skilled engine-room-artificer. What does he become? A cook. A cordon bleu chef? A gunner.' He waved his hand much as Petersen had done. 'So, in their all-knowing wisdom, they gave me this. Dr Tremino, ferryman, first class. Considering the state of the ferry, make that second class. Come in, come in.' A knock had come on the door.

The young woman who stepped over the low coaming – she could have been anything between twenty and thirty-five – was of medium height, slender and dressed in a jersey, jacket and skirt, all in blue. Pale-complexioned, without a trace of make-up, she was grave and unsmiling. Her hair was black as night and swooped low, like a raven's wing, over the left forehead, quite obscuring the left eyebrow. The pockmarking, for such it seemed to be, high up on the left cheekbone, served only to accentuate, not diminish, the classical, timeless beauty of the features: twenty years on, just as conceivably thirty, she would still be as beautiful as she was at that moment. Nor, it seemed certain, would time ever change the appearance of the man who followed her into the cabin, but the sculpted perfection of features had nothing to do with this. A tall, solidly built, fair-haired character, he was irredeemably ugly. Nature had had no hand in this. From the evidence offered by ears, cheeks, chin, nose and teeth he had been in frequent and violent contact with a variety of objects, both blunt and razor-edged, in the course of what must have been a remarkably chequered career. It was, withal, an attractive face, largely because of the genuine warmth of his smile: as with Carlos, an almost irrepressible cheerfulness was never far from the surface.

'This,' Carlos said, 'is Lorraine and Giacomo.' He introduced Petersen and the other four in turn. Lorraine's voice was soft and low, in tone and timbre remarkably like that of Sarina: Giacomo's, predictably, was neither soft nor low and his hand-clasp fearsome except when it came to Sarina: her fingers he took in his finger and thumb and gallantly kissed the back of her hand. Such a gesture from such a man should have appeared both affected and stagey: oddly

550

enough, it did neither. Sarina didn't seem to think so either. She said nothing, just smiled at him, the first genuine smile Petersen had seen from her: it came as no surprise that her teeth would have been a dentist's delight or despair, depending upon whether aesthetic or financial considerations were uppermost in his mind.

'Help yourselves,' Carlos gestured to the wicker basket. Giacomo, leaving no doubt that he was decisive both as to cast of mind and action, needed no second urging. He poured a glass of Pellegrino for Lorraine, evidence enough that this was not the first time he had met her and that she shared the von Karajans' aversion towards alcohol, and then half-filled a tumbler with scotch, topping it up with water. He took a seat and beamed around the company.

'Health to all.' He raised his brimming glass. 'And confusion to our enemies.'

'Any particular enemies?' Carlos said.

'It would take too long.' Giacomo tried to look sad but failed. 'I have too many.' He drank deeply to his own toast. 'You have called us to a conference, Captain Carlos?'

'Conference, Giacomo? Goodness me, no.' It didn't require any great deductive powers, Petersen reflected, to realize that those two had met before and not just that day. 'Why should I hold a conference? My job is to get you where you're going and you can't help me in that. After you land I can't help you in whatever you're going to do. Nothing to confer about. As a ferryman, I'm a great believer in introductions. People in your line of business are apt to react overquickly if, rightly or wrongly, they sense danger in meeting an unknown on a dark deck at night. No such danger now. And there are three things I want to mention briefly.

'First, accommodation. Lorraine and Giacomo have a cabin each, if you can call something the size of a telephone box a cabin. Only fair. First come, first served. I have two other cabins, one for three, one for two.' He looked at

551

Michael. 'You and – yes, Sarina – are brother and sister?'

'Who told you?' Michael probably didn't mean to sound truculent, but his nervous system had suffered from his encounter with Petersen and his friends, and that was the way it came out.

Carlos lowered his head briefly, looked up and said, not smiling, 'The good Lord gave me eyes and they say "twins".'

'No problem.' Giacomo bowed towards the embarrassed girl. 'The young lady will do me the honour of switching cabins with me?'

She smiled and nodded. 'You are very kind.'

'Second. Food. You could eat aboard but I don't recommend it. Giovanni cooks only under duress and protest. I don't blame him. He's our engineer. Everything that comes out of that galley, even the coffee, tastes and smells of oil. There's a passable café close by – well, barely passable, but they do know me.' He half-smiled at the two women in turn. 'It will be a hardship and a sacrifice but I think I'll join you.

'Third. You're free to go ashore whenever you wish, although I can't imagine why anyone should want to go ashore on a night like this – except, of course, to escape Giovanni's cooking. There are police patrols but their enthusiasm usually drops with the temperature. If you do run into any, just say you're from the *Colombo*: the worst that can happen is that they'll escort you back here to check.'

'I think I'll take my chance on both weather and the police,' Petersen said. 'Advancing years or too many hours in that damned truck or maybe both, but I'm as stiff as a board.'

'Back inside an hour, please, then we'll leave for the meal.' He looked at the bulkhead clock. 'We should be back at ten. We sail at one o'clock in the morning.'

'Not till then?' Michael looked his astonishment. 'Why, that's hours away. Why don't we –'

'We sail at 1.00 a.m.' Carlos was patient.

552

'But the wind's getting stronger. It must be rough now. It'll be getting rougher.'

'It will not be too comfortable. Are you a bad sailor, Michael?' The words were sympathetic, the expression not.

'No. Yes. I don't know. I don't see – I mean, I can't understand –'

'Michael.' It was Petersen, his voice gentle. 'It really doesn't matter what you can't see or can't understand. Lieutenant Tremino is the captain. The captain makes the decisions. No-one *ever* questions the captain.'

'It's very simple, really.' It was noticeable that Carlos spoke to Petersen not Michael. 'The garrison that guard such port installations as they have at Ploče are not first-line troops. As soldiers go, they are either superannuated or very very young. In both cases they're nervous and trigger-happy and the fact that they have radio notification of my arrival seems to have no effect on them. Experience and a few lucky escapes have taught me that the wisest thing is to arrive at sunrise so that even the most rheumy eyes can see that the gallant Captain Tremino is flying the biggest Italian flag in the Adriatic.'

The wind, as Michael had said, had indeed strengthened, and was bitingly cold but Petersen and his two companions were not exposed to it for long, for George's homing instinct was unerring. The tavern in which they fetched up was no more or less dingy than any other dockside tavern and it was at least warm.

'A very short stroll for such stiff legs,' George observed.

'Nothing wrong with my legs. I just wanted to talk.'

'What was wrong with our cabin? Carlos has more wine and grappa and slivovitz than he can possibly use –'

'Colonel Lunz, as we've said, has a long arm.'

'Ah! So! A bug?'

'Would you put anything past him? This could be awkward.'

'Alas, I'm afraid I know what you mean.'

'I don't.' Alex wore his suspicious expression.

'Carlos,' Petersen said. 'I know him. Rather, I know who he is. I knew his father, a retired naval captain but on the reserve list: almost certainly on the active list now, a cruiser captain or such. He became a reserve Italian naval captain at the same time as my father became a reserve Yugoslav army colonel. Both men loved the sea and both men set up chandlers' businesses: both were highly successful. Inevitably, almost, their paths crossed and they became very good friends. They met frequently, usually in Trieste and I was with them on several occasions. Photographs were taken. Carlos may well have seen them.'

'If he has seen them,' George said, 'let it be our pious hope that the ravages of time and the dissipation of years make it difficult for Carlos to identify Major Petersen with the carefree youth of yesteryear.'

Alex said: 'Why is it so important?'

'I have known Colonel Petersen for many years,' George said. 'Unlike his son, he is, or was, a very outspoken man.'

'Ah!'

'A pity about Carlos, a great pity.' George sounded, and may well have been, profoundly sad. 'An eminently likeable young man. And you can say the same about Giacomo – except, of course, not so young. An excellent pair to have by one's side, one would have thought, in moments of trouble and strife, which are the only ones we seem to have.' He shook his head. 'Where, oh where, are my ivory towers?'

'You should be grateful for this touch of realism, George. Exactly the counter-balance you academics need. What do you make of Giacomo? An Italian counterpart of the British commando?'

'Giacomo has been savagely beaten up or savagely tortured

or perhaps both at the same time. Commando material unquestionably. But not Italian. Montenegrin.'

'Montenegrin!'

'You know. Montenegro.' George, on occasion, was capable of elaborate sarcasm, an unfortunate gift honed and refined by a lifetime in the groves of academe. 'A province in our native Yugoslavia.'

'With that fair hair and impeccable Italian?'

'Fair hair is not unknown in Montenegro and though his Italian is very good the accent overlay is unmistakable.'

Petersen didn't doubt him for a moment. George's ear for languages, dialects, accents and nuances of accent was, in philological circles, a byword far beyond the Balkans.

The evening meal was more than passable, the café more than presentable. Carlos was not only known there, as he had said, but treated with some deference. Lorraine spoke only occasionally and then to no-one except Carlos, who sat beside her. She, too, had, it seemed been born in Pescara. Predictably, neither Alex nor Michael nor Sarina contributed a word to the conversation but that didn't matter. Both Carlos and Petersen were relaxed and easy talkers but even that didn't matter very much: when Giacomo and George were in full cry, more often than not at the same time, even the possibility of a conversational hiatus seemed preposterous: both men talked a great deal without saying anything at all.

On the way back to the ship they had to face not only a perceptibly stronger wind but a thinly driving snow. Carlos, who had drunk little enough, was not so sure on his feet as he thought or, more likely, would have others think. After the second stumble he was seen to be walking arm in arm with Lorraine: who had taken whose arm could only be guessed at. When they arrived at the gangway, the *Colombo* was rocking perceptibly at its moorings: the harbour swell responsible bespoke much worse conditions outside.

555

To Petersen's surprise and an ill-concealed irritation that amounted almost to anger, five more men were awaiting their arrival down below. Their leader, who was introduced as Alessandro, and for whom Carlos showed an unusual degree of respect, was a tall, thin, grey-haired man with a beaked nose, bloodless lips and only the rudimentary vestiges of eyebrows. Three of his four men, all about half his age, were introduced as Franco, Cola and Sepp, which names were presumably abbreviations for Francesco, Nicholas and Giuseppe: the fourth was called Guido. Like their leader, they wore nondescript civilian clothes. Like their leader they gave the distinct impression that they would have been much happier in uniform: like their leader they had cold, hard, expressionless faces.

Petersen glanced briefly at George, turned and left the cabin, George following with Alex, inevitably, close behind. Petersen had barely begun to speak when Carlos appeared in the passage-way and walked quickly towards them.

'You are upset, Major Petersen?' No 'Peter'. The trace of anxiety was faint but it was there.

'I'm unhappy. It is true, as I told Michael, that one never questions the captain's decisions but this is a different matter entirely. I take it those men are also passengers to Ploče?' Carlos nodded. 'Where are they sleeping?'

'We have a dormitory for five in the bows. I did not think that worth mentioning, any more than I thought their arrival worth mentioning.'

'I am also unhappy at the fact that Rome gave me the distinct impression that we would be travelling alone. I did not bargain for the fact that we would be travelling with five – seven now – people who are totally unknown to me.

'I am unhappy about the fact that you know them or, at least, Alessandro.' Carlos made to speak but Petersen waved him to silence. 'I'm sure you wouldn't think me such a fool as to deny it. It's just not in your nature to show a deference amounting almost to apprehension towards a total stranger.

'Finally, I'm unhappy about the fact that they have the appearance of being a bunch of hired, professional assassins, tough ruthless killers. They are, of course, nothing of the kind, they only think they are, which is why I use the word "appearance". Their only danger lies in their lack of predictability. For your true assassin, no such word as unpredictability exists in his vocabulary. He does precisely what he intends to do. And it is to be borne in mind, when it comes to the far from gentle art of premeditated and authorized murder, your true assassin never, never, never looks like one.'

'You seem to know a lot about assassins.' Carlos smiled faintly. 'I could be speaking to three of them.'

'Preposterous!' George was incapable of snorting but he came close.

'Giacomo, then?'

'One is left with the impression that Giacomo is a one-man panzer division,' Petersen said. 'Cold-blooded stealth is not his forte. He doesn't even begin to qualify. You should know – you know him much better than we do.'

'What makes you say that?'

'Because acting isn't *your* forte.'

'So our school drama teacher said. Lorraine?'

'You're mad.' George spoke with conviction.

'He doesn't mean you are.' Petersen smiled. 'Just the suggestion. Classically beautiful women almost never have gentle eyes.'

Carlos confirmed what seemed to be the growing opinion that he was indeed no actor. He was pleased, and not obscurely. He said: 'If you're unhappy, then I apologize for that although I really don't know why I'm apologizing. I have orders to carry out and it's my duty to follow orders. Beyond that, I know nothing.' He still wasn't a very good actor, Petersen thought, but there was nothing to be gained in saying so. 'Won't you come back to my cabin? Three hours before we sail yet. Ample time for a nightcap. Or two. Alessandro and his men, as you say, aren't so ferocious as they look.'

'Thank you,' Petersen said. 'But no. I think we'll just take a turn on the upper deck and then retire. So we'll say goodnight now.'

'The upper deck? This weather? You'll freeze.'

'Cold is an old friend of ours.'

'I prefer other company. But as you wish, gentlemen.' He reached out a steadying hand as the *Colombo* lurched sharply. 'A rather rough passage tonight, I'm afraid. Torpedo boats may have their good points – I may find one some day – but they are rather less than sea-kindly. I hope you are also on friendly terms with Father Neptune.'

'Our next of kin,' George said.

'That apart, I can promise you a quiet and uneventful trip. Never had a mutiny yet.'

In the lee of the superstructure Petersen said: 'Well?'

'Well?' George said heavily. 'All is not well. Seven total strangers aboard this boat and the worthy young Carlos seems to know all seven of them. Every man's hand against us. Not, of course, that that's anything new.' The tip of his nauseous cigar glowed redly in the gloom. 'Would it be naïve of me to wonder whether or not our good friend Colonel Lunz is acquainted with the passenger list of the *Colombo*?'

'Yes.'

'We are, of course, prepared for all eventualities?'

'Certainly. Which ones did you have in mind?'

'None. We take turns to keep watch in our cabin?'

'Of course. If we stay in our cabin.'

'Ah! We have a plan?'

'We have no plan. What do you think about Lorraine?'

'Charming. I speak unhesitatingly. A delightful young lady.'

'I've told you before, George. About your advanced years and susceptibility. That wasn't what I meant. Her presence aboard puzzles me. I can't see that she belongs in any way to this motley bunch that Carlos is transporting to Ploče.'

'Motley, eh? First time I've ever been called motley. How does she differ?'

'Because every other passenger on this vessel is up to no good or I strongly suspect them of being up to no good. I suspect her of nothing.'

'My word!' George spoke in tones of what were meant to be genuine awe. 'That makes her unique.'

'Carlos let us know – he could have been at pains to let us know – that she, too, came from Pescara. Do you think she comes from Pescara, George?'

'How the devil should I tell? She could come from Timbuktu for all I know.'

'You disappoint me, George. Or wilfully misunderstand me. I shall be patient. Your unmatched command of the nuances of all those European languages. Was she born or brought up in Pescara?'

'Neither.'

'But she is Italian?'

'No.'

'So we're back in Yugoslavia again?'

'Maybe you are. I'm not. I'm in England.'

'What! England?'

'The overlay of what it pleases the British Broadcasting Corporation to call Southern Standard English is unmistakable.' George coughed modestly, his smugness could occasionally verge on the infuriating. 'To the trained ear, of course.'

THREE

Both Alex and Carlos had made predictions and both had
turned out to be wrong or, in Alex's case, half wrong. He had
said, gloomily and accurately, that it was going to be very very
cold and at three a.m. that morning none of the passengers on
the *Colombo* would have disagreed with him. The driving
snow, so heavy as to reduce visibility to virtually zero, had
an uncommonly chilling effect on the torpedo boat, which
would have been of no concern to those in an adequately
central-heated boat but on this particular one the central-
heating unit, as became practically everything else aboard,
was functioning at about only one-third degree efficiency
and, moreover, had been of a pathetically ancient design in
the first place so that for the shivering passengers – and crew
– the snow had become a matter for intense concern.

Alex had been wrong, even if only slightly – and what he
had said had been a statement, really, not a fact – when he
spoke of an east-north-east wind. It was a north-east wind.
To a layman or, indeed, anybody not aboard an elderly
torpedo boat, a paltry twenty-three degree difference in wind
direction might seem negligible: to a person actually aboard
such a boat the difference is crucial, marking, as it did for
those with inbuilt queasiness, the border-line between the
uncomfortable and the intolerable. Had the *Colombo* been
head-on to wind and seas, the pitching would have been
uncomfortable: had the seas been on the beam, the rolling

would have been even more uncomfortable: but, that night, with the seas two points off the port bow, the resultant wicked cork-screwing was, for the less fortunate, the last straw. For some people aboard the torpedo boat that night, the degree of sea-sickness ranged from the unpleasant to the acute.

Carlos had predicted that the trip would be quiet and uneventful. At least two people, both, at least outwardly, immune to the effects of sea and cold, did not share Carlos' confidence. The door to the bo'sun's store, which lay to the port hand of the stairway leading down to the engine-room, had been hooked open and Petersen and Alex, standing two feet back in the unlit store, were only dimly visible. There was just enough light to see that Alex was carrying a semi-automatic machine-pistol while Petersen, using one hand to steady himself on the lurching deck had the other in his coat pocket. Petersen had long ago learned that with Alex by his side when confronting minimal forces, it was quite superfluous for him to carry a weapon of any kind.

Their little cabin, almost directly opposite them on the starboard side of the ill but sufficiently lit passage-way, had its door closed. George, Petersen knew, was still behind that door: and George, Petersen also knew, would be as wide awake as themselves. Petersen looked at his luminous watch. For just over ninety minutes he and Alex had been on station with no signs of weariness or boredom or awareness of the cold and certainly with no signs of their relaxed vigilance weakening at any time: a hundred times they had waited thus on the bleak and often icy mountains of Bosnia and Serbia and Montenegro, most commonly for much longer periods than this: and always they had survived. But that night was going to be one of their shorter and more comfortable vigils.

It was in the ninety-third minute that two men appeared at the for'ard end of the passage-way. They moved swiftly aft, crouched low as if making a stealthy approach, an attempt in which they were rather handicapped by being flung from

561

bulkhead to bulkhead with every lurch of the *Colombo*: they had tried to compensate for this by removing their boots, no doubt to reduce the noise level of their approach, a rather ludicrous tactic in the circumstances because the torpedo boat was banging and crashing about to such a high decibel extent that they could have marched purposefully along in hob-nailed boots without anyone being any way the wiser. Each had a pistol stuck in his belt: more ominously, each carried in his right hand an object that looked suspiciously like a hand-grenade.

They were Franco and Cola and neither was looking particularly happy. That their expressions were due to the nature of the errand on hand or to twinges of conscience Petersen did not for a moment believe: quite simply, neither had been born with the call of the sea in his ear and, from the lack of colour in their strained faces, both would have been quite happy never to hear it again. On the logical assumption that Alessandro would have picked his two fittest young lieutenants for the job on hand, Petersen thought, their appearance didn't say too much for the condition of those who had been left behind. Their cabin was right up in the bows of the vessel and in a cork-screwing sea that was the place to be avoided above all. They halted outside the door behind which George was lurking and looked at each other. Petersen waited until the boat was on even keel, bringing with it a comparative, if brief, period of silence.

'Don't move!'

Franco, at least, had some sense: he didn't move. Cola, on the other hand, amply demonstrated Petersen's assertion that they weren't hired assassins but only tried to look like ones, by dropping his grenade – he had to be right-handed – reaching for his pistol and swinging round, all in what he plainly hoped was one swift coordinated movement: for a man like Alex it was a scene in pathetically slow motion. Cola had just cleared the pistol from his left waistband when Alex

562

fired, just once, the sound of the shot shockingly loud in the metallic confines. Cola dropped his gun, looked uncomprehendingly at his shattered right shoulder then, back to the bulkhead, he slid to the deck in a sitting position.

'They never learn,' Alex said gloomily. Alex was not one to derive childish pleasure from such childishly simply exercises.

'Maybe he's never had the chance to learn,' Petersen said. He relieved Franco of his armoury and had just picked up Cola's pistol and grenade when George appeared in the cabin doorway. He, too, carried a weapon but had had no expectation of using it: he held his semi-automatic loosely by the stock, its muzzle pointing towards the deck. He shook his head just once, resignedly, but said nothing.

Petersen said: 'Mind our backs, George.'

'You are going to return those unfortunates to the bosom of their family?' Petersen nodded. 'A Christian act. They're not fit to be out alone.'

Petersen and Alex moved back up the passage-way preceded by Franco and Cola, the former supporting his stricken comrade. They had taken only four steps whe . a door on the port side, just aft of where George was standing, opened and Giacomo stepped out into the passage-way, brandishing a Biretta.

'Put that thing away,' George said. His machine-pistol was still pointing at the deck. 'Don't you think there has been enough noise already?'

'That's why I'm here.' Giacomo had already lowered his gun. 'The noise, I mean.'

'Took your time, didn't you?'

'I had to get dressed first,' Giacomo said with some dignity. He was clad only in a pair of khaki trousers, displaying a tanned chest rather impressively criss-crossed with scars. 'But I notice you are fully dressed, so I take it you were expecting whatever did happen.' He looked in the

563

direction of the quartet making their slow way along the passage-way. 'What exactly did happen?'

'Alex has just shot Cola.'

'Good for Alex.' If Giacomo was moved by the news he hid it well. 'Hardly worth wakening a man for.'

'Cola might view matters differently.' George coughed delicately. 'You are not, then, one of them?'

'You must be mad.'

'Not really. I don't know any of you, do I? But you don't *look* like them.'

'You're very kind, George. And now?'

'We won't find out just by standing here.'

They caught up with the others in just a matter of seconds which was easily enough done as the now moaning Cola could barely drag his feet along. A moment afterwards a door at the for'ard end of the passage-way opened and an armed figure came – or lurched – into view. It was Sepp and he wasn't looking at all like the ruthless killer of a few hours ago. It required no imagination to see the slightly greenish pallor on his face, for slightly green he indisputably was: time and the seaway had wrought its effect. It was not difficult to understand why Alessandro had selected Franco and Cola for the mission.

'Sepp.' Petersen's tone was almost kindly. 'We have no wish to kill you. Before you can reach us, you would have to kill your two friends, Franco and Cola. That would be bad enough, wouldn't it, Sepp?' From Sepp's pallor and general demeanour of uncertainty it seemed, that for him, things were quite bad enough as they were. 'Even worse, Sepp, before you could get around to killing the second of your friends, you yourself would be dead. Drop that gun, Sepp.'

Whatever other parts of Sepp's physiology were in a state of temporary dysfunction there was nothing wrong with his hearing. His elderly Lee Enfield .303 clattered to the deck.

'Who fired that shot?' Carlos, his habitual smile in momentary abeyance, had come limping up behind them, a pistol in hand. 'What goes on?'

'It would help if you could tell us.' Petersen looked at the gun in Carlos' hand. 'You don't require that.'

'I require it as long as I am the master of this vessel. I asked' – he broke off with an exclamation of pain as George's massive hand closed over his gun-wrist. He struggled to free his hand, an expression of incomprehension spread over his face and he bit his lips as if to hold back another cry of pain. George removed the gun from the suddenly nerveless fingers.

'So that's it,' Carlos said. His face, not without reason, was pale. 'So I was right. *You* are the assassins. It is your intention to take over my vessel, perhaps?'

'Goodness gracious, no.' It was George who answered. 'Your forefinger has gone white at the knuckles. Precipitate action isn't going to help anyone.' He handed the pistol back to Carlos and went on pontifically: 'Unnecessary violence never helped anyone.'

Carlos took the pistol, hesitated, stuck it in his waistband and began to massage his right wrist. The demonstration of pacific intentions had had an unsettling effect. He said uncertainly: 'I still don't understand –'

'Neither do we, Carlos,' Petersen said, 'neither do we. That's what we're trying to do at this moment – understand. Perhaps you could help us. Those two men, Franco and Cola – Cola, I'm afraid is going to require your peacetime professional skills quite soon – came to attack us. Perhaps they came to kill us but I don't think so. They bungled it.'

'Amateurs,' George said by way of explanation.

'Amateurs, agreed. But the effect of an amateur bullet can be just as permanent as a professional one. I want to know why those two came for us in the first place. Perhaps you can help explain this, Carlos?'

565

'How should I be able to help you?'

'Because you know Alessandro.'

'I do but not well. I have no idea why he should seek to do you harm. I do not permit my passengers to carry out guerrilla warfare.'

'I'm sure you don't. But I'm equally sure that you know who Alessandro is and what he does.'

'I don't know.'

'I don't believe you. I suppose I should sigh and say how much trouble it would save all round if you were to tell the truth. Not, of course, that you are telling lies. You're just not telling anything. Well, if you don't help us, I'll just have to help myself.' Petersen raised his voice. 'Alessandro!'

Seconds passed without reply.

'Alessandro. I have three of your men prisoner, one of them badly injured. I want to know why those men came to attack us.' Alessandro made no reply and Petersen went on: 'You don't leave me any option. In wartime, people are either friends or enemies. Friends are friends and enemies die. If you're a friend, step out into the passage-way: if you're not, then you'll just have to stay there and die.'

Petersen didn't show any particular emotion but his tone sounded implacable enough. Carlos, his pain forgotten, laid a hand on Petersen's forearm.

'People don't commit murder aboard my ship.'

'Haven't committed. And murder is for peacetime. In wartime we call it execution.' For those listening inside the cabin the tone of his voice could have lent little encouragement. 'George, Alex. Help Franco and Sepp into the cabin. Keep out of any line of fire.'

Franco and Sepp didn't need any kind of helping. Execution chamber or not they couldn't get inside it fast enough. The door banged shut and a watertight clip came down. Petersen examined the pear-shaped object in his hand.

Carlos said apprehensively: 'What's that?'

'You can see. A hand-grenade of sorts. George?' George didn't need telling what to do. He never did. He took up position by the cabin door, his hand reaching up for the closed watertight clip. With one hand Petersen took a grip on the door handle, with the other he pressed a lever on the bottom of the grenade as he glanced at George who immediately opened the clip. Petersen jerked open the door the requisite few inches, dropped the grenade inside and banged shut the door as George closed the clip again. They could have rehearsed it a hundred times.

'Jesus!' Carlos' face was white. 'In that confined space –' He stopped, his face puzzled now, and said: 'The explosion. The bang.'

'Gas-grenades don't go bang. They go hiss. Reactions, George?' George had taken his hand away from the clip.

'Five seconds and then whoever it was gave up. Quick-acting stuff, is it not?'

Carlos was still almost distraught. 'What's the difference? Explosives or poison gas –'

Petersen spoke with patience. 'It was not poison gas. George.' He spoke a few words in the ear of his giant lieutenant, who smiled and moved quickly aft. Petersen turned to Carlos. 'Is it your intention to let your friend Cola die?'

'He's not my friend and he's in no danger of dying.' He turned to the elder Pietro who had just arrived on the scene. 'Get my medicine box and bring along two of your boys.' To Petersen he said: 'I'll give a sedative, a knockout one. Then a coagulant. A few minutes later and I'll bandage him up. There'll be a broken bone or bones. It may be that his shoulder is shattered beyond repair, but whatever it is there's nothing I can do about it in this seaway.' He glanced aft, passed his hand over his forehead and looked as if he would like to moan. 'More trouble.'

Michael von Karajan was approaching them, closely followed by George. Michael was trying to look indignant and truculent but succeeded only in looking miserable and frightened. George was beaming.

'By heavens, Major, there's nothing wrong with this new generation of ours. You have to admire their selfless spirit. Here we are with the good ship *Colombo* trying to turn somersaults but does that stop our Michael in the polishing of his skills? Not a bit of it. There he was, crouched over his transceiver in this appalling weather, headphones clamped over his ears –'

Petersen held up his hand. When he spoke his face was as cold as his voice. 'Is this true, von Karajan?'

'No. What I mean is –'

'You're a liar. If George says it's true, it's true. What message were you sending?'

'I wasn't sending any message. I –'

'George?'

'He wasn't transmitting any message when I arrived.'

'He would hardly have had time to,' Giacomo said. 'Not between the time I left our cabin and when George got there.' He eyed the now visibly shaking Michael with open distaste. 'He's not only a coward, he's a fool. How was he to know that I wasn't going to return at any moment? Why didn't he lock his door to make sure that he wasn't disturbed?'

Petersen said: 'What message were you going to transmit?'

'I wasn't going to transmit any –'

'That makes you doubly a liar. Who were you transmitting to or about to transmit to?'

'I wasn't going to –'

'Oh, do be quiet. That makes you three times a liar. George, confiscate his equipment. For good measure confiscate his sister's as well.'

'You can't do that.' Michael was aghast. 'Take away our radios? They're our equipment.'

568

'Good God in heaven!' Petersen stared at him in disbelief. Whether the disbelief were real or affected didn't matter. The effect was the same. 'I'm your commanding officer, you young fool. I can not only lock up your equipment, I can lock you up too, on charges of mutiny. In irons, if need be.' Petersen shook his head. '"Can't", he says, "can't". Another thing, von Karajan. Can it be that you're so stupid as not to know that, in wartime at sea, the use of radio by unauthorized personnel is a very serious offence.' He turned to Carlos. 'Is that not so, Captain Tremino?' Petersen's use of formal terms lent to his enquiry all the gravity of a court-martial.

'Very much so, I'm afraid.' Carlos wasn't too happy to say it but he said it all the same.

'Is this young fellow authorized personnel?'

'No.'

'You see how it is, von Karajan? The Captain would also be justified in locking you up. George, put the sets in our cabin. No, wait a minute. This is primarily a naval offence.' He looked at Carlos. 'Do you think –'

'I have a very adequate safe in the office,' Carlos said. 'And I have the only key.'

'Splendid.' George moved off, a disconsolate Michael trailing behind him, passing by Pietro, bearing a black metal box and accompanied by two seamen. Carlos opened the medicine chest – it appeared to be immaculately equipped – and administered two injections to the hapless Cola. The box was closed and removed: so was Cola.

'Well, now,' Petersen said. 'Let's see what we have inside.' Alex, not without considerable effort, managed to free the watertight clip – when George heaved a watertight clip home it tended to stay heaved – then levelled his machine-pistol on the door. Giacomo did the same with his pistol, clearly demonstrating that whoever's side, if any, he was on it clearly was not that of Alessandro and his henchmen. Petersen didn't bother about any weapon, although he had a Luger on his person: he just pushed the door open.

The guns were unnecessary. The four men were not unconscious but, on the other hand, they weren't very conscious either, although they would be very soon. No coughing, no spluttering, no tears running down their cheeks: they were just slightly dazed, slightly woozy, slightly apathetic. Alex laid down his machine-pistol, collected the several weapons that were lying around, then searched the four men thoroughly, coming up with two more hand-guns and no fewer than four very unpleasant knives. All these he threw out into the passage-way.

'Well.' Carlos was almost smiling. 'That wasn't very clever of me, was it? I mean, if you had wished to dispose of all of them you'd have thrown Cola in here, too. I missed that.' He sniffed the air professionally. 'Nitrous oxide, I'd say. You know, laughing gas.'

'Not bad for a doctor,' Petersen said. 'I thought that gas was confined only to dentists' surgeries. Nitrous oxide, a refined form of.. With this, you don't come out of the anaesthetic with tears in your eyes, laughing, singing and generally making a fool of yourself. Normally, you don't come out of it at all, by which I mean you'd just keep on sleeping until you woke up at your usual time, quite unaware that anything untoward had happened to you. But I'm told that if you've recently undergone some sort of traumatic experience immediately before you've been gassed, the tendency is to wake up directly the effects of the gas have worn off. They also say that if you had something weighing on your mind, such as a nagging conscience, the same thing happens.'

Carlos said: 'That's a strange sort of thing for a soldier to know about.'

'I'm a strange sort of soldier. Alex, take up your gun while I have a look around.'

'Look around?' Carlos did just that. The cabin, if one could call it such, held five canvas cots and that was all: there wasn't as much as even a cupboard for clothes. 'There's nothing to look around for.'

Petersen didn't bother to reply. He ripped blankets from the cots and flung them on the deck. Nothing had lain beneath the blankets. He picked up a rucksack – there were five of them in the cabin – and unceremoniously dumped the contents on a cot. They were innocuous. Among some clothes and a rudimentary toilet kit there was a considerable amount of ammunition, some loose, some in magazines, but those, too, Petersen considered innocuous: he would have expected nothing else. The second rucksack yielded the same results. The third was padlocked. Petersen looked at Alessandro, who was sitting on the deck, his ravaged face expressionless: the effect was chilling, even a hint of balefulness would have been preferable to this emptiness but Petersen was not the man to be moved by expressions or lack of them.

'Well, now, Alessandro, that wasn't very clever, was it? If you want to hide a thing you do it inconspicuously: a padlock is conspicuous. The key.'

Alessandro spat on the deck and remained silent.

'Spitting.' Petersen shook his head. 'Unpleasant, for second-rate villains. Alex.'

'Search him?'

'Don't bother. Your knife.'

Alex's knife, as one would have expected of Alex, was razor sharp. It sliced through the tough canvas of the rucksack as if through paper. Petersen peered at the contents.

'Yes, indeed, twinges of conscience.' He extracted a very small butane burner and an equally small kettle. The kettle had no top – the spout had a screwed top. Petersen shook the kettle: the glugging of water inside was unmistakable. Petersen turned to Carlos.

571

'Doesn't say much for the hospitality of the *Colombo*, does it, when a man has to bring along his own equipment for making tea or coffee or whatever.'

Carlos looked slightly puzzled. 'Any passenger aboard this ship can have as much tea or coffee or any other drink that he wants.' Then his face cleared. 'For shore use, of course.'

'Of course.' Petersen tipped the remainder of the contents of the rucksack on to another cot, rummaged briefly around, then straightened. 'Although, mind you, it's difficult to see how we can make any of those refreshing beverages without any tea or coffee to make them. I've found out all I want to know even although I knew in advance anyway.' He turned his attention to the fourth rucksack.

Carlos said: 'If you've already found out what you want to know why keep on?'

'Natural curiosity together with the fact that Alessandro, I'm afraid, is not a very trustworthy man. Who knows, this bag might contain a nest of vipers.'

There were no vipers but there were two more gas-grenades and a Walther with a screwed-on silencer.

'And a stealthy killer to boot,' Petersen said. 'I've always wanted one of those.' He put it in his pocket and opened up the last rucksack: this yielded only a small metal case about half the size of a shoe-box. Petersen turned to the nearest of his prisoners who happened to be Franco.

'You know what's inside this?'

Franco didn't say whether he did not not.

Petersen sighed, placed the muzzle of his Luger against Franco's knee-cap and said: 'Captain Tremino, if I pull the trigger, will he walk again?'

'Good God!' Carlos was used to war but not this kind of war. 'He might. He'll be a cripple for life.'

Petersen took two steps back. Franco looked at Alessandro but Alessandro wasn't looking at him. Franco looked at Petersen and the levelled Luger.

Franco said: 'I know.'

'Open it.'

Franco released two brass clips and swung back the lid. There was no explosion, no release of gas.

Carlos said: 'Why didn't *you* open it?'

'Because the world is full of untrustworthy people. Lots of these boxes of tricks around. If an unauthorized opener doesn't know where a secret switch or button is he's going to inhale a very nasty gas. Most of the latest safes incorporate some such device.' He took the box from Franco. The interior was shaped and lined with velvet and contained glass ampoules, two round boxes and two small hypodermic syringes. Petersen took out one of the round boxes and shook it: it rattled. Petersen handed the box to Carlos.

'Should interest a medical man. At a guess, a variety of liquids and tablets to render the victim temporarily or permanently unconscious, by which I mean dead. Seven ampoules, you observe. One green, three blue, three pink. At a guess, the green is scopolamine, an aid to flagging memories. As for the difference in colour in the other six ampoules, there can be only one reason. Three are lethal, three non-lethal. Wouldn't you agree, Captain?'

'It's possible.' It was Carlos' night for being unhappy and Petersen was no longer as surprised by his unhappiness as he had been earlier, nor at the obvious apprehension in which he held Alessandro. 'There's no means of telling one from the other, of course.'

'I wouldn't bet on that,' Petersen said. He turned round as George came through the doorway. 'All is well?'

'A little trouble with the young lady,' George said. 'She put up a surprisingly spirited resistance to the confiscation of her radio.'

'Nothing surprising about that. Fortunately, you're bigger than she is.'

'I'm hardly proud of that. The radios are in the captain's

573

cabin.' George looked around the cabin which looked as if a small tornado had lately passed by. 'Untidy lot, aren't they?'

'I helped a little.' Petersen took the box from Carlos and handed it to George. 'What do you make of that?'

It is difficult to conceive of a beaming, plump and cherubic face changing in an instant to one of graven stone but that was what happened to George's.

'Those are death capsules.'

'I know.'

'Alessandro's?'

'Yes.'

George looked at Alessandro for some seconds, nodded, and turned back to Petersen. 'I think perhaps we should have a talk with our friend.'

'You're making a mistake.' Carlos' voice was not quite as steady as it could have been. 'I'm a doctor. You don't know human nature. Alessandro will never talk.'

George faced him. His expression hadn't changed and Carlos visibly recoiled.

'Be quiet, little man. Five minutes alone with me, ten at the most, and any man in the world will talk. Alessandro is a five minute man.'

'It may come to that,' Petersen said. 'It probably will. But first things first. Apart from the capsules, we picked up one or two other interesting objects. This silenced gun, for instance.' He showed George the Walther. 'Two gas-grenades and a spirit burner and kettle and about two hundred rounds of ammunition. What do you think the kettle was for?'

'One thing only. He was going to gas us, steal some real or imagined document, steam open the envelope – odd, that he should be convinced that there was an envelope around – study the contents, reseal the envelope, return it to our cabin, gas us again, wait a few seconds, replace the envelope,

574

remove the gas-canister and leave. When we woke up in the morning we almost certainly wouldn't be aware that anything had happened.'

'That's the only way it could have happened or was intended to happen. There are three questions. Why was Alessandro so interested in us? What were his future plans? And who sent him?'

'We'll find all that out easily enough,' George said.

'Of course we will.'

'Not aboard this ship,' Carlos said.

George studied him with mild interest. 'Why not?'

'There will be no torture aboard any vessel I command.' The words sounded more resolute than the tone of the voice.

'Carlos,' Petersen said. 'Don't make things any more difficult for yourself – or us – than you can help. Nothing easier than to lock you up with this bunch of villains: you're not the only person who can find his way to Ploče. We don't want to nor do we intend to. We realize you find yourself in an invidious situation through no fault of your own. No torture. We promise.'

'You've just said you'll find out.'

'Psychology.'

'Drugs?' Carlos was immediately suspicious. 'Injections?'

'Neither. Subject closed. I had another question but the answer is obvious – why did Alessandro choose to surround himself with such a bunch of incompetents? Camouflage. A dangerous man might well be tempted to surround himself with other dangerous men. Alessandro's too smart.' Petersen looked around. 'No heavy metal objects and only a cat could get out of that port-hole. Carlos, would you have one of your men bring us a sledge-hammer or as near to it as you have aboard.'

The suspicion returned. 'What do you want a sledge-hammer for?'

575

'To beat out Alessandro's brains,' George said patiently. 'Before we start asking questions.'

'To close this door from the outside,' Petersen said. 'The clips, you understand.'

'Ah!' Carlos stepped into the passage-way, gave an order and returned. 'I'll go and have a look at the fallen hero. Not much I can do for him, I'm afraid.'

'A favour, Carlos. When we leave, may we go up to your cabin or whatever you call the place we met you first?'

'Certainly. May one ask why?'

'If you'd been standing frozen in that damned passage-way for an hour and a half you'd understand why.'

'Of course. Restoratives. Help yourselves, gentlemen. I'll step by and let you know how Cola is.' He paused then added drily: 'That should give you plenty of time to prepare your intensive interrogation of me.'

He left almost immediately to be replaced by Pietro, bearing a small sledge-hammer. They closed the door and secured one of the eight water-tight clips. One was enough. George struck it with one blow of the hammer. That, too, was enough – not even a gorilla could now have opened that clip from the inside. They left the sledge-hammer in the passage-way and went directly to the engine-room, which was unmanned, as they had known it would be: all controls were operated from the wheelhouse. It took them less than a minute to find what they were looking for. They made a brief excursion to the upper deck then repaired to Carlos' cabin.

'A thirsty night's work,' George said. He was on his second, or it could have been third, glass of grappa. He looked at the von Karajans' radios on the deck beside him. 'These would have been safer in our cabins. Why have them here?'

'They'd have been too safe in our cabins. Young Michael would never have dared to try to get at them there.'

'Don't try to tell me that he might try to get at them here.'

'Unlikely, I admit. Michael, it is clear, is not cast in the heroic mould. He might, of course, be a consummate actor, but I don't see him as an actor any more than a hero. However, if he's desperate enough – and he must have been desperate to try to get off a message at the time and place he did – he might try.'

'But the radios will be in the safe as soon as Carlos returns. And Carlos has the only key.'

'Carlos might give him that key.'

'Oh! So that's the way our devious mind works. So we keep an eye on our Michael for the remainder of the night? Not that there's all that much left of it. And if he does try to recover the radios, what does that prove except that there is a connection between him and Carlos?'

'That's all I want to prove. I don't expect either would say or admit to anything. They don't have to. At least, Michael doesn't have to. I can have him detained in Ploče for disobedience of orders and suspicion of trying to communicate with the enemy.'

'You really suspect him of that?'

'Good Lord, no. But, no question, he's been trying to communicate with someone and that someone might as well be a spy. It'll look better on a charge sheet. All I want to see is if there's any connection between him and Carlos.'

'And if there is you're prepared to clap him into durance vile?'

'Sure.'

'And his sister?'

'She's done nothing. She can come along with us, hang around Ploče or join him in, as you say, durance vile. Up to her.'

'The very flower of chivalry.' George shook his head and reached for the grappa. 'So we may or may not suspect a connection between Carlos and Michael but we do suspect one between Carlos and Alessandro.'

'I don't. I do think that Carlos knows a great deal more about Alessandro than we do but I don't think he knows what Alessandro is up to on this passage. A very simple point. If Carlos were privy to Alessandro's plans then he, Alessandro, wouldn't have bothered to bring along a kettle and burner: he'd just have gone to the galley and steamed the envelope open.' He turned round as Carlos entered. 'How's Cola?'

'He'll be all right. Well, no danger. His shoulder is a mess. Even if it were a flat calm I wouldn't touch it. It needs a surgeon or an osteologist and I'm neither.' He unlocked a safe, put the radio gear inside then relocked the door. 'Well, no hurry for you, gentlemen, but I must return to the wheelhouse.'

'A moment, please.'

'Yes, Peter?' Carlos smiled. 'The interrogation?'

'No. A few questions. You could save us a lot of time and trouble.'

'What? In interrogating Alessandro? You promised me no torture.'

'I still promise. Alessandro tried to assault us and steal some papers tonight. Did you, do you know about this?'

'No.'

'I believe you.' Carlos raised his eyebrows a little but said nothing. 'You don't seem unduly concerned that your fellow-Italian has been made a prisoner by a bunch of uncivilized Yugoslavs, do you?'

'If you mean does he mean anything personally to me, no.'

'But his reputation does.'

Carlos said nothing.

'You know something about his background, his associations, the nature of his business that we don't. Is that not so?'

'That could be. You can't expect me to divulge anything of that nature.'

'Not expect. Hope.'

'No hope. You wouldn't break the Geneva Conventions to extract that information from me.'

Petersen rose. 'Certainly not. Thank you for your hospitality.'

Petersen was carrying a canvas chair and the metal box of capsules when he entered the cabin in which Alessandro and his three men were imprisoned. George was carrying two lengths of heaving line and the sledge-hammer with which he had just released the outside clip. Alex was carrying only his machine-pistol. Petersen unfolded the chair, sat on it and watched with apparent interest as George hammered home a clip.

'We'd rather not have any interruptions, you see,' Petersen said. He looked at Franco, Sepp and Guido. 'Get into that corner there. If anyone moves Alex will kill him. Take your jacket off, Alessandro.'

Alessandro spat on the floor.

'Take your jacket off,' George said pleasantly, 'or I'll knock you out of it.'

Alessandro, not a man of a very original turn of mind, spat again. George hit him somewhere in the region of the solar plexus, not a very hard blow, it seemed, but enough to make Alessandro double up, whooshing in agony. George removed the jacket.

'Tie him up.'

George set about tying him up. When Alessandro had recovered a little from his initial bout of gasping, he tried to offer some resistance, but an absent-minded cuff from George to the side of the jaw convinced him of the unwisdom of this. George tied him in such a fashion that both arms were lashed immovably to his sides. His knees and ankles were bound together and then, for good measure, George used the second heaving line to lash Alessandro to the cot. No chicken was ever so securely trussed, so immobile, as Alessandro was then.

George surveyed his handiwork with some satisfaction then turned to Petersen: 'Isn't there something in the Geneva Conventions about this?'

'Could be, could be. Truth is, I've never read them.' He opened the metal box and looked at Alessandro. 'In the interests of science, you understand. This shouldn't take any time at all.' The words were light enough but Alessandro wasn't listening to the words, he was looking at the implacable face above and not liking at all what he saw. 'Here we have three blue ampoules and three pink. We think, and Captain Tremino who is also a doctor agrees with us, that three of these are lethal and three non-lethal. Unfortunately, we don't know which is which and there's only one simple, logical way to find out. I'm going to inject you with one of these. If you survive it, then we'll know it's a non-lethal ampoule. If you don't, we'll know it's the other ones that are non-lethal.' Petersen held up two ampoules, one blue, one pink. 'Which would you suggest, George?'

George rubbed his chin thoughtfully. 'A big responsibility. A man's life could hang on my decision. Well, it's not all that big a responsibility. No loss to mankind, anyway. The blue one.'

'Blue it shall be.' Petersen broke the ampoule into a test tube, inserted the needle of the hypodermic and began to withdraw the plunger. Alessandro stared in terrified fascination as the blue liquid seeped up into the hypodermic.

'I'm afraid I'm not very good at this job.' Petersen's conversational calm was more terrifying than any sibilant threats could ever have hoped to be. 'If you're careless an air bubble can get in and an air bubble in the blood stream can be very unpleasant. I mean, it can kill you. However, in your case, I don't think it's going to make very much difference one way or another.'

Alessandro's eyes were staring, his whitened lips drawn back in a rictus of terror. Petersen touched the inside of Alessandro's right elbow. 'Seems a suitable vein to me.' He pinched the vein and advanced the syringe.

'No! No! No!' Alessandro's voice was an inhuman scream torn from his throat. 'God, no! No!'

'You've nothing to worry about,' Petersen said soothingly. 'If it's a non-lethal dose you'll just slip away from us and come back in a few minutes. If it's a lethal dose, you'll just slip away.' He paused. 'Just a minute, though. He just might die in screaming agony.' He brought out a pad of white linen cloth and handed it to George. 'Just in case. But watch your hand, though. When a dying man's teeth clench they stay clenched. Worse, if he draws blood you'll get infected too.'

Petersen pinched the vein between fingers and thumb. Alessandro screamed. George applied the pad to his mouth. After a few seconds, at a nod from Petersen, he withdrew the pad. Alessandro had stopped screaming now and a weird moaning noise came from deep in his throat. He was struggling insanely against his bonds, his face was a mask of madness and a seizure, a heart attack, seemed imminent. Petersen looked at George: the big man's face was masked in sweat.

Petersen said in a quiet voice: 'This is the killer dose, isn't it?' Alessandro didn't hear him. Petersen had to repeat the questions twice before the question penetrated the fear-crazed mind.

'It's the killer dose! It's the killer dose.' He repeated the words several times, the words a babble of near-incoherent terror.

'And you die in agony?'

'Yes, yes! Yes, yes!' He was gasping for breath like a man in the final stages of suffocation. 'Agony! Agony!'

'Which means you have administered this yourself. There can be no pity, Alessandro, no mercy. Besides, you could still

581

be telling a lie.' He touched the tip of the needle against the skin. Alessandro screamed again and again. George applied the clamp.

'Who sent you?' Twice Petersen repeated the question before Alessandro rolled his eyes. George removed the pad.

'Cipriano.' The voice was a barely distinguishable croak. 'Major Cipriano.'

'That's a lie. No major could authorize this.' Careful not to touch the plunger Petersen inserted the tip of the needle just outside the vein. Alessandro opened his mouth to scream again but George cut him off before he could make a sound. 'Who authorized this? The needle's inside the vein now, Alessandro. All I have to do is press the plunger. Who authorized this?'

George removed the pad. For a moment it seemed that Alessandro had lost consciousness. Then his eyes rolled again.

'Granelli.' The voice was a faint whisper. 'General Granelli.' Granelli was the much-feared, much-hated Chief of Italian Intelligence.

'The needle is still inside the vein, my hand is still on the plunger. Does Colonel Lunz know of this?'

'No. I swear it. No!'

'General von Löhr?'

'No.'

'Then how did Granelli know I was on board?'

'Colonel Lunz told him.'

'Well, well. The usual trusting faith between the loyal allies. What did you want from my cabin tonight?'

'A paper. A message.'

'Perhaps you'd better withdraw that syringe,' George said. 'I think he's going to faint. Or die. Or something.'

'What were you going to do with it, Alessandro?' The tip of the needle had remained where it was.

'Compare it with a message.' Alessandro really did look very ill indeed. 'My jacket.'

Petersen found the message in the inside pocket of the jacket. It was the duplicate of the one he had in his cabin. He refolded the paper and put it in his own inside pocket.

'Odd,' George said. 'I do believe he's fainted.'

'I'll bet his victims never had a chance to faint. I wish,' Petersen said with genuine regret, 'that I had pressed that plunger. No question our friend here is – was – a one-man extermination squad.' Petersen sniffed at the test-tube, dropped it and the ampoule to the deck, crushed them both beneath his heel and then squirted the contents of the hypodermic on the deck.

'Spirit-based,' Petersen said. 'It will evaporate quickly enough. Well, that's it.'

In the passage-way, George mopped his forehead. 'I wouldn't care to go through that again. Neither, I'm sure, would Alessandro.'

'Me neither,' Petersen said. 'How do you feel about it, Alex?'

'I wish,' Alex said morosely, 'that you had pushed that plunger. I could have shot him as easy as a wink.'

'That would have been an idea. At least he'd have gone without the agony. In any event, he's all washed up as an operative of any kind or will be as soon as he gets back to Termoli. Or even to Ploče. Let's fix this door.'

All eight water-tight clips were engaged and with each clip in turn, to muffle sound, Alex held in position the pad that had been so lately used for another purpose, while George hammered home the clip. When the eighth had been so dealt with, George said: 'That should hold it for a while. Especially if we throw this hammer overboard.'

'Let's make sure,' Petersen said. He left and returned within a minute with a gas cylinder, a welder's rod and a face-mask. Petersen was, at best, but an amateur welder but

583

what he lacked in expertise he made up in enthusiasm. The completed result would have won him no prizes for finesse but that was unimportant. What was important was that for all practical purposes that door was sealed for life.

'What I'd like to do now,' Petersen said, 'is to have a word with Carlos and Michael. But first, I think, a pause for reflection.'

'How does this sound,' Petersen said. He was seated at Carlos' desk, a scotch in front of him and, beside it, a message he had just drafted. 'We'll have Michael send it off by and by. Plain language, of course. COLONEL LUNZ. Then his code number. YOUR WOULD-BE ASSASSINS AND/OR EX-TERMINATORS A BUNCH OF INCOMPETENTS STOP ALESS-ANDRO AND OTHER BUNGLERS NOW CONFINED FORE CABIN *COLOMBO* BEHIND WELDED STEEL DOOR STOP SORRY CANNOT CONGRATULATE YOU GENERAL VON LOHR GENERAL GRANELLI MAJOR CIPRIANO ON CHOICE OF OPERATIVES REGARDS ZEPPO. "Zeppo", you may recall, is my code name.'

George steepled his fingers. 'Fair,' he said judicially, 'fair. Not entirely accurate, though. We don't *know* that they are assassins and/or etc.'

'How are they to know that we don't know? Should cause quite a stirring in the dovecote. Not too much billing and cooing, wouldn't you think?'

George smiled broadly. 'Colonel Lunz and General von Löhr are going to be fearfully upset. Alessandro said they knew nothing of this set-up.'

'How are they to know that we didn't know,' Petersen said reasonably. 'They'll be fit to be tied and ready to assume anything. I'd love to be listening in to the heated telephone calls among the named parties later on today. Nothing like spreading confusion, dissension, suspicion and mistrust among the loyal allies. Not a bad night's work, gentlemen. I

584

think we're entitled to a small nightcap before going to have a word with Carlos.'

The wheelhouse was lit only by the dim light from the binnacle and it had taken Petersen and his two companions some time to adjust their eyes to the gloom. Carlos himself was at the wheel – at a discreet word from Petersen the helmsman had taken temporary leave of absence.

Petersen coughed, again discreetly, and said: 'I am surprised, Carlos – I would almost say acutely distressed – to find a simple honest sailorman like yourself associating with such notorious and unscrupulous characters as General Granelli and Major Cipriano.'

Carlos, hands on the wheel, continued to gaze straight ahead and when he spoke his voice was surprisingly calm. 'I have never met either. After tonight, I shall take care that I never shall. Orders are orders but I will never again carry one of Granelli's murderous poisoners. They may threaten court-martial but threats are as far as they will go. I take it that Alessandro has talked?'

'Yes.'

'He is alive?' From the tone of his voice Carlos didn't particularly care whether he were or not.

'Alive and well. No torture, as promised. Simple psychology.'

'You wouldn't and couldn't say so unless it were true. I'll talk to him. By and by.' There was no hint of urgency in his voice.

'Yes. Well. I'm afraid that to talk to him you'll have to have yourself lowered in a bo'sun's chair to his cabin porthole. Door's locked, you see.'

'What's locked can be unlocked.'

'Not in this case. We apologize for having taken liberties with an Italian naval vessel but we thought it prudent to weld the door to the bulkhead.'

585

'Ah, so.' For the first time Carlos looked at Petersen his expression registering, if anything, no more than a polite interest. 'Welded? Unusual.'

'I doubt whether you'll find an oxyacetylene lance in Ploče.'

'I doubt it.'

'You might have to go all the way back to Ancona to have them freed. One would hope you are not sunk before you get there. It would be a terrible thing if Alessandro and his friends were to go to a watery grave.'

'Terrible.'

'We've taken another liberty. You did have an oxyacetylene flame. It's at the bottom of the Adriatic.'

Although he could see no gleam of white teeth, Petersen could have sworn that he was smiling.

FOUR

As the seas had remained rough throughout the crossing and
had hardly moderated when they reached what should have
been the comparative shelter of the Neretva Channel between the island of Pelješac and the Yugoslav mainland, the
seven passengers who were in a position to sit down to have
breakfast did not in fact do so until they had actually tied up
to the quay in Ploče. True to Carlos' prediction, because they
had arrived after dawn and were flying a ludicrously large
Italian flag, the harbour garrison had refrained from firing at
them as they made their approach towards the port that not
even the most uninhibited of travel brochure writers would
have described as the gem of the Adriatic.

Breakfast was unquestionably the handiwork of Giovanni,
the engineer: the indescribable mush of eggs and cheese
seemed to have been cooked in diesel oil, and the coffee made
of it, but the bread was palatable and the sea air lent an edge
to the appetite, more especially for those who had suffered
during the passage.

Giacomo pushed his half-finished plate to one side. He was
freshly shaven and, despite the ghastly meal, as cheerful as
ever. 'Where are Alessandro and his cut-throats? They don't
know what they're missing.'

'Maybe they've had breakfast aboard the *Colombo* before,' Petersen said. 'Or already gone ashore.'

'Nobody's gone ashore. I've been on deck.'

'Prefer their own company, then. A secretive lot.'

Giacomo smiled. 'You have no secrets?'

'Having secrets and being secretive are two different things. But no, no secrets. Too much trouble trying to remember who you are supposed to be and what you are supposed to be saying. Especially, if like me, you have difficulty in remembering. Start a life of deception and you end up by being trapped in it. I believe in the simple, direct life.'

'I could believe that,' Giacomo said. 'Especially if last night's performance was anything to go by.'

'Last night's performance?' Sarina, her face still pale from what had obviously been an unpleasant night, looked at him in puzzlement. 'What does that mean?'

'Didn't you hear the shot last night?'

Sarina nodded towards the other girl. 'Lorraine and I both heard a shot.' She smiled faintly. 'When two people think they are dying they don't pay much attention to a trifle like a shot. What happened?'

'Petersen shot one of Alessandro's men. An unfortunate lad by the name of Cola.'

Sarina looked at Petersen in astonishment. 'Why on earth did you do that?'

'Credit where credit is due. Alex shot him – with, of course, my full approval. Why? He was being secretive, that's why.'

She didn't seem to have heard. 'Is he – is he dead?'

'Goodness me no. Alex doesn't kill people.' Quite a number of ghosts would have testified to the contrary. 'A damaged shoulder.'

'Damaged!' Lorraine's dark eyes were cold, the lips compressed. 'Do you mean shattered?'

'Could be.' Petersen lifted his shoulders in a very small shrug indeed. 'I'm not a doctor.'

'Has Carlos seen him?' It was less a question than a demand.

Petersen looked at her thoughtfully. 'What good would that do?'

'Carlos, well –' She broke off as if in confusion.

'Well, what? Why? What could he do?'

'What could he – he's the Captain, isn't he?'

'Both a stupid answer and a stupid question. Why should he see him? I've seen him and I'm certain I've seen many more gunshot wounds than Carlos has.'

'You're not a doctor?'

'Is Carlos?'

'Carlos? How should I know?'

'Because you do,' Petersen said pleasantly. 'Every time you speak you tread deeper water. You are not a born liar, Lorraine, but you are a lousy one. When first we practise to deceive – you know. Deception again – and it's not your forte, I'm afraid. Sure he's a doctor. He told me. He didn't tell you. How did you know?'

She clenched her fists and her eyes were stormy. 'How dare you cross-examine me like this.'

'Odd,' Petersen said contemplatively. 'You look even more beautiful when you're angry. Well, some women are like that. And why are you angry? Because you've been caught out, that's why.'

'You're smug! You're infuriating! So calm, so reasonable, so sure, so self-satisfied, Mr Clever know-all!'

'My, my. Am I all those things? This must be another Lorraine talking. Why have you taken such offence?'

'But you're not so clever. I *do* know he is a doctor.' She smiled thinly. 'If you were clever you'd remember the conversation in the café last night. You'd remember that it came up that I, too, was born in Pescara. Why should I *not* know him?'

'Lorraine, Lorraine. You're not only treading deep water, you're in over your head. You were not born in Pescara. You weren't born in Italy. You're not even Italian.'

589

There was silence. Petersen's quiet statement carried complete conviction. Then Sarina, as angry as Lorraine had been a few moments earlier, said: 'Lorraine! Don't listen to him. Don't even talk to him. Can't you see what he's trying to do? To needle you? To trap you? To make you say things you don't mean to say, just to satisfy his great big ego.'

'I *am* making friends this morning,' Petersen said sadly. 'My great big ego notices that Lorraine hasn't contradicted me. That's because she knows that I know. She also knows that I know she's a friend of Carlos. But not from Pescara. Tell me if I'm wrong, Lorraine.'

Lorraine didn't tell him anything. She just caught her lower lip and looked down at the table.

Sarina said: 'I think you're *horrible*.'

'If you equate honesty with horror then, sure, I'm horrible.'

Giacomo was smiling. 'You certainly do know a lot, don't you, Peter?'

'Not really. I've just learned to learn enough to stay alive.'

Giacomo was still smiling. 'You'll be telling me next that *I'm* not Italian.'

'Not if you don't want me to.'

'You mean I'm *not* Italian?'

'How can you be if you were born in Yugoslavia? Montenegro, to be precise.'

'Jesus!' Giacomo was no longer smiling, but there was neither rancour nor offence in face or tone. Then he started smiling again.

Sarina looked bleakly at Petersen then turned to Giacomo. 'And what else did this – this –'

'Monster?' Petersen said helpfully.

'This monster. Oh, do be quiet. What other outrage did this man commit last night?'

'Well, now.' Giacomo linked his fingers behind his head and seemed prepared to enjoy himself. 'It all depends upon what you call an outrage. To start with, after he had Cola shot he gassed Alessandro and three other men.'

'*Gassed* them?' She stared at Giacomo in disbelief.

'Gassed. It was their own gas he used. They deserved it.'

'You mean he killed them? *Murdered* them?'

'No, no. They recovered. I know. I was there. Simply,' he added hastily, 'you understand, as an observer. Then he took away their guns, and ammunition, and grenades and a few other nasty things. Then he locked them up. That's all.'

'That's all.' Sarina breathed deeply, twice. 'When you say it quickly it sounds like nothing, doesn't it? Why did he lock them up?'

'Maybe he didn't want them to have breakfast. How should I know. Ask him.' He looked at Petersen. 'A pretty fair old job of locking up, if I may say so. I just happened along that way as we were coming into port.'

'Ah!'

'Ah, indeed.' Giacomo looked at Sarina. 'You didn't smell any smoke during the night, did you?'

'Smoke? Yes, we did.' She shuddered, remembering. 'We were sick enough already when we smelled it. That was really the end. Why?'

'That was your friend Peter and *his* friends at work. They were welding up the door of Alessandro's cabin.'

'Welding up the door?' A faint note of hysteria had crept into her voice. 'With Alessandro and his men inside! Why on earth —' She was suddenly at a loss for words.

'I guess he didn't want them to get out.'

The two girls looked at each other in silence. There was nothing more to say. Petersen cleared his throat in a brisk fashion.

'Well, now that's everything satisfactorily explained.' The two girls turned their heads in slow unison and looked at him in total incredulity. 'The past, as they say, is prologue. We'll be leaving in about half an hour or whatever time it takes to

591

obtain some transport. Time to brush your teeth and pack your gear.' He looked at Giacomo. 'You and your friend coming with us?'

'Lorraine, you mean?'

'Got any other friends aboard? Don't stall.'

'All depends where you're going.'

'Same place as you. Don't be cagey.'

'Where are you going?'

'Up the Neretva.'

'We'll come.'

Petersen made to rise when Carlos entered, a piece of paper in his hand. Like Giacomo, he was shaven, brisk and apparently cheerful. He didn't look like a man who hadn't slept all night but then, in his business, he probably slept enough during the day.

'Good morning. You've had breakfast?'

'Our compliments to the chef. That paper for me?'

'It is. Radio signal just come in. Code, so it doesn't make any sense to me.'

Petersen glanced at it. 'Doesn't make any sense to me either. Not until I get the code book.' He folded the paper and put it in an inside pocket.

'Might it not be urgent?' Carlos said.

'It's from Rome. I've invariably found that whenever Rome thinks something is urgent it's never urgent to me.'

Lorraine said: 'We've just heard that a man has been shot. Is he badly hurt?'

'Cola?' Carlos didn't sound very concerned about Cola's health. 'He thinks he is. I don't. Anyway, I've sent for an ambulance. Should have been here by now.' He looked out of the small window. 'No ambulance. But a couple of soldiers approaching the gangway. If, that is, you could call them soldiers. One's about ninety, the other ten. Probably for you.'

'We'll see.'

Carlos had exaggerated the age disparity between the two soldiers but not by much: the younger was indeed a beardless youth, the older well stricken in years. The latter saluted as smartly as his arthritic bones would permit.

'Captain Tremino. You have a Yugoslav army officer among your passengers?'

Carlos waved a hand. 'Major Petersen.'

'That's the name.' The ancient saluted again. 'Commandant's compliments, sir, and would you be so kind as to see him in his office. You and your two men.'

'Do you know why?'

'The Commandant does not confide in me, sir.'

'How far is it?'

'A few hundred metres. Five minutes.'

'Right away.' Petersen stood and picked up his machine-pistol. George and Alex did the same. The older soldier coughed politely.

'The commandant doesn't like guns in his office.'

'No guns? There is a war in progress, this is a military post, and the commandant doesn't like guns.' He looked at George and Alex, then slipped off his machine-pistol. 'He's probably in his dotage. Let's humour him.'

They left. Carlos watched through the window as they descended the gangway to the quayside. He sighed.

'I can't bear it. I can't. As an Italian, I can't bear it. It's like sending a toothless old hound and a frisky puppy to round up three timber wolves. Sabre-toothed tigers, more like.' He raised his voice. 'Giovanni!'

Sarina said hesitatingly: 'Are they really like that? I mean, I heard a man in Rome yesterday call them that.'

'Ah! My old friend Colonel Lunz, no doubt.'

'You know the Colonel?' There was surprise in her voice. 'I thought – well, everybody seems to know everything around here. Except me.'

'Of course I know him.' He turned as the lean, dyspeptic

593

looking engineer-chef appeared in the doorway. 'Breakfast, Giovanni, if you would.'

Giacomo said wonderingly: 'You can really eat that stuff?'

'Atrophied taste-buds, a zinc-lined stomach, a little imagination and you could be in Maxim's. Sarina, one does not approach me at the quayside at Termoli, jerk a thumb towards the east and ask for a lift to Yugoslavia. Do you think you'd be aboard the *Colombo* if I didn't know the Colonel? Do you have to be suspicious about everyone?'

'I'm suspicious about our Major Petersen. I don't trust him an inch.'

'That's a fine thing to say about a fellow-countryman.' Carlos sat and buttered bread. 'Honest and straightforward sort of fellow, one would have thought.'

'One would have – look, we've got to go up into the mountains with that man!'

'He seems to know his way around. In fact, I know he does. You should reach your destination all right.'

'Oh, I'm sure. Whose destination – his or ours?'

Carlos looked at her in mild exasperation. 'Do you have any option?'

'No.'

'Then why don't you stop wasting your breath?'

'Carlos! How can you talk to her like that?' Lorraine's voice was sharp enough to bring a slightly thoughtful look to Giacomo's face. 'She's worried. Of course she's worried. I'm worried, too. We're both going up into the mountains with that man. You're not.' She was either nervous or had a low temper flash-point. 'It's all very well for you sitting safe and sound here aboard the *Colombo*.'

'Oh, come now,' Giacomo said easily. 'I don't think that's being too fair. I'm quite sure, Carlos, that she didn't mean what she implied.' He looked at Lorraine in mock-reproval. 'I'm sure Carlos would willingly leave his safe and sound ship

594

and accompany you into the mountains. But there are two inhibiting factors. Duty and a tin leg.'

'I *am* sorry.' She was genuinely contrite and put her hand on Carlos' shoulder to show it: Carlos, who was addressing himself to the confection that Giovanni had just brought, looked up at her and smiled amiably. 'Giacomo's right' she said. 'Of course I didn't mean it. It's just that – well, Sarina and I feel so helpless.'

'Giacomo is in the same position. He doesn't look in the slightest bit helpless to me.'

She shook his shoulder in exasperation. 'Please. You don't understand. We don't know what's going on. We don't know *anything*. He seems to know everything.'

'He? Peter?'

'Who else would I be talking about?' For so patrician-looking a lady she could be very snappish. 'Perhaps I can shake you out of your complacency. Do you know that he knows where Giacomo and I are going? Do you know that he seems to know about my background? Do you know that he knows I'm not Italian? That he knows that you and I knew each other in the past, but not in Pescara?'

If Carlos was shaken he concealed it masterfully. 'Peter knows a great number of things that you wouldn't expect him to. Or so Colonel Lunz tells me. For all I know Colonel Lunz told him about you and Giacomo, although that wouldn't be like the Colonel. He may have expected you aboard. He didn't seem annoyed by your presence.'

'He was annoyed enough by Alessandro's presence.'

'He wouldn't know about Alessandro. Alessandro is controlled by another agency.'

She said quickly: 'How do you know that?'

'He – Peter – told me.'

She removed her hand and straightened. 'So. You and Peter have your little secrets too.' She turned to Sarina. 'We can trust everybody, can't we?'

Giacomo said: 'Carlos, you're beginning to look like a hen-pecked husband.'

'I'm beginning to feel like one, too. My dear girl, I only learnt this during the night. What did you expect me to do? Come hammering on your cabin door at four in the morning to announce this earth-shaking news to you and Sarina?' He looked up as the dyspeptic engineer-chef appeared again in the doorway.

'Breakfast has been served, Carlos.'

'Thank you, Giovanni.' He looked at Lorraine. 'And before you start getting suspicious of Giovanni he only means that he's given food to our friends in the fore cabin.'

'I thought the door was locked.'

'Oh dear, oh dear.' Carlos laid down knife and fork. 'Suspicious again. The door *is* locked. Breakfast was lowered in a bucket to their cabin porthole.'

'When are you going to see them?'

'When I'm ready. When I've had breakfast.' Carlos picked up his knife and fork again. 'If I get peace to eat it, that is.'

George said: 'Took a bit of a risk back there, didn't you? Chanced your arm, as they say, pretending you knew all about their plans and backgrounds when you knew nothing.'

'Credit's all yours, George. Just based on a couple of remarks of yours about ethnic background. Couldn't very well tell them that, though. Besides, Lorraine gave away more than I extracted. I don't think she'd make a very good espionage agent.'

They were threading their way through cranes, trucks, both army and civilian, and scattered dock buildings, a few yards behind the two Italian soldiers. The snow had stopped now, the Rilić hills were sheltering them from the north-east wind but the temperature was still below freezing point. There were few enough people around, the early hour and the cold were not such as to encourage outdoor activity. The soldiers, as Carlos had said, were either reservists or youths. The few civilians around were in the same age categorics. There didn't seem to be a young or middle-aged man in the port.

'At least,' George said, 'you've established a kind of moral ascendancy over them. Well, over the young ladies, anyway. Giacomo doesn't lend himself to that sort of thing. That paper Carlos gave you – a message from our Roman allies?'

'Yes. We are requested to remain in Ploče and await further orders.'

'Ridiculous.'

'Isn't it?'

'You think sending that cablegram was wise? We might have expected this.'

'I did. I hoped to precipitate exactly this. We know what to expect and we've got the initiative. If we'd got clear of the port without trouble and then were stopped by a couple of tanks up the valley road we'd have lost the initiative. Our two guards in front there – they're not very bright, are they?'

'You mean they didn't search us for hand-guns? One's too old to care, the other's too inexperienced to know. Besides, look at our honest faces.'

The two guards led the way to a low wooden hut, obviously a temporary affair, up some steps and, after knocking, into a small room about as spartan and primitive as the exterior of the hut – cracked linoleum on the floor, two metal filing cabinets, a radio transceiver, a telephone, a table and some chairs. The officer behind the table rose at their entrance. He was a tall thin man, middle-aged, with pebble glasses which explained clearly enough why he wasn't at the front. He peered at them myopically over the tops of his glasses.

'Major Petersen?'

'Yes. Glad to meet you, Commandant.'

'Oh. I see. I wonder.' He cleared his throat. 'I have just received a detention order –'

597

'Ssh!' Petersen had a finger to his lips. He lowered his voice. 'Are we alone?'

'We are.'

'Quite sure?'

'Quite sure.'

'In that case put your hands up.'

Carlos pushed his chair back and rose. 'Excuse me. I must have a look at that cabin door.'

Lorraine said: 'You mean you haven't seen it yet?'

'No. If Peter says it's welded, then it is. I should imagine one welded door looks very much like another. Curiosity, really.'

He was back in just over a minute.

'A welded door is a welded door and the only way to open it is with an oxyacetylene flame-cutter. I've sent Pietro ashore to try and find one. I don't have much hope. We had one but Peter and his friends dropped it over the side.'

Lorraine said: 'You don't seem worried about it.'

'I don't get worried about trifles.'

'And if you can't get them out?'

'They'll have to stay there till we get back to Termoli. Plenty of facilities there.'

'You could be sunk before you get there. Have you thought of that?'

'Yes. That would upset me.'

'Well, that's better. A little compassion, at least.'

'It would upset me because I've really grown quite fond of this old boat. I would hate to think it would be Alessandro's tomb.' Carlos' face and voice were cold. 'Compassion? Compassion for that monster? Compassion for a murderer, a hired assassin, a poisoner who travels with hypodermics and ampoules of lethal liquids? Compassion for a psychopath who would just love to inject you or Sarina there and giggle his evil head off as you screamed your way to death? Peter

598

spared him: I wish he'd killed him. Compassion!' He turned and walked out.

'And now you've upset him,' Giacomo said. 'Nag, nag, nag. It's bloody marvellous. People – well, Peter and Carlos – tried, judged and condemned when you don't have the faintest idea what you're talking about.'

'I didn't mean anything.' She seemed bewildered.

'It's not what you mean. It's what you say. You could always try watching your tongue.' He rose and left.

Lorraine stared at the empty doorway, her face woebegone. Two large tears trickled slowly down her cheeks. Sarina put her arm around her shoulders.

'It's all right,' she said. 'It really is. They don't understand. I do.'

Ten minutes later Petersen and his two companions arrived. Petersen was driving an elderly truck, civilian not army, with a hooped canvas roof and canvas flaps at the rear. Petersen jumped down from the driving seat and looked at the five on the deck of the *Colombo* – Carlos, Giacomo, Lorraine, Michael and Sarina, the last four with their rucksacks and radios beside them.

'Well, we're ready when you are,' Petersen said. He seemed in excellent spirits. 'We'll just come aboard for our gear.'

'No need,' Carlos said. 'The two Pietros are bringing that.'

'And our guns?'

'I wouldn't want you to feel undressed.' Carlos led the way down the gangway. 'How did things go?'

'Couldn't have been better. Very friendly, cooperative and helpful.' He produced two papers. 'A military pass and a permit for me to drive this vehicle. Only as far as Metković but it will at least get us on the way. Both signed by Major Massamo. Would you two young ladies come up front with me? It's much more comfortable and the cab is heated. The back is not.'

'Thank you,' Lorraine said. 'I'd rather sit in the back.'

'Oh, no, she wouldn't,' Sarina said. 'I'm not putting up with this walking inquisition all by myself.' She took Lorraine's arm and whispered in her ear while Petersen lifted patient eyes to heaven. At first Lorraine shook her head vigorously, then reluctantly nodded.

They shook hands with Carlos, thanked him and said goodbye. All except Lorraine – she just stood there, her eyes on the dockside. Carlos looked at her in exasperation then said: 'All right. You upset me and I, forgetting that I'm supposed to be an officer and a gentleman, upset you.' He put his arm round her shoulders, gave her a brief hug and kissed her none too lightly on the cheek. 'That's by way of apology and goodbye.'

Petersen started up the rather asthmatic engine and drove off. The elderly guard at the gate ignored Petersen's proffered papers and lackadaisically waved them on: he probably didn't want to leave the brazier in his sentry-box. As he drove on, Petersen glanced to his right. Lorraine, at the far end of the seat was staring straight ahead: her face was masked in tears. Petersen, frowning, leaned forward and sideways but was brought up short by a far from gentle elbow in the ribs. Sarina, too, was frowning and giving an almost imperceptible shake of the head. Petersen looked at her questioningly, got a stony glance in return and sat back to concentrate on his driving.

In the back of the truck, already heavily polluted by George's cigars, Giacomo kept glancing towards the tarpaulin-covered heap in the front. Eventually, he tapped George on the arm.

'George?'

'Yes.'

'Have you ever seen a tarpaulin moving of its own accord?'

'Can't say that I have.'

'Well, I can see one now.'

George followed the direction of the pointing finger. 'I see what you mean. My goodness, I hope they're not suffocating under that lot.' He pulled back the tarpaulin to reveal three figures lying on their sides, securely bound at wrists and ankles and very effectively gagged. 'They're not suffocating at all. Just getting restless.'

The light inside the back of the truck was dim but sufficient to let Giacomo recognize the elderly soldier and his very junior partner who had come aboard earlier in the morning to collect Petersen and the other two. 'And who's the other person?'

'Major Massamo. Commandant – Deputy Commandant, I believe – of the port.'

Michael, seated with Alex on the opposite side of the truck, said: 'Who are those people? What are they doing here? Why are they tied up?' The questions didn't betray any real interest: the voice was dull as befitted one still in a state of dazed incomprehension. They were the first words he had spoken that day: sea-sickness and the traumatic experience he had undergone during the night had wrought their toll to the extent that he had not even been able to face breakfast.

'The Port Commandant and two of his soldiers,' George said. 'They are here because we couldn't very well leave them behind to raise the alarm the moment we were gone, and we couldn't very well shoot them, could we? And they're bound and gagged because we couldn't very well have them raising a song and dance on the way out of the harbour. You do ask stupid questions, Michael.'

'This is the Major Massamo that Major Petersen mentioned? How did you manage to get him to sign those permits you have?'

601

'You, Michael, have a suspicious mind. It doesn't become you. He didn't sign them. I did. There were lots of notices in his room all signed by him. You don't have to be a skilled forger to copy a signature.'

'What's going to happen to them?'

'We will dispose of them at a convenient time and place.'

'Dispose of them?'

'They'll be back in Ploče, safe and unharmed, this evening. Good heavens, Michael, you don't go around shooting your allies.'

Michael looked at three bound and gagged men. 'Yes. I see. Allies.'

They were stopped at roadblocks at the next two villages but the questioning was very perfunctory and routine. At the third village, Bagalović, Petersen pulled up by a temporary army filling station, descended, gave some papers to the corporal in attendance, waited until the truck had been fuelled, gave the corporal some money for which he was rewarded by a surprised salute, then drove off again.

Sarina said: 'They don't look like soldiers to me. They don't behave like soldiers. They seem so – so – what is the word? – apathetic.'

'A marked lack of enthusiasm, agreed. Their behaviour doesn't show them up in the best of light, does it? The Italians can, in fact, be very very good soldiers, but not in this war. They have no heart for it, in spite of Mussolini's stirring, martial speeches. The people didn't want this war in the first place and they want it less and less as time goes by. Their front-line troops fight well enough, but not from patriotism, just professional pride. But it's convenient for us.'

'What were those papers you gave to that soldier?'

'Diesel coupons. Major Massamo gave them to me.'

602

'Major Massamo gave them to you. Free fuel, of course. That tip you handed to the soldier. I suppose Major Massamo gave you the money as well?'

'Of course not. We don't steal.'

'Just trucks and fuel coupons. Or have you just borrowed those?'

'Temporarily. The truck, anyway.'

'Which, of course, you will return to Major Massamo?'

Petersen spared her a glance. 'You're supposed to be apprehensive, nervous, not full of nosey questions. I don't much care to be cross-examined. We're supposed to be on the same side, remember? As for the truck, I'm afraid the Major won't be seeing it again.'

They drove on in silence and after another fifteen minutes ran into the town of Metković. Petersen parked the truck in the main street and stepped down to the roadway. Sarina said: 'Forgotten something, haven't you?'

'What?'

'Your keys. You've left them in the ignition.'

'Please don't be silly.' Petersen crossed the street and disappeared into a store.

Lorraine spoke for the first time since leaving Ploče. 'What did he mean by that?'

'What he says. He knows so much that he probably knows I can't drive anyway. Certainly not this rackety old monster. Even if I could, what place would I have to drive to?' She touched the back of the cab. 'Wood. I couldn't get five yards – that fearful Alex could shoot through that.' She looked and sounded doleful in the extreme.

Lorraine said: 'Wouldn't it be nice to see him, just once, make a mistake, do something wrong?'

'I'd love it. But I don't think we should want it. I have the feeling that what is good for Major Petersen is good for us. And vice versa.'

Twenty minutes elapsed before Petersen returned. For a man who might have been regarded as being on the run, he was in no hurry. He was carrying a large wicker basket, its contents covered with brown paper. This he took round to the back of the truck. Moments later he was back in the driving seat. He seemed in good humour.

'Well, go on,' he said. 'Ask away.'

Sarina made a moue, but curiosity won. 'The basket.'

'An army marches on its stomach. Stretch a point and you might regard us as part of an army. Provisions. What else would I have been buying in a food store? Bread, cheese, hams, various meats, goulash, fruits, vegetables, tea, coffee, sugar, a spirit stove, kettle and stewpan. I promised Colonel Lunz to deliver you in fairly good condition.'

In spite of herself, she smiled faintly. 'You sound as if you wanted to deliver us in prime condition at a slave market. Overlooked your fat friend, didn't you?'

'My first purchase. George had the top off a litre flask of beer within five seconds. Wine, too.'

They cleared the outskirts of the town. Sarina said: 'I thought the permit took you only as far as Metković?'

'I have two permits. I showed only one to Carlos.'

Half an hour later Petersen recrossed the Neretva and pulled up at a fairly large garage on the outskirts of Čapljina. Petersen went inside and returned in a few minutes.

'Just saying "hallo" to an old friend.'

They passed through the village of Trebižat and not long afterwards Petersen pulled off the highway and turned up a secondary road, climbing fairly steeply as they went. From this they turned on to yet another road which was no more than a grass track, still climbing, until they finally rounded and came to a halt about fifty yards from a low stone building. They could approach no further because the road ended where they were.

604

They dismounted from the cab and went round to the back of the truck. Petersen tweaked back one of the canvas flaps. 'Lunch,' he said.

Perhaps a minute passed without any signs of activity. Sarina and Lorraine looked at each other in a puzzled apprehension which was in no way lessened by Petersen's air of relaxed calm.

'When George ties a knot,' Petersen said cryptically, 'it takes a fair deal of untying.'

Suddenly the flaps were parted and Major Massamo and his two soldiers, untied and ungagged, were lowered from the tailboard. Massamo and the older soldier collapsed dramatically immediately on touching the ground.

'"Who have we here and what have the wicked Petersen and his evil friends done to those poor men",' Petersen said. The young soldier had now joined the two others in a sitting position on the ground. 'Well, the officer is Major Massamo, the Port Commandant, and the other two you have already seen. We have not broken their legs or anything like that. They're just suffering from a temporary loss of circulation.' The other four men in the back of the truck had now jumped to the ground. 'Walk them around a bit, will you?' Petersen said.

George lifted the Major, Giacomo the young soldier, and Michael the elderly soldier. But the last was not only old but fat and didn't seem at all keen to get to his feet. Sarina gave Petersen what was probably intended to be a withering glance and moved to help her brother. Petersen looked at Lorraine and then at George.

'What shall we do?' His voice was low. 'Stab her or club her?'

Not a muscle flickered in George's face. He appeared to ponder. 'Either. Plenty of ravines hereabouts.'

Lorraine looked at them in perplexity: Serbo-Croat, evidently, was not her language.

Petersen said: 'I can understand now why the boyfriend is along. Bodyguard *and* interpeter. I know who she is.'

'So do I.'

Lorraine could be irritated and imperious at the same time and she was good at being both.

'What are you two talking about? It *is* bad manners, you know.' In another day and age she would have stamped her foot.

'It is our native language. No offence. My dear Lorraine, you would make life so much easier for yourself if you stopped being suspicious of everyone. And yes, we were talking about you.'

'I thought as much.' But her voice was a shade less assertive.

'Just try to trust people occasionally.' Petersen smiled to rob his words of any offence. 'We're as much looker-afterers as your Giacomo is. Will you please understand that we want to take care of you. If anything were to happen to you, Jamie Harrison would never forgive us.'

'Jamie Harrison! You know Jamie Harrison.' Her eyes had widened and a half-smile touched her lips. 'I don't believe it. You know Captain Harrison!'

'"Jamie" to you.'

'Jamie.' She looked at George. 'Do you know him?'

'Tush, tush! Suspicions again. If Peter says he knows him then I must know him. Isn't that so?' He smiled as colour touched her cheeks. 'My dear, I don't blame you. Of course I know him. Tall, very tall. Lean. Brown beard.'

'He didn't have a brown beard when I knew him.'

'He has now. And a moustache. Brown hair, anyway. And, as they say in English, he's terribly terribly English. Wears a monocle. Sports it, I should say. Claims he needs it, but he doesn't. Just English.'

She smiled. 'It couldn't be anyone else.'

Major Massamo and his two men, their grimaces bespeaking their still returning circulation, were now at least partially mobile. Petersen retrieved the heavy wicker basket from the back of the truck and led the way up grass-cut steps to the stone hut and produced a key. Sarina looked at the key, then at Petersen but said nothing.

Petersen caught her glance. 'I told you. Friends.' The combination of the creaking hinges as the door swung open and the musty smell from within was indication enough that the place hadn't been used for months. The single room, which made up the entire hut, was icy, bleak and sparsely furnished: a deal table, two benches, a few rickety wooden chairs, a stove and a pile of cordwood.

'Be it ever so humble,' Petersen said briskly. 'First things first.' He looked at George who had just extracted a bottle of beer from the basket. 'You have your priorities right?'

'I have a savage thirst,' George said with dignity. 'I can slake that and light a stove at the same time.'

'You'll look after our guests? I have a call to make.'

'Half an hour. I hope.'

It was an hour later when Petersen returned. George was no believer in doing things by half and by that time the hut was a great deal more than pleasantly warm. The top of the stove glowed a bright cherry red and the room was stiflingly hot. Petersen pointedly left the door open and set on the table a second wicker basket he had brought with him.

'More provisions. Sorry I'm late.'

'We weren't worried,' George said. 'Food's ready when you are. We've eaten.' He peered inside the basket Petersen had brought. 'Took you all that time to get that?'

'I met some friends.'

Sarina said from the doorway. 'Where's the truck?'

'Round the corner. Among trees. Can't be seen from the air.'

'You think they're carrying out an air search for us?'

607

'No. One doesn't take chances.' He sat at the table and made himself a cheese and salami sandwich. 'Anyone who needs some sleep had better have it now. I'm going to have some myself. We didn't have any last night. Two or three hours. Besides, I prefer to travel at night.'

'And I prefer to sleep at night,' George said. He reached out for another bottle. 'Let me be your trusty guard. Enjoy yourself. We did.'

'After Giovanni's cooking anyone would be ravenous.'

.Petersen set about proving that he was no exception. After a few minutes he looked up, looked around and said to George: 'Where have those pesky girls gone to?'

'Just left. For a walk, I suppose.'

Petersen shook his head. 'My fault. I didn't tell you.' He rose and went outside. The two girls were about forty yards away.

'Come back!' he called. They stopped and turned around. He waved a peremptory arm. 'Come back.' They looked at each other and slowly began to retrace their steps.

George was puzzled. 'What's wrong with a harmless walk?'

Petersen lowered his voice so that he couldn't be heard inside the hut. 'I'll tell you what's wrong with a harmless walk.' He told him briefly and George nodded. He stopped talking as the girls approached.

Sarina said: 'What is it? What's wrong?'

Petersen nodded to a small outhouse some yards from the cabin. 'If that's what you're looking for –'

'No. Just a walk. What's the harm?'

'Get inside.'

'If you say so.' Sarina smiled at him sweetly. 'Would it kill you to tell us why?'

'Other ranks don't talk to officers in that tone. The fact that you're females doesn't alter a thing.' Sarina had stopped smiling, Petersen's own tone was not such as to encourage levity. 'I'll tell you why. Because I say so. Because you can't do anything without my permission. Because you're babes in the woods. And because I'll trust you when you trust me.' The two girls looked at each other in incomprehension then went inside without a word.

'A bit harsh, I would have thought,' George said.

'You and your middle-aged susceptibility. Sure, it was a bit harsh. I just wanted them to get the message that they don't wander without permission. They could have made it damned awkward for us.'

'I suppose so. Of course I know they could. But they don't know they could have. For them, you're just a big, bad, bullying wolf and a nasty one to boot. Irrational, they think you are. Orders for orders' sake. Never mind, Peter, when they come to appreciate your sterling qualities, they may yet come to love you.'

Inside the hut, Petersen said: 'Nobody is to go outside, please. George and Alex of course. And, yes, Giacomo.'

Giacomo, seated on a bench by the table, lifted a drowsy head from his folded arms. 'Giacomo's not going anywhere.'

Michael said: 'Not me?'

'No.'

Then why Giacomo?

Petersen was curt. 'You're not Giacomo.'

Petersen woke two hours later and shook his head to clear it. As far as he could tell only the indefatigable George, a beaker of beer to hand, and the three captives were awake. Petersen got up and shook the others.

'We're going shortly. Time for tea, coffee, wine or what you will and then we're off.' He started to feed cordwood into the stove.

Major Massamo, who had kept remarkably quiet since his gag had been taken off, said: 'We're going with you?'

'You're staying here. Bound, but not gagged – you can

609

shout your heads off but no-one will hear you.' He raised a hand to forestall a protest. 'No, you won't perish of cold during the long watches of the night. You'll be more than warm enough until help comes. About an hour after we leave I'll phone the nearest army post – it's only about five kilometres from here – and tell them where you are. They should be here within fifteen minutes of getting the call.'

'You're very kind, I'm sure.' Massamo smiled wanly. 'It's better than being shot out of hand.'

'The Royal Yugoslav Army takes orders from no-one, and that includes Germans and Italians. When our allies prove to be obstructive we're forced to take some action to protect ourselves. But we don't shoot them. We're not barbarians.'

A short time later Petersen looked at the three freshly-bound captives. 'The stove is stoked, there's no possibility of sparks, so you won't burn to death. You'll certainly be freed inside an hour and a half. Goodbye.'

None of the three prisoners said "goodbye" to him.

Petersen led the way down the grassy steps and round the first corner. The truck was standing in a small clearing without a tree near it. Sarina said: 'Ooh! A *new* truck.'

'"Ooh! A *new* truck",' Petersen mimicked. 'Which is exactly what you would have said when you'd come back to the hut after finding it. It's as I say, you can't trust babes in the woods. Major Massamo would just have loved to hear you say that. He would then have known that we had ditched the old truck and would have called off the hunt for the old truck – there must be a search under way by now – and, when freed, ask for a search for another missing truck and broadcast its details. It's most unlikely, but it could have happened and then I'd have been forced to lumber myself with Massamo again.'

Giacomo said: 'Someone might stumble across the old one?'

'Not unless someone takes it into his head to go diving into the freezing Neretva River. And why on earth should anyone be daft enough to do that? I drove it off only a very small cliff but the water is deep there. A local fisherman told me.'

'Can it be seen underwater?'

'No. At this time of year the waters of the Neretva are brown and turgid. In a few months' time, when the snow in the mountains melts, then the river runs green and clear. Who worries about what happens in a few months' time?'

George said: 'What kindly soul gave you this nice new model? Not, I take it, the Italian army?'

'Hardly. My fisherman friend, who also happens to be the proprietor of the garage I stopped at on the way up here. The army has no local repair facilities here and he does the occasional repair job for them. He had a few civilian trucks he could have offered me but we both thought this was much more suitable and official.'

'Won't your friend be held answerable for this?'

'Not at all. We've already wrenched off the padlock at the rear of the garage just in case some soldier happens by tomorrow, which is most unlikely, as it is Sunday. Come Monday morning, as a good collaborator should, he'll go to the Italian army authorities and report a case of breaking, entering and theft of one army motor vehicle. No blame will attach to him. The culprits are obvious. Who else could it be but us?'

Sarina said, 'And come Monday morning? When the search starts?'

'Come Monday morning this truck will probably have joined the old one. Whatever happens, we'll be a long way away from it by then.'

'You *are* devious.'

'You're being silly again. This is what you call forward planning. Get inside.'

The new truck was rather more comfortable and much quieter than the old one. As they drove off, Sarina said: 'I'm

611

not carping or criticizing but – well, you do have rather a cavalier attitude towards the property of your allies.'

Petersen glanced at her then returned his attention to the road. '*Our* allies.'

'What? Oh! Yes, of course. Our allies.'

Petersen kept looking ahead. He could have become suddenly thoughtful but it was impossible to tell. Petersen's expression did what he told it to do. He said: 'That mountain inn yesterday. Lunch-time. Remember what George said?'

'Remember – how could I? He says so much – all the time. Said about what?'

'Our allies.'

'Vaguely.'

'Vaguely.' He clucked his tongue in disapproval. 'This augurs ill. A radio operator – any operative – should remember everything that is said. Our alliance is simply a temporary measure of convenience and expediency. We are fighting *with* the Italians – George said "Germans" but it's the same thing – not *for* them. We are fighting for ourselves. When they have served their purpose it will be time for them to be gone. In the meantime, a conflict of interests has arisen between the Italians and the Germans on the one hand and us on the other. Our interests come first. Pity about the trucks but the loss of one or two isn't going to win or lose the war.'

There was a short silence then Lorraine said: 'Who *is* going to win this dreadful war, Major Petersen?'

'We are. I'd rather you'd just call me Peter. As long as you're otherwise civil, that is.'

The two girls exchanged glances. If Petersen saw the exchange he gave no signs.

In Čapljina, in the deepening dusk, they were halted at an army roadblock. A young officer approached, shone his torch at a piece of paper in his hand, switched it to the truck's plates, then played it across the windscreen. Petersen leaned out of the window.

'Don't shine that damned light in our eyes!' he shouted angrily.

The light beam dipped immediately.

'Sorry, sir. Routine check. Wrong truck.' He stepped back, saluted and waved them on. Petersen drove off.

'I didn't like that,' Sarina said. 'What happens when your luck runs out? And why did he let us through so easily?'

'A young man with taste, sensibility and discretion,' Petersen said. 'Who is he, he said to himself, to interfere with an army officer carrying on a torrid affair with two beautiful young ladies. The hunt, however, is on. The paper he held had the number of the old truck. Then he checked driver and passengers, a most unusual thing. He had been warned to look out for three desperadoes. Anyone can see that I'm perfectly respectable and neither of you could be confused with a fat and thin desperado.'

'But they must know we're with you.'

'No "must" about it. They will, soon enough, but not yet. The only two people who knew that you were aboard the ship were the two who are still tied up in the hut back there.'

'Somebody may have asked questions at the *Colombo*.'

'Possibly. I doubt it. Even if they had, no member of the crew would divulge anything without Carlos' okay. He has that kind of relationship with them.'

Sarina said doubtfully: 'Carlos might tell them.'

'Carlos wouldn't volunteer anything. He might have a struggle with his conscience but it would be a brief one and duty would lose out: he's not going to sell his old girlfriend down the river, especially, as is like enough, there would be shooting.'

Lorraine leaned forward and looked at him. 'Who's supposed to be the girlfriend? Me?'

'A flight of fancy. You know how I ramble on.'

613

Twice more they were stopped at roadblocks, both times without incident. Some minutes after the last check, Petersen pulled into a lay-by.

'I'd like you to get in the back, now, please. It's colder there but my fisherman friend did give me some blankets.'

Sarina said: 'Why?'

'Because from now on you might be recognized. I don't think it likely but let's cater for the unlikely. Your descriptions will be out any minute now.'

'How can they be out until Major Massamo –' She broke off and looked at her watch. 'You said you'd phone the army post at Čapljina in an hour. That was an hour and twenty minutes ago. Those men will freeze. Why did you lie –'

'If you can't think, and you obviously can't, at least shut up. Just a little, white, necessary lie. What would have happened if I phoned now or had done in the past twenty minutes?'

'They'd have sent out a rescue party.'

'That all?'

'What else?'

'Heaven help Yugoslavia. They'd have traced the call and know roughly where I am. The call *was* sent on the hour by my friend. From Gruda, on the Čapljina–Imotski road away to the north-west of here. What more natural than we should be making for Imotski – an Italian division is headquartered there. So they'll concentrate their search on the Imotski area. There's an awful lot of places – buildings, store-houses, trucks – where a person can hide in a divisional headquarters, and as the Italians like the Germans about as much as they like the Yugoslavs – and the order for my detention comes from the German HQ in Rome – I don't suppose they'll conduct the search with any great enthusiasm. They *may* have double-guessed – I don't think they'd even bother trying – but go in the back anyway.'

Petersen descended, saw them safely hoisted aboard the

rear of the truck, returned to the cab and drove off.

He passed two more roadblocks – in both cases he was waved on without stopping – before arriving at the town of Mostar. He drove into the middle of the town, crossed the river, turned right by the Hotel Bristol and two minutes later pulled up and stopped the engine. He went round to the back of the truck.

'Please remain inside,' he said. 'I should be back in fifteen minutes.'

Giacomo said: 'Are we permitted to know where we are?'

'Certainly. In a public car park in Mostar.'

'Isn't that rather a public place?' It was, inevitably, Sarina.

'The more public the better. If you really want to hide, there's no place like hiding in the open.'

George said: 'You won't forget to tell Josip that I've had nothing to eat or drink for days?'

'I don't have to tell him. He's always known that.'

When Petersen returned it was in a small fourteen-seater Fiat bus which had seen its heyday in the middle twenties. The driver was a small, lean man with a swarthy complexion, a ferocious black moustache, glittering eyes and a seemingly boundless source of energy.

' 'This is Josip,' Petersen said. Josip greeted George and Alex with great enthusiasm, they were obviously acquaintances of old standing. Petersen didn't bother to introduce him to the others. 'Get your stuff into the bus. We're using the bus because Josip doesn't care too much to have an Italian army lorry parked outside the front door of his hotel.'

'Hotel?' Sarina said. 'We're going to stay in a *hotel*?'

'When you travel with us,' George said expansively, 'you may expect nothing but the best.'

The hotel, when they arrived there, didn't look like the best. The approach to it could not have been more uninviting. Josip parked the bus in a garage and led the way along a

615

narrow winding lane that was not even wide enough to accommodate a car, fetching up at a heavy wooden door.

'Back entrance,' Petersen said. 'Josip runs a perfectly respectable hotel but he doesn't care to attract too much attention by bringing so many people in at once.'

They passed through a short passage into the reception area, small but bright and clean.

'Now then.' Josip rubbed his hands briskly, he was that kind of man. 'If you'll just bring your luggage, I'll show you to your rooms. Wash and brush up, then dinner.' He spread his hands. 'No Ritz, but at least you won't go to bed hungry.'

'I can't face the stairs, yet,' George said. He nodded towards an archway. 'I think I'll just go and rest quietly in there.'

'Barman's off tonight, Professor. You'll have to help yourself.'

'I can take the rough with the smooth.'

'This way, ladies.'

In the corridor upstairs Sarina turned to Petersen and said in a low voice: 'Why did your friend call George "Professor"?'

'Lots of people call him that. A nickname. You can see why. He's always pontificating.'

Dinner was rather more than Josip had promised it would be but, then, Bosnian innkeepers are renowned for their inventiveness and resourcefulness, not to mention acquisitiveness. Considering the ravaged and war-stricken state of the country, the meal was a near miracle: Dalmatian ham, grey mullet with an excellent Pošip white wine and, astonishingly, venison accompanied by one of the renowned Neretva red wines. George, after remarking, darkly, that one never knew what the uncertain future held for them, thereafter remained silent for an unprecedented fifteen minutes: no mean trencherman at the best of times, his current exercise in gastronomy bordered on the awesome.

Apart from George, his two companions and their host, Marija, Josip's wife, was also at the table. Small, dark and energetic like her husband, she was in other ways in marked contrast to him: he was intense, she was vivacious: he was taciturn, she was talkative to the point of garrulity. She looked at Michael and Sarina, seated some distance away at one small table, and at Giacomo and Lorraine, seated about the same distance away, at another, and lowered her voice.

'Your friends are very quiet.'

George swallowed some venison. 'It's the food.'

'They're talking, all right,' Petersen said. 'You just can't hear them over the champing noise George is making. But you're right, they are talking very softly.'

Josip said: 'Why? Why do they have to murmur or whisper? There's nothing to be afraid of here. Nobody can hear them except us.'

'You heard what George said. They don't know what the future holds for them. This is a whole new experience for them – not, of course, for Giacomo, but for the other three. They're apprehensive and from their point of view they have every right to be. For all they know, tomorrow may be their last day on earth.'

'It could be yours, too,' Josip said. 'The word in the market-place – we hoteliers spend a lot of time in the market-place – is that groups of Partisans have by-passed the Italian garrison at Prozor, moved down the Rama valley and are in the hills overlooking the road between here and Jablanica. They may even be astride the road: they're crazy enough for anything. What are your plans for tomorrow? If, I may add hastily, one may ask.'

'Why ever not? We'll have to take to the mountains by and by of course, but those three young people don't look much like mountain goats to me so we'll stick as long as possible to the truck and the road. The road to Jablanica, that is.'

'And if you run into the Partisans?'

'Tomorrow can look after itself.'

At the end of the meal, Giacomo and Lorraine rose and crossed to the main table. Lorraine said: 'I tried to have a walk, stretch my legs, this afternoon, but you stopped me. I'd like to have one now. Do you mind?'

'Yes. I mean, I do mind. At the moment, this is very much a frontier town. You're young, beautiful and the streets, as the saying goes, are full of licentious soldiery. Even if a patrol stops you, you don't speak a word of the language. Besides, it's bitterly cold.'

'Since when did you begin to worry about my health?' She was back to being her imperious self again. 'Giacomo will look after me. What you mean is, you still don't trust me.'

'Well, yes, there's that to it also.'

'What do you expect me to do? Run away? Report you to — to the authorities? What authorities? There *is* nothing I can do.'

'I know that. I'm concerned solely with your own welfare.'

Beautiful girls are not much given to snorting in disbelief but she came close. 'Thank you.'

'I'll come along with you.'

'No, thank you. I don't want you.'

'You see,' George said, 'she doesn't even like you.' He pushed back his chair. 'But everyone likes George. Big, cheerful, likeable George. I'll come along with you.'

'I don't want you either.'

Petersen coughed. Josip said: 'The Major is right, you know, young lady. This *is* a dangerous town after dark. Your Giacomo looks perfectly capable of protecting anyone, but there are streets in this town where even the army police patrols won't venture. I know where it's safe to go and where it isn't.'

She smiled. 'You are very kind.'

618

Sarina said: 'Mind if we come, too?'

'Of course not.'

All five, Michael included, buttoned up in their heavy coats and went out, leaving Petersen and his two companions behind. George shrugged his shoulders and sighed.

'To think I used to be the most popular person in Yugoslavia. That was before I met you, of course. Shall we retire?'

'So soon?'

'Through the archway, I meant.' George led the way and ensconced himself behind the bar counter. 'Strange young lady. Lorraine, that is. I muse aloud. Why did she sally forth into the dark and dangerous night. She hardly strikes one as a fresh-air fiend or fitness fanatic.'

'Neither does Sarina. Two strange young ladies.'

George reached for a bottle of red wine. 'Let us concede that the vagaries of womankind, especially young womankind, are beyond us and concentrate more profitably on this vintage '38.'

Alex said suddenly: 'I don't think they're all that strange.'

Petersen and George gave him their attention. Alex spoke so seldom, far less ventured an opinion, that he was invariably listened to when he did speak.

George said: 'Can it be, Alex, that you have observed something that has escaped our attention?'

'Yes. You see, I don't talk as much as you do.' The words sounded offensive but weren't meant to be, they were simply by way of explanation. 'When you're talking I look and listen and learn, while you're listening to yourselves talking. The two young ladies seem to have become very friendly. I think they've become too friendly too quickly. Maybe they really like each other, I don't know. What I do know is that they don't trust each other. I am sure that Lorraine went out to learn something. I don't know what. I think Sarina thought the same thing and wanted to find out, so she's gone to watch.'

George nodded a judicious head. 'A closely reasoned

argument. What do you think they both went out to learn?'

'How should I know?' Alex sounded mildly irritable. 'I just watch. You're the ones who are supposed to think.'

The two girls and their escorts were back even before the three men had finished their bottle of wine, which meant that they had returned in very short order indeed. The two girls and Michael were already slightly bluish with cold and Lorraine's teeth were positively chattering.

'Pleasant stroll?' Petersen said politely.

'Very pleasant,' Lorraine said. Clearly, she hadn't forgiven him for whatever sin he was supposed to have committed. 'I've just come to say goodnight. What time do we leave in the morning?'

'Six o'clock.'

'Six o'clock!'

'If that's too late –'

She ignored him and turned to Sarina. 'Coming?'

'In a moment.'

Lorraine left and George said, 'For a nightcap, Sarina, I can recommend this Maraschino from Zadar. After a lifetime –'

She ignored him as Lorraine had ignored Petersen, to whom she now turned and said: 'You lied to me.'

'Dear me. What a thing to say.'

'George here. His "nickname". The Professor. Because, you said, he was loquacious –'

'I did not. "Pontificated" was the word I used.'

'Don't quibble! Nickname! Dean of the Faculty of Languages and Professor of Occidental Languages at Belgrade University!'

'My word!' Petersen said admiringly. 'You *are* clever. How did you find out?'

She smiled. 'I just asked Josip.'

'Well done for you. Must have come as a shock. I mean, you had him down as the janitor, didn't you?'

She stopped smiling and a faint colour touched her cheeks. 'I did not. And why did you lie?'

'No lie, really. It's quite unimportant. It's just that George doesn't like to boast of his modest academic qualifications. He's never reached the dizzying heights of a degree in economics and politics in Cairo University.'

She coloured again, more deeply, then smiled, a faint smile, but a smile. 'I didn't even qualify. I didn't deserve that.'

'That's true. Sorry.'

She turned to George. 'But what are you doing – I mean, a common soldier –'

Behind the bar, George drew himself up with dignity. 'I'm a very uncommon soldier.'

'Yes. But I mean – a dean, a professor –'

George shook his head sadly. 'Hurling pluperfect subjunctives at the enemy trenches never won a battle yet.'

Sarina stared at him then turned to Petersen. 'What on earth does he mean?'

'He's back in the groves of academe.'

'Wherever we're going,' she said with conviction, 'I don't think we're going to get there. You're mad. Both of you. Quite mad.'

FIVE

It was three-thirty in the morning when Petersen woke. His watch said so. He should not have been able to see his watch because he had switched the light off before going to sleep. It was no longer off but it wasn't the light that had wakened him, it was something cold and hard pressed against his right cheek-bone. Careful not to move his head. Petersen swivelled his eyes to take in the man who held the gun and was sitting on a chair beside the bed. Dressed in a well-cut grey suit, he was in his early thirties, had a neatly trimmed black moustache of the type made famous by Ronald Colman before the war, a smooth clear complexion, an engaging smile and very pale blue, very cold eyes. Petersen reached across a slow hand and gently deflected the barrel of the pistol.

'You need to point that thing at my head? With three of your fellow-thugs armed to the teeth?'

There were indeed three other men in the bedroom. Unlike their leader they were a scruffy and villainous looking lot, dressed in vaguely para-military uniforms but their appearance counted little against the fact that each carried a machine-pistol.

'Fellow thugs?' The man on the chair looked pained. 'That makes me a thug too?'

'Only thugs hold pistols against the heads of sleeping men.'

'Oh, come now, Major Petersen. You have the reputation

of being a highly dangerous and very violent man. How are we to know that you are not holding a loaded pistol in your hand under that blanket?'

Petersen slowly withdrew his right hand from under the blanket and turned up his empty palm. 'It's under my pillow.'

'Ah, so.' The man withdrew the gun. 'One respects a professional.'

'How did you get in? My door was locked.'

'Signor Pijade was most cooperative.' "Pijade" was Josip's surname.

'Was he now?'

'You can't trust anyone these days.'

'I've found that out, too.'

'I begin to believe what people say of you. You're not worried, are you? You're not even concerned about who I might be.'

'Why should I be. You're no friend. That's all that matters to me.'

'I may be no friend. Or I may. I don't honestly know yet. I'm Major Cipriano. You may have heard of me.'

'I have. Yesterday, for the first time. I feel sorry for you, Major, I really do, but I wish I were elsewhere. I'm one of those sensitive souls who feel uncomfortable in hospital wards. In the presence of the sick, I mean.'

'Sick?' Cipriano looked mildly astonished but the smile remained. 'Me? I'm as fit as a fiddle.'

'Physically, no doubt. Otherwise a cracked fiddle and one sadly out of tune. Anyone who works as a hatchet-man for that evil and sadistic bastard, General Granelli, has to be sick in the mind: and anyone who employs as *his* hatchet-man the psychopathic poisoner, Alessandro, has to be himself a sadist, a candidate for a maximum-security lunatic asylum.'

'Ah, so! Alessandro.' Cipriano was either not a man easily

623

to take offence or, if he did, too clever to show it. 'He gave a message for you.'

'You surprise me. I thought your poisoner – and poisonous – friend was in no position to give messages. You have seen him, then?'

'Unfortunately, no. He's still welded up in the fore cabin of the *Colombo*. One has to admit, Major Petersen, that you are not a man to do things by half-measures. But I spoke to him. He says that when he meets you again you'll take a long time to die.'

'He won't. I'll gun him down as I would a mad dog with rabies. I don't want to talk any more about your psycho friend. What do you want of me?'

'I'm not quite sure yet. Tell me, why do you keep referring to Alessandro as a poisoner?'

'You don't know?'

'I might. If I knew what you were talking about.'

'You know that he carried knockout gas-grenades with him?'

'Yes.'

'You knew that he carried a nice little surgical kit with him along with hypodermics and liquids in capsules that caused unconsciousness – some form of scopolamine, I believe?'

'Yes.'

'Do you know that he also carried capsules which, when injected, led to the victims dying in screaming agony?'

Cipriano had stopped smiling. 'That's a lie.'

'May I get out of bed?' Cipriano nodded. Petersen crossed to his rucksack, extracted the metal box he had taken from Alessandro, handed it to Cipriano and said: 'Take that back to Rome or wherever and have the contents of those capsules analyzed. I would not drink or self-inject any of them if I were you. I threatened to inject your friend with the contents of the missing capsule and he fainted in terror.'

'I know nothing about this.'

624

'That I believe. Where would Alessandro get hold of such lethal poison?'

'I don't know that either.'

'That I don't believe. Well, what do you want of me?'

'Just come along with us.' Cipriano led the way to the dining-room where Petersen's six companions were already assembled under the watchful eye of a young Italian officer and four armed soldiers. Cipriano said: 'Remain here. I know you're too professional to try anything foolish. We won't be long.'

George, inevitably, was relaxed in a carver chair, a tankard of beer in his hand. Alex was looking quietly murderous. Giacomo just looked thoughtful. Sarina was tight-lipped and pale while the mercurial Lorraine, oddly enough, was expressionless.

Petersen shook his head. 'Well, well, we're a fine lot. Major Cipriano has just said I was a professional. If –'

'That was Major Cipriano?' George said.

'That's what he says.'

'A fast mover. He doesn't *look* like a Major Cipriano.'

'He doesn't talk like one either. As I was about to say, George, if I were a professional, I'd have posted a guard, a patrolling sentry. Mea culpa. I thought we were safe here.'

'Safe!' Sarina spoke with a wealth of contempt.

'Well, no harm done, let's hope.'

'No harm done!'

Petersen spread his hands. 'There are always compensations. You – and Lorraine – wanted to see me in, what shall we say, a disadvantaged position. Well, you see it now. How do you like it?' There was no reply. 'Two things. I'm surprised they got you, Alex. You can hear a leaf fall.'

'They had a gun at Sarina's head.'

'Ah! And where is our good friend Josip?'

'*Your* good friend,' Sarina said acidly, 'will be helping

Cipriano and his men to find whatever they're looking for.'

'My goodness! What a low opinion – what an immediate low opinion – of my friend.'

'Who tipped them off that we were here? Who let them in? Who gave them the keys – or the master key – to the bedrooms?'

'One of these days,' Petersen said mildly, 'someone's going to clobber you, young lady. You've a waspish tongue and you're far too ready to judge and condemn. If that soldier with the gun at your head had taken the second necessary to pull the trigger he'd be dead now. So, of course, would you. But Alex didn't want you to die. Nobody let them in – Josip never locks his front door. Once in, getting the keys would be no trouble. I don't know who tipped them off. I'll find out. It could even have been you.'

'Me!' She stared at him, at first stunned and then furious.

'No-one's above suspicion. You've said more than once that I don't trust you. If you said that, you must have had reasons to think that I have reservations about you. What reasons?'

'You must be out of your mind.' She wasn't mad any more, just bewildered.

'You've turned pale very suddenly. Why have you turned pale?'

'Leave my sister alone!' Michael's voice was an angry shout. 'She's done nothing! Leave her alone. Sarina? A criminal? A traitor? She's right, you must be out of your mind. Stop tormenting her. Who the hell do you think you are?'

'An army officer who wouldn't hesitate to instruct a very raw enlisted man – boy, I should say – in the elements of discipline. Mind you, a show of spirit at last, but I'm afraid it's mistimed and misplaced. Meantime, you should rest content with the knowledge that *you* are not under suspicion.'

'I'm supposed to be pleased with that while Sarina is under suspicion?'

'I don't care whether you're pleased or not.'

'Look here, Petersen –'

'Petersen? Who's Petersen? "Major Petersen" to a ranker. Or "Sir".' Michael made no reply. 'You're not under suspicion because after you'd transmitted this message to Rome yesterday morning I rendered your radio inoperable. You could have used your sister's tonight, but you wouldn't have had the guts, not after being caught out the previous night. I know you're not very bright but the inference is obvious. Alex, a word with you.'

As brother and sister looked at each other in mingled apprehension, incomprehension and dismay, Alex crossed the room and listened as Petersen began talking to him.

'Stop!' The young Italian officer's voice was sharp.

Petersen looked at him patiently. 'Stop what?'

'Stop talking.'

'Why ever should I? You just let me talk to that young man and girl.'

'I understood that. I don't understand Serbo-Croat.'

'Your lack of education doesn't concern me. To compound your ignorance, we're not talking Serbo-Croat but a Slavonic dialect understood only by this soldier here, the fat gentleman with the beer glass and myself. You think, perhaps, that we are planning a suicidal attack on you, three unarmed men against four machine-guns and a pistol? You can't possibly be so crazy as to think we're so crazy. What rank are you?'

'Lieutenant.' He was a very stiff, very correct and very young, lieutenant.

'Lieutenants don't give orders to majors.'

'You're my prisoner.'

'I have yet to be informed of that. Even if I were, which legally I'm not, I'd be Major Cipriano's prisoner and he would regard me as a very important one and one not to be

molested or harmed in any way, so don't bother looking at
your men. If any of them comes over to try to stop or separate
us I'll take his gun from him and break it over his head and
then you might shoot me. You'd be court-martialled,
cashiered and then, by the stipulations of the Geneva Conventions, face a firing squad. But you know that, of course.'
Petersen hoped the lieutenant didn't, for he himself had no
idea, but apparently the young man didn't either for he made
no further attempt to pursue the matter.

Petersen talked to Alex for no more than a minute, went
behind the bar, picked up a wine bottle and glass – this
without even a raised eyebrow from the young lieutenant
who might have been wondering how many men it took to
constitute a firing squad and sat down at the table with
George. They talked in low and seemingly earnest tones and
were still talking when Cipriano returned with his three
soldiers, Josip and his wife, Marija. Cipriano not only looked
less buoyant and confident than he had done when he had left
the dining-room: he was still smiling, because he was an
habitual smiler, but the smile was of such a diminished
quality that he looked positively morose.

'I am glad to see that you are enjoying yourselves.'

'We might be just a little justifiably annoyed at having our
sleep disturbed.' Petersen replenished his glass. 'But we are
of a forgiving nature, happy and relaxed in our carefree
conscience. You will join us in a nightcap? I'm sure it would
help you to frame a more graceful apology.'

'No nightcap, thank you, but you are correct in saying
that an apology is in order. I have just made a telephone
call.'

'To the wise men of your intelligence HQ, of course.'

'Yes. How did you know?'

'Where else does all the misinformation come from? We,
as you know, are in the same line of business and it happens
to us all the time.'

'I am genuinely sorry to have inconvenienced you all over a stupid false alarm.'

'What false alarm?'

'Papers missing from our Rome HQ. Some misguided genius on General Granelli's staff – I don't know, yet, who it was but I'll find out before the day is over – decided that they had fallen, if that's the word, into the hands of either yourself or one of your group. Very important papers, very top-secret.'

'All missing papers are top-secret. I have some papers with me myself, but I assure you they're not stolen and how top-secret or important they may be I don't know.'

'I know about those papers.' Cipriano waved a dismissive hand and smiled. 'As you're probably well aware. Those other, and much more important papers have never left their safe in Rome. A top-secret filing clerk careless about filing top-secret documents.'

'May one ask what they are about?'

'You may and that's all the answer you'd get. I don't know and even if I did I couldn't tell you. I wish you an undisturbed night – or what's left of it. Again, my apologies. Goodbye, Major Petersen.'

'Goodbye.' Petersen took the extended hand. 'My regards to Colonel Lunz.'

'I will.' Cipriano frowned. 'I hardly know the man.'

'In that case, my regards to Alessandro.'

'I'll give him more than that.' He turned to Josip and took his hand. 'Many thanks, Signor Pijade. You have been most helpful. We will not forget.'

It was Sarina, nothing if not resilient, who broke the conversational hiatus that followed the departure of Cipriano and his men. '"Thank you, Signor Pijade. Most helpful, Signor Pijade. We won't forget, Signor Pijade."'

Josip looked at her in puzzlement then turned to Petersen. 'Is the young lady talking to me?'

'I think she's addressing the company.'

'I don't understand.'

'I don't think she does either. The young lady, as you call her, is under the ridiculous impression that you notified Major Cipriano – one assumes she thinks it was by telephone – of our presence and then took him and his men on a guided tour of the premises, distributing keys where necessary. She may, of course, be trying to divert from herself the suspicion that she is the guilty party.'

Sarina made to speak but an outraged Marija gave her no chance. Three quick steps and she was before the suddenly apprehensive Sarina. The ivory-knuckled fists and arms held rigidly by her sides spoke eloquently of her outrage: her eyes were stormy and her clenched teeth remained that way even when she spoke.

'Such a beautiful face, my dear.' It is difficult not to hiss when one's teeth are clenched. 'Such a delicate complexion. And I have long nails. Should I tear your face because you insult the honour of my husband? Or would a few slaps – hard slaps – be enough for a creature like you?' In the technique of expressing contempt, Marija Pijade had nothing to learn from anyone.

Sarina said nothing. The apprehensive expression on her face had given way to one of near shock.

'A soldier – not the Major, he's a civilized man and was not there – pointed a gun at me. Like this.' Dramatically, she swung up her right arm and pressed her forefinger against her neck. 'Not pointed. Pushed. Pushed hard. Three seconds, he said, for my husband to hand over the master key. I am sure he would not have fired but Josip handed over the key at once. Do you blame him for that?'

Slowly, dumbly, Sarina shook her head.

'But do you still think Josip betrayed you?'

'No. I don't know what to think, but I don't think that any more. I just don't know what to think. I'm sorry, Marija, I'm

630

truly sorry.' She smiled wanly. 'A soldier threatened me with a gun, too. He pressed it in my ear. Maybe that doesn't make for very clear thinking.'

The cold fury in Marija's face gave way to speculation then softened into concern. She took an impulsive step forward, put her arms round the girl and began to stroke her hair.

'I don't think any of us is thinking very clearly. George!' This over Sarina's shoulder. 'What are you thinking of?'

'Šljivovica,' George said decisively. 'The universal specific. If you read the label on a Pellegrino bottle –'

'George!'

'Right away.'

Josip rubbed a blue and unshaven chin. 'If Sarina and I are not the culprits, then we're no nearer to an answer. Who did talk? Have you no suspicions, Peter?'

'None. I don't need any. I know who it is.'

'You know –' Josip turned to the bar, picked up a bottle of Šljivovica from a tray George was preparing, filled a small glass, drained it in two gulps and when he'd finished coughing and spluttering said: 'Who?'

'I'm not prepared to say at the moment. That's not because I'm intending to prolong anxiety, increase tension, give the villain enough rope to hang him – or herself – or anything stupid like that. It's because I can't prove it – yet. I'm not even sure I want to prove it. Perhaps the person I have in mind was misguided, or the action may have been unintentional, accidental, inadvertent or even done from the best motives – from, of course, the viewpoint of the person concerned. Unlike Sarina here, I don't go in much for premature judgments and condemnation.'

'Peter!' Marija's voice held a warning, almost peremptory, note. She still had an arm around Sarina's shoulders.

'Sorry, Marija. Sorry, Sarina. Just my natural nastiness surfacing. By the way, if you people want to go to bed, well of course, go. But no hurry now. Change of plan. We won't be leaving until the late forenoon tomorrow. Certainly not before. Giacomo, could I have a quiet word with you?'

'Have I any option?'

'Certainly. You can always say "no".'

Giacomo smiled his broad smile, stood up and put his hand in his pocket. 'Josip, if I could buy a bottle of that excellent red wine –'

Josip was mildly affronted. 'Peter Petersen's friends pay for nothing in my hotel.'

'Maybe I'm not his friend. I mean, maybe he's not my friend.' Giacomo seemed to find the thought highly amusing. 'Thanks all the same.' He picked up a bottle and two glasses from the bar, led the way to a distant table, poured wine and said admiringly: 'That Marija. Quite a girl. Not quite a tartar but no shrinking violet. Changes her mind a bit quick, doesn't she?'

'Mercurial, you'd say?'

'That's the word. Seems to know you pretty well. Has she known you long?'

'She does and she has.' Petersen spoke with some feeling. 'Twenty-six years, three months and some days. The day she was born. My cousin. Why do you ask?'

'Curiosity. I was beginning to wonder if you knew everyone in the valley. Well, on with the inquisition. Incidentally, I would like to say that I'm honoured to be the prime suspect and/or the chosen villain.'

'You're neither a suspect nor villain. Wrong casting. If you wanted, say, to dispose of George or Alex or myself, or get your hands on something you thought we had, you'd use a heavy instrument. Surreptitious phone calls or secret tip-offs are not in your nature. Deviousness is not part of your stock-in-trade.'

'Well, thank you. It's a disappointment, though. I take it you want to ask some questions?'

'If I may.'

632

'About myself, of course. Fire away. No, don't fire away. Let *me* give you my curriculum vitae. Behind me lies a blameless existence. My life is an open book.

'You're right, I'm Montenegrin. Vladimir was my given name. I prefer Giacomo. In England they called me "Johnny". I still prefer Giacomo.'

'You lived in England?'

'I am English. Sounds confusing, but not really. Before the war I was a second officer in the Merchant Navy – the Yugoslav one, I mean. I met a beautiful Canadian girl in Southampton so I left the ship.' He said it as if it had been the most natural thing in the world to do and Petersen could readily understand that for him it had been. 'There was a little difficulty at first at staying on in England but I'd found an excellent and very understanding boss who was working on a diving contract for the Government and who was one experienced diver short. I'd qualified as a diver before joining the merchant marine. By and by I got married –'

'Same girl?'

'Same girl. I became naturalized in August 1939 and joined the services on the outbreak of war the following month. Because I had a master's ocean-going ticket and was a qualified diver who could have been handy at things like sticking limpet mines on to warships in enemy harbours and was a natural for the Navy, it was inevitable, I suppose, that they put me into the infantry. I went to Europe, came back by Dunkirk, then went out to the Middle East.'

'And you've been in those parts ever since. No home leave?'

'No home leave.'

'So you haven't seen your wife in two years. Family?'

'Twin girls. One still-born. The other died at six months. Polio.' Giacomo's tone was matter-of-fact, almost casual. 'In the early summer of '41, my wife was killed in a Luftwaffe attack on Portsmouth.'

633

Petersen nodded and said nothing. There was nothing to say. One wondered why a man like Giacomo smiled so much but one did not wonder long.

'I was with the Eighth Army. Long-Range Desert Group. Then some genius finally discovered that I was really a sailor and not a soldier and I joined Jellicoe's Special Boat Service in the Aegean.' Both those hazardous services called for volunteers, Petersen knew: it was pointless to ask Giacomo why he had volunteered. 'Then the same genius found out some more about me, that I was a Yugoslav, and I was called back to Cairo to escort Lorraine to her destination.'

'And what happens when you've delivered her to her destination?'

'When *you've* delivered her, you mean. Responsibility over, from here on I just sit back and relax and go along for the ride. They thought I was the best man for the job but they weren't to know I was going to have the good luck to meet up with you.' Giacomo poured some more wine, leaned back in his chair and smiled broadly. 'I haven't a single cousin in the whole of Bosnia.'

'If it's luck, I hope it holds. My question, Giacomo.'

'Of course. Afterwards. I'd happily turn back now, conscience clear, but I've got to get a receipt or something from this fellow Mihajlović. I think they want me to take up diving again. Not hard to guess why – must have been the same genius who found out that I was an ex-sailor. As Michael said in that mountain inn, it's a funny old world. I spent over three years fighting the Germans and in a couple of weeks I'll be doing the same thing. This interlude, where I'm more or less fighting with the Germans – although I don't expect I'll ever see a German in Yugoslavia – I don't like one little bit.'

'You heard what George said to Michael. No point in rehashing it. A very brief interlude, Giacomo. You bid your charge a tearful farewell, trying not to smile, then heigh-ho for the Aegean.'

634

'Trying not to smile?' He considered the contents of his glass. 'Well, perhaps. Yes and no. If this is a funny old world, she's a funny young girl in a funny old war. Mercurial – like your cousin. Temperamental. Patrician-looking young lady but sadly deficient in patrician sang-froid. Cool, aloof, even remote at one moment, she can be friendly, even affectionate, the next.'

'The affectionate bit has escaped me so far.'

'A certain lack of rapport between you two has not escaped me either. She can be sweet and bad-tempered at the same time which is no small achievement. Most un-English. I suppose you know she's English. You seem to know quite a bit about her.'

'I know she's English because George told me so. He also told me you were from Montenegro.'

'Ah! Our professor of languages.'

'Remarkable linguist with a remarkable ear. He could probably give you your home address.'

'She tells me you know this Captain Harrison she's going to work for?'

'I know him well.'

'So does she. Used to work for him before. Peacetime. Rome. He was the manager of the Italian branch of an English ball-bearing company. She was his secretary. That's where she learned to speak Italian. She seems to like him a lot.'

'She seems to like men a lot. Period. You haven't fallen into her clutches yet, Giacomo?'

'No.' Again the broad smile. 'But I'm working on it.'

'Well, thanks.' Petersen stood. 'If you'll excuse me.' He crossed to where Sarina was sitting. 'I'd like to talk to you. Alone. I know that sounds ominous, but it isn't, really.'

'What about?'

'That's a silly question. If I want to talk to you privately I don't talk publicly.'

She rose and Michael did the same. He said: 'You're not going to talk to her without me.'

George sighed, rose wearily to his feet, crossed to where Michael was standing, put his two ham-like hands on the young man's shoulders and sat him in his chair as easily as he would have done a little child.

'Michael, you're only a private soldier. If you were in the American army you'd be a private soldier, second class. I'm a Regimental Sergeant-Major. Temporary, mind you, but effective. I don't see why the Major should have to be bothered with you. I don't see why *I* should have to be bothered with you. Why should you bother us? You're not a boy any more.' He reached behind him, picked up a glass of Maraschino from the table and handed it to Michael, who took it sulkily but did not drink. 'If Sarina's kidnapped, we'll all know who did it.'

Petersen took the girl up to her room. He left the door ajar, looked around but not with the air of one expecting to find anything and sniffed the air. Sarina looked at him coldly and spoke the same way.

'What are you looking for? What are you sniffing for? Everything you do, everything you say is unpleasant, nasty, overbearing, superior, humiliating –'

'Oh, come on. I'm your guardian angel. You don't talk to your guardian angel that way.'

'Guardian angel! You also tell lies. You were telling lies in the dining-room. You still think I sent a radio message.'

'I don't and didn't. You're far too nice for anything underhand like that.' She looked at him warily then almost in startlement as he put his hands lightly on her shoulders, but did not try to flinch away. 'You're quick, you're intelligent – unlike your brother but that's not his fault – and I've no doubt you can or could be devious because your face doesn't show much. Except for the one thing that would disqualify you from espionage. You're too transparently honest.'

'That's a kind of left-handed compliment,' she said doubtfully.

'Left or right, it's true.' He dropped to his knees, felt under the foot of the rather ill-fitting door, stood, extracted the key from the inside of the lock and examined it. 'You locked your door last night?'

'Of course.'

'What did you do with the key?'

'I left it in the lock. Half-turned. That way a person with a duplicate key or a master can't push your key through or on to a paper that's been pushed under the door. They taught us that in Cairo.'

'Spare me. Your instructor was probably a ten-year-old schoolboy. See those two tiny bright indentations on either side of the stem of the key?' She nodded. 'Made by an instrument much prized by the better-class burglar who's too sophisticated to batter doors open with a sledge-hammer. A pair of very slender pincers with tips of either Carborundum or titanium stainless steel. Turn any key in a lock. You had a visitor during the night.'

'Somebody took my radio?'

'Somebody sure enough used it. Could have been here.'

'That's impossible. Certainly, I was tired last night but I'm not a heavy sleeper.'

'Maybe you were last night. How did you feel when you woke up this morning – when you were woken, I mean?'

'Well.' She hesitated. 'I felt a bit sick, really. But I thought I was perhaps over-tired and hadn't had enough sleep or I was scared – I'm not a great big coward but I'm not all that brave either and it was the first time anyone had ever pointed a gun at me – or perhaps I just wasn't used to the strange food.'

'You felt dopey, in other words.'

'Yes.'

'You probably were doped. I don't suggest flannel-foot

637

crept stealthily in and applied a chloroform pad or anything of the kind, for the smell of that lingers for hours. Some gas that was injected through the keyhole from a nozzled canister that may well have come from the chemist's joker shop where Alessandro buys his toys. In any event, I can promise you that you won't be disturbed again tonight. And you rest easy in the knowledge that you're not on anyone's black list. Not judged, not condemned, not even suspected. You might at least have the grace to say that I'm not such an awful monster as you thought.'

She smiled faintly. 'Maybe you're not even a monster at all.'

'You're going to sleep, now?' She nodded so he said goodnight and closed the door behind him.

Almost an hour elapsed before Petersen, George and Josip were left together in the dining-room. The others had been in no hurry to depart. The night's events had not been conducive to an immediately renewed slumber and, besides, they were secure in the knowledge that there would be no early morning start.

George, who had returned to his red wine, was making steady inroads on his current uncounted bottle, looked and spoke as if he had been on mineral water all the time. There was, unfortunately, not the same lack of evidence about his cigar-smoking: an evil-smelling blue haze filled the upper half of the room.

'Your friend, Major Cipriano, didn't over-stay his welcome,' Josip said.

'He's no friend of mine,' Petersen said. 'Never seen him before. Appearances mean nothing but he seems a reasonable enough character. For an intelligence agent, that is. Have you known him long?'

'He has been here twice. As a bona-fide traveller. He's no friend. Thanking me for my help was just an attempt to divert suspicion from whoever tipped him off. A feeble attempt, he must have known it would fail but probably the best he could think up at the time. What was his object in coming here?'

'No mystery about that. Both the Germans and Italians are suspicious of me. I have a message to deliver to the leader of the Četniks. On the boat coming across from Italy one of his agents, an unpleasant character called Alessandro, tried to get this message from me. He wanted to see if it was the same as a copy he was carrying. He failed, so Cipriano got worried and came across to Ploče. He was tipped off as to our whereabouts, came up here – almost certainly by light plane – and, when we were herded down here, went through our possessions, steamed open the envelope containing my message, found that it was unchanged and resealed it. Exit Cipriano, baffled but satisfied – for the moment anyway.'

George said: 'Sarina?'

'Someone got into her room in the early hours of this morning. That was after she had been doped. Her radio was used to call up Cipriano. Sarina says she trusts me now. I don't believe her.'

'It is as always,' George said mournfully. 'Every man's – and woman's – hands are against us.'

'Doped?' Josip was incredulous. 'In my hotel? How can anyone be doped in my hotel?'

'How can anyone be doped anywhere?'

'Who was this villain?'

'Villainess. Lorraine.'

'Lorraine! That beautiful girl?'

'Maybe her mind is not as beautiful as the rest of her.'

'Sarina. Now Lorraine.' George shook his head sadly. 'The monstrous regiment of women.'

Josip said: 'But how do you know?'

'Simple arithmetic. Elimination. Lorraine went for a walk tonight and returned very hurriedly. She didn't go for the

639

walk's sake. She went for something else. Information. You went with her, Josip. Do you recall her doing or saying anything odd?'

'She didn't do anything. Just walked. And she said very little.'

'That should make it easy to remember.'

'Well, she said it was odd that I didn't have the name of the hotel outside. I told her I hadn't yet got around to putting it up and that it was the Hotel Eden. She also said it was funny that there were no streets signs up, so I gave her the name of the street. Ah! So she got the name and address, no?'

'Yes.' Petersen rose. 'Bed. I trust you're not going to stay here for the remainder of the night, George.'

'Certainly not.' George fetched a fresh bottle from behind the bar. 'But we academics must have our moments for meditation.'

At noon that day, Petersen and his six companions had still not left the Hotel Eden. Instead, they were just sitting down to a lunch which Josip had insisted they have, a meal that was to prove to be on a par with the dinner they had had the previous evening. But there was one vacant seat.

Josip said: 'Where is the Professor?'

'George,' Petersen said, 'is indisposed. In bed. Acute stomach pains. He thinks it must have been something he had to eat last night.'

'Something he had to eat!' Josip was indignant. 'He had exactly the same to eat as anyone else last night – except of course, a great deal more of it – and nobody else is stricken. My food, indeed! *I* know what ails the Professor. When I came down early this morning, just about two hours after you went to bed, the Professor was still here, still, as he said, meditating.'

'That might help to account for it.'

That might have accounted for it but it didn't account for

640

George's appearance some ten minutes after the meal had commenced. He tried to smile wanly but he didn't look wan.

'Sorry to be late. The Major will have told you I was unwell. However, the cramps have eased a little and I thought I might try a little something. To settle the stomach, you understand.'

By one o'clock George's stomach seemed to have settled in a most remarkable fashion. In the fifty minutes that had intervened since his joining the company he had consumed twice as much as anyone else and effortlessly disposed of two large bottles of wine.

'Congratulations are in order, George,' Giacomo said. 'One moment at death's door and now – well, an incredible performance.'

'It was nothing,' George said modestly. 'In many ways, I am an incredible man.'

Petersen sat on the bed in George's room. 'Well?'

'Satisfactory. In one way, not well. There were two items that one would not have looked for in such an aristocratic young lady's luggage. One was a very small leather case with a few highly professional burglarious tools. The other was a small metal box with some sachets inside, the sachets containing a liquid. When squeezed, the liquid turned into a gas. I sniffed only a very tiny amount. An anaesthetic of some kind, that's certain. The interesting thing is that this little box, though smaller than Alessandro's, was made of and lined with the same materials. What do we do with this young charmer?'

'Leave her be. She's not dangerous. If she were, she wouldn't have made so amateurish a mistake.'

'You said you knew the identity of the miscreant. She's going to wonder why you haven't disclosed it.'

'Let her wonder. What's she going to do about it?'

'There's that,' George said. 'There's that.'

SIX

It was snowing heavily and the temperature was below freezing when Petersen drove the stolen Italian truck out of Mostar shortly after two o'clock that afternoon. The two girls beside him were silent and withdrawn, a circumstance that affected Petersen not at all. Relaxed and untroubled, he drove as unhurriedly as a man with all the time in the world and, after passing unhindered through a check-point at Potoci, slowed down even more, an action dictated not by any change of mood but by the nature of the road. It was narrow, twisting and broken-surfaced and urgently in need of the attentions of road repair gangs who had not passed that way for a long time: more importantly, they had begun to climb, and climb quite steeply, as the Neretva valley narrowed precipitously on either side of the river which sank further and further below the tortuous road until there was an almost sheer drop of several hundred feet to the foaming river that lay beneath them. Given the unstable nature of the road, the fact that there were no crash-barriers or restraining walls to prevent their sliding off the slippery road and the fact that the river itself increasingly disappeared in the thickening snowsqualls, it was not a route to lighten the hearts of those of an imaginative or nervous disposition. Judging by the hand-clenching and highly apprehensive expression of Petersen's two front-seat companions, they clearly came well within that category. Petersen had neither comfort nor cheer to offer them, not through any callous indifference but because on the evidence of their own eyes they wouldn't have believed a word he said anyway.

Their relief was almost palpable when Petersen abruptly turned off the road into a narrow gully which suddenly – and to the two girls, miraculously – appeared in the vertical cliff-side to their right. The road was no road at all, just a convoluted, rutted track that offered only minimal traction for the almost constantly spinning rear wheels, but at least there was no way they could fall off it: high walls of rock pressed in closely on both sides. Perhaps five minutes after leaving the main road, Petersen stopped, cut the engine and dropped down.

'This is as far as we go,' he said. 'As far as we can go in this truck, anyway. Stay here.' He walked round to the back of the truck, parted the curtains, repeated his words and disappeared into the swirling snow.

He was back within a few minutes, sitting beside the driver of a peculiar open vehicle which looked as if it might once have been a small truck that had had both its top and rear sliced off. The driver, clad in British warm – a thick, khaki, woollen overcoat – could have been of any nationality: with a fur cap pulled down to eyebrow level, a luxuriant black beard and moustache and a pair of horn-rimmed sunglasses, there wasn't a single distinguishable feature of his face to be seen except for a nose that could have belonged to anyone. Petersen stepped down as the vehicle came to a halt.

'This is Dominic,' he said. 'He's come to help us along a bit. That's a four-wheel-drive vehicle he's got there. It can go places where this truck can't, but even then it can't go very far, perhaps a couple of kilometres. Dominic will take the two young ladies, all our gear and all our blankets – I can assure you we're going to need those tonight – as far as he can, then come back for the rest of us. We'll start walking.'

Sarina said: 'You mean to tell us you expected this friend of yours to meet us here? And at just this time?'

'Give or take a few minutes. I wouldn't be much of a tour guide, would I, if I got all my connections wrong?'

'This truck,' Giacomo said. 'You're surely not going to leave it here?'

'Why ever not?'

'I thought it was your custom to park unwanted Italian trucks in the Neretva. I saw some lovely parking spots in the god-awful ravine we just came through.'

'A sinful waste. Besides, we might even want it again. What matters, of course, is that our friend Major Cipriano already knows we have it.'

'How would he know that?'

'How would he not know it, you mean. Has it not occurred to you that the informer who tipped him off to our presence in the Hotel Eden would also have given him all the details of our trip from the torpedo boat, including those of this vehicle? Either by radio or before being apparently dragged from an hotel bedroom, it doesn't matter. We passed through a check-point at Potoci about an hour ago and the guard didn't even bother to slow us down. Odd, one might think, except that he had already been given details of our vehicle, recognized it at once and obeyed orders to let us through. Let's get that stuff out quickly. It's turned even colder than I thought it would be.'

It had indeed. A south-east wind had sprung up, a wind from which they would have been sheltered in the Neretva valley, and was steadily strengthening. This would not normally have been a cold wind but this was a wind that paid no attention to meteorological norms: it could have been blowing straight from Siberia. The four-wheel-drive vehicle was loaded with passengers and gear and drove off in a remarkably short time: there could be no doubt that Dominic's sunglasses were, in effect, snow-glasses.

The five men set out on foot and were picked up some fifteen minutes later by the returning Dominic. The ride

644

along an even more bumpy and deteriorating track was, because of the increase in snowdepth and incline, uncomfortable and haphazard to a degree, and only marginally better and faster than walking. None of the passengers was sorry when the truck pulled up at the track's end outside a ramshackle wooden hut which proved to be its garage. Inside, the two girls were sheltering from the snow. They were not alone. There were three men – boys, rather – in vaguely para-military uniforms and five ponies.

Sarina said: 'Where on earth are we?'

'Home, sweet home,' Petersen said. 'Well, an hour and a half's gentle ride and we'll be there. This is the mountain of Prenj, more of a massif, really. The Neretva river makes a big U-turn here and runs around three sides of it, which makes Prenj, in defensive terms, an ideal place to be. Only two bridges cross the river, one to the north-west at Jablanica, the other to the north-east at Konjik, and both of those are easily guarded and defended. It's open to the south-east but no danger threatens from that direction.'

'Gentle ride, you said. Do those horses canter or gallop? I don't like horses.'

'They're ponies, not horses, and, no, they don't canter or gallop. Not on this occasion anyway. They wouldn't be stupid enough to try. It's all uphill and pretty steeply uphill.'

'I don't think I'm going to enjoy this climb.'

'You'll enjoy the view.'

It was half an hour later and she was enjoying neither the climb nor the view. The climb, though not impossibly steep, was a difficult enough one and the view, remarkable though it was, engendered in her only a feeling that lay halfway between fascinated horror and paralysed terror. The path, barely two metres in width and sometimes noticeably less, had been gouged out of the side of a slope so steep as to be virtually a cliff-side, and ascended it by a series, a seemingly endless series, of hairpin twists and turns. With every step the pony took, the floor of the narrow valley, when it could be seen at all through the driving snow, seemed more remotely and vertically distant. Only she and Lorraine had been mounted: the other three ponies carried all their securely strapped gear and blankets. Lorraine was on foot now, clutching Giacomo's arm as if he was her last faint hope on earth.

Petersen, walking beside Sarina's pony, said: 'I'm afraid you're not enjoying this as much as I would like you to.'

'Enjoying it!' She shuddered uncontrollably, not with cold. 'Back in the hotel I told you I wasn't a great big coward. Well, I am, I am! I'm terrified. I keep on telling myself it's silly, it's stupid, but I can't help it.'

Petersen said matter-of-factly: 'You're not a coward. It's been like this since you were a child.'

'Like what? What do you mean?'

'Vertigo is what I mean. Anyone can suffer from it. Some of the bravest men I know, some of the most fearsome fighters I've ever met, won't climb a step-ladder or set foot in a plane.'

'Yes, yes. Always. Do you know about it?'

'I don't get it, but I've seen it too often not to know about it. Dizziness, loss of equilibrium, an almost uncontrollable desire to throw yourself over the edge and, in the present case, a conviction on your part that your pony is about to jump out into space at any moment. That's about it, isn't it?'

She nodded, dumbly. Petersen refrained from saying that if she'd known about her condition and the Yugoslav mountains, she should have stayed in Cairo. Instead he moved round the head of the horse and took her stirrup-leather in his hand.

'These ponies are more sure-footed than we are and by a long way. Even if it should suffer from a bout of vertigo now, and ponies never do, I would be the first over the edge. And even if you felt like throwing yourself over, you can't because I'm between you and the cliff edge and I'd stop you and catch you. And I'll change sides at every corner. That way we'll be sure to make it to the top. I won't be so silly as to tell you to sit back and relax: all I can say is that you'll be feeling a lot better in fifteen minutes or so.'

'We'll be away from this cliff by that time?' The tremor was still in her voice.

'We will, we will.' They wouldn't be, but by that time it would be so dark that she would be unable to see the valley below.

It was quite some time after dark when they passed through the perimeter of what seemed to be a permanent camp of sorts. There were a large number of huts and tents, all close together and nearly all illuminated: not brightly illuminated, for at that remote altitude there was no central power grid and the only small generator available was reserved for the headquarters area: for the rest, the great majority of the guerrilla soldiers and the inevitable camp-followers, there was only the light to be had from oil, tallow or coke braziers. Then there came a quite uninhabited and gently rising slope of perhaps three hundred metres before their small cavalcade fetched up at a large hut with a metal roof and two windows which gave out a surprising amount of light.

'Well, here we are,' Petersen said. 'Home or what you'd better call home until you find a better word for it.' He reached up his hands and swung the shivering girl to the ground. She clung to him as if she were trying to prevent herself from falling to the ground which was what she was indeed trying to do.

'My legs feel all funny.' Her voice was low and husky but at least the tremor had gone.

'Sure they do. I'll bet you've never been on a horse before.'

'You'd win your bet but it's not that. The way I hung on to

647

that horse, clung to it–' She tried to laugh but it was a poor enough attempt. 'I'll be surprised if that poor pony doesn't have bruised ribs for days to come.'

'You did very well.'

'Very well! I'm ashamed of myself. I hope you won't go around telling everyone that you've met up with the most cowardly radio operator in the Balkans.'

'I won't. I won't because I don't go around telling lies. I think you may be the bravest girl I ever met.'

'After that performance!'

'Especially after that performance.'

She was still clinging to him, clearly still not trusting her balance, was silent for a few moments, then said: 'I think you may be the kindest man I've ever met.'

'Good God!' He was genuinely astonished. 'The strain has been too much. After all you've said about me!'

'Especially after everything I said about you.'

She was still holding him, although now only tentatively, when they heard the sound of a heavy fist banging on a wooden door and George's booming voice saying: 'Open up, in the name of the law or common humanity or whatever. We have crossed the burning sands and are dying of thirst.'

The door opened almost immediately and a tall, thin figure appeared, framed in the rectangle of light. He came down the two steps and thrust out a hand.

'It cannot be . . .' He had an excruciatingly languid Oxbridge accent.

'It is.' George took his hand. 'Enough of the formalities. At stake there is nothing less than the sacred name of British hospitality.'

'Goodness gracious!' The man screwed a monocle, an oddly-shaped oval one, into his right eye, advanced towards Lorraine, took her hand, swept it up in a gesture of exquisite gallantry and kissed it. 'Goodness gracious me. Lorraine Chamberlain!' He seemed about to embark upon a speech of some length, caught sight of Petersen and went to meet him. 'Peter, my boy. Once again all those dreadful trials and tribulations lie behind you. My word, I can't tell you how dull and depressing it's been here during the two weeks you've been gone. Dreadful, I tell you. Utterly dreadful.'

Petersen smiled. 'Hello, Jamie. Good to see you again. Things should improve now. George, quite illicitly, of course, has brought you some presents – quite a lot of presents, they almost broke the back of one of the ponies coming up here. Presents that go clink.' He turned to Sarina. 'May I introduce Captain Harrison. Captain Harrison,' he added with a straight face, 'is English. Jamie, this is Sarina von Karajan.'

Harrison shook her hand enthusiastically. 'Delighted, delighted. If only you knew now we miss even the commonest amenities of civilization in these benighted parts. Not, of course,' he added hastily, 'that there's anything common about you. My goodness, I should say not.' He looked at Petersen. 'The Harrisons' ill luck runs true to form again. We were born under an evil and accursed star. Do you mean to tell me that you have had the great fortune, the honour, the pleasure of escorting those two lovely ladies all the way from Italy?'

'Neither of them think there was any fortune, honour or pleasure about it. I didn't know you had the pleasure of knowing Lorraine before.' Giacomo had a sudden but very brief paroxysm of coughing which Petersen ignored.

'Oh, my goodness, yes, indeed. Old friends, very old. Worked together once, don't you know? Tell you some time. Your other new friends?' Petersen introduced Giacomo and Michael whom Harrison welcomed in what was his clearly customary effusive fashion, then said: 'Well, inside, inside. Can't have you all freezing to death in this abominable weather. I'll have your goods and chattels taken in. Inside, inside.'

"Inside" was surprisingly roomy, warm, well-lit and, by guerrilla standards, almost comfortable. There were three bunks running the length of each side of the room, some tall articles of furniture that could have been either cupboards or wardrobes, a deal table, half a dozen pine chairs, the unheard luxury of a couple of rather scruffy arm-chairs and even two strips of worn and faded carpet. At either end of the room were two doors that led, presumably, to further accommodation. Harrison closed the outside door behind him.

'Have a seat, have a seat.' The Captain was much given to repeating himself. 'George, if I may suggest – ah, foolish of me, I might have known that any such suggestion was superfluous.' George had, indeed, lost no time in doubling in his spare-time role of barman. Harrison looked around him with an air of proprietorial pride. 'Not bad, although I say it myself, not bad at all. You won't find many such havens in this strife-torn land. I regret to say that we live in accommodation such as this all too infrequently, but when we do we make the best of it. Electric light, if you please – you can't hear it but we have the only generator in the base apart from the commander. Need it for our big radios.' He pointed to two six-inch diameter pipes angling diagonally upwards along either wall to disappear through the roof. 'Central heating, of course. Actually, they're only the stove-pipes from our coke and wood stove outside. Would have it inside but we'd all be asphyxiated in minutes. And what do we have here, George?' He inspected the contents of a glass George had just handed him.

George shrugged and said diffidently: 'Nothing really. Highland malt whisky.'

'Highland malt whisky.' Harrison reverently surveyed the amber liquid, sipped it delicately and smiled in rapture. 'Where on earth did you get this, George?'

'Friend of mine in Rome.'

'God bless your Roman friends.' This time assuming his

650

beatific expression in advance, Harrison sipped again. 'Well, that's about all the mod cons. That door to the left leads to my radio room. Some nice stuff in there but unfortunately we can't take most of it with us when we travel which, again unfortunately, is most of the time. The other door leads to what I rather splendidly call my sleeping quarters. It's about the size of a couple of telephone boxes but it does have two cots.' Harrison took another sip from his glass and went on gallantly: 'Those quarters, naturally, I will gladly vacate for the night for the two young ladies.'

'You are very kind,' Sarina said doubtfully. 'But I – we – were supposed to report to the Colonel.'

'Nonsense. Not to be thought of. You are exhausted by your travels, your sufferings, your privations. One has only to look at you. I am sure the Colonel will gladly wait until the morning. Is that not so, Peter?'

'Tomorrow will be time enough.'

'Of course. Well, we castaways marooned on a mountain top are always eager for news of the outside world. What of the past fortnight, my friend?'

Petersen put down his untouched glass and rose. 'George will tell you. He's a much better raconteur than I am.'

'Well, yes, you do rather lack his gift for dramatic embellishment. Duty calls?' Petersen nodded.

'Ah! The Colonel?'

'Who else. I won't be long.'

When Petersen returned, he was not alone. The two men accompanying him were, like himself, covered in a heavy coating of snow. While they were brushing this off, Harrison rose courteously and introduced them.

'Good evening, gentlemen. We are honoured.' He turned to the newcomers. 'Let me introduce Major Ranković, Major Metrović, two of the Colonel's senior commanders. You venture forth on a wild night, gentlemen.'

651

'You mean, of course, why have we come?' The speaker, Major Metrović, was a man of medium height, dark, thickset and cheerful. 'Curiosity, of course. Peter's movements are always shrouded in mystery and heaven knows we see little enough of new faces from the outer world.'

'Peter didn't also mention that two of those new faces were young, female and – I speak as a detached observer, of course – rather extraordinarily good-looking?'

'He may have done, he may have done.' Metrović smiled again. 'You know how it is with my colleague and myself. Our minds are invariably preoccupied with military matters. Isn't that so, Marino?'

Marino – Major Ranković – a tall, thin, dark-bearded and rather gloomy character, who looked as if he let Metrović do all the smiling for both of them, didn't say whether it was so or not. He seemed preoccupied and the source of his preoccupation was unquestionably Giacomo.

'I asked them along,' Petersen said. 'I felt it was the least I could do to bring some relief into their cheerless lives.'

'Well, welcome, welcome.' Harrison looked at his watch. 'Won't be long, you said. What do you call short?'

'I wanted to give George a chance to finish his story. Besides, I was detained. Much questioning. And I stopped by at my radio hut to see if you'd made off with anything during my absence. It seems not. Perhaps you mislaid the key.'

'The radio hut?' Sarina glanced at the door at the end of the room. 'But we heard nothing. I mean –'

'My radio hut is fifty metres away. No mystery. There are three radios in the camp. One for the Colonel. One for Captain Harrison. One for me. You will be assigned to the Colonel. Lorraine comes here.'

'You arranged that?'

'I arranged nothing. I take orders, just like anyone else.

The Colonel arranged it, Lorraine's assignation here was arranged weeks ago. There's no secret about it. The Colonel, for reasons that may seem obscure to you but which I understand very well, prefers that Captain Harrison's radio operator, like Captain Harrison himself, should not speak or understand Serbo-Croat. The basis of the Colonel's security beliefs is that one should trust nobody.'

'You must have a lot in common with the Colonel.'

'I think that's rather unfair, young lady.' It was Metrović again and he was still smiling. 'I can confirm what the Major has said. I'm the go-between, the translator, if you like, for the Colonel and Captain Harrison. Like the major, I was partly educated in England.'

'Enough,' Harrison said. 'Let us put unworthy thoughts to one side and concentrate on more important things.'

'Such as hospitality?' George said.

'Such as hospitality, as you say. Be seated, please. What is your choice, gentlemen – and ladies, of course?'

They all told him what they wanted, all, that is, except Major Ranković. He crossed to where Giacomo was seated and said: 'May I ask what your name is?'

Giacomo lifted his eyebrows in slight puzzlement, smiled and said: 'Giacomo.'

'That's an Italian name, isn't it?' ·

'Yes.'

'Giacomo what?'

'Just Giacomo.'

'Just Giacomo.' Ranković's voice was deep and gravelly. 'It suits you to be mysterious?'

'It suits me to mind my own business.'

'What's your rank?'

'That's my business, too.'

'I've seen you before. Not in the army, though. Rijeka, Split, Kotor, some place like that.'

'It's possible.' Giacomo was still smiling but the smile no

653

longer extended to his eyes. 'It's a small enough world. I used to be a sailor.'

'You're a Yugoslav.'

Giacomo, Petersen was aware, could easily have conceded the fact but he knew he wouldn't. Ranković was an able soldier but no psychologist.

'I'm English.'

'You're a liar.'

Petersen stepped forward and tapped Ranković on the shoulder. 'If I were you, Marino, I'd quit while I was ahead. Not, mind you, that I think you are ahead.'

Ranković turned. 'What do you mean?'

'I mean that you're still intact and in one piece. Keep on like this and you'll wake up in hospital wondering if you fell under a train. I can vouch for Giacomo. He is English. He's got so long and so distinguished a war record that he puts any man in this room to shame. While you've been pottering around the mountains he's been fighting in France and Belgium and North Africa and the Aegean and usually on assignments so dangerous that you couldn't even begin to wonder what they were like. Look at his face, Marino. Look at it and you'll look into the face of war.'

Ranković studied Giacomo closely. 'I'm not a fool. I never questioned his qualities as a soldier. I was curious, that is all, and maybe, like the Colonel and yourself, I am not much given to trusting anyone. I did not intend to give offence.'

'And I didn't intend to take any,' Giacomo said. His good humour had returned. 'You're suspicious, I'm touchy. A bad mix. Let me suggest a good mix or rather no mix at all. You never mix malt whisky with anything, do you, George? Not even water?'

'Sacrilege.'

'You were right on one count, Major. I am English but I was born in Yugoslavia. Let us drink to Yugoslavia.'

'A toast no man could quarrel with,' Ranković said. There

654

were no handshakes, no protestations of eternal friendship. It was, at best, a truce. Ranković, no actor, still had his reservations about Giacomo.

Petersen, for his part, had none.

Considerably later in the evening an understandably much more relaxed and mellowed atmosphere had descended upon the company. Some of them had paid a brief visit to a mess four hundred metres distant for an evening meal. Sarina and Lorraine had point-blank – and as it turned out, wisely – refused to brave the near blizzard that was now sweeping by outside. Michael, inevitably, had elected to remain with them and Giacomo, after a quick exchange of glances with Petersen, had announced that he was not hungry. Giacomo did not have to have it spelt out to him that, even among his own people, Petersen was suspicious of practically everybody in sight.

Compared to Josip Pijade's midday offerings, the meal was a gastronomic disaster. It was no fault of the Četnik cooks – as elsewhere through that ravaged country, food was at a premium and fine food almost wholly unobtainable. Still, it was a sad come-down from the flesh-pots of Italy and Mostar and even George could manage no more than two platefuls of the fatty mutton and beans which constituted the main and only course of the evening. They had left as soon as decency permitted.

Back in Harrison's radio hut their relative sufferings were soon forgotten.

'There's no place like home,' Harrison announced to nobody in particular. Although it would have been unfair to call him inebriated, it would have been fair to pass the opinion that he wasn't stone cold sober either.

He bent an appreciative gaze on the glass in his hand. 'Nectar emboldens me. George has given me a very comprehensive account of your activities over the past two weeks.

655

He has not, however, told me *why* you went to Rome in the first place. Nor did you seek to enlighten me on your return.'

'That's because I didn't know myself.'

Harrison nodded sagely. 'That makes sense. You go all the way to Rome and back and you don't know why.'

'I was just carrying a message. I didn't know the contents.'

'Is one permitted to ask if you know the contents now?'

'One is permitted. I do.'

'Ah! Is one further permitted to know the contents?'

'In your own language, Jamie, I don't know whether I'm permitted or not. All I can say is that this is purely a military matter. Strictly, I am not a military man, a commander of troops. I'm an espionage agent. Espionage agents don't wage battles. We're far too clever for that. Or cowardly.'

Harrison looked at Metrović and Ranković in turn. 'You're military men. If I'm to believe half you tell me, you wage battles.'

Metrović smiled. 'We're not as clever as Peter.'

'You know the contents of the message?'

'Of course. Peter's discretion does him credit but it's not really necessary. Within a couple of days the news will be common knowledge throughout the camp. We – the Germans, Italians, ourselves and the Ustaša – are to launch an all-out offensive against the Partisans. We shall annihilate Titoland. The Germans have given the name of the attack "Operation Weiss": the Partisans will doubtless call it the Fourth Offensive.'

Harrison seemed unimpressed. He said, doubtfully: 'That means, of course, that you've made three other offensives already. Those didn't get you very far, did they?'

Metrović was unruffled. 'I know it's easy to say, but this time really will be different. They're cornered. They're trapped. They've no way out, no place left to go. They haven't a single plane, fighter or bomber. We have squadrons upon squadrons. They haven't a tank, not even a single

656

effective anti-aircraft gun. At the most, they have fifteen thousand men, most of them starving, weak, sick and untrained. We have almost a hundred thousand men, well-trained and fit. And Tito's final weakness, his Achilles' heel, you might say, is his lack of mobility: he is known to have at least three thousand wounded men on his hands. It will be no contest. I don't say I look forward to it, but it will be a massacre. Are you a betting man, James?'

'Not against odds like that, I'm not. Like Peter here, I lay no claim to being a military man – I never even *saw* a uniform until three years ago – but if the action is so imminent why are you drinking wine at your leisured ease instead of being hunched over your war maps, sticking flags in here, flags in there, drawing up your battle plans or whatever you're supposed to be doing in cases like this?'

Metrović laughed. 'Three excellent reasons. First, the offensive is not imminent – it's two weeks away yet. Second, all the plans have already been drawn up and all the troops are already in position or will be in a few days. Third, the main assault takes place at Bihać, where the Partisan forces are at present centred, and that's over two hundred kilometres north-west of here. We're not taking part in that: we're staying just where we are in case the Partisans are so foolish, or optimistic or suicidal to try to break out to the south-east: stopping them from crossing the Neretva, in the remote possibility of a few stragglers getting as far as here, would be only a formality.' He paused and gazed at a darkened window. 'There may well be a fourth possibility. If the weather worsens, or even continues like this, the best laid plans of the High Command could well go wrong. A postponement would be inevitable. Nobody's going to be moving around the mountains in those impossible weather conditions for days to come, that's for sure. Days might well become weeks.'

'Well, yes,' Harrison said. 'One sees why you face the

657

future with a certain resigned fortitude. On the basis of what you say the chances are good that you won't even become involved at all. For myself, I hope your prognosis is correct – as I've said I'm no man of war and I've become quite attached to these rather comfortable quarters. And do you, Peter, expect to hibernate along with us?'

'No. If the Colonel has nothing for me in the morning – and he gave no indication tonight that he would have – then I shall be on my way the following morning. Provided, of course, that we're not up to our ears in snowdrifts.'

'Whither away, if one is –'

'Permitted to ask? Yes. A certain Italian intelligence officer is taking an undue amount of interest in me. He's trying either to discredit me or hamper me in my operations. Has tried, I should say. I would like to find out why.'

Metrović said: 'In what way has he tried, Peter?'

'He and a gang of his thugs held us up in a Mostar hotel in the early hours of this morning. Looking for something, I suppose. Whether they found it or not I don't know. Shortly before that, on the boat coming from Italy, some of his minions tried to carry out a night attack on us. They failed, but not for the want of trying, for they were carrying syringes and lethal drugs which they were more than prepared to use.'

'Goodness me.' Harrison looked suitably appalled. 'What happened?'

'It was all quite painless, really,' George said with satisfaction. 'We welded them up in a cabin on the boat. Last heard of they were still there.'

Harrison looked reproachfully at George. 'Missed this out in your stirring account of your activities, didn't you?'

'Discretion, discretion.'

'This Italian intelligence officer,' Metrović said, 'is, of course an ally. With some allies, as we know, you don't need enemies. When you meet up with this ally what are you going to do? Question him or kill him?' The Major seemed to regard that as a very natural query.

'Kill him?' Sarina looked and was shocked. 'That nice man. Kill him! I thought you rather liked him.'

'Liked him? He's reasonable, personable, smiling, open-faced, has a firm handshake and looks you straight in the eye – anyone can tell at once that he's a member of the criminal classes. He was prepared to kill me, by proxy, mind you, through his hatchet-man Alessandro – which, if anything, makes it an even more heinous intention on his part – so why shouldn't I be prepared to pre-empt him? But I won't, at least not right away. I just want to ask him a few questions.'

'But – but you might not even be able to find him.'

'I'll find him.'

'And if he refuses to answer?'

'He'll answer.' There was the same chilling certainty in the voice.

She touched her lips with the back of her hand and fell silent. Metrović, his face thoughtful, said: 'You're not the man to ask questions unless you're pretty certain of the answers in advance. You're after confirmation of something. Could you not have obtained this confirmation at the hotel you mentioned?'

'Certainly. But I didn't want the place littered with corpses, not all of which might have been theirs. I'd promised to deliver this lot intact first. Everything in its due turn. Confirmation? I want confirmation of why Italy is planning to pull out of this war. That they want out I don't for a moment doubt. Their people never wanted this war. Their army, navy and air force never wanted it. Remember when Wavell's army in North Africa overwhelmed the Italians? There was a picture taken just after the last battle, a picture that was to become world-famous. It showed about a thousand Italian prisoners being marched off to their barbed

659

wire cages escorted by three British soldiers. The sun was so hot that the soldiers had given their rifles to three of the prisoners to carry. That about sums up the Italian attitude to the war.

'Given a cause that is close to their hearts, the Italians can fight as gallantly as any people on earth. This cause is not close to their hearts – it couldn't be further away from it. This is Germany's war and they don't like fighting Germany's war because, basically, they don't like the Germans. It has been repeatedly claimed, both by the Italians and the British that the Italians are, at bottom, pro-British. The truth is, of course, that they're just pro-Italian.

'No-one is more acutely aware of this than the Italian high command. But there's more to it of course than just patriotism. There's no lack of first-class minds in the Italian high command and it's my belief that they are convinced, even at this early stage, that the Germans are going to lose the war.' Petersen looked round the room. 'It may not be your belief, it may not be my belief, but that's irrelevant. What matters is that I'm convinced it is their belief and that they are even now figuring out a way to arrive at an accommodation – for want of a better word – with the British and Americans. This accommodation, of course, would take the form of a full-scale surrender but, of course, it would be nothing of the sort. It would involve full-scale cooperation upon the part of the Italians with every aspect of the British and American forces just short of the front-line engagement of their troops in the front line.'

'You seem very sure about this, Peter,' Metrović said. 'How can you be so sure?'

'Because I have access to sources and information that none of you has. I am in constant touch with both Italian and German forces in this country and, as you know, I'm a frequent visitor to Italy and have talked to literally hundreds of Italians there, both military men and civilians. I am neither literally deaf nor figuratively dumb. I know, for instance. that Italian Intelligence and German Intelligence are barely on civil speaking terms with each other and most certainly do not trust each other round the nearest corner in the street.

'General Granelli, Head of Italian Intelligence and Cipriano's boss – Cipriano is this Intelligence Major I was talking about – is an evil and warped character but out-and-out brilliant. He knows the situation and the options as well as anyone and is in no doubt that the Germans are going to go down in dust and flames and has no intention of joining them there. He's also pretty certain that I know quite well what the true situation is and that if I start voicing my doubts – my convictions, rather – out loud I could be a positive danger to him. I think he's been twice on the point of having me eliminated and has twice changed his mind at the last minute. I know there's going to be a third time which is one reason why I want to get out of here – before Cipriano or some other comes, in the guise of a loyal ally, naturally, and arranges for an accident to happen to me. But the main reason, of course, for my departure is to get to their link-man before he gets to me.'

'Link-man? Link-man?' Harrison shook his head in bafflement. 'You speak in riddles, Peter.'

'A riddle with a childishly easy answer. If the Germans go down who else is going to go down with them?'

'Ah-ha!'

'As you've just said, ah-ha. All those who have fought with them, that's who. Including us. If you were General Granelli and with Granelli's keen eye to the future, which of the opposing forces in Yugoslavia would you back?'

'Good Lord!' Harrison sounded slightly stunned. He looked around the room. The others, if not quite stunned, looked for the most part deeply pensive, not least Ranković and Metrović. 'What you are saying is that Granelli and this

Major Cipriano are working hand-in-hand with the Partisans and that Cipriano is the master double-agent?'

Petersen rubbed his chin with his hand, glanced briefly at Harrison, sighed, poured himself some more red wine and did not deign to answer.

Petersen's radio shack did not begin to compare in magnificence with Harrison's, which they had left only a few moments previously, a premature departure arising directly from the conversational hiatus that had ensued immediately after Harrison's last words, a lacuna that went on and on and on. Harrison and the two Četnik officers were sunk in profound reverie, Sarina and Lorraine, by their expressions not by words, had made it clear that their aversion to Petersen had not only returned but was in fuller flood than ever and Alex and Michael, as ever, had nothing to say. Those two master conversationalists, George and Giacomo, had battled bravely but only briefly on. It was a lost cause.

The hut would have been big enough to serve as a one-car garage, if the car were small enough. Three beds, a table, three chairs, a cooking stove and that was all: the radio room was a tiny office next door.

'I am sad and disturbed,' George said. 'Profoundly disturbed.' He poured himself a large glass of wine and drank half of it in one apparently endless gulp just to show how profoundly disturbed he was. 'Sad, perhaps, is a better word. The realization that one's life and one's lifework has been a failure is a bitter pill to swallow. The damage to one's pride and self-esteem is irreparable. The effect, overall, is crushing.'

'I know what you mean,' Petersen said sympathetically. 'I've felt that myself.'

George might not have heard him. 'You will not have forgotten the days when you were my student in Belgrade?'

'Who could, ever? As you said yourself, not more than a

hundred times, a walk with you through the rose-arboured groves of academe was an experience to remain with one always.'

'Remember the precepts I preached, the eternal verities I cherished? Honour, honesty, straightforwardness, the pure in mind, the open heart, the outright contempt for deceit, deception, dishonesty: we were, remember, to go through the darkness of this world guided solely by the light of the everlasting flame of truth?'

'Yes, George.'

'I am a broken man.'

'I'm sorry, George.'

SEVEN

There were six of them in all, and six tougher looking and more villainous characters it would have been almost impossible to imagine, far less find. There was a curious likeness about them. They were all just over medium height, all lean and broad-shouldered, all clad exactly alike: khaki trousers tucked into high boots, belted khaki canvas jacket over a khaki tunic, and khaki forage caps. They carried no badges, no identification marks. All were armed in precisely the same fashion: machine-pistols in hands, a revolver at waist level and hunting knives stuck into a sheath on the right boot. Their faces were dark and still, their eyes quiet and watchful. They were dangerous men.

Surprise had been complete, resistance – even the thought of a token resistance – unthinkable. The same company as had been in Harrison's hut the previous evening, had been there just a few minutes before eight that evening when the outside door had burst open and three men had been inside the door with levelled guns before anyone could even react. Now there were six inside, and the door was closed. One of the intruders, a little shorter and a little broader than the others, took a pace forward.

'My name is Crni.' It was the Serbo-Croat word for black. 'You will take off your weapons, one by one, and place them on the floor.' He nodded at Metrović. 'You begin.'

Within a minute every gun in the room – at least every visible gun – was lying on the floor. Crni beckoned Lorraine.

'Pick up those guns and put them on that table there. You will not, of course, be so stupid as to even think of firing any of them.'

Lorraine had no thought of firing any of them, her hands were shaking so much that she had some difficulty in picking them up. When they were on the table Crni said: 'Are either of you two young ladies armed?'

'They're not,' Petersen said. 'I guarantee it. If you find a weapon on their persons or in their bags you can shoot me.'

Crni looked at him almost quizzically, reached under his canvas jacket and produced a piece of paper from his tunic. 'What's your name?'

'Petersen.'

'Ah! Major Peter Petersen. At the very top of the list. One can see they're not carrying a weapon on their persons. But their bags?'

'I've searched them.'

The two girls momentarily stopped being apprehenisve and exchanged indignant glances. Crni smiled slightly.

'You should have told them. I believe you. If any man here is carrying a gun on his person and conceals the fact, then if I find it I'll shoot him. Through the heart.' Crni's matter-of-fact tone carried an unpleasant degree of conviction.

'There's no need to go around making all those ludicrous threats,' George said complainingly. 'If it's cooperation you want, I'm your man.' He produced an automatic from the depths of his clothing and nudged Alex in the ribs. 'Don't be foolish. I don't think this fellow Crni has any sense of humour.' Alex scowled and threw a similar automatic on the table.

'Thank you.' Crni consulted his list. 'You, of course, have to be the learned Professor, number two on our list.' He looked up at Alex. 'And you must be number three. It says here "Alex brackets assassin". Not much of a character reference. We'll bear that in mind.' He turned to one of his men. 'Edvard. Those coats hanging there. Search them.'

'No need,' Petersen said. 'Just the one on the left. That's mine. Right-hand pocket.'

'You are cooperative,' Crni said.

'I'm a professional, too.'

'I know that. I know quite a lot about you. Rather, I've been told quite a lot.' He looked at the gun Edvard had brought him. 'I didn't know they issued silenced Lugers to the Royal Yugoslav Army.'

'They don't. A friend gave it to me.'

'Of course. I have five other names on this list.' He looked at Harrison. 'You must be Captain James Harrison.'

'Why must I?'

'There are two officers in Yugoslavia who wear monocles? And you must be Giacomo. Just the one name. Giacomo.'

'Same question.'

'Description.'

Giacomo smiled. 'Flattering?'

'No. Just accurate.' He looked at Michael. 'And you, by elimination, must be Michael von Karajan. Two ladies.' He looked at Lorraine. 'You're Lorraine Chamberlain.'

'Yes.' She smiled wanly. 'You have my description, too?'

'Sarina von Karajan bears a remarkable resemblance to her twin brother,' Crni said patiently. 'You eight are coming with me.'

George said: 'May I ask a question?'

'No.'

'I think that's downright uncivil,' George said plaintively. 'And unfair. What if I wanted to go to the toilet?'

'I take it you are the resident comedian,' Crni said coldly. 'I hope your sense of humour bears with you in the days to come. Major, I'm going to hold you personally responsible for the conduct of your group.'

Petersen smiled. 'If anyone tries to run away, you'll shoot me?'

'I wouldn't have put it as crudely as that, Major.'

'Major this, Major that. Major Crni? Captain Crni?'

'Captain,' he said briefly. 'I prefer Crni. Do I have to be an officer?'

'They don't send a mess-boy to bring in apparently notorious criminals.'

'Nobody's said you're a criminal. Not yet.' He looked at the two Četnick officers. 'Your names?'

Metrović said: 'I'm Major Metrović. This is Major Ranković.'

'I've heard of you.' He turned to Petersen. 'You eight will be taking your baggage with you.'

'That's nice,' George said.

'What is?'

'Well,' George said reasonably, 'if we're taking our baggage with us it's hardly likely that you're going to shoot us out of hand.'

'To be a comedian is bad enough. To be a buffoon, insufferable.' He turned back to Petersen. 'How many of the eight have their baggage here? Men and women, I mean?'

'Five. Three of us have our baggage in a hut about fifty yards away – myself and those two gentlemen here.'

'Slavko. Sava.' This to two of his men. 'This man Alex will show you where the hut is. Bring the baggage back. Search it very carefully first. And be just as careful in watching this man. He has an appalling record.' For a fleeting moment the expression on Alex's face made Crni's statement more than credible. 'Hurry nothing, watch everything.' He looked at his watch. 'We have forty minutes left.'

In less than half that time all the luggage had been packed and collected. George said: 'I know I'm not allowed to ask a question so may I make a statement? Oh, that's a question, too. I want to make a statement.'

'What?'

'I'm thirsty.'

'I see no harm.'

'Thank you.' George had opened a bottle and downed a glass of wine in what appeared near-impossible time.

'Try that other bottle,' Crni suggested. George blinked, frowned, but willingly did what he was told. 'Seems satisfactory. My men could do with a specific against the cold.'

'Seems satisfactory?' George stared at him. 'You suggest that I could have doctored some bottles, poisoned bottles, against just such an impossible eventuality? Me? A faculty dean? A learned academic? A – a –'

'Some academics are more learned than others. You'd have done the same.' Three of his men took a glass: the other two held their unwavering guns. There was a discouraging certainty about everything Crni said and did: he seemed to take the minutest precautions against anything untoward, including, as George had said, the impossible eventuality.

Metrović said: 'What happens to Major Ranković and myself?'

'You remain behind.'

'Dead?'

'Alive. Bound and gagged but alive. We are not Četniks. We do not murder helpless soldiers, far less helpless civilians.'

'Nor do we.'

'Of course not. Those thousands of Muslims who perished in south Serbia died by their own hands. Cowards, were they not?'

Metrović made no reply.

'And how many more thousand Serbians – men, women and children – were massacred in Croatia, with the most bestial atrocities ever recorded in the Balkans, just because of their religion?'

'We had no hand in that. The Ustaša are no soldiers, just undisciplined terrorists.'

668

'The Ustaša are your allies. Just as the Germans are your allies. Remember Kragujevac, Major, where the Partisans killed ten Germans and the Germans rounded up and shot five thousand Yugoslav citizens? Marched the children out of schools and shot them in droves until even the execution squads were sickened and mutinied? Your allies. Remember the retreat from Užice where the German tanks rolled backwards and forwards over the fields until all the wounded Partisans lying there had been crushed to death? Your allies. The guilt of your murderous friends is your guilt too. Much as we would like to treat you in the same fashion we will not. I have my orders and, besides, you are at least technically our allies.' Crni's voice was heavy with contempt.

Metrović said: 'You are Partisans.'

'God forbid!' The revulsion in Crni's face was momentary but unmistakable. 'Do we look like guerrilla rabble? We are paratroopers of the Murge division.' The Murge was the best Italian division then operating in south-east Europe. 'Your allies, as I said.' Crni gestured towards the eight prisoners. 'You harbour a nest of vipers. You can't recognize them as such, far less know what to do with them. We can do both.'

Metrović looked at Petersen. 'I think I owe you an apology, Peter. Last night I didn't know whether to believe your assessment or not. It seemed so fantastic. Not any more. You were right.'

'Much good that's done me. My forecast, I mean. I was twenty-four hours out.'

'Tie them up,' Crni said.

Immediately after leaving the hut, to nobody's surprise, they were joined by two other soldiers: Crni was not the man to spend almost an hour inside any place without having a guard posted outside. That those were élite troops was beyond question. It was a bitter night, with driving snow, a biting wind and zero visibility but Crni and his men not only put up

669

with the extreme conditions but seemed positively to revel in them.

Metrović had been wrong more than once the previous night. He had said that nobody was going to be moving around the mountains in those impossible weather conditions for days to come: Crni and his men were there to prove him wrong.

Once they were well clear of the camp Crni and his men produced torches. The prisoners were arranged so that they trudged on in single file through the deepening snow – it was already almost knee-high – while four of the guards walked on either side of them. By and by, at a command from Crni, they halted.

Crni said: 'Here, I'm afraid, we have to tie you up. Your wrists. Behind your backs.'

'I'm surprised you haven't done it before,' Petersen said. 'I'm even more surprised that you want to do it now. You have in mind to kill us all, perhaps?'

'Explain yourself.'

'We are at the head of that track leading down the mountain-side to the valley floor?'

'How do you know?'

'Because the wind hasn't changed since yesterday. You have ponies?'

'Two only. For the ladies. That was all you required yesterday.'

'You are very well informed. And the rest of us are to have our hands bound behind our backs just in case we feel tempted to give you or one of your men a brisk shove over the precipice. Mistake, Captain Crni, mistake. Out of character.'

'Indeed?'

'Two reasons. The surface of that rock is broken and slippery with either ice or hard-packed snow. If a man slips on that surface how is he, with his hands tied behind his back, going to grab at the ground to stop himself sliding over the edge – and how's he going to be able to maintain his balance in the first place with his hands tied? To keep your balance you have to be able to stretch both arms wide. You should know that. It's as good as sending people to their deaths. Second reason is that your men don't have to be anywhere near the prisoners. Four of them well in advance, four well behind, the prisoners, maybe with a couple of torches, in the middle. What positive action could the prisoners take then except commit suicide by jumping off the precipice? I can assure you that none of them is in the least suicidally inclined.'

'I am not a mountaineer, Major Petersen. I take your point.'

'Another request, if I may. Let Giacomo and myself walk alongside the young ladies' ponies. I'm afraid the young ladies don't care too much for heights.'

'I don't want you!' Even the prospect of the descent had brought a note of hysteria into Sarina's voice. 'I don't want you!'

'She doesn't want you,' Crni said drily.

'She doesn't know what she's saying. It's just a personal opinion of mine. She suffers severely from vertigo. What have I to gain by saying so?'

'Nothing that I can see.'

As they lined up by the cliff-top, Giacomo, leading a pony, brushed by Petersen and said, sotto voce: 'That, Major, was quite a performance.' He vanished into the snow with Petersen looking thoughtfully after him.

A steep descent, in treacherous conditions, is always more difficult and dangerous than a steep ascent and so it was to prove in this case. It is also slower and it took them all of forty minutes to reach the valley floor but reach it they did without incident. Sarina spoke for the first time since they had left the plateau.

'We are down?'

'Safe and sound as ever was.'

She gave a long quavering sigh. 'Thank you. You don't need to hold my horse any more.'

'Pony. Whatever you say. I was getting quite attached to the old lady.'

'I'm sorry,' she said quickly. 'I didn't mean it that way. It's just that you're so – so awful and so kind. No, *I'm* the person who is awful. *You're* the person they're after.'

'As is only fitting. My rank.'

'They're going to kill you, aren't they?'

'Kill me? What a thought. Why should they? A little discreet questioning perhaps.'

'You said yourself that General Granelli is an evil man.'

'General Granelli is in Rome. Haven't you given any thought as to what is going to happen to you?'

'No, I haven't.' Her voice was dull. 'I don't think I care what's going to happen to me.'

'That,' said Petersen, 'is what is known as a conversation stopper.'

They moved on in silence, the still heavily falling snow now at their backs, until Crni called a halt. He had the beam of his torch directed at the Italian army truck Petersen had stolen two days previously.

'It was thoughtful of you, Major, to leave transport so conveniently at hand.'

'If we can help our allies – you didn't arrive by this.'

'It was thoughtful, but not necessary.' Crni moved the beam of the torch. Another, even larger Italian truck, was parked close by. 'All of you, into that truck. Edvard, come with me.'

The eight prisoners were ushered into the larger truck and made to sit on the floor crowded up against the cab. Five soldiers followed them and sat on side benches towards the rear. Five torch beams were directed forwards and in the light of the beams it was possible to see that an equal number of machine-pistol barrels were pointed in the same direction. The engine started up and the truck jolted off. Five minutes later they turned right on to the main Neretva road.

'Ah!' Harrison said. 'Bound for the bright lights of Jablanica, I see.'

'On this road, where else?' Petersen said. 'After that the road divides. We could be going anywhere. I would guess that Jablanica is as far as we go. It's getting late. Even Crni and his men have to sleep.'

Shortly afterwards the driver stopped both the truck and the engine.

'I don't see any bright lights around here,' Harrison said. 'What are those devils up to now?'

'Nothing that concerns us,' Petersen said. 'Our driver is just waiting for Crni and his friend Edvard to join him up front.'

'Why? They have their own transport.'

'Had. It's in the Neretva now. That lad who met us yesterday – you remember, Dominic, the driver with the sunglasses – would not have failed to note the make and number of the truck. When and if Ranković and Metrović are discovered and freed – which may not be for hours yet – the proverbial hue and cry may be raised. "May", I say. I doubt it. The Colonel is not a man to publicize the security gaps in his forces. But Crni doesn't strike me as a man to take the slightest chance.'

'Objection,' Giacomo said. 'If your friend Cipriano is the man behind this, he already knows the description of the truck. So what's the point in destroying the truck?'

'Giacomo, you sadden me. We don't *know* that Cipriano is the man behind this but if he is he wouldn't want to leave any clue that would point a finger at him in connection with the abduction. Remember that, officially, he and the Colonel are sworn allies, faithful unto death.'

673

Voices came from up front, a door banged, the engine started again and the truck moved off. 'That must be the way of it,' Giacomo said to no-one in particular. 'Pity about the truck, though.'

They jolted on through the snow-filled night, torch beams and barrels still pointed at them, until suddenly Harrison said: 'At last. Civilization. It's a long time since I've seen city lights.'

Harrison, as was his custom, was exaggerating to a considerable extent. A few dim lights appeared occasionally through the opened back of the truck but hardly enough to lend the impression that they were driving through a metropolis. By and by the truck pulled off on to a side road, climbed briefly, then stopped. The guards apparently knew where they were and did not wait for orders. They jumped down, lined up torches and guns as before and were joined by Crni.

'Down,' he said. 'This is as far as we go tonight.'

They lowered themselves to the ground and looked around them. As far as could be judged from the light of the beams, the building before them appeared to be standing alone and seemed, vaguely, to be shaped like a chalet. But, in the darkness and the snow it could have been just any building.

Crni led the way inside. The hallway presented a pleasant contrast to the swirling cold of the wintry night outside. The furnishings were sparse enough, just a table, a few chairs and a dresser, but it was warm – a small log fire burned in a low hearth – and warmly if not brightly lit: electric power had not yet reached this part of Jablanica and suspended oil lamps were the norm.

'Door to the left is a bathroom,' Crni said. 'Can be used anytime. There will, of course,' he added unnecessarily, 'be a guard in the hall all the time. The other door to the left leads to the main quarters of the house and does not concern you. Neither do those stairs.' He led the way to an opened door on

674

the far right and ushered them inside. 'Your quarters for the night.'

The room was unmistakably such as one would only find in a chalet. It was long, wide and low, with beamed ceiling, knotted pine walls and an oak parquet floor. Cushioned benches ran both sides of the room, there was a table, several arm-chairs, a very commodious dresser, some cupboards and shelves and, best of all, a rather splendid log fire several times the size of the one in the hallway. The only immediately incongruous note was struck by some canvas cots, blankets and pillows stacked neatly in one corner. It was George, inevitably, who discovered the second and not so immediately incongruous note. He pulled back the curtains covering one of the two windows and examined with interest the massive bars on the outside.

'It is part of the general malaise of our times,' he said sadly. 'With the onset of war, the deterioration of standards is as immediate as it is inevitable. The rules of honour, decency and common law go by default and moral degeneracy rears its ugly head.' He let fall the curtains. 'A wise precaution, very wise. One feels sure that the streets of Jablanica are infested by burglars, house-breakers, footpads and other criminals of that ilk.'

Crni ignored him and looked at Petersen who was inspecting the bedding. 'Yes, Major, I can count, too. Only six cots. We have a room upstairs for the two young ladies.'

'Considerate. You were very sure of yourself, weren't you, Captain Crni?'

'Oh, no, he wasn't,' George said disgustedly. 'A blind man could drive a coach and four with bells on through Mihajlović's perimeter.'

For a second time Crni ignored him. He had probably come to the conclusion that this was the only way to treat him.

'We may or may not move on tomorrow. It certainly won't

be early. Depends entirely on the weather. From now on our travel will be mainly on foot. Should you be hungry, there's food in that cupboard there. The contents of that high dresser will be of more interest to the professor.'

'Ah!' George opened the doors and looked appreciatively at what was, in effect, a comprehensively stocked miniature bar. 'The window bars are superfluous, Captain Crni. I shall not be moving on tonight.'

'Even if you could, where would you go? When you ladies want to sleep, let the guard know and I'll show you your room. I may or may not wish to interrogate you later, it depends on a call I have to make.'

'You surprise me,' Petersen said. 'I thought the phone system had ceased to work.'

'Radio, of course. We do have one. In fact, we have four, the other three being yours and those two very modern sets belonging to the von Karajans. I expect the code books will also prove to be useful.'

He left behind him a profound and fairly lengthy silence interrupted only by the sound of a cork being extracted from a bottle. Michael was the first to speak.

'Radios,' he said bitterly. 'Code books.' He looked accusingly at Petersen. 'You know what this means, don't you?'

'Yes. Nothing. Crni was amusing himself. All it means is that we will be put to the trouble of getting ourselves a new code. What else do you think they'll do after they discover the books are missing? They will do this, of course, not to protect themselves against their enemies but against their friends. The Germans have twice broken the code that we use among ourselves.' He looked at Harrison, who had seated himself, cross-legged, in an arm-chair before the fire and was contemplating a glass of wine that George had just handed him. 'For a man who has just been driven from house and home, Jamie, or snatched from it, which comes to the same thing, you don't look all that downcast to me.'

'I'm not,' Harrison said comfortably. 'No reason to be. I never thought I'd find quarters better than my last one but I was wrong. I mean, look, a real log fire. Carpe diem, as the man says. What, Peter, do you think the future holds for us?'

'I wouldn't know how to use a crystal ball.'

'Pity. It would have been nice to think that I might see the white cliffs of Dover again.'

'I don't see why not. No one's after your blood. I mean, you haven't been up to anything, have you, Jamie? Such as sending clandestine radio messages, in codes unknown to us, to parties also unknown to us?'

'Certainly not.' Harrison was unruffled. 'I'm not that kind of person, I don't have any secrets and I'm useless with a radio anyway. So you think I might see the white cliffs again. Do you think I'll be seeing the old homestead on Mount Prenj again?'

'I should think it highly unlikely.'

'Well now. A fairly confident prediction *and* without a crystal ball.'

'For that, I don't need a crystal ball. A person who has occupied the – ah – delicate position you have done will never again be employed in that capacity after he's been captured by the enemy. Torturing, brain-washing, reconversion to a double-agent, that sort of thing. Standard practice. You'd never be trusted again.'

'I say, that's a bit thick, isn't it? A blameless, stainless reputation. It's hardly my fault that I've been captured. It wouldn't have happened if you people had looked after me a bit better. Thank you, George, I will have a little more. Now that I'm happily out of that place, I've no intention of ever returning to it, not unless I'm dragged forcibly back to it, kicking and screaming in the accepted fashion.' He raised his glass. 'Your health, Peter.'

'You have taken an aversion to the people, the Četniks, the Colonel, myself?'

'A profound aversion. Well, not to you, although I must admit I don't care overmuch for what might be called your military politics. You're a total enigma to me, Peter, but I'd rather have you on my side than against me. As for the rest, I despise them. An extraordinary position for an ally to find himself in, is it not?'

'I think I'll have some wine, too, George, if I may. Well, yes, Jamie, it's true, you have made your discontent – I might even say displeasure – rather guardedly evident from time to time but I thought you were doing no more than exercising every soldier's inalienable right to complain loudly and at length about every conceivable aspect of army life.' He sipped his wine thoughtfully. 'One gathers there was something a little more to it than that?'

'A little more? There was a great deal more.' Harrison sipped his wine and gazed at the burning logs, a man relaxed, at peace with himself. 'In spite of the fact that the future looks somewhat uncertain, in some ways I owe our Captain Crni a favour. He's done no more than to pre-empt my decision, my intention, to leave Mount Prenj and its miserable inhabitants at the first convenient opportunity. Had it not been for the unexpected happening of the past couple of hours, you'd have discovered that I'd already made an official request for an official recall. But, of course, as matters stood before the appearance of Captain Crni, I wouldn't have made any such disclosures anyway.'

'I could have misjudged you, Jamie.'

'Indeed you could.' He looked around the room to see if there was anyone else misjudging him, but there was no-one thinking along those lines: a magnet to the iron filings, he had the undivided attention of every person in the room.

'So you didn't – don't – like us?'

'I should have thought that I had made that abundantly

clear. I may be no soldier, and the good Lord knows that I'm not, but I'm no clown either, all appearances to the contrary. I'm educated after a fashion: in practically any intellectual field that matters the average soldier is a virtual illiterate. I'm not educated in the way George is, I don't float around in cloud-cuckoo-land or wander among the groves of academe.' George looked profoundly hurt and reached for the wine bottle. 'I have been educated in a more practical fashion. Wouldn't you agree, Lorraine?'

'I would.' She smiled and said as if by rote: 'B.Sc., M.Sc., A.M.I.E.E., A.M.I.Mech.E. Oh, he's educated, all right. I used to be James's secretary.'

'Well, well, well,' Petersen said. 'The world grows even smaller.' Giacomo covered his face with his hand.

'Bachelor of Science, Master of Science we understand,' George said. 'As for the rest, it sounds as if he was coming down with a terminal illness.'

'Associate Member of the Institute of Electrical Engineers,' Lorraine said. 'Associate Member of the Institute of Mechanical Engineers.'

'It's unimportant.' Harrison was impatient. 'Point is I've been trained to observe, evaluate and analyze. I've been out here less than two months but I can tell you it took only a fraction of that time and a minimum of observation, evaluation and analysis to realize that Britain was backing the wrong horse in the Yugoslav stakes.

'I speak as a British officer. I don't want to sound overly dramatic, but Britain is locked, literally, in mortal combat with Germany. How do we defeat the Germans – by fighting them and killing them. How should we judge our allies or potential allies, what yardstick should we use? One. Only one. Are *they* fighting and killing Germans? Is Mihajlović? Is he hell. He's fighting with the Germans, alongside the Germans. Tito? Every German soldier caught in the sights of a Partisan rifle is a dead man. Yet those fools and dolts and

679

idiots in London keep sending supplies to Mihajlović, a man who is in effect their sworn enemy. I am ashamed for my own people. The only possible reason for this – God knows it's no excuse – is that Britain's war, as far as the Balkans is concerned, is being run by politicians and soldiers, and politicians are almost as naïve and illiterate as soldiers.'

George said: 'You speak harsh words about your own people, James.'

'Shut up! No, sorry, George, I didn't mean that, but in spite or maybe because of your vast education you're just as naïve and illiterate as any of them. Harsh but true. How does this extraordinary situation come about? Mihajlović is a near Machiavellian genius in international diplomacy: Tito is too busy killing Germans to have any time for any such thing.

'As far back as September 1941 Mihajlović and his Cetniks, instead of fighting the Germans, were busy establishing contacts with your precious Royalist government in London. Yes, Peter Petersen, precious I said and precious I did not mean. They don't give a damn about the unimaginable sufferings of the Yugoslav people, all they want to do is to regain royal power and if it's over the bodies of one or two millions of their countrymen, so much the worse for their countrymen. And, of course, Mihajlović, when contacting King Peter and his so-called advisers could hardly help contacting the British government as well. What a bonus! And naturally, at the same time, he contacted the British forces in the Middle East. For all I know the dunderheaded brasshats in Cairo may still regard the Colonel as the great white hope for Yugoslavia.' He gestured towards Sarina and Michael. 'In fact, the dunderheads unquestionably still do. Look at this gullible young couple here, specially trained by the British to come to the aid and comfort of the gallant Cetniks.'

'We're not gullible!' Sarina's voice was strained, her hands twisted together and she could have been close to either anger

680

or tears. 'We weren't trained by the British, we were trained by the Americans. And we *didn't* come to give aid and comfort to the Četniks.'

'There are no American radio operator schools in Cairo. Only British. If you received American training it was because the British wanted it that way.' Harrison's tone was as cool and discouraging as his face. 'I think you're gullible, I think you tell lies and I believe you came to help the Četniks. I also think you're a fine actress.'

'Good for you, Jamie,' Petersen said approvingly. 'You got one thing right there. She *is* a fine actress. But she's not gullible, she doesn't tell lies – well, maybe one or two little white ones – and she didn't come to help us.'

Both Harrison and Sarina stared at him in astonishment. Harrison said: 'How on earth can you say that?'

'Intuition.'

'Intuition!' Harrison, was, for Harrison, being heavily sardonic. 'If your intuition is on a par with your judgment you can mothball the two of them together. And don't try to side-track me. Hasn't it struck you as ironic that when you and your precious Četniks' – Harrison was very fond of the word 'precious' and used it, always in its most derogatory sense, with telling effect – 'were receiving arms and payments from the Germans, Italians and Nedić's quisling Serb régime, that you were simultaneously receiving arms and payments from the western allies – this, mark you, at a time when you were fighting along with the Germans, Italians and Ustaša in an attempt to destroy the Partisans, Britain's only real allies in Yugoslavia?'

'Have some more wine, Jamie.'

'Thank you, George.' Harrison shook his head. 'I confess myself to being totally baffled and, when I say that, I mean baffled all round. By you Četniks and by my own people. Can it really be that there are none so blind as will not see? Are you so gagged and blinkered by your all-consuming and wholly misguided sense of patriotism, by your blind allegiance to a discredited royalty that your myopic eyes are so reduced to a ten-degree field of tunnel vision that you have no concept of the three hundred and fifty degree of peripheral vision that lies beyond? Are my people in London similarly affected? They have to be, they have to be, for what else could explain the inexplicable, the incomprehensible idiocy of keeping on sending supplies to Mihajlović when they have before them incontrovertible evidence that he is actively collaborating with the Germans.'

'I'll bet you couldn't say that again,' Petersen said admiringly. 'All the big words, I mean. As you say, Jamie, it's all probably reduced to a factor of vision, what lies in the eye of the beholder.' He rose, crossed over to the fireplace and sat down beside Sarina. 'This is not really a switch, we're talking about the same thing. How did you enjoy your tête-à-tête with the Colonel this morning?'

'Tête-à-tête? I didn't have any tête-à-tête with him. Michael and I just reported to him. You told us to. Or have you forgotten?'

'I've forgotten nothing. But I think you have. Walls have ears. Not original, but still true.'

She glanced quickly at Michael then back again. 'I don't know what you're talking about.'

'Walls also have eyes.'

'Stop brow-beating my sister!' Michael shouted.

'Brow-beating? Asking a simple question is brow-beating? If that's what you call brow-beating maybe I should start beating you about the brow. You were there, too, of course. You got anything to tell me? You have, you know. I already know what your answer should be. Your truthful answer.'

'I've got nothing to tell you! Nothing! Nothing at all!'

'You're a lousy actor. Also, you're too vehement by half.'

'I've had enough of you, Petersen!' Michael was breathing quickly and shallowly. 'Enough of your bullying my sister and me.' He jumped to his feet. 'If you think I'm going to stand –'

'You're not going to stand, Michael.' George had come up behind Michael and laid his hands on his shoulders. 'You're going to sit.' Michael sat. 'If you can't keep quiet I'll have to tie and gag you. Major Petersen is asking questions.'

'Good Lord!' Harrison was or seemed outraged. 'This *is* a bit thick, George. A bit high-handed, I must say. Peter, I don't think you're any longer in a position to –'

'And if *you* don't keep quiet,' George said with a trace of weariness in his voice, 'I'll do the same thing to you.'

'To me!' No question, this time the outrage was genuine. 'Me? An officer? A Captain in the British Army! By God! Giacomo, you're an Englishman. I appeal to you –'

'Appeal is denied. I wouldn't hurt an officer's feelings by telling him to shut up, but I think the Major is trying to establish something. You may not like his military philosophy but at least you should keep an open mind. And I think Sarina should too. I think you're both being foolish.'

Harrison muttered 'My God' twice and subsided.

Petersen said: 'Thanks, Giacomo. Sarina, if you think I'm trying to hurt you or harm you then you are, as Giacomo says, being foolish. I couldn't and wouldn't. I want to help. Did you and the Colonel have or not have a private conversation?'

'We talked, if that's what you mean.'

'Of *course* you talked. If I sound a bit exasperated, it's pardonable. What did you talk about? Me?'

'No. Yes. I mean, among other things.'

'Among other things,' he mimicked. 'What other things?'

'Just other things. Just generally.'

'That's a lie. You talked just about me and, maybe, a bit about Colonel Lunz. Remember, walls can have both ears and eyes. And you can't remember what you said when you sold me down the river which is where I am now. How many pieces of silver did the good Colonel give you?'

'I never did!' She was breathing quickly now and there were patches of red high up on her cheeks. 'I didn't betray you. I didn't! I didn't!'

'And all for a little piece of paper. I hope you got your due. You earned your thirty pieces. You didn't know that I'd picked up the paper later, did you?' He brought a piece of paper out from his tunic and unfolded it. 'This one.'

She stared at it dully, looked at him equally dully, put her elbows on her knees, her face in her hands. 'I don't know what's going on.' Her voice was muffled. 'I don't know any more. I know you're a bad man, a wicked man, but I didn't betray you.'

'I know you didn't.' He reached out a gentle hand and touched her shoulder. 'But I know what's going on. I have done all along. I'm sorry if I hurt you but I had to get you to say it. Why couldn't you have admitted it in the first place? Or have you forgotten what I said only yesterday morning?'

'Forgotten what?' She took her hands from her face and looked at him. It was difficult to say if the hazel eyes were still dull for there were tears in them.

'That you're far too nice and too transparently honest to do anything underhand. There were three pieces of paper. The one I gave to the Colonel, this one I'd made out before leaving Rome – I never picked anything up after your talk with him – and the one Colonel Lunz had given to you.'

'You *are* clever, aren't you?' She'd wiped the tears from her eyes and they weren't dull any more, just mad.

'Cleverer than you are, anyway,' Petersen said cheerfully. 'For some inexplicable reason Lunz thought that I might be some kind of spy or double agent and change the message, forge a different set of orders. But I didn't, did I? The message I gave the Colonel was the one I received and it checked with the copy Lunz had given you. Paradoxically, of course – you being a woman – this annoyed you. If I had been a spy, a sort of reconverted renegade who had gone over to

684

the other side, you would have been no end pleased, wouldn't you? You might have respected me, even liked me a little. Well, I remained an unreconstructed Četnik. You were aware, of course, that if I *had* changed the orders that Mihajlović would have had me executed?'

A little colour drained from her face and she touched her hand to her lips.

'Of course you were unaware. Not only are you incapable of double-dealing, not only are you incapable of thinking along double-dealing lines, you're not even capable of thinking of the consequences to the double-dealer who has over-played his hand. How an otherwise intelligent girl – well, never mind. As I've said before, in this nasty espionage world, leave the thinking to those who are capable of it. Why did you do it, Sarina?'

'Why did I do what?' All of a sudden she seemed quite defenceless. She said, almost in a monotone: 'What am I going to be accused of now?'

'Nothing, my dear. I promise you. Nothing. I was just wondering, although I'm sure I know why, how it came about that you went along with this underground deal with Colonel Lunz, something so completely alien to your nature. It was because it was your only way into Yugoslavia. If you had refused, he'd have refused you entrance. So I've answered my own question.' Petersen rose. 'Wine, George, wine. All this talk is thirsty work.'

'What is not common knowledge,' George said, 'is that listening is even thirstier work.'

Petersen lifted his replenished glass and turned towards Harrison. 'To your health, Jamie. As a British officer, of course.'

'Yes, yes, of course.' Clutching his glass Harrison struggled to his feet. 'Of course. Your health. Ah. Well. Extenuating circumstances, old boy. How was I –'

'And a gentleman.'

685

'Of course, of course.' He was still confused. 'A gentleman.'

'Were you being a gentleman, Jamie, when you called her a gullible liar, and an aider and comforter to us miserable lot? This lovely and charming lady is not only not that, she's something you've been looking for, something to gladden your patriotic heart, a true blue loyalist and not a true blue Royalist, a patriot in your best sense of the word, what you would call a Yugoslav. As dedicated a Partisan as one can be who has never seen a Partisan in her life. That's why she and her brother came back to this country the hard way, to give – as you would put it in your customary stirring language, Jamie – their services to their country, i.e., the Partisans.'

Harrison put down his glass, crossed to where Sarina was sitting, stooped low, lifted the back of her hand and kissed it. 'Your servant, ma'am.'

'That's an apology?' George said.

'For an English officer,' Petersen said, 'that is – as an English officer would say – a jolly handsome apology.'

'He's not the only one who's due to make an apology.' Michael wasn't actually shuffling his feet but he looked as if he would have liked to. 'Major Petersen, I have –'

'No apology, Michael,' Petersen said hastily. 'No apology. If I'd a sister like that, I wouldn't even talk to her tormentor, in this case, me. I'd clobber him over the head with a two by four. So if I don't apologise to your sister for what I've done to her, don't you apologize to me.'

'Thank you very much, sir.' He hesitated. 'May I ask how long you've known that Sarina and I were – well, what you say we are.'

'From the first time I saw you. Rather, let me say I suspected something was far wrong when I met you in that Rome apartment. You were both stiff, awkward, ill at ease, reserved, even truculent. No smile on the lips, no song in the heart, none of the eagerness, the youthful enthusiasm of

686

those marching off into a glorious future. Ultra-cautious, ultra-suspicious. Wrong attitude altogether. If you'd been flying red flags you couldn't have indicated more clearly that something was weighing heavily on your minds. Your pasts were so blameless, so your concern was obviously with future problems such – as became evident quite soon – how you were going to transfer yourselves to the Partisan camp after you had arrived at our HQ. Your sister lost little time in giving you away – it was in the mountain inn when she tried to convince me of her Royalist sympathies. Told me she was a pal of King Peter's – prince, as he was then.'

'I never did!' Her indignation was unconvincing. 'I just met him a few times.'

'Sarina.' The tone was mildly reproving.

She said nothing.

'How often must I tell you –'

'Oh, all right,' she said.

'She's never met him in her life. She sympathized with me about his club foot. Young lad's as fit as a fiddle. Wouldn't know a club foot if he saw one. Well, all this is of interest but I'm afraid only academic interest.'

'Oh, I don't know,' Giacomo said. 'It's of more than academic interest to me.' He was, as always, smiling, but in the circumstances, it was difficult to say what he was smiling about. 'However, as a matter of academic interest, I'm totally in agreement with those kids – sorry, I mean Sarina and Michael. I don't want to fight – I mean I don't want to fight in those damned mountains; the Aegean and the Royal Navy will do me very nicely, thank you – but if I have to it'll be with the Partisans.'

'You're like Jamie,' Petersen said. 'If you're going to fight anybody it's going to be the Germans?'

'I think I made that pretty clear to you back in the Hotel Eden.'

'You did. It's still only a matter of academic interest. What

687

are you going to do about it? How do you intend going about joining your guerrilla friends?'

Giacomo smiled. 'I'll wait for a break.'

'You could wait for ever.'

'Peter.' There was a note of appeal, almost desperation, in Harrison's voice. 'I know you owe us nothing, that you have no responsibility for us any more. But there must be a way. However different our philosophies, we're all in this together. Come on, Peter. We could settle our differences afterwards. Meantime – well, a man of your infinite resources and –'

'Jamie,' Petersen said gently. 'Can't you see the fence down the middle of this room. George, Alex and I are on one side. You five are on the other. Well, you, the von Karajans and Giacomo are. I don't know about Lorraine. It's a mile high, that fence, Jamie, and not for climbing.'

'I see his point, Captain Harrison,' Giacomo said. 'The fence is not for climbing. Besides, my pride wouldn't let me try it. I must say, Major, it's not like you to leave loose ends lying around. Lorraine, here. Doesn't she fit into a category? For our edification, I mean.'

'Category? I don't know. And not to give you offence, Lorraine, but I don't really care now. It doesn't matter. Not any more.' He sat down, glass in hand, and said no more. As far as anyone could tell, Major Petersen had, for the first time in their experience, lapsed into a brooding silence.

It was a silence, punctuated only by the occasional glug-glug as George topped empty wineglasses, that stretched on and uncomfortably on, until Lorraine said suddenly and sharply: 'What's wrong? Please, what's wrong?'

'Speaking to me?' Petersen said.

'Yes. You're staring at me. You keep on staring at me.'

'Being on the wrong side of a fence doesn't stop a man from having good taste,' Giacomo said.

'I wasn't aware of it,' Petersen said. He smiled. 'Besides,

as Giacomo said, it's no hardship. I'm sorry. I was a long long way away, that's all.'

'And speaking of staring,' Giacomo said cheerfully, 'Sarina's no slouch at it either. Her eyes haven't left your face since you started your Rodin the thinker bit. There are deep currents, hereabouts. Do you know what I think? I think she's thinking.'

'Oh, do be quiet, Giacomo.' She sounded positively cross.

'Well, I suppose we're all thinking one way or another,' Petersen said. 'Heaven knows we've plenty to think about. You, Jamie, you're sunk in a pretty profound gloom. The bright lights? No. The white cliffs? No. Ah! The lights of home.'

Harrison smiled and said nothing.

'What's she like, Jamie?'

'What's she like?' Harrison smiled again, shrugged and looked at Lorraine.

'Jenny's wonderful,' Lorraine said quietly. 'I think she's the most wonderful person in the world. She's my best friend and James doesn't deserve her. She's worth ten of him.'

Harrison smiled like a man who was well-pleased with himself and reached for his wineglass; if he was wounded, he hid it well.

Petersen looked away until his eyes lighted casually on Giacomo, who nodded almost imperceptibly: Petersen smiled slightly and looked away.

Twenty more minutes passed, partly in desultory conversation but mainly in silence, before the door opened and Edvard entered. 'Major Petersen?'

Petersen rose. Giacomo made to speak but Petersen forestalled him. 'Don't say it. Thumb-screws.'

He was back inside five minutes. Giacomo looked disappointed. 'No thumb-screws?'

'No thumb-screws. I would like to say that they're bringing out a rack and that you're next. No rack. But you're next.'

Giacomo left. Harrison said: 'What was it like. What did they want?'

'Very humane. Very civilized. What you would expect of Crni. Lots of questions, some very personal, but I just gave them name, rank and regiment, which is all you're legally required to give. They didn't press the matter.'

Giacomo was back in even less time than Petersen. 'Disappointing,' he said. 'Very disappointing. They'd never have made the Spanish Inquisition. The courtesy of your presence, Captain Harrison.'

Harrison was away a little longer than either but not much. He returned looking very thoughtful. 'You're next, Lorraine.'

'Me?' She stood and hesitated. 'Well, if I don't go I suppose they'll come for me.'

'It would be most unseemly,' Petersen said. 'We've survived. What's a lion's den to an English girl like you?'

She nodded and left, but left reluctantly. Petersen said: 'How was it, Jamie?'

'An urbane lot, as you say. Seemed to know a surprising amount about me. No questions that had any military bearing that I could see.'

Lorraine was absent for at least fifteen minutes. When she returned she was rather pale and although there were no tears on her cheeks it seemed clear that she had been crying. Sarina looked at Petersen, Harrison and Giacomo, shook her head and put her arm round Lorraine's shoulders.

'They're a gallant lot, aren't they, Lorraine? Chivalrous. Concerned.' She gave them a withering glance. 'Maybe they're just shy. Who's next?'

'They didn't ask to see anyone.'

'What did they do to you, Lorraine?'

'Nothing. Do you mean – no, no, they didn't touch me. It

690

was just some of the questions they asked . . .' Her voice trailed off. 'Please, Sarina, I'd rather not talk about it.'

'Maraschino,' George said authoritatively. He took her by the arm, seated her and proffered a small glass. She took it, smiled gratefully and said nothing.

Crni came in accompanied by Edvard. He was, for the first time anyone had seen, relaxed and smiling.

'I have some news for you. I hope you will find it good news.'

'You're not even armed,' George said. 'How do you know we won't break every bone in your bodies? Better still, use you as hostage to escape? We are desperate men.'

'Would you do that, Professor?'

'No. Some wine?'

'Thank you, Professor. Good news, at least I think it's good news, for the von Karajans, Captain Harrison and Giacomo. I am sorry that we have been guilty of a small deception but it was necessary in the circumstances. We are not members of the Murge Division. We are, thank heavens, not even Italians. We are just common-or-garden members of a Partisan reconnaissance group.'

'Partisans.' There was no excitement in Sarina's voice, just incomprehension tinged with disbelief.

Crni smiled. 'It's true.'

'Partisans.' Harrison shook his head. ''Pon my soul. Partisans. Well, now. I mean. Yes.' He shook his head then his voice rose an octave. 'Partisans!'

'Is it true?' Sarina had Crni by the arms and was actually shaking him. 'Is it true?'

'Of course it's true.'

She searched his eyes as if searching for the truth, then suddenly put her arm around him and hugged him. She was very still for a moment then released him and stepped back. 'I'm sorry,' she said. 'I shouldn't have done that.'

He smiled. 'There's no regulation that says that a young

691

recruit, female, may not hug an officer. Not, of course, to make a practice of it.'

'There's that, too, of course.' She smiled uncertainly.

'There's something else?'

'No, not really. We're terribly glad to see you.'

'Glad?' Harrison said. 'Glad!' The initial shock absorbed, he was in a state bordering on euphoria. 'Nothing less than a merciful providence has sent you our way!'

'It wasn't a merciful providence, Captain Harrison. It was a radio message. When my commanding officer says "move", I move. That's the "something else" you wouldn't talk about, Miss von Karajan. Your fears are groundless. Military regulations don't allow me to shoot my boss.'

'Your boss?' She looked at him, then Petersen, then back at Crni. 'I don't understand.'

Crni sighed. 'You're quite right, Peter. You, too Giacomo. No espionage material among this lot. If there were they wouldn't have to be hit over the head with the obvious. We're both Partisans. We're both in intelligence. I am the ranking subordinate officer. He is the deputy chief. I'm sure that makes everything clear.'

'Perfectly,' George said. He handed Crni a glass. 'Your wine, Ivan.' He turned to Sarina. 'He doesn't really like being called Crni. And don't clench your fists. All right, all right, this is life in a nutshell. Decisions, decisions. Do you kiss him or do you hit him?' The bantering note left George's voice. 'If you're mad because you've been fooled, then you're a fool. There was no other way. You and your hurt pride. You've got your Partisans and he hasn't to face a firing squad. Don't you know how to be glad, girl? Or is there no room for emotions like relief and gratitude in the minds of you spoilt young aristocrats?'

'George!' She was shocked, less because of the words than the tone she had never heard before. 'George! I am so selfish?'

'Never.' His good humour instantly restored, he squeezed her shoulders. 'It's just that I thought it would rather spoil the flavour of the moment if you were to give Peter a black eye.' He glanced sideways. Harrison, his forehead on his forearms on the table, was softly pounding the table with his fist and muttering to himself. 'You are not well, Captain Harrison?'

'My God, my God, my God!' The pounding with the fist continued.

'A Šljivovica?' George said.

Harrison lifted his head. 'And the awful thing is that I am cursed with total recall. That,' he added irrelevantly, 'was why I was so good at passing exams. I can remember every word I said in that stirring speech about patriotism and duty and loyalty and myopic idiocy and – I can't go on, I can't.'

'You mustn't reproach yourself, Jamie,' Petersen said. 'Think what it did for our morale.'

'If there was any justice, any compassion in this world,' Harrison said, 'this floor would open up beneath me at this very moment. A British officer, I called myself, thereby meaning there was no other. A highly skilled observer, evaluator, analyzer. Good God! Total recall, I tell you, total recall. It's hell!'

'I'm sorry I missed that speech,' Crni said.

'Pity,' Petersen said. 'Still, you've heard about Jamie's total recall. He can repeat it to you verbatim any time you want.'

'Spare the vanquished,' Harrison said. 'I heard what you said to Sarina, George, but I remain bitter. Fooled, fooled, fooled. And doubly bitter because Peter didn't trust me. But you trusted Giacomo, didn't you? He knew.'

'I told Giacomo nothing,' Petersen said. 'He guessed – he's a soldier.'

'And I'm not? Well, that's for sure. How did you guess, Giacomo?'

'I heard what you heard. I heard the Major telling –

693

suggesting rather, to Captain Crni that his intention to rope us up before descending that cliff path was dangerous. Captain Crni is not the man to take an order or suggestion from anyone. So then I knew.'

'Of course. I missed it. So you didn't trust any of us, did you Peter?'

'I didn't. I had to know where I stood with you all. Lots of odd things have been happening in Rome and ever since we left Rome. I had to know. You'd have done the same.'

'Me? I wouldn't have noticed anything odd in the first place. When did you come to the decision that you were free to talk? And why did you decide to talk? My God, when I come to think of it, when have you ever been free to talk? My word, I can't imagine it, I just can't. Can you, Sarina? Living the life of a lie, surrounded by enemies, one false move, one unconsidered slip, one careless word and pouf! And he spent almost half his time with us!'

'Ah! But I spent the other half with our own people. Holiday, you might say.'

'Oh, God, holiday. I knew – and I haven't known you long – that you were something different, but this – but this – it passes my comprehension. And you, a man like you, you're only the deputy chief. I'd love to meet the man you call chief.'

'I don't call him "chief." I call him lots of other things but not that. As for loving to meet him, you don't have to bother. You've already met him. In fact, you've described him. Big fat clown, naïve and illiterate, who spends his time floating around in cloud-cuckoo-land. Or was it the groves of academe? I don't remember.'

Harrison spilled the contents of his glass on the table. He looked dazed. 'I don't believe it.'

'Nobody does. I'm his right arm, only, in charge of field operations. As you know, he seldom accompanies me. This mission was different but, then, this was an unusually important mission. Couldn't be trusted to bunglers like me.'

694

Michael approached George, a certain awed incredulity in his face. 'But in Mostar you told me you were a Sergeant Major.'

'A tiny prevarication.' George waved his hand in airy dismissal. 'Inevitable in this line of business. Tiny prevarications, I mean. But I did say it was a temporary not substantive rank. Generalmajor.'

'Good God!' Michael was overcome. 'I mean "Sir".'

'It's too much.' Harrison didn't even notice when George courteously refilled his glass. 'It's really too much. Too much for the reeling mind to encompass. Maybe I haven't such a mind after all. Tell me next that I'm Adolph Hitler and I'd seriously consider the possibility.' He looked at George, shook his head and drained half his glass. 'You see before you a man trying to find his way back to reality. Now, where was I? Ah, yes. I was asking you when you came to the decision you were free to talk.'

'When you told me – or Lorraine did – about your Jenny.'

'Ah, yes, of course. Jenny. I see.' It was plain that Harrison was quite baffled. He suddenly, physically, shook himself. 'What the hell has Jenny got to do with this?'

'Nothing, directly.'

'Ah Jenny. Lorraine. The question that Captain Crni asked me through there.'

Lorraine said in a quiet voice: 'What question, James?'

'He asked me if I knew Giancarlo Tremino – you know, Carlos. Of course I said yes, I knew him very well.' He looked down at his glass. 'Perhaps I shouldn't have answered. I mean, they weren't torturing me or anything. Maybe I don't have such a mind after all.'

'It wasn't your fault, James,' Lorraine said. 'You weren't to know. Besides, there's been no harm done.'

'How do you know there's been no harm done, Lorraine?' Sarina sounded bitter. 'I know it wasn't Captain Harrison's fault. And I know it wasn't really Captain Crni who asked the

695

question. Don't you know that Major Petersen *always* finds out what he wants? Are we still to regard ourselves as prisoners in this room, Captain Crni?'

'Good God, no! As far as I'm concerned the house is yours. Anyway, you don't ask me. Major Petersen is in charge.'

'Or you, George?' She smiled faintly. 'Sorry. I'm not used to the Generalmajor yet.'

'Quite frankly, neither am I. George is fine.' He smiled and wagged a finger at her. 'Don't try to spread dissension in the ranks. Outside my head office, which at the moment is a disused shepherd's hut up near Bihać, Peter is in sole charge. I just point in the general direction and then get out of the way. If you know you're not in his class, as I'm wise enough to know, you don't interfere with the best field operative there is.'

'Could I speak to you, Major? In the hall?'

'Ominous,' he said and picked up his glass. 'Very ominous.' He followed her out and closed the door behind them. 'Well?'

She hesitated. 'I don't know quite how to say this. I think –'

'If you don't know what to say and you're still at the thinking stage, why waste my time in this really melo-dramatic fashion?'

'It's not silly. It's not dramatic! And you're not going to make me mad. What you've just said sums you up. Superior, cutting, contemptuous, never making allowances for people's faults and weaknesses: and at the same time you can be the most thoughtful and kind person I know. It's not just that you're unbearable. You're unknowable. Jekyll and Hyde. The Dr Jekyll bit I like and admire. You're brave, George thinks you're brilliant, you take incredible risks that would destroy a person like me and, best of all, you're very good at looking after people. Anyway, I knew last night that you couldn't belong to those people.'

Petersen smiled. 'I won't give you the chance of telling me

again how nasty I am, so I won't say you're being wise after the event.'

'You're wrong,' she said quietly. 'It was something that Major Metrović said last night about Tito's Achilles' heel, his lack of mobility, his three thousand wounded men. In any civilized war – if there is such a thing – those men would be left to the enemy who would treat them in hospital. This is no civilized war. They would be massacred. You could never be a party to that.'

'I have my points. But you did not bring me out here to point those out.'

'I did not. It's the Mr Hyde side – oh, I *don't* want to lecture but I dislike that side, it hurts me and it baffles me. That a man so physically kind can in other ways be so cold, detached, uncaring to the point of not being quite human.'

'Oh, dear. Or, as Jamie would put it, I say, I say.'

'It's true. In order to gain your own ends, you can be – you are – indifferent to people's feelings to the point of cruelty.'

'Lorraine?'

'Yes. Lorraine.'

'Well, well. I thought it was axiomatic that two lovely ladies automatically disliked each other.'

She seized his upper arms. *'Don't* change the subject.'

'I must tell Alex about this.'

'Tell him what?' she said warily.

'He thinks you detest one another.'

'Tell Alex he's a fool. She's a lovely person. And *you* are tearing her to pieces.'

Petersen nodded. 'She's being torn to pieces all right. But I'm not the person who's doing the tearing.'

She looked closely at him, her eyes moving from one of his to the other, as if hoping that would help her find the truth. 'Then who is?'

'If I told you, you'd just go and tell her.' She said nothing, just kept up her intense scrutiny of his face. 'She knows who is. But I don't want her to think that it's public knowledge.'

She looked away. 'Two things. Maybe, deep down, you do have some finer feelings after all.' She looked at his eyes again and half-smiled. 'And you don't trust me.'

'I'd like to.'

'Try.'

'She's a good, honest, patriotic British citizen and she's working for the Italian secret service, specifically for Major Cipriano and she may well be responsible, however indirectly, for the deaths of an untold number of my fellow countrymen.'

'I don't believe it! I don't believe it!' Her eyes were wide and full of horror and her voice shook. 'I don't! I don't! I don't!'

'I know you don't,' he said gently. 'That's because you don't want to believe it. I didn't want to believe it myself. I do now. I can prove it. Do you think I'm so stupid as to say I can prove a thing when I can't. Or don't you believe me either?'

'I don't know what to believe,' she said wildly. 'Yes, I do. I do. I do know what to believe. I don't believe Lorraine could be like that.'

'Too lovely a person, too honest, too good, too true?'

'Yes! Yes! That's what I believe.'

'That's what I believed, too. That's what I still believe.'

Her grip on his arms tightened and she looked at him almost beseechingly. 'Please. Please don't make fun of me.'

'She's being blackmailed.'

'Blackmailed! Blackmailed! How could anyone blackmail Lorraine?' She looked away, was silent for some seconds, then looked back again. 'It's something to do with Carlos, isn't it?'

'Yes. Indirectly.' He looked at her curiously. 'How did you know that?'

'Because she's in love with him,' Sarina said impatiently.

'How do you know *that*?' This time he was openly surprised.

'Because I'm a woman.'

'Ah, well, yes. I suppose that explains it.'

'*And* because you had Captain Crni ask her about Carlos. But I knew before that. Anyone could see it.'

'Here's one who didn't.' He thought. 'Well, hindsight, retrospect, yes. But I said only indirectly. Nobody would be stupid enough to use Carlos as a blackmail weapon. They'd find themselves with a double-edged sword in their hands. But, sure, he's part of it.'

'Well?' She'd actually arrived at the stage where she had started shaking him, no mean feat with a person of Petersen's bulk. 'What's the other part of it?'

'I know, or I think I know, the other part of it. But I haven't any proof.'

'Tell me what you think.'

'You think because she's honest and good and true that she has led a blameless life, that she can't possibly have any guilty secrets?'

'Go on.'

'I don't think she's got any guilty secrets either. Unless you call having an illegitimate child a guilty secret, which I don't.'

She took her right hand away from his arm and touched her lips. She was shocked not by what he had said but because of its implications.

'Carlos is a doctor.' He sounded tired and, for the first time since she had met him, he looked tired. 'He qualified in Rome. Lorraine lived with him during the time she was Jamie Harrison's secretary. They have a son, aged two and a half. It's my belief that he's been kidnapped. I'll find out for sure when I have a knife at Cipriano's throat.'

She stared at him in silence. Two tears trickled slowly down her cheeks.

EIGHT

At nine o'clock the next morning Jablanica looked so much like an idealized Christmas postcard that it was almost unreal, untrue in its breathtaking beauty. The snow had stopped, the clouds were gone, the sun shone from a clear pale blue sky and the air on the windless slopes, where the trees hung heavy with snow, was crisp and pellucid and very cold. It required only the sound of sleigh-bells to complete the illusion. But peace on earth and goodwill to all men were the last considerations in the thoughts of those gathered around the breakfast table that morning.

Petersen, his chin on his hand and his coffee growing cold before him, was obviously lost in contemplation. Harrison, who showed remarkably little after-effects from the considerable amount of wine he had found necessary to drown his chagrin and bring himself once more face to face with reality, said: 'A penny for them, Peter, my boy.'

'My thoughts? They'd be worth a lot more than that to the people I'm thinking about. Not, may I add hastily, that they include any of those sitting around the table.'

'And not only do you look pensive,' Harrison went on, 'but I detect a slight diminution in the usual early morning ebullience, the sparkling cheer. You found sleep hard to come by? The change of beds, perhaps?'

'As I sleep in a different bed practically every night in life that would hardly be a factor, otherwise I'd be dead by this time. Fact is, I was up nearly all night, with either George or Ivan, in the radio room. You couldn't possibly have heard it, but there was a long and violent thunderstorm during the night – that's why we have cloudless skies this morning – and both transmission and reception were close on impossible.'

'Ah! That explains it. Would it be in order to ask who you were talking to during the long watches of the night?'

'Certainly. No secrets, no secrets.' Harrison's expression of disbelief was only fleeting and he made no comment. 'We had, of course, to contact our HQ in Bihać and warn them of the impending attack. That, alone, took almost two hours.'

'You should have used my radio,' Michael said. 'It's got a remarkable range.'

'We did. It was no better than the other.'

'Oh. Then perhaps you should have used me. After all, I do know that equipment.'

'Of course you do. But, then, our people in Bihać don't know Navajo which is the only code you are familiar with.'

Michael looked at him, his mouth fallen slightly open. 'How on earth did you know that? I mean, I've got no code books.' He tapped his head. 'It's all up here.'

'You sent a message just after Colonel Lunz and I had been talking to you. You may be a good radio operator, Michael, but otherwise you shouldn't be allowed out without a minder.'

Sarina said: 'Don't forget I was there also.'

'Two minders. I'll bet you never even checked to see if the room was bugged.'

'Good God!' Michael looked at his sister. 'Bugged! Did you – how could you have known we were going to stay –'

'It could have been bugged. It wasn't. George was listening on the balcony.'

'George!'

'You talked in plain language. George said it wasn't any European language he'd ever heard. You had an American

701

instructor. The Americans labour under the happy delusion that Navajo is unbreakable.'

'Now you tell me,' George said. He seemed in no way upset.

'Sorry. Busy. I forgot.'

'Peter's expertise in espionage is matched only by his expertise in codes. The two go hand-in-glove. Makes up codes all the time. Breaks them, too. Remember he said the Germans had twice broken the Četnik code. *They* didn't. Peter gave them the information. Not that they know that. Nothing like spreading dissension among allies.'

· Harrison said: 'How do you know the Germans didn't monitor and break your transmission last night?'

'Impossible. Only two people know my codes – me and the receiver. Never use the same code twice. You can't break a code on a single transmission.'

'That's fine. But – not trying to be awkward, old boy – will this information be of any use to your Partisans? Won't the Germans know that you've been kidnapped or disappeared or whatever and might pass this message on. If they did, surely they would change their plan of attack.'

'Don't you think I have considered this, Jamie? You simply don't even begin to know the Balkans. How could you, after less than a couple of months? What do you know of the deviousness, the plotting and counter-plotting, the rivalries, the jealousies, the self-seeking, the total regard for one's own power base, the distrusts, the obsession for personal gain, the vast gulf between the Occidental and Byzantine minds? I don't think there's even a remote chance of the Germans finding out.

'Consider. Who knows I've got the plans? As far as the Colonel is concerned, there are only two plans, he's got both and I've never seen a copy. Why should he think so? Metrović will have given him the name of Cipriano but I'll bet the Colonel has never heard of him and even if he has what's he going to tell him? Even if he did tell him Cipriano would be too smart to believe it was the Murge division – a commando unit like Ivan's never discloses their true identity. Again, apart from the fact that the Colonel's pride would probably stop him anyway from letting anyone know that his defences have been breached, he could be Machiavellian enough to want the Germans to be taken by surprise, not, of course in order that they should be defeated but that they should suffer severe casualties. Sure, he wants the Partisans destroyed but, when and if it happens, he wants the Germans out of the country. Basically, they're both his natural enemies.

'And even if the Germans did eventually find out, so what? It's too late to change plans and, anyway, there *are* no other plans they could make. There *is* no alternative.'

'I have to agree,' Harrison said. 'They'll go ahead as planned. Forewarned, one takes it, is forearmed. A satisfactory night's work, no?'

'It was unimportant. They would almost certainly have found out in any case. We have a considerable number of reliable contacts throughout the country. In the areas held by the Germans, Italians, Četniks and Ustaša – and that's most of the country – there are reliable solid citizens, or are so regarded by the Germans, Italians, Četniks and Ustaša, who, while cheerfully collaborating with the enemy, send us regular and up-to-date reports of the latest enemy troop movements. In other words, they are Partisan spies. Their reports are far from complete but enough to give Tito and his staff a fair indication of the enemy's intentions.'

'I suppose that happens in every war,' Harrison said, 'But I didn't know the Partisans had spies in the enemy's camp.'

'We have had from the very beginning. We couldn't have survived otherwise. What took up most of our time last night was the distressing discovery – well, we first suspected it about ten weeks ago – that the enemy have spies in *our* camp.

Even more distressing was the discovery that they had spies in the Partisan HQ. In retrospect, it was naïve of us, we should have suspected the possibility and taken precautions long ago. In fairness to us, we weren't complacent – we were just under the fond misapprehension that every Partisan was a burning patriot. Some, alas, burn less brightly than others. This, and not acting as message boys for General von Löhr, is what has been occupying George, Alex and myself in Italy in the past two weeks. It was a matter of such vital importance that George was actually sufficiently motivated to drag himself away from his snug retreats in Bihać and Mount Prenj. Those spies in our camp had become a major threat to our security: we were trying to uncover the Italian connection.

'That there was, and is, an Italian connection, is beyond dispute. Not German, not Četnik, not Ustaša – specifically Italian, for it has been the Italian Murge division, first-class mountain troops, that have been causing us all the trouble. Our Partisans are as good, probably even better mountain troops, but hundreds of them have been killed by the Murge division in the past few months. Never in pitched battle. Invariably in isolated, one-off, incidents. A patrol, a localized troop movement, a transfer of wounded to a supposedly safer area, a reconnaissance group behind enemy lines – it came to the stage where none of those was immune to a lightning strike by specialized Murge units who apparently knew, always, exactly where to strike, when to strike, how to strike – they even seemed to know the number and composition of the Partisan groups they would be attacking, even the approximate number of the groups themselves. Our small-scale guerrilla movements were becoming very hampered, almost paralysed: and a partisan's army's survival depends almost exclusively on mobility, flexibility and long-range reconnaissance.

'The Murge, of course, were receiving precise advance information of our movements. The information had to be coming from a person or persons in the neighbourhood of our HQ. Those secret messages, messages which led hundreds of men to their deaths, were not of course written down, addressed to the enemy and dropped in the nearest letter-box: they were sent by radio.' Petersen broke off as if to collect his thoughts, his eyes wandering, unseeingly, as it seemed, round the table. Lorraine, he could see, was un-naturally pale: Sarina had her hands clasped tightly together. Petersen appeared to notice nothing.

'I'll carry on for a moment,' George said. 'At this time, you must understand that Peter has been overcome by his habitual modesty. Peter couldn't believe that the traitors could be any long-serving Partisans. Neither could I. Peter suggested that we check the approximate dates of the first transmissions – the times of the first unexpected swoops by the Murge units – with the time of the arrival of the latest recruits to the Partisans. We did and found that this checked with the arrival of an unusually high number of ex-Četniks – Četniks regularly desert to us and it's quite impossible to check out the credentials and good faith of all of them or even a fraction of them.

'Peter and some of his men checked on a small number of those and found two who had access to long-range transmitters hidden in a forest on a hill-side. They wouldn't talk and we don't torture. They were executed. Thereafter the number of unexpected attacks by the Murge fell off rapidly: but they still continued at sporadic intervals. Which, of course, could only mean that there were still some traitors around.'

George helped himself liberally to some beer. It was but breakfast time, but George claimed to be allergic to both tea and coffee.

'So we went to Italy, the three of us. Why? Because we are – or were – Četnik intelligence officers and naturally associated with our Italian counterparts. Why? Because we were convinced that the messages were being relayed through

Italian Intelligence. Why? Because a fighting division has neither the facilities, the ability, the organization nor the cash to mount such an operation. But Italian Intelligence has all of these in abundance.'

'Amidst the welter of "whys", George,' Harrison said, 'why the cash?'

'It's as Peter said,' George said sadly. 'You haven't got the Balkan mentality. Come to that, I doubt whether you have the universal mentality. The Četnik agents, like agents and double-agents the world over, are not motivated simply by altrusim, patriotism or political conviction. The little gears in their minds only mesh efficiently under the influence of the universal lubricant. Money. They are rather highly paid and, considered dispassionately, deserve to be: look what happened to those two unfortunates unmasked by Peter.'

Petersen rose, walked to the window and stood there, gazing down the gentle valley that sloped away from their chalet. He seemed to have lost interest in the conversation.

'All in all,' Harrison said, 'a fair night's work.'

'That wasn't quite all of it,' George said. 'We have located Cipriano.'

'Cipriano!'

'None other. Lorraine, my dear! You look so pale. Are you not well?'

'I feel – I feel a little faint.'

'Maraschino,' George said unhesitatingly. 'Sava!' This to one of Crni's soldiers who rose at once and crossed to the liquor cupboard. 'Yes, indeed. The worthy Major himself.'

'But how on earth –'

'We have our little methods,' George said complacently. 'We have, as Peter told you, our reliable, solid citizens everywhere. Incidentally, you can now forget all that Peter told you – thank you, my boy, just give it to the lady – all he told you about Cipriano working hand-in-glove with the Partisans. I'm afraid he grossly maligned the poor man but at the moment he deemed it prudent to divert any suspicions that Majors Metrović and Ranković might have been harbouring from himself to an absent person. Cipriano was conveniently absent. Our Peter is a very convincing actor, no?'

'He's a very convincing liar,' Sarina said.

'Oh, tush! Hurt pride again. We're just mad because he fooled you, too. Anyway, Cipriano's in Imotski, doubtless closeted with the Murge brigade commander there and hatching fresh devilish schemes against our poor Partisans. I shouldn't have to explain any of this. You will remember that Peter said in Mount Prenj that he wanted to get to the link-man – Cipriano – because he was aiding and abetting the Partisans. What he meant to say was he wanted to get at the link-man because he was a deadly enemy of the Partisans but he couldn't very well say that, could he, in front of Metrović and Ranković? Come, come, my children, you disappoint me: you had all night long to work out something as simple and obvious as that.'

George yawned behind a massive hand. 'Excuse me. Now that I'm breakfasted and am once more at peace with myself, I intend to retire and rest lightly for two or three hours. We will not be moving out until the afternoon at the earliest. We await an urgent communication from Bihać but it will take some time to collect and collate the information we want. Meantime, how do you people propose to spend the morning?' He raised his voice. 'Peter. Those people are free to come and go as they want, inside and out, aren't they?'

'Of course.'

Captain Crni smiled and said: 'May I suggest that you put on your coats and I'll show you around our little town. There's not much to show so it would be a short walk and hardly exhausting. Apart from the fact that it's a lovely morning I know where we can get the best coffee in Bosnia. Far better than that awful swill we've just had.'

Sarina said, 'That way we can still be watched, can't we?'

Captain Crni bowed gallantly. 'It would always be a pleasure to watch you and Miss Chamberlain. If however, you wish to go alone and report to the nearest Italian command post that we are Partisans and have designs on a certain Italian intelligence major, then you are by all means free to do so. That, Miss von Karajan, is the extent to which we trust you.'

'I *am* sorry.' She reached out an impulsive hand and caught his forearm. 'That was a terrible thing to say. Two or three days in this country and I find I can't trust anyone, not even myself.' She smiled. 'Besides, you're the only one who knows where the coffee shop is.'

They left – without Giacomo who had elected to remain behind – shortly afterwards. Petersen said wearily: 'She doesn't trust anyone. God knows I don't blame her. George, I am a hypocritical liar. Even when I say nothing, I'm a hypocritical liar.'

'I know what you mean, Peter. Sometimes a tiny voice reaches down to my conscience – God knows how it ever finds it – and says exactly the same thing. The clarion call to duty strikes a pretty cracked note at times. Sava?'

'General?'

'Go to the window in the front room and watch the road. If they return unexpectedly, call me. I'll be upstairs. I'll let you know when you can stop the watch. Shouldn't be more than a few minutes.'

After lunch a very refreshed-looking Petersen – he'd had four hours' sleep – crossed to where Lorraine sat with Sarina on a bench seat by a window and said: 'Lorraine, please don't start getting worried because there is no need to. George and I would like to talk to you.'

She bit her lip. 'I knew you would. Can – can Sarina come?'

'Certainly.' He looked at Sarina. 'Provided, of course, that you don't say "Oh!" and "Ah!" and "monster" and clench your fists. Promise?'

'Promise.'

Petersen ushered them to an upstairs room where George was already seated, a large tankard on the table before him and a crate, presumably for emergency, on the floor beside him. Petersen said: 'George?'

George shook his head positively. 'Would you come between a man and his thirst.'

'I would have thought you slaked that pretty thoroughly at lunch.'

'This is a post-prandial beer,' George said with dignity. 'Pray proceed.'

'This will be short and painless,' Petersen said to Lorraine. 'I'm not a dentist and you don't have to tell lies. As you must have guessed, we know everything. I can promise you, and George will confirm, that neither retribution nor punishment waits for you. You're a victim and not a villain and acted under extreme duress. Besides, you didn't even know what you were doing. All transmissions were not only in code but in Yugoslav code and you don't understand a word of Serbo-Croat. George's word, of course, carries immense weight in the war councils, almost totally so in cases such as this, and they listen to me a bit, too. No harm will come to you or Carlos or Mario.'

She nodded, almost composedly. 'You know about our son, of course?'

'Yes. When was he kidnapped?'

'Six months ago.'

'You have no idea where he is being held?'

'No. Well, vaguely.' She was no longer composed. 'In this country, I know. Major Cipriano wanted him out of Italy. I don't know why.'

'I can understand. There are certain things that even

709

Cipriano can't do in Italy. How do you know he's in this country?'

'They let Carlos see him twice. That was twice when I said I wasn't going to work for them any more because I was sure he was dead. But I don't know where he is.'

'Yes. I see. It doesn't matter.'

'It doesn't matter!' She was no longer composed and her eyes were masked in tears.

George took his evil-smelling cigar from his mouth. 'What Peter means is that Cipriano will tell him.'

'Cipriano will tell –' She broke off, nodded and shivered involuntarily.

'We have your code books, Lorraine. We searched your room when you were out this morning.'

'You searched her room!' Sarina said indignantly. 'What right –'

Petersen rose and opened the door. 'Out.'

'I'm sorry. I forgot. I –'

'You promised.'

'Don't you ever give anyone a second chance?'

Petersen didn't answer. He closed the door, sat down and said: 'False bottoms to kitbags are really dreadfully passé these days. But, then, I don't suppose either you or Cipriano ever dreamed that you would come under suspicion. No names in your book but we don't need them. There are code numbers, call-up signs and call-up times. It will take us little enough time to trap them.'

'And then?'

George removed his cigar again. 'Don't ask silly questions.'

'Tell me, Lorraine. You had no idea why you had been sent to Mount Prenj? Oh, you knew what you were to do, but not why. Well, Cipriano knew that you knew Jamie Harrison and that he trusted you completely – after all, you *were* his confidential secretary – so that he would never suspect you of

710

double-dealing: transferring messages from our diehard Četnik friends in Bihać to him in Rome or wherever, messages
which he could re-transmit to the Murge regiment. But the
real reason, of course, is that we had destroyed the only two
long-range transmitters they had. With short-range transmitters their contacts with Rome could only be sporadic at
best. But Mount Prenj is only two hundred kilometres from
Bihać. It would be an awfully short range transmitter that
couldn't reach there.' Petersen paused and considered.
'Well, that's all. No, one more thing.' He smiled. 'Yes. One
more thing. Purely personal. Where did you first meet
Carlos?'

'Isle of Wight, where I was born. He was sailing at
Cowes.'

'Of course, of course. He told me that he often went sailing
there before the war. Well, I hope you'll both go sailing there
again after the war.'

'Will – will Carlos be all right, Major Petersen?'

'If you can refer to a Generalmajor as George you can refer
to a Major as Peter. Why shouldn't he be? He's in the clear.
Under both Italian military and civilian law he has committed no criminal offence, aided and abetted no-one. With any
luck we might see him later on tomorrow.'

'What! Carlos?' Her face was transformed.

Petersen looked at Sarina. 'Yes, you were right, no question.' He didn't say what she had been right about. 'Certainly. Carlos. He hasn't been up to any aiding or abetting yet,
but tomorrow he will.'

She didn't seem to hear him or, if she did, her mind was
elsewhere.

'He's still in Ploče?'

'Yes.'

'He hasn't gone back to Italy?'

'Alas, no. Some disaffected citizen has put sugar in his
diesel oil.'

She looked at him for a long moment then smiled slowly. 'It wouldn't have been one of those solid, reliable citizens you talk about, would it?'

He smiled back at her. 'I am not responsible for the actions of solid, reliable citizens.'

At the foot of the stairs Sarina took Petersen's arm and held him back. 'Thank you,' she said. 'Thank you very much. That was very kind.'

He looked at her in amazement. 'What else did you expect me to do?'

'Nothing, I suppose. But it was wonderful. Especially about Carlos.'

'Today I'm not an ogre? Not a monster?'

She smiled and shook her head.

'And tomorrow? When I have to find out where the little boy is? Do you understand what I mean?'

She stopped smiling.

Petersen shook his head sadly. ' "*Souvent femme varie, bien fol est qui s'y fie*".'

'What is that meant to mean?'

'Picked it up from George. Something King Francis I scratched with a diamond on a pane of glass at Chambord. "Often does woman change, and very foolish is he who trusts her".'

'Pfui!' she said. But she was smiling again.

Towards the middle of the afternoon Petersen and Crni walked into the lounge, carrying several machine-pistols and hand-guns.

'Replacement equipment. Ivan here took ours away so it's only fair that he should replace them. We'll be leaving shortly. Ivan, Edvard and Sava are coming with us.' He glanced at his watch. 'Twenty minutes, shall we say? I want to get through the nasty bit of the Neretva gorge in daylight but not to arrive at our destination until it's dark, for the usual reasons.'

'I'm not looking forward to that,' Sarina said.

'Have no fear. I'm not driving. Sava is. He's a truckdriver in civilian life.'

'What destination?' Harrison said.

'Ah! I forgot. A new acquaintance for you, Jamie, but an old friend of ours. The proprietor of the Hotel Eden in Mostar, one Josip Pijade.'

'A solid and reliable citizen,' Lorraine said.

'A very solid, very reliable citizen. You have a faraway look on your face, George. What are you thinking of?'

'Venison.'

NINE

And venison it was. Josip and Marija had excelled themselves and achieved the seemingly impossible – the venison tasted even marginally better than the last time. George excelled himself in a corresponding fashion, but failed to achieve the impossible: halfway through his third massive helping of venison he had to admit defeat. Sleep that night, unlike the last occasion, was undisturbed by unwelcome visitors. Breakfast was a late and leisurely meal.

'I wish we'd had you up in the damned Mount Prenj for the past two months,' Harrison said to Josip after the meal. 'But it's been worth the wait. I wish someone would station me here for the duration. He directed his attention towards Petersen. 'Are we permitted to know our plans – well, your plans – for the day?'

'Of course. They're concerned primarily, though not entirely, with one person – Cipriano, his apprehension and interrogation. The Bihać affair we can consider as being virtually a closed matter. As you know, we failed to make contact yesterday, but Ivan and I had better luck during the small hours – reception, as you know, is always better at night. They've come up with no fewer than sixteen Četnik-turned-Partisan suspects, there can't be more than two, at the most three. We send out a coded message at a certain hour on a certain wavelength and note will be taken as to which of the sixteen is absent at the time. He will not of course be apprehended until the other one or two have been similarly trapped. Routine. Forget it.' That the words were tantamount to a death sentence was evident to everyone, except, apparently, Petersen.

'Cipriano,' Giacomo said. 'Still at Imotski?'

'He is. We have two men up there on a twenty-four hour watch. We're in radio contact. Spoke to them last an hour ago. Cipriano's up and around but shows no sign yet of moving on. He's got quite an entourage with him.' He looked at Alex. 'You might be interested in hearing the description of one of them.'

'Alessandro?' Alex said hopefully.

'No other.'

'Ah.' Just for once Alex registered a trace of expression: it was as near to a happy smile as Alex would ever come.

'Plus, I'm almost certain from the description, Alessandro's three henchmen. Seems that Carlos must have found a flame-cutter somewhere. We don't, of course, know which way the fox is going to jump – there are several different exit routes he can take from Imotski – but we'll be told immediately that is known. He could, of course, be taking a back road to Ploče and hitch-hiking a lift home with Carlos – if the *Colombo*'s diesel lines have been cleared out – but I think that unlikely. I think he'll be heading for the military airfield just outside the town here and the fast way back to Rome. Ivan and I are just going out to the airport to check.'

'Check what?' Harrison asked.

'Whether there's air transport standing by for him.'

'Won't the airfield be guarded?'

'We are two Italian officers. I've just promoted myself to Colonel and will probably outrank anyone there. We'll just walk in and ask them.'

'That won't be necessary, Peter,' Josip Pijade said. 'My cousin, who owns a garage just outside the airport, works there as a part-time repair and maintenance engineer. Not, unfortunately, on the planes, but on the plant, otherwise the

715

Italian air force would be experiencing mysterious crashes. I have but to lift the phone.'

'Thank you, Josip.'

Josip left. Lorraine said: 'Another solid and reliable citizen?'

'Yugoslavia is full of them.'

Josip was back in two minutes. 'There is an Italian plane on standby. *And* it's reserved for Major Cipriano.'

'Thank you.' He nodded to the small transceiver on the table. 'I'll take this with me. Call up if you hear from Imotski. We're almost certain of the route Cipriano will take into town so Ivan and I will go and select an ambush spot. We may take your car, Josip?'

'Take me, too. I know the perfect spot.'

Sarina said: 'We can go into town?'

'I think so. I won't be needing you until nightfall. The only attention you're liable to attract is wolf-whistles from the licentious Italian soldiery.' He looked at Giacomo. 'I'd feel happier if you went along.'

'No sacrifice too great,' Giacomo said.

Sarina smiled. 'We need protection?'

'Only from the licentious soldiery.'

The call came, inevitably enough, when they were halfway through lunch. Marija came in and said: 'They've just left. They're heading for Posušje.'

'The Mostar road. Excuse us,' Petersen said. He rose as did Alex, Crni and Edvard.

George said: 'I wish I were coming with you. But everyone knows I'm not a man of action.'

'What he means,' Petersen said coldly, 'is that his jaws haven't even got out of second gear yet and he's barely touched his first litre of beer.'

Sarina said: 'You will be careful, won't you?'

Petersen smiled and said: 'Coming, Giacomo?'

'Certainly not. That's a public bar through there. The licentious soldiery might come in any moment.'

'There's your answer about being careful, Sarina. If Giacomo thought there was the slightest chance of shooting an Italian full of holes he'd be the first aboard the truck. He knows there's no hope. But thanks all the same.'

Alex, white handkerchief in hand, stood on a low knoll in the rough grazing field opposite the tree-lined lane which led off the main Lištica–Mostar road. In the lane itself, with engine running, Petersen sat in the cab of the Italian army truck which was parked only feet from the entrance to the road.

Alex raised the handkerchief high above his head. Petersen engaged first gear and waited, clutch depressed, accelerator at half-throttle. Alex brought the handkerchief sharply down and, clutch released, the truck moved forward under full throttle. Three seconds later Petersen jammed on the brakes, bringing the truck to an abrupt halt, fair and square across the width of the main highway.

The Italian army command car which, fortunately for its occupants, was travelling at only a moderate speed, had no chance: even as the driver stamped on the foot-brake he must have realized that his options were limited indeed: he could either keep to the road and hit the side of the truck head-on or swerve to his right into the field where Alex was – a swerve to the left would have fetched him up against the trees lining the lane. Prudently, he chose the latter course. Locked tyres screeching on the tarmac, the car bust through a low wooden fence, broke into the field while balanced on only two wheels, teetered for a couple of seconds then came to rest as it fell over on its left side, wheels still spinning slowly in the air.

Within seconds, rifle butts had smashed in the right-hand windows of the car but the need for haste was not there: the five occupants, unhurt except for cuts about their faces, were too dazed to recognize the presence of their assailants, far less

717

offer resistance: when they did recover some sense of awareness, the sight of the four machine-pistol muzzles only inches
from their heads made the thought of offering any resistance
too ludicrous for contemplation.

When Petersen and Crni returned to the hotel they found
George and his companions – inevitably, in George's case – in
the bar. Equally inevitably, George was presiding behind the
counter.

'Good afternoon, gentlemen.' George was at his affable
best.

'You've finished lunch, then?' Petersen said.

'And it wasn't bad. Not bad at all. What shall it be? Beer?'

'Beer is fine.'

'Aren't you going to ask him what happened?' Sarina said
indignantly.

'Ah. Alex and Edvard have been cut off in their prime?'

'They're in the truck and the truck is in the car park.'

'That's what I like. Solicitude. Making sure that the
prisoners are not doing themselves an injury. When do you
propose to bring them inside?'

'When it's dark. I can't very well march them through the
streets, bound and gagged, in broad daylight, can I?'

'True.' George yawned and slid off his stool. 'Siesta.'

'I know,' Petersen said sympathetically. 'Go, go, go all the
time. Wears a man down.'

George left in dignified silence. Sarina said: 'Doesn't go in
much for congratulations, does he?'

'He postponed his siesta. That shows he's deeply moved.'

'So you got Major Cipriano. What do you think of that,
Lorraine?'

'I suppose I should be weeping for joy. I am glad, I'm
terribly glad. But I *knew* he would. I never for a moment
doubted it. Did you?'

'No. It's very irritating.'

'"*Souvent femme varie*"', Petersen said sadly. 'Josip, would you send someone with your hotel wagon to pick up the prisoners' luggage and take it upstairs. No, not upstairs: I can examine it just as well down here.' He turned to Sarina. 'And you keep quiet.'

'I didn't say anything!'

'You were about to tell me that that was something else I was very good at. Examining other people's luggage, I mean.'

The five prisoners were brought in by the back entrance as soon as it was reasonably dark. The hotel doors were locked. Cipriano, Alessandro and the three others were settled in chairs and their gags removed. Their wrists remained bound behind their backs. The normally tranquil and civilized Major Cipriano had undergone a radical transformation. His eyes glared and his face was suffused in anger.

'What is the meaning of this – this abominable outrage, Petersen? Have you gone mad? Stark raving mad? Untie me at once! I'm an officer, an Italian officer, an *allied* officer!'

'You're a murderer. Your rank and nationality is of no importance. Not when you're a mass murderer.'

'Untie me! You're crazy! By God, Petersen, if it's the last thing I do –'

'Has it occurred to you that you may already have done your last thing on earth?'

Cipriano stared at Petersen. His lack of understanding was total. Suddenly, he noticed Josip for the first time.

'Pijade! Pijade! You – *you* are a party to this monstrous outrage!' Cipriano was so clearly nearly bereft of reason that he struggled futilely with his bonds. 'By God, Pijade, you shall pay for this treachery!'

'Treachery.' Petersen laughed without mirth. 'Speak of treachery while you may, Cipriano, because you're going to die for it. Pijade will pay, will he? How will he do that,

Cipriano?' Petersen's voice was very soft. 'Your eternal curses from the bottom of hell where you'll surely be before midnight tonight?'

'You're all mad,' Cipriano whispered. The anger had drained from his face: he had suddenly become aware that he was in mortal danger.

Petersen went on in the same gentle tone: 'Hundreds of my comrades lie dead because of you.'

'You are mad!' His voice was almost a scream. 'You must be mad. I've never touched a Četnik in my life.'

'I am not a Četnik. I'm a Partisan.'

'A Partisan!' Cipriano was back to his husky whispering again. 'A Partisan! Colonel Lunz suspected – I should have listened –' He broke off and then his voice strengthened. 'I have never harmed a Partisan in my life.'

'Come in,' Petersen called.

Lorraine entered.

'Do you still deny, Cipriano, that you have masterminded the deaths of hundreds of my fellow-Partisans? Lorraine has told me everything, Cipriano. Everything.' He produced a small black book from his tunic. 'Lorraine's code book. In your own handwriting. Or perhaps you don't recognize your handwriting, Cipriano, I'm sure you never thought that you would be signing your own death warrant with your own handwriting. I find it ironic, Cipriano. I hope you do too. But irony isn't going to bring all those hundreds back to life, is it? Even although the last of your spies will have been trapped and executed by the end of the week, those men will still be dead, won't they, Cipriano. Where's the little boy, Lorraine's little boy? Where's Mario, Cipriano?'

Cipriano made a noise in his throat, a harsh and guttural and meaningless sound and struggled to his feet. Giacomo glanced at Petersen, correctly interpreted the nod and, with evident satisfaction, hit Cipriano none too gently in the solar

720

plexus. Cipriano collapsed into his chair, harsh retching noises coming deep from his throat.

Petersen said: 'George?'

George emerged from behind the bar, carrying two pieces of rope in his hand. He ambled across the saloon, dropped one piece to the floor and secured Cipriano firmly to his chair with the other. Then he picked up the second rope, already noosed, and dropped it over Alessandro's chest before the man realized what was happening. Seconds later and he was trussed like the proverbial turkey.

'Cipriano isn't going to tell me because Cipriano knows that he's going to die, whatever happens. But you'll tell me where the little boy is, won't you, Alessandro?'

Alessandro spat on the floor.

'Oh dear.' Petersen sighed. 'Those disgusting habits are difficult to eradicate, aren't they?' He reached behind the bar and produced the metal box of syringes and drugs he had taken from Alessandro aboard the *Colombo*. 'Alex.'

Alex produced his razor-sharp knife and slit Alessandro's left sleeve from the shoulder to where the ropes bound him at the elbow level.

'No!' Alessandro's voice was a scream of pure terror. 'No! No! No!'

Cipriano leaned forward and struggled against his bonds, his face suffused dark red as he tried to force words through his still constricted throat. Giacomo tapped him again to ensure his continued silence.

'I'm afraid I cut him a little,' Alex said apologetically. He was hardly exaggerating: Alessendro's arm was, indeed, quite badly gashed.

'No matter.' Petersen picked up the syringe and selected a phial at apparent random. 'Save the trouble of searching for a vein.'

'Ploče!' Alessandro's whispered. His voice was strangled with fear. His breath coming and going faster than once

721

every second. 'Ploče. I can take you there!' 18 Fra Spalato! I swear it! I can take you there!'

Petersen replaced the syringe and phials and closed the lid. He said to the girls: 'Alessandro, I'm afraid, was psychologically disadvantaged. But I never laid a finger on him, did I?'

Both girls stared at him, then looked at each other. As if by some telepathic signal, they shuddered in unison.

When Alessandro's arm had been bandaged and Cipriano recovered, they made ready to leave. As Alex approached him with a gag, Cipriano looked at Petersen with empty eyes and said: 'Why don't you kill me here? Difficult to dispose of the body? But no trouble in the Adriatic, is it? A few lengths of chain.'

'Nobody's going to dispose of you, Cipriano. Not permanently. We never had any intention of killing you. I knew Alessandro would crack but I didn't want to waste time over it. A bit of a pragmatist, is our Alessandro, and he had no intention of sacrificing his life for a man he believed to be already as good as dead. We have every moral justification for killing you but no legal justification. Spies are shot all the time: spy-masters never. Geneva Conventions say so. It does seem unfair. No, Cipriano, you are going into durance vile. A prisoner of war, for however long the war lasts. British Intelligence are just going to love to have a chat with you.'

Cipriano had nothing to say, which was perhaps understandable. When the reprieve comes along just as the guillotine is about to be tripped, suitable comment is hard to come by.

Petersen turned to his cousin as Cipriano's gag was being fastened. 'Marija, I would like you to do me a favour. Would you look after a little boy for a day or two?'

'Mario!' Lorraine said. 'You mean Mario?'

'What other little boy would I be talking about. Well, Marija?'

722

'Peter!' Her voice was full of reproach.

'Well, I had to ask.' He kissed her on the cheek. 'The bane of my life, but I love you.'

'So we part once more,' Jossip said sadly. 'When do we meet again?'

'Dinner-time. George is coming back for the rest of that venison he couldn't finish last night. So am I.'

Edvard stopped the truck several hundred yards short of the entrance to the docks. Alex and Sava dropped down from the back of the truck followed by a now unbound and ungagged Alessandro – they were in the main street and there were a number of people around. The three men turned, without any undue haste, down an unlit side-street.

Crni, seated up front with Petersen, said: 'Do you anticipate any trouble at the control gate?'

'No more than usual. The guards are old, inefficient, not really interested and very susceptible to arrogant and ill-tempered authority. That's us.'

'Cipriano's wrecked command car is bound to have been found some time ago. And the people in charge at the airport must be wondering where he's got to.'

'If a Yugoslav found it, it will have made his day and he would have driven by without stopping. Whether the airport was expecting him I don't know – Cipriano seems an unpredictable fellow who does very much what he wants. Even if it's accepted by now that he's genuinely missing, where are they going to start looking? Ploče's about as unlikely a place as any.'

And so it proved. The sentry didn't even bother to leave his box. Beyond the gate, the docks were deserted – the day's work was over and the freezing temperatures were hardly calculated to encourage night-time strollers. Even so, Petersen told Edvard to stop two hundred metres short of where the *Colombo* was berthed, left the cab, went

723

round to the back, called Lorraine's name and helped her down.

'See that light there? That's the *Colombo*. Go and tell Carlos to switch off his two gangway lights.'

'Yes,' she said. 'Oh, yes.' She ran a few steps then halted abruptly as Petersen called her.

'Walk you clown. No one in Ploče ever runs.'

Three minutes later the gangway lights went out. Two minutes after that the prisoners had made their unobserved way up the unlighted gangway and the truck had disappeared. The gangway lights came on again.

Carlos sat in his usual chair in his cabin, his good left hand tightly held in both of Lorraine's, the expression on his face not so much uncomprehending and stunned but comprehending and still stunned.

'Let me see whether I've got this right or whether I'm just imagining it,' Carlos said. 'You're going to lock up my crew and myself, abscond with Lorraine and Mario, imprison Cipriano and his men aboard and steal my ship?'

'I couldn't have put it more succinctly myself. Except, of course, that I wouldn't have used the word "abscond". Only, of course, if you consent. The decision is entirely up to you. And Lorraine, too. But I think Lorraine has already made up her mind.'

'Yes, I have.' There was no hesitation in her voice.

'I'll be dismissed from the Navy,' Carlos said gloomily. 'No, I won't, I'll be court-martialled and shot.'

'Nothing will happen to you. There is not a chance in the world. George and I have gone over it time and again.'

'My crew will talk and –'

'Talk? Talk what about? They're sitting in the mess-room with machine-pistols at their heads. If you had a machine-pistol at your head would you have any doubt whatsoever that your ship had been taken over by force?'

724

'Cipriano –'

'What of Cipriano. Even if he survives his captivity, which he unfortunately probably will as the British don't shoot prisoners, there's nothing he can do. There is no way your version and that of the crew – and this will become the official version – can be disproved. And he would never dare lay a personal charge against you – by the time peace comes you can call for the testimony of several solid and respected citizens of Yugoslavia who will testify to the fact that Cipriano kidnapped your son. The penalty in Italy for kidnapping is life imprisonment.'

'Oh, do come on, Carlos,' Lorraine said impatiently. 'It's not like you to dilly-dally. There *is* no other way.' She gently touched his chin so that his eyes came round to hers. 'We've got Mario back.'

'True, true.' He smiled at her. 'That's all that matters to you, isn't it?'

'Not all.' She smiled in return. 'You're back too. That matters a little. What's the alternative, Carlos? Peter doesn't want to kill Cipriano, and if Cipriano is free our life is finished. He *has* to be imprisoned in a safe place and that means in British hands, and the only way to get him there is in this boat. Peter doesn't make mistakes.'

'Correction,' Sarina said sweetly. 'Peter *never* makes mistakes.'

' "*Souvent femme varie*" ' Petersen said.

'Oh, do be quiet.'

'If I'm locked up,' Carlos said, 'When will I – and my crew – be released?'

'Tomorrow. An anonymous phone message.'

'And Lorraine and Mario will stay with your friends?'

'Only a few days. Until we provide them with new identity papers. George is a close friend of *the* master forger in the Balkans. Lorraine Tremino, we had thought. In these troublous times you should have no difficulty in establish-

725

ing a long-established family unit. A marriage certificate, George?'

George lowered his tankard. 'For my friend, a trifle. Venue? Rome? Pescara? Cowes? Wherever. We shall see what forms he has available.'

The door opened and Alex entered, Sava close behind him. Alex had a curly-haired little boy by the hand. The boy looked around him, wonderingly, caught a sight of Carlos and ran to him, arms outstretched. Carlos picked him up and set him on his knees. Mario wound his arms round his neck and gazed wonderingly at Lorraine.

'He's only a little boy,' George said comfortingly. 'For a little boy, Lorraine, six months is a long time. He will remember.'

Harrison coughed. 'And I am to go with Giacomo on this perilous voyage, this rendezvous with eternity?'

'Your choice, Jamie, but Giacomo has to have somebody. Besides, you know as well as I do that the Illyrian Alps are not your homeland and that there's no useful function you can perform here any more. More important, as a serving British officer you will lend credulity – total credibility – to Giacomo's story – apart from convincing the British of the true state of affairs out here, about which you feel so strongly.'

'I will go,' Harrison said. 'A twisted smile on my face, but I will go.'

'You'll untwist your smile when the fast Royal Navy patrol boat comes out to meet you. We will radio Cairo. I don't have their call-up sign but you do, don't you, Sarina?'

'Yes.'

'As a final back-up we will give you a letter explaining the situation fully. Do you have a typewriter, Carlos?'

'Next door.' Carlos had handed Mario over to Lorraine. The little boy, while not objecting, still had a suspicious frown on his face.

'This letter will be signed by the Generalmajor and myself. Can you type, Sarina?'

'Of course.'

'Of course. As if it were the most natural thing in the world. Well, I can't. You should, at least, be pleased. A chink in my armour. Come on.'

Carlos said, 'I don't like to say this, Peter, but I think you've missed something. It's a long long way to the south of Italy where I assume this rendezvous will be made.'

'Your diesel lines are cleared? Your tanks are full?'

'Yes. That's not my point. Oh, I'm sure that Giacomo can steer by the sun and the compass but a rendezvous has to be precise. Latitude this, longitude that.'

'Indeed. But there are some things you don't know about Giacomo.'

Carlos smiled. 'I'm sure there are. What?'

'Do *you* have a foreign-going master's ticket?'

'No.' Carlos smiled again. 'Don't tell me. Giacomo has.'

In the tiny cabin next door Petersen said: 'You liked Cairo, didn't you?'

'Yes.' Sarina looked puzzled. 'Yes, I did.' Her puzzlement changed to suspicion. 'Why?'

'Aristocratic young ladies like you are not cut out for this life. All the cold and ice and snow and mountains. Besides, you suffer from vertigo.'

'I'm coming with you.' The tone in her voice was final.

Petersen looked at her for a long moment then smiled. 'A Partisan.'

'I'm coming with you.'

'So is Michael.'

'I'm coming with you in a different way.'

Petersen pondered. 'If things like that have to be said I think that I should really –'

'You talk so much I'd have to wait for ever.'

727

He smiled and touched the auburn hair. 'About this letter.'

'Romance,' she said. 'Life is going to be full of it.'

'One little thing you've overlooked, Peter,' Harrison said.

'Peter never overlooks anything.'

Petersen looked at Sarina and raised his eyes. '*Souvent –*'

'Please.'

'Giacomo and I are going to be alone,' Harrison said. 'We have to sleep. Five dangerous men to be watched. How are we –'

'Alex?'

'Yes, Major?'

'The engine-room.'

'Ah!' A rare, a very rare smile touched Alex's lips. 'The oxyacetylene welder.'